I0831562

THE COLLECTED WORKS OF W. B. YEATS
Richard J. Finneran and George Mills Harper
General Editors

VOLUME I: *The Poems*,
ed. Richard J. Finneran

VOLUME II: *The Plays*,
ed. David R. Clark

VOLUME III: *Autobiographies*,
ed. William H. O'Donnell, Douglas Archibald, J. Fraser Cocks III,
and Gretchen L. Schwenker

VOLUME IV: *Early Essays*,
ed. Warwick Gould and Deirdre Toomey

VOLUME V: *Later Essays*,
ed. William H. O'Donnell

VOLUME VI: *Prefaces and Introductions*,
ed. William H. O'Donnell

VOLUME VII: *Letters to the New Island*,
ed. George Bornstein and Hugh Witemeyer

VOLUME VIII: *The Irish Dramatic Movement*,
ed. Mary FitzGerald

VOLUME IX: *Early Articles and Reviews*,
ed. John P. Frayne

VOLUME X: *Later Articles and Reviews*,
ed. Colton Johnson

VOLUME XI: *Mythologies*,
ed. Warwick Gould, Phillip L. Marcus,
and Michael Sidnell

VOLUME XII: *John Sherman and Dhoya*,
ed. Richard J. Finneran

VOLUME XIII: *A Vision* (1925),
ed. Connie K. Hood and Walter Kelly Hood

VOLUME XIV: *A Vision* (1937),
ed. Connie K. Hood and Walter Kelly Hood

The Collected Works of W. B. Yeats

Volume V

W. B. YEATS

Later Essays

EDITED BY

William H. O'Donnell

With Assistance from

Elizabeth Bergmann Loizeaux

CHARLES SCRIBNER'S SONS

NEW YORK • LONDON •
TORONTO • SYDNEY • TOKYO • SINGAPORE

CHARLES SCRIBNER'S SONS
Rockefeller Center
1230 Avenue of the Americas
New York, New York 10020

Manufactured in the United States of America
1 3 5 7 9 10 8 6 4 2

Library of Congress Cataloging-in-Publication Data
(Revised for vol. 5)

Yeats, W. B. (William Butler), 1865–1939.
The collected works of W.B. Yeats
Includes bibliographical references and indexes.
Contents: v. 1. The poems / edited by Richard J. Finneran— —v. 5. Later essays / edited by William H. O'Donnell—[etc.]—v. 7. Letters to the new island / edited by George Bornstein and Hugh Witemeyer.
I. Finneran, Richard J. II. Harper, George Mills.
PR5900.A2F56 1989 821'.8 88.27365
ISBN 0-02-632701-5 (v. 1)

CONTENTS

EDITOR'S PREFACE

This volume in *The Collected Works of W. B. Yeats* contains the essays that Yeats wrote from 1912 onwards and that he collected in the Cuala Press volume *Essays 1931 to 1936* or that he specifically selected for the collected editions of his works. One essay, 'If I were Four-and-Twenty' (1919), which was collected posthumously in a Cuala Press volume, is included here for convenience because it is not available in *Uncollected Prose* or *Prefaces and Introductions*. One essay from this period, 'Certain Noble Plays of Japan' (1916), is placed in the *Early Essays* volume of this edition because in 1919 Yeats had incorporated that essay in the revised version of an earlier collection, *The Cutting of an Agate* (1912; rev. 1919), and it remained there in *Essays* (1924).

Later Essays opens with *Per Amica Silentia Lunae* (1917) and closes with *On the Boiler* (written 1938; publ. 1939). The essays are arranged generally according to their dates of publication, except that the nine essays of *Essays 1931 to 1936* are kept in the topical order of that collection, together with its brief preface. Yeats placed three essays about Indian topics at the end of *Essays 1931 to 1936,* and I have chosen to follow them with his three other Indian essays: the introductions to *Gitanjali* (1912) by Tagore, *Ten Principal Upanishads* (1937) and *Aphorisms of Yôga* (dated 1937; publ. 1938) by Patanjali. Also included are the two essays that Yeats contributed to *Visions and Beliefs in the West of Ireland* (dated 1914; publ. 1920) by Lady Gregory, 'Swedenborg, Mediums, and the Desolate Places' and 'Witches and Wizards and Irish Folk-Lore', printed here in the sequence according to Yeats's holograph instructions, but which the American printer ignored in 1920. The other essays are Yeats's introduction to *The Oxford Book of Modern Verse* (1936) and two of his introductions (written 1937) for the never-published Charles Scribner's Sons collected edition ('Dublin Edition'). The 'Introduction to Plays', written for Charles Scribner's Sons edition, is placed in the *Plays* volume of this edition.

The simultaneous need for explanatory annotation and for

careful editing of the texts can be demonstrated with two brief examples of textual corruption that stemmed from imperfect understanding of references. One example is in 'Swedenborg, Mediums, and the Desolate Places' (1914), where the typescript (NLI Ms. 30,623, p. 37) and the first printed text correctly refer to 'the juggler Houdin', the French magician Robert Houdin (1805–71), who, as Yeats explains, when 'sent to Morocco by the French Government, was able to break the prestige of the dervishes' (p. 64, ll. 28–29 below). However, in the Cuala Press *Essays 1931 to 1936,* which is the copy-text for the present edition, 'Houdin' was printed wrongly as 'Houdini', a confusion with the American magician Harry Houdini (Ehrich Weiss, 1874–1926)—whose stage name paid homage to Houdin. The incorrect 'Houdini' was retained by Macmillan in *Explorations* (1962) and was also used in the Coole Edition of the Works of Lady Gregory (1970). Another example is a reference to *Baisers,* French short erotic poems about kissing that enjoyed a vogue during the second half of the sixteenth century. Yeats mentions *Baisers* in the introduction to *Aphorisms of Yôga* as a chronological reference and for its sensuality: ' . . . Saint Teresa who lived back somewhere near the Baisers and the sôma drinker' (p. 179, ll. 36–37 below). The manuscript spelling, of which two letters cannot be deciphered confidently, is 'Bais*re*' (NLI Ms. 30,400, fol. 11^{v}). The typist settled for 'Basarid', a completely meaningless term (NLI Ms. 30,148, Ts. p. 9), which was retained, but without capitalisation, in the final typescript (HRC Texas, p. 9) and the Faber and Faber book publication (1938) as 'basarid'.

Explanatory annotation is provided for all quotations, direct references and allusions. Those notes are marked in the text by superscript numerals and are printed on pages 293–460, following the appendices. The numbering of notes restarts in a new series for each essay. Yeats's own notes are printed among the explanatory annotation, prefixed with the notation '[Yeats's note]'. Explanatory notes to Yeats's notes are marked by a superscript letter in the text of his note and are printed immediately following the note to which they relate. His notes to *Visions and Beliefs in the West of Ireland* are given in Appendix 3. Other appendices give sections that had once been published by Yeats but that he later dropped from the copy-text version, and, for interest, unadopted sections from three essays.

The copy-text for each essay is the last version seen by Yeats; they are listed on pages 503–05 below. The textual introductions, on pages 461–501 below, describe the textual history of each essay and the often difficult problem of how much authority should be assigned to decisions made collectively by Mrs Yeats and Thomas Mark of Macmillan, London, after Yeats's death. Those issues are particularly important for *On the Boiler*, which Yeats saw only in an early proof version of the rejected first edition, and for the two introductions for the Charles Scribner's Sons 'Dublin Edition', which Yeats last saw in typescript. The evidence available from manuscripts and typescripts suggests that in many instances Mrs Yeats possessed documentary authority for posthumous emendations. For example, in 1959, when Macmillan, London, copy-edited the typescript '[General] Introduction', which was first received by Macmillan, London, after September 1955, but which had been written and typed in 1937, two of the emendations presumably were confirmed from a manuscript and a preliminary typescript in the possession of Mrs Yeats. The first of those emendations in 1959 corrected a misreading (as 'classes') by the 1937 typist (who, ironically, had been Mrs Yeats herself) of Yeats's holograph word 'clans' (p. 207, 1. 4 below; NLI Ms. 30,798; *E&I* 513). The other emendation corrected her mistyping (or intentional revision, as 'what the newspapers call of my school') of Yeats's holograph, 'of what the newspapers call my school' (p. 208, 11. 30–31 below; NLI Ms. 30,798; *E&I* 515). Similarly, the Macmillan, London, copy-editing in 1959 restored stress markings (p. 214 below) that had been omitted entirely from both the typescripts, and which were available only in the manuscript version. But Macmillan's published 1961 version of that same introduction inserted an emendation that apparently was made solely for the printer's convenience and that contradicts the manuscript, both typescripts and the 1959 page proofs,[1] where the text reads: 'Slievenamon will be more im- [LINE DIVISION] portant than Olympus' (1959 page proofs *E&I* 390, ll. 18–19). Hyphens were added in 'Slieve-na-mon' to standardise its spelling, and then some unidentified person revised 'important' to 'famous', apparently to simplify the printer's work: 'Slieve-na-mon will be more [LINE DIVISION] famous than Olympus' (*E&I* 512, ll. 18–19). The posthumous emendations are not all of one cloth; they should neither be accepted wholesale nor rejected out of hand.

Emendations to the copy-texts are listed near the end of the volume. The listing of 'Emendations to the Copy-Texts' gives the page and line number of the emendation, the reading in this edition, the reading in the copy-text, and a contemporary authority for the emendation. Posthumous and other auxiliary evidence as the authority for an emendation is given within square brackets; the citation 'None' means 'No contemporary documentary authority'. When an essay contains a poem by Yeats, the poem is emended to correspond to the *Poems* volume of this edition, but all differences from the *Later Essays* copy-text are given in the list of 'Emendations to the Copy-Texts'.

Editorial emendation has been kept to a minimum, especially in the eighteen essays and four appendices that had been published during Yeats's lifetime. Those twenty-two items published during his lifetime have a total of only thirty-one editorial emendations that lack contemporary documentary authority, and all but four of those thirty-one emendations are limited to minor corrections of spelling, hyphenation, capitalisation and punctuation. Three of the four emendations of words are straightforward ('Yogi' changed to 'Yoga', 'attains' changed to 'attain' and 'lead' changed to 'led'); the fourth emendation ('shall not prevail' changed to 'shall prevail') is strongly supported by context and also was emended during copy-editing in 1939 by Thomas Mark at Macmillan, London.[2]

The eighteen essays published during Yeats's lifetime have a total of only ten emendations for which I have only posthumous or other auxiliary evidence; eight of those ten are corrections of spelling and two are stanza divisions that were missed in quoted poetry of Dorothy Wellesley and W. J. Turner.

The three essays and three appendices that were not published during Yeats's lifetime have required many more editorial emendations than the essays that he saw through the press. In the typescript '[General] Introduction' and 'Introduction to Essays' (pp. 204–19) that Yeats submitted to Charles Scribner's Sons in 1937, sixty-five of a total of 143 emendations lack a contemporary documentary authority. For *On the Boiler,* which Yeats last saw in a preliminary state of page proofs, 203 of 216 editorial emendations have a contemporary documentary authority or posthumous editorial evidence from a set of page proofs that Mrs Yeats marked within six months of Yeats's death or from the two versions of the book published in 1939.

The conservative limits on emendation of punctuation can be demonstrated by what I consider the most extreme instance, which is the conversion of two commas into semicolons, in order to clarify the division of a very long (sixty-eight-word) sentence that contains a series of three clauses that themselves contain five commas.[3]

The carefully limited extent of the emendations can be illustrated with the following examples. Yeats's misquotations are left standing in the text, and corrections are provided in the explanatory notes. His factual errors are left standing in the text and are mentioned in the explanatory notes, as in 'chlorate of lime' (p. 132 below) rather than 'chloride of lime' (p. 370, note 9), 'Horton' (p. 175 below) rather than 'Haughton' (p. 390, note 1), 'Hutchinson' (p. 119) rather than 'Hitchener' (p. 362, note 12) and 'II' (p. 426, Yeats's note 33) rather than 'I' (p. 426, note 33a). However, where evidence exists that a wrong spelling of a name is simply a typist's or printer's misreading of Yeats's difficult handwriting, the name is emended and the manuscript evidence is cited in the list of 'Emendations to the Copy-Texts'. Similarly, in instances of the standardisation of the spelling of names such as 'Cuchulain', each emendation is recorded. However, I have not emended the consistent use in 'Swedenborg, Mediums, and the Desolate Places' (dated 1914) of an alternate spelling of Joseph Glanvill's name, as 'Glanvil' (two instances) and the single instance in 'My Friend's Book' (1932), even though all seven instances of his name are 'Glanvill' in 'Witches and Wizards and Irish Folk-Lore', the companion essay of 'Swedenborg, Mediums, and the Desolate Places'. Yeats would have encountered the alternate spelling 'Glanvil' on the title page of his copy of *Sadducismus Triumphatus* (O'Shea no. 750) and in his copy of a 1911 edition of Richard Ward's *Life of Henry More* (1710).[4] Similarly, I have not emended the variant transliterations 'Shri', used consistently in two essays (twenty-one instances) and 'Shree', used consistently in two other essays (eight instances).

Except for names, emendation to achieve standardised spelling has been avoided. For example, five essays consistently use a hyphen in 'to-day', but five other essays consistently use the unhyphenated form, 'today'; none has been emended. I have retained minor eccentricities of capitalisation. All ellipses in the text are authorial, unless listed in the 'Emendations to the Copy-

Texts'. All hyphens that occur within a line are authorial. No hyphens at line divisions in this edition are authorial, except for thirty-eight instances in which an authorial hyphen happens to occur at a line division in this edition; those instances are identified, for convenience, in the listing of 'Emendations to the Copy-Texts'.

The following typographical and format conventions are silently adopted in *The Collected Works of W. B. Yeats:*

1. The presentation of headings is standardised. In this volume, the main headings are set in full capitals (capitals and small capitals for subtitles), and include brief details of date and source (for fuller bibliographical information, see the textual introductions and list of copy-texts). Section numbers are in roman capitals. All headings are centered and have no concluding full point.
2. The opening line of each paragraph is indented, except following a displayed heading or section break.
3. All sentences open with a capital letter followed by lower-case letters.
4. British single quotation mark conventions are used.
5. A colon that introduces a quotation is not followed by a dash.
6. Quotations that are set off from the text and indented are not placed within quotation marks.
7. Except in headings, the titles of stories and poems are placed within quotation marks; titles of books, plays, long poems, periodicals, operas, statues, paintings and drawings are set in italics.
8. Contractions (i.e., abbreviations such as 'Mr', 'Mrs' and 'St') that end with the last letter of the abbreviated word are not followed by a full point.
9. Abbreviations such as 'i.e.' are set in roman type.
10. In this volume, a dash—regardless of its length in the copy-text—is set as an unspaced em rule when used as punctuation. When a dash indicates an omission, as in 'J——', a two-em rule is used.
11. Ampersands are expanded to 'and'.
12. Each signature of the author is indented from the left margin, set in upper- and lower-case letters, and ends without punctuation; when present, the place and date

are indented from the left margin, set in italics in upper- and lower-case letters, and end without punctuation.

In this volume, capitalisation of the titles of French books follows the convention of that language.

I am pleased to acknowledge the generous assistance first of Elizabeth Bergmann Loizeaux, who helped with preliminary examination of several manuscripts in the British Library and with information for several of the explanatory notes to *Per Amica Silentia Lunae*. In acknowledging her help and that of the following lengthy list of friends and scholars in a wide range of disciplines, I should remind the reader that the responsibility for any erroneous information in the notes is entirely mine. Among many others, thanks are due to Douglas Archibald, Colby College; Massimo Bacigalupo, University of Genoa; Conrad A. Balliet, Wittenberg University; Jonas A. Barish, University of California, Berkeley; George J. Bornstein, University of Michigan; Edward T. Callan, Western Michigan University; Wayne K. Chapman, Clemson University; David R. Clark, University of Massachusetts; R. W. Desai, University of Delhi; Jean T. and Richard C. Fallis, Syracuse University; Norma M. Field, University of Chicago; Richard J. Finneran, University of Tennessee; Warwick Gould, Royal Holloway and Bedford New College, University of London; Dymphna Halpin, Dublin; George M. Harper, Florida State University; Connie K. and Walter K. Hood, Tennessee Technological University; T. G. Henry James, British Museum; A. Norman Jeffares, Fife Ness, Crail, Scotland; Deborah Journet, University of Louisville; John Kelly, St John's College, Oxford; Mary M. Lago, University of Missouri; Jon Lanham, Harvard University Library; M. M. Liberman, Grinnell College; Phillip L. Marcus, Cornell University; C. D. Narasimhaiah, Bombay; John R. O'Donnell, Red Bank, New Jersey; Dennis Omø, University of Copenhagen; Roger Pineau, Bethesda, Maryland; Mary Powell, University of New Mexico; the late B. L. Reid, Mount Holyoke College; Marsha Keith Manatt Schuchard, Atlanta; W. Ronald Schuchard, Emory University; Peter L. Shillingsburg, Mississippi State University; Shalini Sikka, Jesus and Mary College, University of Delhi; Colin Smythe, Gerrards Cross, Bucks.; Joan and Barry Stahl, Washington; G. Martin Stephen, The Perse School, Cambridge; Craig R. Thompson, University of Pennsylvania; Frances Whistler, Oxford University Press; Hedley P. Wilmott, Royal Military College, Sandhurst; Hugh Witemeyer, University of New Mexico; Anne Yeats, Dublin; Yoshiko Yoshimura, Library of Congress. At the University of Memphis: John Beifuss, Peter Bridson, Kay Easson, Robert Gaia, Florence Halle, James Holland, Graden Kirksey, Scott Langston, Charles Long, Catherine Martin, Hall Peyton, Mark Richardson, Hoke Robinson, Naseeb Shaheen, David Sigsbee, Betsy Taylor, Cherisa Tisdale, Daniel Ray Willbanks and Helen Wussow. At Pennsylvania State University: Steven Andrews, Michael H. Begnal, Daniel Göske, Dana M. Stuchell and Stanley Weintraub. Amherst College library; British Broadcasting Corporation Written Archives Centre (Jackie Kavanagh and Caroline Cornish); British Library; British Library National Sound Archive, London (Jeremy Silver and Simon Robinson); Emory University library (Linda Matthews and Ginger Kane); University of Iowa library; National Library of Ireland (Catherine Fahy and Brian McKenna); University of Kansas library (Alexandra Mason); Library of Congress; University of Massachusetts library; University of Memphis library (Deborah Brackstone, Elizabeth Buck and Janell Rudolph); New York Public Library Annex, Berg Collection, Fine Arts Division, Map Division, Oriental Division (Usha Bhasker), Reference Division and Special Collections; Pennsylvania State University library (Charles Mann, Sandra Stelts and Christine Whittington); Princeton University library (Jean F. Preston and John Delaney); Southern Illinois University library (David Koch); Harry Ransom Humanities Research Center, University of Texas at Austin (Cathy Henderson); Washington University in St Louis library; and Wesleyan University library (Elizabeth Swaim). Research travel for this volume was funded by grants-in-aid from the American Council of Learned Societies, National Endowment for the Humanities, and the College of Arts and Sciences, University of Memphis. The book is dedicated to Gloria, whose eye for editorial detail has been helpful, and to Clare and Kerry. I will be pleased if this edition fully meets the standards that were called for a quarter century ago by the late Marion W. Witt.[5]

For permission to quote from unpublished materials I gratefully acknowledge Anne Yeats; Michael Yeats; the British Library; the National Library of Ireland; Henry W. and Albert A.

Berg Collection, The New York Public Library, Astor, Lenox and Tilden Foundations; Archives of Charles Scribner's Sons, Princeton University Library (published with permission of Princeton University Library); Special Collections, Morris Library, Southern Illinois University at Carbondale; Yeats Microfilm Archive, Frank Melville, Jr, Memorial Library, State University of New York, Stony Brook; and the Harry Ransom Humanities Research Center, University of Texas at Austin. Excerpts from unpublished lyrics by Shree Purohit Swāmi are published with the permission of the Board of the Shree Purohit Swāmi Memorial Trust, Poona, and the Nehru Memorial Library, New Delhi. The introduction to *The Oxford Book of Modern Verse* is published with permission of the Oxford University Press, Oxford.

NOTES TO EDITOR'S PREFACE

1. Yeats's holograph manuscript (p. 4) and typescript corrected by Yeats (p. 5; both NLI Ms. 30,798), the typescript submitted to Scribner's in 1937 and then copy-edited by Macmillan in 1955–59 (p. 4); and the 1959 page proofs of *E&I*, p. 390 (collection of George M. Harper). The passage is p. 206, ll. 28–29 below.
2. Pp. 145, l. 7 ('Yoga'), 148, l. 24 ('attain'), 275, l. 32 ('led') and 106, l. 37 ('shall prevail') above.
3. 4. P. 205, ll. 23–29.
4. Yeats's holograph spelling 'Glanvil' (two instances) in 'Swedenborg, Mediums, and the Desolate Places' and 'My Friend's Book' (one instance) was left standing in the typescripts and the printed versions published during Yeats's lifetime. However, in 'Witches and Wizards and Irish Folk-Lore' (1914) his holograph spelling 'Glanvil' (five instances) was changed to 'Glanvill' (seven instances) in the typescript and the printed version.

   Richard Ward, *The Life of the Learned and Pious Dr Henry More: Late Fellow of Christ's College in Cambridge* (1710), ed. M. F. Howard (London: Theosophical Publishing Society, 1911) (O'Shea no. 2226), pp. 17, 19 *et passim:* 'Glanvil'.
5. 'Yeats: 1865–1965', *PMLA*, 80 (1965): 311–20. Professor Marion Winifred Witt, of Hunter College, City University of New York, died 22 December 1978.

LIST OF ABBREVIATIONS

The following abbreviations are used in the editorial apparatus; additional abbreviations that are confined to the list of emendations to the copy-texts are explained at the head of that list.

Agrippa, *Three Books of Occult Philosophy*
Henry Cornelius Agrippa von Nettesheim, *Three Books of Occult Philosophy* (w. 1509–10; publ. 1531–33), tr. John French (London: Moule, 1651)

Ancient Criminal Trials in Scotland
Ancient Criminal Trials in Scotland, compiled by Robert Pitcairn, 3 vols., Maitland Club Publication no. 19 (Edinburgh: Maitland Club, 1833)

Au W. B. Yeats, *Autobiographies* (London: Macmillan, 1955)

AY *The Aphorisms of Yôga*, by Bhagwān Shree Patanjali, tr. Shree Purohit Swāmi (London: Faber and Faber, 1938)

Balzac, *Séraphita*
Honoré de Balzac, *Séraphita* (1834–35), tr. Clara Bell, *Comédie humaine*, ed. George Saintsbury (London: Dent Edition, 1895–98), repr. as vol. XXXIV of Temple Edition (New York: Macmillan, 1901), (O'Shea no. 106)

BB Joseph M. Hone and Mario M. Rossi, *Bishop Berkeley: His Life, Writings, and Philosophy*, intro. by W. B. Yeats (London: Faber & Faber, 1931)

Bentley, *Blake Records*
G. E. Bentley, Jr., *Blake Records* (Oxford: Clarendon Press, 1969)

Berg NYPL
Henry W. and Albert A. Berg Collection, New York Public Library, Astor, Lenox and Tilden Foundations

Works of Berkeley
The Works of George Berkeley (Dublin: Exshaw, 1784), (O'Shea no. 160)

Berkeley's Commonplace Book
Berkeley's Commonplace Book, ed. G. A. Johnston (London: Faber & Faber, 1930), (O'Shea nos. 159, 159a)

BL British Library

Burnet, *Early Greek Philosophy*
John Burnet, *Early Greek Philosophy* (London and Edinburgh: Black, 1892), (O'Shea no. 308)

Certain Noble Plays of Japan
Certain Noble Plays of Japan: From the Manuscripts of Ernest Fenollosa, Chosen and Finished by Ezra Pound, With an Introduction by William Butler Yeats (Churchtown, Dundrum: Cuala Press, 1916)

CL1 *The Collected Letters of W. B. Yeats*, vol. I, ed. John Kelly, associate ed. Eric Domville (Oxford: Clarendon Press; New York: Oxford University Press, 1986)

CPlays W. B. Yeats, *Collected Plays* (London: Macmillan, 1952)

CSS Princeton
Archives of Charles Scribner's Sons, Princeton University Library

Cuchulain of Muirthemne
Lady Gregory, *Cuchulain of Muirthemne: The Story of the Men of the Red Branch of Ulster* (London: Murray, 1902), (O'Shea no. 792)

E&I W. B. Yeats, *Essays and Introductions* (London and New York: Macmillan, 1961)

Early Italian Poets . . . with Dante's Vita Nuova
The Early Italian Poets from Ciullo d'Alcamo to Dante Alighieri (1100–1200–1300) . . . together with Dante's Vita Nuova, tr. and ed. D. G. Rossetti (London: Smith, Elder, 1861), (O'Shea 1920s list)

Erdman *The Poetry and Prose of William Blake*, ed. David V. Erdman (Garden City, NY: Doubleday, 1965 [4th printing, with revisions])

Ex W. B. Yeats, *Explorations*, sel. Mrs W. B. Yeats (London: Macmillan, 1962; New York: Macmillan, 1963)

EYPR Richard J. Finneran, *Editing Yeats's Poems: A Reconsideration* (London: Macmillan; New York: St Martin's Press, 1990)

FFT *Fairy and Folk Tales of the Irish Peasantry*, ed. W. B. Yeats, Camelot Classics series, no. 32 (London: Scott, 1888)

Glanvill, *Sadducismus Triumphatus*
Joseph Glanvill, *Sadducismus Triumphatus: or, a Full and Plain Evidence, Concerning Witches and Apparitions* [title spelt *Saducismus* . . . in the earlier editions, 1681–1700], 4th ed. (London: Bettesworth and Batley, 1726), (O'Shea no. 750)

Gods and Fighting Men
Lady Gregory, *Gods and Fighting Men: The Story of the Tuatha de Danaan and of the Fianna of Ireland* (London: Murray, 1904), (O'Shea no. 795)

Harper, *Making of A Vision*
George M. Harper, *The Making of Yeats's A Vision: A Study of the Automatic Script*, 2 vols. (London: Macmillan, 1987)

Harper, *Yeats's Golden Dawn*
George M. Harper, *Yeats's Golden Dawn* (London: Macmillan, 1974)

Harper's Dictionary of Hinduism
Margaret and James Stutley, *Harper's Dictionary of Hinduism* (New York: Harper & Row, 1977)

HM Bhagwān Shri Hamsa, *The Holy Mountain: Being the Story of a Pilgrimage to Lake Mānas and of Initiation on Mount Kailās in Tibet*, tr. Shri Purohit Swāmi, intro. by W. B. Yeats (London: Faber and Faber, 1934)

HRC Texas
Harry Ransom Humanities Research Center, University of Texas at Austin

IM Shri Purohit Swāmi, *An Indian Monk: His Life and Adventures*, intro. by W. B. Yeats (London: Macmillan, 1932)

L *The Letters of W. B. Yeats*, ed. Allan Wade (London: Hart-Davis, 1954; New York: Macmillan, 1955)

LDW *Letters on Poetry from W. B. Yeats to Dorothy Wellesley*, ed. Dorothy Wellesley (London, New York and Toronto: Oxford University Press, 1940)

'Leo Africanus' (*c.* 1916?; *YA1*)
'The Manuscript of "Leo Africanus" ' (*c.* 1916?), ed. Steve L. Adams and George Mills Harper in *Yeats Annual No. 1*, ed. Richard J. Finneran (London: Macmillan; Atlantic Highlands, NJ: Humanities Press, 1982), pp. 3–47

Lombroso, *After Death—What?*
Cesare Lombroso, *After Death—What? Spiritistic Phenomena and their Interpretation,* tr. William Sloane Kennedy (London: Unwin; Boston: Small, Maynard, 1909), (O'Shea no. 1145)

LTSM *W. B. Yeats and T. Sturge Moore: Their Correspondence: 1901–1937,* ed. Ursula Bridge (London: Routledge & Kegan Paul; New York: Oxford University Press, 1953)

LTWBY *Letters to W. B. Yeats,* ed. Richard J. Finneran, George Mills Harper and William M. Murphy (London: Macmillan; New York: Columbia University Press, 1977)

Luce, *Life of George Berkeley*
Arthur Aston Luce, *The Life of George Berkeley Bishop of Cloyne* (London: Nelson, 1949)

Mem W. B. Yeats, *Memoirs,* ed. Denis Donoghue (London: Macmillan, 1972; New York: Macmillan, 1973)

More, *The Immortality of the Soul*, in *A Collection*
Henry More, *The Immortality of the Soul* (1659; rev. 1662), in *A Collection of Several Philosophical Writings,* 2nd ed. (London: William Morden, 1662), (O'Shea no. 1377)

Myth W. B. Yeats, *Mythologies* (London and New York: Macmillan, 1959)

NLI National Library of Ireland

OBMV *The Oxford Book of Modern Verse, 1892–1935,* chosen by W. B. Yeats (Oxford: Clarendon Press, 1936)

O'Shea Edward O'Shea, *A Descriptive Catalog of W. B. Yeats's Library* (New York: Garland, 1985) and 'The 1920s Catalogue of W. B. Yeats's Library', *Yeats Annual No. 4,* ed. Warwick Gould (London: Macmillan, 1986) pp. 279–90

O'Shea, *Yeats as Editor*
Edward O'Shea, *Yeats as Editor,* New Yeats Papers 12 (Dublin: Dolmen Press, 1975)

P W. B. Yeats, *The Poems,* revised edition, ed. Richard J. Finneran (New York: Macmillan, 1989; London: Macmillan, 1991)

P&I W. B. Yeats, *Prefaces and Introductions: Uncollected Prefaces and Introductions by Yeats to Works by other Authors and to Anthologies Edited by Yeats,* ed. W. H. O'Donnell (London: Macmillan, 1989; New York: Macmillan, 1990)

PWB — *Poems of William Blake,* ed. W. B. Yeats, Muses' Library, 2nd ed. (London: Routledge; New York: Dutton, 1905)

Rochas, *L'Extériorisation de la motricité*
Albert de Rochas, *L'Extériorisation de la motricité: recueil d'expériences et d'observations* (Paris: Chamuel, 1896) [Yeats owned the augmented 4th ed. (Paris: Bibliothèque Chacornac, 1906), (O'Shea no. 1775).]

Collected Works of Dante Gabriel Rossetti
The Collected Works of Dante Gabriel Rossetti, ed. William Michael Rossetti (1887–88; repr. London: Ellis and Elvey, 1897), (O'Shea no. 1789)

SB — W. B. Yeats, *The Speckled Bird,* ed. W. H. O'Donnell (Toronto: McClelland and Stewart, 1977)

Shelley, *Essays and Letters*
Percy Bysshe Shelley, *Essays and Letters,* ed. Ernest Rhys, Camelot Classics (London: Scott, 1886), (O'Shea no. 1902)

Poems of Shelley, ed. Locock
The Poems of Percy Bysshe Shelley, ed. C. D. Locock (London: Methuen, 1911), (O'Shea no. 1905)

Solovof (Soloviev), *The Justification of the Good*
Vladimir Sergeevich Solovof (or Soloviev or Solovyou), *The Justification of the Good: An Essay on Moral Philosophy* (1898, in Russian), tr. Nathalie A. Duddington (London: Constable, 1918), (O'Shea no. 1958)

Poems of Spenser, ed. W. B. Yeats
(Edinburgh: Jack, 1906), (O'Shea no. 1977)

SS — *The Senate Speeches of W. B. Yeats,* ed. Donald R. Pearce (Bloomington: Indiana University Press, 1960; London: Faber and Faber, 1961)

SUI — Special Collections, Morris Library, Southern Illinois University at Carbondale

SUNY-SB — Yeats Microfilm Archive, Frank Melville, Jr, Memorial Library, State University of New York, Stony Brook

Swedenborg, *Arcana Coelestia*
Emanuel Swedenborg, *Arcana Coelestia. The Heavenly Arcana Contained in the Holy Scripture; or Word of the Lord, Unfolded, in an Exposition of Genesis and Exodus, together with a Revelation of Wonderful Things Seen in the World of Spirits and in the Heaven of Angels* (1749–56 in Latin), tr. John Clowes (1783, vol. I), 13

vols. (1861; repr. London: Swedenborg Society, 1891), (O'Shea no. 2037: vol. I only)

Swedenborg, *Conjugial Love*
Emanuel Swedenborg, *The Delights of Wisdom Pertaining to Conjugial Love; After which follow the Pleasures of Insanity relating to Scortatory Love* (1768), tr. A. H. Searle (1876), rev. R. L. Tafel (1891), (London: Swedenborg Society, 1891), (O'Shea no. 2038)

Swedenborg, *Heaven and . . . Hell*
Emanuel Swedenborg, *Heaven and its Wonders and Hell: from Things Heard and Seen* (1758, in Latin), tr. rev. F. Bayley, Everyman's Library series (1909; repr. London: Dent, 1911), (O'Shea 1920s list [probable identification])

Swedenborg, *Spiritual Diary*
Emanuel Swedenborg, *The Spiritual Diary: Being the Record during Twenty Years of his Supernatural Experience,* tr. George Bush and Rev. John H. Smithson, 5 vols. (London: Speirs, 1883–1902), (O'Shea nos. 2040–40D)

Synge, *Works of John M. Synge*
The Works of John M. Synge, 4 vols. (Dublin: Maunsel, 1910), (O'Shea no. 2076)

TPU *The Ten Principal Upanishads,* tr. Shree Purohit Swāmi and W. B. Yeats (1937; 2nd ed., London: Faber and Faber, 1938)

UP1 *Uncollected Prose by W. B. Yeats,* vol. 1, ed. John P. Frayne (New York: Columbia University Press; London: Macmillan, 1970)

UP2 *Uncollected Prose by W. B. Yeats,* vol. 2, ed. John P. Frayne and Colton Johnson (London: Macmillan, 1975; New York: Columbia University Press, 1976)

V(A) W. B. Yeats, *A Vision* (London: Werner Laurie, title page 1925 [January 1926])

V(B) W. B. Yeats, *A Vision,* 2nd ed. (London: Macmillan, 1937)

V(A)CE *A Critical Edition of Yeats's A Vision (1925),* ed. George Mills Harper and Walter Kelly Hood (London: Macmillan, 1978)

VP *The Variorum Edition of the Poems of W. B. Yeats,* ed. Peter Allt and Russell K. Alspach (New York: Macmillan, 1957; cited from the corrected 3rd printing, 1966, or later printings)

VPl — *The Variorum Edition of the Plays of W. B. Yeats*, ed. Russell K. Alspach (London and New York: Macmillan, 1966; cited from the corrected 2nd printing, 1966, or later printings)

V&B — Lady Augusta Gregory, *Visions and Beliefs in the West of Ireland . . . with Two Essays and Notes by W. B. Yeats*, 2 vols. (New York: Putnam's, 1920)

V&B1970 — Lady Augusta Gregory, *Visions and Beliefs in the West of Ireland*, vol. 1 of the Coole Edition of the Works of Lady Gregory (Gerrards Cross: Smythe, 1970)

Wade — Allan Wade, *A Bibliography of the Writings of W. B. Yeats*, 3rd ed., rev. Russell K. Alspach (London: Hart-Davis, 1968)

Works of George Berkeley — *The Works of George Berkeley, D.D., Late Bishop of Cloyne in Ireland*, 2 vols. (London: G. Robinson; Dublin: John Exshaw, 1784), (O'Shea no. 160)

WWB — *The Works of William Blake: Poetic, Symbolic, and Critical*, ed. Edwin J. Ellis and W. B. Yeats, 3 vols. (London: Quaritch, 1893)

YA — *Yeats Annual*

Yeats on Yeats — Edward Callan, *Yeats on Yeats: The Last Introductions and the 'Dublin' Edition*, New Yeats Papers 20 (Mountrath, Portlaoise: Dolmen Press, 1981)

Per Amica Silentia Lunae[1] (1917)

PROLOGUE

My dear 'Maurice'[2]—You will remember that afternoon in Calvados[3] last summer when your black Persian 'Minoulooshe',[4] who had walked behind us for a good mile, heard a wing flutter in a bramble-bush? For a long time we called him endearing names in vain. He seemed resolute to spend his night among the brambles. He had interrupted a conversation, often interrupted before, upon certain thoughts so long habitual that I may be permitted to call them my convictions. When I came back to London my mind ran again and again to those conversations and I could not rest till I had written out in this little book all that I had said or would have said. Read it some day when 'Minoulooshe' is asleep.

W. B. Yeats
May 11, 1917

EGO DOMINUS TUUS[5]

Hic. On the grey sand beside the shallow stream
Under your old wind-beaten tower, where still
A lamp burns on beside the open book
That Michael Robartes left, you walk in the moon
And though you have passed the best of life still trace,
Enthralled by the unconquerable delusion,
Magical shapes.

Ille. By the help of an image
I call to my own opposite, summon all
That I have handled least, least looked upon.

Hic. And I would find myself and not an image.

Ille. That is our modern hope, and by its light
We have lit upon the gentle, sensitive mind
And lost the old nonchalance of the hand;
Whether we have chosen chisel, pen, or brush
We are but critics, or but half create,
Timid, entangled, empty, and abashed,
Lacking the countenance of our friends.

Hic. And yet
The chief imagination of Christendom,
Dante Alighieri, so utterly found himself
That he has made that hollow face of his
More plain to the mind's eye than any face
But that of Christ.

Ille. And did he find himself
Or was the hunger that had made it hollow
A hunger for the apple on the bough
Most out of reach? and is that spectral image
The man that Lapo and that Guido knew?
I think he fashioned from his opposite
An image that might have been a stony face
Staring upon a Bedouin's horse-hair roof
From doored and windowed cliff, or half upturned
Among the coarse grass and the camel-dung.
He set his chisel to the hardest stone.
Being mocked by Guido for his lecherous life,
Derided and deriding, driven out
To climb that stair and eat that bitter bread,
He found the unpersuadable justice, he found
The most exalted lady loved by a man.

Hic. Yet surely there are men who have made their art
Out of no tragic war, lovers of life,
Impulsive men that look for happiness
And sing when they have found it.

Ille. No, not sing,
For those that love the world serve it in action,
Grow rich, popular and full of influence,
And should they paint or write, still is it action:
The struggle of the fly in marmalade.

The rhetorician would deceive his neighbours,
The sentimentalist himself; while art
Is but a vision of reality.
What portion in the world can the artist have
Who has awakened from the common dream
But dissipation and despair?

Hic. And yet
No one denies to Keats love of the world;
Remember his deliberate happiness.

Ille. His art is happy, but who knows his mind?
I see a schoolboy when I think of him,
With face and nose pressed to a sweet-shop window,
For certainly he sank into his grave
His senses and his heart unsatisfied,
And made—being poor, ailing and ignorant,
Shut out from all the luxury of the world,
The coarse-bred son of a livery-stable keeper—
Luxuriant song.

Hic. Why should you leave the lamp
Burning alone beside an open book,
And trace these characters upon the sands?
A style is found by sedentary toil
And by the imitation of great masters.

Ille. Because I seek an image, not a book.
Those men that in their writings are most wise
Own nothing but their blind, stupefied hearts.
I call to the mysterious one who yet
Shall walk the wet sand by the edge of the stream
And look most like me, being indeed my double,
And prove of all imaginable things
The most unlike, being my anti-self,
And standing by these characters disclose
All that I seek; and whisper it as though
He were afraid the birds, who cry aloud
Their momentary cries before it is dawn,
Would carry it away to blasphemous men.

December 1915

ANIMA HOMINIS[6]

I

When I come home after meeting men who are strange to me, and sometimes even after talking to women, I go over all I have said in gloom and disappointment. Perhaps I have overstated everything from a desire to vex or startle, from hostility that is but fear; or all my natural thoughts have been drowned by an undisciplined sympathy. My fellow-diners have hardly seemed of mixed humanity, and how should I keep my head among images of good and evil, crude allegories?

But when I shut my door and light the candle, I invite a Marmorean Muse,[7] an art, where no thought or emotion has come to mind because another man has thought or felt something different, for now there must be no reaction, action only, and the world must move my heart but to the heart's discovery of itself, and I begin to dream of eyelids that do not quiver before the bayonet: all my thoughts have ease and joy, I am all virtue and confidence. When I come to put in rhyme what I have found it will be a hard toil, but for a moment I believe I have found myself and not my anti-self. It is only the shrinking from toil perhaps that convinces me that I have been no more myself than is the cat the medicinal grass it is eating in the garden.

How could I have mistaken for myself an heroic condition that from early boyhood has made me superstitious? That which comes as complete, as minutely organised, as are those elaborate, brightly lighted buildings and sceneries appearing in a moment, as I lie between sleeping and waking, must come from above me and beyond me. At times I remember that place in Dante where he sees in his chamber the 'Lord of Terrible Aspect', and how, seeming 'to rejoice inwardly that it was a marvel to see, speaking, he said, many things among the which I could understand but few, and of these this: ego dominus tuus';[8] or should the conditions come, not as it were in a gesture—as the image of a man—but in some fine landscape, it is of Boehme, maybe, that I think, and of that country where we 'eternally solace ourselves in the excellent beautiful flourishing of all manner of flowers and forms, both trees and plants, and all kinds of fruit'.[9]

II

When I consider the minds of my friends, among artists and emotional writers, I discover a like contrast. I have sometimes told one close friend that her only fault is a habit of harsh judgement with those who have not her sympathy, and she has written comedies where the wickedest people seem but bold children.[10] She does not know why she has created that world where no one is ever judged, a high celebration of indulgence, but to me it seems that her ideal of beauty is the compensating dream of a nature wearied out by over-much judgement. I know a famous actress[11] who in private life is like the captain of some buccaneer ship holding his crew to good behaviour at the mouth of a blunderbuss, and upon the stage she excels in the representation of women who stir to pity and to desire because they need our protection, and is most adorable as one of those young queens imagined by Maeterlinck who have so little will, so little self, that they are like shadows sighing at the edge of the world.[12] When I last saw her in her own house she lived in a torrent of words and movements, she could not listen, and all about her upon the walls were women drawn by Burne-Jones in his latest period. She had invited me in the hope that I would defend those women, who were always listening, and are as necessary to her as a contemplative Buddha to a Japanese Samurai, against a French critic who would persuade her to take into her heart in their stead a Post-Impressionist picture of a fat, flushed woman lying naked upon a Turkey carpet.[13]

There are indeed certain men whose art is less an opposing virtue than a compensation for some accident of health or circumstance. During the riots over the first production of the *Playboy of the Western World* Synge was confused, without clear thought, and was soon ill—indeed the strain of that week may perhaps have hastened his death—and he was, as is usual with gentle and silent men, scrupulously accurate in all his statements.[14] In his art he made, to delight his ear and his mind's eye, voluble dare-devils who 'go romancing through a romping lifetime . . . to the dawning of the Judgement Day'.[15] At other moments this man, condemned to the life of a monk by bad health, takes an amused pleasure in 'great queens . . .

making themselves matches from the start to the end'.[16] Indeed, in all his imagination he delights in fine physical life, in life when the moon pulls up the tide. The last act of *Deirdre of the Sorrows*, where his art is at its noblest, was written upon his death-bed.[17] He was not sure of any world to come, he was leaving his betrothed and his unwritten play—'Oh, what a waste of time,' he said to me; he hated to die, and in the last speeches of Deirdre and in the middle act he accepted death and dismissed life with a gracious gesture. He gave to Deirdre the emotion that seemed to him most desirable, most difficult, most fitting, and maybe saw in those delighted seven years, now dwindling from her, the fulfilment of his own life.

III

When I think of any great poetical writer of the past (a realist is an historian and obscures the cleavage by the record of his eyes) I comprehend, if I know the lineaments of his life, that the work is the man's flight from his entire horoscope, his blind struggle in the network of the stars. William Morris, a happy, busy, most irascible man, described dim colour and pensive emotion, following, beyond any man of his time, an indolent muse; while Savage Landor topped us all in calm nobility when the pen was in his hand, as in the daily violence of his passion when he had laid it down.[18] He had in his *Imaginary Conversations* reminded us, as it were, that the Venus de Milo is a stone, and yet he wrote when the copies did not come from the printer as soon as he expected: 'I have . . . . had the resolution to tear in pieces all my sketches and projects and to forswear all future undertakings. I have tried to sleep away my time and pass two-thirds of the twenty-four hours in bed. I may speak of myself as a dead man.'[19] I imagine Keats to have been born with that thirst for luxury common to many at the outsetting of the Romantic Movement, and not able, like wealthy Beckford, to slake it with beautiful and strange objects.[20] It drove him to imaginary delights; ignorant, poor, and in poor health, and not perfectly well-bred, he knew himself driven from tangible luxury; meeting Shelley, he was resentful and suspicious because he, as Leigh Hunt recalls, 'being a little too sensitive on the score of his origin, felt inclined to see in every man of birth his natural enemy'.[21]

IV

Some thirty years ago I read a prose allegory by Simeon Solomon, long out of print and unprocurable, and remember or seem to remember a sentence, 'a hollow image of fulfilled desire'.[22] All happy art seems to me that hollow image, but when its lineaments express also the poverty or the exasperation that set its maker to the work, we call it tragic art. Keats but gave us his dream of luxury; but while reading Dante we never long escape the conflict, partly because the verses are at moments a mirror of his history, and yet more because that history is so clear and simple that it has the quality of art. I am no Dante scholar, and I but read him in Shadwell or in Dante Rossetti,[23] but I am always persuaded that he celebrated the most pure lady poet ever sung and the Divine Justice, not merely because death took that lady and Florence banished her singer, but because he had to struggle in his own heart with his unjust anger and his lust; while unlike those of the great poets, who are at peace with the world and at war with themselves, he fought a double war. 'Always,' says Boccaccio, 'both in youth and maturity he found room among his virtues for lechery';[24] or as Matthew Arnold preferred to change the phrase, 'his conduct was exceeding irregular'.[25] Guido Cavalcanti, as Rossetti translates him, finds 'too much baseness' in his friend:

> And still thy speech of me, heartfelt and kind,
> Hath made me treasure up thy poetry;
> But now I dare not, for thy abject life,
> Make manifest that I approve thy rhymes.[26]

And when Dante meets Beatrice in Eden, does she not reproach him because, when she had taken her presence away, he followed in spite of warning dreams, false images, and now, to save him in his own despite, she has 'visited . . . the Portals of the Dead',[27] and chosen Virgil for his courier? While Cino da Pistoia complains that in his *Commedia* his 'lovely heresies . . . beat the right down and let the wrong go free':

> Therefore his vain decrees, wherein he lied,
> Must be like empty nutshells flung aside;
> Yet through the rash false witness set to grow,
> French and Italian vengeance on such pride
> May fall like Anthony on Cicero.[28]

Dante himself sings to Giovanni Guirino 'at the approach of death':

> The King, by whose rich grave his servants be
> With plenty beyond measure set to dwell,
> Ordains that I my bitter wrath dispel,
> And lift mine eyes to the great Consistory.[29]

V

We make out of the quarrel with others, rhetoric, but of the quarrel with ourselves, poetry. Unlike the rhetoricians, who get a confident voice from remembering the crowd they have won or may win, we sing amid our uncertainty; and, smitten even in the presence of the most high beauty by the knowledge of our solitude, our rhythm shudders. I think, too, that no fine poet, no matter how disordered his life, has ever, even in his mere life, had pleasure for his end. Johnson and Dowson, friends of my youth, were dissipated men, the one a drunkard, the other a drunkard and mad about women, and yet they had the gravity of men who had found life out and were awakening from the dream; and both, one in life and art and one in art and less in life, had a continual preoccupation with religion.[30] Nor has any poet I have read of or heard of or met with been a sentimentalist. The other self, the anti-self or the antithetical self, as one may choose to name it, comes but to those who are no longer deceived, whose passion is reality. The sentimentalists are practical men who believe in money, in position, in a marriage bell, and whose understanding of happiness is to be so busy whether at work or at play, that all is forgotten but the momentary aim. They find their pleasure in a cup that is filled from Lethe's wharf, and for the awakening, for the vision, for the revelation of reality, tradition offers us a different word—ecstasy. An old artist wrote to me of his wanderings by the quays of New York, and how he found there a woman nursing a sick child, and drew her story from her. She spoke, too, of other children who had died: a long tragic story. 'I wanted to paint her,' he wrote; 'if I denied myself any of the pain I could not believe in my own ecstasy'.[31] We must not make a false faith by hiding from our thoughts the causes of doubt, for faith is the highest achievement of the human intellect, the only gift man can make to God, and therefore it must be offered in sincerity. Neither must we create, by hiding ugliness, a false beauty as our offering to the world. He only can create the greatest imaginable beauty who has endured all imaginable pangs, for only when we have seen and foreseen what we dread shall we be rewarded by that dazzling unforeseen wing-footed wanderer.[32] We could not find him if he were not in some sense of our being and yet of our being but as water with fire, a noise with silence. He is of all things not impossible the most difficult, for that only which comes easily can never be a portion of our being, 'Soon got, soon gone', as the proverb says. I shall find the dark grow luminous, the void fruitful when I understand I have nothing, that the ringers in the tower have appointed for the hymen of the soul a passing bell.[33]

The last knowledge has often come most quickly to turbulent men, and for a season brought new turbulence. When life puts away her conjuring tricks one by one, those that deceive us longest may well be the wine-cup and the sensual kiss, for our Chambers of Commerce and of Commons have not the divine architecture of the body, nor has their frenzy been ripened by the sun. The poet, because he may not stand within the sacred house but lives amid the whirlwinds that beset its threshold, may find his pardon.

VI

I think the Christian saint and hero, instead of being merely dissatisfied, make deliberate sacrifice. I remember reading once an autobiography of a man who had made a daring journey in disguise to Russian exiles in Siberia, and his telling how, very timid as a child, he schooled himself by wandering at night through dangerous streets.[34] Saint and hero cannot be content to pass at moments to that hollow image and after become their heterogeneous selves, but would always, if they could, resemble the antithetical self. There is a shadow of type on type, for in all great poetical styles there is saint or hero, but when it is all over Dante can return to his chambering and Shakespeare to his 'pottle pot'.[35] They sought no impossible perfection but when they handled paper or parchment. So too will saint or hero, because he works in his own flesh and blood and not in paper or parchment, have more deliberate understanding of that other flesh and blood.

Some years ago I began to believe that our culture, with its doctrine of sincerity and self-realisation, made us gentle and passive, and that the Middle Ages and the Renaissance were right to found theirs upon the imitation of Christ or of some classic hero. St Francis and Caesar Borgia made themselves over-mastering, creative persons by turning from the mirror to meditation upon a mask.[36] When I had this thought I could see nothing else in life. I could not write the play I had planned, for all became allegorical, and though I tore up hundreds of pages in my endeavour to escape from allegory, my imagination became sterile for nearly five years and I only escaped at last when I had mocked in a comedy my own thought.[37] I was always thinking of the element of imitation in style and in life, and of the life beyond heroic imitation. I find in an old diary: 'I think all happiness depends on the energy to assume the mask of some other life, on a re-birth as something not one's self, something created in a moment and perpetually renewed; in playing a game like that of a child where one loses the infinite pain of self-realisation, in a grotesque or solemn painted face put on that one may hide from the terror of judgement. . . . Perhaps all the sins and energies of the world are but the world's flight from an infinite blinding beam';[38] and again at an earlier date: 'If we cannot imagine ourselves as different from what we are, and try to assume that second self, we cannot impose a discipline upon ourselves though we may accept one from others. Active virtue, as distinguished from the passive acceptance of a code, is therefore theatrical, consciously dramatic, the wearing of a mask. . . . Wordsworth, great poet though he be, is so often flat and heavy partly because his moral sense, being a discipline he had not created, a mere obedience, has no theatrical element. This increases his popularity with the better kind of journalists and politicians who have written books.'[39]

VII

I thought the hero found hanging upon some oak of Dodona[40] an ancient mask, where perhaps there lingered something of Egypt, and that he changed it to his fancy, touching it a little here and there, gilding the eyebrows or putting a gilt line where the cheek-bone comes; that when at last he looked out of its eyes he knew another's breath came and went within his breath upon the carven lips, and that his eyes were upon the instant fixed upon a visionary world: how else could the god have come to us in the forest? The good, unlearned books say that He who keeps the distant stars within His fold comes without intermediary,[41] but Plutarch's precepts[42] and the experience of old women in Soho, ministering their witchcraft to servant girls at a shilling a piece, will have it that a strange living man may win for Daemon[43] an illustrious dead man; but now I add another thought: the Daemon comes not as like to like but seeking its own opposite, for man and Daemon feed the hunger in one another's hearts.[44] Because the ghost is simple, the man heterogeneous and confused, they are but knit together when the man has found a mask whose lineaments permit the expression of all the man most lacks, and it may be dreads, and of that only.

The more insatiable in all desire, the more resolute to refuse deception or an easy victory, the more close will be the bond, the more violent and definite the antipathy.

VIII

I think that all religious men have believed that there is a hand not ours in the events of life, and that, as somebody says in *Wilhelm Meister*, accident is destiny;[45] and I think it was Heraclitus who said: the Daemon is our destiny.[46] When I think of life as a struggle with the Daemon who would ever set us to the hardest work among those not impossible, I understand why there is a deep enmity between a man and his destiny, and why a man loves nothing but his destiny. In an Anglo-Saxon poem a certain man is called, as though to call him something that summed up all heroism, 'Doom eager'.[47] I am persuaded that the Daemon delivers and deceives us, and that he wove that netting from the stars and threw the net from his shoulder. Then my imagination runs from Daemon to sweetheart, and I divine an analogy that evades the intellect. I remember that Greek antiquity has bid us look for the principal stars, that govern enemy and sweetheart alike, among those that are about to set, in the Seventh House as the astrologers say;[48] and that it may be 'sexual love', which is 'founded upon spiritual hate', is an image of the warfare of man and Daemon; and I even wonder if there may not be some secret communion, some whispering in the dark between Daemon and sweetheart. I remember how often women when in love, grow superstitious, and believe that they can bring their lovers good luck; and I remember an old Irish story of three young men who went seeking for help in battle into the house of the gods at Slieve-na-mon. 'You must first be married', some god told them, 'because a man's good or evil luck comes to him through a woman'.[49]

I sometimes fence for half an hour at the day's end, and when I close my eyes upon the pillow I see a foil playing before me, the button to my face. We meet always in the deep of the mind, whatever our work, wherever our reverie carries us, that other Will.

IX

The poet finds and makes his mask in disappointment, the hero in defeat. The desire that is satisfied is not a great desire, nor has the shoulder used all its might that an unbreakable gate has never strained. The saint alone is not deceived, neither thrusting with his shoulder nor holding out unsatisfied hands. He would climb without wandering to the antithetical self of the world, the Indian narrowing his thought in meditation or driving it away in contemplation, the Christian copying Christ, the antithetical self of the classic world. For a hero loves the world till it breaks him, and the poet till it has broken faith; but while the world was yet debonair, the saint has turned away, and because he renounced Experience itself, he will wear his mask as he finds it. The poet or the hero, no matter upon what bark they found their mask, so teeming their fancy, somewhat change its lineaments, but the saint, whose life is but a round of customary duty, needs nothing the whole world does not need, and day by day he scourges in his body the Roman and Christian conquerors: Alexander and Caesar are famished in his cell. His nativity is neither in disappointment nor in defeat, but in a temptation like that of Christ in the Wilderness, a contemplation in a single instant perpetually renewed of the Kingdoms of the World; all—because all renounced—continually present showing their empty thrones. Edwin Ellis, remembering that Christ also measured the sacrifice, imagined himself in a fine poem as meeting at Golgotha the phantom of 'Christ the Less', the Christ who might have lived a prosperous life without the knowledge of sin, and who now wanders 'companionless a weary spectre day and night'.

> I saw him go and cried to him
> 'Eli, thou hast forsaken me.'
> The nails were burning through each limb,
> He fled to find felicity.[50]

And yet is the saint spared—despite his martyr's crown and his vigil of desire—defeat, disappointed love, and the sorrow of parting.

> O Night, that did'st lead thus,
> O Night, more lovely than the dawn of light,
> O Night, that broughtest us
> Lover to lover's sight,
> Lover with loved in marriage of delight!
>
> Upon my flowery breast,
> Wholly for him, and save himself for none,
> There did I give sweet rest
> To my beloved one;
> The fanning of the cedars breathed thereon.
>
> When the first morning air
> Blew from the tower, and waved his locks aside,
> His hand, with gentle care,
> Did wound me in the side,
> And in my body all my senses died.
>
> All things I then forgot,
> My cheek on him who for my coming came;
> All ceased and I was not,

Leaving my cares and shame
Among the lilies, and forgetting them.[51]

X

It is not permitted to a man, who takes up pen or chisel, to seek originality, for passion is his only business, and he cannot but mould or sing after a new fashion because no disaster is like another. He is like those phantom lovers in the Japanese play who, compelled to wander side by side and never mingle, cry: 'We neither wake nor sleep and passing our nights in a sorrow which is in the end a vision, what are these scenes of spring to us?'[52] If when we have found a mask we fancy that it will not match our mood till we have touched with gold the cheek, we do it furtively, and only where the oaks of Dodona cast their deepest shadow, for could he see our handiwork the Daemon would fling himself out, being our enemy.

XI

Many years ago I saw, between sleeping and waking, a woman of incredible beauty shooting an arrow into the sky,[53] and from the moment when I made my first guess at her meaning I have thought much of the difference between the winding movement of nature and the straight line, which is called in Balzac's *Séraphita* the 'Mark of Man', but is better described as the mark of saint or sage.[54] I think that we who are poets and artists, not being permitted to shoot beyond the tangible, must go from desire to weariness and so to desire again, and live but for the moment when vision comes to our weariness like terrible lightning, in the humility of the brutes. I do not doubt those heaving circles, those winding arcs, whether in one man's life or in that of an age, are mathematical, and that some in the world, or beyond the world, have foreknown the event and pricked upon the calendar the life-span of a Christ, a Buddha, a Napoleon: that every movement, in feeling or in thought, prepares in the dark by its own increasing clarity and confidence its own executioner. We seek reality with the slow toil of our weakness and are smitten from the boundless and the unforeseen. Only when we are saint or sage, and renounce Experience itself, can we, in imagery of the Christian Cabbala, leave the sudden lightning and the path of the serpent and become the bowman who aims his arrow at the centre of the sun.[55]

XII

The doctors of medicine have discovered that certain dreams of the night, for I do not grant them all, are the day's unfulfilled desire, and that our terror of desires condemned by the conscience has distorted and disturbed our dreams.[56] They have only studied the breaking into dream of elements that have remained unsatisfied without purifying discouragement. We can satisfy in life a few of our passions and each passion but a little, and our characters indeed but differ because no two men bargain alike. The bargain, the compromise, is always threatened, and when it is broken we become mad or hysterical or are in some way deluded; and so when a starved or banished passion shows in a dream we, before awaking, break the logic that had given it the capacity of action and throw it into chaos again. But the passions, when we know that they cannot find fulfilment, become vision; and a vision, whether we wake or sleep, prolongs its power by rhythm and pattern, the wheel where the world is butterfly. We need no protection but it does, for if we become interested in ourselves, in our own lives, we pass out of the vision. Whether it is we or the vision that create the pattern, who set the wheel turning, it is hard to say, but certainly we have a hundred ways of keeping it near us: we select our images from past times, we turn from our own age and try to feel Chaucer nearer than the daily paper. It compels us to cover all it cannot incorporate, and would carry us when it comes in sleep to that moment when even sleep closes her eyes and dreams begin to dream; and we are taken up into a clear light and are forgetful even of our own names and actions and yet in perfect possession of ourselves murmur like Faust, 'Stay, moment', and murmur in vain.[57]

XIII

A poet, when he is growing old, will ask himself if he cannot keep his mask and his vision without new bitterness, new disappointment. Could he if he would, knowing how frail his vigour from youth up, copy Landor who lived loving and hating, ridiculous and unconquered, into extreme old age, all lost but the favour of his muses?

> The mother of the muses we are taught
> Is memory; she has left me; they remain
> And shake my shoulder urging me to sing.[58]

Surely, he may think, now that I have found vision and mask I need not suffer any longer. He will buy perhaps some small old house where like Ariosto he can dig his garden,[59] and think that in the return of birds and leaves, or moon and sun, and in the evening flight of the rooks he may discover rhythm and pattern like those in sleep and so never awake out of vision. Then he will remember Wordsworth withering into eighty years, honoured and empty-witted, and climb to some waste room and find, forgotten there by youth, some bitter crust.

February 25, 1917

ANIMA MUNDI[60]

I

I have always sought to bring my mind close to the mind of Indian and Japanese poets, old women in Connaught, mediums in Soho, lay brothers whom I imagine dreaming in some mediaeval monastery the dreams of their village, learned authors who refer all to antiquity; to immerse it in the general mind where that mind is scarce separable from what we have begun to call 'the subconscious'[61]; to liberate it from all that comes of councils and committees, from the world as it is seen from universities or from populous towns; and that I might so believe I have murmured evocations and frequented mediums, delighted in all that displayed great problems through sensuous images, or exciting phrases, accepting from abstract schools but a few technical words that are so old they seem but broken architraves fallen amid bramble and grass, and have put myself to school where all things are seen: *A Tenedo Tacitae per Amica Silentia Lunae.*[62] At one time I thought to prove my conclusions by quoting from diaries where I have recorded certain strange events the moment they happened, but now I have changed my mind—I will but say like the Arab boy that became Vizier: 'O brother, I have taken stock in the desert sand and of the sayings of antiquity.'[63]

II

There is a letter of Goethe's, though I cannot remember where, that explains evocation, though he was but thinking of literature. He described some friend who had complained of literary sterility as too intelligent. One must allow the images to form with all their associations before one criticises. 'If one is critical too soon', he wrote, 'they will not form at all'.[64] If you suspend the critical faculty, I have discovered, either as the result of training, or, if you have the gift, by passing into a slight trance, images pass rapidly before you. If you can suspend also desire, and let them form at their own will, your absorption becomes more complete and they are more clear in colour, more precise in articulation, and you and they begin to move in the midst of what seems a powerful light. But the images pass before you linked by certain associations, and indeed in the first instance you have called them up by their association with traditional forms and sounds.[65] You have discovered how, if you can but suspend will and intellect, to bring up from the 'subconscious' anything you already possess a fragment of. Those who follow the old rule keep their bodies still and their minds awake and clear, dreading especially any confusion between the images of the mind and the objects of sense; they seek to become, as it were, polished mirrors.

I had no natural gift for this clear quiet, as I soon discovered, for my mind is abnormally restless; and I was seldom delighted by that sudden luminous definition of form which makes one understand almost in spite of oneself that one is not merely imagining. I therefore invented a new process. I had found that after evocation my sleep became at moments full of light and form, all that I had failed to find while awake; and I elaborated a symbolism of natural objects that I might give myself dreams during sleep, or rather visions, for they had none of the confusion of dreams, by laying upon my pillow or beside my bed certain flowers or leaves. Even to-day, after twenty years, the exaltations and the messages that came to me from bits of hawthorn or some other plant seem of all moments of my life the happiest and the wisest. After a time, perhaps because the novelty wearing off the symbol lost its power, or because my work at the Irish Theatre became too exciting, my sleep lost its responsiveness. I had fellow-scholars, and now it was I and now they who made some discovery. Before the mind's eye whether in sleep or waking, came images that one was to discover presently in some book one had never read, and after looking in vain for explanation to the current theory of forgotten personal memory, I came to believe in a great memory passing on from generation to generation. But that was not enough, for these images showed intention and choice. They had a relation to what one knew and yet were an extension of one's knowledge. If no mind was there, why should I suddenly come upon salt and antimony, upon the liquefaction of the gold, as they were understood by the alchemists,[66] or upon some detail of Cabbalistic symbolism verified at last by a learned scholar from his never-published manuscripts, and who can have put together so ingeniously, working by some law of association and yet with clear intention and personal application, certain mythological images. They had shown themselves to several minds, a fragment at a time, and had only shown their meaning when the puzzle picture had been put together. The thought was again and again before me that this study had created a contact or mingling with minds who had followed a like study in some other age, and that these minds still saw and thought and chose. Our daily thought was certainly but the line of foam at the shallow edge of a vast luminous sea; Henry More's *Anima Mundi*[67], Wordsworth's 'immortal sea which brought us hither . . . and near whose edge the children sport'[68], and in that sea there were some who swam or sailed, explorers who perhaps knew all its shores.

III

I had always to compel myself to fix the imagination upon the minds behind the personifications, and yet the personifications were themselves living and vivid. The minds that swayed these seemingly fluid images had doubtless form, and those images themselves seemed, as it were, mirrored in a living substance whose form is but change of form. From tradition and perception, one thought of one's own life as symbolised by earth, the place of heterogeneous things, the images as mirrored in water and the images themselves one could divine but as air; and beyond it all there was, I felt confident, certain aims and governing loves, the fire that makes all simple. Yet the images themselves were fourfold, and one judged their meaning in part from the predominance of one out of the four elements, or that of the fifth element, the veil hiding another four, a bird born out of the fire.[69]

IV

We longed to know something—even if it were but the family and Christian names—of those minds that we could divine, and that yet remained always as it seemed impersonal. The sense of contact came perhaps but two or three times with clearness and certainty, but it left among all to whom it came some trace, a sudden silence, as it were, in the midst of thought or perhaps at moments of crisis a faint voice. Were our masters right when they declared so solidly that we should be content to know these presences that seemed friendly and near but as 'the phantom' in Coleridge's poem, and to think of them perhaps, as having, as St Thomas says,[70] entered upon the eternal possession of themselves in one single moment?

All look and likeness caught from earth,
All accident of kin and birth,
Had passed away. There was no trace
Of ought on that illumined face,
Upraised beneath the rifted stone,
But of one spirit all her own;
She, she herself and only she,
Shone through her body visibly.[71]

V

One night I heard a voice that said: 'The love of God for every human soul is infinite, for every human soul is unique; no other can satisfy the same need in God'.[72] Our masters had not denied that personality outlives the body or even that its rougher shape may cling to us a while after death, but only that we should seek it in those who are dead. Yet when I went among the country people, I found that they sought and found the old fragilities, infirmities, physiognomies that living stirred affection. The Spiddal knowledgeable man, who had his knowledge from his sister's ghost, noticed every hallowe'en, when he met her at the end of the garden, that her hair was greyer.[73] Had she perhaps to exhaust her allotted years in the neighbourhood of her home, having died before her time? Because no authority seemed greater than that of this knowledge running backward to the beginning of the world, I began that study of spiritism so despised by Stanislas de Guaïta, the one eloquent learned scholar who has written of magic in our generation.[74]

VI

I know much that I could never have known had I not learnt to consider in the after life what, there as here, is rough and disjointed; nor have I found that the mediums in Connaught and Soho have anything I cannot find some light on in Henry More, who was called during his life the holiest man now walking upon the earth.[75]

All souls have a vehicle or body, and when one has said that, with More and the Platonists[76] one has escaped from the abstract schools who seek always the power of some church or institution, and found oneself with great poetry, and superstition which is but popular poetry, in a pleasant dangerous world. Beauty is indeed but bodily life in some ideal condition. The vehicle of the human soul is what used to be called the animal spirits, and Henry More quotes from Hippocrates this sentence: 'The mind of man is . . . not nourished from meats and drinks from the belly, but by a clear luminous substance that redounds by separation from the blood'.[77] These animal spirits fill up all parts of the body and make up the body of air, as certain writers of the seventeenth century have called it.[78] The soul has a plastic power, and can after death, or during life, should the vehicle leave the body for a while, mould it to any shape it will by an act of imagination, though the more unlike to the habitual that shape is, the greater the effort.[79] To living and dead alike, the purity and abundance of the animal spirits are a chief power. The soul can mould from these an apparition clothed as if in life, and make it visible by showing it to our mind's eye, or by building into its substance certain particles drawn from the body of a medium till it is as visible and tangible as any other object. To help that building the ancients offered sheaves of corn, fragrant gum, and the odour of fruit and flowers, and the blood of victims. The half-materialised vehicle slowly exudes from the skin in dull luminous drops or condenses from a luminous cloud, the light fading as weight and density increase. The witch, going beyond the medium, offered to the slowly animating phantom certain drops of her blood. The vehicle once separate from the living man or woman may be moulded by the souls of others as readily as by its own soul, and even it seems by the souls of the living.[80] It becomes a part for a while of that stream of images which I have compared to reflections upon water. But how does it follow that souls who never have handled the modelling tool or the brush, make perfect images? Those materialisations who imprint their powerful faces upon paraffin wax, leave there sculpture that would have taken a good artist, making and imagining, many hours.[81] How did it follow that an ignorant woman could, as Henry More believed, project her vehicle in so good a likeness of a hare, that horse and hound and huntsman followed with the bugle blowing?[82] Is not the problem the same as of those finely articulated scenes and patterns that come out of the dark, seemingly completed in the winking of an eye, as we are lying half asleep, and of all those elaborate images that drift in moments of inspiration or evocation before the mind's eye? Our animal spirits or vehicles are but as it were a condensation of the vehicle of *Anima Mundi*, and give substance to its images in the faint materialisation of our common thought, or more grossly when a ghost is our visitor. It should be no great feat, once those images have dipped into our vehicle, to take their portraits in the photographic camera.[83] Henry More will have it that a hen scared by a hawk when the cock is treading, hatches out a hawk-headed chicken (I am no stickler for the fact), because before the soul of the unborn bird could give the shape 'the deeply impassioned fancy of the mother' called from the general cistern of form a competing image. 'The soul of the world', he runs on, 'interposes and insinuates into all generations of things while the matter is fluid and yielding, which would induce a man to believe that she may not stand idle in the transformation of the vehicle of the daemons, but assist the fancies and desires, and so help to clothe them and to utter them according to their own pleasures; or it may be sometimes against their wills as the unwieldiness of the mother's fancy forces upon her a monstrous birth'.[84] Though images appear to flow and drift, it may be that we but change in our relation to them, now losing, now finding with the shifting of our minds; and certainly Henry More speaks by the book, in claiming that those images may be hard to the right touch as 'pillars of crystal' and as solidly coloured as our own to the right eyes.[85] Shelley, a good Platonist, seems in his earliest work to set this general soul in the place of God,[86] an opinion, one may find from More's friend Cudworth[87] now affirmed, now combated by classic authority; but More would steady us with a definition. The general soul as apart from its vehicle is 'a substance incorporeal but without sense and animadversion pervading the whole matter of the universe and exercising a plastic power therein, according to the sundry predispositions and occasions, in the parts it works upon, raising such phenomena in the world, by directing the parts of the matter and their motion as cannot be resolved into mere mechanical powers'.[88] I must assume that 'sense and animadversion', perception and direction, are always faculties of individual soul, and that, as Blake said, 'God only acts or is in existing beings or men'.[89]

VII

The old theological conception of the individual soul as bodiless or abstract led to what Henry More calls 'contradictory debate' as to how many angels 'could dance booted and spurred upon the point of a needle',[90] and made it possible for rationalist physiology to persuade us that our thought has no corporeal existence but in the molecules of the brain. Shelley was of opinion that the 'thoughts which are called real or external objects' differed but in regularity of occurrence from 'hallucinations, dreams and ideas of madmen', and noticed that he had dreamed, therefore lessening the difference, 'three several times between intervals of two or more years the same precise dream'.[91] If all our mental images no less than apparitions (and I see no reason to distinguish) are forms existing in the general vehicle of *Anima Mundi*, and mirrored in our particular vehicle, many crooked things are made straight. I am persuaded that a logical process, or a series of related images, has body and period, and I think of

Anima Mundi as a great pool or garden where it moves through its allotted growth like a great water plant or fragrantly branches in the air.[92] Indeed as Spenser's Garden of Adonis:

> There is the first seminary
> Of all things that are born to live and die
> According to their kynds.[93]

The soul by changes of 'vital congruity', More says,[94] draws to it a certain thought, and this thought draws by its association the sequence of many thoughts, endowing them with a life in the vehicle meted out according to the intensity of the first perception. A seed is set growing, and this growth may go on apart from the power, apart even from the knowledge of the soul. If I wish to 'transfer' a thought I may think, let us say, of Cinderella's slipper, and my subject may see an old woman coming out of a chimney; or going to sleep I may wish to wake at seven o'clock and, though I never think of it again, I shall wake upon the instant. The thought has completed itself, certain acts of logic, turns, and knots in the stem have been accomplished out of sight and out of reach as it were. We are always starting these parasitic vegetables and letting them coil beyond our knowledge, and may become, like that lady in Balzac who, after a life of sanctity, plans upon her deathbed to fly with her renounced lover.[95] After death a dream, a desire she had perhaps ceased to believe in, perhaps ceased almost to remember, must have recurred again and again with its anguish and its happiness. We can only refuse to start the wandering sequence or, if start it does, hold it in the intellectual light where time gallops, and so keep it from slipping down into the sluggish vehicle. The toil of the living is to free themselves from an endless sequence of objects, and that of the dead to free themselves from an endless sequence of thoughts. One sequence begets another, and these have power because of all those things we do, not for their own sake but for an imagined good.

VIII

Spiritism, whether of folk-lore or of the séance room, the visions of Swedenborg, and the speculation of the Platonists and Japanese plays, will have it that we may see at certain roads and in certain houses old murders acted over again, and in certain fields dead huntsmen riding with horse and hound, or ancient armies fighting above bones or ashes.[96] We carry to *Anima Mundi* our memory, and that memory is for a time our external world; and all passionate moments recur again and again, for passion desires its own recurrence more than any event, and whatever there is of corresponding complacency or remorse is our beginning of judgement; nor do we remember only the events of life, for thoughts bred of longing and of fear, all those parasitic vegetables that have slipped through our fingers, come again like a rope's end to smite us upon the face; and as Cornelius Agrippa writes: 'We may dream ourselves to be consumed in flame and persecuted by daemons,'[97] and certain spirits have complained that they would be hard put to it to arouse those who died, believing they could not awake till a trumpet shrilled. A ghost in a Japanese play is set afire by a fantastic scruple, and though a Buddhist priest explains that the fire would go out of itself if the ghost but ceased to believe in it, it cannot cease to believe.[98] Cornelius Agrippa called such dreaming souls hobgoblins, and when Hamlet refused the bare bodkin because of what dreams may come, it was from no mere literary fancy.[99] The soul can indeed, it appears, change these objects built about us by the memory, as it may change its shape; but the greater the change, the greater the effort and the sooner the return to the habitual images.[100] Doubtless in either case the effort is often beyond its power. Years ago I was present when a woman consulted Madame Blavatsky for a friend who saw her newly-dead husband nightly as a decaying corpse and smelt the odour of the grave. 'When he was dying', said Madame Blavatsky, 'he thought the grave the end, and now that he is dead cannot throw off that imagination'.[101] A Brahmin once told an actress friend of mine that he disliked acting, because if a man died playing Hamlet, he would be Hamlet in eternity.[102] Yet after a time the soul partly frees itself and becomes 'the shape changer' of the legends, and can cast, like the mediaeval magician, what illusions it would. There is an Irish country-man in one of Lady Gregory's books who had eaten with a stranger on the road, and some while later vomited, to discover he had but eaten chopped-up grass.[103] One thinks, too, of the spirits that show themselves in the images of wild creatures.

IX

The dead, as the passionate necessity wears out, come into a measure of freedom and may turn the impulse of events, started while living, in some new direction, but they cannot originate except through the living. Then gradually they perceive, although they are still but living in their memories, harmonies, symbols, and patterns, as though all were being refashioned by an artist, and they are moved by emotions, sweet for no imagined good but in themselves, like those of children dancing in a ring; and I do not doubt that they make love in that union which Swedenborg has said is of the whole body and seems from far off an incandescence.[104] Hitherto shade has communicated with shade in moments of common memory that recur like the figures of a dance in terror or in joy, but now they run together like to like, and their Covens and Fleets have rhythm and pattern. This running together and running of all to a centre and yet without loss of identity, has been prepared for by their exploration of their moral life, of its beneficiaries and its victims, and even of all its untrodden paths, and all their thoughts have moulded the vehicle and become event and circumstance.

X

There are two realities, the terrestrial and the condition of fire.[105] All power is from the terrestrial condition, for there all opposites meet and there only is the extreme of choice possible, full freedom. And there the heterogeneous is, and evil, for evil is the strain one upon another of opposites; but in the condition of fire is all music and all rest. Between is the condition of air where images have but a borrowed life, that of memory or that reflected upon them when they symbolise colours and intensities of fire: the place of shades who are 'in the whirl of those who are fading', and who cry like those amorous shades in the Japanese play:

That we may acquire power
Even in our faint substance,
We will show forth even now,
And though it be but in a dream,
Our form of repentance.[106]

After so many rhythmic beats the soul must cease to desire its images, and can, as it were, close its eyes.

When all sequence comes to an end, time comes to an end, and the soul puts on the rhythmic or spiritual body or luminous body and contemplates all the events of its memory and every possible impulse in an eternal possession of itself in one single moment.[107] That condition is alone animate, all the rest is phantasy, and from thence come all the passions, and some have held, the very heat of the body.

> Time drops in decay,
> Like a candle burnt out,
> And the mountains and woods
> Have their day, have their day;
> What one in the rout
> Of the fire-born moods
> Has fallen away?[108]

XI

The soul cannot have much knowledge till it has shaken off the habit of time and of place, but till that hour it must fix its attention upon what is near, thinking of objects one after another as we run the eye or the finger over them. Its intellectual power cannot but increase and alter as its perceptions grow simultaneous. Yet even now we seem at moments to escape from time in what we call prevision, and from place when we see distant things in a dream and in concurrent dreams. A couple of years ago, while in meditation, my head seemed surrounded by a conventional sun's rays, and when I went to bed I had a long dream of a woman with her hair on fire. I awoke and lit a candle, and discovered presently from the odour that in doing so I had set my own hair on fire.[109] I dreamed very lately that I was writing a story, and at the same time I dreamed that I was one of the characters in that story and seeking to touch the heart of some girl in defiance of the author's intention; and concurrently with all that, I was as another self trying to strike with the button of a foil a great china jar. The obscurity of the prophetic books of William Blake,[110] which were composed in a state of vision, comes almost wholly from these concurrent dreams. Everybody has some story or some experience of the sudden knowledge in sleep or waking of some event, a misfortune for the most part happening to some friend far off.

XII

The dead living in their memories are, I am persuaded, the source of all that we call instinct, and it is their love and their desire, all unknowing, that make us drive beyond our reason, or in defiance of our interest it may be; and it is the dream martens that, all unknowing, are master-masons to the living martens building about church windows their elaborate nests;[111] and in their turn, the phantoms are stung to a keener delight from a concord between their luminous pure vehicle and our strong senses. It were to reproach the power or the beneficence of God, to believe those children of Alexander, who died wretchedly,[112] could not throw an urnful to the heap, nor Caesarion[113] murdered in childhood, whom Cleopatra bore to Caesar, nor the brief-lived younger Pericles Aspasia bore[114]—being so nobly born.

XIII

Because even the most wise dead can but arrange their memories as we arrange pieces upon a chess-board and obey remembered words alone, he who would turn magician is forbidden by the Zoroastrian oracle to change 'barbarous words' of invocation.[115] Communication with *Anima Mundi* is through the association of thoughts or images or objects; and the famous dead and those of whom but a faint memory lingers, can still—and it is for no other end, that all unknowing, we value posthumous fame—tread the corridor and take the empty chair. A glove and a name can call their bearer; the shadows come to our elbow amid their old undisturbed habitations, and 'materialisation' itself is easier, it may be, among walls, or by rocks and trees, that bring before their memory some moment of emotion while they had still animate bodies.

Certainly the mother returns from the grave, and with arms that may be visible and solid, for a hurried moment, can comfort a neglected child or set the cradle rocking; and in all ages men have known and affirmed that when the soul is troubled, those that are a shade and a song

live there,
And live like winds of light on dark or stormy air.[116]

XIV

Awhile they live again those passionate moments, not knowing they are dead, and then they know and may awake or half awake to be our visitors. How is their dream changed as Time drops away and their senses multiply? Does their stature alter, do their eyes grow more brilliant? Certainly the dreams stay the longer, the greater their passion when alive: Helen may still open her chamber door to Paris or watch him from the wall, and know she is dreaming but because nights and days are poignant or the stars unreckonably bright. Surely of the passionate dead we can but cry in words Ben Jonson meant for none but Shakespeare: 'So rammed' are they 'with life they can but grow in life with being'.[117]

XV

The inflowing from their mirrored life, who themselves receive it from the Condition of Fire, falls upon the winding path called the Path of the Serpent,[118] and that inflowing coming alike to men and to animals is called natural. There is another inflow which is not natural but intellectual, and is from the fire; and it descends through souls who pass for a lengthy or a brief period out of the mirror life, as we in sleep out of the bodily life, and though it may fall upon a sleeping serpent, it falls principally upon straight paths. In so far as a man is like all other men, the inflow finds him upon the winding path, and in so far as he is a saint or sage, upon the straight path.

XVI

The Daemon, by using his mediatorial shades, brings man again and again to the place of choice, heightening temptation that the choice may be as final as possible, imposing his own lucidity upon events, leading his victim to whatever among works not impossible is the most difficult. He suffers with man as some firm-souled man suffers with the woman he but loves the better because she is extravagant and fickle. His descending power is neither the winding nor the straight line but zigzag, illuminating the passive and active properties, the tree's two sorts of fruit: it is the sudden lightning,[119] for all his acts of power are instantaneous. We perceive in a pulsation of the artery,[120] and after slowly decline.

XVII

Each Daemon is drawn to whatever man or, if its nature is more general, to whatever nation it most differs from, and it shapes into its own image the antithetical dream of man or nation. The Jews had already shown by the precious metals, by the ostentatious wealth of Solomon's temple, the passion that has made them the money-lenders of the modern world. If they had not been rapacious, lustful, narrow, and persecuting beyond the people of their time, the incarnation had been impossible; but it was an intellectual impulse from the Condition of Fire that shaped their antithetical self into that of the classic world. So always it is an impulse from some Daemon that gives to our vague, unsatisfied desire, beauty, a meaning, and a form all can accept.

XVIII

Only in rapid and subtle thought, or in faint accents heard in the quiet of the mind, can the thought of the spirit come to us but little changed; for a mind, that grasps objects simultaneously according to the degree of its liberation, does not think the same thought with the mind that sees objects one after another. The purpose of most religious teaching, of the insistence upon the submission to God's will above all, is to make certain of the passivity of the vehicle where it is most pure and most tenuous. When we are passive where the vehicle is coarse, we become mediumistic, and the spirits who mould themselves in that coarse vehicle can only rarely and with great difficulty speak their own thoughts and keep their own memory. They are subject to a kind of drunkenness and are stupefied, old writers said, as if with honey, and readily mistake our memory for their own, and believe themselves whom and what we please. We bewilder and overmaster them, for once they are among the perceptions of successive objects, our reason, being but an instrument created and sharpened by those objects, is stronger than their intellect, and they can but repeat with brief glimpses from another state, our knowledge and our words.[121]

XIX

A friend once dreamed that she saw many dragons climbing upon the steep side of a cliff and continually falling.[122] Henry More thought that those who, after centuries of life, failed to find the rhythmic body and to pass into the Condition of Fire, were born again.[123] Edmund Spenser, who was among More's masters, affirmed that nativity without giving it a cause:

After that they againe retourned beene,
They in that garden planted be agayne,
And grow afresh, as they had never seene
Fleshy corruption, nor mortal payne.
Some thousand years so doen they ther remayne,
And then of him are clad with other hew,
Or sent into the chaungeful world agayne,
Till thither they retourn where first they grew:
So like a wheele, around they roam from old to new.[124]

XX

But certainly it is always to the Condition of Fire, where emotion is not brought to any sudden stop, where there is neither wall nor gate, that we would rise; and the mask plucked from the oak-tree is but my imagination of rhythmic body. We may pray to that last condition by any name so long as we do not pray to it as a thing or a thought, and most prayers call it man or woman or child:

For mercy has a human heart,
Pity a human face.[125]

Within ourselves Reason and Will, who are the man and woman, hold out towards a hidden altar, a laughing or crying child.

XXI

When I remember that Shelley calls our minds 'mirrors of the fire for which all thirst',[126] I cannot but ask the question all have asked, 'What or who has cracked the mirror?' I begin to study the only self that I can know, myself, and to wind the thread upon the perne again.

At certain moments, always unforeseen, I become happy, most commonly when at hazard I have opened some book of verse. Sometimes it is my own verse when, instead of discovering new technical flaws, I read with all the excitement of the first writing. Perhaps I am sitting in some crowded restaurant, the open book beside me, or closed, my excitement having over-brimmed the page. I look at the strangers near as if I had known them all my life, and it seems strange that I cannot speak to them: everything fills me with affection, I have no longer any fears or any needs; I do not even remember that this happy mood must come to an end.[127] It seems as if the vehicle had suddenly grown pure and far extended and so luminous that the images from *Anima Mundi*, embodied there and drunk with that sweetness, would, like a country drunkard who has thrown a wisp into his own thatch, burn up time.

It may be an hour before the mood passes, but latterly I seem to understand that I enter upon it the moment I cease to hate. I think the common condition of our life is hatred—I know that this is so with me—irritation with public or private events or persons. There is no great matter in forgetfulness of servants, or the delays of tradesmen, but how forgive the ill-breeding of Carlyle, or the rhetoric of Swinburne,[128] or that woman who murmurs over the dinner-table the opinion of her daily paper? And only a week ago last Sunday, I hated the spaniel who disturbed a partridge on her nest, a trout who took my bait and yet broke away unhooked. The books say that our happiness comes from the opposite of hate, but I am not certain, for we may love unhappily. And plainly, when I have closed a book too stirred to go on reading, and in those brief intense visions of sleep, I have something about me that, though it makes me love, is more like innocence. I am in the place where the Daemon is, but I do not think he is with me until I begin to make a new personality, selecting among those images, seeking always to satisfy a hunger grown out of conceit with daily diet;

and yet as I write the words 'I select', I am full of uncertainty not knowing when I am the finger, when the clay. Once, twenty years ago, I seemed to awake from sleep to find my body rigid, and to hear a strange voice speaking these words through my lips as through lips of stone: 'We make an image of him who sleeps, and it is not him who sleeps, and we call it Emmanuel.'[129]

XXII

As I go up and down my stair and pass the gilded Moorish wedding-chest where I keep my 'barbarous words', I wonder will I take to them once more, for I am baffled by those voices that still speak as to Odysseus but as the bats;[130] or now that I shall in a little be growing old, to some kind of simple piety like that of an old woman.

May 9, 1917

EPILOGUE

My dear 'Maurice'—I was often in France before you were born or when you were but a little child.[131] When I went for the first or second time Mallarmé had just written: 'All our age is full of the trembling of the veil of the temple.'[132] One met everywhere young men of letters who talked of magic. A distinguished English man of letters asked me to call with him on Stanislas de Guaïta because he did not dare go alone to that mysterious house.[133] I met from time to time with the German poet Dauthendey, a grave Swede whom I only discovered after years to have been Strindberg, then looking for the philosopher's stone in a lodging near the Luxembourg;[134] and one day in the chambers of Stuart Merrill the poet, I spoke with a young Arabic scholar who displayed a large, roughly-made gold ring which had grown to the shape of his finger. Its gold had no hardening alloy, he said, because it was made by his master, a Jewish Rabbi, of alchemical gold.[135] My critical mind—was it friend or enemy?—mocked, and yet I was delighted. Paris was as legendary as Connaught. This new pride, that of the adept, was added to the pride of the artist. Villiers de l'Isle Adam, the haughtiest of men, had but lately died. I had read his *Axël* slowly and laboriously as one reads a sacred book—my French was very bad—and had applauded it upon the stage. As I could not follow the spoken words, I was not bored even when Axël and the Commander discussed philosophy for a half-hour instead of beginning their duel. If I felt impatient it was only that they delayed the coming of the adept Janus, for I hoped to recognise the moment when Axël cries: 'I know that lamp, it was burning before Solomon'; or that other when he cries: 'As for living, our servants will do that for us.'[136]

The movement of letters had been haughty even before Magic had touched it. Rimbaud had sung: 'Am I an old maid that I should fear the embrace of death?'[137] And everywhere in Paris and in London young men boasted of the garret, and claimed to have no need of what the crowd values.

Last summer you, who were at the age I was when first I heard of Mallarmé and of Verlaine,[138] spoke much of the French poets young men and women read to-day. Claudel I already somewhat knew, but you read to me for the first time from Jammes a dialogue between a poet and a bird, that made us cry, and a whole volume of Péguy's *Mystère de la Charité de Jeanne d'Arc.*[139] Nothing remained the same but the preoccupation with religion, for these poets submitted everything to the Pope, and all, even Claudel, a proud oratorical man, affirmed that they saw the world with the eyes of vine-dressers and charcoal-burners.[140] It was no longer the soul, self-moving and self-teaching—the magical soul—but Mother France and Mother Church.

Have not my thoughts run through a like round, though I have not found my tradition in the Catholic Church, which was not the church of my childhood, but where the tradition is, as I believe, more universal and more ancient?

W.B.Y.
May 11, 1917

If I were Four-and-Twenty (1919)

I

When I was asked to become a director of *The Irish Statesman*[1] I agreed, because for many years I have been hoping for some Irish review, able and willing to submit our life and thought to a constant, precise, unexaggerated, passionate criticism. No organ of the popular party could do that; it would have too many people to please; but *The Irish Statesman* has done it from the first; and now I have begun to examine my own hope, to see if we can construct as well as criticize. I dislike responsibility so much that I shall have little to say to board meetings, and, besides, my thoughts are wild. I shall be content to ask myself what I would do if I were four-and-twenty, and not four-and-fifty, indolent and discouraged, with but one settled habit—that of writing verse.

I would set out once again to found a little school of Irish thought, but this time I would not confine myself to literature and to drama. One day when I was twenty-three or twenty-four this sentence seemed to form in my head, without my willing it, much as sentences form when we are half-asleep: 'Hammer your thoughts into unity.'[2] For days I could think of nothing else, and for years I tested all I did by that sentence. I had three interests: interest in a form of literature, in a form of philosophy, and a belief in nationality. None of these seemed to have anything to do with the other, but gradually my love of literature and my belief in nationality came together. Then for years I said to myself that these two had nothing to do with my form of philosophy, but that I had only to be sincere and to keep from constraining one by the other and they would become one interest. Now all three are, I think, one, or rather all three are a discrete expression of a single conviction. I think that each has behind it my whole character and has gained thereby a certain newness—for is not every man's character peculiar to himself? —and that I have become a cultivated man. Certainly a cultivated man is not a man who can read difficult books or pass well at the Intermediate,[3] but a man who brings to general converse, and business, character that informs varied intellect.

It is just the same with a nation—it is only a cultivated nation when it has related its main interests one to another. We are a religious nation. The priest of the ancient chapel of St Michel, on Mont-Saint-Michel, where Montaigne's old woman offered a candle to the Dragon and a candle to the Saint, said to a certain friend of mine, 'What faith you Irish have!' on finding her early in the morning praying for the governing body of the National University.[4] Yet is there any nation that has a more irreligious intellect, or that keeps its political thought so distinct from its religious thought? It is, indeed, this distinction that makes our priests and our politicians distrust one another.

II

I spent two summers of the war on the coast of Normandy, and a friend read out to me *Le Mystère de la charité de Jeanne d'Arc*, by Péguy, and certain poems of Jammes.[5] Claudel I had already read myself.[6] A school of literature, which owed something perhaps to Huysmans' exposition of the symbolism of Chartres Cathedral,[7] had begun to make Christianity French, and in Péguy's heroic patriotism had prepared young France for the struggle with Germany. These writers are full of history and of the scenery of France. The Eucharist in a continually repeated symbol makes them remember the wheat-fields and the vineyards of France; and, when Joan of Arc is told that the Apostles fled from Christ before the crucifixion, she, to that moment the docile shepherd girl, cries: 'The men of France would not have betrayed Him, the men of Lorraine would not have betrayed Him.' It is in vain that the nun Gervaise tells her that these were the greatest of all saints and apostles, and that her words are wicked: she repeats, with half-sullen obstinacy, 'The men of France would not have betrayed Him, the men of Lorraine would not have betrayed Him.'[8] Péguy—a peasant born of peasants—can, for hundreds of pages, speak as the thirteenth century spoke, and use no thought that is of our time, yet it was amidst Socialist and Dreyfusard controversy that he discovered his belief, and it was so much a passion, so little an opinion, that somebody told me in Paris that he was always reminding himself to go to church and get married, or to go to church and get a child baptized, and always forgetting it.[9]

Now, if I were four-and-twenty, I think I would write or persuade others to write such accounts, as our young writers might read, of these men in whom an intellectual patriotism is not distinct from religion; and I would raise such a lively agitation that the Abbey or the Drama League would find an audience for Claudel's *L'Annonce faite à Marie* or his *L'Otage*.[10] I do not think Claudel as pure a talent as Péguy, and do not like him with my whole heart, for he is prepense, deliberate—I am sure he never forgot his religious duties—oratorical, discursive, loving resounding words, vast sentiments, situations half melodrama and half religious ritual. He impresses me a little against my will, but then his intellect is powerful and it searches deep. Perhaps we would learn more at this moment of our history from Claudel than from Péguy. I would also, I think, read a paper to some little circle of poets on Jammes, and I would tell them that when he introduces a volume of little lyrics with a preface, repudiating beforehand any heretical conclusions that may be deduced from it, and submits all to the Pope, he is certainly poking fun.[11] I think, indeed, that the school—in its fine moments—has been compelled to speak all that it shares with religion and patriotism by a purely literary development. There has been a development in various forms of literature—in French '*unanisme*'[12] for instance—towards the expression, through an intellectual difference, of an emotional agreement with some historical or local group or crowd: towards the celebration, for instance, not of oneself but of one's neighbours, of the countryside or the street where one lives. Many have grown weary of the individualism of the nineteenth century, which now seems less able in creation than in criticism. Intellectual agreements, propagandas, dogmas, we have always had, but emotional agreements, which are so much more lasting and put no constraint upon the soul, we have long lacked.

But if I were four-and-twenty, and without rheumatism, I should not, I think, be content with getting up performances of French plays and with reading papers. I think I would go—though certainly I am no Catholic and never shall be one—upon both of our great pilgrimages, to Croagh Patrick and to Lough Derg.[13] Our churches have been unroofed or stripped; the stained glass of St Canice, once famous throughout Europe, was destroyed three centuries ago, and Christ Church looks as clean and unhistorical as a Methodist chapel, its sculptured tombs and tablets broken up or heaped one on t'other in the crypt; no congregation has climbed to the Rock of Cashel since the stout Church of Ireland bishop took the lead roof from the Gothic church to save his legs:[14] but Europe has nothing older than our pilgrimages. In many little lyrics I would claim that stony mountain for all Christian and pagan faith in Ireland, believing, in the exultation of my youth, that in three generations I should have made it as vivid in the memory of all imaginative men among us, as the sacred mountain of Japan is in that of the collectors of prints; and I would, being but four-and-twenty and a lover of lost causes, memorialize the bishops to open once again that Lough Derg cave of vision once beset by an evil spirit in the form of a long-legged bird with no feathers on its wings.[15]

A few years ago Bernard Shaw explained, what he called 'the vulgarity and the savagery' of his writing, by saying that he had sat once upon a time every Sunday morning in an Irish Protestant church.[16] But mountain and lough have not grown raw and common; pillage and ravage could not abate their beauty; and the impulse that gathers these great companies in every year has outlasted armorial stone.

Then, too, I would associate that doctrine of purgatory, which Christianity has shared with Neo-Platonism, with the countryman's belief in the nearness of his dead 'working out their penance' in rath[17] or at garden end: and I would find in the psychical research of our day detail to make the association convincing to intellect and emotion. I would try to create a type of man whose most moving religious experience, though it came to him in some distant country, and though his intellect were wholly personal, would bring with it imagery to connect it with an Irish multitude now and in past time.

III

We need also a logical unity. When I was a boy William Morris came to Dublin to preach us into Socialism. After an appeal from the chairman, on the ground of national hospitality, an unwilling audience heard him out, and after gave itself to mockery, till somebody quenched the light.[18] Now our young men sing 'The Red Flag',[19] for any bloody catastrophe seems welcome that promises an Irish Republic. They condemned Morris's doctrine without examination. Now for the most part they applaud it without examination; but that will change, for the execution of Connolly[20] has given him many readers. I have already noticed Karl Marx's *Kapital* in the same window with Mitchel's *Jail Journal* and with *Speeches from the Dock*; and, being an indolent man of four-and-fifty, with no settled habit but the writing of verse, I did not remind the bookseller that he was a regular church-goer and suggest that he display also Soloviev's *Justification of the Good, Distributive Justice*, and some of those little works edited by Father Plater of Oxford.[21]

I admit that it is a spirited action to applaud the economics of Lenin—in which I notice much that I applauded as a boy when Morris was the speaker—when we do it to affront our national enemy; but it does not help one to express the character of the nation through varied intellect. No man is less like an Englishman because he takes his opinion from the *Daily Herald* instead of the *Morning Post*;[22] and it is likely that we shall take our opinion from one or the other till we have swung the hammer. 'Hammer your thoughts into unity'—but for my disabilities I think I would, in exposition of that sentence, persuade some of the Sinn Féin[23] branches, which find it hard to fill up their evenings, to study the writers I have named and perhaps, if some local library would collect enough translations, I might set some exceptional young man, some writer perhaps of Abbey plays, to what once changed all my thought: the reading of the whole *Comédie humaine*.[24]

IV

When I was a child I heard the names of men whose lives had been changed by Balzac, perhaps because he cleared them of Utopian vapours, then very prevalent; and I can remember someone saying to an old lion-painter:[25] 'If you had to choose, would you give up Shakespeare or Balzac?' and his answering, 'I would keep the yellow backs.' Balzac is the only modern mind which has made a synthesis comparable to that of Dante, and, though certain of his books are on the Index, his whole purpose was to expound the doctrine of his Church as it is displayed, not in decrees and manuals, but in the institutions of Christendom. Yet Nietzsche might have taken, and perhaps did take, his conception of the superman in history from his *Catherine de Medici*, and he has explained and proved, even more thoroughly than Darwin, the doctrine of the survival of the fittest, though as a creator of social, not of biological, species.[26] Only, I think, when one has mastered his whole vast scheme can one understand clearly that his social order is the creation of two struggles, that of family with family, that of individual with individual, and that our politics depend upon which of the two struggles has most affected our imagination. If it has been most affected by the individual struggle we insist upon equality of opportunity, 'the career open to talent',[27] and consider rank and wealth fortuitous and unjust; and if it is most affected by the struggles of families, we insist upon all that preserves what that struggle has earned, upon social privilege, upon the rights of property.

Throughout the *Comédie humaine* one finds—and in this Balzac was perhaps conscious of contradicting the cloudy Utopian genius of Hugo[28]—that the more noble and stable qualities, those that are spread through the personality, and not isolated in a faculty, are the results of victory in the family struggle, while those qualities of logic and of will, all those qualities of toil rather than of power, belong most to the individual struggle. For a long time after closing the last novel one finds it hard to admire deeply any individual strength that has not family strength behind it. He has shown us so many men of talent, to whom we have denied our sympathy because of their lack of breeding, and has refused to show us even Napoleon apart from his Corsican stock, its strong roots running backward to the Middle Ages.[29]

For a while, at any rate, we must believe—and it is the doctrine of his Church—that we discover what is most lasting in ourselves in labouring for old men, for children, for the unborn, for those whom we have not even chosen. His beautiful ladies and their lovers, his old statesmen, and some occasional artist to whom he has given his heart, children of a double strength, all those who seek the perfection of some quality, love or unpersuadable justice, often have seemed to me like those great blossoming plants that rise through the gloom of some Cingalese[30] forest to open their blossoms above the tops of the trees. He, too, so does he love all bitter things, cannot leave undescribed that gloom, that struggle, which had made them their own legislators, from the founder or renovator of their house, from some obscure toiler or notorious speculator, and often as not the beginning of it all has been some stroke of lawless rapacity. Perhaps he considers that the will is by its very nature an antagonist of the social order; if we can say 'he considers' of one in whom creation itself wrote and thought. I forget who has written of him: 'If I meet him at midday he is a very ignorant man, but at midnight, when he sits beside a cup of black coffee, he knows everything in the world.'[31]

Here and there one meets among his two thousand characters certain men, who do not interest him, and whom he is perhaps too impatient to understand, the '*Fourieristes*'[32] and insurrectionists who would abate or abolish the struggle. I remember some artist of his who has made an absurd allegorical statue of regenerate mankind and who expects to be the most famous sculptor in the world, after the revolution; a figure of diluted emotion and a chiropodist noted for skill and delicacy of touch, who while cutting the corns of some famous man speaks of the coming abolition of all privilege—'genius too is a privilege we shall abolish.'[33]

In the world that Balzac has created it is the intensity of the struggle—an intensity beyond that of real life—which makes his common soldiers, his valets, his commercial travellers, all men of genius: and I doubt if law had for him any purpose but that of preserving the wine when the grapes had been trodden, and seeing to it that the treaders know their treads. 'The passionate minded', says an Indian saying, 'love bitter food.'[34]

V

When I close my eyes and pronounce the word 'Christianity' and await its unconscious suggestion, I do not see Christ crucified, or the good Shepherd from the catacombs, but a father and mother and their children, a picture by Leonardo da Vinci most often.[35] While Europe had still Christianity for its chief preoccupation men painted little but that scene. Yet what Christian economists said of the family seemed to me conventional and sentimental till I had met with Balzac. Now I understand them. Soloviev writes that every industrious man has a right to certain necessities and decencies of life; and I think he would not object to Aristotle's proposed limitation of fortunes, however much he might object to us, who are jealous and still lack philosophy, fixing the limit.[36] But that the community should do more for a man than secure him these necessities and decencies he denounces for devil's work. The desire of the father to see his child better off than himself, socially, financially, morally, according to his nature, is, he claims, the main cause of all social progress, of all improvements in civilization. Yet all the while his attention is too much fixed upon the direct conscious effects—he sees the world as child, father, grandfather, and all virtues as derivable from our veneration for the past we inherit from, or our compassion for the future that inherits from us—and not enough upon its indirect unconscious effects, upon the creation of social species each bound together by its emotional quality.

Yesterday I came upon a little wayside well planted about with roses, a sight I had not seen before in Ireland, and it brought to mind all that planting of flowers, all that cleanness and neatness that the countryman's ownership of his farm has brought with it in Ireland, and also the curious doctrine of Soloviev, that no family has the full condition of perfection that cannot share in what he calls 'the spiritualization of the soil'[37]—a doctrine derivable, perhaps, from the truth that all emotional unities find their definition through the image, unlike those of the intellect, which are defined in the logical process. However, Soloviev is a dry ascetic, half-man, and may see nothing beyond a round of the more obvious virtues approved by his Greek Church. I understand by 'soil' all the matter in which the soul works, the walls of our houses, the serving up of our meals, and the chairs and tables of our rooms, and the instincts of our bodies; and by 'family' all institutions, classes, orders, nations that arise out of the family and are held together, not by a logical process, but by historical association, and possess a personality for whose lack men are 'sheep without a shepherd when the snow shuts out the sun'.[38]

Men, who did not share their privileges, have died for and lived for all these, and judged them little. Certainly no simple age has denied to monk or nun their leisure, nor thought that the monk's lamp and the nun's prayer, though from the first came truth and from the second denial of self, were not recompense enough, nor has any accomplished age begrudged the expensive leisure of women, knowing that they gave back more than they received in giving courtesy.

VI

If, as these writers affirm, the family is the unit of social life, and the origin of civilization which but exists to preserve it, and almost the sole cause of progress, it seems more natural than it did before that its ecstatic moment, the sexual choice of man and woman, should be the greater part of all poetry. A single wrong choice may destroy a family, dissipating its tradition or its biological force, and the great sculptors, painters, and poets are there that instinct may find its lamp. When a young man imagines the woman of his hope, shaped for all the uses of life, mother and mistress and yet fitted to carry a bow in the wilderness, how little of it all is mere instinct, how much has come from chisel and brush. Educationists and statesmen, servants of the logical process, do their worst, but they are not the matchmakers who bring together the fathers and mothers of the generations, nor shall the type they plan survive.

VII

When we compare any modern writer, except Balzac, with the writers of an older world, with, let us say, Dante, Villon, Shakespeare, Cervantes, we are in the presence of something slight and shadowy.[39] It is natural for a man who believes that man finds his happiness here on earth, or not at all, to make light of all obstacles to that happiness and to deny altogether the insuperable obstacles seen by religious philosophy. The strength and weight of Shakespeare, of Villon, of Dante, even of Cervantes, come from their preoccupation with evil. In Shelley, in Ruskin, in Wordsworth, who for all his formal belief was, as Blake saw, a descendant of Rousseau,[40] there is a constant resolution to dwell upon good only; and from this comes their lack of the sense of character, which is defined always by its defects or its incapacity, and their lack of the dramatic sense; for them human nature has lost its antagonist. William Morris was and is my chief of men; but how would that strong, rich nature have grasped and held the world had he not denied all that forbade the millennium he longed for? He had to believe that men needed no spur of necessity and that men, not merely those who, in the language of the Platonists, had attained to freedom and so become self-moving, but all men, would do all necessary work with no compulsion but a little argument. He was perhaps himself half aware of his lack, for in *News from Nowhere* he makes a crotchety old man complain that the novelists are not as powerful as before Socialism was established.[41]

Bernard Shaw, compelled to believe, not as Morris did, that men will slaughter cattle and skin dead horses for a pastime, but that men can be found to force them to it, and yet neither bully, nor accept bribes, nor put the wrong man to the work, has invented a drama where ideas and not men are the combatants, and so dislikes whatever is harsh or incomprehensible that he complains of Shakespeare's 'ghosts and murders' and of Ibsen's 'morbid terror of death'.[42] It has been the lot of both men, the one a great many-sided man, and the other a logician without rancour, and both lovers of the best, to delight the Garden City mind.[43] To the Garden City mind the slightness and shadowiness may well seem that of the clouds of dawn; but how can it seem to us in Ireland who have faith—whether heathen or Christian—who have believed from our cradle in original sin, and that man lives under a curse, and so must earn his bread with the sweat of his face, but what comes from blotting out one half of life?

When I went every Sunday to the little lecture hall at the side of William Morris's house, Lionel Johnson said to me, his tongue unloosed by slight intoxication, 'I wish those who deny the eternity of punishment could realize their unspeakable vulgarity.'[44] I remember laughing when he said it, but for years I turned it over in my mind and it always made me uneasy. I do not think I believe in the eternity of punishment, and yet I am still drawn to a man that does—Swedenborg for instance[45]—and rather repelled by those who have never thought it possible. I remember, too, old John O'Leary's contempt for a philanthropist, a contempt he could never explain.[46] Is it that these men, who believe what they wish, can never be quite sincere and so live in a world of half belief? But no man believes willingly in evil or in suffering, above all in eternal suffering. How much of the strength and weight of Dante and of Balzac comes from unwilling belief, from the lack of it how much of the rhetoric and vagueness of all Shelley that does not arise from personal feeling?

VIII

Logic is loose again, as once in Calvin and Knox, or in the hysterical rhetoric of Savonarola,[47] or in Christianity itself in its first raw centuries, and because it must always draw its deductions from what every dolt can understand, the wild beast cannot but destroy mysterious life. We do not the less need, because it is an economic and not a theological process, those Christian writers whose roots are in permanent human nature. They, too, have their solution of the social question. To Balzac indeed it was but personal charity, the village providence of the eighteenth century, but Soloviev and the economists are more scientific, and have fostered a movement which, instead of attacking property, distributes it as widely as possible, and this movement has been in practice co-operation, and there Ireland is not Russia's pupil, but her teacher. Their design is always to guard and strengthen family ambition; content to be the midwife of Nature and not a juggling mechanist who would substitute an automaton for her living child.

A family is part of history and a part of the soil, and it seems to me a natural thing that co-operative Denmark should have invented the phrase: 'to understand the peasant by the saga and the saga by the peasant.'[48] Socialism is as international as Capital or as Calvinism, and I have never met a Socialist who did not believe he could carry his oratory from London to Paris and from Paris to Jericho and there find himself at home.

If we could but unite our economics and our nationalism with our religion, that, too, would become philosophic—and the religion that does not become philosophic, as religion is in the East, will die out of modern Europe—and we, our three great interests made but one, would at last be face to face with the great riddle, and might, it may be, hit the answer. Yet no man can hit the answer till certain discoveries have had time to change the direction of speculation and research. To take but one straw from a haystack, I have known a dream to pass through a whole house—I can never blind myself to the implications of that fact—

but what I do not know is whether it so passed because all were under one roof, or because all shared certain general interests, or because all had various degrees of affection for one another. Now all these writers of economics overrate the importance of work. Every man has a profound instinct that idleness is the true reward of work, even if it only come at the end of life, or if generations have to die before it comes at all, and literature and art are often little but its preparation that it may be an intensity. I have no doubt that the idleness, let us say, of a man devoted to his collection of Chinese paintings affects the mind even of men who do physical labour without spoken or written word, and all the more because physical labour increases mental pursuits.

I have studied the influence as it were in the laboratory, and I cannot exclude this fact, to which the world may not be converted for fifty years, from my judgment of the social system and its reformers; but I do not know if this influence would be strengthened, if labourer and idler used churches, or furniture, or listened to or read stories, and wore clothes which had all, as let us say in Minoan or Egyptian civilization, a common character. Albert de Rochas suspected something of the kind,[49] and I do not know how large a portion of our day's thought—though I suspect the greater portion—has its direction or its intensity from such influence.

Did some perception of this create among primitive people the conviction that ordinary men had no immortality, but obtained it through a magical bond with some chief or king? Perhaps it may be possible in a few years to apportion the values of idleness by a science that traces the connections of thought and by a religion that judges the result. With Christianity came the realization that a man must surrender his particular will to an implacable will, not his, though within his, and perhaps we are restless because we approach a realization that our general will must surrender itself to another will within it, interpreted by certain men, at once economists, patriots, and inquisitors. As all realization is through opposites, men coming to believe the subjective opposite of what they do and think, we may be about to accept the most implacable authority the world has known.

Do I desire it or dread it, loving as I do the gambling table of Nature where many are ruined but none is judged, and where all is fortuitous, unforeseen?

IX

When Dr Hyde delivered in 1894 his lecture on the necessity of 'the de-anglicization of Ireland', to a society that was a youthful indiscretion of my own, I heard an enthusiastic hearer say: 'This lecture begins a new epoch in Ireland.'[50] It did that, and if I were not four-and-fifty, with no settled habit but the writing of verse, rheumatic, indolent, discouraged, and about to move to the Far East, I would begin another epoch by recommending to the Nation a new doctrine, that of unity of being.[51]

W. B. Yeats

Swedenborg, Mediums, and the Desolate Places

(w. 1914), in *Visions and Beliefs in the West of Ireland,* by Lady Gregory (1920)

I

Some fifteen years ago I was in bad health and could not work, and Lady Gregory brought me from cottage to cottage while she began to collect the stories in this book, and presently when I was at work again she went on with her collection alone till it grew to be, so far as I know, the most considerable book of its kind. Except that I had heard some story of 'The Battle of the Friends' at Aran and had divined that it might be the legendary common accompaniment of death, she was not guided by any theory of mine, but recorded what came, writing it out at each day's end and in the country dialect. It was at this time mainly she got the knowledge of words that makes her little comedies of country life so beautiful and so amusing. As that ancient system of belief unfolded before us, with unforeseen probabilities and plausibilities, it was as though we had begun to live in a dream, and one day Lady Gregory said to me when we had passed an old man in the wood: 'That old man may know the secret of the ages.'[1]

I had noticed many analogies in modern spiritism and began a more careful comparison, going a good deal to séances for the first time and reading all writers of any reputation I could find in English or French. I found much that was moving, when I had climbed to the top story of some house in Soho or Holloway, and, having paid my shilling, awaited, among servant girls, the wisdom of some fat old medium.[2] That is an absorbing drama, though if my readers begin to seek it they will spoil it, for its gravity and simplicity depends on all, or all but all, believing that their dead are near.

I did not go there for evidence of the kind the Society for Psychical Research would value, any more than I would seek it in Galway or in Aran. I was comparing one form of belief with another, and like Paracelsus, who claimed to have collected his knowledge from midwife and hangman, I was discovering a philosophy.[3] Certain things had happened to me when alone in my own room which had convinced me that there are spiritual intelligences which can warn us and advise us, and, as Anatole France has said, if one believes that the Devil can walk the streets of Lisbon, it is not difficult to believe that he can reach his arm over the river and light Don Juan's cigarette.[4] And yet I do not think I have been easily convinced, for I know we make a false beauty by a denial of ugliness and that if we deny the causes of doubt we make a false faith, and that we must excite the whole being into activity if we would offer to God what is, it may be, the one thing germane to the matter, a consenting of all our faculties. Not but that I doubt at times, with the animal doubt of the Middle Ages that I have found even in pious country-women when they have seen some life come to an end like the stopping of a clock, or that all the perceptions of the soul, or the weightiest intellectual deductions, are not at whiles but a feather in the daily show.

I pieced together stray thoughts written out after questioning the familiar of a trance medium or automatic writer, by Allan Kardec,[5] or by some American, or by myself, or arranged the fragments into some pattern, till I believed myself the discoverer of a vast generalization. I lived in excitement, amused to make Holloway interpret Aran, and constantly comparing my discoveries with what I have learned of mediaeval tradition among fellow students, with the reveries of a Neoplatonist, of a seventeenth-century Platonist, of Paracelsus or a Japanese poet. Then one day I opened *The Spiritual Diary* of Swedenborg, which I had not taken down for twenty years, and found all there, even certain thoughts I had not set on paper because they had seemed fantastic from the lack of some traditional foundation. It was strange I should have forgotten so completely a writer I had read with some care before the fascination of Blake and Boehme had led me away.[6]

II

It was indeed Swedenborg who affirmed for the modern world, as against the abstract reasoning of the learned, the doctrine and practice of the desolate places, of shepherds and of midwives, and discovered a world of spirits where there was a scenery like that of earth, human forms, grotesque or beautiful, senses that knew pleasure and pain, marriage and war, all that could be painted upon canvas, or put into stories to make one's hair stand up. He had mastered the science of his time, he had written innumerable scientific works in Latin, had been the first to formulate the nebular hypothesis and wrote a cold abstract style, the result it may be of preoccupation with stones and metals, for he had been assessor of mines to the Swedish Government, and of continual composition in a dead language.[7]

In his fifty-eighth year he was sitting in an inn in London, where he had gone about the publication of a book, when a spirit appeared before him who was, he believed, Christ himself, and told him that henceforth he could commune with spirits and angels. From that moment he was a mysterious man describing distant events as if they were before his eyes, and knowing dead men's secrets, if we are to accept testimony that seemed convincing to Immanuel Kant. The sailors who carried him upon his many voyages spoke of the charming of the waves and of favouring winds that brought them sooner than ever before to their journey's end, and an ambassador described how a queen, he himself looking on, fainted when Swedenborg whispered in her ear some secret known only to her and to her dead brother.[8] And all this happened to a man without egotism, without drama, without a sense of the picturesque, and who wrote a dry language, lacking fire and emotion, and who to William Blake seemed but an arranger and putter away of the old Church, a Samson shorn by the churches, an author not of a book, but of an index.[9] He considered heaven and hell and God, the angels, the whole destiny of man, as if he were sitting before a large table in a Government office putting little pieces of mineral ore into small square boxes for an assistant to pack away in drawers.

All angels were once men, he says, and it is therefore men who have entered into what he calls the Celestial State and become angels, who attend us immediately after death, and communicate to us their thoughts, not by speaking, but by looking us in the face as they sit beside the head of our body. When they find their thoughts are communicated they know the time has come to separate the spiritual from the physical body. If a man begins to feel that he can endure them no longer, as he doubtless will, for in their presence he can think and feel but sees nothing, lesser angels who belong to truth more than to love take their place and he is in the light again, but in all likelihood these angels also will be too high and he will slip from state to state until he finds himself after a few days 'with those who are in accord with his life in the world; with them he finds his life, and, wonderful to relate, he then leads a life similar to that he led in the world'. This first state of shifting and readjustment seems to correspond with a state of sleep more modern seers discover to follow upon death. It is characteristic of his whole religious system, the slow drifting of like to like. Then follows a period which may last but a short time or many years, while the soul lives a life so like that of the world that it may not even believe that it has died, for 'when what is spiritual touches and sees what is spiritual the effect is the same as when what is natural touches what is natural'.[10] It is the other world of the early races, of those whose dead are in the rath or the faery hill,[11] of all who see no place of reward and punishment but a continuance of this life, with cattle and sheep, markets and war. He describes what he has seen, and only partly explains it, for, unlike science which is founded upon past experience, his work, by the very nature of his gift, looks for the clearing away of obscurities to unrecorded experience. He is revealing something and that which is revealed, so long as it remains modest and simple, has the same right with the child in the cradle to put off to the future the testimony of its worth. This earth-resembling life is the creation of the image-making power of the mind, plucked naked from the body, and mainly of the images in the memory. All our work has gone with us, the books we have written can be opened and read or put away for later use, even though their print and paper have been sold to the buttermen; and reading his description one notices, a discovery one had thought peculiar to the last generation, that the 'most minute particulars which enter the memory remain there and are never obliterated', and there as here we do not always know all that is in our memory, but at need angelic spirits who act upon us there as here, widening and deepening the consciousness at will, can draw forth all the past, and make us live again all our transgressions and see our victims 'as if they were present, together with the place, words, and motives'; and that suddenly, 'as when a scene bursts upon the sight' and yet continues 'for hours together',[12] and like the transgressions, all the pleasure and pain of sensible life awaken again and again, all our passionate events rush up about us and not as seeming imagination, for imagination is now the world. And yet another impulse comes and goes, flitting through all, a preparation for the spiritual abyss, for out of the celestial world, immediately beyond the world of form, fall certain seeds as it were that exfoliate through us into forms, elaborate scenes, buildings, alterations of form that are related by 'correspondence' or 'signature' to celestial incomprehensible realities.[13] Meanwhile those who have loved or fought see one another in the unfolding of a dream, believing it may be that they wound one another or kill one another, severing arms or hands, or that their lips are joined in a kiss, and the countryman has need but of Swedenborg's keen ears and eagle sight to hear a noise of swords in the empty valley, or to meet the old master hunting with all his hounds upon the stroke of midnight among the moonlit fields. But gradually we begin to change and possess only those memories we have related to our emotion or our thought; all that was accidental or habitual dies away and we begin an active present life, for apart from that calling up of the past we are not punished or rewarded for our actions when in the world but only for what we do when out of it. Up till now we have disguised our real selves and those who have lived well for fear or favour have walked with holy men and women, and the wise man and the dunce have been associated in common learning, but now the ruling love has begun to remake circumstance and our body.

Swedenborg had spoken with shades that had been learned Latinists, or notable Hebrew scholars, and found, because they had done everything from the memory and nothing from thought and emotion, they had become but simple men. We have already met our friends, but if we were to meet them now for the first time we should not recognize them, for all has been kneaded up anew, arrayed in order and made one piece. 'Every man has many loves, but still they all have reference to his ruling love and make one with it or together compose it',[14] and our surrender to that love, as to supreme good, is no new thought, for Villiers de l'Isle Adam quotes Thomas Aquinas as having said, 'Eternity is the possession of one's self, as in a single moment.'[15] During the fusing and rending man flits, as it were, from one flock of the dead to another, seeking always those who are like himself, for as he puts off disguise he becomes unable to endure what is unrelated to his love, even becoming insane among things that are too fine for him.

So heaven and hell are built always anew and in hell or heaven all do what they please and all are surrounded by scenes and circumstances which are the expression of their natures and the creation of their thought. Swedenborg because he belongs to an eighteenth century not yet touched by the romantic revival feels horror amid rocky uninhabited places, and so believes that the evil are in such places while the good are amid smooth grass and garden walks and the clear sunlight of Claude Lorraine.[16] He describes all in matter-of-fact words, his meeting with this or that dead man, and the place where he found him, and yet we are not to understand him literally, for space as we know it has come to an end and a difference of state has begun to take its place, and wherever a spirit's thought is, the spirit cannot help but be. Nor should we think of spirit as divided from spirit, as men are from each other, for they share each other's thoughts and life, and those whom he has called celestial angels, while themselves mediums to those above, commune with men and lower spirits, through orders of mediatorial spirits, not by a conveyance of messages, but as though a hand were thrust within a hundred gloves,[17] one glove outside another, and so there is a continual influx from God to man. It flows to us through the evil angels as through the good, for the dark fire is the perversion of God's life and the evil angels have their office in the equilibrium that is our freedom, in the building of that fabulous bridge made out of the edge of a sword.[18]

To the eyes of those that are in the high heaven 'all things laugh, sport, and live',[19] and not merely because they are beautiful things but because they arouse by a minute correspondence of form and emotion the heart's activity, and being founded, as it were, in this changing heart, all things continually change and shimmer. The garments of all befit minutely their affections, those that have most wisdom and most love being the most nobly garmented, in ascending order from shimmering white, through garments of many colours and garments that are like flame, to the angels of the highest heaven that are naked.

In the west of Ireland the country people say that after death every man grows upward or downward to the likeness of thirty years, perhaps because at that age Christ began his ministry, and stays always in that likeness; and these angels move always towards 'the springtime of their life' and grow more and more beautiful, 'the more thousand years they live', and women who have died infirm with age, and yet lived in faith and charity, and true love towards husband or lover, come 'after a succession of years' to an adolescence that was not in Helen's Mirror, 'for to grow old in heaven is to grow young'.[20]

There went on about Swedenborg an intermittent 'Battle of the Friends' and on certain occasions had not the good fought upon his side, the evil troop, by some carriage accident or the like, would have caused his death, for all associations of good spirits have an answering mob, whose members grow more hateful to look on through the centuries. 'Their faces in general are horrible, and empty of life like corpses, those of some are black, of some fiery like torches, of some hideous with pimples, boils, and ulcers; with many no face appears, but in its place a something hairy or bony, and in some one can but see the teeth.' And yet among themselves they are seeming men and but show their right appearance when the light of heaven, which of all things they most dread, beats upon them; and seem to live in a malignant gaiety, and they burn always in a fire that is God's love and wisdom, changed into their own hunger and misbelief.[21]

III

In Lady Gregory's stories there is a man who heard the newly dropped lambs of faery crying in November,[22] and much evidence to show a topsy-turvydom of seasons, our spring being their autumn, our winter their summer, and Mary Battle, my Uncle George Pollexfen's old servant, was accustomed to say that no dream had a true meaning after the rise of the sap; and Lady Gregory learned somewhere on Slieve Ochte that if one told one's dreams to the trees fasting the trees would wither.[23] Swedenborg saw some like opposition of the worlds, for what hides the spirits from our sight and touch, as he explains, is that their light and heat are darkness and cold to us and our light and heat darkness and cold to them, but they can see the world through our eyes and so make our light their light. He seems however to warn us against a movement whose philosophy he announced or created, when he tells us to seek no conscious intercourse with any that fall short of the celestial rank. At ordinary times they do not see us or know that we are near, but when we speak to them we are in danger of their deceits. 'They have a passion for inventing', and do not always know that they invent.[24] 'It has been shown me many times that the spirits speaking with me did not know but that they were the men and women I was thinking of; neither did other spirits know the contrary. Thus yesterday and today one known of me in life was personated. The personation was so like him in all respects, so far as known to me, that nothing could be more like. For there are genera and species of spirits of similar faculty (? as the dead whom we seek), and when like things are called up in the memory of men and so are represented to them they think they are the same persons. At other times they enter into the fantasy of other spirits and think that they are them,[25] and sometimes they will even believe themselves to be the Holy Spirit', and as they identify themselves with a man's affection or enthusiasm they may drive him to ruin, and even an angel will join himself so completely to a man that he scarcely knows 'that he does not know of himself what the man knows', and when they speak with a man they can but speak in that man's mother tongue, and this they can do without taking thought, for 'it is almost as when a man is speaking and thinks nothing about his words'. Yet when they leave the man 'they are in their own angelical or spiritual language and know nothing of the language of the man'. They are not even permitted to talk to a man from their own memory for did they do so the man would not know 'but that the things he would then think were his when yet they would belong to the spirit',[26] and it is these sudden memories occurring sometimes by accident, and without God's permission that gave the Greeks the idea they had lived before. They have bodies as plastic as their minds that flow so readily into the mould of ours and he remembers having seen the face of a spirit change continuously and yet keep always a certain generic likeness. It had but run through the features of the individual ghosts of the fleet it belonged to, of those bound into the one mediatorial communion.

He speaks too, again and again, of seeing palaces and mountain ranges and all manner of scenery built up in a moment, and even believes in imponderable troops of magicians that build the like out of some deceit or in malicious sport.[27]

IV

There is in Swedenborg's manner of expression a seeming superficiality. We follow an easy narrative, sometimes incredulous, but always, as we think, understanding, for his moral conceptions are simple, his technical terms continually repeated, and for the most part we need but turn for his 'correspondence', his symbolism as we would say, to the index of his *Arcana Coelestia.*[28] Presently, however, we discover that he treads upon this surface by an achievement of power almost as full of astonishment as if he should walk upon water charmed to stillness by some halcyon; while his disciple and antagonist Blake is like a man swimming in a tumbling sea, surface giving way to surface and deep showing under broken deep. A later mystic has said of Swedenborg that he but half felt, half saw, half tasted the kingdom of heaven, and his abstraction, his dryness, his habit of seeing but one element in everything, his lack of moral speculation have made him the founder of a church,[29] while William Blake, who grows always more exciting with every year of life, grows also more obscure. An impulse towards what is definite and sensuous, and an indifference towards the abstract and the general, are the lineaments, as I understand the world, of all that comes not from the learned, but out of common antiquity, out of the 'folk' as we say, and in certain languages, Irish for instance—and these languages are all poetry—it is not possible to speak an abstract thought. This impulse went out of Swedenborg when he turned from vision. It was inseparable from this primitive faculty, but was not a part of his daily bread, whereas Blake carried it to a passion and made it the foundation of his thought. Blake was put into a rage by all painting where detail is generalized away, and complained that Englishmen after the French Revolution became as like one another as the dots and lozenges in the mechanical engraving of his time, and he hated histories that gave us reasoning and deduction in place of the events, and St Paul's Cathedral because it came from a mathematical mind, and told Crabb Robinson that he preferred to any others a happy, thoughtless person. Unlike Swedenborg he believed that the antiquities of all peoples were as sacred as those of the Jews, and so rejecting authority and claiming that the same law for the lion and the ox was oppression, he could believe 'all that lives is holy', and say that a man if he but cultivated the power of vision would see the truth in a way suited 'to his imaginative energy', and with only so much resemblance to the way it showed in for other men, as there is between different human forms.[30] Born when Swedenborg was a new excitement, growing up with a Swedenborgian brother, who annoyed him 'with bread and cheese advice', and having, it may be, for nearest friend the Swedenborgian Flaxman with whom he would presently quarrel,[31] he answered the just translated *Heaven and Hell* with the paradoxical violence of *The Marriage of Heaven and Hell.* Swedenborg was but 'the linen clothes folded up' or the angel sitting by the tomb, after Christ, the human imagination, had arisen.[32] His own memory being full of images from painting and from poetry he discovered more profound 'correspondences', yet always in his boys and girls walking or dancing on smooth grass and in golden light, as in pastoral scenes cut upon wood or copper by his disciples Palmer and Calvert one notices the peaceful Swedenborgian heaven.[33] We come there, however, by no obedience but by the energy that 'is eternal delight', for 'the treasures of heaven are not negations of passion but realities of intellect from which the passions emanate uncurbed in their eternal glory'. He would have us talk no more 'of the good man and the bad', but only of 'the wise man and the foolish', and he cries, 'Go put off holiness and put on intellect.'[34]

Higher than all souls that seem to theology to have found a final state, above good and evil, neither accused, not yet accusing, live those, who have come to freedom, their senses sharpened by eternity, piping or dancing or 'like the gay fishes on the wave when the moon sucks up the dew'.[35] Merlin, who in the verses of Chrétien de Troyes was laid in the one tomb with dead lovers, is very near and the saints are far away.[36] Believing too that crucifixion and resurrection were the soul's diary and no mere historical events, which had been transacted in vain should a man come again from the womb and forget his salvation,[37] he could cleave to the heroic doctrine the angel in the crystal made Sir Thomas Kelly renounce[38] and have a 'vague memory' of having been 'with Christ and Socrates'; and stirred as deeply by hill and tree as by human beauty, he saw all Merlin's people, spirits 'of vegetable nature' and faeries whom we 'call accident and chance'.[39] He made possible a religious life to those who had seen the painters and poets of the romantic movement succeed to theology, but the shepherd and the midwife had they known him would have celebrated him in stories, and turned away from his thought, understanding that he was upon an errand to their masters. Like Swedenborg he believed that heaven came from 'an improvement of sensual enjoyment', for sight and hearing, taste and touch grow with the angelic years, but unlike him he could convey to others 'enlarged and numerous senses', and the mass of men know instinctively they are safer with an abstract and an index.[40]

V

It was, I believe, the Frenchman Allan Kardec[41] and an American shoemaker's clerk called Jackson Davis, who first adapted to the séance room the philosophy of Swedenborg. I find Davis whose style is vague, voluble, and pretentious, almost unreadable, and yet his books have gone to many editions[42] and are full of stories that had been charming or exciting had he lived in Connaught or any place else, where the general mass of the people has an imaginative tongue. His mother was learned in country superstition, and had called in a knowledgeable man when she believed a neighbour had bewitched a cow, but it was not till his fifteenth year that he discovered his faculty, when his native village, Poughkeepsie, was visited by a travelling mesmerist. He was fascinated by the new marvel, and mesmerized by a neighbour he became clairvoyant, describing the diseases of those present and reading watches he could not see with his eyes. One night the neighbour failed to awake him completely from the trance and he stumbled out into the street and went to his bed ill and stupefied. In the middle of the night he heard a voice telling him to get up and dress himself and follow. He wandered for miles, now wondering at what seemed the unusual brightness of the stars and once passing a visionary shepherd and his flock of sheep, and then again stumbling in cold and darkness. He crossed the frozen Hudson and became unconscious. He awoke in a mountain valley to see once more the visionary shepherd and his flock, and a very little, handsome, old man who showed him a scroll and told him to write his name upon it.

A little later he passed, as he believed, from this mesmeric condition and found that he was among the Catskill Mountains and more than forty miles from home. Having crossed the Hudson again he felt the trance coming upon him and began to run. He ran, as he thought, many miles and as he ran became unconscious. When he awoke he was sitting upon a gravestone in a graveyard surrounded by a wood and a high wall. Many of the gravestones were old and broken. After much conversation with two stately phantoms, he went stumbling on his way. Presently he found himself at home again. It was evening and the mesmerist was questioning him as to where he had been since they lost him the night before. He was very hungry and had a vague memory of his return, of country roads passing before his eyes in brief moments of wakefulness. He now seemed to know that one of the phantoms with whom he had spoken in the graveyard was the physician Galen, and the other, Swedenborg.[43]

From that hour the two phantoms came to him again and again, the one advising him in the diagnosis of disease, and the other in philosophy. He quoted a passage from Swedenborg, and it seemed impossible that any copy of the newly translated book that contained it could have come into his hands, for a Swedenborgian minister in New York traced every copy which had reached America.[44]

Swedenborg himself had gone upon more than one somnambulistic journey, and they occur a number of times in Lady Gregory's stories, one woman saying that when she was among the faeries she was often glad to eat the food from the pigs' troughs.[45]

Once in childhood, Davis, while hurrying home through a wood, heard footsteps behind him and began to run, but the footsteps, though they did not seem to come more quickly and were still the regular pace of a man walking, came nearer. Presently he saw an old, white-haired man beside him who said: 'You cannot run away from life,' and asked him where he was going. 'I'm going home,' he said, and the phantom answered, 'I also am going home,' and then vanished. Twice in later childhood, and a third time when he had grown to be a young man, he was overtaken by the same phantom and the same words were spoken, but the last time he asked why it had vanished so suddenly. It said that it had not, but that he had supposed that 'changes of state' in himself were 'appearance and disappearance'. It then touched him with one finger upon the side of his head, and the place where he was touched remained ever after without feeling, like those places always searched for at the witches' trials. One remembers 'the touch' and 'the stroke' in the Irish stories.[46]

VI

Allan Kardec, whose books are much more readable than those of Davis, had himself no mediumistic gifts.[47] He gathered the opinions, as he believed, of spirits speaking through a great number of automatists and trance speakers, and all the essential thought of Swedenborg remains, but like Davis, these spirits do not believe in an eternal Hell, and like Blake they describe unhuman races, powers of the elements, and declare that the soul is no creature of the womb, having lived many lives upon the earth. The sorrow of death, they tell us again and again, is not so bitter as the sorrow of birth, and had our ears the subtlety we could listen amid the joy of lovers and the pleasure that comes with sleep to the wailing of the spirit betrayed into a cradle. Who was it that wrote: 'O Pythagoras, so good, so wise, so eloquent, upon my last voyage, I taught thee, a soft lad, to splice a rope'?[48]

This belief, common among continental spiritists, is denied by those of England and America, and if one question the voices at a séance they take sides according to the medium's nationality. I have even heard what professed to be the shade of an old English naval officer denying it with a fine phrase: 'I did not leave my oars crossed; I left them side by side.'[49]

VII

Much as a hashish eater will discover in the folds of a curtain a figure beautifully drawn and full of delicate detail all built up out of shadows that show to other eyes, or later to his own, a different form or none, Swedenborg discovered in the Bible the personal symbolism of his vision. If the Bible was upon his side, as it seemed, he had no need of other evidence, but had he lived when modern criticism had lessened its authority, even had he been compelled to say that the primitive beliefs of all peoples were as sacred, he could but have run to his own gift for evidence. He might even have held of some importance his powers of discovering the personal secrets of the dead and set up as medium. Yet it is more likely he had refused, for the medium has his gift from no heightening of all the emotions and intellectual faculties till they seem as it were to take fire, but commonly because they are altogether or in part extinguished while another mind controls his body. He is greatly subject to trance and awakes to remember nothing, whereas the mystic and the saint plead unbroken consciousness. Indeed the author of *Sidonia the Sorceress*, a really learned authority, considered this lack of memory a certain sign of possession by the devil,[50] though this is too absolute. Only yesterday, while walking in a field, I made up a good sentence with an emotion of triumph, and half a minute after could not even remember what it was about, and several minutes had gone by before I as suddenly found it. For the most part, though not always, it is this unconscious condition of mediumship, a dangerous condition it may be, that seems to make possible 'physical phenomena' and that over-shadowing of the memory by some spirit memory, which Swedenborg thought an accident and unlawful.[51]

In describing and explaining this mediumship and so making intelligible the stories of Aran and Galway I shall say very seldom, 'it is said,' or 'Mr So-and-So reports,' or 'it is claimed by the best authors'. I shall write as if what I describe were everywhere established, everywhere accepted, and I had only to remind my reader of what he already knows. Even if incredulous he will give me his fancy for certain minutes, for at the worst I can show him a gorgon or chimera that has never lacked gazers, alleging nothing (and I do not write out of a little knowledge) that is not among the sober beliefs of many men, or obvious inference from those beliefs, and if he wants more—well, he will find it in the best authors.[52]

VIII

All spirits for some time after death, and the 'earth-bound', as they are called, the larvae, as Beaumont, the seventeenth-century Platonist, preferred to call them,[53] those who cannot become disentangled from old habits and desires, for many years, it may be for centuries, keep the shape of their earthly bodies and carry on their old activities, wooing or quarrelling, or totting figures on a table, in a round of dull duties or passionate events. Today while the great battle in Northern France is still undecided,[54] should I climb to the top of that old house in Soho where a medium is sitting among servant girls, some one would, it may be, ask for news of Gordon Highlander or Munster Fusilier,[55] and the fat old woman would tell in Cockney language how the dead do not yet know they are dead, but stumble on amid visionary smoke and noise, and how angelic spirits seem to awaken them but still in vain.

Those who have attained to nobler form, when they appear in the séance room, create temporary bodies, commonly like to those they wore when living, through some unconscious constraint of memory, or deliberately, that they may be recognized. Davis, in his literal way, said the first sixty feet of the atmosphere was a reflector and that in almost every case it was mere images we spoke with in the séance room, the spirit itself being far away.[56] The images are made of a substance drawn from the medium who loses weight, and in a less degree from all present, and for this light must be extinguished or dimmed or shaded with red as in a photographer's room. The image will begin outside the medium's body as a luminous cloud, or in a sort of luminous mud forced from the body, out of the mouth it may be, from the side or from the lower parts of the body.[57] One may see a vague cloud condense and diminish into a head or arm or a whole figure of a man, or to some animal shape.[58]

I remember a story told me by a friend's steward in Galway of the faeries playing at hurley in a field and going in and out of the bodies of two men who stood at either goal.[59] Out of the medium will come perhaps a cripple or a man bent with years and sometimes the apparition will explain that, but for some family portrait, or for what it lit on while rummaging in our memories, it had not remembered its customary clothes or features, or cough or limp or crutch. Sometimes, indeed, there is a strange regularity of feature and we suspect the presence of an image that may never have lived, an artificial beauty that may have shown itself in the Greek mysteries. Has some cast in the Vatican, or at Bloomsbury been the model? Or there may float before our eyes a mask as strange and powerful as the lineaments of the Servian's *Frowning Man* or of Rodin's *Man with the Broken Nose.*[60] And once a rumour ran among the séance rooms to the bewilderment of simple believers, that a heavy middle-aged man who took snuff, and wore the costume of a past time, had appeared while a French medium was in his trance, and somebody had recognized the Tartuffe of the Comédie Française.[61] There will be few complete forms, for the dead are economical, and a head, or just enough of the body for recognition, may show itself above hanging folds of drapery that do not seem to cover solid limbs, or a hand or foot is lacking, or it may be that some *Revenant* has seized the half-made image of another, and a young girl's arm will be thrust from the withered body of an old man. Nor is every form a breathing and pulsing thing, for some may have a distribution of light and shade not that of the séance room, flat pictures whose eyes gleam and move; and sometimes material objects are thrown together (drifted in from some neighbour's wardrobe, it may be, and drifted thither again) and an appearance kneaded up out of these and that luminous mud or vapour almost as vivid as are those pictures of Antonio Mancini which have fragments of his paint tubes embedded for the high lights into the heavy masses of the paint.[62] Sometimes there are animals, bears frequently for some unknown reason, but most often birds and dogs. If an image speak it will seldom seem very able or alert, for they come for recognition only, and their minds are strained and fragmentary; and should the dogs bark, a man who knows the language of our dogs may not be able to say if they are hungry or afraid or glad to meet their master again. All may seem histrionic or a hollow show. We are the spectators of a phantasmagoria that affects the photographic plate or leaves its moulded image in a preparation of paraffin.[63] We have come to understand why the Platonists of the sixteenth and seventeenth centuries, and visionaries like Boehme and Paracelsus confused imagination with magic, and why Boehme will have it that it 'creates and substantiates as it goes'.[64]

Most commonly, however, especially of recent years, no form will show itself, or but vaguely and faintly and in no way ponderable, and instead there will be voices flitting here and there in darkness, or in the half-light, or it will be the medium himself fallen into trance who will speak, or without a trance write from a knowledge and intelligence not his own. Glanvil, the seventeenth-century Platonist, said that the higher spirits were those least capable of showing material effects,[65] and it seems plain from certain Polish experiments that the intelligence of the communicators increases with their economy of substance and energy.[66] Often now among these faint effects one will seem to speak with the very dead. They will speak or write some tongue that the medium does not know and give correctly their forgotten names, or describe events one only verifies after weeks of labour. Here and there amongst them one discovers a wise and benevolent mind that knows a little of the future and can give good advice. They have made, one imagines, from some finer substance than a phosphorescent mud, or cobweb vapour that we can see or handle, images not wholly different from themselves, figures in a galanty show[67] not too strained or too extravagant to speak their very thought.

Yet we never long escape the phantasmagoria nor can long forget that we are among the shape-changers. Sometimes our own minds shape that mysterious substance, which may be life itself, according to desire or constrained by memory, and the dead no longer remembering their own names become the characters in the drama we ourselves have invented. John King, who has delighted melodramatic minds for hundreds of séances with his career on earth as Henry Morgan the buccaneer, will tell more scientific visitors that he is merely a force, while some phantom long accustomed to a decent name, questioned by some pious Catholic, will admit very cheerfully that he is the devil.[68] Nor is it only present minds that perplex the shades with phantasy, for friends of Count Albert de Rochas once wrote out names and incidents but to discover that though the surname of the shade that spoke had been historical, Christian name and incidents were from a romance running at the time in some clerical newspaper no one there had ever opened.[69]

All these shadows have drunk from the pool of blood and become delirious.[70] Sometimes they will use the very word and say that we force delirium upon them because we do not still our minds, or that minds not stupefied with the body force them more subtly, for now and again one will withdraw what he has said, saying that he was constrained by the neighbourhood of some more powerful shade.

When I was a boy at Sligo, a stable boy met his late master

going round the yard, and having told him to go and haunt the lighthouse, was dismissed by his mistress for sending her husband to haunt so inclement a spot.[71] Ghosts, I was told, must go where they are bid, and all those threatenings by the old *grimoires* to drown some disobedient spirit at the bottom of the Red Sea, and indeed all exorcism and conjuration affirm that our imagination is king. *Revenants* are, to use the modern term, 'suggestable', and may be studied in the 'trance personalities' of hypnosis and in our dreams which are but hypnosis turned inside out, a modeller's clay for our suggestions, or, if we follow *The Spiritual Diary*, for those of invisible beings. Swedenborg has written that we are each in the midst of a group of associated spirits who sleep when we sleep and become the *dramatis personae* of our dreams, and are always the other will that wrestles with our thought, shaping it to our despite.[72]

IX

We speak, it may be, of the Proteus of antiquity which has to be held or it will refuse its prophecy, and there are many warnings in our ears. 'Stoop not down', says the Chaldaean Oracle, 'to the darkly splendid world wherein continually lieth a faithless depth and Hades wrapped in cloud, delighting in unintelligible images',[73] and amid that caprice, among those clouds, there is always legerdemain; we juggle, or lose our money with the same pack of cards that may reveal the future. The magicians who astonished the Middle Ages with power as incalculable as the fall of a meteor were not so numerous as the more amusing jugglers who could do their marvels at will; and in our own day the juggler Houdin, sent to Morocco by the French Government, was able to break the prestige of the dervishes whose fragile wonders were but worked by fasting and prayer.[74]

Sometimes, indeed, a man would be magician, jester, and juggler. In an Irish story a stranger lays three rushes upon the flat of his hand and promises to blow away the inner and leave the others unmoved, and thereupon puts two fingers of his other hand upon the outer ones and blows. However, he will do a more wonderful trick. There are many who can wag both ears, but he can wag one and not the other, and thereafter, when he has everybody's attention, he takes one ear between finger and thumb. But now that the audience are friendly and laughing the moment of miracle has come. He takes out of a bag a skein of silk thread and throws it into the air, until it seems as though one end were made fast to a cloud. Then he takes out of his bag first a hare and then a dog and then a young man and then 'a beautiful, well-dressed young woman' and sends them all running up the thread.[75] Nor, the old writers tell us, does the association of juggler and magician cease after death, which only gives to legerdemain greater power and subtlety. Those who would live again in us, becoming a part of our thoughts and passion have, it seems, their sport to keep us in good humour, and a young girl who has astonished herself and her friends in some dark séance may, when we have persuaded her to become entranced in a lighted room, tell us that some shade is touching her face, while we can see her touching it with her own hand, or we may discover her, while her eyes are still closed, in some jugglery that implies an incredible mastery of muscular movement. Perhaps too in the fragmentary middle world there are souls that remain always upon the brink, always children. Dr Ochorowicz finds his experiments upset by a naked girl, one foot one inch high, who is constantly visible to his medium and who claims never to have lived upon the earth. He has photographed her by leaving a camera in an empty room where she had promised to show herself, but is so doubtful of her honesty that he is not sure she did not hold up a print from an illustrated paper in front of the camera.[76] In one of Lady Gregory's stories a countryman is given by a stranger he meets upon the road what seems wholesome and pleasant food, but a little later his stomach turns and he finds that he has eaten chopped grass, and one remembers Robin Goodfellow and his joint stool, and witches' gold that is but dried cow dung.[77] It is only, one does not doubt, because of our preoccupation with a single problem, our survival of the body, and with the affection that binds us to the dead, that all the gnomes and nymphs of antiquity have not begun their tricks again.

X

Plutarch, in his essay on the daemon, describes how the souls of enlightened men return to be the schoolmasters of the living, whom they influence unseen;[78] and the mediums, should we ask how they escape the illusions of that world, claim the protection of their guides. One will tell you that when she was a little girl she was minding geese upon some American farm and an old man came towards her with a queer coat upon him, and how at first she took him for a living man. He said perhaps a few words of pious commonplace or practical advice and vanished. He had come again and again, and now that she has to earn her living by her gift, he warns her against deceiving spirits, or if she is working too hard, but sometimes she will not listen and gets into trouble. The old witch doctor of Lady Gregory's story learned his cures from his dead sister whom he met from time to time, but especially at Hallowe'en, at the end of the garden, but he had other helpers harsher than she, and once he was beaten for disobedience.[79]

Reginald Scot gives a fine plan for picking a guide. You promise some dying man to pray for the repose of his soul if he will but come to you after death and give what help you need, while stories of mothers who come at night to be among their orphan children are as common among spiritists as in Galway or in Mayo.[80] A French servant girl once said to a friend of mine who helped her in some love affair: 'You have your studies, we have only our affections'; and this I think is why the walls are broken less often among us than among the poor. Yet according to the doctrine of Soho and Holloway and in Plutarch, those studies that have lessened in us the sap of the world may bring to us good, learned, masterful men who return to see their own or some like work carried to a finish. 'I do think', wrote Sir Thomas Browne, 'that many mysteries ascribed to our own invention have been the courteous revelations of spirits; for those noble essences in heaven bear a friendly regard unto their fellow creatures on earth.'[81]

XI

Much that Lady Gregory has gathered seems but the broken bread of old philosophers, or else of the one sort with the dough they made into their loaves. Were I not ignorant, my Greek gone and my meagre Latin all but gone, I do not doubt that I could find much to the point in Greek, perhaps in old writers on medicine, much in Renaissance or Medieval Latin. As it is, I must be content with what has been translated or with the seventeenth-century Platonists who are the handier for my purpose because they found in the affidavits and confessions of the witch trials, descriptions like those in our Connaught stories. I have Henry More in his verse and in his prose and I have Henry More's two friends, Joseph Glanvil, and Cudworth in his *Intellectual System of the Universe*, three volumes violently annotated by an opposed theologian; and two essays by Mr G. R. S. Mead clipped out of his magazine, *The Quest*.[82] These writers quote much from Plotinus and Porphyry and Plato and from later writers, especially Synesius and John Philoponus in whom the School of Plato came to an end in the seventh century.[83]

We should not suppose that our souls began at birth, for as Henry More has said, a man might as well think 'from souls new souls' to bring as 'to press the sunbeams in his fist' or 'wring the rainbow till it dye his hands'. We have within us an 'airy body' or 'spirit body' which was our only body before our birth as it will be again when we are dead and its 'plastic power' has shaped our terrestrial body as some day it may shape apparition and ghost.[84] Porphyry is quoted by Mr Mead as saying that 'Souls who love the body attach a moist spirit to them and condense it like a cloud', and so become visible,[85] and so are all apparitions of the dead made visible; though necromancers, according to Henry More, can ease and quicken this condensation 'with reek of oil, meal, milk, and such like gear, wine, water, honey'.[86] One remembers that Dr Ochorowicz's naked imp once described how she filled out an appearance of herself by putting a piece of blotting paper where her stomach should have been and that the blotting paper became damp because, as she said, a materialization, until it is completed, is a damp vapour.[87] This airy body which so compresses vapour, Philoponus says, 'takes the shape of the physical body as water takes the shape of the vessel that it has been frozen in', but it is capable of endless transformations, for 'in itself it has no especial form',[88] but Henry More believes that it has an especial form, for 'its plastic power' cannot but find the human form most 'natural', though 'vehemency of desire to alter the figure into another representation may make the appearance to resemble some other creature; but no forced thing can last long'. 'The better genii' therefore prefer to show 'in a human shape yet not it may be with all the lineaments' but with such as are 'fit for this separate state' (separate from the body that is) or are 'requisite to perfect the visible features of a person', desire and imagination adding clothes and ornament. The materialization, as we would say, has but enough likeness for recognition.[89] It may be that More but copies Philoponus who thought the shade's habitual form, the image that it was as it were frozen in for a time, could be again 'coloured and shaped by fantasy', and that 'it is probable that when the soul desires to manifest it shapes itself, setting its own imagination in movement, or even that it is probable with the help of daemonic co-operation that it appears and again becomes invisible, becoming condensed and rarefied'. Porphyry, Philoponus adds, gives Homer as his authority for the belief that souls after death live among images of their experience upon earth, phantasms impressed upon the spirit body.[90] While Synesius, who lived at the end of the fourth century and had Hypatia among his friends, also describes the spirit body as capable of taking any form and so of enabling us after death to work out our purgation; and says that for this reason the oracles have likened the state after death to the images of a dream.[91] The seventeenth century English translation of Cornelius Agrippa's *De Occulta Philosophia* was once so famous that it found its way into the hands of Irish farmers and wandering Irish tinkers, and it may be that Agrippa influenced the common thought when he wrote that the evil dead see represented 'in the fantastic reason' those shapes of life that are 'the more turbulent and furious . . . sometimes of the heavens falling upon their heads, sometimes of their being consumed with the violence of flames, sometimes of being drowned in a gulf, sometimes of being swallowed up in the earth, sometimes of being changed into divers kinds of beasts . . . and sometimes of being taken and tormented by demons . . . as if they were in a dream'. The ancients, he writes, have called these souls 'hobgoblins', and Orpheus has called them 'the people of dreams' saying 'the gates of Pluto cannot be unlocked; within is a people of dreams'.[92] They are a dream indeed that has place and weight and measure, and seeing that their bodies are of an actual air, they cannot, it was held, but travel in wind and set the straws and the dust twirling; though being of the wind's weight they need not, Dr Henry More considers, so much as feel its ruffling, or if they should do so, they can shelter in a house or behind a wall, or gather into themselves as it were, out of the gross wind and vapour.[93] But there are good dreams among the airy people, though we cannot properly name that a dream which is but analogical of the deep unimaginable virtues and has, therefore, stability and a common measure. Henry More stays himself in the midst of the dry learned and abstract writing of his treatise *The Immortality of the Soul* to praise 'their comely carriage . . . their graceful dancing, their melodious singing and playing with an accent so sweet and soft as if we should imagine air itself to compose lessons and send forth musical sounds without the help of any terrestrial instrument' and imagines them at their revels in the thin upper air where the earth can but seem 'a fleecy and milky light' as the moon to us, and he cries out that they 'sing and play and dance together, reaping the lawful pleasures of the very animal life, in a far higher degree than we are capable of in this world, for everything here does, as it were, taste of the cask and has some measure of foulness in it'.

There is, however, another birth or death when we pass from the airy to the shining or ethereal body, and 'in the airy the soul may inhabit for many ages and in the ethereal for ever', and indeed it is the ethereal body which is the root 'of all that natural warmth in all generations' though in us it can no longer shine. It lives while in its true condition an unimaginable life and is sometimes described as of 'a round or oval figure' and as always circling among gods and among the stars, and sometimes as having more dimensions than our penury can comprehend.[94]

Last winter Mr Ezra Pound was editing the late Professor Fenollosa's translations of the Noh Drama of Japan, and read me a great deal of what he was doing. Nearly all that my fat old woman in Soho learns from her familiars is there in an unsurpassed lyric poetry and in strange and poignant fables once danced or sung in the houses of nobles. In one a priest asks his way of some girls who are gathering herbs. He asks if it is a long road to town; and the girls begin to lament over their hard lot gathering cress in a cold wet bog where they sink up to their knees and to compare themselves with ladies in the big town who only pull the cress in sport, and need not when the cold wind is flapping their sleeves. He asks what village he has come to and if a road near by leads to the village of Ono. A girl replies that nobody can know that name without knowing the road, and another says: 'Who would not know that name, written on so many pictures, and know the pine trees they are always drawing.' Presently the cold drives away all the girls but one and she tells the priest she is a spirit and has taken solid form that she may speak with him and ask his help. It is her tomb that has made Ono so famous. Conscience-struck at having allowed two young men to fall in love with her she refused to choose between them. Her father said he would give her to the best archer. At the match to settle it both sent their arrows through the same wing of a mallard and were declared equal. She being ashamed and miserable because she had caused so much trouble and for the death of the mallard, took her own life. That, she thought, would end the trouble, but her lovers killed themselves beside her tomb, and now she suffered all manner of horrible punishments. She had but to lay her hand upon a pillar to make it burst into flame; she was perpetually burning. The priest tells her that if she can but cease to believe in her punishments they will cease to exist. She listens in gratitude but she cannot cease to believe, and while she is speaking they come upon her and she rushes away enfolded in flames.[95] Her imagination has created all those terrors out of a scruple, and one remembers how Lake Harris, who led Laurence Oliphant such a dance, once said to a shade, 'How did you know you were damned?' and that it answered, 'I saw my own thoughts going past me like blazing ships.'[96]

In a play still more rich in lyric poetry a priest is wandering in a certain ancient village. He describes the journey and the scene, and from time to time the chorus sitting at the side of the stage sings its comment. He meets with two ghosts, the one holding a red stick, the other a piece of coarse cloth and both dressed in the fashion of a past age, but as he is a stranger he supposes them villagers wearing the village fashion. They sing as if muttering, 'We are entangled up—whose fault was it, dear? Tangled up as the grass patterns are tangled up in this coarse cloth, or that insect which lives and chirrups in dried seaweed. We do not know where are today our tears in the undergrowth of this eternal wilderness. We neither wake nor sleep and passing our nights in sorrow, which is in the end a vision, what are these scenes of spring to us? This thinking in sleep for some one who has no thought for you, is it more than a dream? And yet surely it is the natural way of love. In our hearts there is much, and in our bodies nothing, and we do nothing at all, and only the waters of the river of tears flow quickly.' To the priest they seem two married people, but he cannot understand why they carry the red stick and the coarse cloth. They ask him to listen to a story. Two young people had lived in that village long ago and night after night for three years the young man had offered a charmed red stick, the token of love, at the young girl's window, but she pretended not to see and went on weaving. So the young man died and was buried in a cave with his charmed red sticks, and presently the girl died too, and now because they were never married in life they were unmarried in their death. The priest, who does not yet understand that it is their own tale, asks to be shown the cave, and says it will be a fine tale to tell when he goes home. The chorus describes the journey to the cave. The lovers go in front, the priest follows. They are all day pushing through long grasses that hide the narrow paths. They ask the way of a farmer who is mowing. Then night falls and it is cold and frosty. It is stormy and the leaves are falling and their feet sink into the muddy places made by the autumn showers; there is a long shadow on the slope of the mountain, and an owl in the ivy of the pine tree. They have found the cave and it is dyed with the red sticks of love to the colour of 'the orchids and chrysanthemums which hide the mouth of a fox's hole'; and now the two lovers have 'slipped into the shadow of the cave'. Left alone and too cold to sleep the priest decides to spend the night in prayer. He prays that the lovers may at last be one. Presently he sees to his wonder that the cave is lighted up 'where people are talking and setting up looms for spinning and painted red sticks'. The ghosts creep out and thank him for his prayer and say that through his pity 'the love promises of long past incarnations' find fulfilment in a dream. Then he sees the love story unfolded in a vision and the chorus compares the sound of weaving to the clicking of crickets. A little later he is shown the bridal room and the lovers drinking from the bridal cup. The dawn is coming. It is reflected in the bridal cup and now singers, cloth, and stick break and dissolve like a dream, and there is nothing but 'a deserted grave on a hill where morning winds are blowing through the pine'.[97]

I remember that Aran story of the lovers who came after death to the priest for marriage.[98] It is not uncommon for a ghost, 'a control' as we say, to come to a medium to discover some old earthly link to fit into a new chain. It wishes to meet a ghostly enemy to win pardon or to renew an old friendship. Our service to the dead is not narrowed to our prayers, but may be as wide as our imagination. I have known a control to warn a medium to unsay her promise to an old man, to whom, that she might be rid of him, she had promised herself after death. What is promised here in our loves or in a witch's bond may be fulfilled in a life which is a dream. If our terrestrial condition is, as it seems the territory of choice and of cause, the one ground for all seed sowing, it is plain why our imagination has command over the dead and why they must keep from sight and earshot. At the British Museum at the end of the Egyptian Room and near the stairs are two statues, one an august decoration, one a most accurate looking naturalistic portrait. The august decoration was for a public site, the other, like all the naturalistic art of the epoch, for burial beside a mummy. So buried it was believed, the Egyptologists tell us, to be of service to the dead. I have no doubt it helped a dead man to build out of his spirit-body a recognizable apparition, and that all boats or horses or weapons or their models buried in ancient tombs were helps for a flagging memory or a too weak fancy to imagine and so substantiate the old surroundings.[99] A shepherd at Doneraile told me some years ago[100] of an aunt of his who showed herself after death stark naked and bid her relatives to make clothes and to give them to a beggar, the while remembering her.[101] Presently she appeared again wearing the clothes and thanked them.

XII

Certainly in most writings before our time the body of an apparition was held for a brief, artificial, dreamy, half-living thing. One is always meeting such phrases as Sir Thomas Browne's 'they steal or contrive a body'.[102] A passage in the *Paradiso* comes to mind describing Dante in conversation with the blessed among their spheres, although they are but in appearance there, being in truth in the petals of the yellow rose;[103] and another in the *Odyssey* where Odysseus speaks not with 'the mighty Heracles', but with his phantom, for he himself 'hath joy at the banquet among the deathless gods and hath to wife Hebe of the fair ankles, child of Zeus and Here of the golden sandals', while all about the phantom 'there was a clamour of the dead, as it were fowls flying everywhere in fear and he, like black night with bow uncased, and shaft upon the string, fiercely glancing around like one in the act to shoot'.[104]

W.B.Y.
14th October, 1914

Witches and Wizards and Irish Folk-Lore

(w. 1914), in *Visions and Beliefs in the West of Ireland,* by Lady Gregory (1920)

I

Ireland was not separated from general European speculation when much of that was concerned with the supernatural. Dr Adam Clarke tells in his unfinished autobiography how, when he was at school in Antrim towards the end of the eighteenth century, a schoolfellow told him of Cornelius Agrippa's book on Magic and that it had to be chained or it would fly away of itself. Presently he heard of a farmer who had a copy and after that made friends with a wandering tinker who had another.[1] Lady Gregory and I spoke of a friend's visions to an old countryman. He said 'he must belong to a society'; and the people often attribute magical powers to Orangemen and to Freemasons, and I have heard a shepherd at Doneraile speak of a magic wand with Tetragramaton Agla written upon it.[2] The visions and speculations of Ireland differ much from those of England and France, for in Ireland, as in Highland Scotland, we are never far from the old Celtic mythology; but there is more likeness than difference. Lady Gregory's story of the witch who in semblance of a hare, leads the hounds such a dance, is the best remembered of all witch stories.[3] It is told, I should imagine, in every countryside where there is even a fading memory of witchcraft. One finds it in a sworn testimony given at the trial of Julian Cox, an old woman indicted for witchcraft at Taunton in Somersetshire in 1663 and quoted by Joseph Glanvill. 'The first witness was a huntsman, who swore that he went out with a pack of hounds to hunt a hare, and not far from Julian Cox her house he at last started a hare: the dogs hunted her very close, and the third ring hunted her in view, till at last the huntsman perceiving the hare almost spent and making towards a great bush, he ran on the other side of the bush to take her up and preserve her from the dogs; but as soon as he laid hands on her, it proved to be Julian Cox, who had her head grovelling on the ground, and her globes (as he expressed it) upward. He knowing her, was so affrighted that his hair on his head stood an end; and yet spake to her, and ask'd her what brought her there; but she was so far out of breath that she could not make him any answer; his dogs also came up full cry to recover the game, and smelled at her and so left off hunting any further. And the huntsman with his dogs went home presently sadly affrighted.'[4] Dr Henry More, the Platonist, who considers the story in a letter to Glanvill, explains that Julian Cox was not turned into a hare, but that 'Ludicrous Daemons exhibited to the sight of this huntsman and his dogs, the shape of a hare, one of them turning himself into such a form, another hurrying on the body of Julian near the same place', making her invisible till the right moment had come. 'As I have heard of some painters that have drawn the sky in a huge landscape, so lively, that the birds have flown against it, thinking it free air, and so have fallen down. And if painters and jugglers, by the tricks of legerdemain can do such strange feats to the deceiving of the sight, it is no wonder that these aerie invisible spirits have far surpassed them in all such prestigious doings, as the air surpasses the earth for subtlety.'[5] Glanvill has given his own explanation of such cases elsewhere. He thinks that the sidereal or airy body is the foundation of the marvel, and Albert de Rochas has found a like foundation for the marvels of spiritism. 'The transformation of witches', writes Glanvill, 'into the shapes of other animals . . . is very conceivable; since then, 'tis easy enough to imagine, that the power of imagination may form those passive and pliable vehicles into those shapes', and then goes on to account for the stories where an injury, say to the witch hare, is found afterwards upon the witch's body precisely as a French hypnotist would account for the stigmata of a saint. 'When they feel the hurts in their gross bodies, that they receive in their airy vehicles, they must be supposed to have been really present, at least in these latter; and 'tis no more difficult to apprehend, how the hurts of those should be translated upon their other bodies, than how diseases should be inflicted by the imagination, or how the fancy of the mother should wound the foetus, as several credible relations do attest.'[6]

All magical or Platonic writers of the times speak much of the transformation or projection of the sidereal body of witch or wizard. Once the soul escapes from the natural body, though but for a moment, it passes into the body of air and can transform itself as it please or even dream itself into some shape it has not willed.

> Chameleon-like thus they their colour change,
> And size contract and then dilate again.[7]

One of their favourite stories is of some famous man, John Heydon says Socrates, falling asleep among his friends, who presently see a mouse running from his mouth and towards a little stream. Somebody lays a sword across the stream that it may pass, and after a little while it returns across the sword and to the sleeper's mouth again. When he awakens he tells them that he has dreamed of himself crossing a wide river by a great iron bridge.[8]

But the witch's wandering and disguised double was not the worst shape one might meet in the fields or roads about a witch's house. She was not a true witch unless there was a compact (or so it seems) between her and an evil spirit who called himself the devil, though Bodin believes that he was often, and Glanvill always, 'some human soul forsaken of God', for 'the devil is a body politic'.[9] The ghost or devil promised revenge on her enemies and that she would never want, and she upon her side let the devil suck her blood nightly or at need.

When Elizabeth Style made a confession of witchcraft before the Justice of Somerset in 1664, the Justice appointed three men, William Thick and William Read and Nicholas Lambert, to watch her, and Glanvill publishes an affidavit of the evidence of Nicholas Lambert. 'About three of the clock in the morning there came from her head a glistering bright fly, about an inch in length which pitched at first in the chimney and then vanished.' Then two smaller flies came and vanished. 'He, looking steadfastly then on Style, perceived her countenance to change, and to become very black and ghastly and the fire also at the same time changing its colour; whereupon the Examinant, Thick and Read, conceiving that her familiar was then about her, looked to her poll, and seeing her hair shake very strangely, took it up and then a fly like a great miller flew out from the place and pitched on the table board and then vanished away. Upon this the Examinant and the other two persons, looking again in Style's poll, found it very red and like raw beef. The Examinant ask'd her what it was that went out of her poll, she said it was a butterfly, and asked them why they had not caught it. Lambert said, they could not. I think so too, answered she. A little while after, the informant and the others, looking again into her poll, found the place to be of its former colour. The Examinant asked again what the fly was, she confessed it was her familiar and that she felt it tickle in her poll, and that was the usual time for her familiar to come to her.' These sucking devils alike when at their meal, or when they went here and there to do her will or about their own business, had the shapes of pole-cat or cat or greyhound or of some moth or bird.[10] At the trials of certain witches in Essex in 1645 reported in the English state trials a principal witness was one 'Matthew Hopkins, gent.' Bishop Hutchinson, writing in 1730, describes him as he appeared to those who laughed at witchcraft and had brought the witch trials to an end. 'Hopkins went on searching and swimming poor creatures, till some gentlemen, out of indignation of the barbarity, took him, and tied his own thumbs and toes as he used to tie others, and when he was put into the water he himself swam as they did. That cleared the country of him and it was great pity that they did not think of the experiment sooner.'[11] Floating when thrown into the water was taken for a sign of witchcraft. Matthew Hopkins's testimony, however, is uncommonly like that of the countryman who told Lady Gregory that he had seen his dog and some shadow fighting.[12] A certain Mrs Edwards of Manningtree in Essex had her hogs killed by witchcraft, and 'going from the house of the said Mrs Edwards to his own house, about nine or ten of the clock that night, with his greyhound with him, he saw the greyhound suddenly give a jump, and run as she had been in full course after a hare; and that when this informant had made haste to see what his greyhound so eagerly pursued, he espied a white thing, about the bigness of a kitlyn, and the greyhound standing aloof from it; and that by and by the said white imp or kitlyn danced about the greyhound, and by all likelihood bit off a piece of the flesh of the shoulder of the said greyhound; for the greyhound came shrieking and crying to the informant, with a piece of flesh torn from her shoulder. And the informant further saith, that coming into his own yard that night, he espied a black thing proportioned like a cat, only it was thrice as big, sitting on a strawberry bed, and fixing the eyes on this informant, and when he went towards it, it leaped over the pale towards this informant, as he thought, but ran through the yard, with his greyhound after it, to a great gate, which was underset with a pair of tumble strings, and did throw the said gate wide open, and then vanished; and the said greyhound returned again to this informant, shaking and trembling exceedingly.' At the same trial Sir Thomas Bowes, Knight, affirmed 'that a very honest man of Manningtree, whom he knew would not speak an untruth, affirmed unto him, that very early one morning, as he passed by the said Anne West's door' (this is the witch on trial) 'about four o'clock, it being a moonlight night, and perceiving her door to be open so early in the morning, looked into the house and presently there came three or four little things, in the shape of black rabbits, leaping and skipping about him, who, having a good stick in his hand, struck at them, thinking to kill them, but could not; but at last caught one of them in his hand, and holding it by the body of it, he beat the head of it against his stick, intending to beat out the brains of it; but when he could not kill it that way, he took the body of it in one hand and the head of it in another, and endeavoured to wring off the head; and as he wrung and stretched the neck of it, it came out between his hands like a lock of wool; yet he would not give over his intended purpose, but knowing of a spring not far off, he went to drown it; but still as he went he fell down and could not go, but down he fell again, so that he at last crept upon his hands and knees till he came at the water, and holding it fast in his hand, he put his hand down into the water up to the elbow, and held it under water a good space till he conceived it was drowned, and then letting go his hand, it sprung out of the water up into the air, and so vanished away.'[13] However, the sucking imps were not always invulnerable for Glanvill tells how one John Mompesson, whose house was haunted by such a familiar, 'seeing some wood move that was in the chimney of a room, where he was, as if of itself, discharged a pistol into it after which they found several drops of blood on the hearth and in divers places of the stairs.'[14] I remember the old Aran man who heard fighting in the air and found blood in a fish-box and scattered through the room, and I remember the measure of blood Odysseus poured out for the shades.[15]

The English witch trials are like the popular poetry of England, matter-of-fact and unimaginative. The witch desires to kill some one and when she takes the devil for her husband he as likely as not will seem dull and domestic. Rebecca West told Matthew Hopkins that the devil appeared to her as she was going to bed and told her he would marry her. He kissed her but was as cold as clay, and he promised to be 'her loving husband till death', although she had, as it seems, but one leg.[16] But the Scotch trials are as wild and passionate as is the Scottish poetry, and we find ourselves in the presence of a mythology that differs little, if at all, from that of Ireland. There are orgies of lust and of hatred and there is a wild shamelessness that would be fine material for poets and romance writers if the world should come once more to half-believe the tale. They are divided into troops of thirteen, with the youngest witch for leader in every troop, and though they complain that the embraces of the devil are as cold as ice, the young witches prefer him to their husbands. He gives them money, but they must spend it quickly, for it will be but dry cow dung in two circles of the clock. They go often to Elfhame or Faeryland and the mountains open before them and as they go out and in they are terrified by the 'rowtling and skoylling' of the great 'elf bulls'. They sometimes confess to trooping in the shape of cats and to finding upon their terrestrial bodies when they awake in the morning the scratches they had made upon one another in the night's wandering, or should they have wandered in the images of hares the bites of dogs. Isobell Godie who was tried at Lochlay in 1662 confessed that 'We put besoms in our beds with our husbands till we return again to them . . . and then we would fly away where we would be, even as straws would fly upon a highway. We will fly like straws when we please; wild straws and corn straws will be horses to us, and we put them betwixt our feet and say horse and hillock in the devil's name. And when any see these straws in a whirlwind and do not sanctify themselves, we may shoot them dead at our pleasure.'[17] When they kill people, she goes on to say, the souls escape them 'but their bodies remain with us and will fly as horses to us all as small as straws'. It is plain that it is the 'airy body' they take possession of; those 'animal spirits' perhaps which Henry More thought to be the link between soul and body and the seat of all vital function.[18] The trials were more unjust than those of England, where there was a continual criticism from sceptics; torture was used again and again to distort confessions, and innocent people certainly suffered; some who had but believed too much in their own dreams and some who had but cured the sick at some vision's prompting. Alison Pearson who was burnt in 1588 might have been Biddy Early or any other knowledgeable woman in Ireland today. She was convicted 'for haunting and repairing with the Good Neighbours and queen of Elfhame, these divers years and bypast, as she had confessed in her depositions, declaring that she could not say readily how long she was with them; and that she had friends in that court who were of her own blood and who had great acquaintance of the queen of Elfhame. That when she went to bed she never knew where she would be carried before dawn.' When they worked cures they had the same doctrine of the penalty that one finds in Lady Gregory's stories. One who made her confession before James I was convicted for 'taking the sick party's pains and sicknesses upon herself for a time and then translating them to a third person.'[19]

II

There are more women than men mediums today; and there have been or seem to have been more witches than wizards. The wizards of the sixteenth and seventeenth centuries relied more upon their conjuring book than the witches whose visions and experiences seem but half voluntary, and when voluntary called up by some childish rhyme:

> Hare, hare, God send thee care;
> I am in a hare's likeness now,
> But I shall be a woman even now;
> Hare, hare, God send thee care.[20]

More often than not the wizards were learned men, alchemists or mystics, and if they dealt with the devil at times, or some spirit they called by that name, they had amongst them ascetics and heretical saints. Our chemistry, our metallurgy, and our medicine are often but accidents that befell in their pursuit of the philosopher's stone, the elixir of life. They were bound together in secret societies and had, it may be, some forgotten practice for liberating the soul from the body and sending it to fetch and carry them divine knowledge. Cornelius Agrippa in a letter quoted by Beaumont has hints of such a practice. Yet, like the witches, they worked many wonders by the power of the imagination, perhaps one should say by their power of calling up vivid pictures in the mind's eye. The Arabian philosophers have taught, writes Beaumont, 'that the soul by the power of the imagination can perform what it pleases; as penetrate the heavens, force the elements, demolish mountains, raise valleys to mountains, and do with all material forms as it pleases'.[21]

He shewed hym, er he wente to sopeer,
Forestes, parkes ful of wilde deer;
Ther saugh he hertes with hir hornes hye,
The gretteste that evere were seyn with yë.
. . . . .
Tho saugh he knyghtes justing in a playn;
And after this, he dide hym swich plaisaunce,
That he hym shewed his lady on a daunce
On which hymself he daunced, as hym thoughte.
And whan this maister, that this magyk wroughte,
Saugh it was tyme, he clapte his handes two,
And, farewel! al our revel was ago.[22]

One has not as careful a record as one has of the works of witches, for but few English wizards came before the court, the only society for psychical research in those days. The translation, however, of Cornelius Agrippa's *De Occulta Philosophia* in the seventeenth century, with the addition of a spurious fourth book full of conjurations, seems to have filled England and Ireland with whole or half wizards.[23] In 1703, the Reverend Arthur Bedford of Bristol who is quoted by Sibley in his big book on astrology wrote to the Bishop of Gloucester telling how a certain Thomas Perks had been to consult him. Thomas Perks lived with his father, a gunsmith, and devoted his leisure to mathematics, astronomy, and the discovery of perpetual motion. One day he asked the clergyman if it was wrong to commune with spirits, and said that he himself held that 'there was an innocent society with them which a man might use, if he made no compacts with them, did no harm by their means, and were not curious in prying into hidden things, and he himself had discoursed with them and heard them sing to his great satisfaction.' He then told how it was his custom to go to a crossway with lantern and candle consecrated for the purpose, according to the directions in a book he had, and having also consecrated chalk for making a circle. The spirits appeared to him 'in the likeness of little maidens about a foot and a half high . . . they spoke with a very shrill voice like an ancient woman' and when he begged them to sing, 'they went to some distance behind a bush from whence he could hear a perfect concert of such exquisite music as he never before heard; and in the upper part he heard something very harsh and shrill like a reed but as it was managed did give a particular grace to the rest.' The Reverend Arthur Bedford refused an introduction to the spirits for himself and a friend and warned him very solemnly. Having some doubt of his sanity, he set him a difficult mathematical problem, but finding that he worked it easily, concluded him sane. A quarter of a year later, the young man came again, but showed by his face and his eyes that he was very ill and lamented that he had not followed the clergyman's advice for his conjurations would bring him to his death. He had decided to get a familiar and had read in his magical book what he should do. He was to make a book of virgin parchment, consecrate it, and bring it to the cross-road, and having called up his spirits, ask the first of them for its name and write that name on the first page of the book and then question another and write that name on the second page and so on till he had enough familiars. He had got the first name easily enough and it was in Hebrew, but after that they came in fearful shapes, lions and bears and the like, or hurled at him balls of fire. He had to stay there among those terrifying visions till the dawn broke and would not be the better of it till he died.[24] I have read in some eighteenth-century book whose name I cannot recall of two men who made a magic circle and who invoked the spirits of the moon and saw them trampling about the circle as great bulls, or rolling about it as flocks of wool. One of Lady Gregory's story-tellers considered a flock of wool one of the worst shapes that a spirit could take.[25]

There must have been many like experimenters in Ireland. An Irish alchemist called Butler was supposed to have made successful transmutations in London early in the eighteenth century, and in the *Life of Dr Adam Clarke*, published in 1833, are several letters from a Dublin maker of stained glass describing a transmutation and a conjuration into a tumbler of water of large lizards. The alchemist was an unknown man who had called to see him and claimed to do all by the help of the devil 'who was the friend of all ingenious gentlemen'.[26]

W.B.Y.
1914

Preface to *Essays 1931 to 1936* (1937)

In this book I have put whatever critical essays I have written since the war, except those in *Wheels and Butterflies*, the long introduction to *The Oxford Book of Modern Verse*, and one or two notes rather than essays that seemed too slight in effort or in achievement.[1] Nothing in this book is journalism; nothing was written to please a friend or satisfy an editor, or even to earn money. When I introduced a book it was some book I had awaited with excitement; nor was anything written out of the fullness of knowledge; why should I write what I knew? I wrote always that when I laid down my pen I might be less ignorant than when I took it up. I think my head has grown clearer.

The poem about Parnell was first published in a Cuala *Broadside* a few months ago, but the essay is new. 'Modern Poetry' was broadcasted from the London B.B.C. in October of last year. 'Bishop Berkeley' introduced Rossi and Hone's life of that writer published in 1931. 'My Friend's Book' was published in *The Spectator* in April 1932, 'Prometheus Unbound' and 'Louis Lambert' in *The Spectator* and *The Mercury* three or four years ago, in what month I cannot recall, 'An Indian Monk' and 'The Holy Mountain' in 1932 and 1934 as introductions to books bearing those names, and the 'Introduction to a short Upanishad' in *The Criterion* in 1935.[2]

Parnell (w. 1936; publ. 1937)

In the late Eighties I read in the newspapers that an Oxford undergraduate, Henry Harrison, had been tried, and whether condemned or acquitted I do not remember, for some gallant reckless action at an eviction in Donegal.[1] Years afterwards I came to know him slightly, met him perhaps half a dozen times. Two or three weeks ago he walked into my garden, a man broken by time, and sat by my wheeled chair. He had, I knew, a life-long devotion to Parnell's memory, had helped his widow and children with legal and financial advice, had been asked to write an official 'Life' which was never written. He brought me his book *Parnell Vindicated*[2] and asked my help to make it known in Dublin; Ensor, in his book *England, 1870-1914* had spoken of it as 'the main, final source of information',[3] but Irish newspapers had ignored it, seemed to prefer the story told in the undefended divorce case of a seduced wife and a deceived husband. I asked what I could do, for who listened to a poet until he was dead, but he insisted that words of mine would reach somebody or other he could not. A couple of days ago the verses at the end of this note came into my head, and I thought that they might suggest to somebody that there was nothing discreditable in Parnell's love for his mistress and his wife.[4]

Parnell Vindicated proves beyond controversy that when Parnell met her Mrs O'Shea was 'a free woman'; that while a rich old woman lived she could not seek divorce; that Captain O'Shea knew of their liaison from the first; that he sold his wife for money and for other substantial advantages; that for £20,000, could Parnell have raised that sum, he was ready to let the divorce proceedings go, not against Parnell, but himself;[5] that he extracted money from Parnell and Parnell's widow; that a well-known book signed by her, but only here and there her work whenever it put him in a better light was 'forgery . . . no less hurtful to Parnell's honour' than the Piggot Letters;[6] that the Irish leaders knew all about the liaison after a certain election in the middle Eighties if not sooner; that the Liberal leaders knew from May 1882 when Sir William Harcourt told the Cabinet, apparently upon the evidence of his detectives.[7]

I was once enough of a politician to contemplate politics ever since with amusement. The leading articles, the speeches, the resolutions of the shocked Irish and English politicians, the sudden reversal of all the barrel-organs, the alphabets running back from Z to A, sycophantic fiction become libel, eulogy vituperation, what could be more amusing? Henry Harrison does not ask if Gladstone knew and his biographers deny it. I have no doubt that he did; he used Mrs O'Shea as an intermediary while negotiating with Parnell. Leveson-Gower, after consultation with Lord Granville, drew his attention to the rumours, but Gladstone, who, in Mr Ensor's words 'shared with many Victorians a dislike to hearing or repeating scandal, treated this as idle gossip'. But he must have heard more than rumours from the mouth of his own Home Secretary in 1882.[8] A great Victorian once said to me 'There are things that may be done but never spoken of.'[9] Gladstone was in his private life, what he could not be in his public, a tolerant man of the world. Wilfrid Blunt brought him to see a well-known courtesan, the 'Esther' of the sonnets, and Gladstone, charmed by a charming woman, returned alone some days later with no profligate intention but to present forty pounds of tea.[10] They were all tolerant men of the world except the peasant born Irish members; toleration is most often found beside ornamental waters, upon smooth lawns, amid conversations that have no object but pleasure. But all were caught in that public insincerity which was about to bring such discredit upon democracy. All over the world men are turning to Dictators, Communist or Fascist. Who can keep company with the Goddess Astrea if both eyes are upon the brindled cat?[11]

I cannot however look upon Captain O'Shea as merely amusing. I am not sufficiently unselfish. He has endangered the future of Irish dramatic literature by making melodrama too easy, and I am a theatre director; for drama one must imagine, and I cannot imagine what Captain O'Shea thought of himself when he looked into the mirror. The complacent husband may have charm and dignity like the old French painter who called upon some friends of mine to say that he was taking his wife into the country for a change: 'I always knew that Persian lover would turn out badly, I do hope she will choose better next time,' and then two or three years later to say he had falsified her age upon her tombstone: 'She never liked people to know her age.'[12] But what of the complacent husband who is 'in effect a black-mailer' (Ensor, page 565)[13] and yet is such a dashing figure that a Cabinet Minister considering a duel consults him upon the point of honour? There is something interesting there, but too much is left to the imagination. Those who knew him in his vigorous years are underground or over ninety.

COME GATHER ROUND ME PARNELLITES

Come gather round me Parnellites
And praise our chosen man,
Stand upright on your legs awhile,
Stand upright while you can,
For soon we lie where he is laid
And he is underground;
Come fill up all those glasses
And pass the bottle round.

And here's a cogent reason
And I have many more,
He fought the might of England
And saved the Irish poor,
Whatever good a farmer's got
He brought it all to pass;
And here's another reason,
That Parnell loved a lass.

And here's a final reason,
He was of such a kind
Every man that sings a song
Keeps Parnell in his mind
For Parnell was a proud man,
No prouder trod the ground,
And a proud man's a lovely man
So pass the bottle round.

The Bishops and the Party
That tragic story made,
A husband that had sold his wife
And after that betrayed;
But stories that live longest
Are sung above the glass,
And Parnell loved his country
And Parnell loved his lass.

August, 1936

Modern Poetry: A Broadcast (1936)

The period from the death of Tennyson until the present moment[1] has, it seems, more good lyric poets than any similar period since the seventeenth century—no great overpowering figures, but many poets who have written some three or four lyrics apiece which may be permanent in our literature. It did not always seem so; even two years ago I should have said the opposite; I should have named three or four poets and said there was nobody else who mattered. Then I gave all my time to the study of that poetry. There was a club of poets—you may know its name, 'The Rhymers' Club'—which first met, I think, a few months before the death of Tennyson and lasted seven or eight years. It met in a Fleet Street tavern called 'The Cheshire Cheese'.[2] Two members of the club are vivid in my memory: Ernest Dowson, timid, silent, a little melancholy, lax in body, vague in attitude; Lionel Johnson, determined, erect, his few words dogmatic, almost a dwarf but beautifully made, his features cut in ivory. His thought dominated the scene and gave the club its character. Nothing of importance could be discovered, he would say, science must be confined to the kitchen or the workshop; only philosophy and religion could solve the great secret, and they said all their say years ago; a gentleman was a man who understood Greek. I was full of crude speculation that made me ashamed. I remember praying that I might get my imagination fixed upon life itself, like the imagination of Chaucer. In those days I was a convinced ascetic, yet I envied Dowson his dissipated life. I thought it must be easy to think like Chaucer when you lived among those morbid, elegant, tragic women suggested by Dowson's poetry, painted and drawn by his friends Conder and Beardsley. You must all know those famous lines that are in so many anthologies:

> Wine and women and song,
> To us they belong,
> To us the bitter and gay.[3]

When I repeated those beautiful lines it never occurred to me to wonder why the Dowson I knew seemed neither gay nor bitter. A provincial, conscious of clumsiness and lack of self-possession, I still more envied Lionel Johnson who had met, as I believed, everybody of importance. If one spoke of some famous ecclesiastic or statesman he would say: 'I know him intimately', and quote some conversation that laid bare that man's soul. He was never a satirist, being too courteous, too just, for that distortion. One felt that these conversations had happened exactly as he said. Years were to pass before I discovered that Dowson's life, except when he came to the Rhymers' or called upon some friend selected for an extreme respectability, was a sordid round of drink and cheap harlots; that Lionel Johnson had never met those famous men, that he never met anybody because he got up at nightfall, got drunk at a public house or worked half the night, sat the other half, a glass of whiskey at his elbow, staring at the brown corduroy curtains that protected from dust the books that lined his walls, imagining the puppets that were the true companions of his mind. He met Dowson, but then Dowson was nobody and he was convinced that he did Dowson good. He had no interest in women, and on that subject was perhaps eloquent. Some friends of mine saw them one moonlight night returning from 'The Crown' public house which had just closed, their zigzagging feet requiring the whole width of Oxford Street, Lionel Johnson talking. My friend stood still eavesdropping; Lionel Johnson was expounding a Father of the Church.[4] Their piety, in Dowson a penitential sadness, in Lionel Johnson more often a noble ecstasy, was, as I think, illuminated and intensified by their contrasting puppet shows, those elegant, tragic penitents, those great men in their triumph. You may know Lionel Johnson's poem on the statue of King Charles, or that characteristic poem that begins: 'Ah, see the fair chivalry come, the Companions of Christ'.[5] In my present mood, remembering his scholarship; remembering that his religious sense was never divided from his sense of the past; I recall most vividly his 'Church of a Dream':

Sadly the dead leaves rustle in the whistling wind,
Around the weather-worn, grey church, low down the vale:
The Saints in golden vesture shake before the gale;
The glorious windows shake, where still they dwell enshrined;

Old Saints by long-dead, shrivelled hands, long since designed:
There still, although the world autumnal be, and pale,
Still in their golden vesture the old Saints prevail;
Alone with Christ, desolate else, left by mankind.

Only one ancient priest offers the Sacrifice,
Murmuring holy Latin immemorial:
Swaying with tremulous hands the old censer full of spice,
In grey, sweet incense clouds; blue, sweet clouds mystical:
To him, in place of men, for he is old, suffice
Melancholy remembrances and vesperal.[6]

There were other poets, generally a few years younger, who having escaped that first wave of excitement lived tame and orderly lives. But they, too, were in reaction against everything Victorian.

A church in the style of Inigo Jones opens on to a grass lawn a few hundred yards from the Marble Arch. It was designed by a member of 'The Rhymers' Club,' whose architecture, like his poetry, seemed to exist less for his own sake than to illustrate his genius as a connoisseur. I have sometimes thought that masterpiece, perhaps the smallest church in London, the most appropriate symbol of all that was most characteristic in the art of my friends.[7] Their poems seemed to say: 'You will remember us the longer because we are very small, very unambitious'. Yet my friends were most ambitious men; they wished to express life at its intense moments, those moments that are brief because of their intensity, and at those moments alone. In the Victorian era the most famous poetry was often a passage in a poem of some length, perhaps of great length, a poem full of thoughts that might have been expressed in prose. A short lyric seemed an accident, an interruption amid more serious work. Somebody has quoted Browning as saying that he could have written many lyrics had he thought them worth the trouble.[8] The aim of my friends, my own aim, if it sometimes made us prefer the acorn to the oak, the small to the great, freed us from many things that we thought an impurity. Swinburne, Tennyson, Arnold, Browning, had admitted so much psychology, science, moral fervour. Had not Verlaine said of 'In Memoriam', 'when he should have been broken-hearted he had many reminiscences'.[9] We tried to write like the poets of the Greek Anthology, or like Catullus, or like the Jacobean Lyrists, men who wrote while poetry was still pure.[10] We did not look forward or look outward, we left that to the prose writers; we looked back. We thought it was in the very nature of poetry to look back, to resemble those Swedenborgian angels who are described as moving forever towards the dayspring of their youth.[11] In this we were all, orderly and disorderly alike, in full agreement.

When I think of 'The Rhymers' Club' and grow weary of those luckless men, I think of another circle that was in full agreement. It gathered round Charles Ricketts, one of the greatest connoisseurs of any age, an artist whose woodcuts prolonged the inspiration of Rossetti, whose painting mirrored the rich colouring of Delacroix.[12] When we studied his art we studied our double. We, too, thought always that style should be proud of its ancestry, of its traditional high breeding, that an ostentatious originality was out of place whether in the arts or in good manners. When 'The Rhymers' Club' was breaking up I read enthusiastic reviews of the first book of Sturge Moore[13] and grew jealous. He did not belong to 'The Rhymers' Club' and I wanted to believe that we had all the good poets; but one evening Charles Ricketts brought me to a riverside house at Richmond and introduced me to Edith Cooper. She put into my unwilling hands Sturge Moore's book and made me read out and discuss certain poems. I surrendered. I took back all I had said against him. I was most moved by his poem called 'The Dying Swan'.

O silver-throated Swan
Struck, struck! a golden dart
Clean through thy breast has gone
Home to thy heart.
Thrill, thrill, O silver throat!
O silver trumpet, pour
Love for defiance back
On him who smote!
And brim, brim o'er
With love; and ruby-dye thy track
Down thy last living reach
Of river, sail the golden light . . .
Enter the sun's heart . . . even teach,

O wondrous-gifted Pain, teach thou
The god to love, let him learn how.[14]

Edith Cooper herself seemed a dry, precise, precious, pious, finicking old maid; with an aunt, a Miss Bradley, she had written under the name of 'Michael Field' tragedies in the Elizabethan manner, which I seem to remember after forty or fifty years as occasionally powerful but spoilt by strained emotion and laboured metaphor; they had already fallen into oblivion,[15] but under the influence of Charles Ricketts she had studied Greek and found a new character, a second youth. She had begun, though I did not know it for many years, a series of little poems, masterpieces of simplicity, which resemble certain of Landor's lyrics, though her voice is not so deep, but high, thin and sweet.

Thine elder that I am, thou must not cling
To me, nor mournful for my love entreat:
And yet, Alcaeus, as the sudden spring
Is love, yea, and to veiled Demeter sweet.

Sweeter than tone of harp, more gold than gold
Is thy young voice to me; yet, ah, the pain
To learn I am beloved now I am old,
Who, in my youth, loved, as thou must, in vain.[16]

And here is another, which because it hints at so much more than it says, is very moving.

They bring me gifts, they honour me,
Now I am growing old;
And wondering youth crowds round my knee,
As if I had a mystery
And worship to unfold.

To me the tender, blushing bride
Doth come with lips that fail;
I feel her heart beat at my side
And cry: 'Like Ares in his pride,
Hail, noble bridegroom, hail!'[17]

My generation, because it disliked Victorian rhetorical moral fervour, came to dislike all rhetoric. In France, where there was a similar movement, a poet had written: 'Take rhetoric and wring its neck'.[18] People began to imitate old ballads because an old ballad is never rhetorical. I think of *The Shropshire Lad*, of certain poems by Hardy, of Kipling's 'Saint Helena Lullaby', and his 'The Looking-Glass'.[19] I will not read any of that famous poetry but a poem nobody ever heard of. When I was a young man, York Powell, an Oxford Don, was renowned for his miraculous learning, but only his few intimates, perhaps only those much younger than himself, knew that he was not the dry man he seemed. From the top of a bus, somewhere between Victoria and Walham Green he pointed out to me a pawnshop he had once found very useful; I was in his rooms at Oxford when he replied to somebody who had asked him to become Proctor that the older he grew the less and less difference could he see between right and wrong. He used to frequent prize-fights with my brother, a lad in his twenties, and it was in a Broadside, a mixture of hand-coloured prints and poetry published by my brother, and now long out of print, that I discovered the poem I am now about to read. It is a translation from the French of Paul Fort.

The pretty maid she died, she died, in love-bed as she lay;
They took her to the church-yard; all at the break of day;
They laid her all alone there: all in her white array;
They laid her all alone there: a'coffin'd in the clay:
And they came back so merrily: all at the dawn of day;
A'singing all so merrily: '*The dog must have his day!*'
The pretty maid is dead, is dead; in love-bed as she lay
And they are off a-field to work: as they do every day.[20]

The poems I have read resemble in certain characteristics all modern poetry up to the Great War. The centaurs and amazons of Sturge Moore, the Tristram and Isoult of Binyon's noble poem—there were always some long poems; my Deirdre, my Cuchulain had been written about for centuries and our public wished for nothing else.[21] Here and there some young revolutionist would boast that his eyes were on the present or the future, or even denounce all poetry back to Dante, but we were content; we wrote as men had always written. Then established things were shaken by the Great War. All civilised men had believed in progress, in a warless future, in always-increasing wealth, but now influential young men began to wonder if anything could last or if anything were worth fighting for. In the third year of the War came the most revolutionary man in poetry during my life-time, though his revolution was stylistic alone—T. S. Eliot published his first book.[22] No romantic word or sound, nothing reminiscent, nothing in the least like the painting of Ricketts could be permitted henceforth. Poetry must resemble prose, and both must accept the vocabulary of their time; nor must there be any special subject-matter. Tristram and Isoult were not a more suitable theme than Paddington Railway Station. The past had deceived us: let us accept the worthless present.

> The morning comes to consciousness
> Of faint stale smells of beer
> From the saw-dust-trampled street
> With all its muddy feet that press
> To early coffee stands. . . .
> One thinks of all the hands
> That are raising dingy shades
> In a thousand furnished rooms.[23]

We older writers disliked this new poetry, but were forced to admit its satiric intensity. It was in Eliot that certain revolutionary War poets,[24] young men who felt they had been dragged away from their studies, from their pleasant life, by the blundering frenzy of old men, found the greater part of their style. They were too near their subject-matter to do, as I think, work of permanent importance, but their social passion, their sense of tragedy, their modernity, have passed into young influential poets of today: Auden, Spender, MacNeice, Day Lewis, and others.[25] Some of these poets are Communists, but even in those who are not, there is an overwhelming social bitterness. Some speak of the War in which none were old enough to have served:

> I've heard them lilting at loom and belting,
> Lasses lilting before dawn of day;
> But now they are silent, not gamesome and gallant—
> The flowers of the town are rotting away.

There was laughing and loving in the lanes at evening;
Handsome were the boys then, and girls were gay.
But lost in Flanders by medalled commanders
The lads of the village are melted away.[26]

This poetry is supported by critics who think it the poetry of the future—in my youth I heard much of the music of the future—and attack all not of their school. A poet of an older school has named them 'the racketeers'.[27] Sometimes they attack Miss Edith Sitwell, who seems to me an important poet, shaped as they are by the disillusionment that followed the Great War. Among her fauns, cats, columbines, clowns, wicked fairies, into that phantasmagoria which reminds me of a ballet called *The Sleeping Beauty*, loved by the last of the Tsars, she interjects a nightmare horror of death and decay. I commend to you 'The Hambone and the Heart', and 'The Lament of Edward Blastock', as among the most tragic poems of our time.[28] Her language is the traditional language of literature, but twisted, torn, complicated, jerked here and there by strained resemblances, unnatural contacts, forced upon it by terror or by some violence beating in her blood, some primitive obsession that civilisation can no longer exorcise. I find her obscure, exasperating, delightful. I think I like her best when she seems a child, terrified and delighted by the story it is inventing. I will read you a little poem she has called 'Ass-face', but first I must explain its imagery which has taken me a couple of minutes to puzzle out, not because it is obscure, but because image follows image too quickly to be understood at a first hearing. I prefer to think of Ass-face as a personality invented by some child at a nursery window after dark. The starry heavens are the lighted bars and saloons of public houses, and the descending light is asses' milk which makes Ass-face drunk. But this light is thought of the next moment as bright threads floating down in spirals to make a dress for Columbine, and the next moment after that as milk squirting on the sands of the sea—one thinks of the glittering foam—a sea which brays like an ass, and is covered because it is a rough sea by an ass's hide. Along the shore there are trees, and under these trees beavers are building Babel, and these beavers think that the noise Ass-face makes in his drunkenness is Cain and Abel fighting. Then somehow as the vision ends the starlight has turned into the houses that the beavers are building. But their Babel and their houses are like white lace, and we are told that Ass-face will spoil them all.

When you listen to this poem, you should become two people, one a sage who thinks perhaps that Ass-face is the stupefying frenzy of nature, one a child listening to a poem as irrational as a 'Sing a Song of Sixpence':[29]

> Ass-face drank
> The asses' milk of the stars . . .
> The milky spirals as they sank
> From heaven's saloons and golden bars,
> Made a gown
> For Columbine,
> Spiriting down on sands divine
> By the asses' hide of the sea
> (With each tide braying free).
> And the beavers building Babel
> Beneath each tree's thin beard,
> Said, 'Is it Cain and Abel
> Fighting again we heard?,
> It is Ass-face, Ass-face,
> Drunk on the milk of the stars,
> Who will spoil their houses of white lace—
> Expelled from the golden bars![30]

I think profound philosophy must come from terror. An abyss opens under our feet; inherited convictions, the presuppositions of our thoughts, those Fathers of the Church Lionel Johnson expounded, drop into the abyss. Whether we will or no we must ask the ancient questions: Is there reality anywhere? Is there a God? Is there a Soul? We cry with the Indian Sacred Book: 'They have put a golden stopper into the neck of the bottle; pull it! Let out reality!'[31]

Some seven years after the close of the War, seven years of meditation, came Turner's *Seven Days of the Sun*, Dorothy Wellesley's 'Matrix', Herbert Read's 'Mutations of the Phoenix', T. S. Eliot's *Waste Land*;[32] long philosophical poems; and even now the young communist poets complicate their short lyrics with difficult metaphysics.

If you are lovers of poetry, and it is for such that I speak, you know *The Waste Land*, but perhaps not the other poems that I have named, though you will certainly know Dorothy Wellesley's poem in praise of horses, and probably Turner's praise of a mountain in Mexico with a romantic name.[33] To three, perhaps to all four of these writers, what we call the solid earth was manufactured by the human mind from unknown raw material. They do not think this because of Kant and Berkeley, who are an old story, but because of something that has got into the air since a famous French mathematician wrote 'space is a creation of our ancestors'.[34] Eliot's historical and scholarly mind seems to have added this further thought, probably from Nicholas of Cusa: reality is expressed in a series of contradictions, or is that unknowable something that supports the centre of the see-saw.[35]

At the still point of the turning world. Neither flesh nor fleshless;
Neither from nor towards; at the still point, there the dance is,
But neither arrest nor movement. And do not call it fixity.
Where past and future are gathered. Neither movement from nor towards,
Neither ascent nor decline. Except for the point, the still point,
There would be no dance, and there is only the dance.[36]

All are pessimists; Dorothy Wellesley thinks that the 'unconceived', as she calls those that have not yet been melted into that subjective creation we call the world, are alone happy. They are a part of the unknown raw material which the manufacturer has neglected. They have escaped the torture of the senses, the boredom of that automatic return of the same sensation Eliot has described. I will read you a passage from her poem 'Matrix':

Where then are the unborn ones?
Do they eternally go,
Cloud wracks of souls tormented,
Through ether for ever?

No such ventures theirs, no.

They crowd in the core of the earth;
They lie in the loam,
Laid backwards by slice of the plough;

They sit in the rock:
In a matrix of amethyst crouches a man,
Pygmy, a part of the womb,
Of the stone,
For ever, for all time, now.

All things there are his own:
The light on water, the leaves,
The spray of the wild yellow rose;
Beautiful as to the born
Are the stars to the unconceived;
The twilight, the morn, of their sight,
Are lovelier than to the born.[37]

Turner, the poet, mathematician, musician, thinks that the horror of the world is in its beauty. Beautiful forms deceive us, because if we grasp them, they dissolve into what he calls 'confused sensation';[38] and destroy us because they drag us under the machinery of nature; if it were possible he would, like a Buddhist, or a connoisseur, kill, or suspend desire. He does not see men and women as the puppets of Eliot's poetry, repeating over and over the same trivial movements, but as the reflections of a terrible Olympus. I will read you his poem upon the procession of the mannequins.

I have seen mannequins,
As white and gold as lilies,
Swaying their tall bodies across the burnished floor
Of *Reville* or *Paquin*;
Writhing in colour and line,
Curved tropical flowers
As bright as thunderbolts.
Or hooded in dark furs
The sun's pale splash
In English autumn woods.

And I have watched these soft explosions of life
As astronomers watch the combustion of stars.

The violence of supernatural power
Upon their faces,

White orbits
Of incalculable forces.

And I have had no desire for their bodies
But have felt the whiteness of a lily
Upon my palate;
And the solidity of their slender curves
Like a beautiful mathematical proposition
In my brain.

But in the expression of their faces
Terror.

Cruelty in the eyes, nostrils, and lips—

Pain
thou passion-flower, thou wreath, thou orbit,
thou spiritual rotation,
thou smile upon a pedestal
Peony of the garden of Paradise![39]

Many Irish men and women must be listening, and they may wonder why I have said nothing of modern Irish poetry. I have not done so because it moves in a different direction and belongs to a different story. Modern Irish poetry began in the midst of that rediscovery of folk thought I described when quoting York Powell's translation from Paul Fort. The English movement, checked by the realism of Eliot, the social passion of the war poets, gave way to an impersonal philosophical poetry. Because Ireland has a still living folk tradition, her poets cannot get it out of their heads that they themselves, good-tempered or bad-tempered, tall or short, will be remembered by the common people. Instead of turning to impersonal philosophy, they have hardened and deepened their personalities. I could have taken as examples Synge or James Stephens,[40] men I have never ceased to delight in. But I prefer to quote poetry of which you have probably never heard, though it is among the greatest lyric poetry of our time.

Some twelve years ago political enemies came to Senator Gogarty's house while they knew he would be in his bath and so unable to reach his revolver, made him dress, brought him to an empty house on the edge of the Liffey. They told him nothing, but he felt certain he was to be kept as hostage and shot after the inevitable execution of a certain man then in prison. Self-possessed and daring, he escaped, and while swimming the cold December river, vowed two swans to it if it would land him safely. I was present some weeks later when, in the presence of the Head of the State and other notables the two swans were launched. That story shows the man—scholar, wit, poet, gay adventurer. In one poem, written years afterwards, the man who dedicated the swans dedicates the poems, and the mood has not changed:

> Tall unpopular men,
> Slim proud women who move
> As women walked in the islands when
> Temples were built to Love,
> I sing to you. With you
> Beauty at best can live,
> Beauty that dwells with the rare and few,
> Cold and imperative.
> He who had Caesar's ear
> Sang to the lonely and strong.
> Virgil made an austere
> Venus Muse of his song.[41]

Here is another poem characteristic of those poems which have restored the emotion of heroism to lyric poetry:

> Our friends go with us as we go
>   Down the long path where Beauty wends,
> Where all we love forgathers, so
>   Why should we fear to join our friends?
>
> Who would survive them to outlast
>   His children; to outwear his fame—
> Left when the Triumph has gone past—
>   To win from Age, not Time, a name?
>
> Then do not shudder at the knife
>   That Death's indifferent hand drives home,
> But with the Strivers leave the Strife,
>   Nor, after Caesar, skulk in Rome.[42]

When I have read you a poem I have tried to read it rhythmically; I may be a bad reader; or read badly because I am out of sorts, or self-conscious; but there is no other method. A poem is an elaboration of the rhythms of common speech and their association with profound feeling. To read a poem like prose, that hearers unaccustomed to poetry may find it easy to understand, is to turn it into bad, florid prose. If anybody reads or recites poetry as if it were prose from some public platform, I ask you, speaking for poets, living, dead or unborn, to protest in whatever way occurs to your perhaps youthful minds; if they recite or read by wireless, I ask you to express your indignation by letter. William Morris, coming out of a hall where somebody had read or recited his *Sigurd the Volsung* said: 'It cost me a lot of damned hard work to get that thing into verse.'[43]

1936

Bishop Berkeley

Introduction to *Bishop Berkeley*,[1] by Joseph M. Hone and Mario M. Rossi (1931)

I

Imagination, whether in literature, painting or sculpture, sank after the death of Shakespeare. Supreme intensity had passed to another faculty; it was as though Shakespeare, Dante, Michelangelo, had been re-born with all their old sublimity, their old vastness of conception, but speaking a harsh, almost unintelligible language. Two or three generations hence, when men accept the inventions of science as a commonplace and understand that it is limited by its method to appearance, no educated man will doubt that the movement of philosophy from Spinoza to Hegel[2] is the greatest of all works of intellect.

II

I delight in that fierce young man, whose student years passed when the battle of the Boyne fought, as Molyneux said, to change not an English but an Irish crown, was a recent memory;[3] who established with Molyneux's son for secretary a secret society to examine the philosophy of a 'neighbouring nation';[4] who defined that philosophy, the philosophy of Newton and Locke, in three sentences, wrote after each that Irishmen thought otherwise, and on the next page that he must publish to find if men elsewhere agreed with Irishmen.[5] What he then was, solitary, talkative, ecstatic, destructive, he showed through all his later years though but in glimpses or as something divined or inferred. It is not the fault of his biographer but of the inanimate record, or of his own inanimate pose that he is not there in all his blood and state. But after all when we search our own experience whether of life or letters how many stand solidly? At this moment I but recall four or five intimate friends, an old woman that I never spoke to, seen at a public assembly in America, an image met ten years ago in a sudden blaze of light under my closed eyelids, William Morris, and the half symbolic image of Jonathan Swift.[6] Yet I am indebted to Joseph Hone that Berkeley moves among those images, though not with their solidity, that when the pattern has changed, when some of its elements have gone, he will still move there. Furthermore I understand now what I once but vaguely guessed that these two images, standing and sounding together, Swift and Berkeley, concern all those who feel a responsibility for the thought of modern Ireland that can take away their sleep.

III

I hate what I remember of his portrait in the Fellows Room at Trinity College;[7] it wears a mask kept by engravers and painters from the middle of the eighteenth century for certain admired men; Phillips' Blake, contradicted by the powerful lines of the life mask, wears it too,[8] and the statue of the Prince Consort on Leinster Lawn;[9] the smooth gregarious mask of Goldsmith's *Goodnatured Man*,[10] an abstraction that slipped away unexamined when Swift and Berkeley examined and mocked its kind. The portrait attributed to Vanderbank is more amusing; the painter overpowered by the admired man turns the ecclesiastical sleeves into those great sleeves worn by Titian's women, and rounds the face to a vague half-animal Venetian loveliness. One turns one's eyes from the gods and satyrs in the background—the engraved figures are too small for my sight—to peer under the bowl of the fountain or behind the chair expecting to discover one of those little dogs brought into fashion by Venetian courtesans.[11] I reject with less liking and equal incredulity the Berkeley come down to us in the correspondence of his day; the sage as imagined by gentlemen of fortune—a role accepted by Berkeley that he might not be left to starve in some garret by a generation terrified of religious scepticism and political anarchy, and loved because it hid from himself and others his own anarchy and scepticism. The *Commonplace Book* is there to show that he did not accept it without hesitation or love it with his whole heart. 'N. B. To use utmost caution not to give the least handle of offence to the Church or churchmen . . . even to speak somewhat well of the Schoolmen . . .' 'N. B. To rein in your satirical nature.'[12] The something unreal about his public life made him the more attractive to his contemporaries, was an essential element perhaps of his incredible persuasiveness as if he were some hieratic image; only in those speculations, that seemed the lovable foible of a great man, is he altogether real. One looks in vain for some different life lived among friends and pupils, wonders what habits of secrecy still remained. What did he say in those three sermons to under-graduates that brought so much suspicion upon him, not perhaps what he says in the long unreadable essay upon utilitarian ethics written to save his face?[13] Was the Bermuda project, with its learned city so carefully mapped out, a steeple in the centre, a market in each corner, more than a theme for discourse? He had left behind those earnest Fellows of Trinity College who had offered their service and might have liked converting American-Indians—there is a Trinity College Mission to savage parts—and brought to America a portrait-painter and a couple of pleasant young men of fortune, and associated there with fox-hunters and immaterialist disciples.[14] Or did he think that if he could stop all thought with his Utopian drug—what thinker has not felt the temptation—the mask might become real? He that cannot live must dream. Did tar-water, a cure-all learnt from American-Indians, suggest that though he could not quiet men's minds he might give their bodies quiet, and so bring to life that incredible benign image, the dream of a time that after the anarchy of the religious wars, the spiritual torture of Donne, of El Greco and Spinoza, longed to be protected and flattered.[15] The first great imaginative wave had sunk, the second had not yet risen.

I think of my father, of one friend or another, even of a drunken countryman who tumbled into my carriage out of the corridor one summer night, men born into our Irish solitude, of their curiosity, their rich discourse, their explosive passion, their sense of mystery as they grew old, their readiness to dress up at the suggestion of others though never quite certain what dress they wore, their occasional childish worldliness. In our eighteenth century four or five such men had genius, two or three have genius today.

IV

It is customary to praise English empirical genius, English sense of reality, and yet throughout the eighteenth century when her Indian Empire was founded England lived for certain great constructions that were true only in relation to the will. I spoke in the Irish Senate on the Catholic refusal of divorce and assumed that all lovers who ignored Priest or Registrar were immoral; upon education,[16] and assumed that everybody who could not read the newspaper was a poor degraded creature; and had I been sent there by some religious organisation must have assumed that a child captured by a rival faith lost its soul; and had my country been at war—but who does not serve these abstractions? Without them corporate life would be impossible. They are as serviceable as those leaf-like shapes of tin that mould the ornament for the apple pie, and we give them belief, service, devotion. How can we believe in truth that is always moth-like and fluttering and yet can terrify?—A friend and I, both grown men talked ourselves once into terror of a little white moth in Burnham Beeches.[17] And of all these the most comprehensive, the most useful, was invented by Locke when he separated the primary and secondary qualities;[18] and from that day to this the conception of a physical world without colour, sound, taste, tangibility, though indicted by Berkeley as Burke was to indict Warren Hastings fifty years later,[19] and proved mere abstract extension, a mere category[20] of the mind, has remained the assumption of science, the ground-work of every text book. It worked, and the mechanical inventions of the next age, its symbols that seemed its confirmation, worked even better, and it worked best of all in England where Edmund Spenser's inscription over the gates of his magic city seemed to end 'Do not believe too much':[21] elsewhere it is the grosser half of that dialectical materialism, the socialist Prince Mirski calls 'the firm foundation-rock of European socialism',[22] and works all the mischief Berkeley foretold.

V

The sense for what is permanent, as distinct from what is useful, for what is unique and different, for the truth that shall prevail, for what antiquity called the sphere as distinct from the gyre, comes from solitaries or from communities where the solitaries flourish, Indians with a begging bowl, monks where their occupation is an adventure, men escaped out of machinery, improvident men that sit by the roadside and feel responsible for all that exists:

Do not thou grieve or blush to be
As all inspired and tuneful men
And all thy great forefathers were from Homer down to Ben.[23]

Born in such community Berkeley with his belief in perception, that abstract ideas are mere words, Swift with his love of perfect nature, of the Houyhnhnms, his disbelief in Newton's system and every sort of machine, Goldsmith and his delight in the particulars of common life that shocked his contemporaries, Burke with his conviction that all states not grown slowly like a forest tree are tyrannies, found in England an opposite that stung their own thought into expression and made it lucid.[24]

VI

If J. W. Dunne's *Experiment with Time*[25] is well founded, if our nightly dreams are in part a mixture of past and future events; if with little effort we can think the like dreams awake; and my own experience supports him; I may perhaps regard the speculations of men caught in the machinery of life as mere prophecy, perhaps even suggest that we honour the prophetic afflatus before every other afflatus because it is so gregarious. Berkeley had his disciples, but they came in twos and threes, were far apart in time and place, no man until many years had passed lived the heartier because he shared their theme.

VII

Berkeley thought the Seven Days not the creation of sun and moon, beast and man, but their entrance into time, or into human perception, or into that of some spirit; that his study table when the room seemed empty existed in the mind of some spirit or went back into eternity.[26] Though he could not describe mystery—his age had no fitting language—his suave glittering sentences suggest it; we feel perhaps for the first time that eternity is always at our heels or hidden from our eyes by the thickness of a door. Something of this depends upon his use of common words,[27] his sparing use of exact definitions, his conviction that he must as far as possible accept our point of view, upon his remaining, no matter what the theme, a conversationalist, an easy travelled man whose attention flatters us; upon those three dialogues of Hylas and Philonous, the only philosophical arguments since Plotinus that are works of art, being so well-bred, so sensible.[28] What does it matter when we are in such good company if Michael's trumpet blares on every threshold?

VIII

I published some pages from a diary a few years back in which this quotation occurs: 'A few days ago my sister Lolly dreamed that she saw three dead bodies on a bed. One had its face to the wall, one had a pink mask like a child's toy mask, and before she could look at the third, somebody had put a mask on that too. While she was looking at them the body with its face to the wall suddenly moved. The same night J—— dreamed that she saw three very long funerals and that she saw what she thought a body on a bed. She thought it the body of a brother of hers who had died lately. She lay down on the bed by it and it suddenly moved. The same night my sister Lily dreamed that she had received three telegrams.'[29]

I draw J. W. Dunne's attention to these dreams that he may look right and left and not merely before and behind, and I assure him that if he experiments he will discover simultaneous correspondential reveries, as he did prophetic reveries even in waking life, that there is as much warp as woof. They may be as new to psychology as his own discoveries but that should not deter him.[30]

The romantic movement seems related to the idealist philosophy; the naturalistic movement, Stendhal's mirror dawdling down a lane,[31] to Locke's mechanical philosophy as simultaneous correspondential dreams are related; not merely where there is some traceable influence but through their whole substance, and I remember that monks in the Thebaid or was it by the Mariotic Sea, claimed 'To keep the ramparts',[32] meaning perhaps that all men whose thoughts skimmed the 'unconscious', God-abetting affected others according to their state, that what some feel others think, what some think others do. When I speak of idealist philosophy I think more of Kant than of Berkeley who was idealist and realist alike, more of Hegel and his successors than of Kant, and when I speak of the romantic movement I think more of Manfred, more of Shelley's Prometheus, more of Jean Valjean, than of those traditional figures, Browning's Pope, the fakir-like pedlar in *The Excursion.*[33]

IX

The romantic movement with its turbulent heroism, its self-assertion, is over, superseded by a new naturalism that leaves man helpless before the contents of his own mind. One thinks of Joyce's *Anna Livia Plurabelle*, Pound's *Cantos*, works of an heroic sincerity, the man, his active faculties in suspense, one finger beating time to a bell sounding and echoing in the depths of his own mind; of Proust who still fascinated by Stendhal's fixed frame-work seems about to close his eyes and gaze upon the pattern under his lids.[34] This new art which has arisen in different countries simultaneously seems related, as were the three telegrams to the three bodies, to that form of the new realist philosophy which thinks that the secondary and primary qualities alike are independent of consciousness;[35] that an object can at the same moment have contradictory qualities. This philosophy seems about to follow the analogy of an art that has more rapidly completed itself, and after deciding that a penny is bright and dark, oblong and round, hot and cold, dumb and ringing in its own right; to think of the calculations it incites, our distaste or pleasure at its sight, the decision that made us pitch it, our preference for head or tail, as independent of a consciousness that has shrunk back, grown intermittent and accidental, into the looking-glass. Some Indian Buddhists would have thought so had they pitched pennies instead of dice.

If you ask me why I do not accept a doctrine so respectable and convenient, its cruder forms so obviously resurrected to get science down from Berkeley's roasting-spit, I can but answer like Zarathustra, 'Am I a barrel of memories that I should give you my reasons?';[36] somewhere among those memories something compels me to reject whatever—to borrow a metaphor of

Coleridge's—drives mind into the quick-silver.[37] And why should I, whose ancestors never accepted the anarchic subjectivity of the nineteenth century, accept its recoil; why should men's heads ache that never drank? I admit there are, especially in America, such signs of prophetic afflatus about this new movement in philosophy, so much consonant with the political and social movements of the time, or so readily transformable into a desire to fall back or sink in on some thing or being, that it may be the morning cock-crow of our Hellenistic Age.

X

Berkeley wrote in his *Commonplace Book*—'The Spirit—the active thing—that which is soul and God—is the will alone'; and then remembering the mask that he must never lay aside, added: 'The concrete of the will and understanding I must call mind, not person, lest offence be given, there being but one volition acknowledged to be God. Mem. carefully to omit defining Person, or making much mention of it.'[38] Then remembering that some member of his secret society had asked if our separate personalities were united in a single will, a question considered by Plotinus in the Fourth Ennead but dangerous in the eighteenth century, he wrote, 'What you ask is merely about a word, unite is no more.'[39] Number had no existence being like all abstract ideas a part of language. It is plain however from his later writings that he thought of God as a pure indivisible act, personal because at once will and understanding, which unlike the Pure Act of Italian philosophy creates passive 'ideas'—sensations—thrusts them as it were outside itself; and in this act all beings—from the hierarchy of heaven to man and woman and doubtless to all that lives[40]—share in the measure of their worth: not the God of Protestant theology but a God that leaves room for human pride. As I enumerate these thoughts I forget the gregarious episcopal mask and remember a Berkeley that asked the Red Indian for his drugs, an angry, unscrupulous[41] solitary that I can test by my favourite quotations and find neither temporal nor trivial—'An old hunter talking with gods, or a high-crested chief, sailing with troops of friends to Tenedos,'[42] and the last great oracle of Delphi commemorating the dead Plotinus, 'That wave-washed shore . . . the golden race of mighty Zeus . . . the just Aeacus, Plato, stately Pythagoras, and all the choir of immortal love'.[43]

XI

Only where the mind partakes of a pure activity can art or life attain swiftness, volume, unity; that contemplation lost we picture some slow-moving event, turn the mind's eye from everything else that we may experience to the full our own passivity, our personal tragedy; or like the spider in Swift's parable mistake for great possessions what we spit out of our guts and deride the bee that has nothing but its hum and its wings, its wax and its honey, its sweetness and light.[44] 'God', 'Heaven', 'Immortality', those words and their associated myths define that contemplation. Philosophy can deny them all meaning, some of the greatest human works are such denial, but we think it vulgar and jejune if it do so without despair; and history shows that it must return again and again to the problem that they set. Giambattista Vico has said that we should reject all philosophy that does not begin in myth,[45] and it is impossible to pronounce those three words without becoming as simple as a camel-driver or a pilgrim.

XII

Berkeley in his youth described the *summum bonum* and the reality of heaven as physical pleasure, and thought this conception made both more intelligible to simple men.[46] And though he abandoned it in later life, and not merely because incompatible with the mask, one returns to it remembering Blake's talk of 'enlarged and numerous senses', his description of heaven as an improvement of sense,[47] Lake Harris' denunciation of Swedenborg as a half man 'that half saw, half felt, half tasted the Kingdom of Heaven'.[48] Berkeley was fumbling his way backward to some simple age. I think of the Zen monk's expectation though maybe but as an inducement to passivity, of an odour of unknown flowers as contemplation reached its climax; of the Zen painter gathering into the same powerful rhythm all those things that in the work of his predecessor stood so solidly as themselves.[49]

When Berkeley abandoned that first opinion he did not exalt in place of perception some abstract thought or law but some always undefined apprehension of spirits and their relations. Looking for a clue I think of Coleridge's contrast between Juliet's nurse and Hamlet,[50] remember that Shakespeare drew the nurse from observation, from passive sense-impression, but Hamlet, the court, the whole work of art, out of himself in a pure indivisible act. There have been mystics no doubt who thought they knew by a knowledge as direct the creatures of their neighbourhood, partaking as it were the timeless act of their creation, and I once visited a Cabbalist who spent the day trying to look out of the eyes of his canary; he announced at nightfall that all things had for it colour but nothing outline. His method of contemplation was probably in error.[51]

XIII

Forty years ago intellectual young men dissatisfied with the political poetry of Young Ireland, once the foundation of Irish politics, substituted an interest in old stories and modern peasants,[52] and now the young men are dissatisfied again. The hereditary political aim has been accomplished; their country does not need their help; the question I have heard put again and again 'What would he sacrifice?' is put no more, everything is upside down; it is their aims that are unaccomplished, they that need help; they have begun to ask if their country has anything to give. Joseph Hone draws their attention to that eighteenth century when its mind became so clear that it changed the world.

July, 1931

My Friend's Book

(1932) Review of *Song and its Fountains*, by AE (George Russell)

I

One opens a friend's book with dread, every trick of style has its associations, we wonder perpetually—such hatred is in friendship—how a man we have buckled to our heart can have so little sense. Admiration can but feed hatred, and if we have known the man for five-and-forty years and met him once a week for the last ten, and must write about his book—and what else can be so interesting?—it may seem best to touch upon some one aspect and ignore the rest. Yet, in writing about AE's *Song and its Fountains* I cannot do so; I must face all my associations, merely stating at the outset that my hatred has won the right to call itself friendship.[1]

II

Towards the end of my Dublin schooldays an elderly servant of my mother's took an interest in a schoolboy who passed our windows daily. None of us knew his name, nor did he interest my sisters or myself or seem in any way unusual, but our servant called him 'the strayed angel'. Then I went to the Art schools and found him, turning his study of the nude into a Saint John in the Desert, with some reminiscence of da Vinci perhaps obstructing his sight. I soon discovered that he possessed a faculty dormant elsewhere since the time of Swedenborg.[2] If he sat silent for a while on the Two Rock Mountain,[3] or any spot where man was absent, the scene would change; unknown, beautiful people would move among the rocks and trees; but his vision, unlike that of Swedenborg, remained always what seemed an unexplained, external, sensuous panorama. Another student, devout and Catholic, cried to him once in a moment of excitement, 'You will drift into a penumbra,' yet it was he himself who became unbalanced, wandering about Dublin in clothes of sack-cloth stitched by his own unskilful hands, full of queer tricks to gather an audience for his moral exhortations,[4] AE, as George Russell names himself, becoming that influential journalist and economist Dublin knows so well. My criticism varied, sometimes calling those images a subjective intensification of such reminiscences as that which transformed his nude study, but when I had confirmed from the obscure symbolism of alchemy an explanation of the Scourging of Christ[5] implicit in some visionary scene I had to change my tune.

III

Three or four years later our disputes began in earnest. I insisted that these images, whether symbols projected by the subconscious, or physical facts, should be made to explain themselves; sometimes I broke off abruptly, afraid that he might never speak to me again. Sometimes I quarrelled with something said or done in the ordinary affairs of life which could not have been said or done, as I thought, had he not encountered the Magical Emblems and the Sick King and refused to ask questions that might have made the soil fruitful again.[6]

That he should question, as Swedenborg had questioned, seemed to me of the first importance. Locke based himself upon the formula, 'Nothing in mind that has not come from sense'—sense as the seventeenth century understood it—and Leibnitz commented, 'Nothing except mind.'[7] But what if Henry More was right when he contended that men and animals drew not only universals but particulars from a supersensual source?[8] May we not be compelled to change all our conceptions should it be proved that, in some crisis of life perhaps, we have access to the detailed circumstantial knowledge of other minds, or to the wisdom that has such knowledge for a foundation; or, as Henry More believed—unless I have forgotten his long essay on *The Immortality of the Soul*, toiled through some fifteen years ago—that the bees and birds learn to make nest and comb from that *Anima Mundi* which contains the knowledge of all dead bees and birds?[9] What if the modern accentuation of individuality is what the Buddhists call, we are told, 'separateness' and in intellect as in morality an error? I think of *An Adventure* by those two Oxford ladies, heads of Colleges who found themselves of a sudden in the Court of Marie Antoinette; of Dunne's *Experiment with Time* where the visions are of the future—to name but two books from a voluminous literature from which no man has as yet deduced the consequences.[10]

'Nothing in mind that has not come from sense except mind.' If that is the foundation even of our most profound thought do not contemporary schools of opinion resemble a ghastly sight of childhood: turkeys running round the yard with their heads off?

IV

In this book AE attempts to describe and explain some part of his experience. Swedenborg, metallurgical expert, scientific speculator, was a man of boundless curiosity, but the author of *Song and its Fountains*—landscape painter and pastellist, when his visions were still a novelty[11]—escapes with difficulty from mere pleasure and astonishment at the varied scene. I began by hating the book for its language. My friend, whose English at the close of the civil war was so vigorous and modern—I remember an article which found its way into the prisons and stopped a hunger strike[12]—writes as though he were living in the 'nineties, seems convinced that spiritual truth requires a dead language. He writes 'dream' where other men write 'dreams', a trick he and I once shared, picked up from William Sharp[13] perhaps when the romantic movement was in its last contortions. Renaissance Platonism had ebbed out in poetic diction, isolating certain words and phrases as if they were Platonic Ideas. He has heaped up metaphors that seem to me like those wax flowers of a still older time I saw in childhood melted on the side towards the window. Yet I came to love the book for its thought.

It is almost wholly an illustration and commentary upon Plato's doctrine of pre-natal memory. It traces back AE's dominating ideas to certain impressions, the colour of a wild flower, an image from a child's story, something somebody told him about a neighbour,[14] a vision seen under closed eyelids; always, it seems, to single images, single events, which opened as it were sluice-gates into the will. A poet, he contends, does not transmute into song what he has learned in experience. He reverses the order and says that the poet first imagines and that later the imagination attracts its affinities. The more we study those affinities as distinct from the first impulse the more realistic is our art, which explains why a certain novelist of my acquaintance who can describe with the most convincing detail the clothes, houses, tricks of speech of his characters, is yet the most unobservant of men. The author of *Song and its Fountains*, shows the origin of certain of his poems and believes that we can all trace back our lives as a whole from event to event to those first acts of the mind, and those acts through vision to the pre-natal life. While so engaged he came upon a moral idea which seems to me both beautiful and terrible. He had an intuition that in some pre-natal life there had been 'downfall and tragic defeat'; he had begun a 'concentration upon that intuition'[15] and almost at once became terrified. He seemed to be warned away from some knowledge he could not have endured, a warning which may have preserved his sanity while confining vision to a seemingly sensuous and external panorama, and substituting an emotional apprehension for analysis. He thinks that when a man is to attain great wisdom he first learns all the evil of his past, assumes responsibility for his share in that evil, follows out with a complete knowledge the consequence of every act, repents the sin of twenty thousand years, unified at last in thought, and only when this agony has been exhausted can he recall what was 'lovely and beloved'.[16] We do not re-live the past, for our life is always our own, always novel, but dream back or think back to that first purity. Is not all spiritual knowledge perhaps a reversal, a return? Or, as he sums up in one of those quotations from his own verse which give the book its chief beauty:

I know when I come to my own immortal I will find there
In a myriad instant all that the soul found fair,
Empires that never crumbled and thrones all glorious yet
And hearts ere they were broken and eyes ere they were wet.[17]

Plotinus had not this thought; the Cambridge Platonists, the more exhaustive ethical logic of Christianity spurring them on, might have discovered it had not the soul's re-birth, though it fascinated Glanvil, been a dangerous theme.[18] Now, however, that McTaggart has made that doctrine the foundation of the first English systematic philosophy, one can invite attention to what may bring all past ages into the circle of conscience.

V

I turn the pages once more and find that my friend has excused his lack of questioning curiosity better than I had thought. 'The Spirit', as he calls the ultimate reality, gave to some 'the infinite vision', but he had been content 'to know that it was there', and through that knowledge was 'often happy'; had he stirred 'it would have vanished';[19] and then he cries out in an unrhymed poem that seems to me new:

> If I would stay thee
> Thou art gone inward, and thy light as lost
> As the flying fish is, a pearly shadow that leaps
> From the dark blue to slide in the dark blue.

He cannot follow, he adds, the stern passage of sanctity ascending from anguish to delight, nor worship Spirit under some majestic form:

> My secret was thy gentleness. I know
> No nurse has ever crooned a lullaby
> So softly as thou the music that guides the loud
> Tempest in its going forth.[20]

Prometheus Unbound (w. 1932; publ. 1933)

I

When I was a young man I wrote two essays calling Shelley's dominant symbol the Morning Star, his poetry the poetry of desire.[1] I had meant to explain *Prometheus Unbound*, but some passing difficulty turned me from a task that began to seem impossible. What does Shelley mean by Demogorgon? It lives in the centre of the earth, the sphere of Parmenides perhaps, in a darkness that sends forth 'rays of gloom' as 'light from the meridian sun';[2] it names itself 'eternity'.[3] When it has succeeded Jupiter, 'the supreme of living things', as he did Saturn, when it and Jupiter have gone to lie 'henceforth in darkness',[4] Prometheus is set free, nature purified. Shelley the political revolutionary expected miracle, the Kingdom of God in the twinkling of an eye like some Christian of the first century. He had accepted Berkeley's philosophy as expounded in Sir William Drummond's *Academical Questions*.[5] The ultimate reality is not thought, for thought cannot create, but 'can only perceive';[6] the created world is a stream of images in the human mind, the stream and cavern of his symbolism; this stream is Time. Eternity is the abyss which receives and creates. Sometimes the soul is a boat, and in this boat Asia sails against the current from age to youth, from youth to infancy, and so to the pre-natal condition 'peopled by shapes too bright to see'.[7] In the fourth act this condition, man's first happiness and his last, sings its ecstatic song: and yet although the first and last it is always near at hand, 'Tír-na-nÓg is not far from any of you', as a countrywoman said to me:

That garden sweet, that lady fair,
And all sweet shapes and odours there,
In truth, have never passed away;
'Tis we; 'tis ours are changed; not they.[8]

Why then does Demogorgon, whose task is beneficent, who lies in wait behind 'The mighty portal . . . whence the oracular vapour is hurled up which lonely men drink wandering in their youth',[9] bear so terrible a shape, and not to the eyes of Jupiter, external necessity, alone, but to those of Asia, who is identical with the Venus-Urania of the 'Athanase'.[10] Why is Shelley terrified of the Last Day like a Victorian child? It was not terrible to Blake, 'For the cherub with the flaming sword is hereby commanded to leave his guard at the Tree of Life: and when he does the whole creation will be consumed and appear infinite and holy, whereas it now appears finite and corrupt.'[11]

II

Demogorgon made his plot incoherent, its interpretation impossible, it was thrust there by that something which again and again forced him to balance the object of desire conceived as miraculous and superhuman, with nightmare. Shelley told his friends of attempts upon his life or his liberty, elaborating details between delusion and deceit, believed himself infected with elephantiasis because he had sat opposite a fat woman in an omnibus, encountered terrifying apparitions, one woman with eyes in her breasts; nor did his friendships escape obsession, his admired Elizabeth Hutchinson[12] became 'the brown demon . . . an artful, superficial, ugly, hermaphroditical beast of a woman'; nor was *Prometheus* the only nightmare-ridden work; there is nothing in *Swellfoot the Tyrant*[13] but the cold rhetoric of obsession; *The Cenci*[14] for all its magnificent construction is made unendurable upon the stage by an artificial character, the scapegoat of his unconscious hatred. When somebody asked Aubrey Beardsley towards the end of his life why he secreted indecencies in odd corners of his designs, more than once necessitating the destruction of a plate, he answered 'Something compels me to sacrifice to Priapus.' Shelley, whose art is allied to that of the Salome drawings[15] where sex is sublimated to an unearthly receptivity, though more ardent and positive, imagined under a like compulsion whatever seemed dark, destructive, indefinite. Blake, though he had his brown demons, kept his freedom in essentials; he had encountered with what seemed his physical eyes but one nightmare; 'scaly, speckled, very awful'[16] and thought such could visit but seldom imaginative men.

III

Shelley was not a mystic, his system of thought was constructed by his logical faculty to satisfy desire, not a symbolical revelation received after the suspension of all desire. He could neither say with Dante 'Thy will is my peace',[17] nor with Finn in the Irish story 'the best music is what happens'.[18]

There is a form of mediation which permits an image or symbol to generate itself, and the images and symbols so generated build themselves up into coherent structures often beautiful and startling. When a young man I made an exhaustive study of this condition in myself and in others, choosing as a rule for the initiatory symbol a name or form associated with the Cabbalistic Sephiroth, or with one of the five traditional elements.[19] Sometimes, though not in my own case, trance intervened and the structure attained a seeming physical solidity, this however seldom happened and was considered undesirable. Almost always, after some days or weeks of meditation, a form emerged in sleep or amid the ordinary affairs of life to show or speak some significant message, or at some moment a strange hidden will controlled the unconscious movements of the body. If the experimentalist had an impassioned purpose, some propaganda, let us say, and no critical sense, he might become obsessed by images, voices, that had, it seemed, for their sole object to guard his purpose or to express its contrary and to threaten. The mystic on the other hand is in no such danger, he so lives whether in east or west, whether he be Ramakrishna or Boehme,[20] as to dedicate his initiatory image, and its generated images, not to his own but to the Divine Purpose, and after certain years attains the Saint's miraculous life. There have been others unfitted for such a life by nature or station, who could yet dedicate their actions and acquire what William Morris has called lucky eyes; 'all that he does unwitting he does well.'[21] There is much curious evidence to show that the Divine Purpose so invoked descends into the mind at moments of inspiration, not as spiritual life alone but as what seems a physical brightness. Perhaps everybody that pursues that life for however short a time, even, as it were, but touches it, experiences now and again during sleep bright coherent dreams where something is shown or spoken that grows in meaning with the passage of time. Blake spoke of this 'stronger and better light', called its source 'the human form divine',[22] Shelley's 'harmonious soul of many a soul',[23] or, as we might say, the Divine Purpose. The stationary, joyous energy of certain among his figures, *Christ Blessing*[24] for instance, or of his own life when we regard it as a whole as contrasted with the sadness and disquiet of Shelley's, suggests radiating light. We understand why the first Christian painters encircled certain heads with light. Because this source or purpose is always an action, never a system of thought, its man can attend, as Shelley would not, to the whole drama of life, simplicities, banalities, intoxications, even lie upon his left side and eat dung, set free 'from a multitude of opinions'.[25]

It was as a mystic that Blake wrote 'Sweet joy befall thee', 'Soft deceit and idleness', 'The Holy Word walks among the ancient trees.'[26] Shelley's art shows that he was an unconverted man though certainly a visionary, what people call 'psychic'; his landscapes are vaporised and generalised by his purpose, his spirits have not the separated existence even of those that in *Manfred* curse and yet have 'sweet and melancholy' voices.[27] He was the tyrant of his own being, nor was it in all likelihood a part of the plan that it should find freedom, seeing that he worked as did Keats and Marlowe, uncorrecting and unhesitating, as though he knew the shortness of his life.[28] That life, and all lives would be unintelligible to me did I not think of them as an exfoliation prolonged from life to life; he sang of something beginning.

IV

When I was in my early twenties Shelley was much talked about, London had its important 'Shelley Society', *The Cenci* had been performed and forbidden, provincial sketching clubs displayed pictures by young women of the burning of Shelley's body. The orthodox religion, as our mothers had taught it, was no longer credible, those who could not substitute connoisseurship, or some humanitarian or scientific pursuit, found a substitute in Shelley. He had shared our curiosities, our political problems, our conviction that despite all experience to the contrary, love is enough; and unlike Blake, isolated by an arbitrary symbolism, he seemed to sum up all that was metaphysical in English poetry. When in middle life I looked back I found that he and not Blake, whom I had studied more and with more approval, had shaped my life, and when I thought of the tumultuous and often tragic lives of friends or acquaintances I attributed to his direct or indirect influence their Jacobin frenzies, their brown demons.

V

Another study of that time, less general, more confined to exceptional men, was that of Balzac as a social philosopher.[29] When I was thirteen or fourteen I heard somebody say that he changed men's lives, nor can I think it a coincidence that an epoch founded in such thought as Shelley's ended with an art of solidity and complexity. Me at any rate he saved from the pursuit of a beauty that seeming at once absolute and external requires, to strike a balance, hatred as absolute. Yet Balzac is no complete solution for that can be found in religion alone. One of the sensations of my childhood was a description of a now lost design of Nettleship's, *God creating Evil*, a vast terrifying face, a woman and a tiger rising from the forehead. Why did it seem so blasphemous and so profound?[30] It was many years before I understood that we must not demand even the welfare of the human race, nor traffic with divinity in our prayers. Divinity moves outside our antinomies, it may be our lot to worship in terror; 'Did He who made the lamb make thee?'[31]

Louis Lambert (w. 1933; publ. 1934)

I

Sometimes I meet somebody who read *Louis Lambert*[1] in his 'teens and find that he and I have put it among our sacred books, those books that expound destiny with such a mysterious authority that they furnish texts for pious meditation. Yet *Louis Lambert* is more or less materialistic; all things originate in a substance which is the common element of electricity, heat and light. In the brain the animal transforms it, in proportion to the strength of the brain, into will. This will creates out of itself thought and sense and by their means absorbs more and more of the parent substance. Though we speak of five senses there is only one, light, for tasting, hearing, smelling are light or sight transformed by different mutations of the substance. Balzac, who describes his own schooldays when he describes Louis Lambert's, may have found in that library at the Vendôme College, founded by learned Oratorians,[2] the works of Bonaventura and of his contemporary Grosseteste, for to Bonaventura hearing, tasting, smelling are forms of light,[3] while to Grosseteste light confers form upon the First Matter. Light is corporeality, he declares, or that of which corporeality is made, a point from which spheral space or corporeality flows as from nothing; a miracle repeated whenever our candle is lit.[4] *Louis Lambert* gives, as it seems, this ancient doctrine, Greek in origin, a materialistic turn by substituting for that first formless matter something that is less the ether of science which began to take its place at the close of the seventeenth century than the common element without attributes described by Crookes: that material Absolute sought by Balthasar Claës in crucible and retort.[5] Berkeley, Balzac's opposite physically and mentally, substituted God, and in *Siris*, like Grosseteste, made light or visibility (our principal perception or sensation) the common form of all particular objects.[6]

II

There is no evidence that Balzac knew that things exist in being perceived, or, to adopt the formula of a later idealism, that they exist in being thought, his powerful body, his imagination which saw everywhere weight and magnitude, the science of his day, made him, like Descartes, consider matter as independent of mind.[7] What then drove him half-way back to the mediaeval hypothesis? At some time of life, probably while still at college, before or during the composition of that *Treatise upon the Will*, which he attributes to Louis Lambert, he must have had, or met in others, supernormal experiences resembling those that occur again and again in the *Comédie humaine*.[8] Passages in *Séraphita* suggest familiarity with a state known to me in youth, a state transcending sleep when forms, often of great beauty, appear minutely articulated in brilliant light, forms that express by word or action some spiritual idea and are so moulded or tinted that they make all human flesh seem unhealthy. Then he must have known of, or had some vision of objects distant in time or place, perhaps in the remote past like that vision seen by Lucien de Rubempré before his death.[9] Something more profound, more rooted in the blood than mere speculation, drove him to Swedenborg,[10] perhaps to Bonaventura and Grosseteste; constrained him to think of the human mind as capable, during some emotional crisis, or, as in the case of Louis Lambert by an accident of genius, of containing within itself all that is significant in human history and of relating that history to timeless reality. He was able to do this by considering light, or fire, not as the child but as the parent or grandparent of the physical senses[11] by reviving the old doctrine of the animal spirits. 'In the *Timaeus* of Plato', writes Berkeley, 'there is something like a net of fire, and rays of fire in the human body. Doth this not seem to mean the animal spirit flowing, or rather darting, through the nerves?'[12] This fire is certainly that energy which in *Séraphita* is distinguished from will, and it is doubtless through its agency that will can rise above the human lot, or act beyond the range of the normal senses. 'If we believe Diogenes Laërtius,' writes Berkeley, 'the Pythagorean philosophers thought there was a certain pure heat or fire which had something divine in it, by the participation whereof man becomes allied to the Gods. And according to the Platonists, Heaven is not defined so much by its local situation as by its purity. The purest and most excellent fire, that is Heaven, saith Ficinus.'[13]

III

Louis Lambert's withdrawal into a state of dumb helpless wisdom on the day before what should have been his happy marriage, or into that madness which was an escape from the conflict between his desire of eternity and his sexual desire, suggests certain experiments of Balzac's day. As the mesmeric trance deepened the subject attained, not merely that vision of distant scenes described in *Ursule Mirouët*,[14] but wisdom. Perhaps, too, a Desplein or a Bianchon had pointed out that at times during such experiments the body became icy-cold as though its heat had come not from itself but from the now absent soul; an ancient doctrine Mr Carrington has supported by a curious book. The body, he contends, does not draw its heat from the combustion of food but during sleep from an unknown source.[15] Balzac, could he have known our modern psychical research, would have noticed that the medium passing into trance is cold, that the thermometer may register a chill in the air, that now and again some 'spirit' describes those brilliant lights that flit so silently about the room as the source of the energy used in the levitation of objects or in the production of voices, nor would he have failed to interest himself in Ochorowicz's suggestion that certain luminous egg-shaped objects, appearing and disappearing suddenly in the darkness, were the irreducible physical minimum of personality.[16]

IV

Louis Lambert, having attributed to man two natures, one that of an angel, hesitates; perhaps, he says, man has not two natures, perhaps, though merely men, we are capable of incomprehensible acts which we, in our admiration for the incomprehensible, attribute to spiritual beings.[17] Here are the two doctrines which dominate our psychical research—spiritualism and animism—the first in Anglo-Saxon countries where the Fox Sisters had so great an effect,[18] the second upon the continent where the Mesmerists, perhaps more through Balzac, George Sand, Dumas than by direct influence, have accustomed students to think that a personal illumination or state of power can be aroused by experimental means. When Balzac speaks through Séraphita or describes the Duchesse de Longuet playing upon the organ, he thinks of the choir of Heaven, when he creates a Desplein or a Bianchon he is, as I think, both animist and materialist.[19]

Will, having drawn to itself, one of Louis Lambert's aphorisms explains, a sufficient quantity of the substance (light or matter), becomes a most powerful mechanism, for it is like some great stream drawing to itself lesser streams, it may even acquire the qualities of the substance, 'the swiftness of light, the penetrating power of electricity', or it becomes aware of an 'X', an unknown something which consumes and burns, the Word which is forever generating the substance.[20] Here, though, but for a moment, Balzac's thought and that of Berkeley coincide. The Word is that which turns number into movement, but number (division, magnitude, enumeration) is described by Séraphita as unreal and as involving in unreality all our science. Two and two cannot be four, for nature has no two things alike. Every part is a separate thing and therefore itself a whole and so on. Is movement reality or does it share the unreality of number, its source?[21] Balzac but touches and passes on absorbed in drama. One could fill the gaps in his thought, substitute definition for his vague suggestion, were not that to lose the bull-necked man, the great eater, whose work resembles his body, the mechanist and materialist who wrote upon the darkness with a burnt stick such sacred and exciting symbols.

A modern painter, who thinks, like Whistler, that a picture must be perfect from the first sketch, growing in richness of detail but not in unity,[22] knows that a work of art must remain fluid to the finish, that an alteration in some minor character or in some detail of colour compels alteration elsewhere. He knows, too, having learnt in disappointment and fatigue, that if his first sketch lacks unity he will not know how to finish. But what is true of the work of art is true of the painter's or dramatist's own life, and if the work is not to be a closed circuit that first sketch has been shaped by desires and alarms arising from another sketch, made not for art but for life. The specialist may add fact to fact, postponing synthesis till greater knowledge, but the man cannot, for, lacking it, he can neither understand nor see correctly. Jane Austen, Scott, Fielding, inherited that other sketch in its clearest and simplest form,[23] but Balzac had to find it in his own mind. His sketch is *Louis Lambert,* the demonstration of its truth is that it made possible the *Comédie humaine.*

In the *Comédie humaine* society is seen as a struggle for survival, each character an expression of will, the struggle Darwin was to describe a few years later, without what our instinct repudiates, Darwin's exaltation of accidental variations.[24] Privilege, pride, the rights of property, are seen preserving the family against individual man armed with Liberty, Equality, Fraternity; and because the French Revolution was recent, he seems to prefer that wing of the Historical Antinomy that best fosters fine manners, minds set too high for intrigue and fear. He could be just to Catherine de Medici who preserved the State, personification of the family, to Napoleon who created the State; but, dreading, as I think, that hatred might infect his thought, brought into the action no great figure of the Revolution; personifying in the distant figure of Calvin, what he called the war of ideas with the State.[25] Will, or passion which is but blind will, is always at crisis, or approaching crisis; everything else seems eliminated, or is made fantastic or violent that the will, without seeming to do so, may exceed nature. Charles Grandet when the story is near its climax slips away to the Indies, earns a large fortune, is back again before we have turned the page;[26] Balzac, who invents detail with so much ease, knows that here it would slacken the pulse. Then, too, always somewhere in the background must lurk Vautrin, Séraphita, the Thirteen.[27] He creates the impossible that all may seem possible. He is like those painters who set patches of pure colour side by side, knowing that they will combine in the eye into the glitter of a wave, into the sober brown of a grass seed.[28] And this world of his, where everything happens in a blaze of light, and not the France of the historians, is early nineteenth-century France to thousands all over Europe.

V

Twenty years ago I read Tolstoi, Dostoieffsky, Flaubert with delight, but never opened them again.[29] I belong to a generation that returns to Balzac alone. The Russians make us debate some point of view peculiar to the author, Flaubert etherializes all with his conviction that life is no better than a smell of cooking through a grating. But Balzac leaves us when the book is closed amid the crowd that fills the boxes and the galleries of grand opera; even after hearing Séraphita amid her snows, we return to that crowd which is always right because there is so much history in its veins, to those kings, generals, diplomats, beautiful ladies, to that young Bianchon, to that young Desplein, to all those shabby students of the arts sitting in the Galleries.[30] Tolstoi, Dostoieffsky, Flaubert draw to their support scholars and sectaries, their readers stand above the theme or beside it, they judge and they reject; but there in the crowded theatre are Balzac's readers and his theme, seen with his eyes they have become philosophy without ceasing to be history. They do not make this impression upon us because of their multitude, there is almost a comparable multitude in *War and Peace*, but because that first sketch that gives unity is an adaption to his need and time of all that moulded Europe. Stendhal created a modern art; the seminary in *Rouge et noir*, unlike that described by Balzac in *Louis Lambert*, is of his own time and is judged according to its standards, is wholly reflected in the dawdling mirror that was to empty modern literature;[31] but something compelled Balzac while still at school to travel backward, as did the mind of Louis Lambert, to accept all that lay hidden in his blood and in his nerves. Here and there in Blake, in Keats, in Blunt, in Browning, for I cannot judge the rhythm of words in any language but my own, there is a deep masculine resonance, that comes, I think, from a perfect accord between intellect and blood, lacking elsewhere since the death of Cowley.[32] These men, whose rhythm seems to combine the bull and the nightingale were not modern, one had rejected us, two had ignored us, one had surpassed us. I find what seems their match in those passages in the *Comédie humaine* that suddenly startle us with a wisdom deeper than intellect and seem to demand an audience of the daring and the powerful. I have lived from boyhood in the shadow, as it were, of that enumeration of famous women in *La Recherche de l'absolu* ending with the sentence, 'Blessed are the imperfect for theirs is the Kingdom of Love.'[33] Dante might have made it or some great mediaeval monk, preaching in Rheims, where the French kings lie buried.[34]

VI

When I lectured in America the other day, I always invited questions and was constantly asked about books I had never heard of, books everybody was reading. Once I said, 'Lionel Johnson held that a man should have read through all good books before he was forty and after that be satisfied with six.' Then somebody asked what would be my six books and I said I wanted six authors not six books and I named four authors, choosing not from those that should, but from those that did most move me, and said I had forgotten the names of the other two. 'First comes Shakespeare,' I said. 'Then the *Arabian Nights* in its latest English version, then William Morris, who gives me all the great stories Homer and the Sagas included, then Balzac who saved me from Jacobin and Jacobite.'[35]

Introduction to *An Indian Monk*

An Indian Monk: His Life and Adventures, by Shri Purohit Swami (1932)

I

I wrote an introduction to the beautiful *Gitanjali* of Tagore,[1] and now, twenty years afterwards, draw attention to a book that may prove of comparable importance. A little more than a year ago I met its author, but lately arrived in Europe, at Mr Sturge Moore's house.[2] He had been sent by his Master, or spiritual director, that he might interpret the religious life of India, but had no fixed plan. Perhaps he should publish his poems, perhaps, like Vivekānanda, go to America.[3] He had gone to Rome thinking it was but courteous to pay his respects to the Holy Father, but though the Abbots of the most orthodox Hindu Shrines had given him their blessing, and 'the organiser of the Bhārat-Dharma Mahāmandal . . . a general letter of introduction', he was not received.[4] Then he had come to England and called upon the Poet Laureate,[5] who entertained him. He is a man of fifty, broken in health by the austerities of his religious life; he must have been a stalwart man and he is still handsome. He makes one think of some Catholic theologian who has lived in the best society, confessed people out of Henry James' novels, had some position at Court where he could engage the most absorbed attention without raising his voice, but that is only at first sight. He is something much simpler, more childlike and ancient. During lunch he and I, Sturge Moore, and an attaché from the Egyptian Legation,[6] exceedingly well read in European literature, discussed his plans and ideas. The attaché, born into a Jewish family that had lived among Mohammedans for generations, seemed more Christian in his point of view than Moore or myself. Presently the attaché said: 'Well, I suppose what matters is to do all the good one can.' 'By no means,' said the monk. 'If you have that object you may help some few people, but you will have a bankrupt soul. I must do what my Master bids, the responsibility is His.' That sentence, spoken without any desire to startle, interested me the more because I had heard the like from other Indians. Once when I stayed at Wilfrid Blunt's I talked to an exceedingly religious Mohammedan, kept there that he might not run himself into political trouble in India.[7] He spoke of the coming independence of India, but declared that India would never organise. 'There are only three eternal nations,' he said, 'India, Persia, China; Greece organised and Greece is dead.' I remembered too that an able Indian doctor I met when questioning London Indians about Tagore said of a certain Indian leader:[8] 'We do not think him sincere; he taught virtues merely because he thought them necessary to India.' This care for the spontaneity of the soul seems to me Asia at its finest and where it is most different from Europe, the explanation perhaps why it has confronted our moral earnestness and our control of Nature with its asceticism and its courtesy.

We sat on for a couple of hours after lunch while the monk, in answer to my questions, told of his childhood, his life at the University, of spiritual forms that he had seen, of seven years meditation in his house, of nine years wandering with his begging-bowl. Presently I said: 'The ideas of India have been expounded again and again, nor do we lack ideas of our own; discussion has been exhausted, but we lack experience. Write what you have just told us; keep out all philosophy, unless it interprets something seen or done.'

I found afterwards that I had startled and shocked him, for an Indian monk who speaks of himself contradicts all tradition, but that after much examination of his conscience he came to the conclusion that those traditions were no longer binding, and that besides, as he explained to Sturge Moore, a monk, a certain stage of initiation reached, is bound by nothing but the will of his Master. He took my advice and brought his book, chapter by chapter, to Sturge Moore for correction. Sturge Moore one of our finest critics, would say: 'You have told us too much of this, or too little of that; you must make us see that temple more clearly,' or he would cross something out, or alter a word, helping him to master our European sense of form.

II

The book lies before me complete; it seems to me something I have waited for since I was seventeen years old. About that age, bored by an Irish Protestant point of view that suggested by its blank abstraction chlorate of lime,[9] I began to question the country-people about apparitions. Some dozen years later Lady Gregory collected with my help the stories in her *Visions and Beliefs*.[10] Again and again, she and I felt that we had got down, as it were, into some fibrous darkness, into some matrix out of which everything has come, some condition that brought together as though into a single scheme 'exultations, agonies',[11] and the apparitions seen by dogs and horses; but there was always something lacking. We came upon visionaries of whom it was impossible to say whether they were Christian or Pagan, found memories of jugglers like those of India, found fragments of a belief that associated Eternity with field and road, not with buildings; but these visionaries, memories, fragments, were eccentric, alien, shut off as it were under the plate glass of a museum; I had found something of what I wanted but not all, the explanatory intellect had disappeared. When Shri Purohit Swami described his journey up those seven thousand steps at Mount Girnār, that creaking bed, that sound of pattens in the little old half-forgotten temple, and fitted everything into an ancient discipline, a philosophy that satisfied the intellect, I found all I wanted.[12]

III

Byzantine mystical theologians, Simeon, Callistus, Ignatius, and many others, taught a form of prayer or mental discipline resembling his. The devotee must say continually, even though his thought be elsewhere, 'Lord Jesus Christ, have mercy upon us';[13] a modern Russian pilgrim[14] of their school repeated those words daily twelve thousand times, 'Lord Jesus Christ' as he drew in his breath, 'have mercy upon us' as he breathed it out, until they had grown automatic and were repeated in his sleep;[15] he became, as he said, not speaker but listener.[16] Shri Purohit Swami writes: 'I repeated the Gāyitri, the most sacred mantram, was so habituated that even in my dreams I continued. When talking with others my mind went on unconsciously muttering

"We meditate on the supreme splendour of that Divine Being, may it illuminate our intellects".'[17] The Russian pilgrim begged dry bread from door to door; a monk of Mount Athos is at this moment travelling through the world and living upon 'fifty acorns a day'.[18] My Indian monk's habitual diet is milk and fruit, but his austerity at times has been greater; he writes of a certain pilgrimage: 'I refused to take either milk or fruit by the way and only drank water from time to time; my friend sang the glory of the Master' (their divine Lord Dattātreya) 'whenever I sat for rest under the shade of a tree, and would try to find and bring water to me.'[19]

IV

The prayers, however, are unlike, for the Russian's prayer implies original sin, that of the Indian asks for an inspired intellect; and this unlikeness is fundamental, the source perhaps of all other differences. The Russian, like most European mystics, distrusts visions though he admits their reality, seems indifferent to Nature, may perhaps dread it like Saint Bernard, who passed the Italian Lakes with averted eyes.[20] The Indian, upon the other hand, approaches God through a vision, speaks continually of the beauty and terror of the great mountains, interrupts his prayer to listen to the song of birds, remembers with delight the nightingale that disturbed his meditation by alighting upon his head and singing there, recalls after many years the whiteness of a sheet, the softness of a pillow, the gold embroidery upon a shoe. These things are indeed part of the 'splendour of that Being'.[21] The first four Christian centuries shared his thought; Byzantine theologians that named their great church 'The Holy Wisdom'[22] sang it; so, too, did those Irish monks who made innumerable poems about bird and beast, and spread the doctrine that Christ was the most beautiful of men. Some Irish saint, whose name I have forgotten, sang 'There is one among the beasts that is perfect, one among the fish, one perfect among men.'[23]

V

'And there are also many other things which Jesus did, the which, if they should be written every one, I suppose that even the world itself could not contain the books that should be written',[24] but Christendom has based itself upon four short books and for long insisted that all must interpret them in the same way. It was at times dangerous for a painter to vary, however slightly, the position of the Nails upon the Cross. The greatest saints have had their books examined by the Holy Office, for East and West seem each other's contraries—the East so independent spiritually, so ready to submit to the conqueror; the West independent politically, so ready to submit to its Church. The West impregnated an East full of spiritual turbulence, and that turbulence brought forth a child Western in complexion and in feature. Since the Renaissance, literature, science and the fine arts have left the Church and sought elsewhere the variety necessary to their existence; perhaps the converse impregnation has begun, the East as male. Being most impressed by arts that I have myself practised, I remember our selection for admiration of old masterpieces where 'tonal values' or the sense of weight and bulk that is the particular discovery of Europe are the least apparent: some flower of Botticelli's,[25] perhaps, that seems a separate intellectual existence. Then I think of the sensuous deliberation Spenser brought into English literature, of the magic of *Christabel*, or *Kubla Khan*, of the wise pedlar in the *Excursion*, of Ahasuerus in *Hellas*, and wisdom, magic, sensation, seem Asiatic.[26] We have borrowed directly from the East and selected for admiration or repetition everything in our own past that is least European, as though groping backward towards our common mother.

VI

Perhaps dogmatism was the necessary check upon European violence, asceticism upon the Asiatic fecundity. When Christ said: 'I and my Father are One',[27] it is possible to interpret Him as Shri Purohit Swami interprets his Master's 'I am Brahma'. The One is present in all numbers, Brahma in all men though self-conscious in the ascetic alone; and the plain man admits the evidence, for, beat the pupil and the ascetic's back is scored, and the ascetic, if he please, can exhaust in his own body an epidemic that might have swept away the village. Nor can a single image, that of Christ, Krishna or Buddha, represent God to the exclusion of other images. Shri Purohit Swami worshipped God at first as represented in a certain religious picture with an exciting history and no artistic merit, come to him through some accident of his personal history, but before the ascent of Mount Girnār his Master, though he has forgotten to record the incident in this book, transferred to him by a glance 'the vision of the formless'; after that he could still worship God under an image, but an image chosen by himself.[28] That initiation with its final freedom is itself an epitome of the soul's gradual escape, in its passage through many incarnations, from all that is external and predestined.

The Swami is a minstrel and story-teller where all popular literature is religion; yet all his poems are love-songs, lullabies or songs of loyalty to friend or master, for in his belief and in that of his hearers he can but offer to God the service learnt in service of man or woman; nor can any single service symbolise man's relation to God. He must be sung as the soul's husband, bride, child and friend. I asked for translations of these songs, which he sings in a sweet, not very strong voice, to a music which seems to employ intervals smaller than those of European music, especially for translations of those in Marāthi, his native tongue, for what poet is at his best out of his native tongue? He has, however, sent me translations of his poems in Urdu and Hindi as well, for his pilgrimage as it encircles India expends but two months in his native State, and everywhere he must sing.[29] The English hymn-writer, writing not as himself but as the congregation, is a rhetorician; but the Indian convention, founded upon the most poignant personal emotion, should make poets. The Swami has beautiful dramatic ideas, but only somebody born into one of those three tongues can say whether he has added that irrational element which has made 'Sing a Song of Sixpence'[30] immortal. This is from Marāthi:

Sweet are His eyes, sweet His looks,
The love they look exceeding sweet,
Sweet are His lips, sweet His kiss,
The love displayed exceeding sweet,
Sweet His words, His promise sweet,
Presence and absence both are sweet,
The pangs of love exceeding sweet.

This is from Hindi:

I know that I am a great sinner,
That there is no remedy,
But let Thy will be done.
If my Lord wishes he need not speak to me.
All I ask is that of His bounty
He walk by my side through my life.
I will behave well
Though He never embrace me—
O Lord, Thou art my Master
And I Thy slave.

This is from Urdu:

Shall I do this?
Shall I do that?
My hands are empty,
All that talk amounts to nothing.
Never will I do anything,
Never, never will I do anything;
Having been commanded to woo Thee
I should keep myself wide awake
Or else sleep away my life.
I am unfit to do the first,
But I can sleep with open eyes,
And I can always pretend to laugh,
And I can weep for the state I am in;
But my laugh has gone for good,
And gone the charm of tears.

And this too is from Urdu:

A miracle indeed!
Thou art Lord of All Power.
I asked a little power,
Thou gavest me a begging-bowl.[31]

VII

Our moral indignation, our uniform law, perhaps even our public spirit, may come from the Christian conviction that the soul has but one life to find or lose salvation in: the Asiatic courtesy from the conviction that there are many lives. There are Indian courtesans that meditate many hours a day awaiting without sense of sin their moment, perhaps many lives hence, to leave man for God. For the present they are efficient courtesans. Ascetics, as this book tells, have lived in their houses and received pilgrims there. Kings, princes, beggars, soldiers, courtesans and the fool by the wayside are equal to the eye of sanctity, for everybody's road is different, everybody awaits his moment.

VIII

The reader of the lives of European devotees may at first be disappointed in this book; the author's life is modelled upon no sacred example, ordered by no well-tried conventual discipline. He is pleased to remember that he learnt his book quickly at the college, that he overcame the wrestler, that he showed courage before the assassin's knife;[32] and yet, though he display our foibles and vanities, he has what we have not, though we once had it—heroic ecstatic passion prolonged through years, through many vicissitudes. Certain Indian, Chinese, and Japanese representations of the Buddha, and of other Divine beings, have a little round lump on the centre of the forehead;[33] ecstatics have sometimes received, as it were from the seal of the God, a similar mark. It corresponds to the wounds made as though by nails upon the hands and feet of some Christian saint, but the symbolism differs. The wounds signify God's sacrifice for man—'Jesus Christ, have mercy upon us'—that round mark the third eye, no physical organ but the mind's direct apprehension of the truth, above all antinomies, as the mark itself is above eyes, ears, nostrils, in their duality—'splendour of that Divine Being'. During our first meetings, whether within doors or without, Shri Purohit Swami's orange turban hid his forehead to the eyes, but he took it off one hot day during lunch, and I saw the little round lump. Marks somewhat resembling those made by nails have been produced upon the hands and feet of patients in a French hospital by hypnotic suggestion,[34] and it is usual, although the wounds of the Saints seen by credible witnesses were deeper, more painful, more disfiguring, to attribute those wounds to auto-suggestion. My own studies, which have not been brief or superficial, compel me to admit suggestion, but to deny with a fervour like that of some humble ignorant Catholic that it can come out of the mind of the ecstatic. Some day I shall ask Shri Purohit Swami if the mark first appeared upon his forehead when he lay unconscious upon the top of Mount Girnār.

Introduction to *The Holy Mountain*

The Holy Mountain: Being the Story of a Pilgrimage to Lake Mānas and of Initiation on Mount Kailās in Tibet, by Bhagwān Shri Hamsa, tr. Shri Purohit Swāmi (1934)

I

'I know nothing but the novels of Balzac, and the aphorisms of Patanjali.[1] I once knew other things, but I am an old man with a poor memory.' There must be some reason why I wanted to write that lying sentence, for it has been in my head for weeks. Is it that whenever I have been tempted to go to Japan, China or India for my philosophy, Balzac has brought me back, reminded me of my preoccupation with national, social, personal problems, convinced me that I cannot escape from our *Comédie humaine*?[2] We philosophise that we may reduce our minds to a single energy, and thereby save our souls and feed our bodies. We prove what we must and assume the rest upon hearsay. No two civilisations prove or assume the same things, but behind both hides the unchanging experience of simple men and women. When I read the travels of Purohit Swāmi, or of his Master, Bhagwān Shri Hamsa,[3] I am among familiar things. *Séraphita*[4] has prepared me for those adventures, those apparitions, and I remember that the knights and hermits who prepared the ground for our *Comédie humaine* preferred, it may be, such adventures to philosophy, such apparitions to dogma:

> One wise friend and one
> Better than wise being fair.[5]

II

Shri Purohit Swāmi[6] at the beginning of this century was a Mr Purohit, student of the University of Bombay. He had inherited from his Marāthā fathers the worship of Dattātreya, the first

Yogi, spiritual Father of all Yogis since, or, as we would say, their patron saint. He had seen him in his dreams, but such knowledge is insufficient; dream words are few and hard to understand; he needed for guide some man who could point out from personal experience what meditations enrich the waking mind. For a time he ceased to read. When he fixed his attention upon the Lord Dattātreya even the *Bhagavad-Geetā* distracted him.[7]

The students had come to associate scholarship with a weak body and shabby clothes, and there was a reaction towards athletics; he had prided himself on being scholar, athlete, dandy, but because women, notorious disturbers of meditation, attracted him, and were attracted, he ate little, grew a beard and dressed out of the fashion. Finding that among holy people his mind grew quiet, he frequented temples and places of pilgrimage; because contact with a supernatural being is never attained through the waking mind, but through the act of what is called the 'unconscious mind', he repeated thousands of times every day: 'We meditate upon the splendour of that Being. May it illuminate our intellects,' until he spoke those words in his sleep, or silently while engaged in conversation.[8] At a temple in Narsobā Wādi[9] he met a beautiful courtesan who had come seeking a cure for some ailment, found the cure, but whenever she attempted to return to her lover, fell sick at the border of the territory, and now sat there, and would while life lasted, dressed in a white robe, praising her Divine Master to the notes of her lute. She had prayed, not foreseeing its consequence, not only for physical, but for spiritual health, and the 'unconscious mind' had heard her prayer.

III

But because he could not persuade those Masters he found acceptable to accept him, he sank into despair. He sat weeping in his room; a friend knocked at the door, asked him to meet a certain Shri Nātēkār Swāmi, now known as Bhagwān Shri Hamsa, who had just arrived. 'We ascended the stairs of Keertikar building', he writes, 'and were admitted into a small room at the top floor. As I entered, the Swāmi, who was sitting upon a tiger's skin, rose. Our eyes met.'[10] And Shri Nātēkār Swāmi, though so far as Mr Purohit knew they had never seen each other, said: 'We meet again after a long time.'[11] He was the elder by four years. He came of a wealthy family, and his father, dreading that his son would become a wandering monk, as had uncles and ancestors, had made him marry at the age of sixteen; but one day while he sat reading upon a river bank, his soul awoke, and throwing book and European clothes into the river, he began a life of austerity. The country people account for his sanctity with a story as incredible to modern ears as any told of the childhood of some European saint, but symbolising an alliance between body and soul our theology rejects. A certain beautiful married woman at the age of twenty had, with her husband's consent, become a pilgrim. After wandering from Himālayān shrine to shrine for many years, she had found a home in a ruined temple at Brahmāvarta.[12] Some called her the mad woman, and some, because of the cotton mat that covered her loins, 'the Lady of the Mat'. She had but two possessions, that cotton mat and her lute. Shri Nātēkār Swāmi's father went on pilgrimage to Brahmāvarta with his son, then but a child. Father and son visited the Lady of the Mat.[13] The child climbed on to her knees. She said: 'Leave him with me; I will take care of him.' The father did not dare to disobey, but was alarmed because she had no food but a daily piece of bread brought her by a water-carrier. When he returned next day with food, the child would not touch it, because the Saint had fed him from her breast. She fed him for a fortnight, then gave him back to his father, saying: 'He will know when a grown man what I have done for him.' One day the Saint called the water-carrier, told him that she was about to leave the world. Because he wept, she gave him her mat as a relic, told him that he must bring her lute to the boy she had fed. Then as she played and sang, the waters of the Ganges became disturbed; first little waves, then great waves; the more she sang, the greater grew the waves. When they touched her feet, she handed the lute to the water-carrier. A moment later they had swept her away; then, upon the instant, all was still.

Mr Purohit took up once more the life of a student. When he had passed, to please his father, his final law examination, he was summoned by Dattātreya in a dream. He and his Master set out for Mount Girnār, where the footprints of Dattātreya are shown upon a rock. He repeated all day: 'We meditate upon the splendour of that Being.' At the foot of the Mountain, he vowed to throw himself from the cliff if his Divine Master remained hidden. As they climbed the seven thousand steps, he neither ate nor drank, though he had starved himself for weeks, and he had constantly to lie down to rest. At the full moon of 25 December 1907, the birthday of Dattātreya, they reached the summit. He fell asleep upon the sacred footsteps as the sun set, and did not awake till the moon was in the sky. As he awoke he knew that Dattātreya had in his sleep accepted him,[14] and when he felt his forehead, he found in the centre the first trace of that small mound that is the Indian equivalent to the Christian Stigmata.[15] He had attained *Sushupti* or unconscious *Samādhi*, a dreamless sleep that differs from that of every sleeper in some part of the night, every insect in the chrysalis, every hibernating animal, every soul between death and birth, because attained through the sacrifice of the physical senses, and through meditation upon a divine personality, a personality at once historical and yet his own spiritual Self.[16] Henceforth that personality, that Self, would be able, though always without his knowledge, to employ his senses and, as in the East the bodily movements are classified as senses, to direct his life. He was not isolated, however, as are men of genius or intellect, for henceforth all those in whom that Self had awakened were his neighbours.

Already while his attainment was incomplete, when he had not even reached the top of the steps, he had seen a beautiful slender woman, with dark bright eyes and red lips, leaning against a tree, and as she vanished, received her benediction,[17] and now as he descended, another of the Masters of Wisdom, a bright-eyed man, appeared.[18]

Although accepted, although henceforth not Mr Purohit but Shri Purohit Swāmi, he refused to accompany his friend who had in a meditation known as *Savikalpa-Samādhi* been ordered to seek *Turiyā*, the greater or conscious *Samādhi*, at Mount Kailās, the legendary Meru; he thought himself unworthy, that he had not freed himself from the World, and could but carry it upon the journey.[19]

IV

Sometimes they came in contact with that Europeanised India England has created with a higher education, which is always conducted in the English language. Shri Purohit Swāmi saw to his Master's comforts, left him stretched out for sleep in a first-class carriage, went to find a third-class carriage for himself, but there was not even standing room. He decided to return to his Master, but found an empty carriage. His Master had left the train and was sitting upon a bench, naked but for a loin cloth. A Europeanised Indian had denounced him for wearing silk and travelling first class, and all monks and pilgrims for bringing discredit upon India by their superstitions and idleness. So he stripped off his silk clothes, saying that though they seemed to have come with his destiny, they were of no importance. Then, because the stranger was still unsatisfied, had given him his luggage and his ticket. They were able, however, to continue their journey, for just when the train was about to start, the Europeanised Indian returned and threw clothes, luggage and ticket into the carriage. He had been attacked by remorse. When they reached their destination, Shri Nātākār Swāmi sat down in the prescribed attitude, passed into *Samādhi*, and Shri Purohit Swāmi, openly rejoicing, sang his praises—Divine and Human Master, one in that dark or bright meditation:

> Lead me to that Kingdom of Thine
> Where there is no pleasure of union
> Nor displeasure of separation,
> Where the self is in eternal happiness.
> Thou alone can thither lead the ailing soul[20]

—verse after verse, until his Master came out of meditation with a cry: 'Victory, victory to the Lord Dattātreya.'

V

Much Chinese and Japanese painting is a celebration of mountains, and so sacred were those mountains that Japanese artists, down to the invention of the colour print, constantly recomposed the characters of Chinese mountain scenery, as though they were the letters of an alphabet, into great masterpieces, traditional and spontaneous. I think of the face of the Virgin in Siennese painting, preserving, after the supporting saints had lost it, a Byzantine character.[21]

To Indians, Chinese and Mongols, mountains from the earliest times have been the dwelling places of the Gods. Their kings before any great decision have climbed some mountain, and of all these mountains Kailās, or Mount Meru, as it is called in the *Mahābhārata*, was the most famous.[22] Sven Hedin calls it the most famous of all mountains, pointing out that Mont Blanc is unknown to the crowded nations of the East.[23] Thousands of Hindu, Tibetan and Chinese pilgrims, Vedāntin, or Buddhist, or of some older faith have encircled it, some bowing at every step, some falling prostrate, measuring the ground with their bodies; an outer ring for all, an inner and more perilous for those called by the priests to its greater penance. On another ring, higher yet, inaccessible to human feet, the Gods move in adoration. Still greater numbers have known it from the *Mahābhārata* or from the poetry of Kalidās, known that a tree covered with miraculous fruit rises from the lake at its foot, that sacred swans sing there, that the four great rivers of India rise there, with sands of gold, silver, emerald and ruby, that at certain seasons from the lake—here Dattātreya is himself the speaker—springs a golden Phallos.[24] Mānas Sarowar, the lake's full name, means 'The great intellectual Lake',[25] and in this Mountain, this Lake, a dozen races find the birth-place of their Gods and of themselves. We too have learnt from Dante to imagine our Eden, or Earthly Paradise, upon a mountain, penitential rings upon the slope.

VI

Shri Nātēkār Swāmi visited other sacred places in the Himālayās before starting for Mount Kailās, travelling sometimes alone and almost always by unfrequented routes. He recalls the narrow escape of himself and his Nepālese guide in the Dehrādun Forest from an infuriated elephant, by dropping from a precipice to lie stunned at its foot;[26] but once he had started, his travels record local customs, his pleasure in scenery, some occasional hardship—for a time little that one does not find in Ekai Kawaguchi's *Three Years in Tibet*.[27] Sometimes he and his three coolies sleep on the ground, sometimes in a temple or cave; sometimes there is difficulty about food, or about a mule or ass to carry it; sometimes he notices that the guest-house is full of fleas; once he is so cold he has to surround himself with lambs, two at his head, two at his back, and six or seven about the rest of his body. Sometimes he forms a brief friendship with a Tibetan official or fellow-pilgrim. Pilgrims for untold years doubtless have had such adventures. Now and then something reminds us that we accompany a holy man. Once he and his coolies were caught by a score of mounted robbers. For a moment he was dumb with terror, then he became suddenly calm, closed his eyes, turned towards Mount Kailās, bowed in adoration of his Master, sat down in the Yoga posture that is called *Padmāsan*[28] and waited in silence. The robbers fell silent also. Then one, the strongest and fiercest, asked his name and business, and what money he carried. He explained, or tried to explain by signs, that he was a pilgrim and had no money. The robber called four of the other robbers, said he would kill him and his coolies and take their clothes. Whereat Shri Nātēkār Swāmi called upon the name of his Master, thrust his neck forward to await the blow of the sword, and went into meditation. When he awoke, his eyes wet with tears of adoration, the robber was kneeling before him, his head upon his thumbs; the other robbers, their swords sheathed, were fanning the swooning coolies.[29]

At Lake Mānas Sarowar the supernatural begins to stir the pot. He had, according to his vow, to spend two weeks upon its bank, bathing twice a day in its icy water, taking but one meal a day, and at that nothing but the tea Tibetans mix with butter, and speaking not a word. At five in the morning of the last day of penance he heard a voice towards the west, the direction of Mount Kailās,[30] a woman's voice as it seemed, singing the Māndukya Upanishad's description of the four states of the soul: the waking state corresponding to the letter 'A', where physical objects are present; the dreaming state corresponding to the letter 'U', where mental objects are present; the state of dreamless sleep corresponding to the letter 'M' where all seems darkness to the soul, because all there is lost in Brahma, creator of mental and physical objects; the final state corresponding to the whole sacred word 'AUM',[31] consciousness bound to no object, bliss bound to no aim, *Turiyā,* pure personality. He searched the shore but could find no one; even his binoculars showed it empty. He sent his coolies to inquire at the neighbouring monastery, but nobody could tell them of the singer. Then he paced the sands, thinking of the voice, but when he had gone a hundred yards, was startled to see before him the print of a human foot. He told his coolies that they must gather up the baggage and follow, that he had set out for Mount Kailās. He followed the footprints for two or three miles along the south shore, but near the rocky western shore they grew indistinct and disappeared. He went on in the direction they had taken till stopped by an ascent too steep for his exhausted body.[32]

After two days travelling, one day through storm and hail, spending the nights in a cave and in a foul hut made out of loose stones piled up on four sides, a great single slab for roof, he began his penitential circuit. At the eastern side the guide, pointing to a cave a thousand feet above his head, said that a great Hindu saint lived there, but that he knew no way to reach it. Shri Nātēkār Swāmi and the guide began to climb, but before they had gone a quarter of the way the guide was taken ill. The Swāmi told him to return to the coolies, that he and they must remain a week in a Buddhist guest-house, then if they heard nothing of their master, return to India.[33]

The ice began fifty yards below the cave; that past, came a perpendicular cliff with notches for hand and foot cut in the rock, and seven feet from the bottom the mouth of the cave. He climbed, and crawling through darkness, found a dim lamp and an oldish naked man, sitting upon a tiger's skin. He prostrated himself in reverence and said: 'Lord, it is your grace that has brought this servant to your hallowed feet.' The naked man laughed and said: *'Acha, Vatsa, Uthake baitho'*, which means—'My darling, get up!'[34] He was told that he might ask anything except for age, name and parentage. He asked in Hindi, Marāthi, in English, and the answer came always in the same language, perfect in grammar and accent. He noticed that whatever the language, that language alone was used, no foreign word admitted, and became convinced that his host knew all languages. It was he who had sung the Māndukya Upanishad and made those footprints on the sand, and it was because of that old acquaintance that he had called him darling. Shri Nātēkār Swāmi stayed there for three days, eating nothing, but drinking water, and during those three days his host neither ate nor drank. Then he returned to his coolies, and having told them to await for a week, set out alone for Gaurikund, a little lake high up upon Mount Kailās,[35] wherein he was to cast sand from the southernmost point of India and so complete his pilgrimage.[36] Pilgrims such as he perpetually encircle that religious India, which keeps Mount Kailās within its borders, that all the land may be blessed by their passing feet.

After two nights spent in hollows of the ice, his overcoat about his head, his feet drawn up to his ribs, he came back defeated, but set out again the next day, and after a climb of five thousand feet, reached the lake, and there, twenty feet from the shore, broke through five feet of ice, cast in the sand, sat down, passed into meditation awaiting the object of his pilgrimage, the physical presence of his Divine Master, Dattātreya. He has described his uncertainty as to whether he would live or die, recorded the exact placing of his staff, what points of the compass he had first looked at, what words he spoke, his different postures, a tiger's skin that he had brought for his seat; details all settled by tradition. For three days he remained in meditation, gradually the mental image of his Master grew dim, voices spoke. Three times he heard the words: 'O my child, O my dear',[37] but he knew that if he opened his eyes while the mental image remained he would fail. What were voices to him if he could not see the physical form? At last the mental image suddenly vanished. He opened his eyes, and Dattātreya stood before him, made him perform certain further ceremonies, admitted him to the Giri order of Sanyāsins,[38] promised to keep his heart from straying to physical things, and named him Hamsa,[39] which means 'soul', but is also the name of those emblems of the soul, the white-winged, red-beaked, red-legged water-birds of Lake Mānas Sarowar.

VII

Shri Purohit Swāmi claims that his Master gained at that mountain lake, *Turiyā*, whereas he himself had but gained upon Mount Girnār a dreamless sleep, *Sushupti*. The philosophy and technique of both of these states are described in the *Yoga-Sutras* or aphorisms of Patanjali, written somewhere between the third and fifth centuries of our era, but containing a far older tradition, or in the voluminous commentaries, written between the middle of the seventh and the ninth centuries.[40] The Spirit, the Self that is in all selves, the pure mirror, is the source of intelligence, but Matter is the source of all energy, all creative power, all that separates one thing from another, not Matter as understood by Hobbes and his Mechanists, Matter as understood in Russia, where the Government has silenced the Mechanist, but interpreted with profound logic, almost what Schopenhauer understood by Will.[41] If I think of the table on which I am writing, my mental image is as much Matter as the table itself, though of 'a subtler kind',[42] and I am able to think correctly, because the Matter I call Mind takes the shape of this or that physical object, and this Matter, physical and mental, has three aspects—'*Tamas*', darkness, frustration, '*Rajas*', activity, passion, '*Satva*', brightness, wisdom.[43] In one of the Patanjali commentaries there is a detailed analysis of the stages of concentration that would be Hegelian did they include the Self in their dialectic.[44] The first is the fixing of attention upon some place or object, the navel, the tip of the tongue. Any object will serve so long as it belongs to oneself and is an immediate perception, not something inferred or heard of; or one may fix attention upon the form of some God, for a God is but the Self. But one cannot fix attention without some stream of thought, so if the object be the tongue, one thinks of the tongue as symbol or function. As I write the word, I think at once of Blake's 'False Tongue' which is the 'vegetative' sense, then I remember that according to Patanjali meditation upon the tongue awakens the perception of taste or colour or sound.[45] The taste, colour and sound so perceived attain supernormal perfection as fact and idea draw together. Should one choose a God as the theme of meditation, the majesty of his face, or the beauty of his ear-rings, may, as trance deepens, express all majesty, all beauty. The second stage is this identity between idea and fact, between thought and sense; an identity that recalls the description of dreams in the Upanishads.[46] The third stage is *Sushupti*, a complete disappearance of all but this identity. Nothing exists but that ravening tongue,[47] or that majesty, that beauty; the man has disappeared as the sculptor in his statue, the musician in his music.[48] One remembers the Japanese philosopher's saying, 'What the artist perceives through a medium, the saint perceives immediately.'[49]

In the fourth stage the ascetic enters one or more of these stages at will and retains his complete memory when he returns; this is *Turiyā*, but as yet only in the form called *Savikalpa*; full *Turiyā* or 'seedless' *Samādhi* comes when all these states are as a single timeless act, and that act is pure or unimpeded personality, all existence brought into the words: 'I am.'[50] It resembles that last Greek number, a multiple of all numbers because there is nothing outside it, nothing to make a new beginning.[51] It is not only seedless but objectless because objects are lost in complete light. Darkness is the causal body of existence. Objects are its serrates and dentures. One remembers those lines of Coleridge:

> Resembles life what once was deemed of light,
> Too ample in itself for human sight?
> An absolute self—an element ungrounded—
> All that we see, all colours of all shade,
> By encroachment of darkness made?[52]

VIII

If *Turiyā* be attained, the ascetic may remain in Life until the results of past lives are exhausted or because he would serve his fellows. While such binding to the past remains, or duty to the living, it must, one would think, be incomplete, something less than absolute Self. Probably such an ascetic regards complete 'seedless' *Samādhi* as an ideal form, an all but unattainable ideal that he must approach through life after life: a central experience, touched or it may be but symbolised at some moment when some quality of life flowers.

The life of an ascetic is a preparation for meditation. He repeats the name of some God thousands of times a day, frequents a shrine, is convinced that he must offer there all the devotion, all the passion aroused in his present life, or in his past lives by friend, master, child and wife. If he finds it impossible at once to transform sexual into spiritual desire, he may beseech the God to come as a woman. The God may send some strange woman as his emblem, but should he come himself, the ascetic wakes at dawn to find his empty bed fragrant with some temple incense, or patches of saffron paste upon his breast; but, whether the God send or come, every need soon fades, except that for unity with God. Nor is supernormal sense confined to the moments of concentration; he will suddenly smell amid the ordinary occupations of life, perhaps in the middle of winter, an odour of spring flowers, or have an unimaginable sense of physical well-being that is described as a transformation of the sense of touch, or meet in empty places melodious sound, or a fine sight. I have been told that somewhere in India sits a musician into whose mouth pupils put food and drink. He was accustomed to listen to such sounds and imitate them, but one day the hand he had thrust out towards the string stopped in mid-air and became rigid; from that day he has remained drunk and lost in *Sushupti*.

The ascetic who has not freed his mind of ambition and passion may pass not into *Sushupti,* but into a distortion of the second stage of concentration, analogous to that of dreaming-sleep; sense and thought are one, but the bond between that unity and his ego remains unbroken. He is in the condition of the witches who project afar their passion-driven souls in some animal shape, while their bodies lie at home, or of that woman in Murasaki's book who killed, without knowing it, her enemy in a dream.[53] On the other hand, the ascetic who has attained *Turiyā* enters this second stage wide awake, and as there is nothing outside his will, he can shape a new body to his need, or use the body of another. The old ascetic of the cavern was in this stage when he sang and left his footsteps on the sand. Those who have attained 'seedless' *Samādhi,* are said to be physically immortal; they do not die, but make themselves invisible. The story-tellers describe them dissolving their bodies while they seem to bathe, or leaving, like Christ, an empty tomb: at will, they pass into the Source.[54]

An ascetic who has rid himself of passion may, though unfitted for *Turiyā,* seek, like many Greeks, wisdom through those self-luminous and coherent dreams that seem to surround, like a ring of foam, the dark pool of dreamless sleep.[55] If devoted to some God, or to some other image of the Universal Self, he may pass that ring, obtain *Sushupti* in its highest form, the dreamless sleep of the soul in God. When he returns to waking life, he is still an instrument of that other Will; those upon whom his attention falls may grow more fortunate, but his own fortune will be no better; a miracle may happen under his eyes, but, because it must be as though waking he still slept, he neither knows nor may enquire whether his sacrifice has played a part. He may even, as I imagine, be ignorant of common things, be somewhat childish as though he cannot see by daylight, resemble in all things the pure fool of European tradition. After death indeed he attains liberation, becoming one of those spirits that have no life but to obey that Self, who creates all things in dreamless sleep:

> There is in God some say,
> A deep but dazzling darkness: as men here
> Say it is late and dusky, because they
> See not all clear.
> O for that Night, when I in him
> Might live invisible and dim![56]

The ascetic seeking *Savikalpa-Samādhi* identifies it with *Satva*, but calls *Sushupti*, which he identifies with *Tamas*, the *Samādhi* of a fool, because in that state he is ignorant, and because he is liable to fall back upon it, as though sinking into lethargy, but he who thinks *Sushupti* the supreme self-surrender, must, I am persuaded, identify *Sushupti* with *Satva*, the waking life of sense with *Tamas*. *Savikalpa-Samādhi* is, as it were, ringed with the activities of life, *Sushupti* ringed with dreams, and both rings are *Rajas*, while *Savikalpa-Samādhi* and *Sushupti* are alternatively light and darkness. Neither is in itself the final deliverance or return into the Source, for *Rajas, Tamas, Satva* constitute 'matter', or 'nature' without beginning, without reality. The Vedānt philosophers, unlike Buddha, direct our attention to bright or intelligible perfection, but seek timeless perfection, seedless *Samādhi*, beyond it in the isolated Soul, that is yet in all souls.[57]

IX

In 1818 Hegel, his head full of the intellectual pride of the eighteenth century, was expounding History. Indifferent, as always, to the individual soul, he had taken for his theme the rise and fall of nations. Greece, he explained, first delivered mankind from nature; the Egyptian Sphinx, for all its human face, was Asiatic and animal; but when Oedipus answered the riddle, that Sphinx was compelled to leap into the abyss; the riddle, 'What goes first on four legs, then upon two, then upon three?' called up man. Nature is bondage, its virtue no more than the custom of clan or race, a plant rooted outside man, a law blindly obeyed. From that moment on, intellect or Spirit, that which has value in itself, began to prevail, and now in Hegel's own day, the climax had come, not crippled age but wisdom; there had been many rehearsals, for every civilisation, no matter where its birth, began with Asia, but the play itself had been saved up for our patronage. A few years more and religion would be absorbed in the State, art in philosophy, God's Will proved to be man's will.[58]

I can imagine Balzac, that great eater, his medieval humility greater than his pride, answering: 'Man's intellect or Spirit can do nothing but bear witness; Nature alone is active—I have heard the clergy talk of Grace, but that is beyond my knowledge—I refuse to confine Nature to claw, paw and hoof. It is the irrational glory that reaches perfection at the mid-moment, at the Renaissance of every civilisation. Raphael and Michelangelo closed our sixth century, for our civilisation began when Romanesque displaced Byzantine architecture.[59] Great empires are founded by lovers of women and of money; they are destroyed by men of ideas. There is a continual conflict—I too have my dialectic—the perfection of Nature is the decline of Spirit, the perfection of Spirit is the decline of Nature. In the Spiritual dawn when Raphael painted the Camera della Segnatura, and the Medician Popes dreamed of uniting Christianity and Paganism,[60] all that was sacred with all that was secular, Europe might have made its plan, begun the solution of its problems, but individualism came instead; the egg instead of hatching, burst. The *Peau de chagrin*[61] *and Catherine de Medici* contain my philosophy of History. Genius and talent have torn Europe to pieces. *Divina Commedia* summed up and closed the Europe that created Mont-Saint-Michel, Chartres Cathedral, the Europe that went upon its knees or upon all fours. *Comédie humaine* has closed the counter-movement, that kept her upon two legs. In my open letter to the Duchesse de Castries I foretell the future.[62] What was before man stood up, an impulse in our blood, returns as an external necessity. We shall become one through violence or imitation; and, because we can no longer create, gather, as Rome did, the treasures of the world in some one place. As we grow old we accumulate abstract substitutes for experience, commodities of all kinds, but an old pensioner that taps upon the ground where he once crawled is no whit the wiser for all his proverbs. You should have gone to Hugo[63] with that romantic dream. When I was young I wanted to take opium—Paris had just discovered it—but I could not, because I would not surrender my will. My *Comédie humaine* will cure the world of all Utopias, but you were born too soon.'

That last sentence would have been untrue. Balzac's influence has reached some exceptional men and women. Hegel's Philosophy of History dominates the masses, though they have not heard his name, as Rousseau's philosophy did in the nineteenth and later eighteenth centuries, and has shed more blood.[64]

X

Here and there in the Upanishads mention is made of the moon's bright fortnight, the nights from the new to the full moon, and of the dark fortnight of the moon's decline. He that lives in the first becomes fire or an eater; he that lives in the second becomes fuel and food to the living (Schopenhauer's essay upon Love[65] reversed). He that moves towards the full moon may, if wise, go to the Gods (expressed or symbolised in the senses) and share their long lives, or if to Brahma's question—'Who are you?' he can answer 'Yourself', pass out of those three penitential circles, that of common men, that of gifted men, that of the Gods, and find some cavern upon Meru, and so pass out of all life. Upon the other hand, those that move towards the dark of the moon, if they are pious, as the crowd is pious, if they can offer the right sacrifices, pray at the right temples, can go to the blessed Ghosts, to the Heaven of their fathers, find what peace can be found between death and birth. The Upanishads denied any escape for these.[66] The new thinkers arrayed their asceticism, their complete individuality against the tribal dancers, spirit mediums, ritual poetry, orgiastic ceremonies, soma-drinking priests of the popular religion: 'As for living, our servants will do that for us.'[67]

The bright fortnight's escape is *Turiyā,* and in the dark fortnight, the ascetic who, unlike the common people, asks nothing of God or Ghost, may, though unworthy of *Turiyā,* find *Sushupti* an absorption in God, as if the Soul were His food or fuel.

Man is born into 'a mortal birth of twelve months or thirteen months',[68] into the lunar year that sometimes requires an extra month that it may keep the proper seasons, from which it is plain that every incarnation is divided into twelve or thirteen cycles. As the first and last crescents are nearest the Sun, the visionary must have seen in those cycles a conflict between Moon and Sun, or when Greek astronomy had reached India, between a Moon that has taken the Sun's light into itself, 'I am yourself,' and the Moon lost in the Sun's light, between Sun in

Moon and Moon in Sun. The Eastern poet saw the Moon as the Sun's bride; now in solitude; now offered to her Bridegroom in a self-abandonment unknown to our poetry. A European would think perhaps of the moonlit and moonless nights alone, call the increasing moon man's personality, as it fills into the round and becomes perfect, overthrowing the black night of oblivion. Am I not justified in discovering there the conflict between subjectivity and objectivity, between Self and Not-Self, between waking life and dreamless sleep?

The year of twelve or thirteen months that constitutes a single lifetime was thought of as a day or night in a still greater year, and that year divided in its turn into months, and so on until we reach some greatest year. One must imagine everywhere enclosed one within another, circles of Sun in Moon, Moon in Sun. Mixed with these mythological or symbolic periods were others founded upon the astronomical phantasy of Greece. Certain cycles must have begun when all the planets stood toeing a line like young athletes. If the equinoctial Sun encircles the Zodiac in thirty-six thousand years, as Alexandrian Greece imagined,[69] why not consider that but one month in a still greater year? Indifferent to history, India delighted in vast periods, which solemnised the mind, seeming to unite it to the ageless Heavens. The Indian would have understood the dialectic of Balzac, but not that of Hegel—what could he have made of Hegel's optimism?—but never cared to discover in those great periods a conflict of civilisations and of nations. Even the Great Year of Proclus, though that is cold and abstract compared with the conception that has begun to flit before modern minds, was impossible to the Indian's imagination.[70] Preoccupied with the seeds of action, discoverable by those who have rejected all that is not themselves, he left to Europe the study and creation of civilisation. This he could do, perhaps because the villages that nurtured his childhood were subject to no change but that of the seasons—their life, as it were, the symbolical syntax wherein we may write the History of the World.

XI

Greek and Roman speculation generally made the Great Year solar, but the symbolism is little different. The two extremes correspond to the Sun's passage through Capricorn and Cancer.

In the first the world was nourished by water—Philolaus called it 'the lunar water'; in the second by the 'Fire of Heaven'.[71]

I find my imagination setting in one line *Turiyā*—full moon, mirror-like bright water, Mount Meru; and in the other *Sushupti,* moonless night, 'dazzling darkness'—Mount Girnār.

Does not every civilisation as it approaches or recedes from its full moon seem as it were to shiver into the premonition of some perfection born out of itself, perhaps even of some return to its first Source? Does not one discover in the faces of Madonnas and holy women painted by Raphael or da Vinci, if never before or since, a condition of soul where all is still and finished, all experience wound up upon a bobbin? Does one not hear those lips murmur that, despite whatever illusion we cherish, we came from no immaturity, but out of our own perfection like ships that 'all their swelling canvas wear'.[72] Does not every new civilisation, upon the other hand, imagine that it was born in revelation, or that it comes from dependence upon dark or unknown powers, that it can but open its eyes with difficulty after some long night's sleep or winter's hibernation?

For this one thing above all I would be praised as a man,
That in my words and my deeds I have kept those laws in mind
Olympian Zeus and this high clear Empyrean
Fashioned, and not some man or people of mankind,
Even those sacred laws nor age nor sleep can blind.

. . . should a man forget
The holy image, the Delphian Sybil's trance
And the world's navel stone, and not be punished for it
And seem most fortunate, or even blesséd perchance,
Who could honour the Gods, or join the sacred dance.[73]

P.S.—I have made much use during the writing of this essay of Shri Purohit Swāmi's *An Indian Monk* (Macmillan), of his unpublished translation of the *Yoga-Sutras* of Patanjali, and of the standard translation of the same work published by Harvard University.[74] I thank Shri Purohit Swāmi for answering many questions.

Introduction to 'Mandukya Upanishad'

(1935)

I

When I wrote my introduction to *The Holy Mountain*, I did not analyse Bhagwān Shri Hamsa's vision by the frozen lake,[1] and that has been heavy on my conscience. The culmination of the pilgrimage, it should have been the culmination of my argument, but I shied away from it. Then after the publication of the book I asked Shri Purohit Swāmi if a passerby, were one possible amid such desolation, could have seen the God. He said 'No', and now that I was not compelled to assume a materialization like that which showed the medium and itself side by side and permitted Sir William Crookes to feel its beating heart,[2] my intellect could begin its analysis. Analysis seemed important because of the connection, still vague in my imagination, between pilgrimage and vision, scenery and the pilgrim's salvation.

Forty years ago my closest friend planned a walk through Ireland, a long stick with a head like the letter 'T' in his hand, that he might preach the return of those ancient gods that seemed a part of the soil and the blood. Alarmed for his life; Irish Christianity is not gentle; I brought him to Sir Horace Plunkett who made him a successful organizer of co-operative banks.[3] I have since regretted an action that entangled in practical discussion a mind ripe for spiritual theory. Judea had, he said, robbed all countries; men once thought their own neighbourhood holy, but had now to discover their Holy Land in an atlas. Yet all might be changed could he but discover three old men who lived somewhere in Ireland in a white thatched cottage, beside a telegraph post; or could he but lie upon certain mountains until his soul sank down into the great lakes of spiritual fire under his feet.[4] Was he a German Christian born too soon, or a Swedenborg[5] I had turned from the road before his vision clarified? He was not as strange as he seems in memory; such ideas were in other Irish minds; I had made a map of ancient Ireland with the sacred places marked upon it in red ink, and Standish O'Grady had announced in his weekly review that Slievenamon would yet be more famous than Olympus.[6] An old Tory uncle used to say 'everything that comes to Ireland becomes a reality';[7] the modern interest in folk-lore, a scientific curiosity elsewhere, had transformed our thought. And now compelled by that transfiguration, I must ask why Bhagwān Shri Hamsa had to go that pilgrimage and no other, and to meet his God amid such desolation upon Kailās.[8]

II

Bhagwān Shri Hamsa, almost at the end of his journey, heard a spiritual voice:

'At 5 A.M. I heard strains of melodious music sung by a human voice coming from the west. In rapt attention I listened and thought it the voice of a woman. I decided, a little later, that the chant of Shri Māndukya Upanishad was being sung. Through the binocular I searched in the direction from whence came the melodious sound, but saw no human figure on that beach of sand. I strained my eyes and gazed all round, but there was no trace of any human figure. The music lasted half an hour, then it ceased, and the incident began to trouble me. What could have been the meaning of this sweet chant of the Māndukya Upanishad in this solitary region?'[9]

Two days later a naked ascetic in a cavern claimed to have been present, singing, in his spiritual body. That shortest and the most comprehensive of the Upanishads examines the sacred syllables: 'the word *"Aum"* is the imperishable Spirit. This universe is the manifestation. The past, the present, the future, everything, is *"Aum"*, and whatever transcends this division of time, that too is *"Aum"*.'[10] Then the short paragraphs describe the letters; '*A*' is the physical or waking state; '*U*' the dream state, where only mental substances appear; '*M*' is deep sleep, where man 'feels no desire, creates no dream', yet is this sleep called 'conscious' because he is now united to sleepless Self, creator of all, source of all, unknowable, unthinkable, ungraspable, a union with it sole proof of its existence. The Self, whereto man is now united, expressed by our articulation of the whole word, is the fourth state.

I have already compared these four states with the four stages of concentration described by a commentator upon Patanjali;[11] the first with the selection of some place, object or image, as the theme of meditation; the second with the mutual transformation, the drawing, as it were, together, of theme and thought, fact and idea; the dreamer creating his dream, the sculptor toiling to set free the imprisoned image; the third with the union of theme and thought, fact and idea so complete, that there is nothing more to do, nothing left but statue and dream; the sculptor has gone, the dreamer has gone, there is nobody even to remember that statue and dream are there; the mind is plunged in *Sushupti,* unconscious *Samādhi.*[12] In its fourth state symbolical of or relevant to the Self, the mind can enter all or any of the previous states at will; joyous, unobstructed, it can transform itself, dissolve itself, create itself. It has found conscious *Samādhi,* passed beyond generation that is rooted always in the unconscious, found seedless *Samādhi.* It is the old theme of philosophy, the union of Self and Not-Self, but in the conflagration of that union there is, as in the biblical vision, 'the form of the fourth'.[13]

III

At last, after a climb of 5000 feet Bhagwān Shri Hamsa sat by the frozen lake, awaiting initiation:

'My ideal was to have a sight of the physical form of the Lord Dattātreya Himself, and to get myself initiated into the realisation of the Self. I was determined either to realise this or to die in meditation while sitting in Yogic posture.

'I began by looking in all four directions and then spread my tiger's skin on the icy floor of the lake, planting my staff on the right. I again looked at the sky and at Mount Kailās, crying "Victory, Victory to the Lord, my Master!" I stood for a few minutes facing the north. After this I sat on the tiger's skin in the Siddhāsana posture, with my face towards the north. In short, I began to face the final ordeal. It was sunset. I closed my eyes and passed into meditation, all along trying to fix the mind steadily on a mental image of the Lord Dattātreya in the centre between my eyebrows.

'The first night I experienced terrible hardships. Bitter cold, piercing winds, incessant snow, inordinate hunger and deadly solitude combined to harass the mind; the body became numb and unable to bear the pangs. Snow covered me up to my breast and, till after midnight, I was fighting desperately with my mind. . . .

'Every moment increased the intensity of my yearning to see my Master, and it was while I was in this state that I thought I heard a voice. I did not leave my meditation. Later on I found that the image which formed the subject of my meditation grew more and more dim. Yet I refused to allow my mind to leave its point of concentration; instead I fixed it there with added determination.

' "O my child! O my dear!" I heard these words thrice, but did not open my eyes, for the mental image of my Master was still there between the eyebrows. I wanted to see the Lord Dattātreya in physical form, and naturally it was impossible for me to be satisfied with His voice alone. Moreover, no sight of a physical form was possible until the mental one had disappeared. As I was so keen about the physical sight, I did not leave my meditation, though I heard the call three times.

'At last, all of a sudden, the mental form disappeared. Automatically my eyes were opened and I saw, standing before me, the Lord Dattātreya, my Master, in his physical form. At once I prostrated myself on the icy ground like a staff and placed my head on His lotus-feet.

'Three days had passed like three moments for me! My Master lifted me up like the Divine Mother and hugged me to His breast and caressed me all over the body. Thereafter He gave me the Mantra (sacred words) and initiated me into the realisation of the Self. What a great bliss it was! I cannot describe that joy, as it is beyond any description through words.'[14]

IV

This final vision is that form completed in the third state, the third stage, not as it appears in dreamless sleep but as it appears in the fourth state, the fourth stage, or to conscious man. When the ascetic meditates upon the tip of his tongue, let us say, he begins with an object, and this object slowly transforms and is transformed by his thought until they are one. When he meditates upon an image of God, he begins with thought, God subjectively conceived, and this thought is slowly transformed by, and transforms its object, divine reality, until suddenly superseded by the unity of thought and fact. Yet he is not aware of all this, there is a voice that would persuade him to open his eyes too soon, the event is unforeseen, has taken place in what we call, because we sit in the stalls and watch the play, the unconscious. The Indian, upon the other hand, calls it the conscious, because, whereas we are fragmentary, forgetting, remembering, sleeping, waking, spread out into past, present, future, permitting to our leg, to our finger, to our intestines, partly or completely separate consciousness, it is the 'unbroken consciousness of the Self',[15] the Self that never sleeps, that is never divided, but even when our thought transforms it, is still the same. It is the Universal Self but also that of a civilisation; to Bhagwān Shri Hamsa, Dattātreya is the object, or goal, not of his pilgrimage only, but of his whole life. But we must not think of it as a target, as something struck or seized when subject or object unite, but as the sole being that is completely alive, completely active; our approach is revelation. The pilgrim has meditated, prayed, fasted, almost met his death in snow and ice, strained his heroic will to the utmost, fragments of his consciousness have lived in suffering for months, perhaps for years, but the Self has brought the event, the supreme drama, out of its freedom, and this revelation, because the work of unlimited power, has been sudden. The Mantra, the sacred fire that he must presently light, the caress given to all parts of his body, are from the memory of the race, the immemorial ritual; but 'the initiation into the reality of the Self'[16] is wordless, unique, an act of the unbroken consciousness alone. For this initiation Bhagwān Shri Hamsa finds only technical language:

'Manas (mind) merged into Antahkarana (heart); the Antahkarana with the Manas merged into the Chitta (mind-stuff); the Chitta along with Antahkarana and Manas merged into Buddhi (intellect); the Buddhi with Chitta, Antahkarana and Manas merged into Ahankar (egoism); and the Ahankar along with Buddhi, Chitta, Antahkarana and Manas—all merged into the

Absolute Brahma! I found myself reflected everywhere in the whole Universe!'[17]

V

The Heart is unity, harmony. The Mind is no more to be occupied with external events, it must, as it seems, turn upon itself, be occupied with itself, but that is impossible, for the Discursive Mind must by its nature pursue something, find something. It seemed as if its separation from external things, its union with itself, must be accompanied rather than followed by its union with Chitta. It is Chitta, perhaps, which most separates Indian from European thought. We think of man, his ideas and concepts facing external nature, or as fashioning that nature according to those ideas and concepts from unknown material or from nothing. Chitta is mental substance, mind-stuff is the more usual translation, and this substance must always take its shape from something; it is, as we would say, suggestible, it must copy some external object or symbolize the universal Self. If I shut my eyes and try to recall table and chair, I see them as transformations of the Chitta. Indeed, the actual table and chair are but the Chitta posited by the mind, the personality, in space, where because two things cannot occupy the same place, there is discord and suffering. By withdrawing into our own mind we discover the Chitta united to Heart and therefore pure. It is divided into Tamas, or heaviness, exhaustion; Rajas, or passion, violence, movement; Satva, or wisdom, peace, beauty.[18] Or we can sum up all as darkness, lightning, light, Boehme's three.[19] Because Satva reflects the Self, from it, or from it united to Rajas come all works of wisdom and beauty. When those dreams created by recent or present physical events are absent from our dreams Discursive Mind is united to Chitta, and this Chitta is not isolated, as we think subjective mind is isolated; in so far as Satva reflects the Self, it is common to all whose minds contain the same reflection: the images of the gods can pass from mind to mind, our closed eyes may look upon a world shared, as the physical world is shared, though difference in the degree of purity has been substituted for difference of place.

Buddhi is described as that which 'distinguishes' between Tamas, Rajas, Satva that it may cling to Satva, but 'distinguishes' suggests Discursive Mind; perhaps it instantly recognises and clings. But it is confined to form, for even when most transparent, Chitta is form, the third state, the third concentration, are still in form. Then Manas, Heart, Chitta, Buddhi, are united to egoism, or personality, as it should be called. Personality is first of all the man as he has been made by his Karma;[20] he is set in the external world because that, too, has been made by his Karma. Even though initiation be complete, his nature so gathered up into itself that he can create no new Karma, he must await the exhaustion of the old. In pure personality, seedless Samādhi, there is nothing but that bare 'I am' which is Brahma. The initiate, all old Karma exhausted is 'The Human Form Divine' of Blake,[21] that Unity of Being Dante compared to a perfectly proportioned human body;[22] henceforth he is self-creating. But the Universal Self is a fountain, not a cistern, the Supreme Good must perpetually give itself. The world is necessary to the Self, must receive 'the excess of its delights',[23] and in this Self all delivered selves are present, ordering all things, from the pole star to the passing wind. They are indeed those spirits Shelley imagined in his *Adonais* as visiting the inspired and the innocent.[24]

VI

Bhagwān Shri Hamsa knew that he must not open his eyes while 'the mental image' of his Master 'was still there between the eyebrows',[25] though that Master himself, trying him to the utmost, spoke endearing words. Had he opened his eyes too soon, he would have seen nothing. Before we can see objective truth we must exhaust subjective. This exhaustion, expressed in the drama of master and disciple, had been going on all his life, the perilous pilgrimage but a climax. To seek God too soon is not less sinful than to seek God too late; we must love, man, woman, or child, we must exhaust ambition, intellect, desire, dedicating all things as they pass, or we come to God with empty hands.

VII

An Indian devotee may recognise that he approaches the Self through a transfiguration of sexual desire; he repeats thousands of times a day words of adoration, calls before his eyes a thousand times the divine image. He is not always solitary, there is another method, that of the Tantric philosophy,[26] where a man and woman, when in sexual union, transfigure each other's images into the masculine and feminine characters of God, but the man must not finish, vitality must not pass beyond his body, beyond his being. There are married people who though they do not forbid the passage of the seed practise, not necessarily at the moment of union, a meditation, wherein the man seeks the divine Self as present in his wife, the wife the divine Self as present in the man. There may be trance, and the presence of one with another though a great distance separates. If one alone meditates, the other knows; one may call for and receive through the other, divine protection. Did this worship, this meditation, establish among us romantic love, was it prevalent in Northern Europe during the twelfth century? In the German epic *Parsifal* Gawain drives a dagger through his hand without knowing it during his love-trance, Parsifal falls into such a trance when a drop of blood upon snow recalls to his mind a tear upon his wife's cheek, and before he awakes overthrows many knights. When riding into battle he prays not to God but to his wife, and she, falling into trance, protects him.[27] One thinks too, of that mysterious poem by Chrétien de Troyes, wherein Vivien having laid Merlin, personification of wisdom, by the side of dead lovers, closes their tomb.[28]

VIII

I think it certain that Europeans, travelling the same way, enduring the same fasts, saying the same prayers, would have received nothing but perhaps a few broken dreams. Bhagwān Shri Hamsa's evocation of 'the conscious', of 'the unconscious', depended in part upon innumerable associations from childhood on, in part upon race memory. I have read somewhere that the Aryan race, afterwards the creator of the Vedas and the Upanishads, lingered long, perhaps for many generations, in the country about Kailās, or Mount Meru as it is called in the Vedas, certainly longer than the Children of Israel about Sinai.[29] Who knows what beginning, what act of creation, is commemorated in that legend of a golden phallus rising once in every year from the waters of Mānas Sarowar,[30] or to what source Bhagwān Shri Hamsa, like many before, like many that will come after, made his perilous journey, not what his dreams, or his undreaming sleep recalled?

Though I have to thank Shri Purohit Swāmi for answering many questions, he must not be held responsible for my conclusions.

Gitanjali

Introduction to *Gitanjali* (*Song Offerings*), by Rabindranath Tagore (1912)

I

A few days ago I said to a distinguished Bengali doctor of medicine,[1] 'I know no German, yet if a translation of a German poet had moved me, I would go to the British Museum and find books in English that would tell me something of his life, and of the history of his thought. But though these prose translations from Rabindranath Tagore have stirred my blood as nothing has for years, I shall not know anything of his life, and of the movements of thought that have made them possible, if some Indian traveller will not tell me.' It seemed to him natural that I should be moved, for he said, 'I read Rabindranath every day; to read one line of his is to forget all the troubles of the world.' I said, 'An Englishman living in London in the reign of Richard the Second, had he been shown translations from Petrarch or from Dante, would have found no books to answer his questions, but would have questioned some Florentine banker or Lombard merchant as I question you.[2] For all I know, so abundant and simple is this poetry, the new Renaissance has been born in your country and I shall never know of it except by hearsay.' He answered, 'We have other poets, but none that are his equal; we call this the epoch of Rabindranath. No poet seems to me as famous in Europe as he is among us. He is as great in music as in poetry, and his songs are sung from the west of India into Burma wherever Bengali is spoken. He was already famous at nineteen when he wrote his first novel; and plays, written when he was but little older, are still played in Calcutta.[3] I so much admire the completeness of his life; when he was very young he wrote much of natural objects, he would sit all day in his garden; from his twenty-fifth year or so to his thirty-fifth perhaps, when he had a great sorrow, he wrote the most beautiful love poetry in our language'; and then he said with deep emotion, 'Words can never express what I owed at seventeen to his love poetry. After that his art grew deeper, it became religious and philosophical; all the aspirations of mankind are in his hymns.[4] He is the first among our saints who has not refused to live, but has spoken out of Life itself, and that is why we give him our love.' I may have changed his well-chosen words in my memory but not his thought. 'A little while ago he was to read divine service in one of our churches—we of the Brahma Samaj use your word "church" in English—it was the largest in Calcutta and not only was it crowded, people even standing in the windows, but the streets were all but impassable because of the people.'[5]

Other Indians came to see me and their reverence for this man sounded strange in our world, where we hide great and little things under the same veil of obvious comedy and half-serious depreciation. When we were making the cathedrals had we a like reverence for our great men? 'Every morning at three—I know, for I have seen it'—one said to me, 'he sits immovable in contemplation, and for two hours does not awake from his reverie upon the nature of God. His father, the Maha Rishi, would sometimes sit there all through the next day; once, upon a river, he fell into contemplation because of the beauty of the landscape, and the rowers waited for eight hours before they could continue their journey.'[6] He then told me of Mr Tagore's family and how for generations great men have come out of its cradles. 'To-day', he said, 'there are Gaganendranath and Abanindranath Tagore, who are artists; and Dwijendranath, Rabindranath's brother, who is a great philosopher.[7] The squirrels come from the boughs and climb on to his knees and the birds alight upon his hands.' I notice in these men's thought a sense of visible beauty and meaning as though they held that doctrine of Nietzsche that we must not believe in the moral or intellectual beauty which does not sooner or later impress itself upon physical things.[8] I said, 'In the East you know how to keep a family illustrious. The other day the curator of a museum pointed out to me a little dark-skinned man who was arranging their Chinese prints and said, "That is the hereditary connoisseur of the Mikado, he is the fourteenth of his family to hold the post."'[9] He answered, 'When Rabindranath was a boy he had all round him in his home literature and music.' I thought of the abundance, of the simplicity of the poems, and said, 'In your country is there much propagandist writing, much criticism? We have to do so much, especially in my own country, that our minds gradually cease to be creative, and yet we cannot help it. If our life was not a continual warfare, we would not have taste, we would not know what is good, we would not find hearers and readers. Four-fifths of our energy is spent in the quarrel with bad taste, whether in our own minds or in the minds of others.'[10] 'I understand,' he replied, 'we too have our propagandist writing. In the villages they recite long mythological poems adapted from the Sanscrit in the Middle Ages, and they often insert passages telling the people that they must do their duties.'

II

I have carried the manuscript of these translations about with me for days, reading it in railway trains, or on the top of omnibuses and in restaurants, and I have often had to close it lest some stranger would see how much it moved me. These lyrics—which are in the original, my Indians tell me, full of subtlety of rhythm, of untranslatable delicacies of colour, of metrical invention—display in their thought a world I have dreamed of all my life long. The work of a supreme culture, they yet appear as much the growth of the common soil as the grass and the rushes. A tradition, where poetry and religion are the same thing, has passed through the centuries, gathering from learned and unlearned metaphor and emotion, and carried back again to the multitude the thought of the scholar and of the noble. If the civilization of Bengal remains unbroken, if that common mind which—as one divines—runs through all, is not, as with us, broken into a dozen minds that know nothing of each other, something even of what is most subtle in these verses will have come, in a few generations, to the beggar on the roads. When there was but one mind in England Chaucer wrote his *Troilus and Criseyde*,[11] and though he had written to be read, or to be read out—for our time was coming on apace—he was sung by minstrels for a while. Rabindranath Tagore, like Chaucer's forerunners, writes music for his words, and one understands at every moment that he is so abundant, so spontaneous, so daring in his passion, so full of surprise, because he is doing something which has never seemed strange, unnatural, or in need of defence. These verses will not lie in little well-printed books upon ladies' tables, who turn the pages with indolent hands that they may sigh over a life without meaning, which is yet all they can know of life, or be carried about by students at the university to be laid aside when the work of life begins, but as the generations pass, travellers will hum them on the highway and men rowing upon rivers. Lovers, while they await one another, shall find, in murmuring them, this love of God a magic gulf wherein their own more bitter passion may bathe and renew its youth. At every moment the heart of this poet flows outward to these without derogation or condescension, for it has known that they will understand; and it has filled itself with the circumstance of their lives. The traveller in the red-brown clothes that he wears that dust may not show upon him, the girl searching in her bed for the petals fallen from the wreath of her royal lover, the servant or the bride awaiting the master's home-coming in the empty house, are images of the heart turning to God.[12] Flowers and rivers, the blowing of conch shells, the heavy rain of the Indian July, or the parching heat, are images of the moods of that heart in union or in separation; and a man sitting in a boat upon a river playing upon a lute, like one of those figures full of mysterious meaning in a Chinese picture, is God Himself.[13] A whole people, a whole civilization, immeasurably strange to us, seems to have been taken up into this imagination; and yet we are not moved because of its strangeness, but because we have met our own image, as though we had walked in Rossetti's willow wood,[14] or heard, perhaps for the first time in literature, our voice as in a dream.

Since the Renaissance the writing of European saints—however familiar their metaphor and the general structure of their thought—has ceased to hold our attention. We know that we must at last forsake the world, and we are accustomed in moments of weariness or exaltation to consider a voluntary forsaking; but how can we, who have read so much poetry, seen so many paintings, listened to so much music, where the cry of the flesh and the cry of the soul seem one, forsake it harshly and rudely? What have we in common with St Bernard covering his eyes that they may not dwell upon the beauty of the lakes of Switzerland,[15] or with the violent rhetoric of the Book of Revelation? We would, if we might, find, as in this book, words full of courtesy. 'I have got my leave. Bid me farewell, my brothers! I bow to you all and take my departure. Here I give back the keys of my door—and I give up all claims to my house. I only ask for last kind words from you. We were neighbours for long, but I received more than I could give. Now the day has dawned and the lamp that lit my dark corner is out. A summons has come and I am ready for my journey.'[16] And it is our own mood, when it is furthest from À Kempis or John of the Cross,[17] that cries, 'And because I love this life, I know I shall love death as well.'[18] Yet it is not only in our thoughts of the parting that this book fathoms all. We had not known that we loved God, hardly it may be that we believed in Him; yet looking backward upon our life we discover, in our exploration of the pathways of woods, in our delight in the lonely places of hills, in that mysterious claim that we have made, unavailingly, on the women that we have loved, the emotion that created this insidious sweetness. 'Entering my heart unbidden even as one of the common crowd, unknown to me, my king, thou didst press the signet of eternity upon many a fleeting moment.'[19] This is no longer the sanctity of the cell and of the scourge; being but a lifting up, as it were, into a greater intensity of the mood of the painter, painting the dust and the sunlight, and we go for a like voice to St Francis and to William Blake who have seemed so alien in our violent history.[20]

III

We write long books where no page perhaps has any quality to make writing a pleasure, being confident in some general design, just as we fight and make money and fill our heads with politics—all dull things in the doing—while Mr Tagore, like the Indian civilization itself, has been content to discover the soul and surrender himself to its spontaneity. He often seems to contrast his life with that of those who have lived more after our fashion, and have more seeming weight in the world, and always humbly as though he were only sure his way is best for him: 'Men going home glance at me and smile and fill me with shame. I sit like a beggar maid, drawing my skirt over my face, and when they ask me what it is I want, I drop my eyes and answer them not.'[21] At another time, remembering how his life had once a different shape, he will say, 'Many an hour have I spent in the strife of the good and the evil, but now it is the pleasure of my playmate of the empty days to draw my heart on to him; and I know not why is this sudden call to what useless inconsequence.'[22] An innocence, a simplicity that one does not find elsewhere in literature makes the birds and the leaves seem as near to him as they are near to children, and the changes of the seasons great events as before our thoughts had arisen between them and us. At times I wonder if he has it from the literature of Bengal or from religion, and at other times, remembering the birds alighting on his brother's hands, I find pleasure in thinking it hereditary, a mystery that was growing through the centuries like the courtesy of a Tristram or a Pellinore.[23] Indeed, when he is speaking of children, so much a part of himself this quality seems, one is not certain that he is not also speaking of the saints, 'They build their houses with sand and they play with empty shells. With withered leaves they weave their boats and smilingly float them on the vast deep. Children have their play on the seashore of worlds. They know not how to swim, they know not how to cast nets. Pearl fishers dive for pearls, merchants sail in their ships, while children gather pebbles and scatter them again. They seek not for hidden treasures, they know not how to cast nets.'[24]

W. B. Yeats
September 1912

The Ten Principal Upanishads

(w. 1936, dated 1937) Preface to *The Ten Principal Upanishads*, tr. Shree Purohit Swāmi and W. B. Yeats (1937)

Incompetent to expound Indian philosophy, I shall illustrate some few things that have to be said from my own daily thoughts and contemporary poetry.

Shree Purohit Swāmi has asked me to introduce what is twice as much his as mine, for he knows Sanskrit and English, I but English. Before, after and during his nine years' pilgrimage round India[1] he has sung in Sanskrit every morning the Awadhoota Gēeta, attributed to Dattātreya, an ancient Sage to whom he pays particular devotion,[2] and two Upanishads, the Sadguru, his own composition, and the Māndookya;[3] and perhaps at night to entertain or edify his hosts, songs of his own composition; those in Mārāthi or Hindi among the unlearned, those in Sanskrit among the learned. Sanskrit has been a familiar speech, not changing from place to place, but always on his tongue.

For some forty years my friend George Russell ('AE') has quoted me passages from some Upanishad,[4] and for those forty years I have said to myself—some day I will find out if he knows what he is talking about. Between us existed from the beginning the antagonism that unites dear friends. More than once I asked him the name of some translator and even bought the book, but the most eminent scholars left me incredulous. Could latinised words, hyphenated words; could polyglot phrases, sedentary distortions of unnatural English—'However many Gods in Thee, All-Knower, adversely slay desires of a person'—could muddles, muddied by 'Lo! Verily' and 'Forsooth',[5] represent what grass farmers sang thousands of years ago, what their descendants sing today? So when I met Shree Purohit Swāmi I proposed that we should go to India and make a translation that would read as though the original had been written in common English: 'To write well,' said Aristotle, 'express yourself like the common people, but think like a wise man', a favourite quotation of Lady Gregory's—I quote her diary from memory.[6] Then when lack of health and money made India impossible we chose Majorca to escape telephones and foul weather, and there the work was done, not, as I had planned, in ease and leisure, but in the interstices left me by a long illness.[7] Yet I am satisfied; I have escaped that polyglot, hyphenated, latinised, muddied muddle of distortion that froze belief. Can we believe or disbelieve until we have put our thought into a language wherein we are accustomed to express love and hate and all the shades between? When belief comes we stand up, walk up and down, laugh or swing an arm; a mathematician gets drunk, finding that which is the prerogative of men of action.

I have not worked to confound George Russell, though often saddened by the thought that I could not—he died some months ago[8] —but to confound something in myself. He expressed in his ceaseless vague preoccupation with the East a need and curiosity of our time. Psychical research, which must some day deeply concern religious philosophy, for its evidences surround the pilgrim and the devotee though they never take the centre of the stage, has already proved the existence of faculties that would, combined into one man, make of that man a miracle-working Yogi. More and more too does it seem to approach a main thought of the Upanishads. Continental investigators, who reject the spiritism of Lodge and Crookes, but accept their phenomena, postulate an individual self possessed of such power and knowledge[9] that they seem at every moment about to identify it with that Self without limitation and sorrow, containing and contained by all, and to seek there not only the living but the dead.[10]

But our need and curiosity have no one source. Between 1922 and 1925 English literature, wherever most intense, cast off its preoccupation with social problems and began to create myths like those of antiquity, and to ask the most profound questions. I recall poems by T. S. Eliot,[11] *Those Barren Leaves* by Aldous Huxley, where there is a Buddhistic hatred of life,[12] or a hatred Schopenhauer did not so much find in as deduce from a Latin translation of a Persian translation of the Upanishads:[13] certain poems—*The Seven Days of the Sun*, 'Matrix', 'The Mutations of the Phoenix', by W. J. Turner, by Dorothy Wellesley, by Herbert Read,[14] which have displayed in myths, not as might some writer of my youth for the sake of romantic suggestion but urged by the most recent thought, the world emerging from the human mind. A still younger generation has brought a more minute psychological curiosity, suggesting an eye where a goldsmith's magnifying glass is screwed, to like preoccupations.

In their pursuit of meaning, Day Lewis, MacNeice, Auden, Laura Riding[15] have thrown off too much, as I think, the old metaphors, the sensuous tradition of the poets:

> High on some mountain shelf
> Huddle the pitiless abstractions bald about the neck;[16]

but have found, perhaps the more easily for that sacrifice, a neighbourhood where some new Upanishad, some half-Asiatic masterpiece, may start up amid our averted eyes.

When I was young we talked much of tradition, and those emotional young men, Francis Thompson, Lionel Johnson, John Gray, found it in Christianity.[17] But now that *The Golden Bough* has made Christianity look modern and fragmentary[18] we study Confucius with Ezra Pound,[19] or like T. S. Eliot find in Christianity a convenient symbolism for some older or newer thought, or say with Henry Airbubble, 'I am a member of the Church of England but not a Christian.'[20] Shree Purohit Swāmi and I offer to some young man seeking, like Shakespeare, Dante, Milton, vast sentiments and generalisations, the oldest philosophical compositions of the world, compositions, not writings, for they were sung long before they were written down. European scholarship with many doubts has fixed their date, or the date of the most important, as a little before 600 B.C. when Buddha was born, but Indian scholarship prefers a far earlier date. Whatever the date, those forest Sages began everything;[21] no fundamental problem of philosophy, nothing that has disturbed the schools to controversy, escaped their notice.

It pleases me to fancy that when we turn towards the East, in or out of church, we are turning not less to the ancient west and north; the one fragment of pagan Irish philosophy come down, 'the Song of Amergin', seems Asiatic;[22] that a system of thought like that of these books, though perhaps less perfectly organised, once overspread the world, as ours today;[23] that our genuflections discover in that East something ancestral in ourselves, something we must bring into the light before we can appease a religious instinct that for the first time in our civilisation demands the satisfaction of the whole man.

Upanishad is doctrine or wisdom (literally 'At the feet of', meaning thereby 'At the feet of some Master'), the doctrine or wisdom of the Wedas.[24] Each is attached to some section and sometimes is named from the section. The Katha-Upanishad for instance is part of the Kāthak Brāhman section in the Yajur-Weda. Shree Purohit Swāmi has omitted the usual first five chapters of the Chāndôgya-Upanishad because they are so intermixed with ritual that they are no longer studied, though still sung. For the same reason he has selected from Brihadāranyaka-Upanishad such passages as contain no such intermixture. A few passages have been omitted, not because descriptions of ritual but because repetitions of what is said and said as well elsewhere.[25] Their order wherein the Upanishads should be studied, according to tradition, is that in which they are printed in this book.

W. B. Yeats
1937

Aphorisms of Yoga

Introduction to *Aphorisms of Yôga*, by Bhagwān Shree Patanjali, tr. Shree Purohit Swāmi (1938)

I

Some years ago I bought *The Yôga-System of Patanjali*, translated and edited by James Horton Woods and published by the Harvard Press. It is the standard edition, final, impeccable in scholastic eyes,[1] even in the eyes of a famous poet and student of Samskrit,[2] who used it as a dictionary. But then the poet was at his university, but lately out of school, had not learned to hate all scholar's cant and class-room slang, nor was he an old man in a hurry.

Certainly before the Ajantā Caverns[3] were painted, almost certainly before the ribbed dome and bell columns of Kārli[4] were carved, naked ascetics had put what they believed an ancient wisdom into short aphorisms for their pupils to get by heart and put in practice. I come in my turn, no grammarian, but a man engaged in that endless research into life, death, God, that is every man's revery. I want to hear the talk of those naked men, and I am certain they never said 'The subliminal impression produced this (super reflective balanced state)'[5] nor talked of 'predicate relations'.[6] Then I found among some typed papers on various subjects a first draft of Shree Purohit Swāmi's translation and was moderately content. A little later he said he was engaged on a commentary, and when we had finished *The Ten Principal Upanishads*[7] he began to read it out. Now and then I would stop him to simplify or condense a phrase, or to ask him this or that. He had practised certain meditations, had certain experiences described or implied by Patanjali, and as a Brāhman monk had encircled India for nine years.[8] He knew what he wrote about, he knew it in his bones as no European scholar could, and now after a couple of years I re-read with excitement.

With his consent I lent the manuscript to the only Indian scholar in my circle,[9] and though her excitement was not less than mine she objected to the anecdotes, the personal experiences that seemed to her to break the logical tension. If they are a fault, the fault is mine, for I begged the Swāmi to be as anecdotal, biographical, as he could, because we know nothing of those who study and put in practice the Aphorisms of Patanjali.[10]

II

Some scholars attribute the Aphorisms to a certain Patanjali who lived in the second century B.C., others to a man of the same name who lived in the third, fourth or fifth century A.D.; others have held that these two men were one man who lived at an unknown date. All are agreed that he but recorded or systematised an ancient knowledge. The most famous of the commentaries were written apparently between the third and the ninth centuries A.D. Shree Purohit Swāmi has made some use of them, and the more important are fully translated by James Horton Woods.[11]

III

In all civilisations comes a moment when mass feeling and the dominant images that excite it weaken; when poetic certainty recedes before doubt and analysis. In the *Brihadāranyaka-Upanishad* there is a certain Yādnyawalkya into whose mouth are put profound thoughts, litanies, variations upon a theme: 'Thunder is the honey of all beings; all beings the honey of thunder. The bright eternal Self that is in thunder, the bright eternal Self that lives in the voice, are one and the same; that is immortality, that is Spirit, that is all.'[12] He lived, according to some European scholars, about 600 B.C. before the composition of most of the Wedic Hymns,[13] though Indian scholars put all these events much earlier. Like Pythagoras, who occupied the same place in Greek civilisation, he substituted philosophic reason for custom and mythology, put an end to the Golden Age and began that of the Sophists, an intellectual anarchy that found its Socrates in Buddha.[14] He had substituted the eternal Self for all the gods.[15]

The little I know of India has come to me in the main by word of mouth. A man from Malabār[16] described that age of the sophists, 'thought and action became ends in themselves, the forest Brāhmans,[17] each with his group of students, thought of nothing but wrangling, the military caste in the towns thought of nothing but their military business. They would let out a horse and any town that stopped the horse had to fight. Buddha tried to put down both Brāhman and soldier, failed against the Brāhman, was too successful against the soldier for he destroyed our power of self-protection. We have been conquered by race after race, Syrian, Persian, French, English.'

IV

Somewhere in this Sophistic period came Patanjali and his Aphorisms. Unlike Buddha he turned from ordinary men; he sought truth not by the logic or the moral precepts that draw the crowd, but by methods of meditation and contemplation that purify the soul. The truth cannot be found by argument, the soul itself is truth, it is that Self praised by Yādnyawalkya which is all Selves.[18] The school of Yādnyawalkya and its historical preparation replaced the trance of the sôma drinkers (I think of the mescal of certain Mexican tribes),[19] or that induced by beaten drums, or by ceremonial dancing before the image of a god, by a science that seems to me as reasonable as it must have seemed to its first discoverer. Through states analogous to self-induced hypnotic sleep the devotee attains a final state of complete wakefulness called, now conscious Samādhi, now Tureeyā, where the soul, purified of all that is not itself, comes into possession of its own timelessness.[20] Matter, or the soul's relation to time has disappeared; souls that have found like freedom in the remote past, or will find it in the future, enter into it or are entered by it at will, nor is it bound to any part of space, nor to any process, it depends only upon itself, is Spirit, that which has value in itself.[21]

V

That experience, accessible to all who adopt a traditional technique and habit of life, has become the central experience of Indian civilisation, perhaps of all Far-Eastern civilisation, that wherein all thoughts and all emotions expect their satisfaction and rest. The technique in China and Japan is different, but not that experience. In the Upanishads and in Patanjali the Self and the One are reality. There are other books, Indian or Chinese, where the Self or the Not-Self, the One and the Many, are alike illusion. Whatever is known to the logical intellect is this and not that, here and not there, before and not after, or confined to one wing or another of some antinomy. It became no longer possible to identify the One and the Self with reality, the method of meditation had to be changed. Some years ago, that I might understand its influence upon Chinese and Japanese landscape painting, I sought that method in vain through encyclopedias and histories; it certainly prepared an escape from all that intellect holds true, and that escape, as described in the Scriptures and the legends of Zen Buddhism, is precipitated by shock, often produced artificially by the teacher.[22] A young monk said to the Abbot, 'I have noticed that when anybody has asked about Nirwāna you merely raise your right hand and lower it again, and now when I am asked I answer in the same way.' The Abbot seized his hand and cut off a finger. The young monk ran away screaming, then stopped and looked back. The Abbot raised his hand and lowered it, and at that moment the young monk attained the supreme joy.[23] 'No more does the young man come from behind the embroidered curtain amid the sweet clouds of incense; he goes among his friends, he goes among the flute players, something very nice has happened to the young man, but he can only tell it to his sweetheart.'[24]

VI

Before Humanism, before the Renaissance, the popular intellect found rest and satisfaction in the adoration of God imagined as the figure on the Cross, or the Child upon its Mother's knee, but to the Humanist this must have seemed as alien as did the mythology of early India or Greece to the followers of Yādnyawalkya or Pythagoras, but no Zen Buddhism, no Yôga practice, no Neo-Platonic discipline, came to find a substitute. Our mechanical science intervened.

Goethe alone among men of genius has attempted to become wise, as the ancients understood that word. I who owed as much in youth to *Wilhelm Meister* as in later years to the *Comédie humaine*,[25] join in the general admiration. In *Faust* he sought to experience, and tried to express, a moment acceptable to reason where our thoughts and emotions could find satisfaction or rest. Faust, in the first part, refuses to say 'In the beginning was the Word', and substitutes 'In the beginning was the Act',[26] and when at last he almost cries 'Stay Moment!'[27] it is in contemplation of men struggling to save a small patch of cultivated land from inundation. He may have thought of nothing but his dislike for all abstract, or disembodied thought, of his conviction that culture (was that the cultivated land?) and its creation and defence was the only good, yet I think he meant more than that. He is vague, he does not cry 'Stay Moment!' but says that he might cry it, and there seems no reason for this distinction. Perhaps thought failed, as I think, his life failed, before what seemed the supreme test of his philosophy. He sought unity, that unity which Dante compared to a perfectly proportioned human body,[28] and but turned from one occupation to another. As he approached what seemed to him success his poetry dissolved in abstraction and complexity. Had he died in 1800 *Faust*, including what was already written of the second part, would have remained, though fragmentary, a work of art throughout. Gentile, the Italian Hegelian philosopher, finds in those words of Faust a conviction that ultimate reality is the Pure Act, the actor and the thing acted upon, the puncher and the punching-ball, consumed away.[29] If Goethe failed, he failed because neither he nor his audience knew of any science or philosophy that sought, not a change of opinion, but a different level of consciousness; knowing nothing of white heat he sought truth in the cold iron.

VII

In the seventeenth century conscious Samādhi re-appeared in the 'walking trance' of Boehme, when truth fell upon him 'like a bursting shower',[30] and in the eighteenth, much contaminated by belief in the literal inspiration of Scripture, in the visions of Swedenborg. Possibly I should deny to the visions of Swedenborg, as I do to those of Saint Theresa who lived back somewhere near the Baisers and the sôma drinker,[31] the character of conscious Samādhi; conscious Samādhi, Tureeyā as Patanjali or the Upanishads understand that term is a sovereign condition and cannot accept a limit. 'You ask me what is my religion and I hit you upon the mouth,' wrote a Japanese monk upon attaining Nirwāna.[32] But we may, I think, concede to Swedenborg an impure Samādhi. Boehme had great influence upon the theology of the seventeenth century and some on modern German philosophy; Swedenborg gave what there is of anatomy to the sentimental body of spiritualistic theory, but 'walking trance' and vision were themselves uninvestigated. In the first half of the nineteenth century French hypnotists, or as they were then called, mesmerists, investigated the Yôga sleep from outside, discovering as they believed, a series of spiritual states from man to God, and were the first to study clairvoyance and foreknowledge. From America in the middle of the century came the Yôga sleep of the spirit medium. So great had been the influence of the French hypnotists, largely, as I think, through the incorporation of their discoveries in the novels of Balzac, Dumas, Georges Sand,[33] that there are two interpretations of psychic phenomena. In England and America it is attributed to spirits, whereas almost without exception, Continental investigators discover its origin in some hitherto unimagined power of the individual mind and body.[34] These points of view, spiritism and animism, are not in the eyes of the student of Yôga contradictory; to quote the *Chāndôgya-Upanishad*, 'the wise man sees in Self those that are alive and those that are dead'.[35]

W. B. Yeats
Dublin 1937

Introduction to *The Oxford Book of Modern Verse* (1936)

I

I have tried to include in this book all good poets who have lived or died from three years before the death of Tennyson to the present moment, except some two or three who belong through the character of their work to an earlier period. Even a long-lived man has the right to call his own contemporaries modern. To the generation which began to think and read in the late eighties of the last century the four poets whose work begins this book were unknown, or, if known, of an earlier generation that did not stir its sympathy. Gerard Hopkins remained unpublished for thirty years.[1] Fifty-odd years ago I met him in my father's studio on different occasions, but remember almost nothing. A boy of seventeen, Walt Whitman in his pocket, had little interest in a querulous, sensitive scholar. Thomas Hardy's poems were unwritten or unpublished.[2] Robert Bridges seemed a small Victorian poet whose poetry, published in expensive hand-printed books, one could find behind glass doors in the houses of wealthy friends.[3] I will consider the genius of these three when the development of schools gives them great influence. Wilfrid Blunt one knew through the report of friends as a fashionable amateur who had sacrificed a capacity for literature and the visible arts to personal adventure. Some ten years had to pass before anybody understood that certain sonnets, lyrics, stanzas of his were permanent in our literature.[4] A young man, London bred or just arrived there, would have felt himself repelled by the hard, cold energy of Henley's verse, called it rhetoric, or associated it in some way with that propaganda whereby Henley, through the vehicle of a weekly review and a magazine that were financial failures, had turned the young men at Oxford and Cambridge into imperialists. 'Why should I respect Henley?' said to me Clement Shorter. 'I sell two hundred thousand copies a week of *The Sphere;* the circulation of *The National Observer* fell to two hundred at the end.'[5] Henley lay upon the sofa, crippled by his incautious youth, dragged his body, crutch-supported, between two rooms, imagining imperial might. For a young man, struggling for expression, despairing of achievement, he remained hidden behind his too obvious effectiveness. Nor would that young man have felt anything but contempt for the poetry of Oscar Wilde, considering it an exaggeration of every Victorian fault, nor, except in the case of one poem not then written, has time corrected the verdict. Wilde, a man of action, a born dramatist, finding himself overshadowed by old famous men he could not attack, for he was of their time and shared its admirations, tricked and clowned to draw attention to himself. Even when disaster struck him down it could not wholly clear his soul. Now that I have plucked from the *Ballad of Reading Gaol* its foreign feathers it shows a stark realism akin to that of Thomas Hardy, the contrary to all its author deliberately sought. I plucked out even famous lines because, effective in themselves, put into the *Ballad* they become artificial, trivial, arbitrary; a work of art can have but one subject.

> Yet each man kills the thing he loves,
>   By each let this be heard,
> Some do it with a bitter look,
>   Some with a flattering word.
> The coward does it with a kiss,
>   The brave man with a sword!
>
> Some kill their love when they are young,
>   And some when they are old;
> Some strangle with the hands of Lust,
>   Some with the hands of Gold:
> The kindest use a knife, because
>   The dead so soon grow cold.[6]

I have stood in judgement upon Wilde, bringing into the light a great, or almost great poem, as he himself had done had he lived; my work gave me that privilege.

II

All these writers were, in the eye of the new generation, in so far as they were known, Victorian, and the new generation was in revolt. But one writer, almost unknown to the general public—I remember somebody saying at his death 'no newspaper has given him an obituary notice'—had its entire uncritical admiration, Walter Pater. That is why I begin this book with the famous passage from his essay on Leonardo da Vinci. Only by printing it in *vers libre* can one show its revolutionary importance. Pater was accustomed to give each sentence a separate page of manuscript, isolating and analysing its rhythm;[7] Henley wrote certain 'hospital poems',[8] not included in this book, in *vers libre*, thinking of his dramatic, everyday material, in that an innovator, but did not permit a poem to arise out of its own rhythm as do Turner and Pound[9] at their best and as, I contend, Pater did. I shall presently discuss the meaning of this passage which dominated a generation, a domination so great that all over Europe from that day to this men shrink from Leonardo's masterpiece as from an over-flattered woman. For the moment I am content to recall one later writer:

O wha's been here afore me, lass,
And hoo did he get in?[10]

The revolt against Victorianism meant to the young poet a revolt against irrelevant descriptions of nature, the scientific and moral discursiveness of *In Memoriam*—'When he should have been broken-hearted', said Verlaine, 'he had many reminiscences'[11]—the political eloquence of Swinburne, the psychological curiosity of Browning, and the poetical diction of everybody. Poets said to one another over their black coffee—a recently imported fashion—'We must purify poetry of all that is not poetry', and by poetry they meant poetry as it had been written by Catullus, a great name at that time, by the Jacobean writers, by Verlaine, by Baudelaire.[12] Poetry was a tradition like religion and liable to corruption, and it seemed that they could best restore it by writing lyrics technically perfect, their emotion pitched high, and as Pater offered instead of moral earnestness life lived as 'a hard gem-like flame'[13] all accepted him for master.

But every light has its shadow, we tumble out of one pickle into another, the 'hard gem-like flame' was an insufficient motive; the sons of men who had admired Garibaldi or applauded the speeches of John Bright,[14] picked Ophelias out of the gutter, who knew exactly what they wanted and had no intention of committing suicide. My father gave these young men their right name. When I had described a supper with Count Stenbock, scholar, connoisseur, drunkard, poet, pervert, most charming of men,[15] he said 'they are the Hamlets of our age'. Some of these Hamlets went mad, some drank, drinking not as happy men drink but in solitude, all had courage, all suffered public opprobrium—generally for their virtues or for sins they did not commit—all had good manners. Good manners in written and spoken word were an essential part of their tradition—'Life', said Lionel Johnson, 'must be a ritual';[16] all in the presence of women or even with one another put aside their perplexities; all had gaiety, some had wit:

> Unto us they belong,
> To us the bitter and gay,
> Wine and woman and song.[17]

Some turned Catholic—that too was a tradition. I read out at a meeting of the Rhymers' Club[18] a letter describing Meynell's discovery of Francis Thompson, at that time still bedded under his railway arch, then his still unpublished 'Ode to the Setting Sun'.[19] But Francis Thompson had been born a Catholic; Lionel Johnson was the first convert; Dowson adopted a Catholic point of view without, I think, joining that church, an act requiring energy and decision.

Occasionally at some evening party some young woman asked a poet what he thought of strikes, or declared that to paint pictures or write poetry at such a moment was to resemble the fiddler Nero, for great meetings of revolutionary Socialists were disturbing Trafalgar Square on Sunday afternoons; a young man known to most of us told some such party that he had stood before a desk in an office not far from Southampton Row resolved to protect it with his life because it contained documents that would hang William Morris, and wound up by promising a revolution in six months.[20] Shelley must have had some such immediate circle when he wrote to friends urging them to withdraw their money from the Funds.[21] We poets continued to write verse and read it out at 'The Cheshire Cheese', convinced that to take part in such movements would be only less disgraceful than to write for the newspapers.

III

Then in 1900 everybody got down off his stilts; henceforth nobody drank absinthe with his black coffee; nobody went mad; nobody committed suicide; nobody joined the Catholic church; or if they did I have forgotten.

Victorianism had been defeated, though two writers dominated the moment who had never heard of that defeat or did not believe in it: Rudyard Kipling and William Watson. Indian residence and associations had isolated the first, he was full of opinions, of politics, of impurities—to use our word—and the word must have been right, for he interests a critical audience to-day by the grotesque tragedy of 'Danny Deever', the matter but not the form of old street ballads, and by songs traditional in matter and form like the 'St Helena Lullaby'.[22] The second had reached maturity before the revolt began, his first book had been published in the early eighties.[23] 'Wring the neck of rhetoric,' Verlaine had said,[24] and the public soon turned against William Watson, forgetting that at his best he had not rhetoric but noble eloquence. As I turn his pages I find verse after verse read long ago and still unforgettable, this to some journalist who, intoxicated perhaps by William Archer's translations from Ibsen,[25] had described, it may be, some lyric elaborating or deepening its own tradition as of 'no importance to the age':

> Great Heaven! When these with clamour shrill
>   Drift out to Lethe's harbour bar
> A verse of Lovelace shall be still
>   As vivid as a pulsing star:

this, received from some Miltonic cliff that had it from a Roman voice:

> The august, inhospitable, inhuman night
> Glittering magnificently unperturbed.[26]

IV

Conflict bequeathed its bias. Folk-song, unknown to the Victorians as their attempts to imitate it show, must, because never declamatory or eloquent, fill the scene. If anybody will turn these pages attending to poets born in the 'fifties, 'sixties, and 'seventies, he will find how successful are their folk-songs and their imitations. In Ireland, where still lives almost undisturbed the last folk tradition of western Europe, the songs of Campbell and Colum[27] draw from that tradition their themes, return to it, and are sung to Irish airs by boys and girls who have never heard the names of the authors; but the reaction from rhetoric, from all that was prepense and artificial, has forced upon these writers now and again, as upon my own early work, a facile charm, a too soft simplicity. In England came like temptations. The *Shropshire Lad*[28] is worthy of its fame, but a mile further and all had been marsh. Thomas Hardy, though his work lacked technical accomplishment, made the necessary correction through his mastery of the impersonal objective scene. John Synge brought back masculinity to Irish verse with his harsh disillusionment, and later, when the folk movement seemed to support vague political mass excitement, certain poets began to create passionate masterful personality.

V

We remembered the Gaelic poets of the seventeenth and early eighteenth centuries wandering, after the flight of the Catholic nobility, among the boorish and the ignorant, singing their loneliness and their rage; James Stephens, Frank O'Connor made them symbols of our pride:

> The periwinkle, and the tough dog-fish
> At eventide have got into my dish!
> The great, where are they now! the great had said—
> This is not seemly, bring to him instead
> That which serves his and serves our dignity—
> And that was done.
>
> I am O'Rahilly:
> Here in a distant place I hold my tongue,
> Who once said all his say, when he was young![29]

I showed Lady Gregory a few weeks before her death a book by Day Lewis. 'I prefer', she said, 'those poems translated by Frank O'Connor because they come out of original sin.'[30] A distinguished Irish poet said a month back—I had read him a poem by Turner—'We cannot become philosophic like the English, our lives are too exciting.' He was not thinking of such passing episodes as civil war, his own imprisonment, but of an always inflamed public opinion that made sonnet or play almost equally perilous; yet civil war has had its effect. Twelve years ago Oliver Gogarty was captured by his enemies, imprisoned in a deserted house on the edge of the Liffey with every prospect of death. Pleading a natural necessity he got into the garden, plunged under a shower of revolver bullets and as he swam the ice-cold December stream promised it, should it land him in safety, two swans. I was present when he fulfilled that vow. His poetry fits the incident, a gay, stoical—no, I will not withhold the word—heroic song. Irish by tradition and many ancestors, I love, though I have nothing to offer but the philosophy they deride, swashbucklers, horsemen, swift indifferent men; yet I do not think that is the sole reason, good reason though it is, why I gave him considerable space, and think him one of the great lyric poets of our age.[31]

VI

We have more affinity with Henley and Blunt than with other modern English poets, but have not felt their influence; we are what we are because almost without exception we have had some part in public life in a country where public life is simple and exciting. We are not many; Ireland has had few poets of any kind outside Gaelic. I think England has had more good poets from 1900 to the present day than during any period of the same length since the early seventeenth century. There are no predominant figures, no Browning, no Tennyson, no Swinburne, but more than I have found room for have written two, three, or half a dozen lyrics that may be permanent.

During the first years of the century the best known were celebrators of the country-side or of the life of ships; I think of Davies and of Masefield; some few wrote in the manner of the traditional country ballad. Others, descended not from Homer but from Virgil, wrote what the young communist scornfully calls 'Belles-lettres': Binyon when at his best, as I think, of Tristram and Isoult; Sturge Moore of centaurs, amazons, gazelles copied from a Persian picture; De la Mare short lyrics that carry us back through *Christabel* or *Kubla Khan*.

> Through what wild centuries
> Roves back the rose?[32]

The younger of the two ladies who wrote under the name of 'Michael Field' made personal lyrics in the manner of Walter Savage Landor and the Greek anthology.[33]

None of these were innovators; they preferred to keep all the past their rival; their fame will increase with time. They have been joined of late years by Sacheverell Sitwell with his *Canons of Giant Art*, written in the recently rediscovered 'sprung verse', his main theme changes of colour, or historical phase, in Greece, Crete, India. 'Agamemnon's Tomb', however, describes our horror at the presence and circumstance of death and rises to great intensity.[34]

VII

Robert Bridges seemed for a time, through his influence on Laurence Binyon and others less known, the patron saint of the movement.[35] His influence—practice, not theory—was never deadening; he gave to lyric poetry a new cadence, a distinction as deliberate as that of Whistler's painting,[36] an impulse moulded and checked like that in certain poems of Landor, but different, more in the nerves, less in the blood, more birdlike, less human; words often commonplace made unforgettable by some trick of speeding and slowing,

> A glitter of pleasure
> And a dark tomb,[37]

or by some trick of simplicity, not the impulsive simplicity of youth but that of age, much impulse examined and rejected:

> I heard a linnet courting
> His lady in the spring!

His mates were idly sporting,
Nor stayed to hear him sing
His song of love.—
I fear my speech distorting
His tender love.[38]

Every metaphor, every thought a commonplace, emptiness everywhere, the whole magnificent.

VIII

A modern writer is beset by what Rossetti called 'the soulless self-reflections of man's skill';[39] the more vivid his nature, the greater his boredom, a boredom no Greek, no Elizabethan, knew in like degree, if at all. He may escape to the classics with the writers I have just described, or with much loss of self-control and coherence force language against its will into a powerful, artificial vividness. Edith Sitwell has a temperament of a strangeness so high-pitched that only through this artifice could it find expression. One cannot think of her in any other age or country. She has transformed with her metrical virtuosity traditional metres reborn not to be read but spoken, exaggerated metaphors into mythology, carrying them from poem to poem, compelling us to go backward to some first usage for the birth of the myth; if the storm suggest the bellowing of elephants, some later poem will display 'The elephant trunks of the sea'.[40] Nature appears before us in a hashish-eater's dream. This dream is double; in its first half, through separated metaphor, through mythology, she creates, amid crowds and scenery that suggest the Russian Ballet and Aubrey Beardsley's final phase, a perpetual metamorphosis that seems an elegant, artificial childhood; in the other half, driven by a necessity of contrast, a nightmare vision like that of Webster, of the emblems of mortality.[41] A group of writers have often a persistent image. There are 'stars' in poem after poem of certain writers of the 'nineties as though to symbolize an aspiration towards what is inviolate and fixed; and now in poem after poem by Edith Sitwell or later writers are 'bones'—'the anguish of the skeleton', 'the terrible Gehenna of the bone';[42] Eliot has:

No contact possible to flesh
Allayed the fever of the bone.[43]

and Elinor Wylie, an American whose exquisite work is slighter than that of her English contemporaries because she has not their full receptivity to the profound hereditary sadness of English genius:

Live like the velvet mole:
Go burrow underground,

And there hold intercourse
With roots of trees and stones,
With rivers at their source
And disembodied bones.[44]

Laurence Binyon, Sturge Moore, knew nothing of this image; it seems most persistent among those who, throwing aside tradition, seek something somebody has called 'essential form' in the theme itself.[45] A fairly well-known woman painter in September drew my house, at that season almost hidden in foliage; she reduced the trees to skeletons as though it were mid-winter, in pursuit of 'essential form'.[46] Does not intellectual analysis in one of its moods identify man with that which is most persistent in his body? The poets are haunted once again by the Elizabethan image, but there is a difference. Since Poincaré said 'space is the creation of our ancestors',[47] we have found it more and more difficult to separate ourselves from the dead when we commit them to the grave; the bones are not dead but accursed, accursed because unchanging.

The small bones built in the womb
The womb that loathed the bones
And cast out the soul.[48]

Perhaps in this new, profound poetry, the symbol itself is contradictory, horror of life, horror of death.

IX

Eliot has produced his great effect upon his generation because he has described men and women that get out of bed or into it from mere habit;[49] in describing this life that has lost heart his own art seems grey, cold, dry. He is an Alexander Pope, working without apparent imagination, producing his effects by a rejection of all rhythms and metaphors used by the more popular romantics rather than by the discovery of his own, this rejection giving his work an unexaggerated plainness that has the effect of novelty. He has the rhythmical flatness of the 'Essay on Man'—despite Miss Sitwell's advocacy I see Pope as Blake and Keats saw him[50]—later, in *The Waste Land*, amid much that is moving in symbol and imagery there is much monotony of accent:

> When lovely woman stoops to folly and
> Paces about her room again, alone,
> She smooths her hair with automatic hand,
> And puts a record on the gramophone.[51]

I was affected, as I am by these lines, when I saw for the first time a painting by Manet. I longed for the vivid colour and light of Rousseau and Courbet,[52] I could not endure the grey middle-tint—and even to-day Manet gives me an incomplete pleasure; he had left the procession. Nor can I put the Eliot of these poems among those that descend from Shakespeare and the translators of the Bible. I think of him as satirist rather than poet. Once only does that early work speak in the great manner:

> The host with someone indistinct
> Converses at the door apart,
> The nightingales are singing near
> The Convent of the Sacred Heart,
>
> And sang within the bloody wood
> When Agamemnon cried aloud,
> And let their liquid siftings fall
> To stain the stiff dishonoured shroud.[53]

Not until 'The Hollow Men' and 'Ash Wednesday', where he is helped by the short lines, and in the dramatic poems where his remarkable sense of actor, chanter, scene, sweeps him away, is there rhythmical animation. Two or three of my friends attribute the change to an emotional enrichment from religion, but his religion compared to that of John Gray, Francis Thompson, Lionel Johnson in 'The Dark Angel', lacks all strong emotion; a New England Protestant by descent, there is little self-surrender in his personal relation to God and the soul.[54] *Murder in the Cathedral* is a powerful stage play because the actor, the monkish habit, certain repeated words, symbolize what we know, not what the author knows. Nowhere has the author explained how Becket and the King differ in aim; Becket's people have been robbed and persecuted in his absence; like the King he demands strong government. Speaking through Becket's mouth Eliot confronts a world growing always more terrible with a religion like that of some great statesman, a pity not less poignant because it tempers the prayer book with the results of mathematical philosophy.

Peace. And let them be, in their exaltation.
They speak better than they know, and beyond your understanding,
They know and do not know, that acting is suffering
And suffering is action. Neither does the actor suffer
Nor the patient act. But both are fixed
In an eternal action, an eternal patience
To which all must consent that it may be willed
And which all must suffer that they may will it,
That the pattern may subsist, for the pattern is the action
And the suffering, that the wheel may turn and still
Be forever still.[55]

X

Ezra Pound has made flux his theme; plot, characterization, logical discourse, seem to him abstractions unsuitable to a man of his generation. He is mid-way in an immense poem in *vers libre* called for the moment *The Cantos*, where the metamorphosis of Dionysus, the descent of Odysseus into Hades, repeat themselves in various disguises, always in association with some third that is not repeated. Hades may become the hell where whatever modern men he most disapproves of suffer damnation, the metamorphosis petty frauds practised by Jews at Gibraltar.[56] The relation of all the elements to one another, repeated or unrepeated, is to become apparent when the whole is finished. There is no transmission through time, we pass without comment from ancient Greece to modern England, from modern England to medieval China; the symphony, the pattern, is timeless, flux eternal and therefore without movement. Like other readers I discover at present merely exquisite or grotesque fragments. He hopes to give the impression that all is living, that there are no edges, no convexities, nothing to check the flow; but can such a poem have a mathematical structure? Can impressions that are in part visual, in part metrical, be related like the notes of a symphony; has the author been carried beyond reason by a theoretical conception? His belief in his own conception is so great that since the appearance of the first Canto I have tried to suspend judgement.

When I consider his work as a whole I find more style than form; at moments more style, more deliberate nobility and the means to convey it than in any contemporary poet known to me, but it is constantly interrupted, broken, twisted into nothing by its direct opposite, nervous obsession, nightmare, stammering confusion; he is an economist, poet, politician, raging at malignants with inexplicable characters and motives, grotesque figures out of a child's book of beasts. This loss of self-control, common among uneducated revolutionists, is rare—Shelley had it in some degree—among men of Ezra Pound's culture and erudition. Style and its opposite can alternate, but form must be full, sphere-like, single. Even where there is no interruption he is often content, if certain verses and lines have style, to leave unbridged transitions, unexplained ejaculations, that make his meaning unintelligible. He has great influence, more perhaps than any contemporary except Eliot, is probably the source of that lack of form and consequent obscurity which is the main defect of Auden, Day Lewis, and their school, a school which, as will presently be seen, I greatly admire.[57] Even where the style is sustained throughout one gets an impression, especially when he is writing in *vers libre,* that he has not got all the wine into the bowl, that he is a brilliant improvisator translating at sight from an unknown Greek masterpiece:

> See, they return; ah, see the tentative
> Movements, and the slow feet,
> The trouble in the pace and the uncertain
> Wavering!

See, they return, one, and by one,
With fear, as half-awakened;
As if the snow should hesitate
And murmur in the wind,
and half turn back;

These were the Wing'd-with-awe,
Inviolable.
Gods of the winged shoe!
With them the silver hounds,
sniffing the trace of air![58]

XI

When my generation denounced scientific humanitarian pre-occupation, psychological curiosity, rhetoric, we had not found what ailed Victorian literature. The Elizabethans had all these things, especially rhetoric. A friend writes 'all bravado went out of English literature when Falstaff turned into Oliver Cromwell, into England's bad conscience';[59] but he is wrong. Dryden's plays are full of it. The mischief began at the end of the seventeenth century when man became passive before a mechanized nature; that lasted to our own day with the exception of a brief period between Smart's *Song to David* and the death of Byron,[60] wherein imprisoned man beat upon the door. Or I may dismiss all that ancient history and say it began when Stendhal described a masterpiece as a 'mirror dawdling down a lane'.[61] There are only two long poems in Victorian literature that caught public attention; *The Ring and the Book* where great intellect analyses the suffering of one passive soul, weighs the persecutor's guilt, and the *Idylls of the King* where a poetry in itself an exquisite passivity is built about an allegory where a characterless king represents the soul.[62] I read few modern novels, but I think I am right in saying that in every novel that has created an intellectual fashion from Huysmans's *La Cathédrale* to Ernest Hemingway's *Farewell to Arms*,[63] the chief character is a mirror. It has sometimes seemed of late years, though not in the poems I have selected for this book, as if the poet could at any moment write a poem by recording the fortuitous scene or thought, perhaps it might be enough to put into some fashionable rhythm—'I am sitting in a chair, there are three dead flies on a corner of the ceiling.'

Change has come suddenly, the despair of my friends in the 'nineties part of its preparation. Nature, steel-bound or stone-built in the nineteenth century, became a flux where man drowned or swam; the moment had come for some poet to cry 'the flux is in my own mind'.

XII

It was Turner who raised that cry,[64] to gain upon the instant a control of plastic material, a power of emotional construction, Pound has always lacked. At his rare best he competes with Eliot in precision, but Eliot's genius is human, mundane, impeccable, it seems to say 'this man will never disappoint, never be out of character. He moves among objects for which he accepts no responsibility, among the mapped and measured.' Generations must pass before man recovers control of event and circumstance; mind has recognized its responsibility, that is all; Turner himself seems the symbol of an incomplete discovery. After clearing up some metaphysical obscurity he leaves obscure what a moment's thought would have cleared; author of a suave, sophisticated comedy he can talk about 'snivelling majorities';[65] a rich-natured friendly man he has in his satirical Platonic dialogue *The Aesthetes* shot upon forbidden ground.[66] The first romantic poets, Blake, Coleridge, Shelley, dazed by new suddenly opening vistas, had equal though different inconsistencies. I think of him as the first poet to read a mathematical equation, a musical score, a book of verse, with an equal understanding; he seems to ride in an observation balloon, blue heaven above, earth beneath an abstract pattern.[67]

We know nothing but abstract patterns, generalizations, mathematical equations, though such the havoc wrought by newspaper articles and government statistics, two abstractions may sit down to lunch. But what about the imagery we call nature, the sensual scene? Perhaps we are always awake and asleep at the same time; after all going to bed is but a habit; is not sleep by the testimony of the poets our common mother? In *The Seven Days of the Sun*, where there is much exciting thought, I find:

But to me the landscape is like a sea
The waves of the hills
And the bubbles of bush and flower
And the springtide breaking into white foam!

It is a slow sea,
Mare tranquillum,
And a thousand years of wind
Cannot raise a dwarf billow to the moonlight.

But the bosom of the landscape lifts and falls
With its own leaden tide,
That tide whose sparkles are the lilliputian stars.

It is that slow sea
That sea of adamantine languor,
Sleep![68]

I recall Pater's description of the Mona Lisa; had the individual soul of da Vinci's sitter gone down with the pearl divers or trafficked for strange webs? or did Pater foreshadow a poetry, a philosophy, where the individual is nothing, the flux of *The Cantos* of Ezra Pound, objects without contour as in 'Le Chef-d'oeuvre Inconnu',[69] human experience no longer shut into brief lives, cut off into this place and that place, the flux of Turner's poetry that within our minds enriches itself, re-dreams itself, yet only in seeming—for time cannot be divided? Yet one theme perplexes Turner, whether in comedy, dialogue, poem. Somewhere in the middle of it all da Vinci's sitter had private reality like that of the Dark Lady among the women Shakespeare had imagined,[70] but because that private soul is always behind our knowledge, though always hidden it must be the sole source of pain, stupefaction, evil. A musician, he imagines Heaven as a musical composition, a mathematician, as a relation of curves, a poet, as a dark, inhuman sea.

The sea carves innumerable shells
Rolling itself into crystalline curves
The cressets of its faintest sighs

Flickering into filigreed whorls,
Its lustre into mother-of-pearl
Its mystery into fishes' eyes
Its billowing abundance into whales
Around and under the Poles.[71]

XIII

In 'The Mutations of the Phoenix' Herbert Read discovers that the flux is in the mind, not of it perhaps, but in it. The Phoenix is finite mind rising in a nest of light from the sea or infinite; the discovery of Berkeley in *Siris* where light is 'perception', of Grosseteste, twelfth-century philosopher, who defines it as 'corporeality, or that of which corporeality is made'.[72]

All existence
  past, present and to be
  is in this sea fringe.
There is no other temporal scene.

The Phoenix burns spiritually
  among the fierce stars
  and in the docile brain's recesses.
Its ultimate spark
you cannot trace . . .

Light burns the world in the focus of an eye.[73]

XIV

To Dorothy Wellesley nature is a womb, a darkness; its surface is sleep, upon sleep we walk, into sleep drive the plough, and there lie the happy, the wise, the unconceived;

They lie in the loam
Laid backward by slice of the plough;
They sit in the rock;
In a matrix of amethyst crouches a man . . .[74]

but unlike Turner or Read she need not prove or define, that was all done before she began to write and think. As though it were the tale of Mother Hubbard or the results of the last general election, she accepts what Turner and Read accept, sings her joy or sorrow in its presence, at times facile and clumsy, at times magnificent in her masculine rhythm, in the precision of her style. Eliot and Edith Sitwell have much of their intensity from a deliberate re-moulding or checking of past impulse, Turner much of his from a deliberate rejection of current belief, but here is no criticism at all. A new positive belief has given to her, as it gave to Shelley, an uncheckable impulse, and this belief is all the more positive because found, not sought; like certain characters in William Morris she has 'lucky eyes',[75] her sail is full.

I knew nothing of her until a few months ago I read the opening passage in *Horses,* delighted by its changes in pace, abrupt assertion, then a long sweeping line, by its vocabulary modern and precise;

> Who, in the garden-pony carrying skeps
> Of grass or fallen leaves, his knees gone slack,
> Round belly, hollow back,
> Sees the Mongolian Tarpan of the Steppes?
> Or, in the Shire with plaits and feathered feet,
> The war-horse like the wind the Tartar knew?
> Or, in the Suffolk Punch, spells out anew
> The wild grey asses fleet
> With stripe from head to tail, and moderate ears?[76]

The swing from Stendhal has passed Turner; the individual soul, the betrayal of the unconceived at birth, are among her principal themes, it must go further still; that soul must become its own betrayer, its own deliverer, the one activity, the mirror turn lamp. Not that the old conception is untrue, new literature better than old. In the greater nations every phase has characteristic beauty—has not Nicholas of Cusa said reality is expressed through contradiction?[77] Yet for me, a man of my time, through my poetical faculty living its history, after much meat fish seems the only possible diet. I have indeed read certain poems by Turner, by Dorothy Wellesley, with more than all the excitement that came upon me when, a very young man, I heard somebody read out in a London tavern the poems of Ernest Dowson's despair—that too living history.

XV

I have a distaste for certain poems written in the midst of the great war; they are in all anthologies, but I have substituted Herbert Read's *End of a War* written long after.[78] The writers of these poems were invariably officers of exceptional courage and capacity, one a man constantly selected for dangerous work, all, I think, had the Military Cross;[79] their letters are vivid and humorous, they were not without joy—for all skill is joyful—but felt bound, in the words of the best known, to plead the suffering of their men.[80] In poems that had for a time considerable fame, written in the first person, they made that suffering their own. I have rejected these poems for the same reason that made Arnold withdraw his *Empedocles on Etna* from circulation; passive suffering is not a theme for poetry.[81] In all the great tragedies, tragedy is a joy to the man who dies; in Greece the tragic chorus danced. When man has withdrawn into the quicksilver at the back of the mirror no great event becomes luminous in his mind; it is no longer possible to write *The Persians, Agincourt, Chevy Chase*: some blunderer has driven his car on to the wrong side of the road—that is all.[82]

If war is necessary, or necessary in our time and place, it is best to forget its suffering as we do the discomfort of fever, remembering our comfort at midnight when our temperature fell, or as we forget the worst moments of more painful disease. Florence Farr returning third class from Ireland found herself among Connaught Rangers just returned from the Boer War who described an incident over and over, and always with loud laughter: an unpopular sergeant struck by a shell turned round and round like a dancer wound in his own entrails.[83] That too may be a right way of seeing war, if war is necessary; the way of the Cockney slums, of Patrick Street, of the 'Kilmainham Minut', of 'Johnny I hardly knew ye', of the medieval *Dance of Death*.[84]

XVI

Ten years after the war certain poets combined the modern vocabulary, the accurate record of the relevant facts learnt from Eliot, with the sense of suffering of the war poets, that sense of suffering no longer passive, no longer an obsession of the nerves;

philosophy had made it part of all the mind. Edith Sitwell with her Russian Ballet, Turner with his '*Mare tranquillum*', Dorothy Wellesley with her ancient names—'Heraclitus added fire'—her moths, horses and serpents, Pound with his descent into Hades, his Chinese classics, are too romantic to seem modern.[85] Browning, that he might seem modern, created an ejaculating man-of-the-world good humour; but Day Lewis, Madge, MacNeice, are modern through the character of their intellectual passion. We have been gradually approaching this art through that cult of sincerity, that refusal to multiply personality which is characteristic of our time. They may seem obscure, confused, because of their concentrated passion, their interest in associations hitherto untravelled; it is as though their words and rhythms remained gummed to one another instead of separating and falling into order. I can seldom find more than half a dozen lyrics that I like, yet in this moment of sympathy I prefer them to Eliot, to myself—I too have tried to be modern. They have pulled off the mask, the manner writers hitherto assumed, Shelley in relation to his dream, Byron, Henley, to their adventure, their action. Here stands not this or that man but man's naked mind.

Although I have preferred, and shall again, constrained by a different nationality, a man so many years old, fixed to some one place, known to friends and enemies, full of mortal frailty, expressing all things not made mysterious by nature with impatient clarity, I have read with some excitement poets I had approached with distaste, delighted in their pure spiritual objectivity as in something long foretold.

Much of the war poetry was pacificist, revolutionary; it was easier to look at suffering if you had somebody to blame for it, or some remedy in mind. Many of these poets have called themselves communists, though I find in their work no trace of the recognized communist philosophy and the practising communist rejects them.[86] The Russian government in 1930 silenced its Mechanists, put Spinoza on his head and claimed him for grandfather;[87] but the men who created the communism of the masses had Stendhal's mirror for a contemporary, believed that religion, art, philosophy, expressed economic change, that the shell secreted the fish. Perhaps all that the masses accept is obsolete—the Orangeman beats his drum every Twelfth of July[88]—perhaps fringes, wigs, furbelows, hoops, patches, stocks,

Wellington boots, start up as armed men; but were a poet sensitive to the best thought of his time to accept that belief, when time is restoring the soul's autonomy, it would be as though he had swallowed a stone and kept it in his bowels. None of these men have accepted it, communism is their *deus ex machina*, their Santa Claus, their happy ending, but speaking as a poet I prefer tragedy to tragi-comedy. No matter how great a reformer's energy a still greater is required to face, all activities expended in vain, the unreformed. 'God', said an old country-woman, 'smiles alike when regarding the good and condemning the lost.'[89] MacNeice, the anti-communist, expecting some descent of barbarism next turn of the wheel, contemplates the modern world with even greater horror than the communist Day Lewis, although with less lyrical beauty. More often I cannot tell whether the poet is communist or anti-communist. On what side is Madge? Indeed I know of no school where the poets so closely resemble each other. Spender has said that the poetry of belief must supersede that of personality,[90] and it is perhaps a belief shared that has created their intensity, their resemblance; but this belief is not political. If I understand aright this difficult art the contemplation of suffering has compelled them to seek beyond the flux something unchanging, inviolate, that country where no ghost haunts, no beloved lures because it has neither past nor future.

This lunar beauty
Has no history
Is complete and early;
If beauty later
Bear any feature
It had a lover
And is another.[91]

XVII

I read Gerard Hopkins with great difficulty, I cannot keep my attention fixed for more than a few minutes; I suspect a bias born when I began to think. He is typical of his generation where most opposed to mine. His meaning is like some faint sound that strains the ear, comes out of words, passes to and fro between them, goes back into words, his manner a last development of poetical diction. My generation began that search for hard positive subject-matter, still a predominant purpose. Yet the publication of his work in 1918 made 'sprung verse' the fashion, and now his influence has replaced that of Hardy and Bridges.[92] In sprung verse a foot may have one or many syllables without altering the metre, we count stress not syllable, it is the metre of the *Samson Agonistes* chorus[93] and has given new vitality to much contemporary verse. It enables a poet to employ words taken over from science or the newspaper without stressing the more unmusical syllables, or to suggest hurried conversation where only one or two words in a sentence are important, to bring about a change in poetical writing like that in the modern speech of the stage where only those words which affect the situation are important. In syllabic verse, lyric, narrative, dramatic, all syllables are important. Hopkins would have disliked increase of realism; this stoppage and sudden onrush of syllables were to him a necessary expression of his slight constant excitement. The defect or limitation of 'sprung verse', especially in five-stress lines, is that it may not be certain at first glance where the stress falls. I have to read lines in *The End of a War*[94] as in *Samson Agonistes* several times before I am certain.

XVIII

That I might follow a theme I have given but a bare mention or none at all to writers I greatly admire. There have, for instance, been notable translators. Ezra Pound's *Cathay* created the manner followed with more learning but with less subtlety of rhythm by Arthur Waley in many volumes; Tagore's translation from his own Bengali I have praised elsewhere.[95] AE (George Russell) found in Vedantic philosophy the emotional satisfaction found by Lionel Johnson, John Gray, Francis Thompson in Catholicism and seems despite this identity of aim, and the originality and beauty of his best work, to stand among the translators, so little has he in common with his time. He went to the Upanishads, both for imagery and belief.[96] I have been able to say but little of translations and interpretations of modern and medieval Gaelic literature by Lady Gregory, James Stephens, Frank O'Connor.[97] Then again there are certain poets I have left aside because they stand between two or more schools and might have confused the story—Richard Hughes, Robert

Nichols, Hugh M'Diarmid.[98] I would, if I could, have dealt at some length with George Barker,[99] who like MacNeice, Auden, Day Lewis, handled the traditional metres with a new freedom—*vers libre* lost much of its vogue some five years ago—but has not their social passion, their sense of suffering. There are one or two writers who are not in my story because they seem to be born out of time. When I was young there were almost as many religious poets as love poets and no philosophers. After a search for religious poetry, among the new poets I have found a poem by Force Stead, until lately chaplain of Worcester, and half a dozen little poems, which remind me of Emily Brontë, by Margot Ruddock,[100] a young actress well known on the provincial stage. I have said nothing of my own work,[101] not from modesty, but because writing through fifty years I have been now of the same school with John Synge and James Stephens, now in that of Sturge Moore and the younger 'Michael Field'; and though the concentration of philosophy and social passion of the school of Day Lewis and in MacNeice lay beyond my desire, I would, but for a failure of talent, have been in that of Turner and Dorothy Wellesley.

A distinguished American poet urged me not to attempt a representative selection of American poetry; he pointed out that I could not hope to acquire the necessary knowledge: 'If your selection looks representative you will commit acts of injustice.' I have therefore, though with a sense of loss, confined my selections to those American poets who by subject, or by long residence in Europe, seem to English readers a part of their own literature.[102]

September, 1936

Introduction

(w. 1937) For the never-published Charles Scribner's Sons 'Dublin Edition' of W. B. Yeats; published in *Essays and Introductions* (1961) as 'A General Introduction for my Work'

I
The First Principle

A poet writes always of his personal life, in his finest work out of its tragedies, whatever it be, remorse, lost love or mere loneliness; he never speaks directly as to someone at the breakfast table, there is always a phantasmagoria. Dante and Milton had mythologies, Shakespeare the characters of English history, of traditional romance; even when the poet seems most himself, when Raleigh and gives potentates the lie,[1] or Shelley 'a nerve o'er which do creep the else unfelt oppressions of mankind',[2] or Byron when 'the heart wears out the breast as the sword wears out the sheath',[3] he is never the bundle of accident and incoherence that sits down to breakfast; he has been re-born as an idea, something intended, complete. A novelist might describe his accidence, his incoherence, he must not, he is more type than man, more passion than type. He is Lear, Romeo, Oedipus, Tiresias; he has stepped out of a play and even the woman he loves is Rosalind, Cleopatra, never The Dark Lady.[4] He is part of his own phantasmagoria and we adore him because nature has grown intelligible, and by so doing a part of our creative power. 'When mind is lost in the light of the Self', says the Prashna Upanishad, 'it dreams no more; still in the body it is lost in happiness.' 'A wise man seeks in Self', says the Chāndôgya Upanishad, 'those that are alive and those that are dead and gets what the world cannot give.'[5] The world knows nothing because it has made nothing, we know everything because we have made everything.

II

Subject-Matter

It was through the old Fenian leader John O'Leary I found my theme. His long imprisonment, his longer banishment, his magnificent head, his scholarship, his pride, his integrity, all that aristocratic dream nourished amid little shops and little farms, had drawn round him a group of young men; I was but eighteen or nineteen[6] and I had already under the influence of *The Faerie Queene* and *The Sad Shepherd* written a pastoral play,[7] and under that of Shelley's *Prometheus Unbound* two plays, one staged somewhere in the Caucasus, the other in a crater of the moon;[8] and I knew myself to be vague and incoherent. He gave me the poems of Thomas Davis, said they were not good poetry but had changed his life when a young man, spoke of other poets associated with Davis and *The Nation* newspaper, probably lent me their books.[9] I saw even more clearly than O'Leary that they were not good poetry; I read nothing but romantic literature, hated that dry eighteenth-century rhetoric; but they had one quality I admired and admire. They were not separated individual men, they spoke or tried to speak out of a people to a people, behind them stretched the generations. I knew, though but now and then as young men know things, that I must turn from that modern literature Jonathan Swift compared to the web a spider draws out of its bowels;[10] I hated and still hate with an ever growing hatred the literature of the point of view; I wanted, if my ignorance permitted, to get back to Homer, to those that fed at his table. I wanted to cry as all men cried, to laugh as all men laughed, and the Young Ireland poets when not writing mere politics had the same want, but they did not know that the common and its befitting language is the research of a lifetime and when found may lack popular recognition. Then somebody, not O'Leary, told me of Standish O'Grady and his interpretation of Irish legends. O'Leary had sent me to O'Curry but his unarranged and uninterpreted history defeated my boyish indolence.[11]

A generation before *The Nation* newspaper was founded the Royal Irish Academy had begun the study of ancient Irish literature. That study was as much a gift from that Protestant aristocracy which had created the Parliament as *The Nation* and its school, though Davis and Mitchel[12] were Protestants, was a gift from the Catholic middle classes who were to create the Irish Free State. The Academy persuaded the English government to finance an ordnance survey on a large scale; scholars, including that great scholar O'Donovan, were sent from village to village recording names and their legends.[13] Perhaps it was the last moment when such work could be well done, the memory of the people was still intact, the collectors themselves had perhaps heard or seen the banshee;[14] the Royal Irish Academy and its public with equal enthusiasm welcomed pagan and Christian—thought the Round Towers a commemoration of Persian fire-worship.[15] There was little orthodoxy to take alarm; the Catholics were crushed and cowed; an honoured great-uncle of mine, his portrait by some forgotten master hangs upon my bedroom wall, a Church of Ireland rector, would upon occasion boast that you could not ask a question he could not answer with a perfectly appropriate blasphemy or indecency.[16] When several counties had been surveyed but nothing published, the government, afraid of rousing dangerous patriotic emotion, withdrew support; large manuscript volumes remain containing much picturesque correspondence between scholars.[17]

When modern Irish literature began, O'Grady's influence predominated. He could delight us with an extravagance we were too critical to share; a day will come, he said, when Slievenamon will be more important than Olympus;[18] yet he was no Nationalist as we understood the word, but in rebellion, as he was fond of explaining, against the House of Commons, not against the King. His cousin, that great scholar Hayes O'Grady, would not join our non-political Irish Literary Society because he considered it a Fenian body,[19] but boasted that although he had lived in England for forty years he had never made an English friend. He worked at the British Museum compiling their Gaelic catalogue and translating our heroic tales in an eighteenth-century frenzy; his heroine 'fractured her heart', his hero 'ascended to the apex of the eminence' and there 'vibrated his javelin', and afterwards took ship upon 'colossal ocean's superficies'.[20] Both O'Gradys considered themselves as representing the old Irish land-owning aristocracy; both probably, Standish O'Grady certainly, thought that England, because decadent and democratic, had betrayed their order. It was another member of that order, Lady Gregory, who was to do for the heroic legends in *Gods and Fighting Men* and in *Cuchulain of Muirthemne* what Lady Charlotte Guest's *Mabinogion* had done with less beauty and style for those of Wales.[21] Standish O'Grady had much modern sentiment, his style, like that of John Mitchel forty years before, shaped by Carlyle;[22] she formed her style upon the Anglo-Irish dialect of her neighbourhood, an old vivid speech with a partly Tudor vocabulary, a syntax partly moulded by men who still thought in Gaelic.

I had heard in Sligo cottages or from pilots at Rosses Point endless stories of apparitions, whether of the recent dead, or of the people of history and legend, of that Queen Maeve whose reputed cairn stands on the mountain over the bay.[23] Then at the British Museum I read stories Irish writers of the forties and fifties had written of such apparitions, but they enraged me more than pleased because they turned the country visions into a joke.[24] But when I went from cottage to cottage with Lady Gregory and watched her hand recording that great collection she has called *Visions and Beliefs* I escaped disfiguring humour.[25]

Behind all Irish history hangs a great tapestry, even Christianity had to accept it and be itself pictured there. Nobody looking at its dim folds can say where Christianity begins and Druidism ends; 'There is one perfect among the birds, one perfect among the fish and one among men that is perfect.'[26] I can only explain by that suggestion of recent scholars—Professor Burkitt of Cambridge commended it to my attention—that St Patrick came to Ireland not in the fifth century but towards the end of the second. The great controversies had not begun; Easter was still the first full moon after the Equinox.[27] Upon that day the world had been created, the Ark rested upon Ararat, Moses led the Israelites out of Egypt; the umbilical cord which united Christianity to the ancient world had not yet been cut, Christ was still the half-brother of Dionysus. A man just tonsured by the Druids[28] could learn from the nearest Christian neighbour to sign himself with the Cross without sense of incongruity, nor would his children acquire that sense. The organised clans weakened Church organisation, they could accept the monk but not the bishop.[29]

A modern man, *The Golden Bough* and *Human Personality* in his head, finds much that is congenial in St Patrick's Creed as recorded in his Confessions, and nothing to reject except the word 'soon' in the statement that Christ will soon judge the quick and the dead.[30] He can repeat it, believe it even, without a thought of the historic Christ, or ancient Judea, or of anything subject to historical conjecture and shifting evidence; I repeat it, I think of 'the Self' in the Upanishads.[31] Into this tradition, oral and written, went in later years fragments of Neo-Platonism, Cabbalistic words—I have heard the words Tetragrammaton Agla in Doneraile,[32]—the floating debris of mediaeval thought, but nothing that did not please the solitary mind, even the religious equivalent for Baroque and Rococo could not come to us as thought, perhaps because Gaelic is incapable of abstraction—it came as cruelty.[33] That tapestry filled the scene at the birth of modern Irish literature, it is there in the Synge of *The Well of the Saints*, in James Stephens, and in Lady Gregory throughout, in all of George Russell that did not come from the Upanishads,[34] and in all but my later poetry.

Sometimes I am told in commendation, if the newspaper is Irish, in condemnation if English, that my movement perished under the firing squads of 1916;[35] sometimes that those firing squads made our realistic movement possible. If that statement is true, and it is only so in part, for romance was everywhere receding, it is because in the imagination of Pearse and his fellow soldiers the Sacrifice of the Mass had found the Red Branch in the tapestry; they went out to die calling upon Cuchulain:[36]

> Fall, Hercules, from Heaven in tempests hurled
> To cleanse the beastly stable of this world.[37]

In one sense the poets of 1916 were not of what the newspapers call my school. The Gaelic League, made timid by a modern popularisation of Catholicism sprung from the aspidistra and not from the root of Jesse,[38] dreaded intellectual daring and stuck to dictionary and grammar. Pearse and MacDonagh and others among the executed men would have done, or attempted, in Gaelic what we did, or attempted, in English.

Our mythology, our legends, differ from those of other European countries because down to the end of the seventeenth century they had the attention, perhaps the unquestioned belief, of peasant and noble alike; Homer belongs to sedentary men, even today our ancient queens, our mediaeval soldiers and lovers, can make a pedlar shudder. I can put my own thought, despair perhaps from the study of present circumstance in the light of ancient philosophy, into the mouth of rambling poets of the seventeenth century, or even of some imagined ballad singer of today, and the deeper my thought the more credible, the more peasant-like, are ballad singer and rambling poet. Some modern poets contend that jazz and music hall songs are the folk art of our time, that we should mould our art upon them; we Irish poets, modern men also, reject every folk art that does not go back to Olympus. Give me time and a little youth and I will prove that even 'Johnny I hardly knew ye' goes back.[39]

Mr Arnold Toynbee in an appendix to the second volume of *The Study of History* describes the birth and decay of what he calls the Far Western Christian culture; it lost at the Council of Whitby[40] its chance of mastering Europe, suffered 'final ecclesiastical defeat' in the twelfth century with 'the thorough-going incorporation of the Irish Christendom into the Roman Church, in the political and literary spheres it lasted unbroken till the seventeenth century'. He then insists that if 'Jewish Zionism and Irish Nationalism succeed in achieving their aims, then Jewry and Irishry will each fit into its own tiny niche . . . among sixty or seventy national communities', find life somewhat easier, but cease to be 'the relic of an independent society . . . the romance of ancient Ireland has at last come to an end . . . modern Ireland has made up its mind in our generation to find her level as a willing inmate in a work-a-day modern world.'

If Irish literature goes on as my generation planned it, it may do something to keep the 'Irishry' living, nor will the work of the realists hinder, nor the figures they imagine, nor those described in memoirs of the revolution. These last especially, like certain great political predecessors, Parnell, Swift, Lord Edward,[41] have stepped back into the tapestry. It may be indeed that certain characteristics of the 'Irishry' must grow in importance. When Lady Gregory asked me to annotate her *Visions and Beliefs* I began,[42] that I might understand what she had taken down in Galway, an investigation of contemporary spiritualism. For several years I frequented those mediums who in various poor parts of London instruct artisans or their wives for a few pence upon their relations to their dead, to their employers and their children; then I compared what we had heard in Galway, or I in London, with the visions of Swedenborg, and, after my inadequate notes had been published, with Indian belief. If Lady Gregory had not said when we passed an old man in the woods, 'That man may know the secret of the ages,'[43] I might never have talked with Shree Purohit Swāmi nor made him translate his Master's travels in Tibet, nor helped him translate the Upanishads.[44] I think I now know why the gamekeeper at Coole heard the footsteps of a deer on the edge of the lake where no deer had passed for a hundred years, and why a certain cracked old priest said that nobody had been to hell or Heaven in his time, meaning thereby that the rath[45] had got them all; that the dead stayed where they had lived, or near it, sought no abstract region of blessing or punishment but retreated, as it were, into the hidden character of their neighbourhood. I am convinced that in two or three generations it will become generally known that the mechanical theory has no reality, that the natural and supernatural are knit together, that to escape a dangerous fanaticism we must study a new science; at that moment Europeans may find something attractive in a Christ posed against a background not of Judaism but of Druidism, not shut off in dead history, but flowing, concrete, phenomenal.

I was born into this faith, have lived in it, and shall die in it; my Christ, a legitimate deduction from the Creed of St Patrick as I think, is that Unity of Being Dante compared to a perfectly proportioned human body,[46] Blake's 'Imagination',[47] what the Upanishads have named 'Self': nor is this unity distant and therefore intellectually understandable, but imminent,[48] differing from man to man and age to age, taking upon itself pain and ugliness, 'eye of newt, and leg of frog'.[49]

Subconscious preoccupation with this theme brought me *A Vision,* its harsh geometry[50] an incomplete interpretation. The 'Irishry' have preserved their ancient 'deposit' through wars which, during the sixteenth and seventeenth centuries, became wars of extermination; no people, Lecky said at the opening of his *Ireland in the Eighteenth Century,* have undergone greater persecution, nor did that persecution altogether cease up to our own day.[51] No people hate as we do in whom that past is always alive; there are moments when hatred poisons my life and I accuse myself of effeminacy because I have not given it adequate expression. It is not enough to have put it into the mouth of a rambling peasant poet.[52] Then I remind myself that, though mine is the first English marriage I know of in the direct line, all my family names are English and that I owe my soul to Shakespeare, to Spenser and to Blake, perhaps to William Morris,[53] and to the English language in which I think, speak and write, that everything I love has come to me through English; my hatred tortures me with love, my love with hate. I am like the Tibetan monk who dreams at his initiation that he is eaten by a wild beast and learns on waking that he himself is eater and eaten.[54] This is Irish hatred and solitude, the hatred of human life that made Swift write *Gulliver* and the epitaph upon his tomb,[55] that can still make us wag between extremes and doubt our sanity.

Again and again I am asked why I do not write in Gaelic; some four or five years ago I was invited to dinner by a London society and found myself among London journalists, Indian students and foreign political refugees. An Indian paper says it was a dinner in my honour, I hope not; I have forgotten though I have a clear memory of my own angry mind.[56] I should have spoken as men are expected to speak at public dinners; I should have paid and been paid conventional compliments; then they would speak of the refugees, from that on all would be lively and topical, foreign tyranny would be arraigned, England seem even to those confused Indians the protector of liberty; I grew angrier and angrier; Wordsworth, that typical Englishman, had published his famous sonnet to François Dominique Toussaint, a Santo Domingo negro:

> There's not a breathing of the common wind
> That will forget thee

in the year when Emmet conspired and died, and he remembered that rebellion as little as the half hanging and the pitch cap that preceded it by half a dozen years.[57] That there might be no topical speeches I denounced the oppression of the people of India; being a man of letters, not a politician, I told how they had been forced to learn everything, even their own Sanscrit, through the vehicle of English till the first discoverers of wisdom had become bywords for vague abstract facility. I begged the Indian writers present to remember that no man can think or write with music and vigour except in his mother tongue. I turned a friendly audience hostile, yet when I think of that scene I am unrepentant and angry.

I could no more have written in Gaelic than can those Indians write in English; Gaelic is my national language, but it is not my mother tongue.

III
Style and Attitude

Style is almost unconscious. I know what I have tried to do, little what I have done. Contemporary lyric poems, even those that moved me—'The Stream's Secret', 'Dolores'—seemed too long, but an Irish preference for a swift current might be mere indolence, yet Burns may have felt the same when he read Thomson and Cowper. The English mind is meditative, rich, deliberate; it may remember the Thames valley.[58] I planned to write short lyrics or poetic drama where every speech [would] be short and concentrated, knit by dramatic tension, and I did so with more confidence because young English poets were at that time writing out of emotion at the moment of crisis, though their old slow-moving meditation returned almost at once. Then, and in this English poetry has followed my lead, I tried to make the language of poetry coincide with that of passionate, normal speech. I wanted to write in whatever language comes most naturally when we soliloquise, as I do all day long, upon the events of our own lives or of any life where we can see ourselves for the moment. I sometimes compare myself with the mad old slum women I hear denouncing and remembering; 'how dare you,' I heard one say of some imaginary suitor, 'and you without health or a home'. If I spoke my thoughts aloud they might be as angry and as wild. It was a long time before I had made a language to my liking; I began to make it when I discovered some twenty years ago that I must seek, not as Wordsworth thought words in common use,[59] but a powerful and passionate syntax, and a complete coincidence between period and stanza. Because I need a passionate syntax for passionate subject-matter I compel myself to accept those traditional metres that have developed with the language. Ezra Pound, Turner, Lawrence, wrote admirable free verse, I could not.[60] I would lose myself, become joyless like those mad old women. The translators of the Bible, Sir Thomas Browne,[61] certain translators from the Greek when translators still bothered about rhythm,[62] created a form midway between prose and verse that seems natural to impersonal meditation; but all that is personal soon rots; it must be packed in ice or salt. Once when I was in delirium from pneumonia I dictated a letter to George Moore telling him to eat salt because it was a symbol of eternity;[63] the delirium passed, I had no memory of that letter, but I must have meant what I now mean. If I wrote of personal love or sorrow in free verse, or in any rhythm that left it unchanged, amid all its accident, I would be full of self-contempt because of my egotism and indiscretion, and I foresee the boredom of my reader. I must choose a traditional stanza, even what I alter must seem traditional. I commit my emotion to shepherds, herdsmen, camel-drivers, learned men, Milton's or Shelley's Platonist, that tower Palmer drew.[64] Talk to me of originality and I will turn on you with rage. I am a crowd, I am a lonely man, I am nothing. Ancient salt is best packing. The heroes of Shakespeare convey to us through their looks, or through the metaphorical patterns of their speech, the sudden enlargement of their vision, their ecstasy at the approach of death, 'She should have died hereafter', 'Of many million kisses, the poor last', 'Absent thee from felicity awhile'; they have become God or Mother Goddess, the pelican, 'My baby at my breast', but all must be cold;[65] no actress has ever sobbed when she played Cleopatra, even the shallow brain of a producer has never thought of such a thing. The supernatural is present, cold winds blow across our hands, upon our faces, the thermometer falls, and because of that cold we are hated by journalists and groundlings. There may be in this or that detail painful tragedy, but in the whole work none. I have heard Lady Gregory say, rejecting some play in the modern manner sent to the Abbey Theatre, 'Tragedy must be a joy to the man who dies.'[66] Nor is it any different with lyrics, songs, narrative poems; neither scholars nor the populace have sung or read anything generation after generation because of its pain. The maid of honour whose tragedy they sing must be lifted out of history with timeless pattern, she is one of the four Maries,[67] the rhythm is old and familiar, imagination must dance, must be carried beyond feeling into the aboriginal ice. Is ice the correct word? I once boasted, copying the phrase from a letter of my father's, that I would write a poem 'cold and passionate as the dawn'.[68]

When I wrote in blank verse I was dissatisfied; my vaguely mediaeval *Countess Cathleen* fitted the measure, but our Heroic Age went better, or so I fancied, in the ballad metre of *The Green Helmet*.[69] There was something in what I felt about Deirdre, about Cuchulain, that rejected the Renaissance and its characteristic metres, and this was a principal reason why I created in dance plays the form that varies blank verse with lyric metres.[70] When I speak blank verse and analyse my feelings I stand at a moment of history when instinct, its traditional songs and dances, its general agreement, is of the past. I have been cast up out of the whale's belly though I still remember the sound and sway that came from beyond its ribs, and, like the Queen in Paul Fort's ballad, I smell of the fish of the sea.[71] The contrapuntal structure of the verse, to employ a term adopted by Robert Bridges,[72] combines the past and present. If I repeat the first line of *Paradise Lost* so as to emphasise its five feet I am among the folk singers, 'Of mán's first dísobédience ánd the frúit', but speak it as I should I cross it with another emphasis, that of passionate prose, 'Of mán's first disobédience and the frúit', or 'Of mán's first dísobedience and the frúit', the folk song is still there, but a ghostly voice, an unvariable possibility, an unconscious norm. What moves me and my hearer is a vivid speech that has no laws except that it must not exorcise the ghostly voice. I am awake and asleep, at my moment of revelation, self-possessed in self-surrender; there is no rhyme, no echo of the beaten drum, the dancing foot, that would overset my balance. When I was a boy I wrote a poem upon dancing that had one good line: 'They snatch with their hands at the sleep of the skies.'[73] If I sat down and thought for a year I would discover that but for certain syllabic limitations, a rejection or acceptance of certain elisions, I must wake or sleep.

The Countess Cathleen could speak a blank verse which I had loosened, almost put out of joint, for her need, because I thought of her as mediaeval and thereby connected her with the general

European movement. For Deirdre and Cuchulain and all the other figures of Irish legend are still in the whale's belly.

IV

Whither?

The young English poets reject dream and personal emotion; they have thought out opinions that join them to this or that political party; they employ an intricate psychology, action in character, not as in the ballads character in action, and all consider that they have a right to the same close attention that men pay to the mathematician and the metaphysician. One of the more distinguished has just explained that man has hitherto slept but must now awake.[74] They are determined to express the factory, the metropolis, that they may be modern. Young men teaching school in some picturesque cathedral town, or settled for life in Capri or in Sicily, defend their type of metaphor by saying that it comes naturally to a man who travels to his work by Tube.[75] I am indebted to a man of this school who went through my work at my request, crossing out all conventional metaphors,[76] but they seem to me to have rejected also those dream associations which were the whole art of Mallarmé.[77] He had topped a previous wave. As they express not what the Upanishads call 'that ancient Self'[78] but individual intellect, they have the right to choose the man in the Tube because of his objective importance. They attempt to kill the whale, push the Renaissance higher yet, out-think Leonardo;[79] their verse kills the folk ghost and yet would remain verse. I am joined to the 'Irishry' and I expect a counter-Renaissance. No doubt it is part of the game to push that Renaissance; I make no complaint; I am accustomed to the geometrical arrangement of history in *A Vision*, but I go deeper than 'custom' for my convictions. When I stand upon O'Connell Bridge[80] in the half-light and notice that discordant architecture, all those electric signs, where modern heterogeneity has taken physical form, a vague hatred comes up out of my own dark and I am certain that wherever in Europe there are minds strong enough to lead others the same vague hatred rises; in four or five or in less generations this hatred will have issued in violence and imposed some kind of rule of kindred. I cannot know the nature of that rule, for its opposite fills the light; all I can do to bring it nearer is to intensify my hatred. I am no Nationalist, except in Ireland for passing reasons; State and Nation are the work of intellect, and when you consider what comes before and after them they are, as Victor Hugo said of something or other, not worth the blade of grass God gives for the nest of the linnet.[81]

Introduction to Essays

(w. 1937) For the never-published Charles Scribner's Sons 'Dublin Edition' of W. B. Yeats; published in *Essays and Introductions* (1961)

When I was thirty I thought the best of modern pictures were four or five portraits by Watts (I disliked his allegorical pictures—had not allegory spoiled Edmund Spenser); four or five pictures by Madox Brown; four or five early Millaises; four or five Rossettis where there are several figures engaged in some dramatic action; and an indefinite number of engravings by William Blake, who was my particular study.[1] When I was thirty-five or so a woman of genius asked me to defend her against a German connoisseur. She had made her beautiful house a shrine for certain late Burne-Joneses[2]—'that faun's head'

The Burne-Jones Cartons
Have preserved her eyes.[3]

When I arrived he had firmly planted on a drawing-room chair a picture by Renoir perhaps or an imitator, of a fat naked woman lying on a Turkey carpet and had begun to call Burne-Jones empty and obsolete.[4] She took me to another room and reproached me for keeping silent, but excused me as I must be upset by the connoisseur's 'over-dressed wife'. I could not excuse myself because I admired that slight, elegant, pale lady.

A little later poets younger than myself, especially the one I knew best,[5] began to curse that romantic subject-matter which English literature seemed to share with all great literature, those traditional metres which seemed to have grown up with the language, and still, though getting much angrier, I was silent. I was silent because I am a timid man except before a piece of paper or rioters at the Abbey Theatre,[6] and even there my courage is limited to certain topics. Perhaps I am a better man than I think, perhaps some part of my timidity is a dread of speaking ill-chosen words, of reproving Mr Wells, let us say, with the voice of Bulwer-Lytton;[7] or perhaps there is some censorship like that of the psycho-analysts—yes, there must be a censorship. Now that I have all my critical prose before me, much seems an evasion, a deliberate turning away. Can I do better now that I am almost beyond caring?

I have never said clearly that I condemn all that is not tradition, that there is a subject-matter which has descended like that 'deposit' certain philosophers speak of.[8] At the end of his essay upon 'Style' Pater says that a book written according to the principles he has laid down will be well written, but whether it is a great book or not depends upon subject-matter.[9] This subject-matter is something I have received from the generations, part of that compact with my fellow-men made in my name before I was born; I cannot break from it without breaking from some part of my own nature; and sometimes it has come to me in supernormal experience; I have met with ancient myths in my dreams, brightly lit; and I think it allied to the wisdom or instinct that guides a migratory bird.

A table of values, heroic joy always, intellectual curiosity and so on—and a public theme: in Japan the mountain scenery of China, in Greece its cyclic tales, in Europe the Christian mythology, this or that national theme. I speak of poets and imaginative writers; the great realistic novelists almost without exception describe familiar scenes and people; realism is always topical, it has for public theme the public itself. Flaubert excused the failure of the principal character in his *Salammbô* in the words 'I could not visit her'.[10] I think of the German actress who said to a reporter, 'To know a man you must talk with him, eat with him, sleep with him. That is how I know Mr Bernard Shaw.'[11] Then too I would have all the arts draw together; recover their ancient association, the painter painting what the poet has written, the musician setting the poet's words to simple airs, that the horseman and the engine-driver may sing them at their work. Nor am I for a changeless tradition. I would rejoice if a rich betrothed man asked Mr T. S. Eliot and the dancer Ninette de Valois[12] to pick a musician and compose a new marriage service, for such a service might restore a lost subject-matter to the imaginative arts and be good for the clergy. I admit other themes, even those that have no tradition; I have never blamed the brothers Carracci for painting the butcher's shop they came from,[13] and why should not that fat naked woman look like pork? But those themes we share and inherit so long as they engage our emotions come first.

When that is no longer possible we are broken off and separate, some sort of dry faggot, and the time has come to read criticism and talk of our point of view. I thought when I was young—Walt Whitman had something to do with it—that the poet, painter and musician should do nothing but express themselves.[14] When the laboratories, pulpits and newspapers had imposed themselves in the place of tradition the thought was our protection. It may be so still in the provinces, but sometimes when the provinces are out of earshot I may speak the truth. A poet is justified [not] by the expression of himself, but by the public he finds or creates, a public made by others ready to his hand if he is a mere popular poet, but a new public, a new form of life, if he is a man of genius. Somebody saw a woman of exuberant beauty coming from a public house with a pot of beer and commended her to Rossetti;[15] twenty years later Mrs Langtry called upon Watts and delighted him with her simplicity. Lady Gregory had the story from Watts himself.[16] Two painters created their public; two types of beauty decided what strains of blood would most prevail.

I say against all the faggots that it is our first business to paint, or describe, desirable people, places, states of mind. Rimbaud showed in a famous poem that the picking of lice was a good lawful theme for the Silver Age; the radical critics encourage our painters to decorate the walls with those cubes, triangles, ovoids, that are all stiff under the touch, or with gods and goddesses, distorted by Rubensesque exaggeration, dulled by hard doll-like faces that they may chill desire.[17] We have arrived at that point where in every civilisation Caesar is killed, Alexander catches some complaint and dies; personality is exhausted, that conscious desirous shaping fate rules.[18] But a relative of mine wears silver, many rings, and turns from gold with indifference; there are poetry societies that understand what I never could, books of prosody, and the art schools are more intelligent every day. (I have written of all these things in *A Vision,* but that book is intended, to use a phrase of Jacob Boehme's, for my 'schoolmates only'.)[19]

On the Boiler (w. 1938; publ. 1939)

PREFACE

Many years ago I brought out an occasional publication called, according to the season, *Beltaine* or *Samhain*; it contained my defence of the Abbey Theatre, its actors and its plays. Though I wrote most of it, Synge's *Riders to the Sea,* some of Lady Gregory's little comedies, as well as my *Cathleen ni Houlihan*, appeared first in its pages. In this new publication I shall write whatever interests me at the moment, trying however to keep some kind of unity, and only including poem or play that has something to do with my main theme. *Purgatory* was first produced at the Abbey Theatre, Dublin, on August 10, 1938, with Michael Dolan as the Old Man and Liam Redmond as the Boy.[1]

W. B. Yeats
October, 1938

THE NAME

When I was a child and wandering about the Sligo Quays I saw a printed, or was it a painted notice: on such-and-such a day 'the great McCoy will speak on the old boiler'. I knew the old boiler, very big, very high, the top far out of reach, and all red rust. I wanted to go and hear him for the boiler's sake, but nobody encouraged me. I was told then or later that he was a mad ship's carpenter, very good at his trade if he would stick to it, but he went to bed from autumn to spring and during his working months broke off from time to time to read the Scriptures and denounce his neighbours. Then I saw him at a Rosses Point[2] regatta alone in a boat, sculling it in whenever he saw a crowd, then, bow to seaward, denouncing the general wickedness, then sculling it out amid a shower of stones.

Why should not old men be mad?
Some have known a likely lad
That had a sound fly fisher's wrist
Turn to a drunken journalist;
A girl that knew all Dante once
Live to bear children to a dunce;
A Helen of social welfare dream
Climb on a wagonette to scream.
Some think it matter of course that chance
Should starve good men and bad advance,
That if their neighbours figured plain,
As though upon a lighted screen,
No single story would they find
Of an unbroken happy mind,
A finish worthy of the start.
Young men know nothing of this sort
Observant old men know it well;
And when they know what old books tell
And that no better can be had
Know why an old man should be mad.[3]

PRELIMINARIES

I

Last year the Lord Mayor sent out an intelligent Christmas card, an eighteenth-century print of some Dublin street; but this year his card had a drawing of the Mansion House as it is to-day.[4] It is clear that architecture interests him. Let him threaten to resign if the Corporation will not tell the City Architect to scrape off the stucco, pull down the cast-iron porch, lift out the plate glass, and get the Mansion House into its eighteenth-century state. It would only cost a few hundred pounds, for the side walls and their windows are as they should be, and Dublin would have one more dignified ancestral building. All Catholic Ireland, as it was before the National University and a victory in the field had swept the penal laws[5] out of its bones, swells out in that pretentious front. Old historic bricks and window-panes obliterated or destroyed, its porch invented when England was elaborating the architecture and interior decoration of the gin-palace, its sole fitting inhabitant that cringing firbolg Tom Moore cast by some ironmonger—bronze costs money—now standing on the other side of Trinity College near the urinal.[6]

This has not occurred to the Lord Mayor, a good, amiable, clever man I am told, because he thinks like English royalty that his duty is to make himself popular among the common people, and architectural taste is at present articulate only in the few. His time is taken up opening crèches, talking everything but politics, presiding at dinners, going sober to bed. The whole State should be so constructed that the people should think it their duty to grow popular with King and Lord Mayor instead of King and Lord Mayor growing popular with them; yet, as it is even, I have known some two or three men and women who never, apart from the day's natural kindness, gave the people a thought, or who despised them with that old Shakespearean contempt and were worshipped after their death or even while they lived. Try to be popular and you think another man's thought, sink into that slow, slothful, inanimate, semi-hypocritical thinking Dante symbolised by hoods and cloaks of lead.[7]

II

I read in the *Irish Times* of October 20th, 1937, that the Galway Library Committee is indignant and has written to a firm of publishers to protest. John Eglinton said in his memoir of AE that a mob had broken into a public library, taken out the books of certain eminent authors and burnt them in the street. The committee did not require, it seems, the dictation of a mob to do its duty. They had some years ago discussed whether 'the works of Mr Bernard Shaw were works which should be kept in a public library, and on a division it was decided that the books of Shaw be not kept. It was suggested at the time that any book which was offensive should be burned. There was no other way of getting rid of them.'[8] I do not mention this incident because of its importance, there have been similar burnings elsewhere in Ireland, but that I may stand between these men and their critics. They are probably clever, far-seeing men when ploughing their fields, selling porter, or, if they make their living by teaching class, when they have shut the school doors behind them, but show them a book and they buzz like a bee in a bottle. I know nothing of them except those few printed words, but it seems probable that many men in Irish public life should not have been taught to read and write, and would not have been in any country before the middle of the nineteenth century. Some of the Galway committee may have a family tradition of some grandfather, or grandfather's cousin or nephew, who set out to seek learning supported by the contributions of relations and friends and found at the journey's end, if he had reasonable luck, not a government-appointed dunce, but a man who loved his book and taught something of great people and great literature. Thackeray heard two ragged boys leaning over the Liffey parapet discussing 'wan of the Ptolemies'.[9] Forcing reading and writing on those who wanted neither was a worst part of the violence which for two centuries has been creating that hell wherein we suffer, unless indeed the spoilt priest in *John Bull's Other Island* was right and the world itself is hell.[10] I once travelled up from Limerick with an old priest and a girl of thirteen or fourteen. He had written an essay on Gladstone and it lay upon his knees. He began talking to the girl about it. 'Who was Gladstone?' 'I don't know, Father.' 'Was he at the Siege of Limerick?' 'Yes, Father,' this with a sudden brightening. When he asked about Parnell and the Land Bill and found that she had heard of neither he turned to me with 'Sir, if you ever meet anyone of importance please tell them that this kind of ignorance is spreading everywhere from the schools.'[11]

Perhaps now they learn these names by rote, but I see nowhere evidence that ignorance has abated. Our representative system has given Ireland to the incompetent. There are no districts in County Galway of any size without a Catholic curate, a young shopkeeper, a land-owner, a sawyer, with enough general knowledge to make a good library committee. I remember the volunteers who policed the country, dealt out justice, and had all men's respect.

III

When I was first a member of the Irish Senate I discovered to my surprise that one learned in three months more about every Senator's character and capacity than could have been learned from years of ordinary life. I came to know the Ministers more slowly, for each attended only when his own department was concerned. The thirty men nominated by President Cosgrave were plainly the most able and the most educated. I attached myself to a small group led by an old friend of my father's, Andrew Jameson, for I knew that he would leave me free to speak my mind.[12] The few able men among the elected Senators had been nominated for election by Ministers. As the nominated element began to die out—almost all were old men—the Senate declined in ability and prestige. In its early days some old banker or lawyer would dominate the House, leaning upon the back of the chair in front, always speaking with undisturbed self-possession as at some table in a board-room. My imagination sets up against him some typical elected man, emotional as a youthful chimpanzee, hot and vague, always disturbed, always hating something or other.

The Ministers had not been elected. They had destroyed a system of election and established another, made terrible decisions, the ablest had signed the death warrant of his dearest friend.[13] They seemed men of skill and mother-wit, men who had survived hatred. But their minds knew no play that my mind could play at; I felt that I could never know them. One of the most notable said he had long wanted to meet me. We met, but my conversation shocked and embarrassed him. No, neither Gogarty[14] nor I, with our habit of outrageous conversation, could get near those men. Yet their descendants, if they grow rich enough for the travel and leisure that make a finished man, will constitute our ruling class, and date their origin from the Post Office as American families date theirs from the *Mayflower*.[15] They have already intermarried, able stocks have begun to appear, and recent statistics have shown that men of talent everywhere are much linked through marriage and descent. The Far East has dynasties of painters, dancers, politicians, merchants, but with us the dancer may be the politician's mother, though I cannot think of any example, the painter his rebellious son.

I was six years in the Irish Senate; I am not ignorant of politics elsewhere, and on other grounds I have some right to speak. I say to those that shall rule here: 'If ever Ireland again seems molten wax, reverse the process of revolution. Do not try to pour Ireland into any political system. Think first how many able men with public minds the country has, how many it can hope to have in the near future, and mould your system upon those men. It does not matter how you get them, but get them. Republics, Kingdoms, Soviets, Corporate States, Parliaments, are trash, as Hugo said of something else, "not worth one blade of grass that God gives for the nest of the linnet".[16] These men, whether six or six thousand, are the core of Ireland, are Ireland itself.'

IV

As I write these words the Abbey Players are finishing a successful American tour.[17] These tours, and Irish songs and novels, when they come from a deeper life than their nineteenth-century predecessors, are taking the place of political speakers, political organisations, in holding together the twenty scattered millions conscious of their Irish blood. The attitude towards life of Irish writers and dramatists at this moment will have historical importance. The success of the Abbey Theatre has grown out of a single conviction of its founders: I was the spokesman because I was born arrogant and had learnt an artist's arrogance—'Not what you want but what we want'—and we were the first modern theatre that said it. I did not speak for John Synge, Augusta Gregory and myself alone, but for all the dramatists of the theatre. Again and again somebody speaking for our audience, for an influential newspaper or political organisation, has demanded more of this kind of play or less, or none, of that. They have not understood that we cannot, and if we could would not comply; the moment any dramatist has some dramatic sense and applies it to our Irish theme he is played. We may help him with his technique or to clear his mind of the second-hand or the second-rate in their cruder forms, but beyond that we can do nothing. He must find himself and mould his dramatic form to his nature after his own fashion, and that is why we have produced some of the best plays of modern times, and a far greater number of the worst. And what I have said of the dramatists is true of the actors, though there the bad comedians do not reach our principal company. I have seen English producers turn their players into mimics; but all our producers do for theirs, or so it was in my day and I suppose it is still the same, is to help them to understand the play and their own natures.

Yet the theatre has not, apart from this one quality, gone my way or in any way I wanted it to go, and often looking back I have wondered if I did right in giving so much of my life to the expression of other men's genius. According to the Indians a man may do much good yet lose his own soul. Then I say to myself, I have had greater luck than any other modern English-speaking dramatist; I have aimed at tragic ecstasy, and here and there in my own work and in the work of my friends I have seen it greatly played. What does it matter that it belongs to a dead art and to a time when a man spoke out of an experience and a culture that were not of his time alone, but held his time, as it were, at arm's length, that he might be a spectator of the ages. I am haunted by certain moments: Miss O'Neill in the last act of Synge's *Deirdre* 'Stand a little further off with the quarrelling of fools'; Kerrigan and Miss O'Neill playing in a private house that scene in Augusta Gregory's *Full Moon* where the young mad people in their helpless joy sing 'The Boys of Queen Anne'; Frank Fay's entrance in the last act of *The Well of the Saints*; William Fay at the end of *On Baile's Strand*; Mrs Patrick Campbell in my *Deirdre*, passionate and solitary; and in later years that great artist Ninette de Valois in *Fighting the Waves*.[18] These things will, it may be, haunt me on my deathbed; what matter if the people prefer another art, I have had my fill.

TO-MORROW'S REVOLUTION

I

When I was in my 'teens I admired my father above all men; from him I learnt to admire Balzac and to set certain passages in Shakespeare above all else in literature, but when I was twenty-three or twenty-four I read Ruskin's *Unto This Last*, of which I do not remember a word, and we began to quarrel, for he was John Stuart Mill's disciple. Once he threw me against a picture with such violence that I broke the glass with the back of my head.[19] But it was not only with my father that I quarrelled, nor were economics the only theme. There was no dominant opinion I could accept. Then finding out that I (having no clear case—my opponent's case had been clarifying itself for centuries) had become both boor and bore, I invented a patter, allowing myself an easy man's insincerity, and for honesty's sake a little malice, and now it seems that I can talk nothing else. But I think I have succeeded, and that none of my friends know that I am a fanatic. My reader may say that it was all natural, that every generation is against its predecessor, but that conflict is superficial, an exaltation of the individual life that had little importance before modern journalism; that other war, where opposites die each other's life, live each other's death, is a slow-moving thing. We who are the opposites of our times should for the most part work at our art and for good manners' sake be silent. What matter if our art or science lack hearty acquiescence, seem narrow and traditional? Horne built the smallest church in London, went to Italy and became the foremost authority upon Botticelli.[20] Ricketts made pictures that suggest Delacroix by their colour and remind us by their theatrical composition that Talma once invoked the thunderbolt;[21] Synge fled to the Aran Islands to escape 'the squalor of the poor and the nullity of the rich,'[22] and found among forgotten people a mirror for his bitterness. I gave certain years to writing plays in Shakespearean blank verse about Irish kings for whom nobody cared a farthing.[23] After all, Asiatic conquerors before battle invoked their ancestors, and a few years ago a Japanese admiral thanked his for guiding the torpedoes.[24]

II

But now I must, if I can, put away my patter, speak to the young men before the ox treads on my tongue.[25] Here is my text; I take it from *The Anatomy of Melancholy*.[26]

'So many different ways are we plagued and punished for our fathers' defaults: in so much that, as Fernelius truly saith, "it is the greatest part of our felicity to be well born, and it were happy for human kind, if only such parents as are sound of body and mind should be suffered to marry."[27] An husbandman will sow none but the best and choicest seed upon his land; he will not rear a bull or an horse except he be right shapen in all parts, or permit him to cover a mare, except he be well assured of his breed; we make choice of the best rams for our sheep, rear the neatest kine, and keep the best dogs, *quanto id diligentius in procreandis liberis observandum!* And how careful then should we be in begetting our children! In former times some[28] countries have been so chary in this behalf, so stern, that, if a child were crooked or deformed in mind or body, they made him away; so did the Indians of old by the relation of Curtius,[29] and many other well-governed commonwealths, according to the discipline of those times. Heretofore in Scotland, saith Hect. Boethius, if any were visited with the falling sickness, madness, gout, leprosy, or any such dangerous diseases, which was likely to be propagated from the father to the son, he was instantly gelded: a woman kept from all company of men; and if by chance, having some such disease, she were found to be with child, she and her brood were buried alive:[30] and this was done for the common good, lest the whole nation should be injured or corrupted. A severe doom, you will say, and not to be used among Christians, yet more to be looked into than it is. For now by our too much facility in this kind, in giving way for all to marry that will, too much liberty and indulgence in tolerating all sorts, there is a vast confusion of hereditary diseases, no family secure, no man almost free from some grievous infirmity or other. When no choice is had, but still the eldest must marry, as so many stallions of the race; or if rich, be they fools or dizzards, lame or maimed, inable, intemperate, dissolute, exhaust through riot, as he said, *jure haereditario sapere jubentur*, they must be wise and able by inheritance;[31] it comes to pass that our generation is corrupt, we have many weak persons, both in body and mind, many feral diseases raging amongst us, crazed families, *parentes peremptores*;[32] our fathers bad, and we are like to be worse.'[33]

III

Though well-known specialists are convinced that the principal European nations are degenerating in body and in mind,[34] their evidence remains almost unknown because a politician and newspaper that gave it adequate exposition would lose, the one his constituency, the other its circulation.

That upon which success in life in the main depends may be called co-ordination or a capacity for sustained purpose,[35] and this capacity, this innate intelligence or mother-wit, can be measured, in children especially, with great accuracy. The curious and elaborate tests are unlike school examinations because they eliminate, or almost eliminate, the child's acquired knowledge.[36] This mother-wit is not everything and may have been the same in Bluebeard and St Augustine; Gray's 'Milton' remained for lack of acquired knowledge 'mute, inglorious';[37] but it outweighs everything else by, let us say, six to one, and is hereditary like the speed of a dog or a horse. Take a pair of twins and educate one in wealth, the other in poverty, test from time to time: their mother-wit will be the same. Pick a group of slum children, examine for mother-wit, move half the children to some other neighbourhood where they have better food, light and air, and after several months or years re-examine. Except for the increase which comes with age—it increases until we are seventeen and declines after thirty-five—there will be little or no difference.[38] Furthermore, if you arrange an ascending scale from the unemployed to skilled labour, from skilled labour to shopkeepers and clerks, from shopkeepers and clerks to professional men,[39] there is not only an increase of mother-wit but of the size of the body and its freedom from constitutional defects.[40] Intelligence and bodily vigour are not in themselves connected, but those who in their mating have sought intelligence have sought vigour also. As intelligence and freedom from bodily defect increase, wealth increases in exact measure until enough for the necessities of life is reached—fixed by Cattell at £140 a year—and after that, with many exceptions, for men have other goals.[41] There are exceptions throughout; clever men are born among dunces, dunces among clever men, and here and there a dunce earns much money, but in every country the statistics work out the same average.

But this ascending scale has another character which may, or must, turn all politics upside down; the families grow smaller as we ascend; among the unemployed they average between four and five, among the professional classes between two and three; among the unemployed there are still families of twelve and thirteen, but when we reach skilled labour, families of six have come to an end, and this is true of all Western Europe, Catholic and Protestant alike. Since about 1900 the better stocks have not been replacing their numbers, while the stupider and less healthy have been more than replacing theirs.[42] Unless there is a change in the public mind every rank above the lowest must degenerate, and, as inferior men push up into its gaps, degenerate more and more quickly. The results are already visible in the degeneration of literature, newspapers, amusements (there was once a stock company playing Shakespeare in every considerable town), and, I am convinced, in benefactions like that of Lord Nuffield, a self-made man, to Oxford, which must gradually substitute applied science for ancient wisdom.[43] Not that it will matter much what they teach. Mr Bernard Shaw, contemplating the impressive English school system, has remarked that his old nurse was right when she said that you couldn't make a silk purse out of a sow's ear.[44] Then, too, think of the growing cohesiveness, the growing frenzy, everybody thinking like everybody else, preoccupation of all sorts with 'the youthful chimpanzee'.[45] Any notable eighteenth-century orator contrasts with Lloyd George, as an orator of the great period in Greece and Rome with the Emperor Julian among his troops in Gaul.[46]

IV

The United States organised their troops sent to Europe in the Great War by tests of mother-wit, 'intelligence tests', and yet differ little from other democratic nations in their daily practice; and the new-formed democratic parliaments of India will doubtless destroy, if they can, the caste system that has saved Indian intellect.[47] The Fascist countries know that civilisation has reached a crisis, and found their eloquence upon that knowledge, but from dread of attack or because they must feed their uneducatable masses, put quantity before quality; any hale man can dig or march. They offer bounties for the seventh, eighth or ninth baby, and accelerate degeneration. In Russia, where the most intelligent families restrict their numbers as elsewhere, the stupidest man can earn a bounty by going to bed.[48] Government there has the necessary authority, but as it thinks the social problem economic and not eugenic and ethnic—what was Karl Marx but Macaulay with his heels in the air?—it is the least likely to act.[49] One nation has solved the problem in its chief city: in Stockholm all families are small; but the greater the intelligence the larger the family. Plato's Republic with machines instead of slaves may dawn there,[50] but like the other Scandinavian countries Sweden has spent on education far more than the great nations can afford with their imperial responsibilities and ambitions, their always increasing social services and public works. That increase, too, can be calculated mathematically. But even if all Europe becomes sufficiently educated to follow the Swedish example, can it, or can Sweden itself, escape violence? If some financial reorganisation such as Major Douglas plans,[51] and that better organisation of agriculture and industry which many economists expect, enable everybody without effort to procure all necessities of life and so remove the last check upon the multiplication of the uneducatable masses, it will become the duty of the educated classes to seize and control one or more of those necessities. The drilled and docile masses may submit, but a prolonged civil war seems more likely, with the victory of the skilful, riding their machines as did the feudal knights their armoured horses. During the Great War Germany had four hundred submarine commanders, and sixty per cent of the damage done was the work of twenty-four men.[52] The danger is that there will be no war, that the skilled will attempt nothing, that the European civilisation, like those older civilisations that saw the triumph of their gangrel[53] stocks, will accept decay. When I was writing *A Vision* I had constantly the word 'terror' impressed upon me, and once the old Stoic prophecy of earthquake, fire and flood at the end of an age, but this I did not take literally. It was because of that indefinable impression that I made Michael Robartes say in *A Vision*: 'Dear predatory birds, prepare for war, prepare your children and all that you can reach . . . test art, morality, custom, thought, by Thermopylae, make rich and poor act so to one another that they can stand together there. Love war because of its horror, that belief may be changed, civilisation renewed. We desire belief and lack it. Belief comes from shock and is not desired.'[54]

V

The American intelligence tests put the Irish immigrant lowest in the scale, the English, the German and the Swede highest.[55] Skilled men leave the industrial countries attracted by higher wages; what Irish go there are unskilled men driven by necessity, those that succeed are the few who, as a successful Irish-American lawyer[56] said to me, escape from toil before it has killed them. These immigrants are our unemployed, and balance those that go to posts all over the British Empire as doctors, lawyers, soldiers, civil servants, or drift away drawn to the lights of London. In the opinion of most sociologists the level of mother-wit in all West-European countries is still much the same. But we are threatened as they are, already we have almost twice as many madmen as England for every hundred thousand.[57] Sooner or later we must limit the families of the unintelligent classes, and if our Government cannot send them doctor and clinic it must, till it gets tired of it, send monk and confession-box. We cannot go back as some dreamers would have us, to the old way of big families everywhere, even if the intelligent classes would consent, because that old way worked through lack of science and consequent great mortality among the children of those least fitted for modern civilisation.

Some of the inferiority of our emigrants in the United States and in Scotland may depend upon difference of historical phase. The tests usually employed are appropriate to a civilisation dominated by towns, by their objectivity and curiosity. Some of the tests are rectilinear mazes of increasing difficulty. The child marks with a pointer the way in, the way out at the other side, avoiding if he can turnings that lead nowhere. Probably he thinks of neighbouring streets where every turn is a right angle; an Achill[58] child having no such image would probably fail through lack of attention. Other tests consist of fitting certain objects into pictures, but pictures are almost or wholly unknown in our remote districts. A Canadian artist told me that she once lodged with French-Canadian farmers and, noticing the thought they gave in planting a tree to the composition of the landscape, she gave the farmer's wife a picture. When she returned a year later the farmer's wife said, 'I made this apron out of that bit of canvas, but it took hours of scrubbing to get the dirt off.'[59] Then, we Irish are nearer than the English to the Mythic Age. Once, coming up from Cork, I got into talk with a fellow-traveller and learned that he lived in County Cork, and as there was nothing noticeable about his accent I assumed that he was a Cork man. Presently he said, 'We have passed through three climates since we started; first our breath congealed on the glass, and then it ceased to do so, and now it congeals again.' I said, 'You are English?' He said, 'Yes, but how did you find out?' I said, 'No Irishman would have made that observation.' I forget what more I said, but it may have been that we are not disinterested observers, being much taken up with our own thoughts and emotions. The English are an objective people; they have no longer a sense of tragedy in their theatre; pity, which is fed by observation instead of experience, has taken its place; their poets are psychological, looking at their own minds from without. Ninette de Valois, herself a Dublin woman,[60] protested the other day because somebody had called the theatre the province of the Jews and the Irish. 'The Irish', she said, 'are adaptable immigrants, the bigger and emptier a country the better it pleases them. When England fills up they will disappear; they will lunch in bed instead of merely breakfasting there, they will be scared off by the Matriculation papers.'

PRIVATE THOUGHTS
(SHOULD BE SKIPPED BY POLITICIANS AND JOURNALISTS.)

I

I am philosophical, not scientific, which means that observed facts do not mean much until I can make them part of my experience. Now that I am old and live in the past I often think of those ancestors of whom I have some detailed information. Such-and-such a diner-out and a charming man never did anything; such-and-such lost the never very great family fortune in some wild-cat scheme; such-and-such, perhaps deliberately, for he was a strange, deep man, married into a family known for harsh dominating strength of character. Then, as my mood deepens, I discover all these men in my single mind, think that I myself have gone through the same vicissitudes, that I am going through them all at this very moment, and wonder if the balance has come right; then I go beyond those minds and my single mind and discover that I have been describing everybody's struggle, and the gyres turn in my thoughts. Vico was the first modern philosopher to discover in his own mind, and in the European past, all human destiny. 'We can know nothing', he said, 'that we have not made.'[61] Swift, too, Vico's contemporary, in his first political essay[62] saw history as a personal experience, so too did Hegel in his *Philosophy of History*,[63] Balzac in his letter to the Duchesse de Castries, and here and there in *La Peau de chagrin* and *Catherine de Medici*.[64]

When I allow my meditation to expand until the mind of my family merges into everybody's mind, I discover there, not only what Vico and Balzac found, but my own particular amusements and interests. First, no man can do the same thing twice if he has to put much mind into it, as every painter knows. Just when some school of painting has become popular, reproductions in every print-shop window, millionaires outbidding one another, everybody's affection stirred, painters wear out their nerves establishing something else, and this something else must be the other side of the penny—for Heraclitus was in the right. Opposites are everywhere face to face, dying each other's life, living each other's death.[65] When a man loves a girl it should be because her face and character offer what he lacks; the more profound his nature, the more should he realise his lack and the greater be the difference. It is as though he wanted to take his own death into his arms and beget a stronger life upon that death. We should count men and women who pick, as it were, the dam or sire of a Derby winner from between the shafts of a cab, among persons of genius, for this genius makes all other kinds possible.

II

Our present civilisation began about the first Crusade, reached its mid-point in the Italian Renaissance; just when that point was passing Castiglione recorded in his *Courtier* what was said in the Court of Urbino somewhere about the first decade of the sixteenth century.[66] These admirable conversationalists knew that the old spontaneous life had gone, and what a man must do to retain unity of being, mother-wit expressed in its perfection; he must know so many foreign tongues, know how to dance and sing, talk well, walk well, and be always in love. Elsewhere Titian was painting great figures of the old, simple generations; a little later came Van Dyck and his sensitive fashionable faces where the impulse of life was fading.[67] Somebody has written, 'There can be no wisdom without leisure',[68] and those rich men of leisure still kept war and government for perquisites, and all else was done under their patronage. A City Father of a defeated Spanish town said that he could not understand it because their commander was not less well born than his opponent.[69] They were at times great architects, they travelled everywhere, read the classic authorities and designed buildings that still stir our admiration. When Bishop Berkeley was asked to help design the façade of Speaker Conolly's fine house at Celbridge, he refused because too many country gentlemen were already at the task.[70] Meanwhile a famous event happened with much notoriety: Sir Richard Temple and certain of his distinguished friends had affirmed the genuineness of the letters of Phalaris, and the coarse, arrogant Bentley had proved them in the wrong;[71] culture, unity of being, no longer sufficed, and the specialists were already there. Swift, when little more than a boy, satirised what *Gulliver* would satirise:

But what does our proud ignorance Learning call?
    We oddly Plato's paradox make good,
Our knowledge is but mere remembrance all;
    Remembrance is our treasure and our food;
Nature's fair table-book, our tender souls,
We scrawl all o'er with old and empty rules,
    Stale memorandums of the schools:
    For Learning's mighty treasures look
        In that deep grave a book;
    Think that she there does all her treasures hide,
And that her troubled ghost still haunts there since she dy'd.
Confine her walks to colleges and schools;
    Her priest, her train, and followers show
    As if they all were spectres too!
    They purchase knowledge at th' expense
    Of common breeding, common sense,
    And grow at once scholars and fools;
    Affect ill-manner'd pedantry,
Rudeness, ill-nature, incivility,
    And, sick with dregs of knowledge grown,
    Which greedily they swallow down,
Still cast it up, and nauseate company.[72]

The leisured men had still a characteristic work to do. During the eighteenth century they bred cattle instead of men, turning the fence-jumping, climbing, muscular cow and sheep of antiquity into fat and slothful butcher's meat. And now, their great task done, as it seems, they live the life of pleasure, taking what comes, marrying what's there, but now and again married by some reigning beauty, daughter of a barmaid man-picker who had doubled her own mettle with that of a man whose name she had forgotten or never known.

The specialist's job is anybody's job, seeing that for the most part he is made, not born. My best-informed relative says: 'Because Ireland is a backward country everybody is unique and knows that if he tumbles down somebody will pick him up. But an Englishman must be terrified, for there is a man exactly like him at every street corner.'[73] A poet in an old Irish poem, travelling from great house to great house on his poet's business, meets a woman poet and asks for a child because a child of theirs would be a great poet. Parted, they died of love.[74] The hero Finn, wishing for a son not less strong of body, stood on the top of a hill and said he would marry the first woman that reached him. According to the tale, two thousand started level;[75] but why should Jones of Twickenham bother?[76]

We cannot do the same thing twice, and the new thing must employ a new set of nerves or muscles. When a civilisation ends, task having led to task until everybody was bored, the whole turns bottom upwards, Nietszche's 'transvaluation of all values'.[77] As we approach the phoenix nest the old classes, with their power of co-ordinating events, evaporate, the mere multitude is everywhere with its empty photographic eyes. Yet we who have hated the age are joyous and happy. The new discipline wherever enforced or thought will recall forgotten beautiful faces. Whenever we or our forefathers have been most Christian—not the Christ of Byzantine mosaic but the soft, domesticated Christ of the painter's brush—perhaps even when we have felt ourselves abounding and yielding like the too friendly man who blabs all his secrets, we have been haunted by those faces dark with mystery,[78] cast up by that other power that has ever more and more wrestled with ours, each living the other's death, dying the other's life. A woman's face, though she be lost or childless, may foretell a transformation of the people, be a more dire or beneficent omen than those trumpets heard by Etruscan seers in middle air.[79]

III

But if I would escape from patter I must touch upon things too deep for my intellect and my knowledge, and besides I want to make my readers understand that explanations of the world lie one inside another, each complete in itself, like those perforated

Chinese ivory balls. The mathematician Poincaré, according to Henry Adams, described space as the creation of our ancestors,[80] meaning, I conclude, that mind split itself into mind and space. Space was to antiquity mind's inseparable 'other', coincident with objects, the table not the place it occupies. During the seventeenth century it was separated from mind and objects alike, and thought of as a nothing yet a reality, the place not the table, with material objects separated from taste, smell, sound, from all the mathematician could not measure, for its sole inhabitants, and this new matter and space, men were told, had preceded mind and would live after. Nature or reality as known to poets and tinkers has no moment, no impression, no perception like another, everything is unique, and nothing unique is measurable.

A line, whether made with rule and plummet or with a compass, must start somewhere. How convenient if men were but those dots, all exactly alike, all pushable, arrangeable, or, as Blake said, all intermeasurable by one another.[81] Two and two must make four, though no two things are alike. A time had come when man must have certainty, and man knows what he has made. Man has made mathematics, but God reality. Instead of hierarchical society, where all men are different, came democracy; instead of a science which had re-discovered *Anima Mundi*, its experiments and observations confirming the speculations of Henry More, came materialism: all that Whiggish world Swift stared on till he became a raging man. The ancient foundations had scarcely dispersed when Swift's young acquaintance Berkeley destroyed the new for all that would listen, created modern philosophy and established for ever the subjectivity of space.[82] No educated man to-day accepts the objective matter and space of popular science, and yet deductions made by those who believed in both dominate the world, make possible the stimulation and condonation of revolutionary massacre and the multiplication of murderous weapons by substituting for the old humanity with its unique irreplaceable individuals something that can be chopped and measured like a piece of cheese; compel denial of the immortality of the soul by hiding from the mass of the people that the grave-diggers have no place to bury us but in the human mind.

When I began to grow old I could no longer spend all my time amid masterpieces and in trying to make the like. I gave part of every day to mere entertainment, and it seemed when I was ill that great genius was 'mad as the mist and snow'.[83] Already in mid-Renaissance the world was weary of wisdom, science began to appear in the elaborate perspectives of its painters, in their sense of weight and tangibility; man was looking for some block where he could lay his head. But better than that, with Jacob's dream[84] threatening, get rid of man himself. Civilisation slept in the masses, wisdom in science. Is it criminal to sleep? I do not know; I do not say it.

IV

Among those our civilisation must reject, or leave unrewarded at some level below that co-ordination that modern civilisation finds essential, exist precious faculties. When I was seven or eight I used to run about with a little negro girl, the only person at Rosses Point who could find a plover's nest, and I have noticed that clairvoyance, prevision, and allied gifts, rare among the educated classes, are common among peasants. Among those peasants there is much of Asia, where Hegel has said every civilisation begins.[85] Yet we must hold to what we have that the next civilisation may be born, not from a virgin's womb, nor a tomb without a body, not from a void, but of our own rich experience. These gifts must return, not in the mediumistic sleep dreaming or dreamless, but when we are wide awake. Eugenical and psychical research are the revolutionary movements with that element of novelty and sensation which sooner or later stir men to action. It may be, or it must be, that the best bred from the best shall claim again their ancient omens. And the serving women 'shrank in their rejoicing before the eyes of the child', and 'the hour seemed awful to them' as they brought the child to its mother:

> And she said: 'Now one of the earthly on the eyes of my
> child has gazed
> Nor shrunk before their glory, nor stayed her love amazed:
> I behold thee as Sigmund beholdeth—and I was the home
> of thine heart—
> Woe's me for the day when thou wert not, and the hour
> when we shall part.'[86]

V

In Ireland there is some talk of the counter-Renaissance and a proposal to teach Greek in association with Gaelic was opposed by a well-known Cork Professor on the ground that it would strengthen the influence of the Renaissance. I am about to repeat and amplify the proposal whether first made by Father Patrick Browne of Maynooth or myself I do not know, and precisely because it would strengthen the influence of the Renaissance.[87] I detest the Renaissance because it made the human mind inorganic; I adore the Renaissance because it clarified form and created freedom. I too expect the counter-Renaissance, but if we do not hold to freedom and form it will come, not as an inspiration in the head, but as an obstruction in the bowels.

IRELAND AFTER THE REVOLUTION

I

I assume that some tragic crisis shall so alter Europe and all opinion that the Irish Government will teach the great majority of its school-children nothing but ploughing, harrowing, sowing, curry-combing, bicycle-cleaning, drill-driving, parcel-making, bale-pushing, tin-can-soldering, door-knob-polishing, threshold-whitening, coat-cleaning, trouser-patching, and playing upon the squiffer,[88] all things that serve human dignity, unless indeed it decide that these things are better taught at home, in which case it can leave the poor children at peace.

Having settled that matter I return to more important things. Teach nothing but Greek, Gaelic, mathematics, and perhaps one modern language. I reject Latin because it was a language of the Greco-Roman decadence, all imitation and manner and other feminine tricks; the much or little Latin necessary for a priest, doctor or lawyer should be part of professional training and come later. D'Arbois de Jubainville worked on old Irish for thirty years because it brought him back to the civilisation immediately behind that of Homer,[89] and when I prepared *Oedipus at Colonus* for the Abbey stage I saw that the wood of the Furies in the opening scene[90] was any Irish haunted wood. No passing beggar or fiddler or benighted countryman has ever trembled or been awe-struck by nymph-haunted or Fury-haunted wood described in Roman poetry. Roman poetry is founded upon documents, not upon belief.

Translate into modern Irish all that is most beautiful in old and middle Irish, what Frank O'Connor and Augusta Gregory, let us say, have translated into English;[91] let every schoolmaster point out where in his neighbourhood this or that thing happened, or is said to have happened, but teach Irish and Greek together, make the pupil translate Greek into Irish, Irish into Greek. The old Irish poets lay in a formless matrix; the Greek poets kept the richness of those dreams and yet were completely awake. Sleep has no bottom, waking no top. Irish can give our children love of the soil underfoot; but only Greek, coordination or intensity.

When I was a very young man, fresh from my first study of Elizabethan drama, I began to puzzle my elders with the question: 'Why has the audience deteriorated?' I would go on to explain that the modern theatre audience was as inferior to the Elizabethan as that was to the Greek; I spoke of the difficult transition from topic to topic in Shakespearean dialogue, of the still more difficult in those long speeches of Chapman; we could not give that close attention to-day. And then I would compare the Elizabethan plot broken up into farce and spectacle with the elaborate unity of Greek drama; no Elizabethan had the Greek intensity.[92] No one could answer my question, nor could I myself, for I still half-believed in progress. But I can answer it now: civilisation rose to its high tide mark in Greece, fell, rose again in the Renaissance but not to the same level. But we may, if we choose, not now or soon but at the next turn of the wheel, push ourselves up, being ourselves the tide, beyond that first mark. But no, these things are fated; we may be pushed up.

Mathematics should be taught because being certainty without reality it is the modern key to power, but not till the child is thirteen or fourteen years old and has begun to reason. Children before that age are the only born mimics, and they learn all through mimicry and should be taught languages and nothing else, though not so many that they will lose intensity of expression in their own, and these languages should be taught by word of mouth. Greek and Irish they should speak as fluently as they now speak English.[93] If Irish is to become the national tongue the change must come slowly, almost imperceptibly; a sudden or forced change of language may be the ruin of the soul. England has forced English upon the schools and colleges of India, and now after generations of teaching no Indian can write or speak animated English and his mother-tongue is despised and corrupted. Catholic Ireland is but slowly recovering from its change of language in the eighteenth century. Irishmen learn English at their mother's knee, English is now their mother-tongue, and a sudden change would bring a long barren epoch.

Let schools teach what is too difficult for grown men but is easy to the imitation or docility of childhood; English, history, and geography and those pleasant easy things which are the most important of all should be taught by father and mother, ancestral tradition, and the child's own reading, and if the child lack this teaching let father, mother and child be ashamed, as they are if it lack breeding and manners. I would restore the responsibilities of the family.

II

Armament comes next to education. The country must take over the entire defence of its shores.[94] The formation of military families should be encouraged. I know enough of my countrymen to know that, once democratic plausibility has gone, their small army will be efficient and self-reliant, highly trained though not highly disciplined. Armed with modern weapons, officered by men from such schools as I have described, it could throw back from our shores the disciplined uneducated masses of the commercial nations.

If human violence is not embodied in our institutions the young will not give them their affection, nor the young and old their loyalty. A government is legitimate because some instinct has compelled us to give it the right to take life in defence of its laws and its shores.

Desire some just war, that big house and hovel, college and public house, civil servant—his Gaelic certificate in his pocket—and international bridge-playing woman, may know that they belong to one nation.

I write with two certainties in mind: first that a hundred men, their creative power wrought to the highest pitch, their will trained but not broken, can do more for the welfare of a people, whether in war or peace, than a million of any lesser sort no matter how expensive their education, and that although the

Irish masses are vague and excitable because they have not yet been moulded and cast, we have as good blood as there is in Europe. Berkeley, Swift, Burke, Grattan, Parnell, Augusta Gregory, Synge, Kevin O'Higgins, are the true Irish people, and there is nothing too hard for such as these. If the Catholic names are few history will soon fill the gap.[95] My imagination goes back to those Catholic exiled gentlemen of whom Swift said that their bravery exceeded that of all nations.[96]

III

The recognition of the Crown should be the minimum the law requires, there must be no royal visits; a royal opening of the Dail might be too great a price to pay for the Unity of Ireland.[97] The English royal family must always embody an English ideal. I have been told that King George V asked that the Russian royal family should be brought to England. The English Prime Minister refused, fearing the effect upon the English working classes.[98] That story may be no more true than other stories spoken by word of mouth, but it will serve for an example. The average Englishman would think King George's submission, his abandonment of his relations to a fate already foreseen, if proved, a necessary, even a noble sacrifice. It was indeed his submission, his correctness as a constitutional sovereign that made his popularity so unbounded that he became a part of the English educational system. Some thousands of examination papers were distributed to schoolchildren in a Northern industrial district with the question, 'Who was the best man who ever lived?' The vast majority answered, 'King George the Fifth'. Christ was runner-up.[99]

We, upon the other hand, would think that he showed lack of personality, of manhood even, because he did not abdicate. No propaganda must be permitted which might recommend a sovereign who cannot boast in the words of a Sophoclean chorus:

. . . I would be praised as a man,
That in my words and my deeds I have kept those laws in mind
Olympian Zeus, and that high, clear Empyrean,
Fashioned, and not some man or people of mankind,
Even those sacred laws nor age nor sleep can blind.[100]

Indeed I beg our governments to exclude all alien appeal to mass instinct. The Irish mind has still, in country rapscallion or in Bernard Shaw, an ancient, cold, explosive, detonating impartiality. The English mind, excited by its newspaper proprietors and its schoolmasters, has turned into a bed-hot harlot.

IV

I am tired of cursing the Bishop
(Said Crazy Jane)
Nine books or nine hats
Would not make him a man.
I have found something worse
To meditate on.
A King had some beautiful cousins
But where are they gone?
Battered to death in a cellar
And he stuck to his throne.
Last night I lay on the mountain
(Said Crazy Jane)
There in a two horsed carriage
That on two wheels ran
Great bladdered Emer sat,
Her violent man
Cuchulain, sat at her side,
Thereupon,
Propped upon my two knees,
I kissed a stone;
I lay stretched out in the dirt
And I cried tears down.[101]

V

The old man on the boiler has been silent about religion, but soon this occasional publication, probably in its next number, will print his words upon that subject without tact or discretion. He holds that the whole nation must be convinced by some new argument that death is but passing from one room into another, for lacking that there can be no great lasting quality.

OTHER MATTERS

I

As there is no Dublin criticism I propose to criticise plays produced by the Abbey, books published or written by members of my family or by my friends, Cuala embroidery, or whatever else I have a mind to. The reader can make allowances for my bias, and certainly I am a biassed man.

II

Some years ago I voted for the production by the Abbey Theatre of a play that I disliked because I thought the author had won the right to decide upon the merits of his own work. A few weeks ago I saw that play upon the stage for the first time,[102] and certainly if I had understood how performance would solidify its demerits I would, despite all theory to the contrary, have voted and spoken against it. It displayed a series of base actions without anything to show that its author disapproved or expected us to do so. I left before the finish, feeling that neither I nor anyone else in that audience could help transferring to the author himself the horror inspired by his characters. Yet that was unreasonable, for his other plays are charming and amusing and there all are judged as we would have them judged. The wicked should be punished, the innocent rewarded, marriage bells sound for no evil man, unless an author calls his characters before a more private tribunal and has so much intellect and culture that we respect it as though it were our own. Shakespeare and the ballads judge as we would have them judge. In Jonson's *Volpone,* one of the greatest satiric comedies, Volpone goes to his doom, but innocence is not rewarded, the young people who have gone through so much suffering together leave in the end for their fathers' houses with no hint of marriage, and this excites us because it makes us share in Jonson's cold implacability.[103] His tribunal is private, that of Shakespeare public.

I have learnt much of Ireland as a reader for the Abbey Theatre, perhaps as much as a priest learns in the confessional. During our first years we sometimes rejected plays because they were incoherent or commonplace imitations of Boucicault or of old Queen's Theatre melodrama.[104] There was little vulgarity, tradition was still unshaken, the sixpence had worn thin but it was still silver.[105] But of recent years a form of jocularity incompatible with personal fastidiousness has begun to replace or degrade characterisation, and I was glad when infirmity permitted me to leave to others the search for some quality that could be separated from what seemed the comic paragraphs of some base penny newspaper or the inscriptions on the walls of a Corporation urinal. I once drew the attention of some member of the Executive Council to this disappearance from great spaces of the public mind of the old idealistic tradition, and as political revolution and thirty years of Gaelic grammar had been in vain, I asked for such drastic thought as that of the Abbey Theatre at its best.[106]

III

Two or three recent plays have gone to the other extreme. The persons sit around in a circle and talk, and, that unreality as of a glass chandelier which lifts certain plays of Shaw into philosophic dialogue altogether lacking, turn some question over and over. The pit stays at home, but those who educate themselves through the circulating libraries are delighted; they congratulate the Abbey Board upon its belated discovery that thought is more important than action.[107] But thought is not more important than action; masterpieces, whether of the stage or study, excel in their action, their visibility—who can forget Odysseus, Don Quixote, Hamlet, Lear, Faust, all figures in a peep-show?—and we are not coherent to ourselves through thought but because our visible image changes slowly. English producers slur over that scene where Hamlet changes the letters and sends Rosencrantz and Guildenstern to their deaths, because they define him through his thought and think that scene but old folk material incompatible with Shakespeare's *Hamlet.*[108] Yet no imaginative man has ever complained, and Shakespeare when he made Hamlet kill the father of Fortinbras in single combat[109] showed that he meant it. Hamlet's hesitations are hesitations of thought, and are concerned with certain persons on whom his attention is fixed; outside that he is a mediaeval man of action. Take some seemingly average man or woman, touch some psychological gadget and they turn to angel or devil. Our bodies are nearer to our coherence because nearer to the 'unconscious' than our thought. Sargent once said to me, 'All people are exactly what they look. I have just painted a woman who thinks herself completely serious; here is her portrait, I show her as she looks and is, completely frivolous.'[110] This new art, this art of the circulating libraries, has no interest in anything that cannot be understood through opinion: unlike ancient art, it is urban, it belongs not to the small ancient town serrated by its green gardens but to the great modern town where meditation is impossible, where action is a mechanical routine, where the chest narrows and the stature sinks, where 'individuality' or intellectual coherence is the sole distinction left.

IV

Our Abbey Theatre some years ago took over from the English repertory theatre a play which failed with our audience and is bound to fail with every audience which has not been educated out of its instincts. Flecker's *Santorin* is almost the most moving and romantic of modern lyrics, but in *Hassan* I can discover nothing but the perversity and petulance of the disease of which its author was already fading.[111] I find it even more horrible than the vulgar jocularity of certain ignorant Irish dramatists. With them tradition is dying because neither the old folk-feeling nor the superficial ideality of Young Ireland[112] can resist a contagion from English and American slums. But this play was written during those ten years before the war when the English urban mind was turning against culture as Arnold defined it, the knowledge of the best that is said and thought in the world,[113] and seeking to substitute contemporary thought merely because contemporary. It began with a distaste for romantic subject-matter. Presently would come a desire for a contemporary urban style. In Flecker subject-matter and style were unchanged, but in his illness he seems to have suddenly accepted everything else in the point of view of his critics. In *Hassan* he assumed that at least one masterpiece was already forgotten. We know Harun al Raschid through the *Arabian Nights* alone, and there he is the greatest of all traditional images of generosity and magnanimity. In one beautiful story he finds that a young girl of his harem loves a certain young man, and though he himself loves that girl he sets her free and arranges her marriage;[114] and there are other stories of like import. Considered as history *Hassan* is a forgery, as literature an impertinence, for it makes him put two such lovers to death with every horror of cruelty. One feels that its nightmare-ridden author longed to make Galahad lecherous, Lancelot a coward and Adam impotent; to employ against them, because they are still in some sense reigning sovereigns, all the revolutionist's baser tricks. But even if we could condone its false history we must condemn it as a work of art, for there is nothing there but wanton, morbid cruelty.

The arts are all the bridal chambers of joy. No tragedy is legitimate unless it leads some great character to his final joy. Polonius may go out wretchedly, but I can hear the dance music in 'Absent thee from felicity awhile', or in Hamlet's speech over the dead Ophelia, and what of Cleopatra's last farewells, Lear's rage under the lightning, Oedipus sinking down at the story's end into an earth 'riven' by love?[115] Some Frenchman has said that farce is the struggle against a ridiculous object, comedy against a movable object, tragedy against an immovable; and because the will, or energy, is greatest in tragedy, tragedy is the more noble; but I add that 'will or energy is eternal delight', and when its limit is reached it may become a pure, aimless joy, though the man, the shade, still mourns his lost object.[116] It has, as it were, thrust up its arms towards those angels who have, as Villiers de l'Isle Adam quotes from St Thomas Aquinas, returned into themselves in an eternal moment.[117]

V

The Cuala Press has published during the past few years two series of *Broadsides,* twelve numbers in each.[118] The first contained traditional Irish songs and songs by modern Irish poets, with their music; the second, songs by modern Irish and English poets with their music. There were no accompaniments, for they were intended to be sung, as the country people sing Gaelic words, mainly for the sake of the words. When our modern movement began it attempted not only dramatic literature but new popular songs. Songs by Colum, by Campbell, and one song of mine, became so well known, largely through McCormack's singing, that they have almost the currency of folk songs.[119] They had however been put to tunes musicians thought suitable for the concert platform, and were sung there more for their notes than their words. F. R. Higgins, Dorothy Wellesley and I in editing these new *Broadsides* have thought mainly of the words and not at all of the concert platform. We live in the country or in Dublin where one can see the mountains through a gap between two houses, and the largest audience we think of is a dinner of the Irish Academy of Letters, some group of friends in a public house, or else some house-party like that which saw the first performance of Milton's *Comus.*[120] Those who listen must be few that the words may keep their natural intonation, and those few must share a knowledge of good literature, and sometimes, where the poem is Irish of Irish national tradition, no churl must be present. We, like all good poets, turn our backs on the heterogeneous, seek out our own kindred. We expect no rapid success or development, no John McCormacks.

VI

I have described in some diary pages, and later in an essay on Berkeley, a dream or nightmare that went through my sisters' house. My sisters and their maid dreamt different events complementary to one another.[121] Another such dream affected my wife, my daughter and her nurse. My wife dreamt of a cat, daughter and nurse had a rat and a mouse between them. Events in time come upon us head-on like waves, each wave in some main character the opposite of its predecessor. But there are other events that lie side by side in space, complements one of another. Of late I have tried to understand in its practical details the falsehood that is in all knowledge, science more false than philosophy, but that too false. Yet, unless we cling to knowledge, until we have examined its main joints, it comes at us with staring eyes. Should we drive it away at last, we must enter the Buddhist monastery in Auden's play and for the reason there given.[122] And now comes my brother's extreme book, *The Charmed Life*. He does not care that few will read it, still fewer recognise its genius; it is his book, his *Faust*, his pursuit of all that through its unpredictable, unarrangeable reality, least resembles knowledge. His style fits his purpose, for every sentence has its own taste, tint and smell.[123]

VII

I undertook to find designers for my sister's needle, but found nothing altogether suitable until a friend brought me Diana Murphy. I put her to making designs from my own poetry; four are made or in making, *Innisfree, The Happy Townland, The Land of Youth* from my early poetry and prose, and either *Sailing to Byzantium* or *Byzantium*. My sister will have put the first three into needlework before this paragraph is published. Sold or unsold they will lodge somewhere to keep the name of the designer and the Yeats name in memory.[124]

I delight in Diana Murphy's work with one reservation. Of recent years artists, to clear their minds of what Rossetti called 'the soulless self-reflections of man's skill'[125] depicted in commercial posters and on the covers of magazines, have exaggerated anatomical details. Miss Murphy's forms are deliberately thick and heavy, and I urge upon her the exclusion of all exaggerations, a return to the elegance of Puvis de Chavannes.[126] There are moments when I am certain that art must once again accept those Greek proportions which carry into plastic art the Pythagorean numbers, those faces which are divine because all there is empty and measured. Europe was not born when Greek galleys defeated the Persian hordes at Salamis, but when the Doric studios sent out those broad-backed marble statues against the multiform, vague, expressive Asiatic sea.[127] They gave to the sexual instinct of Europe its goal, its fixed type. In the warm sea of the French and Italian Riviera I can still see it. I recall a Swedish actress standing upon some boat's edge between Portofino and Rapallo, or riding the foam upon a plank towed behind a speed boat,[128] but one finds it wherever the lucky or the well-born uncover their sunburnt bodies. There, too, are doubtless flesh-tints that Greek painters loved as have all the greatest since; nowhere upon any beautiful body, whether of man or woman, those red patches whereby our democratic painters prove that they have really studied from the life.

VIII

In my savage youth I was accustomed to say that no man should be permitted to open his mouth in Parliament until he had sung or written his *Utopia*, for lacking that we could not know where he was taking us, and I still think that artists of all kinds should once again praise or represent great or happy people.[129] Here in Monte Carlo, where I am writing, somebody talked of a man with a monkey and some sort of stringed instrument, and it has pleased me to imagine him a great politician. I will make him sing to the sort of tune that goes well with my early sentimental poems.

I lived among great houses,
Riches drove out rank,
Base drove out the better blood,
And mind and body shrank.
No Oscar ruled the table,
But I'd a troop of friends
That knowing better talk had gone
Talked of odds and ends.
Some knew what ailed the world
But never said a thing
So I have picked a better trade
And night and morning sing:
Tall dames go walking in grass green Avalon.

Am I a great Lord Chancellor
That slept upon the Sack?
Commanding officer that tore
The khaki from his back?
Or am I de Valera,
Or the King of Greece,
Or the man that made the motors?
Ach, call me what you please!
Here's a Montenegrin lute
And its old sole string
Makes me sweet music
And I delight to sing:
Tall dames go walking in grass green Avalon.

With boys and girls about him,
With any sort of clothes,
With a hat out of fashion,
With old patched shoes,
With a ragged bandit cloak,

With an eye like a hawk,
With a stiff straight back,
With a strutting turkey walk,
With a bag full of pennies,
With a monkey on a chain,
With a great cock's feather,
With an old foul tune.
Tall dames go walking in grass green Avalon.[130]

APPENDICES

Appendix 1 'Epilogue' (unadopted manuscript, *c.* 1917) to *Per Amica Silentia Lunae*

A monk and a lay brother and a pilgrim were on their way through Connaught to St Patrick's Purgatory.[1] The pilgrim had been to the Holy Land, and had found there or upon the way heresies so old that nobody could remember their condemnation and others so new they had not yet been condemned. The lay brother was watching the meat they were roasting at a wayside fire. The monk [wanted] to meet at the Purgatory the soul of his old master in theology that he might put to him certain difficult questions.

The Monk said, 'St Thomas says that the Father is power, and the Son truth and that the Holy Spirit the good. The world being the chief act of power, one may even say that in a special[?] sense[?][2] God the Father, rather than his Son or the Holy Spirit is in [CANCELLED: Nature] the world.'[3]

'As Nature is sin', said the pilgrim, 'God the Father is the creator of evil, while his Son redeems us, and brings us into the rest of the Holy Spirit, or ultimate good.'

'God does not create sin,' said the monk, 'but while we are in the world we are in his wrath, and it is from that we are redeemed.'

'I learned in Damascus', said the pilgrim, 'that we have to live many times before the redemption is complete. When we die, at whatever age, we begin to grow young, and when we are spun[?][4] long we are born again. If we die at a few hours old, in a few hours we are ready to be born, whereas if we die at seventy, we shall linger a long time with our diminishing years. The spirits are at their greatest wisdom when they feel a new summons[?][5] in the blood, and have not yet forgotten their antiquity, but a little before birth [are] fanciful and full of tricks. Brother Pollycarte[?], what have you heard that you keep dipping[?] your ear?'

The lay brother said, 'I hear a voice talking in the hedge, and like the chirping of a bat and it is saying that before the fall man had his head in the fire, his heart in the air, his loins in the water and his feet on the earth, and that after Eve pulled the apple, he now[?] had his feet on the fire, his loins in the air, his heart in the water and his head on[?] the earth.'

'What a lot the dead know,' said the pilgrim. 'I will go home in the morning. What more could I be told at the Purgatory.'

Appendix 2 Alternate ending (unadopted typescript, 1919–20?) for 'If I were Four-and-Twenty'

[. . .] and what has Ireland to do with internationalism?

Our literature and our history have given us, more than any other people, the desire to dig down into the soil we stand on, and this digging is our intensity, and it may yet give us an answer to the riddle. Certainly if we could but unite our economics, and our nationalism, with our religion that too would become philosophic, and the religion that does not become philosophic, as religion is in the East, will die out of Europe. Our three great interests united, we would be face to face with the riddler.

IX

Certainly we shall not think the skinning of a dead horse its own reward, or that the minor government official who chooses or compels the skinner will have no need to rate and to bully; and seeing that we believe in evil, the greater number of us, being somewhat too figurative, in The Father of Evil, I think it likely that we shall accept Balzac's view of the world, and be content to solve our difficulties as they arise without great confidence in any plan made by logic. It may be indeed that we shall not only reject any plan, that would establish some committee of despotic men, at once economists, patriots, and inquisitors, but declare our liking enthusiastically, seeing that 'spoil-five' has been played under all our hedge-rows,[1] for the old gambling table of nature where many are ruined but none is judged.

X

The very hunger of our age for truth, more acknowledged and acute than that of any previous age, implies like all hunger an empty belly; and yet an eighteenth-century fanaticism, born, when philosophy was lost, and science not yet discovered would to-day (all the greatest problems visible but unsolved) change the design of the world. Those who would so change it are like some fourth rate artist, who imposes upon his work a symmetry, not born out of his subject, or his own mind, but anonymous and superficial, because he has not patience in discovery, nor the courage to look confusion in the face without flinching. Certain preliminary decisions, we may indeed arrive at for ourselves for they need but little special knowledge. We can decide whether some Marquise de Cinq-Cygne in her idleness, or that busy journalist M. Raoul Nathan, whose lapses from good taste we forgive for the sake of his energy has earned the better right to meat and wine; while admitting that Balzac's cutter of corns, who certainly approved the Communist Manifesto of 1848, would like one as little as the other; but what of those problems of the relative importance of heredity and environment?[2] How many years must pass before men have unravelled all that Austrian Monk discovered in his bed of sweet peas? And there are other problems, from which I have scarcely escaped for one whole day and night these twenty years. What if the age of objective science itself be brought to an end through its own discoveries? through a new conception of civilisation, making possible a science as subjective—I use the word in its most modern sense—as that of Thomas Aquinas, through an understanding of the interaction of all minds by unspoken thoughts and emotions.[3]

XI

When I was a boy I went to a travelling circus, outside a little Connaught town, and noticed that there were two audiences, an audience within the great lighted tent, moved to continual unanimity of laughter and applause, and one upon the outside that judged what had happened by the confused sound, and by the movements of heads that made the canvas bulge and quiver, and by what could be seen when lying upon one's stomach and peering under the canvas. Our objective study of mankind, the entire basis of our politics, and our economics hitherto has been like that of this second audience; while the recorded evidence for the existence of 'Telepathy' and the growing recognition of this evidence, brings near a moment when, after wandering, as it were, round the canvas in our confused darkness, we shall suddenly find ourselves before an open lighted door, our hands gripping the necessary pennies. What if every mind gets always a portion of its thought and emotion from other minds, joined thereto by certain channels of affinity that yet await the exploration of science? The philosophy of early and of Mediaeval Christianity believed it; the hermits of the Thebaid and the Mareotic Lake declared that they 'kept the ramparts'[4] against evil powers that else have infested Rome herself. The Monastic institutions of later centuries found it their universally accepted defence, and only lost their hold upon the world when the belief itself began to die. Once accept it and the whole conception of economic justice is changed, because every class becomes the possible creator, or destroyer of necessary or infesting moieties of the thought and emotion of other classes. 'So and So', said a certain miracle working French priest to me, 'is the victim for my village' meaning thereby that a certain holy woman receives into her soul its sin, and there struggles with the sin.[5]

'There is a Cingalese hermit', said a Cingalese Barrister to me once, 'who has not spoken for years, yet his followers have but to settle in his neighbourhood to get all they need.'[6] We begin to conceive once more a society created not for man, as we have hitherto understood him, but for God, a *Civitas Dei*,[7] or perhaps I should say, (seeing that a certain clergyman has called God 'an obsolete term'[8]) created for its own perfection, every class and occupation having, in addition to its use, a possible perfection. Wisdom, as I see things, is justified of all her children: if the leisure that has enabled some woman to perfect courtesy, or her sanctity, (both a form of self conquest, which the sternest I do not know) has been expensive she need not examine her conscience or, unless her nature impel, organize a society to moralize the poor, for she has the right, except in times of flood and earthquake, to every necessary expense, and even in flood and earthquake there should be some to set her life above their own. Our moralists, incredulous of any secret doors between mind and mind, have been gradually withering the flower of life, which needs an undisturbed attention and for its own sake and not for any too obvious use. The author of *The Anatomy of Melancholy* compares a mind acting thus secretly upon another with a lute that when a string is touched makes a neighbouring lute repeat the note.[9] While Immanuel Kant thought possible, though lacking proof, a more direct interaction than any phenomenon founded upon vibration can illustrate.[10] I think we have now this proof, though certainly there is no general accepted evidence, on which we can found a measurement of the importance and constancy of that interaction, that would justify, lacking other grounds, some change of economic theory. A man who believes that some accident of experience, accompanied by philosophic study, permits him to make or to foresee that others must soon make such measurement, might well however speak his mind something after this fashion. 'We are it seems in the midst of a movement of thought that may come to be known as the counter-Renaissance, and it were well to await a few more years discovery, before re-organizing society according to an abstract theory of justice popularized before the scepticism of the Renaissance had extended itself. Perhaps individual emotional and intellectual abundance (every individual feeding and fed by all) may require a greater variety of personal and hereditary conditions than any admitted of by such a theory. It may be even that certain abundant souls, souls whom the most exact Chinese system of competitive examination could never discover, need leisure from all, even from all self imposed work, because as a certain seventeenth-century Latin author says of the Unicorn, they cannot serve.'[11]

One may even imagine that there is something in that doctrine of certain savage races that the ordinary man has no immortality till he gets it from some priest or King, without thinking imagination has carried one too far from St Thomas à Kempis[12] and his mediaeval masters, authorities who grow more respectable every day.

XII

When Dr Hyde delivered in 1894 his lecture on the necessity of the de-anglicization of Ireland to a society that was a youthful indiscretion of my own, I heard an enthusiastic hearer say: 'This lecture begins a new epoch in Ireland.'[13] It did that, and if I were not four-and-fifty, with no settled habit but the writing of verse, rheumatic, indolent, discouraged, and of late settled in a Cathedral City,[14] I would begin another epoch by recommending to the nation a new doctrine, that of Unity of Being.

Appendix 3 Notes (w. 1914) to *Visions and Beliefs in the West of Ireland*, by Lady Gregory (1920)

Note 1. [To *V&B* I, 8; *V&B1970* 17] THE FAERY PEOPLE. The first detailed account of the Faery People of the Gaelic race was made by the Reverend Robert Kirk in 1691. His book which remained in manuscript till it was discovered by Sir Walter Scott in 1815 was called *The Secret Commonwealth,* an essay 'of the nature of the subterranean (and for the most part invisible people) heretofore going under the names of elves, fays, and faeries'.[1] Kirk was a Gaelic scholar, a translator into Gaelic of the Psalms. He is described upon his tomb as *Lignae hibernae lumen,*[2] for in his day little distinction was made between the Irish and the Scottish-Irish among whom he lived and whose words he has recorded. He died a year after he had finished his manuscript or, as the people of his parish say, was taken by the faeries. The Reverend William Taylor, the present incumbent of Aberfoyle, Kirk's old living, told Mr Wentz that it was generally believed at the time of Kirk's death, that the faeries had carried him off because he had looked too deeply into their secrets. He seems to have fainted while walking upon a faery knoll, a little way from his own door, and to have died immediately. Mr Wentz found one old Gaelic speaker who believed that his spirit had been taken, but others who said there was nothing in the grave but a coffin full of stones, for body and soul had been taken.[3] Mr Lang prints a tradition that Kirk appeared to his cousin Grahame of Duchray and could have been saved if the cousin had dared to throw a knife over the apparition's head.[4]

Kirk describes 'the subterranean people' or 'the abstruse people', as he sometimes calls them, much as they are described today in Galway or in Mayo. He is clear that they are not demons and like Father Sinistrari, a Catholic theologian of Padua, quotes the Scriptures in support of this opinion. The 'abstruse people' are not indeed, without sin though midway between men and angels, but being in no way 'drenched into so gross and dredgy bodies as we, are especially given to the more spiritual and haughty sins'. 'Whatever their own laws, be sure according to ours and equity natural civil and revealed' they do wrong by 'their stealing of nurses to their children and that other sort of Pelaginism in catching our children away (may seem to heir some estate in those invisible dominions) which never return. For the inconvenience of their succubi who tryst with men it is abominable, but for swearing and intemperance they are not observed so subject to this irregularity as to envy, spite, hypocrisy, lying, and simulation.' Some have thought the spirit controls of our best mediums no better. 'They are not subject to sore sickness, but dwindle and decay at a certain period all about ane age' and 'they pass after a long healthy life into one orb and receptacle fitted to their degree till they come under the general cognism at the last day'. They are the 'Sleagh Math or the good people' being called so by the 'Irish' . . . 'to prevent the dint of their ill-attempts' and being 'of a middle nature betwixt man and angel' have 'intelligent, studious spirits, and light changeable bodies (like those called astral) somewhat of the nature of a condensed cloud and best seen in twilight. Their bodies are so pliable through the subtlety of the spirits that agitate them that they can make them appear or disappear at pleasure. Some have bodies or vehicles so spongeous, thin, and desiccate, that they are fed by only sucking into some fine spirituous liquors that pierce like pure air and oil; others feed more gross on the foisone or substance of corns and liquors or corn itself that grows upon the surface of the earth which these faeries steal away, partly invisible, partly preying on the grain as do crows and mice.'[5] Lady Gregory has a story of the crying of new dropped lambs of faery in November and some evidence that there is a reversal of the seasons, our winter being their summer,[6] and some such belief was known to Kirk for 'when we have plenty they have scarcity at their homes; and on the contrary (for they are empowered to catch as much prey everywhere as they please)'. 'Their bodies of congealed air are sometimes carried aloft, other whiles grovel in different shapes and enter into any cranny or cleft of the earth where air enters to their ordinary dwellings, the earth begin full of cavities and cells and there being no place nor creature but is supposed to have other animals greater or lesser, living in or upon it as inhabitants, and no such thing as a pure wilderness in the whole universe' and we must always 'labour for that abstruse people as well as for ourselves'. Unless Kirk is in error, as seems probable, they are unlike the Irish faeries who shift but twice a year in May and in November, when the ancient Irish perhaps shifted from their winter houses to summer pastures or home again, for they have formed the custom to 'remove to other lodgings at the beginning of each quarter of the year, so traversing till doomsday some being impudent [impotent?] of staying in one place and finding some ease by so purning [turning] and changing habitations', and at these times they are much seen when 'their chameleon-like bodies swim in the air near the earth with bag and baggage'. He is evidently puzzled how to place them among the orders and admits that it is uncertain 'what at the last revolution will become of them when they are locked up into ane unchangeable condition'. He even believes that they are so beset with anxiety upon this subject that have they 'any frolic fits of mirth 'tis as the confirmed grinning of a mort head'.

Many of the second-sighted men about him would have nothing of this doctrine and still believed, it seems, the old Celtic theory of the rebirth of the soul, a Manichaean and gnostic doctrine, for being 'unwary in their observations' they believed what the 'abstruse people' themselves declared 'one averring those subterranean people to be departed souls attending awhile in this inferior state and clothed with bodies procured through their alms deeds in this life; fluid, active ethereal vehicles to hold them that they may not scatter or wander or be lost in the totum or the first nothing; but if any were so impious as to have given no alms they say when the souls of such do depart, they sleep in an uncertain state till they resume the terrestrial body'.[7] These bodies, come at by the giving of alms, suggest to one that body of Christ which, as Boehme taught, alone enables the shade to escape from *turba magna* the great wrath and dream-like transformation into the shape of beasts.[8] One remembers also the celestial body of the seventeenth-century Platonists. The power attributed to almsgiving calls to mind those tales of clothes given to the poor in some ghost's name thereby enabling the ghost to be decked out in their double. Lady Gregory has found the idea of rebirth in Aran, but in what seems the Cabbalistic form not the Celtic; and it occurs again and again in the Gaelic romances. Cuchulain was the rebirth of Lug; and Mongan who was killed by Arthur of Britain was the rebirth of Finn Mac Cool.[9] Here and there through the seventeenth-century Platonists, Kirk's contemporaries, one finds some story that might have been in Lady Gregory's book. Glanvill in the second part of his *Sadducismus Triumphatus* published in 1674 has an Irish tale where the dead and the faeries are associated as in Galway today. 'A gentleman in Ireland near to the Earl of Orrery's seat sending his butler one afternoon to buy cards; as he passed a field, he, to his wonder, espied a company of people sitting round a table, with a deal of good cheer before them in the midst of a field. And he going up towards them, they all arose and saluted him, and desired him to sit down with them.' But one of them said these words in his ear: 'Do nothing this company invites you to.' 'He therefore refused to sit down at the table, and immediately the table and all that belonged to it were gone; and the company are now dancing and playing upon musical instruments, and the butler being desired to join himself to them; but he refusing this also, they fall all to work, and he not being to be prevailed with to accompany them in working, any more than in feasting and dancing, they all disappeared, and the butler is now alone.' For some days attempts are made to carry away the butler. During one of these he is levitated in the presence of the Earl of Orrery and certain of his guests. Then the man who warned him to do nothing he was bid, came to his bedside. 'I have been dead,' said the spectre or ghost, 'seven years and you know that I lived a loose life. And ever since have been hurried up and down in a restless condition with the company you saw and shall be till the Day of Judgment.'[10]

Throughout the Middle Ages, there must have been many discussions upon those questions that divided Kirk's Highlanders. Were these beings but the shades of men? Were they a separate race? Were they spirits of evil? Above all, perhaps, were they capable of salvation? Father Sinistrari in *De Daemonialitate et Incubis, et Succubis*, reprinted in Paris with an English translation in 1879, tells a story which must have been familiar through the Irish Middle Ages, and the seed of many discussions. The Abbot Anthony went once upon a journey to visit St Paul, the first hermit. After travelling for some days into the desert, he met a centaur of whom he asked his road and the centaur, muttering barbarous and unintelligible words, pointed to the road with his outstretched hand and galloped away and hid himself in a wood. St Anthony went some way further and presently went into a valley and met there a little man with goat's feet and horns upon his forehead. St Anthony stood still and made the sign of the cross being afraid of some devil's trick. But the sign of the cross did not alarm the little man who went nearer and offered some dates very respectfully as it seemed to make peace. When the old Saint asked him who he was, he said: 'I am a mortal, one of those inhabitants of the desert called fauns, satyrs, and incubi, by the Gentiles. I have come as an ambassador from my people. I ask you to pray for us to our common God who came as we know for the salvation of the world and who is praised throughout the world.' We are not told whether St Anthony prayed but merely that he thought of the glory of Christ and thereafter of Christ's enemies and turning towards Alexandria said: 'Woe upon you harlots worshipping animals as God.'[11] This tale so artfully arranged as it seems to set the pious by the ears may have been the original of a tale one hears in Ireland today. I heard or read that tale somewhere before I was twenty, for it is the subject of one of my first poems. But the priest in the Irish tale, as I remember it, tells the little man that there is no salvation for such as he and it ends with the wailing of the faery host.[12] Sometimes too, one reads in Irish stories of hoof-footed creatures, and it may well be that the Irish theologians who read of St Anthony in Sinistrari's authority, St Hieronymus, thought centaur and homunculus were of like sort with the shades haunting their own raths and barrows.[13] Father Sinistrari draws the moral that those inhabitants of the desert called 'fauns and satyrs and incubi by the Gentiles' had souls that could be shrived,[14] but Irish theologians in a country full of poems very upsetting to youth about the women of the Sidhe who could pass, it may be even monastic walls, may have turned the doubtful tale the other way. Sometimes we are told following the traditions of the eleventh-century poems that the Sidhe are 'the ancient inhabitants of the country' but more often still they are fallen angels who, because they were too bad for heaven and not bad enough for hell, have been sent into the sea and into the waste places. More probably still the question was never settled, sometimes Christ was represented as throwing them into hell till someone said he would empty the whole paradise, and thereupon his hand slackened and some fell in this place and some in that other, as though providence itself were undecided.[15] Father Sinistrari is conscious of weighty opponents but believes that Scripture is upon his side. He quotes St John, Chapter x, verse 16: 'And other sheep I have which are not of this fold; them also I must bring and they shall hear my voice and there shall be one fold and one shepherd.' He argues that the commentators are wrong who say that the fold is the synagogue and the other sheep the Gentiles, because the true church has been from the beginning of the world, and has had nothing to do with Jewish observances, for its revelations were made to the first man and Jews and Gentiles have belonged to it. If the Gentiles were not also of Christ's fold, he would not have sent them prodigies to announce his birth, the star of the Magi, the silencing of their oracle, a miraculous spring of oil at Rome, the falling down of the images of Egyptian gods and so on. The other fold should therefore, he thinks, refer to those 'rational animals' who sent their ambassador to St Anthony and who were to hear Christ's voice 'either directly through Himself or through His apostles'. He argues that they are a race superior to the human and must not be confused with angels and devils who are pure spirits being in a final state of salvation or of judgment. He has written his book as a guide to confessors who have frequently, it seems, to protect men and women, often nuns or monks, who are plagued by spirits or tempted by spirit lovers, and to apportion penalties to those who have fallen. It is a great sin should they confuse their lovers with devils, for then they 'sin through intention', but otherwise it is a venial sin, and seeing that incubi and succubi by reason of their 'rational and immortal' spirits are the equal of man and by reason of their bodies being 'more noble because more subtle', 'more dignified than man', a commerce that does not 'degrade but rather dignify our nature' *(et hoc homo jungens se incubo non vilificat, immo dignificat suam naturam)*. The incubus, (or succuba) however, does, he holds, commit a very great sin considering that we belong to an inferior species. It is difficult to drive them away, for unlike devils they are no more subject to exorcism than we are ourselves, but just as we cannot breathe in the higher peaks of the Alps because of the thinness of the air, so they cannot come near to us if we make certain conditions of the air. They are of different kinds but always one or other of the four elements predominates, and those who are predominantly fiery cannot come if we make the air damp, and those that are watery cannot come if we use hot fumigations and so on. You can generally judge the kind by remembering that a man attracts spirits according to his own temperament, the sanguine, the spirits of fire, and the lymphatic, those of watery nature, and those of a mixed nature, mixed spirits; but it is easy to make mistakes. He tells of the case that came into his own experience. He was asked to drive a spirit away that was troubling a young monk and advised hot fumigations because it was by their means 'a very erudite theologian' drove away a spirit who made passionate love in the form of 'a very handsome young man to a certain young nun' after holy candles burning all night and 'a crowd of relics and many exorcisms' had proved of but as little value as her own vows and fasts. A vessel made of 'glass-like earth' containing 'cubeb seed, roots of both aristolochies, great and small cardamom, ginger, long pepper, caryophylleae, cinnamon, cloves, mace, nutmegs, calamite storax, benzoin, aloes-wood and roots, one ounce of triasandalis and three pounds of half brandy and water', was set upon hot ashes to make it fume, and the door and window of the cell were closed. The young friar, a deacon of the great Carthusian friary of Padua, was further advised to carry about with him perfumes of musk, amber, chive, Peruvian balsam, and the like, and to smoke tobacco and drink brandy perfumed with musk. All was to no purpose for the spirit appeared to him in many forms such as 'a skeleton, a pig, an ass, an angel, a bird' or 'in the figure of one or other of the friars'. These appearances seem to have had no object except that like the Irish faeries the spirit was pleased to make game of somebody. Presently it came in the likeness of the abbot and heard the young deacon's confession and recited with him the psalms *'Exsurgat Deus'* and *'Qui habitat'* and the Gospel according to St John, and bent its knee at the words *'Verbum caro factum est'*, and then after sprinkling with holy water and blessing bed and cell and commanding the spirit to come there no more, it vanished. Presently in the likeness of the young friar, it called at the vicar's room and asked for some tobacco and brandy perfumed with musk of which it was, it said, extremely fond, and having received them 'disappeared in the twinkling of an eye'. Sinistrari, however, having decided that the demon must be igneous or 'at the very least aërial, since he delighted in hot substances' and since the monk's temperament seemed 'choleric and sanguine', advised the vicar to direct his penitent to strew about the cell and hang by the window and door bundles of 'water-lily, liver-wort, spurge, mandrake, house-leek, plantain', and henbane and other herbs of a damp nature which drove the spirit away though it came once to the cell door to speak of Sinistrari all the evil it could. He has other like stories; one to show the uselessness of mere sacred places and objects, describes a woman followed to the steps of the Cathedral altar and there stripped by invisible hands.[16]

One remembers a passage in Plutarch: 'But to believe the gods have carnal knowledge, and do delight in the outward beauty of creatures, that seemeth to carry a very hard belief. Yet the wise Egyptians think it probable enough and likely, that the spirit of the gods hath given original of generation to women, and does beget fruits of their bodies; howbeit they hold that a man can have no corporal company with any divine nature.'[17]

One hears today in Galway, stories of love adventures between countrywomen or countrymen and the People of Faery—there are several in this book and these adventures have been always a principal theme to Gaelic poets. A goddess came to Cuchulain upon the battlefield, but sometimes it is the mortal who must go to them.[18] 'Oh beautiful woman, will you come with me to the wonderful country that is mine? It is pleasant to be looking at the people there: beautiful people without any blemish; their hair is of the colour of the flag flower, their fair body is as white as snow, the colour of the foxglove is on every cheek. The young never grow old there, the fields and the flowers are as pleasant to be looking at as the blackbird's eggs; warm and sweet streams of mead and wine flow through that country; there is no care and no sorrow upon any person; we see others, but we ourselves are not seen.'[19] Did Dame Kyteler, a great lady of Kilkenny who was accused of witchcraft early in the fifteenth century, find such a lover when she offered up the combs of cocks and the bronzed tail feathers of nine peacocks; or had she indeed, as her enemies affirmed at the trial, been enamoured with 'one of the meaner sort of hell'?[20]

Note 2. [To *V&B* I, 9; *V&B1970* 17] This light occurs again and again in modern spiritism as in old legends. It shows in some form in almost every dark séance. Grettir the Strong saw it over buried treasure. It surrounded the head of Hereward the Wake in childhood, and in the middle of the nineteenth century, Baron Reichenbach called it 'odic light' and published much evidence taken down from his 'sensitives' who saw it about crystals, magnets, and one another, and over new-made graves. Holman Hunt represents in his *Flight into Egypt* the souls of the Innocents encircled by creeping and clinging fire.[21] When this fire encircles a good spirit it is generally described as white and brilliant, but about the evil as lurid and smoky.

Note 3. [To *V&B* I, 9; *V&B1970* 17] When I was a boy, there was a countryman in a Sligo madhouse who was sane in all ways except that he saw, in pools and rivers, beings who called and beckoned. I have myself known a landscape painter who after painting a certain stagnant pool was nightly afflicted by a dream of strange shapes, bidding him to drown himself there. The obsession was so strong that he could not throw it off during his waking hours, and for some days struggled with the temptation. I was with him at the time and had noticed his growing gloom and had questioned him about it.[22]

Note 4. [To *V&B* I, 10; *V&B1970* 18] Bran, in the *Voyage of Bran* when sailing, meets Manannan the sea-god. 'And Manannan spoke to him in a song, and it is what he said:

'It is what Bran thinks, he is going in his curragh over the wonderful, beautiful, clear sea; but to me, from far off in my chariot, it is a flowery plain he is riding on.

'What is a clear sea to the good boat Bran is in, is a happy plain with many flowers to me in my two-wheeled chariot.

'It is what Bran sees, many waves beating across the clear sea; it is what I myself see, red flowers without any fault.

'The sea-horses are bright in summer-time, as far as Bran's eyes can reach; there is a wood of beautiful acorns under the head of your little boat.

'A wood with blossom and with fruit, that has the smell of wine; a wood without fault, without withering, with leaves of the colour of gold.' (*Gods and Fighting Men*, by Lady Gregory.)[23]

Note 5. [To *V&B* I, 14; *V&B1970* 20] Swedenborg describes these colours and I have a note of similar visions as seen by a fellow-student of mine at the Dublin Art School. Mrs Besant in her *Ancient Wisdom* and other writers of the modern Theosophical School describe them and moralize about them.[24]

Note 6. [To *V&B* I, 19; *V&B1970* 23] There are constant stories in the history of modern spiritism of people carried through the air often for considerable distances. It is not my business to weigh the evidence at this moment, for I am concerned only with similarity of belief. The medium, Mrs Guppy, somewhere in the 'sixties' was believed to have been carried from Hampstead, a pen in one hand and an account book in the other, and dropped on to the middle of a table in South Conduit Street. Lord Dunraven was one of a number of witnesses who testified to having seen the medium Hume float out of one window of the upper room, where they were sitting, and in at another window. I read the other day in a spiritistic paper, of two boys carried through the air in Italy and dropped in front of a bishop who immediately handed them over to the police.[25] And of course the folk-lore of all countries and the legends of the saints are full of such tales.

Note 7. [To *V&B* I, 20; *V&B1970* 24] The offering to the Sidhe is generally made at Hallowe'en, the old beginning of winter, and upon that night I was told when a boy the offering was still made in the slums of Dublin.

Note 8. [To *V&B* I, 24; *V&B1970* 26] Father Sinistrari speaks of a like commerce between beasts and spirits. '*Et non solum hoc evenit cum mulieribus, sed etiam cum equabus, cum quibus commiscetur; quae si libenter coitum admittunt, ab eo curantur optime, ac ipsarum jubae varie artificiosis et inextricabilibus nodis texuntur; si autem illum adversentur, eas male tractat, percutit, macras reddit, et tandem necat, ut quotidiana constat experientia.*'[26]

Note 9. [To *V&B* I, 25; *V&B1970* 27] Houses built upon faery paths are thought to be unlucky. Often the thatch will be blown away, or their inhabitants die or suffer misfortune.

Note 10. [To *V&B* I, 29; *V&B1970* 29] The number of quotations I can find to prove the universality of the thought that the dead and other spirits change their shape as they please is but lessened by the fewness of the books that are near my hand in the country where I am writing. John Heydon, 'a servant of God and secretary of nature', writing in 1662 in *The Rosie Cross Uncovered* which is the last book of his *Holy Guide* says that a man may become one of the heroes: 'A hero', he writes, 'is a daemon, or good genius, and a genius a partaker of divine things and a companion of the holy company of unbodied souls and immortal angels who live according to their vehicles a versatile life, turning themselves proteus-like into any shape.'[27]

And Mrs Besant, a typical writer of the modern Theosophical School, insists upon these changes of form, especially among those spirits that are most free from the terrestrial body and explains it by saying that, 'astral matter takes form under every impulse of thought'.[28] Swedenborg I have already quoted in my long essay, but to prove that the shape-changer is a part of general literature—I have but Wordsworth and Milton under my hand. When the white doe of Rylstone shows itself at the church door according to its Sunday custom, one has one tale to tell, another another, but an Oxford student will have it that it is the faery that loved a certain 'shepherd-lord'.

'Twas said that she all shapes could wear.[29]

And Milton writes like any Platonist of his time:

For Spirits, when they please,
Can either sex assume, or both; so soft
And uncompounded is their essence pure,
Not ty'd or manacled with joint or limb,
Nor founded on the brittle strength of bones,
Like cumbrous flesh; but, in what shape they choose,
Dilated or condensed, bright or obscure,
Can execute their aery purposes,
And works of love or enmity fulfil.[30]

Note 11. [To *V&B* I, 37; *V&B1970* 32] The seers and healers in this section differ but little from clairvoyants and spirit mediums of the towns, and explain their powers in much the same way. Indeed one of Lady Gregory's story-tellers will have it that America is more full than Ireland of faeries, and describes the mediums there to prove it.[31] It is often through some virtue in these country seers and healers that the faeries or spirits are able to affect men and women and natural objects. Mrs Sheridan says that a child could not have been taken if she had not been looking on, and one hears again and again that even when the faeries fight among themselves or play at hurley, there must be a man upon either side.[32] We are all in a sense mediums, if the village seer speaks truth, for through any unsanctified emotion, love, affection, admiration, the spirits may attain power over a child or horse or whatever is before our eyes, and perhaps, as the controls of mediums will sometimes say, they can only see the world through our eyes. Albert de Rochas, borrowing a theory from the seventeenth century, has suggested with the general assent of spiritists that the fluidic or sidereal body of the medium, the mould upon which the physical body is, it may be, built up, is more detachable than in persons who are not mediums, and that the spirits make themselves visible by transforming it into their own shape or into what shape they please and attain by its means a power over physical objects. (See *L'Extériorisation de la motricité*.)[33] Instead of the expensive crystal of the Bond Street clairvoyant, Biddy Early gazed into her bottle, but that is almost the whole difference. If the dreams and visions of Connacht have more richness and beauty than those of Camberwell, it is that Connacht, having no doubts as to our survival of death, is not always looking for but one sort of evidence, and so can let things happen as they will.[34] The brother or sister or the like who comes to the knowledgeable man or woman after death is but the 'guide' that has been so common in England and America, since the Rochester rappings, and a country form of Plutarch's 'daemon'.[35] At other moments, however, 'seer' or 'healer' resembles a witch or wizard rather than a modern medium.

In one thing, however, they always resemble the medium and not the witch. They seem to have no dealings with the devil. The Irish Trials for witchcraft of the English and continental type took place among the English settlers. I have never come across a case of a 'compact' nor has Lady Gregory, nor have I read of one.

Note 12. [To *V&B* I, 75; *V&B1970* 53] It is almost unthinkable to Lady Gregory and myself, who know Mrs Sheridan, that she can ever have seen a drawbridge in a picture or heard one spoken of. Nor does this instance stand alone. I have had in my own family what seemed the accurate calling up of an unknown past but failing a link of difficult evidence still unfound, coincidence, though exceedingly unlikely, is still a possible explanation. I have come upon a number of other cases which are, though no one case is decisive, a powerful argument taken altogether. In *The Adventure* (Macmillan), an elaborate vision of this kind is recorded in detail and, accepting the record as accurate, the verification is complete. Two ladies found themselves in the garden of the Petit Trianon in the midst of what seemed to be the court of Marie Antoinette, in just the same sudden way in which some countryman finds himself among ladies and gentlemen dressed in what seem the clothes of a long passed time. The record purports to have been made in November and December 1901, whereas the vision occurred in August. This lapse of time does not seem to me to destroy the value of the evidence, if the record was made before its corroboration by long and difficult research.[36] Accepting the good faith of the narrators, both well-known women and of established character, its evidence for some more obscure cause than unconscious memory can only be weakened by the discovery in some book or magazine accessible to the visionaries before their visit to the Trianon, of historical information on such minute points as the dress Marie Antoinette wore in a particular month, and the position of ornamental buildings and rock work not now in existence. There is a great mass of similar evidence in Denton's *Soul of Things* though its value is weakened by his not sufficiently allowing for thought transference from his own mind to that of his sensitives.[37]

A 'theosophist' or 'occultist' of almost any modern school explains such visions by saying they are 'pictures in the astral light' and that all objects and events leave their images in the astral light as upon a photographic plate, and that we must distinguish between spirits and these unintelligent pictures. I was once at Madame Blavatsky's when she tried to explain predestination, our freedom and God's full knowledge of the use that we should make of it. All things past and to come were present to the mind of God and yet all things were free. She soon saw that she had carried us out of our depth and said to one of her followers with a mischievous, mocking voice: 'You with your impudence and your spectacles will be sitting there in the Akasa to all eternity' and then in a more meditative voice, 'No, not to all eternity for a day will come when even the Akasa will pass away and there will be nothing but God, chaos, that which every man is seeking in his heart.' Akasa, she was accustomed to explain as some Indian word for the astral light. Perhaps that theory of the astral pictures came always from the despair of some visionary to find understanding for a more metaphysical theory. It is, however, ancient. To Cornelius Agrippa it is the air that reflects, but the air is something more than what the word means for us. 'It is a vital spirit passing through all beings giving life and substance to all things . . . it immediately receives into itself the influences of all celestial bodies, and then communicates them to the other elements as also to all mixed bodies. Also it receives into itself as if it were a divine looking-glass the species of all things, as well natural as artificial', it enters into men and animals 'through their pores' and 'makes an impression upon them as well when they sleep as when they awake and affords matter to divers strange dreams and divinations. . . . Hence it is that a man passing by a place where a man was slain and the carcase newly laid is moved by fear and dread; because the air in that place being full of the dread species of man-slaughter does being breathed in, move and trouble the spirit of the man with a like species . . . whence it is that many philosophers were of the opinion that the air is the cause of dreams.'[38] Henry More is more precise and philosophical and believes that this air which he calls *Spiritus Mundi* contains all forms, so that the parents when a child is begotten, or a witch when the double is projected as a hare, but as it were, call upon the *Spiritus Mundi* for the form they need.[39] The name 'Astral Light' was given to this air or spirit by the Abbé Constant who wrote under the pseudonym of Éliphas Lévi and like Madame Blavatsky, claimed to be the voice of an ancient magical society. In his *Dogma et rituel de l'haute magie* published in the fifties, he described in vague, eloquent words, influenced perhaps by the recent discovery of the daguerreotype these pictures which we continually confuse with the still animate shades.[40] A more clear exposition of a perhaps always incomprehensible idea is that of Swedenborg who says that when we die, we live over again the events that lie in all their minute detail in our memory, and this is the explanation of the authors of *The Adventure* who believe, as it seems, that they were entangled in the memory of Marie Antoinette. I have met students who claimed to have had knowledge of Lévi's sources and who believed that when at last a spirit has been, as it were, pulled out of its coil, other spirits may use its memory, not only of events but of words and of thoughts. Did Cornelius Agrippa identify soul with memory when, after quoting Ovid to prove that the flesh cleaves to earth, the ghost hovers over the grave, the soul sinks to Orcus, and the spirit rises to the stars, he explains that if the soul has done well it rejoices with the almost faultless spirit, but if it has done ill, the spirit judges it and leaves it for the devil's prey and 'the sad soul wanders about hell without a spirit and like an image?'[41] Remembering these writings and sayings, I find new meaning in that description of death taken down by Lady Gregory in some cottage: 'The shadow goes wandering and the soul is tired and the body is taking a rest.'[42]

I was once talking with Professor James of experiences like to those in *The Adventure* and said that I found it easiest to understand them by believing in a memory of nature distinguished from individual memory, though including and enclosing it. He would, however, have none of my explanation and preferred to think the past, present, and future were only modes of our perception and that all three were in the divine mind, present at once.[43] It was Madame Blavatsky's thought, and Shelley's in the 'Sensitive Plant':

> That garden sweet, that lady fair,
> And all sweet shapes and odours there,
> In truth have never passed away;
> 'Tis we, 'tis ours, are changed, not they.
>
> For love, and beauty, and delight,
> There is no death nor change; their light
> Exceeds our organs, which endure
> No light, being themselves obscure.[44]

Note 13. [To *V&B* I, 77; *V&B1970* 54] The ancient Irish had quadrilateral houses built of logs, and round houses of clay and wattles. O'Sullivan, in his introduction to O'Curry's *Manners and Customs,* writes: 'The houses built in "Duns" and in "stone caiseal", and those surrounded by mounds of earth, were, probably in all cases, round houses.'[45] A 'Bo Aires', or farmer with ten cows was supposed to have a house at least twenty-seven feet wide but the houses of better off men must have made one room of considerable size, a whole household sleeping on beds, sometimes with low partitions between, raying out from the wall like spokes of a wheel. Petrie thought the great quadrilateral banqueting hall of Tara was once ninety feet wide.[46]

Note 14. [To *V&B* I, 79; *V&B1970* 55] In *The Roman Ritual,* there is an exorcism for evil spirits and a ceremony for the succour of the sick (*cura infirmorum*). And in the beginning of the chapter containing this ceremony (Caput IV, verse 12), it is stated that images of Christ, the Virgin, and of saints especially in veneration of the sick man, may cure him if brought into the room. In the ceremony of exorcism, the priest is directed to make numerous signs of the cross over the possessed person (*sic. rubric: Tres cruces sequentes fiant in pectore daemoniaci*). The spirit is commanded to be gone in the name of the Father, of the Son, and of the Holy Spirit. The ceremony with psalms covers twenty-six pages of my copy. The exorcism is described as a driving out of the 'most unclean spirit' of every phantasm and every legion. It commands the 'most evil dragon, in the name of the immaculate lamb who walked upon the asp and the basilisk and cast down the lion and the dragon' to 'go down out of this man'.

In the ceremony for the sick, the priest places his hand on the head of the sick man and says:

'Let them place their hands on the sick and they shall be well [*Super aegros manus imponent, et bene habebunt*]. May Christ Son of Mary, Saviour of the world and Lord, by the merits and intercession of his holy apostles Peter and Paul and of all the saints be clement and propitious to you.'

The ceremony is ten pages and contains various psalms and selections from the Gospels.[47]

Round these two ceremonies have gathered in the minds of the country people, at least, many traditional ideas. When any one is cured, there is a victim, some other human being or some animal will die. If one remembers that diseases were very commonly considered to be the work of demons, one sees how the story of the Gadarene swine[48] would support the tradition. I know not into what subtlety the dreaming mind may not carry the thought, for some few months ago in France, an excommunicated miracle-working priest said in my hearing: 'There is always a victim; so-and-so was the victim for France', naming a holy Italian nun who had just died. 'And so-and-so', naming a living holy woman, 'is the victim for my own village'.[49] Various medieval saints, and even certain witches, cured sick persons by taking the disease upon themselves.

Christian Scientists and Mental Healers are often afraid of themselves acquiring the disease which they drive out of their patient; they sometimes speak of the effort that it costs them to shake it off. I was told a story the other day, which I have proved not to be true, but which is evidence of the belief. A woman said to me some such words as these: 'My friend so-and-so, who is a Mental Healer, was staying in the country. She saw a woman there with a strange look. She asked what was wrong, and found that this woman was expecting a periodical fit of madness. She offered to undertake her cure, and brought her to her own house. The patient became violent, but my friend was able by faith and prayer to soothe her till she fell asleep. My friend went downstairs exhausted, and lay upon the sofa. Presently she saw strange shadows coming into the room and knew they had come from the patient upstairs, and these shadows, taking the form of swine, threw themselves upon her and only after a long struggle could she throw them off.' The swine and their attack were all moonshine, but the healer, whom I found and questioned, did believe that she saw shadows leaving the patient.

The transference of disease was a generally recognized part of medieval and ancient medicine; and Albert de Rochas gives considerable space to it in his *L'Extériorisation de la sensibilité*, Paris, 1909. He quotes from a seventeenth-century writer, Abbé de Vallemort, many examples from medical and scientific writers of that time who believed themselves to have transferred diseases from their patients to animals and to trees and to various substances, 'Mumia' as they called them, which absorb *des esprits qui résident dans le sang* and then describes various experiments made in 1885 by Dr Babinski 'Chef de Clinique de M. Charcot' in transferring now by magnets, now by suggestion various forms of nervous disease from one patient to another. Where these diseases were produced in the first instance by suggestion, the patient from whom the disease was transferred, was freed from it, but where the disease was natural and the cause of the patient being at the hospital, there was no cure although in one case there was improvement. Albert de Rochas then quotes as follows from a lecture given by Dr Luys to la Société de Biologie in 1894.[50]

'M. d'Arsonval has, according to a communication from an English physician, given an account at the last meeting of the Société de Biologie, of the persistent action in a magnetized iron bar of the magnetic fluid, which to a certain extent, kept a memory of its former state.

'My researches of the same kind have given me proofs some time since of analogous phenomena with the help of magnetized crowns placed on the head of a subject in an hypnotic state.

'In this case, it is a question not only of storing vibrations of magnetic nature, but of really living nature, of real cerebral vibrations through the coating of the brain, stored in a magnetic crown, in which they remain for a greater or less length of time.

'To arrive at this phenomenon, instead of using an unresponsive physical instrument, I use a reacting living being—an hypnotized subject, who has thus become sensitive to living magnetic vibrations. I am presenting to the Society the magnetized crown, like several other models which I have already shown. It is adapted to the head by means of a system of straps, encircles it and leaves the frontal region free.

'It also forms a bent magnet with a positive and a negative pole. This crown was put, more than a year ago, on the head of a woman suffering from melancholia with ideas of persecution, agitation, and a tendency to suicide, etc. The application of the crown led to the patient's getting slowly better after five or six séances; and at the end of ten days I thought I could send her back to the hospital without any danger. At the end of a fortnight, the crown having been isolated, the idea came to me quite empirically of placing it on the head of the "subject" now before you.

'He is a male, hypnotizable, *hystérique*, given to frequent fits of lethargy. What was my surprise to see this subject, put into the somnambulistic state, complaining in exactly the same terms as those the cured patient had used a fortnight before.

'*He* first of all took on the sex of the patient; *he* spoke in the feminine gender; *he* complained of violent headache; *he* said he was going mad, that his neighbours came into his room to do him harm. In a word, the hypnotic subject had, thanks to the magnetized crown, taken on the cerebral state of the melancholic patient. The magnetized crown had been powerful enough to draw off the morbid cerebral influx of the patient (who got well), which had persisted, like a memory, in the intimate (or innermost) texture of the magnetic strip of metal.

'This is a phenomenon we have produced many times, for several years; not only with the subject now present, but with others.

'This communication is, amongst physiological phenomena, on a line with M. d'Arsonval's on the persistence of certain anterior states in inorganic bodies; it will no doubt cause much astonishment and scepticism amongst those who are not accustomed to hypnologic research.

'Doubts will be cast on the sincerity of the subject, on his tendency to produce wonders, to being carried away, and also on what may perhaps seem too easy an acquiescence on the part of the operator.

'To all these objections I will only answer: that this phenomenon of the transmission of the psychical states of a subject by means of a magnetized crown which keeps given impressions is quite in the order of the phenomena formerly communicated by M. d'Arsonval. And, further, the first time I made this experiment, it was done without my knowing, in an entirely empirical way. The impregnated crown was put on the head of the hypnotic subject about a fortnight after it had been put on the patient's head. There has therefore necessarily been a first operation, of which I did not foreknow the results; for we did not know any more than the hypnotized subject, what was going to happen, and the subject reacted, *motu proprio*,[51] without any excitant other than the magnetic crown.

'So one can assert, without trying to draw any other conclusions, that certain vibratory states of the brain, and probably of the nervous system, are capable of storing themselves in a magnetized bent strip of metal, as the magnetic fluid is stored in the soft bar of iron, and of leaving persistent traces; still further, that one can only destroy this persistent magnetic property by fire.

The crown has to be red-hot before it ceases to act, as M. d'Arsonval found to be the case with the iron bar.'

Albert de Rochas makes this notable comment:

'The same phenomenon would certainly have been produced had the patient been dead, and so one might by this means have a sort of evocation of a personality no longer of this world.'[52]

Note 15. [To *V&B* I, 80; *V&B1970* 56] As late as the sixteenth and seventeenth centuries the Irish were accustomed to leave their houses on the plains and valleys in spring and live with their cattle on the uplands, returning to the valleys and plains in time to reap the harvest. Before tillage became general they may not have returned till the chill of autumn. From this perhaps came the faery flittings of May and November.

Note 16. [To *V&B* I, 82; *V&B1970* 57] The pictures shown were drawings of spirits 'A.E.' made from his own visions. The yellow thing upon the head was, I suppose, some sort of crown. These countrywomen have seen so little gold that they do not describe anything as 'of gold' or 'like gold'. They will say of yellow hair that it is 'bright like silver'.

Note 17. [To *V&B* I, 84; *V&B1970* 58] The death-coach or more properly *coiste-bodhar* or 'deaf-coach', so called from its rumbling sound. It is usually an omen of death.

Note 18. [To *V&B* I, 84; *V&B1970* 58] The thing 'yellow and slippery, not hair but like marble' is evidently a crown of gold. Are these spirits in dress of ancient authority the shepherds of the more recent dead?

Note 19. [To *V&B* I, 85; *V&B1970* 58] I have read somewhere, but cannot remember where, that ragweed was once used to make some medicine for horses. This would account for its association with them in the half-fantasy, half-vision of the country seers. In the same way, the mushroom ring of the faeries is, it seems, a memory of some intoxicating liquor made of mushrooms, when intoxication was mysterious. The story-teller speaks of 'those red flowers', showing how vague her sense of colour, or her knowledge of English, for ragweed is, of course, yellow.

Note 20. [To *V&B* I, 88; *V&B1970* 61] 'Bracket' is Irish for 'speckled' and seems to me a description of the plaids and stripes of medieval Ireland.

Note 21. [To *V&B* I, 89; *V&B1970* 61] Bodin in his *De Magorum Daemonomania* speaks of salt as a spell against spirits because a 'symbol of eternity'.[53]

Note 22. [To *V&B* I, 91; *V&B1970* 62] Tir-na-n-og, the country of the young, the paradise of the ancient Irish. It is sometimes described as under the earth, sometimes all about us, and sometimes as an enchanted island. This island paradise has given rise to many legends; sailors have bragged of meeting it. A Dutch pilot settled in Dublin in 1614, claimed to have seen it off the coast of Greenland in 61° of latitude. It vanished as he came near, but sailing in an opposite direction he came upon it once more,[54] but Giraldus Cambrensis claimed that shortly before he came to Ireland such a phantom island was discovered off the west coast of Ireland and made habitable. Some young men saw it from the shore; when they came near it, it sank into the water. The next day it reappeared and again mocked the same youths with the like delusion. At length, on their rowing towards it on the third day, they followed the advice of an older man, and let fly an arrow, barbed with red-hot steel, against the island; and then landing, found it stationary and habitable.[55]

Note 23. [To *V&B* I, 93; *V&B1970* 63] Supernatural strength is often spoken of by the people as a sign of faery power. It is also enumerated in *The Roman Ritual* among the signs of possession.[56] I have read somewhere that the priests of Apollo showed it in their religious transports.

Note 24. [To *V&B* I, 94; *V&B1970* 64] 'Materializations' are generally imperfect. The spirit makes just enough of mind and form for its purpose. Even when the form is only visible to the clairvoyant there may still be materialization, though not carried far enough to affect ordinary sight.

Note 25. [To *V&B* I, 95; *V&B1970* 64] The picture was made by 'A.E.' of one of the forms he sees in vision.

Note 26. [To *V&B* I, 96; *V&B1970* 65] The barrel which contained a brew that made the spirits invisible is probably the cauldron of the god Dagda, called 'The Undry' 'because it was never empty'. The Tuatha-de-Danaan, the old Irish divine race, brought with them to Ireland four talismans, the sword, the spear, the stone, and the cauldron. Rhys, in his *Celtic Heathendom,* compares it with the Irish well of wisdom, overhung by nine hazels, and the Welsh 'Cauldron of the Head of Hades', set over a fire, blown into a flame by the breath of nine young girls. Girls and hazels were alike, he thinks, symbols of time because of the nine days of the old Celtic week, and comparable with the nine Muses, daughters of Memory. Nutt thought the Celtic cauldron the first form of the Holy Grail.[57]

Note 27. [To *V&B* I, 99; *V&B1970* 67] In my record of this conversation I find a sentence that has dropped out in Lady Gregory's. The old man used these words: 'And I took down a fork from the rafters and asked her was it a broom and she said it was', and it was that answer that proved her in the power of the faeries. She was 'suggestible' and probably in a state of trance.

Note 28. [To *V&B* I, 100; *V&B1970* 67] The Dundonians are, of course, the Tuatha-de-Danaan, and those with the bag are the 'firbolg' or 'bag-men', we have now, it may be, a true explanation of a name Professor Rhys has interpreted with intricate mythology. I wonder if these bags are related to the Sporran of the Highlanders.[58]

Note 29. [To *V&B* I, 106; *V&B1970* 70] Here though maybe but in seeming, spiritism and folk-lore are at issue with one another. The spirit of the séance room is described as growing to maturity and remaining in that state. In Swedenborg it moves toward 'the day-spring of its youth'.[59] Among the country people too, one sometimes hears of the dead growing to the likeness of thirty years in heaven and remaining so. Thirty years, I suppose, because at that age Christ began his ministry. The idea that underlies Mrs Fagan's statement seems to be that we have a certain measure of life to live out on earth or in some intermediate state.[60] Are the inhabitants of this 'intermediate state' the 'earthbound' of the spiritists?

Note 30. [To *V&B* I, 108; *V&B1970* 71] Professor Lombroso quotes from Professor Faifofer the following description of how he received news of the death of Carducci: 'On the 18th of February, in the evening, our spirit-friends did not at once give us notice of their presence at our sitting, and we waited for them about half an hour. "Remigo", on being asked the reason why they had delayed, replied: "We are in a state of agitation and confusion here. We have just come from a festival—of grief for you and joy for us. We have been present at the death-bed of Carducci." He had died that day and in that very hour and the news had not yet arrived by the ordinary channels.'[61]

Note 31. [To *V&B* I, 108; *V&B1970* 71] I was the patient; it seemed to be the only way of coming to intimate speech with the knowledgeable man.

Note 32. [To *V&B* I, 109; *V&B1970* 72] The ghosts of 'spiritism' are constantly changing place or state. Sometimes for this reason they must say 'goodbye' to a medium. That they are passing to a 'higher state' seems to be the usual phrase. See for instance the account signed by A. I. Smart and a number of witnesses, published in *The Medium and Daybreak*, of June 15, 1877.[62]

Note 33. [To *V&B* I, 110; *V&B1970* 72] I have been several times told that a great battle for the potatoes preceded the great famine. What decays with us seems to come out, as it were, on the other side of the picture and is spirits' property.

Note 34. [To *V&B* I, 110; *V&B1970* 72] This is true but he might have guessed it from the difference of my glasses; one is plain glass.

Note 35. [To *V&B* I, 115; *V&B1970* 74] They are only small when 'upon certain errands', but when small, three feet or thereabouts seems to be the almost invariable height. Mary Battle, my uncle George Pollexfen's second-sighted servant, told me that 'it is something in our eyes makes them big or little'. People in trance often see objects reduced. Mrs Piper when half awakened will sometimes see the people about her very small.[63]

Note 36. [To *V&B* I, 123; *V&B1970* 79] The same story as that in one of the most beautiful of the 'Noh' plays of Japan. I tell the Japanese story in my long terminal essay.[64]

Note 37. [To *V&B* I, 129; *V&B1970* 81] Mediums have often said that the spirits see this world through our eyes. John Heydon, upon the other hand, calls good spirits 'The eyes and ears of God'.[65]

Note 38. [To *V&B* I, 155; *V&B1970* 96] The herbs were gathered before dawn, probably that the dew might be upon them. Dew, a signature or symbol of the philosopher's stone, was held once to be a secretion from dawning light.

Note 39. [To *V&B* I, 172; *V&B1970* 105] The most puzzling thing in Irish folk-lore is the number of countrymen and countrywomen who are 'away'. A man or woman or child will suddenly take to the bed, and from that on, perhaps for a few weeks, perhaps for a lifetime, will be at times unconscious, in a state of dream, in trance, as we say. According to the peasant theory these persons are, during these times, with the faeries, riding through the country, eating or dancing, or suckling children. They may even, in that other world, marry, bring forth, and beget, and may when cured of their trances mourn for the loss of their children in faery. This state generally commences by their being 'touched' or 'struck' by a spirit. The country people do not say that the soul is away and the body in the bed, as a spiritist would, but that body and soul have been taken and somebody or something put in their place so bewitched that we do not know the difference. This thing may be some old person who was taken years ago and having come near his allotted term is put back to get the rites of the church, or as a substitute for some more youthful and more helpful person. The old man may have grown too infirm even to drive cattle. On the other hand, the thing may be a broomstick or a heap of shavings. I imagine that an explanatory myth arose at a very early age when men had not learned to distinguish between the body and the soul, and was perhaps once universal. The fact itself is certainly 'possession' and 'trance' precisely as we meet them in spiritism, and was perhaps once an inseparable part of religion. Mrs Piper surrenders her body to the control of her trance personality but her soul, separated from the body has a life of its own, of which, however, she is little if at all conscious.[66]

There are two books which describe with considerable detail a like experience in China and Japan respectively: *Demon Possession and Allied Themes,* by the Rev. John L. Nevius, D.D. (Fleming H. Revell & Co., 1894); *Occult Japan,* by Percival Lowell (Houghton, Mifflin, 1895). In both countries, however, the dualism of body and soul is recognized, and the theory is therefore identical with that of spiritism. Dr Nevius is a missionary who gradually became convinced, after much doubt and perplexity, of the reality of possession by what he believes to be evil spirits precisely similar to that described in the New Testament. These spirits take possession of some Chinese man or woman who falls suddenly into a trance, and announce through their medium's mouth, that when they lived on earth they had such and such a name, sometimes if they think a false name will make them more pleasing they will give a false name and history. They demand certain offerings and explain that they are seeking a home; and if the offerings are refused, and the medium seeks to drive them from body and house they turn persecutors; the house may catch fire suddenly; but if they have their way, they are ready to be useful, especially to heal the sick. The missionaries expel them in the name of Christ, but the Chinese exorcists adopt a method familiar to the west of Ireland—tortures or threats of torture. They will light tapers which they stick upon the fingers. They wish to make the body uncomfortable for its tenant.[67] As they believe in the division of soul and body they are not likely to go too far. A man actually did burn his wife to death, in Tipperary a few years ago, and is no doubt still in prison for it.[68] My uncle, George Pollexfen, had an old servant Mary Battle, and when she spoke of the case to me, she described that man as very superstitious. I asked what she meant by that and she explained that everybody knew that you must only threaten, for whatever injury you did to the changeling the faeries would do to the living person they had carried away. In fact mankind and spiritkind have each their hostage. These explanatory myths are not a speculative but a practical wisdom. And one can count perhaps, when they are rightly remembered, upon their preventing the more gross practical errors. The Tipperary witch-burner only half knew his own belief. 'I stand here in the door,' said Mary Battle, 'and I hear them singing over there in the field, but I have never given in to them yet.' And by 'giving in' I understood her to mean losing her head.

The form of possession described in Lowell's book is not involuntary like that the missionary describes. And the possessing spirits are believed to be those of holy hermits or of the gods. He saw it for the first time on a pilgrimage to the top of Mount Ontaké. Close on the border of the snow he came to a rest house which was arranged to enclose the path, that all, it would seem, might stop and rest and eat and give something to its keeper. Presently he saw three young men dressed in white who passed on in spite of the entreaties of the keeper. He followed and presently found them praying before a shrine cut in the side of a cliff. When the prayer was finished one of them took from his sleeve a stick that had hanging from it pieces of zigzag paper, and sat himself on a bench opposite the shrine.

One of the others sat facing upon another bench, clasping his hands over his breast and closing his eyes. Then the first young man began a long evocation, chanting and twisting and untwisting his fingers all the time. Presently he put the wand with the zigzag paper into the other's hands and the other's hands began to twitch, and that twitching grew more and more. The man was possessed. A spirit spoke through his mouth and called itself the God, Hakkai.

Now the evoker became very respectful and asked if the peak would be clear of clouds, and the pilgrimage a lucky one, and if the god would take care of those left at home. The god answered that the peak would be clear until the afternoon of the day following and all else go well. The voice ceased and the evoker offered a prayer of adoration. The entranced man was awakened by being touched on the breast and slapped upon the back and now another of the three took his place. And all was gone through afresh; and when that was over the third young man was entranced in his turn.[69]

Mr Lowell made considerable further investigation and records many cases, and was told that the god or spirit would sometimes speak in a tongue unknown to the possessed man, or gave useful medical advice. He is one of the few Europeans who have witnessed what seems to be an important rite of Shinto religion. Shintoism, or the Way of the Gods, until its revival in the last half of the nineteenth century remained lost and forgotten in the roots of Japanese life. It had been superseded by Buddhism, if Mr Lowell was correctly informed, as completely as this old faery faith of Ireland has been superseded by Christianity. Buddhism, however, having no Christian hostility to friendly spirits, does not seem to have done anything to discourage a revival which was one of the causes that brought Japan under the single rule of the Mikado. It had always indeed in certain of its sects practised ceremonies that had for their object the causing of possession.

There is a story in *The Book of the Dun Cow* which certainly describes a like experience, though Prof. Rhys interprets it as a solar myth. I will take the story from Lady Gregory's *Cuchulain of Muirthemne*. The people of Ulster were celebrating the festival of the beginning of winter, held always at the beginning of November. The first of November is still a very haunted day and night. A flock of wild birds lit upon the waters near to

Cuchulain and certain fair women. 'In all Ireland there were not birds to be seen that were more beautiful.'

One woman said: ' "I must have a bird of these birds on each of my two shoulders." "We must all have the same," said the other women. "If any one is to get them, it is I that must first get them," said Eithne Inguba, who loved Cuchulain. "What shall we do?" said the women. "It is I will tell you that," said Levarcham, "for I will go to Cuchulain from you to ask him to get them." '

So she went to Cuchulain and said: ' "The women of Ulster desire that you will get these birds for them." Cuchulain put his hand upon his sword as if to strike her, and he said: "Have the idle women of Ulster nothing better to do than to send me catching birds today?" "It is not for you", said Levarcham, "to be angry with them; for there are many of them are half blind today with looking at you, from the greatness of their love for you." '

After this Cuchulain catches the birds and divides them amongst the women, and to every woman there are two birds, but when he comes to his mistress, Eithne Inguba, he has no birds left. ' "It is vexed you seem to be", he said, "because I have given the birds to the other women." "You have good reason for that," she said, "for there is not a woman of them but would share her love and her friendship with you; while as for me no person shares my love but you alone." ' Cuchulain promises her whatever birds come, and presently there come two birds who are linked together with a chain of gold and 'singing soft music that went near to put sleep on the whole gathering.' Cuchulain went in their pursuit, though Eithne and his charioteer tried to dissuade him, believing them enchanted. Twice he casts a stone from his sling and misses, and then he throws his spear but merely pierces the wing of one bird. Thereupon the birds dive and he goes away in great vexation, and he lies upon the ground and goes to sleep, and while he sleeps two women come to him and put him under enchantment. In the Connacht stories the enchantment begins with a stroke, or with a touch from some person of faery and it is so the women deal with Cuchulain. 'The woman with the green cloak went up to him and smiled at him and she gave him a stroke of a rod. The other went up to him then and smiled at him and gave him a stroke in the same way; and they went on doing this for a long time, each of them striking him in turn till he was more dead than alive. And then they went away and left him there.' The men of Ulster found him and they carried him to a house and to a bed and there he lay till the next November came round. They were sitting about the bed when a strange man came in and sat amongst them. It was the God, Aengus, and he told how Cuchulain could be healed. A king of the other world, Labraid, wished for Cuchulain's help in a war, and if he would give it, he would have the love of Fand the wife of the sea god Manannan. The women who gave him the strokes of the rods were Fand and her sister Liban, who was Labraid's wife. They had sought his help as the Connacht faeries will ask the help of some good hurler. Were they too like our faeries 'shadows' until they found it? When the god was gone, Cuchulain awoke, and Conahar, the King of Ulster, who had been watching by his bedside, told him that he must go again to the rock where the enchantment was laid upon him. He goes there and sees the woman with the green cloak. She is Liban and pleads with him that he may accept the love of Fand and give his help to Labraid. If he will only promise, he will become strong again. Cuchulain will not go at once but sends his charioteer into the other world. When he has his charioteer's good report, he consents, and wins the fight for Labraid and is the lover of Fand. In the Connacht stories a wife can sometimes get back her husband by throwing some spell-breaking object over the heads of the faery cavalcade that keeps him spellbound. Emir, in much the same way, recovers her husband Cuchulain, for she and her women go armed with knives to the yew tree upon Baile's strand where he had appointed a meeting with Fand and outface Fand and drive her away.[70]

We have here certainly a story of trance and of the soul leaving the body, but probably after it has passed through the minds of story-tellers who have forgotten its original meaning. There is no mention of any one taking Cuchulain's place, but Prof. Rhys in his reconstruction of the original form of the story of 'Cuchulain and the Beetle of Forgetfulness', a visit also to the other world, makes the prince who summoned him to the adventure take his place in the court of Ulster.[71] There are many stories belonging to different countries, of people whose places are taken for a time by angels or spirits or gods, the best known being that of the nun and the Virgin Mary,[72] and all may have once been stories of changelings and entranced persons. Pwyll and Arawyn in the *Mabinogion* change places for a year, Pwyll going to the court of the dead in the shape of Arawyn to overcome his enemies, and Arawyn going to the court of Dyved. Pwyll overcomes Arawyn's enemies with one blow and the changeling's rule at Dyved was marvellous for its wisdom.[73] In all these stories strength comes from men and wisdom from among gods who are but shadows. I have read somewhere of a Norse legend of a false Odin that took the true Odin's place, when the sun of summer became the wintry sun.[74] When we say a man has had a stroke of paralysis or that he is touched we refer perhaps to a once universal faery belief.

Note 40. [To *V&B* I, 175; *V&B1970* 107] I suppose this woman who was glad to 'pick a bit of what was in the pigs' trough' had passed along the roads in a state of semi-trance, living between two worlds. Boehme had for seven days what he called a walking trance that began by his gazing at a gleam of light on a copper pot and in that trance truth fell upon him 'like a bursting shower'.[75]

Note 41. [To *V&B* I, 188; *V&B1970* 114] A village beauty of Ballylee. Raftery praised her in lines quoted in my *Celtic Twilight*, and Lady Gregory speaks of her in her essay on Raftery in *Poets and Dreamers.*[76]

Note 42. [To *V&B* I, 189; *V&B1970* 115] An old, second-sighted servant to an uncle of mine used to say that dreams were no longer true 'when the sap began to rise' and when I asked her how she knew that, she said: 'What is the use of having an intellect unless you know a thing like that.'[77]

Note 43. [To *V&B* I, 230; *V&B1970* 139] 'In the faeries' is plainly a misspeaking of the old phrase 'in faery' that is to say 'in glamour', 'under enchantment'. The word 'faery' as used for an individual is a modern corruption. The right word is 'fay'.

Note 44. [To *V&B* I, 242; *V&B1970* 146] The sudden filling of the air by a sweet odour is a common event of the séance room. It is mentioned several times in the 'Diary' of Stainton Moses.[78]

[Notes to Volume II]

Note 1. [To *V&B* II, 214; *V&B1970* 259 (n. '46' [*sic*])] A woman from the North would probably be a faery woman or at any rate a 'knowledgeable' woman, one who was 'in the faeries' and certainly not necessarily at all a woman from Ulster. The North where the old Celtic other world was thought to lie is the quarter of spells and faeries. A visionary student,[79] who was at the Dublin Art School when I was there, described to me a waking dream of the North Pole. There were luxuriant vegetation and overflowing life though still but ice to the physical eye. He added thereto his conviction that wherever physical life was abundant, the spiritual life was vague and thin, and of the converse truth.

Note 2. [To *V&B* II, 239; *V&B1970* 274 (n. '46')] St Patrick prayed, in 'The Breastplate of St Patrick', to be delivered from the spells of smiths and women.[80]

Appendix 4 Deleted typescript section I, 'Introduction', of 'Swedenborg, Mediums, and the Desolate Places', perhaps originally intended to introduce the entire collection *Visions and Beliefs in the West of Ireland* (w. 1911–14; dated 14 October 1914)

INTRODUCTION

The Faeries, the Gentry, the Sheogue, the Others, as they are called by Irish countrymen, are sometimes described as three feet high, or as of the size of little boys but more often they are of the ordinary size of men and women. They have some among them, the leprecauns or dwarfs, for instance, who seem never to have been human, but for the most part they are the dead and carry beyond the tomb the friendships and animosities of life. When a man dies they are often heard fighting with one another, some to carry him off and some to save him from it, and sometimes he himself in trance or dream may give a blow or take a blow in this battle, which is called 'The Battle of the Friends'. The mother who comes after death to see her children, perhaps to shame a step-mother, comes, not from any region described in sermons, but from the fort, or forth as it is called, while the shade who helps a knowledgeable man to the right herb, is cousin or sister taken before her time. He will perhaps meet her at the garden end by an old thorn tree, for they protect the thorn and gather about it making a habitation there, though when they have a need they can build up a palace in a moment or remake an old stone castle, pulled down by Cromwell, filling it with noise and lights. They dance much in flat places of the rocks, quarrel much and play at hurley, and have a music more beautiful than ours and in every household there is a queen and more dreaded still, the Fool of the Forth Amadan-na-Briona,[1] and they can take all shapes, appearing now in mediaeval many coloured clothes, now in the clothes of our own days, now as bird or beast, barrel or flock of wool or creel of turf. Here and there one comes upon some remnant too of the old Gaelic belief, still common when the author of *The Secret Commonwealth*[2] was driven into the Scottish highlands by 'The Saxon Usurper', that those who have been human shall be so again. Certainly they seem even in their freedom dependent upon the living; 'a shadow', as the saying is, if they have not our help, and always seeing through our eyes, falling into and rising from the body in Shelley's metaphor, with the leap of the flying fish.[3] Since I was a little boy and passed with terror a haunted hole by the riverside at Ballisodare[4] I have thought of Hell and Heaven as somewhere among those sights and sounds that seem to pour up out of desolate and empty places. I never pass a clump of elders, beside the gable of a white-washed cottage in the half-hour after sunset without, because of some childish association with the smell of the elder flower, an emotion of spiritual awe. I have never doubted that old men and women who have told me from my childhood up what they have seen and heard have spoken the truth, though I have tried theories of all sorts, devout and sceptical, according to the changes in my reading and my thoughts, to account for what they have seen.

I am not sorry that the problem of the world has so narrowed itself, for the mind would become more vivid if it discovered its next awakening, or first original, through no dry dialectic nor imagery of Jerusalem nor Zion but beyond the common hedge-row. More than half of all my reading since boyhood has been in the hope of bringing not for this world, I am not so vain, but for my own imagination, this resurrection of the body, as it were, this setting up of Melusine by Mary,[5] this marriage of religion with traditional romance. An Irish country-woman because of a fable that Christ walked all countries between the rolling away of the stone and the Ascension, can tell you of what he has said or done in her own village, as she can point to Slieve-na-nÓr[6] where the priest will bring to an end the last war of the world, raising up the chalice three times. All this, because as Blake said, it is a last judgment, when a fool is put from our company,[7] and Christ may be in every day's work, could be made into poems and plays and stories and with no discomfort of new belief, but lacking the shades and the faeries, the desolate places could but lack inhabitants, and a primrose by the river brim imposes upon us an arbitrary sentimentality. 'God is an abode of spirits.' 'God only acts or is in existing beings or men.'[8]

Appendix 5 Postscript to the introduction to *Bishop Berkeley*, by Joseph M. Hone and Mario M. Rossi (1931)

P.S.—When I had finished these notes I read for the first time what Mario M. Rossi had added to the book. Had I read it earlier—it was not included in Joseph Hone's manuscript when first I saw it—diffidence might have kept me silent. And now I study with excitement this profound critic of philosophy, this scholar learned in all the schools who can make himself intelligible to the running man. He has given me my first full knowledge of Berkeley the philosopher; my knowledge of Berkeley the man I shall always owe to Joseph Hone's understanding of the Irish eighteenth century, his mastery of biographical detail.

W.B.Y.

Appendix 6 'A Biographical Note', in *The Holy Mountain*, by Bhagwān Shri Hamsa, tr. Shri Purohit Swāmi (1934)

Bhagwān Shri Hamsa was born in Dhuliā[1] on the 15th of June 1878. He was the younger son of Pāndu Tātyā Nātēkār, a well-known pleader. As he lost his mother at the age of four, his father and elder brother took care of him. When Pāndu Tāytā learned from an astrologer that his son would become a Yogi, he forbade him to read the *Geetā*[2] and found him a wife. He was married in his sixteenth year. But one day sitting on the banks of the Indrāyani at Dehu,[3] he decided to renounce the world. He threw his European clothes into the river. He began to practise austerities; he read the *Guru-Charitra*, the Life of Dattātreya—repeated the *Gāyatri Mantram*,[4] took milk for his sole food. After three and a half years of this life, he went on pilgrimage encircling the whole of India, and visited once every year Mount Girnār, where the footsteps of Dattātreya are shown to pilgrims. Then in 1908 he made the pilgrimage to Mount Kailās described in the following pages.

Appendix 7

Final paragraph of introduction to *The Oxford Book of Modern Verse* (1936)

[For the 'Dublin Edition' Yeats deleted a final paragraph that was retained in all other editions.]

Certain authors are absent from this selection through circumstances beyond my control. Robert Graves, Laura Riding,[1] and the executors of Canon John Gray and Sir William Watson have refused permission. Two others, Rudyard Kipling and Ezra Pound, are inadequately represented because too expensive even for an anthologist with the ample means the Oxford University Press puts at his disposal.[2]

NOTES

PER AMICA SILENTIA LUNAE

1. In a letter to Lady Gregory, Yeats translated the title as 'Through the friendly silences of the moon' (28 June [1917], NLI Ms. 18,735). The title is from Virgil, *Aeneid*, II.255, where the moon presides over the Greeks' stealthy return and entry into Troy; see also note 62 below.
2. 'Maurice' was a code name used by Yeats, during the First World War, for Iseult Gonne (1894–1954), daughter of Maud Gonne; see, for example, George Yeats to Ezra Pound, 24 May 1918, in 'George, Ezra, Dorothy and Friends: Twenty-Six Letters, 1918–59', ed. Ann Saddlemyer, in *YA7* 8 and note 2.
3. Yeats visited the summer home of Maud and Iseult Gonne in Colleville-sur-Mer (near Vierville-sur-Mer) in Normandy, in July and August 1916.
4. For the cat Minoulooshe (or Minnaloushe) see 'The Cat and the Moon' (1918; *P* 167–68), in the play of the same title (w. 1917, 1926; *VPl* 792–804).
5. 'Ego Dominus Tuus' (w. 1915; publ. 1917) (*P* 160–62); for the title, which translates as 'I am thy master', see note 8 below.
6. 'The Soul of Man'.
7. Yeats described the poetry of his friend the English poet Lionel Johnson (1867–1902) as marmorean (resembling marble) (*Au* 223).
8. Dante, in *La Vita Nuova* (*c.* 1292–93), described his dream vision that occurred soon after he had seen Beatrice the second time, after nine years: '. . . There appeared to be in my room a mist of the colour of fire, within the which I discerned the figure of a lord of terrible aspect to such as should gaze upon him, but who seemed therewithal to rejoice inwardly that it was a marvel to see. Speaking he said many things, among the which I could understand but few; and of these, this: *Ego dominus tuus.*' A footnote by Dante Gabriel Rossetti gives the translation, 'I am thy master.' (*The Early Italian Poets from Ciullo d'Alcamo to Dante Alighieri (1100–1200–1300) . . . together with Dante's Vita Nuova*, tr. and ed. D. G. Rossetti [London: Smith, Elder, 1861], [O'Shea 1920s list] p. 226 and repr. in *The Collected Works of Dante Gabriel Rossetti*, ed. William Michael Rossetti [1887–88; repr. London: Ellis and Elvey, 1897], [O'Shea no. 1789] II, 32 and in *The New Life [La Vita Nuova] of Dante Alighieri*, ed. William Michael Rossetti [London: Ellis and Elvey, 1899], [O'Shea 1920s list] p. 28.)

9. Jacob Boehme (1575–1624), German theosophist and mystic, *The Forty Questions of the Soul [1620] and The Clavis [1624]*, tr. John Sparrow (London: Watkins, 1911), (O'Shea no. 236) p. 257 (thirty-second question: 'What shall the Form, Condition, Joy and Glory of the Soul be, in the Life to come?').
10. The comedies of Lady Augusta Gregory (1852–1932) include *Spreading the News* (perf. 1904; publ. 1905) and *The Rising of the Moon* (publ. 1904; perf. 1907).
11. Mrs Patrick Campbell (1862–1949), English actress.
12. Maurice Maeterlinck (1862–1949), Belgian poet, dramatist and essayist. In 1898, Mrs Patrick Campbell first played what was to become one of her most famous roles, Mélisande in Maeterlinck's *Peléas and Mélisande*. She wore a golden crown and dress designed by Edward Burne-Jones.
13. For Burne-Jones, see p. 418, note 2 below.
14. When it opened for a week's run on 26 January 1907, Synge's play met immediate opposition for its treatment of Irish womanhood and for 'indecent' language. John Millington Synge (b. 1871) died of Hodgkin's disease on 24 March 1909.
15. *The Playboy of the Western World*, in *The Works of John M. Synge* (Dublin: Maunsel, 1910), (O'Shea no. 2076) II, 112 (Act III): '. . . judgment day'.
16. *The Tinker's Wedding* (1907; perf. 1909), in *The Works of John M. Synge*, I, 154 (Act I).
17. *Deirdre of the Sorrows* was begun in 1907 and left in draft form at Synge's death in 1909.
18. William Morris (1834–96), English writer, painter, designer and socialist. Walter Savage Landor (1775–1864), author of *Imaginary Conversations* (1824–62).
19. In Landor's imaginary conversation 'Machiavelli and Michel-Angelo Buonarroti' (1846), Machiavelli talks to Michelangelo about broken statues and mentions the famous *Venus de Milo* (*Aphrodite of Melos*, *c.* 150 B.C.), which was discovered in 1820 and is now in the Louvre (*Imaginary Conversations*, ed. Charles G. Crump [London: Dent, 1909], [O'Shea no. 1081] IV, 192). Walter Savage Landor to Robert Southey, 3 June 1822, quoted in John Forster, *Walter Savage Landor: A Biography* (London: Chapman and Hall, 1869), (O'Shea no. 690) II, 12: '. . . projects, and. . . . I try to . . . time, and. . . . myself as of a dead. . . .'
20. William Beckford (1760–1844), English Gothic novelist, art collector and man of letters.
21. Leigh Hunt (1784–1859), English poet and essayist, recorded the meeting of Percy Bysshe Shelley (1792–1822) and John Keats (1795–1821) in *The Autobiography of Leigh Hunt* (London: Smith, Elder, rev. ed. 1860) p. 267: '. . . birth a sort of natural enemy'.
22. Simeon Solomon (1840–1905), *A Mystery of Love in Sleep* (London: printed for the author and F. S. Ellis, 1871) p. 4: '. . . of unappeased desire.' See Warwick Gould, Editorial Miscellany', *YA*4 274.

23. Charles Lancelot Shadwell translated the *Purgatory* in two parts (1892 and 1899; O'Shea nos. 473–74, but not on the 1920s list) and the *Paradise* (1915). Dante Gabriel Rossetti translated Dante's lyrics and the prose *New Life (Vita Nuova)* (1861; repr. 1897 and 1899; O'Shea no. 1789). At this time Yeats probably also owned Charles Eliot Norton's prose translation of the *Purgatorio* (1892; rev. ed. 1902; O'Shea 1920s list [probable identification]).
24. Giovanni Boccaccio, *Life of Dante* (*Vita di Dante*) (*c.* 1354–55), in Philip Henry Wicksteed, tr., *The Early Lives of Dante* (London: Chatto and Windus; Boston: Luce, 1907) pp. 80–81 (ch. xii): 'Amid all the virtue, amid all the knowledge, that hath been shewn above to have belonged to this wondrous poet, lechery found most ample place not only in the years of his youth but also of his maturity; the which vice, though it be natural, and common, and scarce to be avoided, yet in truth is so far from being commendable that it cannot even be suitably excused.'
25. Matthew Arnold, 'Dante and Beatrice' (1863), collected in *Essays in Criticism, Third Series* (Boston: Ball, 1910) p. 103 and in *The Complete Prose Works of Matthew Arnold*, ed. R. H. Super (Ann Arbor: University of Michigan Press, 1962) III, 9: 'Dante's conduct, even in mature life, was at times exceeding irregular'.
26. Guido Cavalcanti (*c.* 1250–1300), 'To Dante Alighieri. Sonnet: He rebukes Dante for his way of Life, after the Death of Beatrice', ll. 2, 7–10, in *Early Italian Poets . . . with Dante's Vita Nuova*, p. 358 and repr. in *Collected Works of Dante Gabriel Rossetti*, II, 144: '. . . much of baseness. . . / . . . kind, / Had made . . . poetry. / But . . . for thine abject . . . / . . . rhymes;'. D. G. Rossetti's footnote (*Early Italian Poets*, p. 358) to this sonnet reads: 'This interesting sonnet must refer to the same period of Dante's life regarding which he has made Beatrice address him in words of noble reproach when he meets her in Eden. (*Purg.* C. XXX.)'
27. *Purgatorio*, XXX.139: '*Per questo visitai l' uscio dei morti*'; Yeats perhaps drew upon the verse translation of Charles Lancelot Shadwell, *The Purgatory of Dante Alighieri. Part II. The Earthly Paradise (Cantos XXVIII–XXXIII): An Experiment in Literal Verse Translation* (London: Macmillan, 1899), (O'Shea no. 474, but not on 1920s list) p. 47: '. . . the portal of the dead, / . . . I visited' or the prose translation of Thomas Okey, *The Purgatorio of Dante Alighieri*, Temple Classics (1901; repr. London: Dent, 1906) (George Yeats's copy; O'Shea no. 472 and 1920s list) p. 387: '. . . I visited the portal of the dead'.
28. Cino da Pistoia, 'Sonnet. He impugns the verdicts of Dante's Commedia', ll. 2, 6, 9, 11–16, in *Early Italian Poets . . . with Dante's Vita Nuova*, p. 394 and repr. in *Collected Works of Dante Gabriel Rossetti*, II, 176: '. . . lovely heresy, / . . . / . . . beats the . . . down, lets the . . . / . . . aside. / . . . / . . . fall, like Antony's on. . . .' Yeats omitted line 10: 'Fixing folks' nearness to the Fiend their foe,'.
29. 'Dante Alighieri to Giovanni Guirino. Sonnet. He answers the foregoing Sonnet', subtitle [by Dante Gabriel Rossetti] and ll. 1–4, in *Early Italian Poets . . . with Dante's Vita Nuova*, p. 436 and repr. in

Collected Works of Dante Gabriel Rossetti, II, 217: '. . . Death. / . . . King by . . . rich grace His . . . / . . . dwell / . . . dispel / . . . consistory;'.

30. Lionel Johnson (1867–1902), English poet and member of the Rhymers' Club, was received into the Catholic church in 1891. Ernest Dowson (1867–1900), his fellow poet and Rhymer, converted soon afterwards, but proved less dedicated.
31. Adapted from J. B. Yeats to W. B. Yeats, 2 July 1913, in *J. B. Yeats: Letters to his Son W. B. Yeats and Others 1869–1922*, ed. Joseph Hone (London: Faber, 1944) p. 163: 'I regretted that I could not take my canvas and paint a portrait of her and her child. . . . Portraiture in art or poetry [is] the effort to keep the pain alive and intensify it, since out of the heart of the pain comes the solace, as a monk scourges himself to bring an ecstasy.'
32. Hermes (Mercury, in Roman mythology), messenger of the gods, conventionally is shown wearing winged sandals. The ancient Egyptian god of wisdom, Thoth, is equated with Hermes because the Greek translation of Thoth is Hermes Trismegistus (Hermes the Thrice-Greatest). The Hermetic writings, a collection of Greek and Latin texts on magic, astrology, alchemy and philosophy (*c.* A.D. 50–300), traditionally are attributed to Hermes Trismegistus.
33. Vague echo of Genesis 1:1–12 for the dark and the void; for the ringers in the tower, see Shelley's 'Julian and Maddalo' (1818) (ll. 98–103, 120–30).
34. The Russian government, which had been using exile as a punishment since the sixteenth century, sent a large number of revolutionists to the mines of the Trans-Baikal following the assassination of Alexander II in 1881. The reference to a daring journey in disguise to the exiles in Siberia is untraced. Benjamin Douglas Howard (1836–1900), an English-born American surgeon and author on criminology, undertook adventurous travels in Siberia, but with the permission of officials and not in disguise; his books about those travels are *Life with Trans-Siberian Savages* (London: Longmans, Green, 1893), which Yeats owned (O'Shea 1920s list), and *Prisoners of Russia: A Personal Study of Convict Life in Sakhalin and Siberia* (New York: Appleton, 1902).
35. For Dante's lechery, see note 25 above. For pottle pot, a two-quart tankard, see *2 Henry IV*, II.ii.83.
36. St Francis of Assisi (1181/2–1226), founder of the Franciscan order, renounced family ties and worldly goods for a life of poverty and prayer. Caesar (Cesare) Borgia (1475/6–1507), usually considered the model for Machiavelli's intelligent, ruthless and treacherous Renaissance Prince, was reportedly remote and secretive among his friends, but open and loquacious among the people he ruled.
37. Yeats began *The Player Queen* (perf. 1919; publ. 1922) in 1908 as 'a verse tragedy' and then in 1914 converted it into prose as 'a wild comedy, almost a farce' (*VPl* 761; *L* 588). His 1922 note to the play specifically links the early version of the play to *Per Amica Silentia Lunae* and the 'Antithetical Self' (*VPl* 761).

38. *Mem* 191 (18 March 1909): '. . . on having the . . . other self, that all joyous or creative life is a rebirth as . . . not oneself, something . . . renewed in . . . self-realization, a . . . the terrors of judgment. . . .'
39. *Mem* 151 (26 January 1909): '. . . are and . . . ourselves, though . . . virtue as . . . a current code is . . . Wordsworth is . . . sense has no theatrical element, it is an obedience, a discipline which he has not created. This . . . better sort of journalists, the *Spectator* writers, for instance, with all who are part of the machine and yet care for poetry.'
40. Sanctuary of Zeus. The tree (or trees) of Dodona give oracles by interpretation of the rustling of its leaves. See *Odyssey*, XIV.327 and *Iliad*, XVI.234.
41. Distant echoes of Isaiah 40:26 and John 10:16; see also p. 263 below.
42. Plutarch, 'On the Sign of Socrates' ('A Discourse Concerning the Daemon of Socrates'), section XXIV (593D–94A), in *Plutarch's Moralia*, tr. Phillip H. DeLacy and Benedict Einarson, Loeb Classical Library (London: Heinemann; Cambridge: Harvard University Press, 1959) VII, 481–85 and also 'The Obsolescence of Oracles', section XIII (416F), V, 389. Compare Heraclitus, frag. 123, in John Burnet, *Early Greek Philosophy* (London and Edinburgh: Black, 1892), (O'Shea no. 308) p. 141 ('. . . that they rise up and become the guardians of the hosts of the quick and dead.') and Burnet's comment, p. 176, note 83 ('We need not hesitate to ascribe to Herkleitos the view that the dead become guardian demons of the living; it appears already in Hesiod, *Works and Days,* 121').
43. [Yeats's note, dated *February 1924*] I could not distinguish at the time between the permanent Daemon and the impermanent, who may be 'an illustrious dead man', though I knew the distinction was there. I shall deal with the matter in *A Vision.*
44. Compare Heraclitus, frag. 67, in Burnet, *Early Greek Philosophy*, p. 138: 'Mortals are immortals and immortals are mortals, the one living the other's death and dying the other's life.'

    At a séance on 3 May 1909, Yeats learned that his daemon was the spirit of Leo Africanus (al-Hassan ibn-Mohammed al-Wazzan; later, Johannes Leo) (*c.* 1494–1552), Moorish traveller and geographer of North Africa; see 'The Manuscript of "Leo Africanus"' (*c.* 1916?), ed. Steve L. Adams and George M. Harper, *YA1* 3–47.
45. Johann Wolfgang von Goethe (1749–1832), *Wilhelm Meister's Apprenticeship* (1796), tr. Thomas Carlyle, 2 vols. 1895[?] (O'Shea 1920s list); in book I, ch. xvii, the stranger tells Wilhelm, 'The fabric of our life is formed of necessity and chance. . . .'
46. Heraclitus, frag. 121, in Burnet, *Early Greek Philosophy*, p. 141: 'Man's character is his fate.' For an extended discussion of this fragment (which is no. 119 in *Die Fragmente der Vorsokratiker*, ed. Hermann Diels, rev. Walther Kranz), see James Olney, *The Rhizome and the Flower: The Perennial Philosophy—Yeats and Jung* (Berkeley and Los Angeles: University of California Press, 1980) pp. 118–19; Olney prefers the translation 'A man's individuality is his *daimon*' (p. 93) by W. K. C. Guthrie (*A History of Greek Philosophy* [1962]).

47. 'The Wanderer', l. 17: *dōmgeorne*.
48. In the arrangement of twelve astrological houses, the seventh house, which governs marriage, begins at the setting (or West or *Dysis*) point, marked by the zodiacal constellation that is setting in the western sky at the moment of birth. Enemies, however, are governed by the twelfth house.
49. Slieve-na-Mon (elev. 2,368 feet), a mountain in southeastern Co. Tipperary; as Sidhe Femen it was the home of Bodb Dearg, a Tuatha de Danaan; see *Gods and Fighting Men*, pp. 73–74 ('Bodb Dearg') and *P&I* 134. The quotation is untraced.
50. Edwin J. Ellis (1848–1916), 'Himself', ll. 41, 39–40, 49–52, in *Fate in Arcadia and Other Poems* (London: Ward & Bowney, 1892) pp. 158–63: 'companionless, / A . . . spectre night and day' (ll. 39–40), '. . . go, and . . . him, / "Eli . . . me!" / . . . limb: / ' (ll. 49–52). In a review of *Fate in Arcadia* in the *Bookman* (London), September 1892, Yeats described 'Himself' as a 'strange poem, perhaps the most powerful in the book' (*UP2* 235).
51. [Yeats's note] Translated by Arthur Symons from *San Juan de la Cruz*.[a]
51a. St John of the Cross [Juan de Yepis y Alvarez (1542–91), Spanish mystic], 'From San Juan de la Cruz. I. The Obscure Night of the Soul' (ll. 25–44), in Arthur Symons, *Images of Good and Evil* (London: Heinemann, 1899), (O'Shea no. 2056) pp. 121–22 and in *Poems* (London: Heinemann, 1902), (O'Shea no. 2061) I, 189: '. . . night that didst lead . . . / . . . night more . . . / . . . night that . . . us, / . . . . // . . . first moving air / . . . aside. His. . . . // . . . ceased, and. . . .' Yeats later included this translation, by his friend Arthur Symons (1865–1944), in *OBMV* (no. 74).
52. 'Nishikigi, A Play in Two Acts by Motokiyo', in *Certain Noble Plays of Japan: From the Manuscripts of Ernest Fenollosa, Chosen and Finished by Ezra Pound, With an Introduction by William Butler Yeats* (Churchtown, Dundrum: Cuala Press, 1916) p. 2: '. . . sleep, and . . .'
53. See *L* 266 (August 1896). See also *Au* 372–75; *Mem* 100–4; 'In the Seven Woods' (1902; *P* 77); 'Parnell's Funeral' (1932; *P* 279).
54. 'Mark of Man' is not Balzac's phrase, but conveys his sense, in *Séraphita*, p. 112: 'Man alone—he alone here on earth having any consciousness of the infinite—can know the straight line'.
55. In the symbolism of the Christian Cabbala, as Yeats explained, 'the Tree of Life is a geometrical figure made up of ten circles or spheres called Sephiroth joined by straight lines' or paths. 'The winding path of nature or instinct' is associated with a jagged pattern of those paths and is symbolised by the downward path of lightning or by the winding upward path of a serpent. It contrasts with 'the long straight path that goes up through the centre of the tree'. Tiphareth, a Sephiroth at the center of the Cabbalistic tree, is associated with the sun, and the path that leads to it is associated with the constellation Sagittarius, a centaur shooting an arrow. Yeats explained that this straight path to Cabbalistic wisdom is 'interpreted as the path of "deliberate effort" ' and is followed only by those 'who could attain to wisdom

by the study of magic' (*Au* 375; see also *Mem* 102–3; 'Is the Order of R.R. and A.C. to Remain a Magical Order?' [1901], repr. in George M. Harper, *Yeats's Golden Dawn* [London: Macmillan, 1974] p. 261; and *E&I* 288). For diagrams, see Kathleen Raine, *Yeats, the Tarot and the Golden Dawn,* 2nd ed. (Dublin: Dolmen Press, 1976) plates 10–13, 15–16, and S. L. MacGregor Mathers, intro. to *The Kabbalah Unveiled* (London: Redway, 1887), (O'Shea no. 1292a) plates 3, 4.

56. For example, Sigmund Freud, *The Interpretation of Dreams* (1900), tr. A. A. Brill (London: Allen, 1913), (O'Shea 1920s list) pp. 464–83 (ch. vii, section E) and Carl Gustav Jung, 'The Psychology of Dreams' (w. 1914) in *Collected Papers on Analytical Psychology,* tr. Constance E. Long (London: Baillière, Tindall and Cox, 1916), (O'Shea no. 1050) pp. 299–311.

57. *Faust,* ll. 11581–82 (part II, Act V [scene 6; in the great forecourt of the palace]); it echoes Faust's wager with Mephistopheles in ll. 1345–46 (part I [scene 4; in the study]). Thomas E. Webb, tr., *The First Part of the Tragedy of Faust,* 2nd ed. (with 'The Death of Faust' from the Second Part) (London: Longmans, Green, 1898), (O'Shea no. 753) p. 268: '*Then* to the moment I might say, / O tarry yet! Thou art so fair!' The English translation closest to Yeats's 'Stay moment!' ('*Augenblicke . . . / Verweile doch*') is by William Barnard Clarke, *Translation of Goethe's Faust 1st and II Parts* (Freiburg and London: Schmidt, 1865) p. 442: 'To such a moment I should say: / Thou art so fine, a while yet stay!'

58. Walter Savage Landor, 'Memory' (ll. 1–3; in *Heroic Idyls,* 1863), in *Poems, Dialogues in Verse, and Epigrams,* ed. Charles G. Crump (London: Dent, 1909), (O'Shea no. 1083) II, 273: '. . . Muses . . . taught, / Is Memory: she . . . remain, / . . . shoulder, urging. . . .'

59. The Italian poet Lodovico Ariosto (1474–1533), author of *Orlando Furioso* (1516), retired to Ferrara, where, from 1527, he 'made a pleasant garden . . . which became his delight and chief recreation' (Edmund G. Gardner, *The King of Court Poets: A Study of the Work Life and Times of Lodovico Ariosto* [London: Constable, 1906] p. 236).

60. *Anima Mundi*: Soul of the World. See also pp. 22–23 above and note 67 below.

61. See the manuscript 'Leo Africanus' (*c.* 1916?; *YA1* 34, 38), in which Yeats's daemon instructs him: '. . . "Spiritus Mundi" which is perhaps that world, your century has named the unconscious. . . . The Spiritus Mundi is indeed the place of images & of all things [that] have been or yet shall be. . . . We are the unconscious as you say or as I prefer to say the animal spirits freed from the will, & moulded by the images of Spiritus Mundi.' In 1900, Yeats had written of the 'great Memory that renews the world and men's thoughts age after age. . . . the great Memory is also a dwelling-house of symbols, of images that are living souls' (*E&I* 79).

62. *Aeneid,* II.255, in *The Works of Virgil, Literally Translated into English Prose,* tr. C. Davidson, ed. Theodore Alois Buckley, Harper's Classical Library (London: Bell, 1875), (O'Shea no. 2203) p. 136: '. . . from Tenedos . . . by the friendly silence of the quiet moon-

shine'. For Yeats's translation of part of this phrase, 'through the friendly silences of the moon', see note 1 above. Tenedos is the Aegean island to which the Greek fleet withdrew (*Aeneid*, II.21–25); it is near the entrance to the Dardanelles.

63. 'King Wird Khan, his Women and his Wazirs', in *A Plain and Literal Translation of the Arabian Nights Entertainments, Now Intituled The Book of the Thousand Nights and a Night* (Night 925), tr. and ed. Richard F. Burton (Benares: Kamashastra Society, 1885–86) IX, 117; see Warwick Gould, ' "A Lesson for the Circumspect": W. B. Yeats's two versions of *A Vision* and the *Arabian Nights*', in *The Arabian Nights in English Literature: Studies in the Reception of The Thousand and One Nights into British Culture,* ed. Peter L. Caracciolo (London: Macmillan, 1988) pp. 245–46 and 275, note 6.

64. Compare Goethe to Johann Gottfried Herder, 10 July 1772, in which Goethe, acknowledging that the plot of an early drama is too obviously logical and predictable, hopes 'for himself that "when beauty and greatness weave themselves more in thy emotion, then wilt thou act, speak, write, what is good and fair, without knowing why" ' (quoted in Heinrich Düntzer, *Life of Goethe*, tr. Thomas W. Lyster [London: Macmillan, 1883], [O'Shea, no. 592] I, 190). For other references to Goethe, see pp. 11 and 178–79 above.

65. For visions that Yeats invoked during the 1890s, see *SB* 29, *E&I* 28–36, 47–50, *Mem* 100 and note 2, and *Au* 185–86, 252, 372–73. Mrs Yeats told Virginia Moore that 'Yeats believed that only the visions that come in color are *true*' (*The Unicorn: William Butler Yeats' Search for Reality* [New York: Macmillan, 1954] p. 63).

66. In alchemy, from at least the fifteenth century, salt is the third elementary principle (of fixity or solidification); see, for example, a passage in Paracelsus, *A Book about Minerals,* marked by Yeats in *The Hermetic and Alchemical Writings,* ed. and tr. Arthur Edward Waite (London: Elliott, 1894), (O'Shea no. 1533) I, 247. For antimony and the liquefaction of the gold, see Arthur Edward Waite, 'A Short Lexicon of Alchemy', in *Hermetic and Alchemical Writings of Paracelsus* (O'Shea no. 1533) II, 353: 'This philosophical antimony . . . cleanses, purifies, and washes philosophical gold after the same manner that common antimony purifies common gold.'

67. See Henry More (1614–87, English philosopher of the Cambridge Platonist school), *The Immortality of the Soul* (1659; rev. 1662), (book III, ch. xii, section I), in *A Collection of Several Philosophical Writings,* 2nd ed. (London: William Morden, 1662), (O'Shea no. 1377) p. 193.

68. William Wordsworth, 'Ode: Intimations of Immortality from Recollections of Early Childhood' (1802–4, publ. 1807), ll. 163–66, in *The Poetical Works of William Wordsworth,* ed. Edward Dowden, The Aldine Edition of the British Poets (London: George Bell, 1892), (O'Shea no. 2292) V, 168: '. . . sea / Which . . . hither, / Can in a moment travel thither, / And see the Children sport upon the shore'.

69. Henry Cornelius Agrippa von Nettesheim, *Three Books of Occult Philosophy* (w. 1509–10; publ. 1531–33), book I, ch. xiv, tr. John French (London: Moule, 1651) mentions the quintessence, the immaterial

fifth element, and describes two occult hierarchies corresponding to each of four material elements (pp. 32–33).

Phoenix, the legendary bird reborn from its own ashes.

70. St Thomas Aquinas (*c*. 1225–74). Yeats later (pp. 52 and 247 above) identified his source as Villiers de l'Isle Adam, *Axël* (1890) (part I, [section I], scene 6). In that play's first English translation, published in 1925 and for which Yeats wrote a preface, the passage reads: 'For eternity, as Saint Thomas well remarks, is merely the full and entire possession of oneself in one and the same instant' (*Axel*, tr. H. P. R. Finberg [London: Jarrolds, 1925], [O'Shea no. 2201] p. 60). Yeats also used this reference in the manuscript 'Leo Africanus' (*c*. 1916?; *YA1* 37).
71. Samuel Taylor Coleridge, 'Phantom' (1804, publ. 1834), [complete poem], in *The Poems of Samuel Taylor Coleridge*, ed. Ernest Hartley Coleridge (London: Oxford University Press, 1912) p. 393: '. . . / Had pass'd away. . . . / Of aught on . . . / . . . stone / . . . own;—/ She . . . herself, and. . . .'
72. For Yeats's other reports of this incident, which occurred in 1898, see *Myth* 68, *SB* 32, *Mem* 126 and *Au* 378–79; he recorded it in a two-volume journal titled 'Visions, begun July 11, 1898'.
73. In 'Irish Witch Doctors' (1900), Yeats had referred to this 'faery doctor' as 'Kirwan' (*UP1* 219–23); in *V&B* 106 (*V&B1970* 70) he is called 'Fagan'. Spiddal, Co. Galway, is a village on the northern shore of Galway Bay, ten miles west of Galway.
74. Stanislas de Guaïta (1861–97), French poet and occultist, author of *Essai de sciences maudites*: I. *Au seuil du Mystère* (1886, 1890, 1894), II. *Le Serpent de la Genèse*: i. *Le Temple de Satan* (1891), ii. *La Clef de la magie noire* (1897); and *Le Problème du mal* (posthumous). His three volumes of poetry were titled *Les Oiseaux de passage* (1881), *La Muse noire* (1883) and *Rosa mystica* (1885). In 1888 he and Joséphin (Sâr) Péladan founded L'Ordre kabbalistique de la Rose + Croix, in Paris.
75. For Henry More (1614–87), see note 67 above. Richard Ward, *The Life of the Learned and Pious Dr Henry More* (1710), ed. M. F. Howard (London: Theosophical Society, 1911), (O'Shea no. 2226) p. 112: 'The late highly Learned and Pious Dr [William] Outram [1625–79, fellow, from *c*. 1650, of Christ's College, Cambridge, and rector of St Margaret's, Westminster] was heard publickly to say at the Arch-Bishop's Table; "That he look'd upon Dr MORE, as the Holiest Person upon the Face of the Earth." '
76. For the Cambridge Platonists, see p. 328, note 64 below. For Henry More on 'vehicles', see, for example, *The Immortality of the Soul*, book II, ch. xiv, pp. 118–21 and Yeats's note 78 below and p. 22 above. Yeats elsewhere cites Joseph Glanvill (1636–80) and John Heydon (fl. 1662) on 'vehicles' (pp. 76 and 268 above).
77. Henry More, *The Immortality of the Soul* (1659), book II, ch. xiv, section III, p. 114: '*That the Spirits are the immediate Instrument of the Soul in all Vital and Animal functions.*' On p. 95 (book II, ch. viii, section III), More quotes Hippocrates, *Book concerning the Heart*: '*That the Mind of man is in the left Ventricle of his Heart; and that it is not*

nourished from meats and drinks from the belly, but by a clear and luminous Substance that redounds by separation from the blood'; see Magni Hippocratis, *Opera Omnia*, ed. C. G. Kühn, vol. XXI of *Medicorum Graecorum Opera quae Exstant* [Lipsiae: Libraria Car. Cnoblochii, 1825) p. 490. For an explanation of 'animal spirits', see, for example, *The Immortality of the Soul*, book II, ch. viii, section II (p. 95).

78. [Yeats's note, dated *1924*] This passage, I think, correctly represents the thought of Henry More, but it would, I now believe, have corresponded better with facts if I had described this 'clear luminous substance' as a sense-material envelope, moulded upon 'the body of air',[a] or true 'vehicle'; and if I had confined to it the words 'animal spirits'. It must, however, be looked upon as surviving, for a time, the death of the physical body. The spirits do not get from it the material from which their forms are made, but their forms take light from it as one candle takes light from another.

78a. For 'the body of air', see More, *The Immortality of the Soul*, book II, ch. xiv, sections I–VII, pp. 118–19 and book III, ch. iii, sections I–II, pp. 155–56.

79. See More, *The Immortality of the Soul*, book III, ch. ii, section X, p. 150.

80. For accounts and photographs of ectoplasm during séances, see Charles Richet, *Thirty Years of Psychical Research; being, A Treatise on Metapsychics*, tr. Stanley de Brath (London: Collins; New York: Macmillan, 1923), (O'Shea no. 1743) pp. 469–545. In the manuscript 'Leo Africanus' (*c.* 1916?; *YA1* 33), Yeats's daemon explained, 'When the animal spirits withdrew from the man in trance or in death, this formed his airy body, & was in one state as in the other plastic to his or anothers fancy.'

81. For example, Cesare Lombroso, *After Death—What? Spiritistic Phenomena and their Interpretation*, tr. William Sloane Kennedy (London: Unwin; Boston: Small, Maynard, 1909), (O'Shea no. 1145) pp. 267–68: 'In 1879 [in Boston] the experimenter [William] Denton succeeded in securing imprints in paraffine of a fluidic hand, while the medium ([Mary M.] Hardy) was two feet distant from the paraffine. Afterwards he obtained the same when the paraffine was in a box, enclosed in a network covering of iron. The . . . sculptor O'Brien declared that scarcely one in twenty of the famous masters of the art could undertake to finish so admirably a hand like that, and perhaps might not succeed at all. . . .' Numerous paraffin molds of spirit hands were produced in England, beginning in 1876 with William Oxley. The famous Italian medium Eusapia Palladino (1854–1918) produced a large number of imprints of spirit faces and hands, in soft clay; for illustrations, see Lombroso, *After Death—What?* figs. 26, 28, 55a, 55b (facing pp. 70, 72, 270, 276); Léon Demonchy, 'Le Rapport sur les Séances d'Eusapia Palladino à l'Institut Général Psychologique en 1905, 1906, 1907 et 1908', *Annales des Sciences Psychiques*, 19 (1–16 February 1909) 42, fig. 13, and Albert de Rochas, 'The Fluidic Hands of Eusapia', *The Annals of Psychical Science*, 9 (April–June 1909), figs. 5–7, between pp. 220–21, and his *L'Extériorisation de la motricité: re-*

cueil d'expériences et d'observations (Paris: Chamuel, 1896) pp. 131–33 and plate v, facing p. 132 (photographs of two casts of fluidic hands of Eusapia Palladino made at Rome in 1893 [Yeats owned the augmented 4th ed. (Paris: Bibliothèque Chacornac, 1906), (O'Shea no. 1775)]. Yeats owned a clipping (NLI Ms. 30,005) of Hereward Carrington's illustrated article, 'Fluidic Hands: The Latest in Medium Photography', *New York Times,* 28 July 1912, part v, p. 8. A parallel passage in the manuscript 'Leo Africanus' (*c.* 1916?; *YA1* 34) reads: '. . . those grotesque heads impressed suddenly upon the soft parafin [*sic*], during the trance of Eusapia Palladino, & any one of them a good hours work for an excellent sculptor. . . .'

82. See p. 334, note 5 below.
83. For spirit photography, see p. 355, note 35d below.
84. For the hawk-headed chicken, see Henry More, *The Immortality of the Soul* (1659; rev. 1662), book III, ch. vi, sections IV and VIII, in *A Collection of Several Philosophical Writings,* 2nd ed. (London: William Morden, 1662), (O'Shea no. 1377) pp. 170, 172. The quotations are from book III, ch. vi, section VII (p. 172): 'the deeply-impassioned Fancy of the Mother'; and book III, ch. vi, section IX (pp. 172–73): 'the *Soul of the World* . . . things, while the Matter is . . . yielding. Which . . . idle in the transfiguration of the Vehicles of the *Daemons* . . . assist their fancies . . . to cloath them and attire them . . . pleasures: or it be may sometimes . . . Mothers Fancy . . . Monstrous. . . .'
85. More, *The Immortality of the Soul,* book III, ch. ii, section VIII, in *A Collection,* p. 154: 'Pillar of *Crystal*'.
86. See, for example, 'Hymn to Intellectual Beauty' (1816, publ. 1817).
87. Ralph Cudworth (1617–88), English philosopher of the Cambridge Platonist school.
88. More, *The Immortality of the Soul,* book III, ch. xii, section I, in *A Collection,* p. 193: '. . . *incorporeal, but . . . Sense and Animadversion, pervading Matter . . . Universe, and . . . a Plastical power therein according . . . occasions in . . . such* Phaenomena *in the World . . . Matter . . . Motion, as . . . Mechanical. . . .*'
89. Blake, *The Marriage of Heaven and Hell* (1790?–93), plate 16, in *PWB* 186 (Erdman, p. 39: '. . . Acts & Is, in . . . Men.').
90. More, *The Immortality of the Soul,* book III, ch. ii, section I, in *A Collection,* p. 151.
91. Percy Bysshe Shelley, 'Speculations on Metaphysics' in *Essays and Letters,* ed. Ernest Rhys, Camelot Classics (London: Scott, 1886), (O'Shea no. 1902) pp. 114, 120: 'thoughts, which . . . *real,* or *external objects* . . . dreams, and the ideas of madness . . . times, between . . . years, the. . . .'
92. For these symbols, see F. A. C. Wilson, *Yeats's Iconography* (London: Gollancz; New York: Macmillan, 1960) pp. 97–98, who cites More, *The Immortality of the Soul,* book II, ch. xv, section VI, in *A Collection,* p. 125, 'a vast ocean of life' and Yeats's mention of the Byzantine Neoplatonic philosopher Gemistus Pletho (1355?–1450?) in the preface (1932) to *Fighting the Waves* (*VPl* 571), as well as the

garden in Shelley's 'The Sensitive Plant' (1820; quoted p. 272 above).

93. Edmund Spenser, *The Fairie Queene* (1590–96), III.vi.30.3–5, in *Poems of Spenser*, p. 220: 'there . . . / . . . are borne to . . . and dye, /'.

94. See More, *The Immortality of the Soul*, book II, ch. xiv, sections VIII–X, in *A Collection*, pp. 120–21.

95. Mme Blanche-Henriette de Mortsauf and her Platonic lover, Félix de Vandenesse, in Balzac's *The Lily of the Valley* (1835–36), tr. James Waring, *Comédie humaine*, ed. George Saintsbury (London: Dent Edition, 1895–98), repr. as vol. xx of Temple Edition (New York: Macmillan, 1901), (O'Shea no. 92) pp. 275–81.

96. For a Japanese play in which life is reenacted, see Motokiyo, *Nishikigi*, in *Certain Noble Plays*, pp. 1–16, the source for Yeats's own *The Dreaming of the Bones* (publ. 1919, perf. 1931; *VPl* 762–79). See also Yeats's *Purgatory* (perf. 1938; *VPl* 1041–50).

97. The reference to Henry Cornelius Agrippa von Nettesheim (1486?–1535) is perhaps to *Three Books of Occult Philosophy*, book III, ch. xli (pp. 479–80), in a description of souls after bodily death: 'But they are most cruelly tortured in the irascible faculty with the hatred of an imaginary evil . . . and there are represented to them sad representations . . . sometimes of being consumed by the violence of flames . . . and sometimes of being taken, and tormented by devils.'

98. The Noh play *Motome-zuka* (*The Maiden's Tomb*) (14th c.), attributed to Kiyotsugu; see p. 332, note 95 below.

99. Agrippa, *Three Books of Occult Philosophy*, book III, chs. xxxii and xli (pp. 450–51 and 479); see also book III, ch. xvi (p. 393). *Hamlet*, III.i.66–68.

100. More, *The Immortality of the Soul*, book III, ch. vi, sections IX, XII, in *A Collection*, pp. 167–69.

101. Yeats met Helena Petrovna Blavatsky (1831–91) in 1887 and was a member of her Theosophical Society in London until 1890.

102. Florence Farr Emery (1860–1917), English actress and member of the Golden Dawn, emigrated in 1912 to Ceylon, where she was principal of Ramanathan College of Girls, Inuvil, near Chunnakan, Jaffna. The Brahmin, a Hindu of the highest or priestly caste, is not identified. In her letters to Yeats, she mentioned discussions about Hinduism with Sir Ponnambalam Ramanathan. See *LTWBY* 255 and Josephine Johnson, *Florence Farr: Bernard Shaw's 'New Woman'* (Gerrards Cross: Smythe, 1975) pp. 188–90. When Yeats repeated this anecdote in *V(A)* 239 and *V(B)* 222 he named Florence Farr.

103. *V&B* II, 216; *V&B1970* 261.

104. See Emanuel Swedenborg, *The Delights of Wisdom Pertaining to Conjugial Love; After which follow the Pleasures of Insanity relating to Scortatory Love* (1768) (especially no. 75, sections V–IX, and no. 359), tr. A. H. Searle (1876), rev. R. L. Tafel (1891), (London: Swedenborg Society, 1891), (O'Shea no. 2038) pp. 73–75, 320–21. See also nos. 50, 56, 69, 188–89, 358 (pp. 53–54, 59–60, 69, 178–79, 320) and *Heaven and its Wonders and Hell: from Things Heard and Seen* (1758, in

Latin), (no. 382), tr. rev. F. Bayley, Everyman's Library series (1909; repr. London: Dent, 1911), (O'Shea 1920s list [probable identification]) pp. 190–91. Yeats recalled this later in letters to Olivia Shakespear, 21 February and 9 March [1933] (*L* 805, 807).

105. [Yeats's note, dated *1924*] When writing this essay I did not see how complete must be the antithesis between man and Daemon. The repose of man is the choice of the Daemon and the repose of the Daemon the choice of man; and what I have called man's terrestrial state the Daemon's condition of fire. I might have seen this, as it all follows from the words written by the beggar in *The Hour Glass* upon the walls of Babylon.[a]

105a. *The Hour Glass* (1902): ' "There are two living countries, one visible and one invisible, and when it is summer there, it is winter here, and when it is November with us, it is lambing-time there." . . . A beggar wrote it upon the walls of Babylon.' (*VPl* 583)

106. Both quotations are from *Nishikigi*, part II, in *Certain Noble Plays*, p. 13: '. . . power, / '.

107. For this reference to St Thomas Aquinas, see note 70 above.

108. 'The Moods' (1893; *P* 56).

109. Yeats recorded this in an entry written after 16 September 1913 in a manuscript book given to him at Christmas, 1912, by Maud Gonne, who was the woman in the dream (Herbert J. Levine, *Yeats's Daimonic Renewal* [Ann Arbor: UMI Research Press, 1983] p. 154, n. 23).

110. Alexander Gilchrist (*Life of William Blake, 'Pictor Ignotus'* [London: Macmillan, 1863] I, 76) coined the term 'Prophetic Books' to describe Blake's works other than lyrics. Blake variously called them 'visions', 'prophecies', 'songs' and 'poems'. See also *P&I* 74.

111. Yeats here paraphrases More, *The Immortality of the Soul*, book III, ch. xiii, section VIII, in *A Collection*, p. 200.

112. Alexander IV, Aegus (Aigos) (323–310 B.C.), posthumous son of Alexander the Great and Roxana, shared rule with Philip Arrhidaeus, in a series of regencies. Aegus and his mother were imprisoned in 316 B.C. by Cassander (350?–297 B.C.), King of Macedonia (316–297 B.C.), and were murdered by his order in 310 B.C. Alexander the Great's second, Asiatic wife, Barsine, eldest daughter of Darius, bore him a son named Heracles; mother and son were put to death in 309 B.C. by Polysperchon, regent of Macedonia.

113. [Yeats's note] I have no better authority for Caesarion[a] than Landor's play.[b]

113a. Caesarion (47–30 B.C.), Cleopatra's child by Julius Caesar, was put to death by order of Octavian (later Augustus), whom Julius Caesar had adopted in 44 B.C.

113b. Walter Savage Landor, *Anthony and Octavius* (1856), in *Poems Dialogues in Verse and Epigrams*, ed. Charles G. Crump (London: Dent, 1909), (O'Shea no. 1083) I (Dramatic Scenes), 325–67.

114. Pericles the younger, son of the Athenian statesman Pericles (*c.* 490–429 B.C.) and his mistress Aspasia (470?–410 B.C.), was executed in 406 B.C., while still in his early twenties.

115. Nicephorus, Michael Constantine Psellus (eleventh-century Byzantine philosopher), no. 7, in *The Chaldaean Oracles of Zoroaster,* ed. Sapere Aude [William Wynn Westcott], vol. VI of Collectanea Hermetica series (London: Theosophical Publishing Society, 1895) p. 47, no. 155: 'Change not the barbarous Names of Evocation for there are sacred Names in every language which are given by God, having in the Sacred Rites a Power Ineffable.'
116. Percy Bysshe Shelley, 'Adonais', stanza XLIV, ll. 8–9, in *The Poems of Percy Bysshe Shelley,* ed. C. D. Locock (London: Methuen, 1911), (O'Shea no. 1905) II, 35: '. . . there / And move like . . . dark and stormy . . .'; on the misquotation of 'move' as 'live', see Harold Bloom, *Yeats* (New York: Oxford University Press, 1970) pp. 188–89 and Herbert J. Levine, *Yeats's Daimonic Renewal* (Ann Arbor: UMI Research Press, 1983) p. 154, note 26; the misquotation was not corrected in *Essays* (1924).
117. Ben Jonson, *Poetaster* (1601), v.i.136–37, in which Horace praises Virgil: 'And for his *poesie,* 'tis so ramm'd with life, / That it shall gather strength of life, with being . . .' (*Ben Jonson,* eds. C. H. Herford and Percy Simpson [Oxford: Clarendon Press, 1932], [O'Shea no. 1029] IV, 293). In the passage Horace is meant to stand for Jonson, and some readers have thought that Virgil is meant to stand for Shakespeare, although, as Jonas A. Barish points out, the relatively early date of Jonson's play argues against that link with Shakespeare.
118. For this Cabbalistic imagery, see note 55 above.
119. See note 55 above.
120. See William Blake, *Milton* (1804–8?), book I, plate 29, l. 3, in *PWB* 234 'a pulsation of the artery' (Erdman, p. 126: 'a Pulsation of the Artery').
121. Perhaps Swedenborg; compare p. 54 above and p. 319, note 26 below. See also pp. 64 and 66 above.
122. Untraced.
123. More, *The Immortality of the Soul,* book III, ch. xiii, section XI, in *A Collection,* p. 228.
124. Edmund Spenser, *The Fairie Queene,* III.vi.33, in *Poems of Spenser,* p. 221: '. . . that Gardin planted bee agayne, / . . . seene / Fleshly corruption, nor mortall payne. / . . . thousand yeares so . . . they there remayne, / . . . . / . . . the chaungefull world . . . / . . . they retourne where . . . / So, like . . . wheele, arownd they ronne from. . . .' Yeats mentioned this passage in his introduction to that collection (*E&I* 366). The marginalia in Yeats's copy of *The Works of Edmund Spenser,* ed. J. Payne Collier (London: Bell and Daldy, 1862), (O'Shea no. 1978A) here reads (II, 456): 'metempsychosis'.
125. William Blake, 'The Divine Image', ll. 9–10, *Songs of Innocence* (1789), in *PWB* 55: '. . . heart; / Pity, a . . .' (Erdman, p. 12: '. . . Mercy . . . heart, / Pity, a . . .').
126. Percy Bysshe Shelley, 'Adonais', stanza LIV, ll. 7–8, in *Poems of Shelley,* ed. Locock, II, 37: '. . . of / The. . . .'
127. See Yeats, 'Vacillation', section IV (1932; *P* 251).

128. For Yeats's opinions of the Scottish essayist and historian Thomas Carlyle (1795–1881), and of the English poet Algernon Charles Swinburne (1837–1900), see *L* 608, *Au* 317, *V(A)* 49 and *V(B)* 116.
129. Emmanuel: 'God with us' (Matthew 1:23). See *SB* 30 and note 41, *Mem* 126, *Au* 379, *V(B)* 233n and 'Leo Africanus' (*c.* 1916?; *YA1* 30).
130. *Odyssey*, XXIV.5–10.
131. Yeats had first visited France during February 1894; Iseult Gonne, daughter of Maud Gonne, was born 6 August 1894.
132. Stéphane Mallarmé (1842–98), French Symbolist poet whose work and conversation Yeats knew from Arthur Symons (*Mem* 98); the remark is from 'Vers et musique en France', *The National Observer*, 26 March 1892, p. 484 [and later incorporated in 'Crise de vers' (1896)]: '. . . une inquiétude du voile dans le temple, avec des plis significatifs et un peu sa déchirure'; '. . . a fluttering in the temple's veil—meaningful folds and even a little tearing' ('Crisis in Poetry', tr. Bradford Cook, *Mallarmé: Selected Prose Poems, Essays, & Letters* [Baltimore: Johns Hopkins Press, 1956] p. 34). On Yeats's first trip to Paris, in February 1894, he had tried to call on Mallarmé (*CL1* 381). See also *L* 671 and *Au* 109 ('Preface' to *The Trembling of the Veil*), 315.
133. For Stanislas de Guaïta, see note 74 above. In 1892–93 the Sâr Péladan and he were accused of black magic in connection with the death of an unfrocked priest, the Abbé Boullan, in Paris; see Richard Ellmann, *Yeats: The Man and the Masks*, 3rd ed. (New York: Norton, 1979) pp. 92–93. The English man of letters is unidentified.
134. Max Dauthendey (1867–1918), German poet and painter. August Strindberg (1849–1912), Swedish playwright, sought to make alchemical gold in Paris during 1894–95; Yeats's only trip to Paris during those years was in February 1894. Strindberg maintained occult and Swedenborgian interests during the next two years in Paris; Yeats's next trip to Paris was December 1896 to January 1897.
135. Stuart Merrill (1867–1918), American-born French poet. In the account of these incidents in *Au* 347–48 the 'young Arabic scholar' is described as a 'Jewish Persian scholar'. For the softness of alchemical gold, see *SB* 60.
136. Villiers de l'Isle Adam (1838–89). Yeats owned a copy of the first edition of *Axël* (Paris: Maison Quentin, 1890), (O'Shea no. 2200). On 24 February 1894, Yeats attended (and reviewed, *UP1* 320–25) a performance of *Axël* with Maud Gonne, who could have translated for him. For the lines quoted by Yeats, see the first English translation, *Axel*, tr. H. P. R. Finberg, pref. W. B. Yeats (London: Jarrolds, 1925), (O'Shea no. 2201): 'This flame that stares at me has perhaps lighted Solomon!' (part III, section I; p. 218); 'Live? Our servants will do that for us!' (part IV, section II; p. 284). Axël and the Commander discuss philosophy in part II, section III (pp. 161–205).
137. 'Une Saison en enfer' ('A Season in Hell') (1873) in *Oeuvres de Arthur Rimbaud: Vers et prose* (Paris: Mercure de France, 1912) p. 268 ('*Mau-*

vais sang' ['Bad Blood'] section of this prose poem): '*Comme je deviens vieille fille, à manquer du courage d'aimer la mort!*'

138. Yeats probably first heard of Stéphane Mallarmé (1842–98) and Paul Verlaine (1844–96) from Arthur Symons in the early 1890s. On his first trip to Paris, in February 1894, Yeats carried introductions to both poets, but he met only Verlaine.
139. Paul Louis Charles Claudel (1868–1955), French diplomat, poet, and dramatist; Francis Jammes (1868–1938), French poet and novelist; and Charles Pierre Péguy (1873–1914), French poet and essayist. See pp. 35–36 above and pp. 309–10, notes 5, 6 and 8–11 below.
140. For Francis Jammes submitting his work to the Pope, see p. 310, note 11 below. Paul Claudel valued his association with country villages such as his birthplace, Villeneuve-sur-Fère, Ainse, sixty miles northwest of Paris, and La Bresse, Vosges.

IF I WERE FOUR-AND-TWENTY

1. From its first issue, 28 June 1919, the weekly *Irish Statesman* emphasized Irish politics and economics, advocating commonwealth status for Ireland. Its editor, George Russell ('AE'), announced in the inaugural issue (p. 4): 'Our hope is that the *Irish Statesman* will serve as a forum for the best constructive thought of Ireland. . . . While neither literary, artistic, and dramatic criticism nor the publication of creative literature is the *raison d'être* of this paper, we shall be no less jealous of its literary than of its political reputation.' 'If I were Four-and-Twenty' was published in its ninth and tenth issues, 23 and 30 August 1919.
2. According to the records of Yeats's automatic script, on 24 November 1919, more than four months after Yeats had completed this sentence in the manuscript draft of this essay (NLI Ms. 30,493), a spirit named Ameritus used this identical sentence; see George M. Harper, *The Making of Yeats's A Vision: A Study of the Automatic Script* (London: Macmillan, 1987) II, 363.
3. Examinations taken at the end of secondary education; established by the Intermediate Education (Ireland) Act of 1878.
4. The church at Mont-Saint-Michel, on the northwest coast of France, was built in 709 by St Aubert of Avranches (d. *c.* 725), bishop of Avranches, at the site of his three visions of St Michael the Archangel, who is often shown conquering a dragon emblematic of Satan (Revelation 12:7–9).

   Michel Eyquem de Montaigne (1533–92), 'Of Profit and Honesty' (1588), in *Essays of Montaigne,* book III, ch. i, tr. Charles Cotton (1685–86), ed. William Carew Hazlitt (1892; new ed. London: Reeves and Turner, 1902), (O'Shea no. 1343) III, 228: '. . . I should easily, in case of need, hold up one candle to St. Michael and another to his dragon, like the old woman. . . .'

   Yeats visited Mont-Saint-Michel in May 1910 with Maud Gonne, who offered a candle to St Michael and told a priest that she prayed a good deal for the National University of Ireland, which had been established in 1908 (*Mem* 246).

5. In July and August 1916 and August 1917 Yeats visited Maud Gonne MacBride at Colleville-sur-Mer (near Vierville-sur-Mer), Calvados, France, sixty miles north-northeast of Mont-Saint-Michel. See p. 35 above, where Yeats identifies the 'friend' as Iseult Gonne and mentions that she read to him the dramatic poem *Mystère de la Charité de Jeanne d'Arc* (1910) by the French poet and essayist Charles Pierre Péguy (1873–1914); see also notes 8–9 below. She also read to him 'Le Poète et l'oiseau: poème dialogué' (1900), by the French poet and novelist Francis Jammes (1868–1938), in *Le Deuil des primevères, 1898–1900* (1901; repr. Paris: Mercure de France, 1917), (O'Shea no. 1012) pp. 123–43.
6. Paul Louis Charles Claudel (1868–1955), French diplomat, poet, and dramatist. He became a Roman Catholic after a mystical experience in 1886; his works show lyric religious fervour and bold imagery. See note 10 below.
7. Henry Adams, in *Mont-Saint-Michel and Chartres* (1904) (Boston: Houghton Mifflin, 1913), (O'Shea no. 19) pp. 76–77, approves the high praise, if not the religious interpretation, that the French novelist Joris Karl Huysmans (1848–1907), author of *La Cathédrale* (1898), had for the statuary on the West (or Royal) portal (*c.* 1145) of Chartres Cathedral: 'If you want to know what an enthusiast thinks of them, listen to M. Huysmans's "Cathedral." "Beyond a doubt, the most beautiful sculpture in the world is in this place." He can hardly find words to express his admiration for the queens, and particularly for the one on the right of the central doorway. "Never in any period has a more expressive figure been thus wrought by the genius of man; it is the chef-d'oeuvre of infantile grace and holy candour. . . . She is the elder sister of the Prodigal Son, the one of whom Saint Luke does not speak, but who, if she existed, would have pleaded the cause of the absent, and insisted, with the father, that he should kill the fatted calf at his son's return." ' Adams adds, 'The idea is charming . . . but, in truth, the figure is that of a queen; an Eleanor of Guienne; her position there is due to her majesty. . . .' For Huysmans, *La Cathédrale,* see also p. 194 above.
8. Charles Péguy, *Le Mystère de la Charité de Jeanne d'Arc* (1910), in *Oeuvres complètes, 1873–1914* (Paris: Éditions de la Nouvelle Française, 1918), (O'Shea no. 1152) v, 195–96: '. . . *jamais des gens de chez nous ne l'auraient abandonné. Des gens du pays français. Des gens du pays lorrain. . . . Jamais nos Français ne l'auraient abandonné ainsi, jamais nos Français ne l'auraient abandonné. Des gens du pays lorrain, des gens du pays français.*'
9. Charles Péguy's *Le Mystère de la Charité de Jeanne d'Arc* is set in the fifteenth century (1425), not the thirteenth century. Péguy, born a peasant, changed his beliefs from ardent revolutionary socialism to patriotic nationalism and nearly mystical Roman Catholicism, although he never became a practising Roman Catholic. He was deeply

moved by the Dreyfus Affair, in which the conviction of Captain Alfred Dreyfus in 1894 was based on false evidence, as was revealed in 1897. Dreyfus was found innocent by a second court martial, in 1899, although he was not reinstated in the French Army until 1906.

10. Yeats was a founder of the Abbey Theatre (Irish National Theatre Society, 1903–) and of the Dublin Drama League (1918–28); the latter specialised in productions of foreign plays. In 1917 in London he saw an English language production of Claudel's *L'Annonce faite à Marie: Mystère en quatre actes* (*The Annunciation*) (1910) and reported to Lady Gregory, 'It was except for the last scene the most moving play I have seen in years' (*L* 626). Yeats owned a copy of its French script (O'Shea no. 393). *L'Otage* (*The Hostage*) (1911) was produced by the Dublin Drama League, 17 February 1924; see *UP2* 433–34.

11. Francis Jammes, untitled prefatory note dated 26 March 1911, in *Les Géorgiques Chrétiennes* (poems) (Paris: Mercure de France, 1912) p. [5], tr. Amy Lowell, in *Six French Poets* (New York: Macmillan, 1915) pp. 265–66: 'On the threshold of this book I confirm that I am a Roman Catholic, submitting very humbly to all the decisions of my Pope, His Holiness Pius X, who speaks in the name of the True God, and that I do not adhere either closely or at a distance to any schism, and that my faith does not permit any sophism, neither the modernist sophism, nor other sophisms; under no pretence will I separate myself from the most uncompromising and most loved of dogmas: the Roman Catholic dogma which is the truth come from the mouth of our Lord Jesus Christ by his Church. I reprove in advance all forestalling which the ideologues, the philosophers, and the reformers would wish to do with this poem.'

12. The French '*unanisme*' (unanimous) poetic movement was begun by Jules Romains (Louis Farigoule) (1885–1972) with the poems of *La Vie unanime* (1908) and by other young writers. The *unanimistes* emphasized the merging of individuals into a group; they endorsed unadorned poetry.

13. Croagh Patrick (Cro-Patrick) (elev. 2,510 feet), five miles southwest of Westport, Co. Mayo, site of an annual pilgrimage on Garland Sunday (last Sunday in July); on its summit, in the fifth century, tradition holds that St Patrick banished snakes from Ireland.

The cave known as St Patrick's Purgatory, on an island in Lough Derg, Co. Donegal, has been a pilgrimage site since the Middle Ages. According to the tradition, St Patrick performed acts of penance there and had a vision of Purgatory; the cave was known throughout mediaeval Europe as an entrance to Purgatory. For details, see Thomas Wright, *St Patrick's Purgatory; An Essay on the Legends of Purgatory, Hell, and Paradise, Current during the Middle Ages* (London: Smith, 1844) and, for a warmly favourable account, the Reverend Daniel Canon O'Connor, *Lough Derg and its Pilgrimages* (Dublin: Dollard, 1879), 2nd ed., enlarged, as *St Patrick's Purgatory, Lough Derg: Its History, Traditions, Legends, Antiquities, Topography, and Scenic Surroundings* (Dublin: Duffy; New York: Benziger Bros, 1895).

14. The fourteenth-century stained-glass windows of St Canice's Cathedral, Kilkenny, were esteemed by the Papal Nuncio, who offered to purchase them in 1645. Five years later they were destroyed by Cromwell's troops.

    Christ Church Cathedral, Dublin, founded in 1038, contains the tomb of Richard Strongbow (d. 1176). As the Church of Ireland diocesan cathedral for Dublin and Glendalough, it was extensively restored in the nineteenth century. The crypt is the oldest part of the building.

    St Patrick baptised the King of Munster at the Rock of Cashel, Co. Tipperary, in the fifth century, and it was the seat of a succession of king-bishops, including Cormac mac Cuilleanáin. Cormac's Chapel, a small Romanesque church, was consecrated in 1134. The adjacent cathedral, now in ruins, dates from the thirteenth century; a tower over its crossing was added in the fifteenth century. For an aerial photo, see *Ireland: A Cultural Encyclopedia*, ed. Brian de Breffny (London: Thames and Hudson, 1983) p. 56. Most Reverend Arthur Price (1679–1752) was Archbishop of Cashel from 1744. James P. McGarry recounts that in 1749 'His Grace Archbishop Price had the roof of the cathedral stripped and used to roof a new cathedral on the nearby plain because he could not drive his coach and four up the incline of the Rock.' (*Place Names in the Writings of William Butler Yeats* [Gerrards Cross, Bucks.: Smythe, 1976] p. 26.) The account in the *Dictionary of National Biography* defends Price, who lies buried at the new cathedral, St Johns, completed in 1783.
15. The bird mentioned by Yeats is untraced. For St Patrick's Purgatory, Lough Derg, see note 13 above.
16. George Bernard Shaw, 'On Going to Church', *The Savoy*, no. 1 (January 1896) p. 24: '. . . vulgarity, savagery'.
17. Rath: circular, prehistoric Irish hill-fort, traditionally inhabited by fairies.
18. Yeats was twenty years old when he met William Morris (1834–96), the English poet, artist and socialist, during Morris's visit to Dublin, 9–14 April 1886, for lectures at the Dublin branch of the Social Democratic Federation. On the evening of 10 April 1886 an audience of 700 or 800 working men at the Saturday Club noisily objected to Morris about the atheism of other, earlier socialist speakers. A brief notice in the *Irish Times* archly remarked that the 'rough and strong sense of Dublin artisans was overmuch' for Morris, whose ' "ideals" were, however, most unfairly as well as rudely treated when "in the end the gas was turned out" ' (12 April 1888, p. 5, col. 1, and Douglas Hyde's diary, quoted in Dominic Daly, *The Young Douglas Hyde: The Dawn of the Irish Revolution and Renaissance 1874–1893* [Totowa, NJ: Rowman and Littlefield, 1974] pp. 75–77). See also *P&I* 276–77, note 3.
19. James M. Connell (b. 1853, Irish-born socialist in London), 'The Red Flag' (1889) (air: 'White Cockade' and, from 1895, 'O Tannenbaum'):

    The people's flag is deepest red;
    It shrouded oft our martyred dead,

And ere their limbs grew stiff and cold,
Their heart's blood dyed its every fold.
Chorus:
Then raise the scarlet standard high!
Within its shade we'll live or die.
Tho' cowards flinch and traitors sneer,
We'll keep the red flag flying here.

Harry Edward Piggott, ed., *Songs that Made History* (London: Dent, 1937) pp. 68–69.

20. James Connolly (1868–1916), Irish socialist and trade union organiser, a leader of the workers in the lockout in Dublin in 1913, organiser of the Irish Citizen Army, and commander in the General Post Office, Dublin, during the Easter Rising, for which he was executed.

21. Karl Marx, *Das Kapital* (3 vols., 1867–95). John Mitchel, *Jail Journal* (1854); he had been convicted in 1848 of advocating armed resistance to English rule in Ireland; see p. 409, note 12 below, and *UP1* 361, 386.

Speeches from the Dock; or, Protests of Irish Patriotism: Containing Speeches Delivered in the Dock by Theobald Wolfe Tone. . . . (Dublin: Gill, 1800; 2nd ed. 1868; repr. 1881, 1882, 1886, 1890, 1893, 1894).

Vladimir Sergeevich Solovof (or Soloviev or Solovyou), *The Justification of the Good: An Essay on Moral Philosophy* (1898, in Russian), tr. Nathalie A. Duddington, Constable's Russian Library (London: Constable, 1918), (O'Shea no. 1958). In this book, the liberal Russian philosopher and poet (1853–1900), who defined the good as truth and righteousness, presents his system of ethics. See notes 36–37 below.

John Augustine Ryan, *Distributive Justice: The Right and Wrong of Our Present Distribution of Wealth* (New York: Macmillan, 1916). Reverend (later Monsignor) Ryan, D.D. (1869–1945), became a leading American Catholic liberal and labor expert; he taught at the Catholic University of America, Washington, DC. In this book, he argues for private ownership of land, as a natural right, and cites St Thomas Aquinas and Pope Leo XIII's encyclical 'Rerum Novarum: On the Condition of Labor' (1891).

Charles Dominic Plater, S.J., rector (1916–20) of Campion Hall, Oxford (renamed from Plater's Hall in 1918), worked to arouse Catholics to a sense of social needs. Father Plater published pamphlets on topics such as 'Retreats for Working-men' and 'Letters to Catholic Soldiers', through the Catholic Truth Society and the Catholic Social Guild; during four weeks in 1917 he was active in the distribution of 40,000 pamphlets for the Catholic Social Guild on the peace note from Pope Benedict XV.

22. *The Daily Herald*, a popular London daily, was strongly pro-Labour; the *Morning Post* was a conservative London daily.

23. Sinn Féin ('Ourselves' or 'Our Own Thing'): Irish independence movement, founded 1905–8 and reorganised in 1917 when Eamon de Valera became its president.

24. Yeats owned nearly all of a forty-volume English translation (1895–98; repr. 1901; O'Shea nos. 76–111) of Honoré de Balzac's collection of novels and stories, *Comédie humaine* (1842 ff.).
25. John Trivett Nettleship (1841–1903), English artist, a friend of J. B. Yeats.
26. For Friedrich Wilhelm Nietzsche, see note 30 below. Honoré de Balzac, *About Catherine de' Medici* (1841); see p. 368, note 25 below. Charles Darwin, *On the Origin of Species by Means of Natural Selection* (1859).
27. The quotation is untraced. Yeats's opinion here agrees with Friedrich Nietzsche; see *The Will to Power: An Attempted Transvaluation of All Values*, [vol. II], tr. Anthony Ludovici, vol. XV of *The Collected Works of Friedrich Nietzsche*, ed. Oscar Levy (Edinburgh and London: Foulis, 1910), (O'Shea no. 1441) 301 (book IV 'Discipline and Breeding', part I 'The Order of Rank', section II 'The Strong and the Weak', subsection 864).
28. Victor Marie Hugo (1802–85), French novelist, dramatist, poet.
29. Napoleon I, Napoleon Bonaparte (1769–1821), who was born in Corsica, figures in Balzac's story about a Corsican blood-feud, 'La Vendetta', in *At the Sign of the Cat and Racket* (1830).
30. Nietzsche, who was Yeats's source for this image, locates the plant in Java rather than Sri Lanka (Ceylon). Friedrich Nietzsche, *Beyond Good and Evil: A Prelude to a Philosophy of the Future* (1886), section 258, in *Nietzsche as Critic, Philosopher, Poet and Prophet: Choice Selections from his Works*, ed. Thomas Common (London: Grant Richards; New York: Dutton, 1901) p. 118: '. . . Society is *not* entitled to exist for its own sake, but only as a substructure and scaffolding, by means of which a select race of beings may elevate themselves to their higher duties, and, in general, to a higher *existence*—comparable to the sun-seeking, climbing plants in Java (they are called *Sipo matador*), which encircle an oak so long and so often with their arms, until at last, high above it, but still supported by it, they can spread their tops in the open light and manifest their felicity.'
31. Untraced. Balzac would rise at midnight and then write until dawn, drinking strong coffee to stay awake. His essay 'Traité des excitants modernes' (1838) includes a section on coffee (*Études analytiques* [Paris: Les Bibliophiles de l'Originale, 1968] pp. 260–65). Yeats repeated this comment on Balzac in a list of examples of the association of ignorance and genius (*V[A]* 96; *V[B]* 162).
32. François Marie Charles Fourier (1772–1837), French social scientist and reformer, advocated socialist cooperatives.
33. In Balzac's 'The Unconscious Mummers' ('*Les Comédiens sans le savoir*') (1845, publ. 1846), Dubourdieu, an artist who has been 'driven crazy by Fourier's notions', proudly describes his preposterous painting of an 'allegorical figure of Harmony' with six breasts and, at her feet, 'an enormous Savoy cabbage, the Master's symbol of Concord'. A few pages later Balzac introduces an ardent Republican chiropodist, Publicola Masson, who bears 'a certain resemblance to Marat'; while trimming the corns of Léon de Lora, a Parisian landscape painter of a

noble family, Masson says, '. . . Genius is an odious privileged class that receives far too much here in France. We shall be forced to demolish a few of our great men to teach the rest the lesson that they must be simple citizens.' (*The Unconscious Mummers,* tr. Ellen Marriage, *Comédie humaine,* ed. George Saintsbury [London: Dent Edition, 1895–98], repr. as vol. XXXVI of Temple Edition [New York: Macmillan, 1901], [O'Shea no. 108] pp. 46, 44, 45, 62, 63.) In *Samhain* 1908, Yeats had described Dubourdieu as 'a sculptor, a follower of the Socialist Fourier, who has made an allegorical figure of Harmony, and got into his statue the doctrine of his master by giving it six breasts and by putting under its feet an enormous Savoy cabbage' (*Ex* 238).

34. Yeats had cited a fuller version of this proverb in 1886: ' "The food of the passions is bitter, the food of the spirit is sweet," say the wise Indians' (*UP1* 87).

35. Leonardo da Vinci (1452–1519) did not paint a group with father, mother and children; Yeats may have been remembering the serene mood of Leonardo's paintings *The Virgin of the Rocks* (Virgin, young St John, infant Christ and an angel) (two versions: 1483–86, Paris, Louvre; 1503–6, London, National Gallery); *St Anne, the Virgin and the Infant Christ with a Lamb* (1510, Paris, Louvre); or a large cartoon, *St Anne, the Virgin, the Infant Christ and the Young St John* (1498, London, National Gallery).

36. Solovyof (Soloviev), *The Justification of the Good,* e.g., p. 354 (ch. viii, section IX); see note 21 above.

For Aristotle on Distributive Justice, see the *Nicomachean Ethics,* v.ii.12–iii.17.

37. Solovyof (Soloviev), *The Justification of the Good,* discusses the spiritualisation of the soil on pp. 346–47 and 357–58; for his asceticism see pp. 41–58 (ch. ii, 'The Ascetic Principle in Morality').

38. Thomas Davis (1814–45), 'Lament for the Death of Eoghan Ruadh O'Neill', l. 27, in *A Book of Irish Verse Selected from Modern Writers,* ed. W. B. Yeats (London: Methuen, 1895 and 2nd ed., 1900) p. 138: '. . . shepherd, when . . . out the sky'. Owen Roe O'Neill, who was defeated by Cromwell, died 10 November 1649. In a lecture on Thomas Davis, celebrating the Davis centenary, 20 November 1914, Yeats praised this poem and read it, saying 'it moves me always, and by its poetical feeling. . . . It has the intensity of the old ballads and to read it is to remember Parnell and Wolfe Tone, to mourn for every leader who has died among the ruins of the cause he had all but established, and to hear the lamentations of the people.' ('Thomas Davis', *New Ireland,* 17 July 1915, repr. in *Tribute to Thomas Davis* [Cork: Cork University Press; Oxford: Blackwell, 1947] pp. 13–14.)

39. Dante (1265–1321), François Villon (1431–55), Shakespeare (1564–1616), Cervantes (1547–1616).

40. Percy Bysshe Shelley (1792–1822); John Ruskin (1819–1900); William Wordsworth (1770–1850); William Blake (1757–1827); Jean Jacques Rousseau, French philosopher and author (1712–78); see Blake, an-

notation to Wordsworth's *Poems,* p. 3: 'I see in Wordsworth the Natural Man rising up against the Spiritual Man Continually' and Blake, *Jerusalem,* 'To the Deists', plate 52: 'Rousseau thought Men Good by Nature' (Erdman, pp. 654, 199).

41. William Morris, *News from Nowhere* (1890), ch. xxii, in *The Collected Works of William Morris* (London: Longmans Green, 1912), (O'Shea no. 1389) XVI, 149–50.
42. George Bernard Shaw, 'Ibsen' [obituary essay], *The Clarion* (London), no. 756, 1 June 1906, p. 5, col. b: 'murders and combats and ghosts'; 'morbid horror of death'. Yeats first made this point in 'The Subject-Matter of Drama' (1906), in *Discoveries* (*E&I* 283). Shaw's article has been reprinted in *Shaw and Ibsen: Bernard Shaw's The Quintessence of Ibsenism and Related Writings,* ed. J. L. Wisenthal (Toronto: University of Toronto Press, 1979).
43. Garden city: model suburban village or town with park and gardens, organised for healthy living; the term originated with the Garden City Pioneer Company, Ltd in 1903 (OED Supplement).
44. From 1887 until the early 1890s Yeats attended Sunday evening Socialist lectures at the Hammersmith Club, adjacent to the home of William Morris (1834–96), Kelmscott House, Upper Mall, Hammersmith. Yeats probably first met Lionel Johnson in 1889.
45. For example, Swedenborg, *Heaven and . . . Hell,* no. 595 (p. 336): 'the inhabitants of the hells cannot be saved'.
46. For John O'Leary (1830–1907), see p. 408, note 6 below; the philanthropist is unidentified.
47. John Calvin (French, 1509–64) and John Knox (Scottish, 1505–72), Protestant reformers; Girolamo Savonarola (1452–98), zealous religious leader in Florence.
48. Untraced. The quoted phrase expresses part of the ideology of the Danish folk high school movement, founded in 1851 by Kristen Mikkelsen Kold (1816–70); its spiritual father was the Danish theologian, poet and philologist Nikolai F. S. Grundtvig (1783–1872), a student of sagas (and translator of *Beowulf*).
49. Eugène Auguste-Albert Comte de Rochas d'Aiglun (1837–1914), French authority on hypnotism and a psychical investigator. The specific reference is untraced. Yeats owned five of his books (O'Shea nos. 1774–77): *La Science des philosophes et l'art des thaumaturges dans l'antiquité* (1882), 2nd ed. (Paris: Dorbon-Ainé, [1912]) [on Hero of Alexandria and Philo of Byzantium]; *Les états profonds de l'hypnose* (1892), 5th ed. (Paris: Bibliothèque Chacornac, 1904), bound with *Les états superficiels de l'hypnose* (*c.* 1892), 5th ed. (Paris: Chamuel, 1897); *L'extériorisation de la sensibilité: Étude expérimentale et historique* (1895), 6th ed. (Paris: Bibliothèque Chacornac, 1909); and *L'extériorisation de la motricité: Recueil d'expériences et d'observations* (1896), 4th ed. (Paris: Bibliothèque Chacornac, 1906), (O'Shea no. 1175). De Rochas also wrote *Les Forces non définies* (Paris: Masson, 1887); *Le Fluide des magnétiseurs* [on Reichenbach's odic light] (Paris: Carré, 1891) and *Les Vies successives: documents pour l'étude de cette question* (Paris: Bibliothèque Chacornac, 1911).

50. Yeats was a founder of the National Literary Society, Dublin, in the summer 1892. Douglas Hyde's inaugural address as president of the society, on 25 November 1892 (not 1894), was titled 'The Necessity for De-Anglicising Ireland'; that influential speech was published in 1894 in *The Revival of Irish Literature: Addresses by Sir Charles Duffy, K.C.M.G., Dr George Sigerson, and Dr Douglas Hyde* (London: Unwin, 1894) pp. 117–61. See *CL1* 338 and n. 1.
51. In July 1919, when Yeats was finishing this essay, he received an invitation to teach in Japan for two years. For 'unity of being', see p. 383, note 22 below.

SWEDENBORG, MEDIUMS, AND THE DESOLATE PLACES

1. Yeats began collecting folklore with Lady Gregory (1852–1932) (née Isabella Augusta Persse) in 1897 in the vicinity of Coole Park, Co. Galway; see also p. 411, note 25 below.

   In his folklore essay 'Away' (1902), Yeats explained that 'what the Arran people call "the battle of the friends" ' is 'believed to be fought between the friends and enemies of the living among the "others," to decide whether a sick person is to live or die' (*UP2* 282); for an instance at Kiltartan, Co. Galway, see his 'Irish Witch Doctors' (1900; *UP2* 228).

   Yeats admired Lady Gregory's literary adaptation of the local dialect of the Kiltartan barony, which includes her estate, Coole Park; see Yeats to Robert Bridges, 20 July [1901], *L* 354 and especially the original section I of his preface to her *Cuchulain of Muirthemne: The Story of the Men of the Red Branch of Ulster* (1902) (*P&I* 225). Two of the best known of her one-act comedies are *Spreading the News* (perf. 1904) and *Hyacinth Halvey* (perf. 1906).

   For the old man who 'may know the secret of the ages', see also p. 210 above and *Mem* 126.
2. For Yeats's active investigations of spiritism, beginning in autumn 1911, see note 52d below. In the introduction (1934) to his play *The Cat and the Moon* he explained that he chose mediums 'in poor districts where the questioners were small shopkeepers, workmen and workmen's wives' (*VPl* 807–8), although he did not mention specifically the London districts Soho and Holloway.
3. The Society for Psychical Research was founded in London in 1882 by advocates of the scientific study of psychical phenomena.

   Philippus Aureolus Paracelsus (Theophrastus Bombastus von Hohenheim, 1493?–1541), Swiss alchemist and physician, preface to *Liber Paragranum*, tr. and quoted in Franz Hartmann, *The Life of Philippus Theophrastus, Bombast of Hohenheim, Known by the Name of Paracelsus and the Substance of his Teachings concerning Cosmology, Anthropology, Pneumatalogy, Magic and Sorcery, Medicine, Alchemy and Astrology, Phi-*

losophy and Theosophy (London: Redway, 1887) p. 18: 'I have not been ashamed to learn that which seemed useful to me even from vagabonds, executioners, and barbers.' See also Paracelsus, '*Das erste Buch der Grossen Wundarznei*', in *Paracelsus: Selected Writings*, ed. Jalande Jacobi (1942), tr. Norbert Guterman, Bollingen Series XXVIII (1950; 2nd ed., New York: Pantheon Books, 1958) p. 4: 'I went not only to the doctors, but also to barbers, bathkeepers, learned physicians, women, and magicians who pursue the art of healing; I went to alchemists, to monasteries, to nobles and common folk, to the experts and the simple.'

4. For Yeats receiving spiritual information, prior to 1914, see *Mem* 127–28. The remark by Anatole France (pseudonym of Jacques Anatole François Thibault) (1844–1924), French novelist, critic, poet and playwright, is untraced.
5. Allan Kardec (pseudonym of Hippolyte Léon Denizard Rivail) (1803–69) was the author of *Spiritualist Philosophy. The Spirits' Book Containing the Principles of Spiritist Doctrine on the Immortality of the Soul; the Nature of Spirits and their Relations with Men; the Moral Law; the Present Life, the Future Life, and the Destiny of the Human Race* (1857, 1860; Eng. tr. 1875); *Experimental Spiritism. Book on Mediums; or, Guide for Mediums and Invocators* (1861; Eng. tr. 1874); and *Practical Spiritism. Heaven and Hell; or, The Divine Justice Vindicated in the Plurality of Existences* (1865; Eng. tr. 1878).
6. For an instance of the occult 'mediaeval tradition', see *The Kabbalah Unveiled* (London: Redway, 1887), (O'Shea no. 1292a), which was translated and edited by S. L. MacGregor Mathers, a fellow member with Yeats of the Golden Dawn; see also p. 298, note 55 above. For the Neoplatonists Plotinus, Porphyry, Synesius, and John Philoponus, see note 83 below; for Proclus, see p. 380, note 70 below. For the seventeenth-century Cambridge Platonists Ralph Cudworth and Henry More, see, for example, note 82 and p. 361, note 18 below. For Paracelsus, see note 3 above. For Japanese Noh plays, see p. 304, note 98 above and notes 17 and 95 below.

   Emanuel Swedenborg, *The Spiritual Diary: Being the Record during Twenty Years of his Supernatural Experience*, tr. George Bush and Rev. John H. Smithson, 5 vols. (London: Speirs, 1883–1902), (O'Shea nos. 2040–40D); the marginalia in Yeats's copy refer to Blake and probably date from the late 1880s or very early 1890s, when Yeats and Edwin J. Ellis were at work on their three-volume edition and study of Blake, *WWB*. Ellis and Yeats mention Blake's interest in Jacob Boehme (1575–1624), German theosophist and mystical writer.
7. Before 1745, his fifty-eighth year, Swedenborg wrote more than thirty scientific papers and books in Latin, plus another thirty-seven in Swedish, mostly before 1724. The subjects include cosmology, theoretical physics, astronomy, geometry, mathematics, anatomy, mineralogy and engineering. The nebular hypothesis—that the solar system was formed from a rotating nebula—is usually credited to the French astronomer and mathematician Marquis Pierre Simon de La-

place, who stated it in a note to his *Exposition du système du monde* (1796).

8. Immanuel Kant, in *Dreams of a Spirit-Seer, Illustrated by Dreams of Metaphysics* (1766), tr. and ed. Frank Sewall (London: Swan Sonnenschein; New York: Macmillan, 1900), did regard Swedenborg's access to a spirit-world seriously enough to investigate its implications for philosophy, although Kant then dismissed 'the wild chimeras of this worst of all dreamers' (p. 111). Kant reported three anecdotes: Swedenborg in 1761 [sic, 1758] astonished a princess by telling her, in response to a question from her, information that he must have gained from the dead; Swedenborg learned from a dead man that a missing receipt could be found in a hidden partition of a closet; and Swedenborg in 1759 described, while in Gothenburg, a fire occurring at that moment at Stockholm (pp. 93–95). Earlier, in a letter of 10 August [1763], Kant had told the second and third of those anecdotes to Charlotte von Knobloch (pp. 155–59). All of these anecdotes and Kant's letter were collected by J. F. I. Tafel in *Documents concerning the Life and Character of Emanuel Swedenborg*, tr. and ed. I. H. Smithson; rev. ed., George Bush (New York: Allen, 1847) pp. 93–103.
   The anecdote about sailors is based on Swedenborg's voyage, 1–8 September 1766, from England to Stockholm; see Tafel, *Documents*, pp. 63–64 (letter from C. Springer, Swedish Consul at the Port of London to the Abbé Pernetti, librarian to the King of Prussia, 18 January 1783).
9. William Blake, *Milton* (1804–8?), plate 22, l. 50, in Erdman, p. 117, and *The Marriage of Heaven and Hell* (*c.* 1790–93), plate 21, in *PWB* 190 (Erdman, p. 41).
10. Swedenborg, *Heaven and . . . Hell*, nos. 449–50, 461 (pp. 227–29, 236): '. . . world. With . . . his own life and . . . that which he. . . .'; '. . . spiritual, the . . . touches and sees what. . . .' See also *V(B)* 209.
11. Rath: circular, prehistoric hill-fort, traditionally inhabited by faeries.
12. Swedenborg, *Heaven and . . . Hell*, nos. 463, 462A (pp. 240, 239): '. . . memory, remain. . . .'; '. . . the places, words . . . scene is presented to the. . . .'
13. See, for example, Swedenborg, *Heaven and . . . Hell*, nos. 89 (pp. 38–39), 487 (p. 261: '. . . nothing natural exists without something spiritual corresponding to it . . .').
14. Swedenborg, *Heaven and . . . Hell*, no. 477 (p. 251): '. . . it, or. . . .' For his conversations with shades who had been learned scholars but who had become simple, see no. 464 (p. 242).
15. For this reference to St Thomas Aquinas in Villiers de l'Isle Adam's drama *Axël*, see p. 301, note 70 above.
16. Swedenborg, *Heaven and . . . Hell*, nos. 488–89 (pp. 261, 263).
   Claude Lorraine (or Lorrain; professional name of Claude Gellée) (1600–82), French landscape painter.
17. [Yeats's note] The Japanese Noh play *Awoi no Uye* has for its theme the exorcism of a ghost which is itself obsessed by an evil spirit. This evil spirit, drawn forth by the exorcism, is represented by a dancer wearing a 'terrible mask with golden eyes'.[a]

17a. Ujinobu, *Awoi no Uye,* in Ernest Fenollosa and Ezra Pound, *'Noh' or Accomplishment: A Study of the Classical Stage of Japan* (London: Macmillan, title page 1916 [January 1917]), (O'Shea no. 1637) p. 204; for this demonic mask, or *hannya,* see also pp. 53 and 194.

18. See p. 334, note 8 below.

19. Untraced.

20. Swedenborg, *Heaven and . . . Hell,* no. 414 (pp. 209–10): 'the spring-time of life'; '. . . more thousands of years . . .'; 'come in process of time'; 'In a word, to grow old. . . .' See also p. 455, note 59 below.

21. Swedenborg, *Heaven and . . . Hell,* no. 553 (p. 308): 'In general their faces are dreadful and void of life, like those of corpses; but in some instances they are black, and in others gleaming like torches: in others they are disfigured with pimples, warts and large ulcers; some seem to have no face at all, but . . . place something . . . bony; and with some only the teeth are seen.'

22. *V&B* II, 218; *V&B1970* 262.

23. *V&B* I, 189; *V&B1970* 115. Slieve Ochta (Echtge or Slieve Aughty) is a range of mountains east of Gort and south of Loughrea, Co. Galway. For George Pollexfen, see p. 382, note 7 below.

24. Swedenborg, *Spiritual Diary,* no. 1622 (II, 19): 'They are extremely fond of fabricating'.

25. Swedenborg, *Spiritual Diary,* nos. 2860–61, quoted in George Bush and B. F. Barrett, tr., *'Davis' Revelations' Revealed; being A Critical Examination of the Character and Claims of that Work in its relations to the Teachings of Swedenborg* (New York: Allen, 1847) pp. 13–14: ' "This has many times been shown to me, that . . . know otherwise than that . . . men who were the men who were the subject of thought; and neither . . . know otherwise; as yesterday . . . to-day, some one . . . life [was represented by one] who was . . . all things which belonged to him, so . . . as they were known . . . nothing was more like: wherefore, let those who speak with spirits beware lest they be deceived, when they say that they are those whom they know, and that they are dead."

' "For . . . of a like faculty; and when similar things . . . man, and are thus represented to them, they think that they . . . same person: then all the things are called forth from the memory which represent those persons, both the words, the speech, the tone, the gesture, and other things; besides that they are induced to think thus, when other spirits inspire them; for then they are in the phantasy of those, and think that they are the same." ' A later translation by Bush and the Reverend John H. Smithson, which Yeats owned (1883; O'Shea no. 2040A) is more distant.

26. Compare Swedenborg, *Heaven and . . . Hell,* nos. 254, 246, 255–56 (pp. 111, 106–7, 111–12): 'The spirit is then under the impression that he is the Lord. . . .' (no. 254, p. 111); '. . . when an angel or a spirit approaches a man, and by turning towards him comes into association with him, he enters so completely into his whole memory that the languages and all else that the man know seem almost like matters

of his own knowledge. . . . the language of the man appears to them as their own, and so does all his knowledge. . . . I have also spoken . . . with spirits who would not believe that it is the man who speaks, but believed that they were speaking in the man; they believed also that man knows nothing but what they tell him. . . .' (no. 246, pp. 106–7); '. . . they are again in possession of their own angelic and spiritual language and know nothing of the language of man.' (no. 255, p. 111); '. . . then the man would think that the resulting thoughts were his own, whereas they would be the spirit's. . . .' (no. 256, p. 112).

27. See Swedenborg, *Conjugial Love,* no. 182, section 3 (p. 168) and *Heaven and . . . Hell,* nos. 489, 580 (pp. 262, 326). See also Swedenborg, *Spiritual Diary,* no. 4305 (III, 361–62).

28. Emanuel Swedenborg, *Arcana Coelestia. The Heavenly Arcana Contained in the Holy Scripture; or Word of the Lord, Unfolded, in an Exposition of Genesis and Exodus, together with a Revelation of Wonderful Things Seen in the World of Spirits and in the Heaven of Angels* (1749–56 in Latin), tr. John Clowes (1783, vol. I), 13 vols. (1861; repr. London: Swedenborg Society, 1891), (O'Shea no. 2037: vol. I only). The entire last volume is a detailed, comprehensive index.

29. For this reference to Thomas Lake Harris, see p. 358, note 48 below.

Although Swedenborg did not found the Churches of the New Jerusalem, it relies on his writings and accepts spiritualism and other psychic phenomena as manifestations of its fundamental doctrine, 'the correspondence of the natural world to spiritual reality' (*Corpus Dictionary of Western Churches,* ed. Thomas C. O'Brien [Washington: Corpus, 1970] p. 203).

30. Blake to George Cumberland, 12 April 1827; 'Public Address' (*c.* 1810), p. 24; annotation (1798) to R. Watson, *An Apology for the Bible* (1797), p. 11; annotation (*c.* 1820) to Berkeley, *Siris* (1744), p. 214; in Erdman, pp. 707, 571, 606, 653.

Edwin J. Ellis and Yeats, in their edition of Blake in 1893, pointed out that Blake considered the dome of St Paul's an example of 'intellectual error', as opposed to the inspiration that characterises Gothic architecture (*WWB* I, 38); see *P&I* 309–10, note 15 (note by Yeats); see also Blake's celebration of a victory of 'Living Proportion' over 'Mathematic Proportion', in *Milton,* plate 5, l. 44, in Erdman, p. 98.

Blake quoted in Henry Crabb Robinson, 'Diary', 13 June 1826 and 'Reminiscences' (1852), in G. E. Bentley, Jr., *Blake Records* (Oxford: Clarendon Press, 1969) pp. 352, 548. *A Descriptive Catalogue* (1809), no. v, p. 43; *Marriage of Heaven and Hell,* plate 22; *Vala, or The Four Zoas* (1795–1804), Night the Second, p. 34, l. 80; '[Vision of the Last Judgment]' (1810), (Notebook, pp. 69–70), in Erdman, pp. 534, 43, 317 ('every thing that . . .'), 545 ('to my Imaginative Eye').

31. Blake was born 28 November 1757, the year in which Emanuel Swedenborg had a vision of the Last Judgment; Swedenborg died, in London, in 1772. His first work to be translated into English was *Heaven and . . . Hell,* in 1778, when Blake was twenty-one. Blake's eldest brother, James (1753–1827), is the Swedenborgian referred to

here; see Yeats's introduction to *PWB* (*P&I* 79); the quoted phrase is from Frederick Tatham, 'Life of Blake' (ms., *c.* 1832), first publ. in *The Letters of William Blake*, ed. Archibald G. B. Russell (London: Methuen, 1906), transcribed in Bentley, *Blake Records*, p. 509. John Flaxman (1755–1826), English sculptor and draughtsman, met Blake in 1780; Blake broke with him in the winter of 1805–6 (*Blake Records*, pp. 173–74, 232–33).

32. Swedenborg, *Heaven and . . . Hell*. Blake, *The Marriage of Heaven and Hell* (1790?–93), plate 3, para. 1, in *PWB* 177 (Erdman, p. 34).

33. For example, Blake's 'Laughing Song' (1789), 'Nurse's Song' (1789), 'A Little Girl Lost' (1789–94), in *PWB* 53, 59, 68–69 (Erdman, pp. 11, 15, 29); see also Vala's garden in *Vala, or The Four Zoas* (1795–1804), Night the Ninth, ll. 390–557, in Erdman, pp. 380–85.

Yeats purchased thirteen slides of pastoral scenes by the English artists Samuel Palmer (1805–81) and Edward Calvert (1799–1883) to use with a lecture, 'William Blake and his School', that he delivered only once, at the Abbey Theatre, Dublin, 14 April 1918. The seven prints by Calvert, which range in size from 4 x 8 cm. to 11 x 17 cm., are *The Ploughman* [also known as *Christian Ploughing the Last Furrow of Life*] (1827), engraving; *The Bride* (1828), engraving; *The Sheep of His Pasture* (1828), engraving (state I); *Ideal Pastoral Life* (1829), lithograph; *The Brook* (1829), wood-engraving (state I); *The Return Home* (1830), wood-engraving (state I) and *The Chamber Idyll* (1831), wood engraving (state I); for literature and reproductions see Raymond Lister, *Edward Calvert* (London: Bell, 1962) pp. 100–6 and plates XVII [state III] (6), XXIII (8), XXVII [state II] (9A), XXVIII (11), XXX (12A), XXXV (14A), XXXVI (15A), XXXVII (15A), XL [state II] (15A). Five of the prints by Palmer are etchings of pastoral scenes, which range in size from 10 x 8 cm. to 13 x 20 cm.; they are *The Herdsman's Cottage* [also known as *Sunset*] (1850); *Christmas* [also known as *Folding the Last Sheep*] (1850); *The Rising Moon* [also known as *An English Pastoral, A British Pastoral* and *Evening Pastures*] (1857); *The Weary Ploughman* [also known as *The Herdsman* and *Tardus Bubulcus*] (begun 1858) and *The Early Ploughman* [also known as *The Morning Spread upon the Mountains*] (begun before 1861; publ. 1868). The sixth print by Palmer is *The Lonely Tower* [illustration to Milton's 'Il Penseroso'] (completed 1879), etching, 17 x 23 cm. (etched surface). For literature and reproductions of all six see Raymond Lister, *Samuel Palmer and his Etchings* (London: Faber and Faber; New York: Watson-Guptill, 1969), pp. 76–79, 81–87, 100–6, 108 and plates 3, 4, 7–9, 12.

Calvert and Palmer were influenced by Blake's small wood-engravings to Virgil's Eclogue I, seven of which are included in Yeats's slides for the lecture: illustrations to Ambrose Philips, 'Imitation of Eclogue I', in *The Pastorals of Virgil, with a Course of English Reading, Adapted for Schools*, ed. Robert John Thornton, M.D., 3rd ed. (London, 1821) I, facing pp. 14–16 (nos. 2, 3, 5–8, 10), (1820–21) (David Bindman, *The Complete Graphic Works of William Blake* [London: Thames and Hudson, 1978], nos. 603–4, 606–9, 611.

34. Blake, *The Marriage of Heaven and Hell,* plate 4, in *PWB* 178 (Erdman, p. 34 '. . . Eternal Delight'); '[Vision of the Last Judgment]' (Notebook, p. 87), in *PWB* 252: '. . . passion, but . . . intellect, from . . . emanate, uncurbed. . . .' (Erdman, p. 554: 'The Treasures . . . Heaven . . . Negations . . . Passion . . . Realities . . . Intellect . . . which All the Passions Emanate Uncurbed . . . Eternal Glory'); *Jerusalem,* ch. 4, plate 91, ll. 54–57, in Erdman, p. 249: 'I care not whether a Man is Good or Evil; all that I care / Is whether he is a Wise Man or a Fool. Go! put off Holiness / And . . . Intellect'.
35. Blake, *Europe, a Prophecy* (1794), plate 14, l. 3, in Erdman, p. 64: '. . . wave, when the cold moon drinks the dew'.
36. See p. 384, note 28 below.
37. See Blake, *Vala, or The Four Zoas* (1795–1804), Night the Ninth, ll. 1–6, in Erdman, pp. 371–72.
38. Sir Edward (not his brother Thomas) Kelly (or Kelley) (1555–95), an English alchemist who was knighted in Prague, was the scryer (crystal gazer) for Dr John Dee (1527–1608), English mathematician and astrologer. On 1 September 1584, Edward Kelly and Dr Dee saw 'three little Creatures walk up and down in the Sun-shine'. When Kelly announced that he wanted to communicate with them directly, instead of using the crystal, Dr Dee warned him against any departure for their conventional practice of scrying: '. . . In the stone we have warrant that no wicked thing shall enter: but without the stone, Illuders might deal with us, unlesse God prevented it' (*A True and Faithful Relation of What passed for Many Years Between Dr. John Dee and Some Spirits* [London: Garthwait, 1659] p. 228). The angel named Uriel, who appeared in the crystal, often rebuked Kelly for such prideful independence (pp. 230, 366, 373–75).
39. Crabb Robinson's recollection of Blake's conversation, diary for 10 December 1825, quoted in Bentley, *Blake Records,* p. 310: 'I must have had conversations with him [i.e., Socrates]—so I had with Jesus Christ—I have an obscure recollection of having been with both of them' and Alexander Gilchrist, *Life of William Blake,* 2nd ed. (London: Macmillan, 1880) I, 382; *Jerusalem* (1804–20), ch. ii, ll. 23–24; *A Descriptive Catalogue,* no. III, p. 20; *Jerusalem,* ch. ii, plate 32, l. 35; in Erdman, pp. 176 ('Merlin . . . the Vegetative Man & his Immortal Imagination'), 526 ('Shakespeare's Fairies also are the rulers of the vegetable world'), 177 ('Accident & Chance').
40. *The Marriage of Heaven and Hell,* plates 14 and 11, in *PWB* 185, 183 (Erdman, pp. 38, 37 ('enlarged & numerous . . .').
41. For Allan Kardec, see note 5 above.
42. Andrew Jackson Davis (1826–1910), American mesmerist and spiritualist, wrote more than thirty books. Yeats owned four books that were reprinted in 1911 and a compendium published in 1917 (O'Shea 1920s list).
43. Davis described these events in *The Magic Staff; An Autobiography* (New York: Brown, 1857) pp. 110–11, 146–51, 201–10, 227–29, 231, 234–35, 237, 238–40 (speech by Galen), 242–43 (speech by Swedenborg), 246, 248. The travelling mesmerist was Dr J. S. Grimes, in

1843. Davis was first mesmerised by his neighbour, William Livingston. The somnambulistic trance was on 6–7 March 1844.

44. Dr George Bush, professor of Hebrew at the University of New York, in letters to the *New York Tribune,* 15 November 1846 and 10 August 1847, collected in Andrew Jackson Davis, *Events in the Life of a Seer; Being Memoranda of Authentic Facts in Magnetism, Clairvoyance, Spiritualism* (1866), 6th ed. (Boston: Banner of Light Publishing Co., n.d.), (repr. 1911; O'Shea 1920s list) pp. 31–35, 49–53 and summarised in Frank Podmore, *Modern Spiritualism* (London: Methuen, 1902) I, 166. Bush pointed to a detailed account of Swedenborg's *The Economy of the Animal Kingdom, Considered Anatomically, Physically, and Philosophically* (1758 in Latin), ed. J. J. Garth Wilkinson, tr. Rev. Augustus Clissold (London: Newberry; Boston: Clapp, 1846) in Davis's *The Principles of Nature, Her Divine Revelations, and a Voice to Mankind* (dictated 1845–46) (1847; repr. Rochester, NY: Austin, 1911), (O'Shea 1920s list).

45. For example, Swedenborg, *Spiritual Diary,* no. 4437 (III, 419–20). *V&B* I, 175; *V&B1970* 107.

46. Yeats's source for the quoted phrases about Davis is untraced. For the faery 'touch' or 'stroke', see Yeats's folklore essays (*UP2* 80, 174–76, 220, 228–29, 270, 275–76, 281).

47. For Allan Kardec and his books on spiritism, see note 5 above.

48. In *Moby Dick* (ch. 98), Ishmael remarks: '. . . Away we sail to fight some other world, and go through young life's old routine again. Oh! the metempsychosis! Oh! Pythagoras, that in bright Greece, two thousand years ago, did die, so good, so wise, so mild; I sailed with thee along the Peruvian coast last voyage—and, foolish as I am, taught thee, a green simple boy, how to splice a rope!' (Herman Melville, *Moby Dick; or, The Whale,* ed. Harrison Hayford and Hershel Parker [New York: Norton, 1976] p. 423.)

49. Untraced.

50. Johann Wilhelm Meinhold (1797–1851), German theologian and writer, *Sidonia the Sorceress. The Supposed Destroyer of the Whole Reigning Ducal House of Pomerania,* tr. Lady Wilde (Hammersmith: Kelmscott Press, 1893) p. 43: '. . . We find no record in Scripture' of the prophets 'having forgotten the oracles they uttered, like the Pythoness & others inspired by Satan. [Note:] It is well known that somnambulists never remember, upon their recovery, what they have uttered during the crisis.' Also in another edition (London: Reeves and Turner, 1894), (O'Shea no. 1304A [with Anne Yeats bookplate dated 1934]) I, 59.

51. See Swedenborg, *Arcana Coelestia,* nos. 5853, 5857–64, Rotch Edition of *Swedenborg's Works* (Boston and New York: Houghton Mifflin, 1907) X, 429, 431–34 and *Heaven and . . . Hell,* nos. 249, 256 (pp. 108, 112).

52. [Yeats's note] Besides the well-known books of Aksakof, Myers, Lodge, Flammarion, Flournoy, Maxwell, Albert de Rochas, Lombroso, Madame Bisson, Delanne, etc.,[a] I have made considerable use of the researches of Dr Ochorowicz published during the last ten or

twelve years in *Annales des Sciences Psychiques* and in the English *Annals of Psychical Science*,[b] and of those of Professor Hyslop published during the last four years in the *Journal* and *Transactions of the American Society for Psychical Research*.[c] I have myself been a somewhat active investigator.[d]

52a. Alexander Nikolaevich Aksakof (or Aksakov) (1832–1903), Russian spiritualist, translator of Swedenborg and founder of the journal *Psychische Studien* (1874; now titled *Zeitschrift für Parapsychologie*). Because of Russian censorship he published mainly in German and French. Among his many translations and books are *Animismus und Spiritismus* (1890 in German, 1893 in Russian, 1895 in French), *A Case of Partial Dematerialization of the Body of a Medium* (Boston, 1896) and *Der Spiritualismus und die Wissenschaft* (Leipzig, 1898).

Frederic William Henry Myers (1843–1901), English psychical researcher, a founder of the Society for Psychical Research in 1882 and its president in 1900. His books on spiritualism are *Science and a Future Life, and Other Essays* (1893) and *Human Personality and its Survival of Bodily Death* (posthumous, 1903); he was coauthor, with Edmund Gurney and Frank Podmore, of an important study of psychical phenomena, *Phantasms of the Living* (1886).

Sir Oliver J. Lodge (1851–1940), distinguished English physicist and president of the Society for Psychical Research (1901–4 and honorary co-president in 1932). Two of his works on spiritualism were published prior to 1914: *The Survival of Man: A Study in Unrecognised Human Faculty* (1909) and his presidential address, 'Continuity', to the British Association for the Advancement of Science, 1913. Yeats owned one of Lodge's later books, *Raymond; or, Life and Death, with Examples of the Evidence for Survival of Memory and Affection after Death* (O'Shea 1920s list), published in November 1916, which gained extensive public notice.

Camille Flammarion (1842–1925), French astronomer and psychical researcher. His books include *Unknown Natural Forces* (1865), *L'Inconnu et les problèmes psychiques* (1900) and *Mysterious Psychic Forces* (1907). Yeats later owned Flammarion's *Death and its Mystery before Death: Proofs of the Existence of the Soul* (1920; Eng. tr. 1921–23), 3 vols. (O'Shea no. 678).

Théodore Flournoy (1854–1920), Swiss psychologist at the University of Geneva and author of *Métaphysique et psychologie* (1890 and 1919), *Des Indes à la planète Mars: étude sur un cas de somnambulisme* (1900), *Nouvelles observations sur un cas de somnambulisme* (1902), *Esprits et médiums: mélanges de métaphysique et de psychologie* (1911; Eng. tr. 1911 as *Spiritism and Psychology*); see also p. 388, note 9 below.

Joseph Maxwell (1858–1938), French magistrate and psychical investigator, author of *Metapsychical Phenomena: Methods and Observations* (1903; expanded Eng. tr. 1905), *La Magie* (1921), *La Divination* (1927) and *Le Tarot* (1933).

For Albert de Rochas (1837–1914), French authority on hypnotism and a psychical investigator, see p. 315, note 49 above.

Cesare Lombroso (1835–1909), Italian psychiatrist and criminal anthropologist, author of *After Death—What? Spiritistic Phenomena and their Interpretation* (1909), tr. W. S. Kennedy (London: Unwin; Boston: Small, Maynard, 1909), (O'Shea no. 1145).

In May 1914 in Paris, Yeats witnessed ectoplasmic manifestations at several séances at the home of Juliette Alexandre Bisson; he owned her book *Les Phénomènes dits de materialisation: étude expérimentale* (Paris: Librairie Feleix Alcan, 1914), (O'Shea no. 195).

Gabriel Delanne (1857–1926), French engineer and spiritualist, editor of the *Revue scientifique et moderne de spiritisme.* His books include *Le Phénomène spirite* (1893); *Le Spiritisme devant la science* (1895?); *Recherches sur la médiumnité* (1896, 1902); *L'Évolution animique: essais de psychologie physiologique suivant le spiritisme* (1897); *Evidence for a Future Life* (1904; Eng. tr. 1904); and *Les Apparitions matérialisées des vivants & des morts* (2 vols., 1909–11), (O'Shea no. 513, vol. II only: *Les Apparitions des morts* [Paris: Libraire Spirite, 1911]).

52b. Julien Ochorowicz (1850–1917), Polish psychical researcher, psychologist and co-director (from 1907) of the Institut Général Psychologique, Paris. His psychical research, mainly on materialisations by the medium Stanislawa Tomczyk (later Mrs Fielding), are described in six articles, illustrated with photographs, in *Annales des Sciences Psychiques* (Paris), the first of which was translated in *The Annals of Psychical Science* (London) and the second, which includes photographs to which Yeats refers, was partially translated by James Hyslop in the *Journal of the American Society for Psychical Research,* with illustrations. See pp. 65 and 67 above and notes 76 and 87 below. The six articles in French and the two English translations are: (1.) 'Un nouveau phénomène médiumnique', *Annales des Sciences Psychiques,* 13 (1909), 1–10, 45–51, 65–77, 97–105, 129–32; 'A New Mediumistic Phenomenon', *The Annals of Psychical Science,* 8 (April–December 1909), 271–84 (April–June), 333–99, 515–33. (2.) 'Les Phénomènes lumineux et la photographie de l'invisible', *Annales des Sciences Psychiques,* 13 (1909), 193–201 ['Le Portrait de la "Petite Stasia" '], 235–41, 275–82, 298–306, 334–39; excerpts and summaries in 'Experiments of Dr Ochorovics: Report of a Commission of Naturalists', tr. James H. Hyslop, *Journal of the American Society for Psychical Research,* 5 (1911), 678–721. (3.) 'Les Rayons rigides et les Rayons X: Études expérimentales', *Annales des Sciences Psychiques,* 14 (1910), 97–105, 129–35, 172–78, 204–9, 225–30, 257–62, 295–301, 336–43. (4.) 'Nouvelle étude expérimentale sur la nature des "rayons rigides" et du courant médiumnique', *Annales des Sciences Psychiques,* 15 (1911), 161–65, 199–202, 230–35, 276–79. (5.) 'Radiographies des mains: Monographie expérimentale', *Annales des Sciences Psychiques,* 15 (1911), 296–302, 334–41; 16 (1912), 1–8. (6.) 'Les Mains fluidiques et la photographie de la pensée', *Annales des Sciences Psychiques,* 16 (1912), 97–103, 147–52, 164–69, 204–9, 232–39. Also Yeats owned a clipping (NLI Ms. 30,005) of Hereward Carrington's illustrated article, 'Fluidic Hands: The Latest in Medium Photography', *New York Times,* 28 July 1912, part 5, p. 8, which includes the spirit photograph of 'Little Stasia' and a summary of Ochorowicz's psychic investigations with Tomczyk.

52c. James Hervey Hyslop (1854–1920), American philosopher, psychologist and psychical researcher, re-established the American Society for Psychical Research and edited its *Journal* and *Transactions,* both of which began in 1907. He was a principal contributor to each issue of the *Journal* and the *Proceedings,* and he edited the reports, in each issue, of psychical phenomena. Hyslop wrote studies of an American medium, Mrs Minnie Meserve Soule ('Mrs Chenoweth' or 'Mrs C') from 1909; Yeats noted Hyslop's report of a séance in the 1912 *Proceedings of the American Society for Psychical Research* (*Mem* 266, 292–302); for additional details see Arnold Goldman, 'Yeats, Spiritualism, and Psychical Research', in *Yeats and the Occult,* ed. George M. Harper (Toronto: Macmillan, 1975) pp. 109–18. Yeats owned a copy of Hyslop's later book, *Life after Death: Problems of the Future Life and its Nature* (New York: Dutton, 1919), (O'Shea no. 944).

52d. In autumn 1911, during a visit to the United States, Yeats met the medium Mrs Minnie Meserve Soule ('Mrs Chenoweth' or 'Mrs C') (d. 1937), and from then frequently attended séances (e.g., *L* 569). In the spring of 1912 he met Elizabeth Radcliffe in Kent and investigated her automatic writing, especially during the summer of 1913 (Yeats, 'Preliminary Examination of the Script of E[lizabeth] R[adcliffe]' [1913], ed. George M. Harper and John S. Kelly, in *Yeats and the Occult,* pp. 130–71; NLI Ms. 30,358; *L* 581–84); he first encountered the spirit 'Leo Africanus' (see p. 297, note 44 above) on 9 May 1912 at a séance in Wimbledon with the American medium Mrs Etta Wriedt (1860–1942). In February 1913 he joined the Society for Psychical Research. In May 1914 he travelled to France to investigate bleeding oleographs of the Sacred Heart at Mirebeau; see his report, ' "A Subject of Investigation": Miracle at Mirebeau', ed. George M. Harper, in *Yeats and the Occult,* pp. 172–89. During that trip he saw luminous ectoplasmic manifestations at séances in Paris (see note 52a above). In lectures delivered January 1912 and February 1919, Yeats spoke of his interest in spiritism and other psychical phenomena, and in a lecture 'Ghosts and Dreams' (NLI Ms. 30,629), delivered October 1913 and April 1914, he reported that he 'had the strongest reasons to believe that the soul survived death very little changed. . . . When the soul died it went over the most passionate moments in its life. When those passions exhausted themselves it passed into a state of lucidity, which corresponded to the state one entered at rare moments in dreams' (*The Irish Times,* 1 November 1913, p. 7, col. b).

53. John Beaumont, *An Historical, Physiological and Theological Treatise of Spirits, Apparitions, Witchcrafts, and Other Magical Practices . . . With a Refutation of Dr Bekker's World bewitch'd* . . . (London, 1705), (O'Shea no. 138) p. 3: '*Larva*'.

54. The Anglo-French armies met the invading Germans in the 'Battles of the Frontiers', 14–25 August 1914, and then in the Battle of the Marne, east of Paris, 5–11 September, with very heavy casualties on each side. That was followed, 15 September–24 November, by the

'Race to the Sea', a series of battles that eventually settled into trench warfare. Yeats finished this essay on 14 October 1914.

55. The Gordon Highlander and the Royal Munster Fusilier regiments.
56. Untraced; for A. J. Davis, see note 42 above.
57. [Yeats's note] Henry More considered that 'the animal spirits' were 'the immediate instruments of the soul in all vital and animal functions' and quotes Hippocrates, who was contemporary with Plato, as saying, 'that the mind of man is . . . not nourished from meats and drinks from the belly but by a clear and luminous substance that redounds by separation from the blood.'[a] Ochorowicz thought that certain small oval lights were perhaps the root of personality itself.[b]

57a. See p. 301, note 77 above.
57b. For a probable identification of this reference, see p. 367, note 16 below.
58. The three previous sentences on materialisations are based on Cesare Lombroso, *After Death—What?*, pp. 72, 332–33 (also 120), 335–36, 329, 248.

    For spirit photographs, see p. 355, note 35d below.
59. Yeats first published this in 'Mortal Help' (1902) (*Myth* 9–10).
60. Bloomsbury: British Museum. The Serbian (Servian) sculptor Ivan Meštrović (1883–1962), who was heavily influenced by Auguste Rodin, became a favourite of Yeats's. The title *Frowning Man*, which was not used by Meštrović, would be apt for any of these sculptures by Meštrović: *Srdja Zlopogledja* (1908), plaster, twice life-size; *Miloš Obilic* (1908), bronze, 260 cm. height; head of *Kraljevic Marko* (1910), bronze, life-size; studies for equestrian statue of *Kraljevic Marko*, plaster (1909–11) and bronze (1911). All are in the National Museum, Belgrade; for illustrations see Laurence Schmeckebier, *Ivan Meštrović: Sculptor and Patriot* (Syracuse, NY: Syracuse University Press, 1959) plate 9 (*Srdja Zlopogledja*); Duško Kečkemet, *Ivan Meštrović* (New York: McGraw-Hill, 1976) plates 22–24 (*Miloš Obilic*), plates 33–34 (*Kraljevic Marko*); and [Ivan Meštrović], *The Sculpture of Ivan Meštrović* (Syracuse: Syracuse University Press, 1948) plate 5.

    Auguste Rodin, *L'Homme au nez cassé* (1863–64), bronze mask, 24 cm. height; illus. in Albert E. Elsen, *Rodin* (New York: Museum of Modern Art, 1963) p. 106.
61. The title character of Molière's comedy *Le Tartuffe* (1669).
62. The Italian artist Antonio Mancini (1852–1931) drew a pastel portrait of Yeats (1907) and painted oil portraits of Lady Gregory and his patron Hugh Lane. Thomas Bodkin reported, in *Hugh Lane and his Pictures* (1932, repr. Dublin: Browne and Nolan, 1934) facing plate 37: 'In his middle period, staining after excessive high-lights, he was accustomed, so he told me, to incorporate in the actual pigment rough pieces of tinfoil, glass, or mother-of-pearl.' An example of Mancini's sumptuous middle style is his portrait 'The Marquis del Grillo' (retouched and dated 1899), oil on canvas, 2.8 x 1.9 m., Hugh Lane Municipal Gallery of Modern Art, Dublin (Lane collection, group 2); *Hugh Lane and his Pictures*, plate 38.

63. For spirit photographs see p. 355, note 35d below. For the paraffin imprints of materialised spirits at séances of the famous Italian medium Eusapia Palladino (1854–1918), see p. 302, note 81 above.
64. In the sixteenth century, Sir Thomas Elyot (*c.* 1490–1548) and, in the seventeenth century, the Cambridge Platonists: Benjamin Whichcote (1609–83), Henry More (1614–87), Ralph Cudworth (1617–88), John Smith (1618–52) and Nathanael Culverwel (1618–51).

[William Law], 'An *Explication* of some *Latin* and other Words used by *This Author* [Boehme] in a *peculiar Sense*, and occurring in the foregoing *Treatises*' in *The Way to Christ Discovered and Described in . . . Treatises by Jacob Behmen* (Bristol: Mills, 1775) p. 425 (in entry under 'Image. Imagination'): 'The Word *Image* meaneth not only a *Creaturely Resemblance* . . . But signifieth also a *Spiritual Substance*, the *Product* or *Effect* of a *Working Will*, wrought in and by a *Spiritual Being* or *Power*. And *Imagination*, which we are apt errôneously to consider as only an *airy*, *idle*, and *impotent Faculty* of the human Mind, dealing in Fiction, and roving in Fancy or Idea, without producing any powerful or permanent Effects, is the *Magia*, and *Power* of raising and forming such *Images* or *Spiritual Substances*. Now this *Magia*, or *Imaginative Property*, which hath *Desire* for its *Root* or *Mother*, is the greatest *Power* in *Nature*; its Works cannot be hindered, for it *creates* and *substantiates* as it goes, and all things are possible to it.' For a corresponding passage in Boehme, see *The Threefold Life of Man* (1620; Eng. tr. 1650), ch. vi, verse 2, in *The Works of Jacob Behmen: The Teuton Theosopher* (London, 1764), (O'Shea no. 239) II, 58 (separately paginated): '. . . so the *human* Word goeth also forth out of the Center of the Spirit, in shape, property, and form, and it is no other, than that the Spirit maketh such a substance, as the Creation itself is, when it expresseth the form of the Creation.'
65. Joseph Glanvill (Glanvil) (1636–80), English divine and philosopher, admirer of Henry More. See, for example, his *Sadducismus Triumphatus: or, a Full and Plain Evidence, Concerning Witches and Apparitions* [title spelt *Saducismus* . . . in the earlier editions, 1681–1700], part I, sections XI, XII, 4th ed. (London: Bettesworth and Batley, 1726), (O'Shea no. 750) pp. 23–24, 27–28.
66. Untraced. The reference probably is not to Julien Ochorowicz, who conducted experiments at Warsaw with the medium Eusapia Palladino and 'John King' in 1893 and 1894, and with the medium Stanislawa Tomczyk and 'Little Stasia' in 1909; see notes 68 and 76 below and p. 65 above.
67. Galanty show: a shadow pantomime.
68. John King, a spirit 'control' (an intermediary between the medium and the spirit 'communicator') for several mediums, beginning in 1850 with the American brothers Ira E. Davenport (1839–77) and William H. Davenport (1841–1911), and including Mrs Samuel (Agnes Nichol) Guppy (English, d. 1917, see p. 450, note 25 below); Charles Williams (English, fl. 1870s, see p. 450, note 25 below); Helena Petrovna Blavatsky (Russian-born, 1831–91), during her early career as a spiritualist; and Eusapia Palladino (Italian, 1854–1918).

John King claimed to have been Sir Henry Owen Morgan (1635?–88), the Welsh buccaneer and Lieutenant-Governor of Jamaica. For 'control', see also p. 65 below.

69. The specific reference is untraced. For Albert de Rochas (1837–1914), French authority on hypnotism and a psychical investigator, see p. 315, note 49 above.

70. See *Odyssey*, XI.35–43, 95–99, 152–54, etc. William Bedell Stanford, in notes to his edition *The Odyssey of Homer* (2nd ed. [London: Macmillan, 1964] I, 383), has pointed out the parallel with West of Ireland folklore in *Myth* 93.

71. In 1888 Yeats had quoted this from 'an old countryman' (*FFT* 128; *P&I* 17).

72. See Swedenborg, *Spiritual Diary*, nos. 2436, 4236–37, 4244 (II, 248; III, 337, 339). See also *V(B)* 227.

73. Synesius, *On Visions* (*c.* 404), 140, in *The Chaldaean Oracles of Zoroaster*, no. 145, ed. Sapere Aude [William Wynn Westcott], vol. VI of the Collectanea Hermetica series (London: Theosophical Publishing Society, 1895) p. 46: '. . . down unto the Darkly-Splendid World; wherein . . . Depth, and . . . in clouds, delighting. . . .' See also George Robert Stow Mead, *The Chaldaean Oracles* [vols. VIII–IX of *Echoes from the Gnosis*] (London: Theosophical Society, 1908), (O'Shea 1920s list) II, 86; Mead, 'The Augoeides or Radiant Body', *The Quest* (London), 1 (July 1910), (O'Shea no. 1299) 719; and note 88 below.

74. In 1856 the French magician Robert Houdin (1805–71) used illusionist tricks to persuade Algerian chieftains that his sorcery, sponsored by the French colonial government, was more powerful than that of the fanatical Arab wonder-workers (Marabouts), who were inciting Algerian tribes to revolt.

75. Untraced.

76. Julien Ochorowicz considered but then rejected the possibility that a picture was placed in front of the lens, in 'Les Phénomènes lumineux et la photographie de l'invisible', *Annales des Sciences Psychiques*, 13 (1909), 197, col. a; see 193–201 ['Le Portrait de la "Petite Stasia" '], with a reproduction (p. 196). For an English translation by James Hyslop, see 'Experiments of Dr Ochorovics: Report of a Commission of Naturalists', *Journal of the American Society for Psychical Research*, 5 (1911), 704 and figure VIII (p. 729). Yeats owned a newspaper clipping (NLI Ms. 30,005) of Hereward Carrington's illustrated article, 'Fluidic Hands: The Latest in Medium Photography', *New York Times*, 28 July 1912 (part 5, p. 8), which includes the spirit photograph of 'Little Stasia' and a summary of Ochorowicz's psychic investigations with his medium, Stanislawa Tomczyk; for them, see note 52b above; for spirit photographs, see p. 355, note 35d below.

77. *V&B* II, 216; *V&B1970* 261. For the mischievous, shape-changing sprite Robin Goodfellow as a 'three-foot stool', see Shakespeare, *Midsummer Night's Dream* (II.i.52). For witches' gold as dried cow dung, see *V&B* I, 77, 85, 196; II, 41; *V&B1970* 54, 59, 120, 169.

78. 'On the Sign of Socrates' ('A Discourse Concerning the Daemon of Socrates'), section XXIV (593D–94A), in *Plutarch's Moralia*, tr. Phillip H. DeLacy and Benedict Einarson, Loeb Classical Library (London: Heinemann; Cambridge: Harvard University Press, 1959) VII, 481–85. See also page 11 above.
79. *V&B* I, 106–7, 109–10; *V&B1970* 70, 72; see also Yeats's essay 'Irish Witch Doctors' (1900), *UP2* 222.
80. Reginald Scot (1541–99), *The Discoverie of Witchcraft* (1584), ed. Brinsley Nicholson (London: Stock, 1886), (O'Shea no. 1857) pp. 356–57 (book XIV, ch. xvii), see also pp. 335–36 (book XV, ch. viii).
81. *Religio Medici* (part I, section XXXI), in *Religio Medici, and Urn-Burial*, Temple Classics, ed. Israel Gollancz (London: Dent, 1896), (O'Shea no. 289) p. 46: '. . . own inventions have . . . Spirits; (for . . . Heaven . . . fellow Natures on Earth;)'.
82. For testimony from witchcraft trials, see pp. 74–80 above. At this time Yeats owned at least the following works by Henry More (1614–87) (O'Shea nos. 1377–79): *A Collection of Several Philosophical Writings . . . as Namely, his An Antidote against Atheism [1652; 3rd ed., 1662]. A Brief Discourse of the Nature, Causes, Kinds and Cure of Enthusiasm [1656]. Epistolae Quator ad Renatum Des-Cartes [1662]. The Immortality of the Soul [1659]. Conjectura Cabalistica [1653]*, 2nd ed. (London, 1662); *The Immortality of the Soul, So Farre Forth as it is Demonstrable from the Knowledge of Nature and the Light of Reason* (London, 1659); *The Theological Works [An Explanation of the Grand Mystery of Godliness. An Enquiry into the Mystery of Iniquity. A Prophetical Exposition of the Epistles to the Seven Churches in Asia. A Discourse of the Grounds of Faith in Points of Religion. An Antidote against Idolatry. Divine Hymns]* (London: Downing, 1708). He later acquired More's *Philosophical Poems, Comprising Psychozoia and Minor Poems*, ed. Geoffrey Bullough (Manchester: Manchester University Press, 1931), (O'Shea no. 1379).

    Joseph Glanvill (Glanvil), *Saddducismus Triumphatus* (O'Shea no. 750); see note 65 above.

    Ralph Cudworth (1617–88), *The True Intellectual System of the Universe. The First Part; wherein, All the Reason and Philosophy of Atheism is Confuted* (1678), 3 vols. (London: Tegg, 1845), (O'Shea no. 454); Yeats also owned the one-volume London 1678 edition, which he received as a gift on 26 March 1917 (O'Shea no. 453).

    George Robert Stow Mead (1863–1933), English theosophist and writer, was editor of the London quarterly *The Quest*. The two essays are 'The Spirit-Body: An Excursion into Alexandrian Psycho-Physiology', *The Quest*, 1 (April 1910), (O'Shea no. 1298) 472–88, and 'The Augoeides or Radiant Body', *The Quest*, 1 (July 1910), (O'Shea no. 1299) 705–26. Earlier, Mead had served as private secretary to Madame Blavatsky (from 1887) and then as general secretary of the Theosophical Society and editor of its journal (1890–98).
83. Plato (427?–347 B.C.); Plotinus (205?–270), Egyptian Neoplatonic philosopher; Porphyry (232?–304?), Syrian Neoplatonic philosopher; Synesius (365–430?), Neoplatonic philosopher and (later) bishop of

Ptolemais; John Philoponus (7th c.), Neoplatonic philosopher at Alexandria.

84. Untraced; compare Henry More, *Immortality of the Soul* (1659), book I, ch. vii and book II, chs. v–vii, in *A Collection of Several Philosophical Writings*, 2nd ed. (London: William Morden, 1662), (O'Shea no. 1377) pp. 31–33, 164–79.

85. George Robert Stow Mead paraphrases Porphyry (*De Antro Nympharium*, xi) in 'The Spirit-Body: An Excursion into Alexandrian Psycho-Physiology', *The Quest: A Quarterly Review*, 1 (April 1910), (O'Shea no. 1298) 483: 'souls . . . them, and. . . .'

86. Henry More, *The Præexistency of the Soul* (1647), stanza 58, ll. 4–5, in *The Complete Poems of Dr Henry More (1614–1687)*, ed. Alexander B. Grosart (Blackburn, 1878) p. 124: '. . . of oyl, meal . . . water, hony'.

87. Julien Ochorowicz, 'Les Phénomènes lumineux et la photographie de l'invisible', *Annales des Sciences Psychiques*, 13 (1909), 201; for an English translation by James Hyslop, see 'Experiments of Dr Ochorovics: Report of a Commission of Naturalists', *Journal of the American Society for Psychical Research*, 5 (1911), 714–15. See also notes 52b and 76 above.

88. John Philoponus, *Aristotelis de Anima*, tr. George Robert Stow Mead, in 'The Spirit-Body: An Excursion into Alexandrian Psycho-Psychology', *The Quest*, 1 (April 1910), (O'Shea no. 1298) 485 and 481: 'It is readily "moulded into the shape of its surrounding body, just as happens with ice, which takes the shape of the vessels in which it is formed" ' and 'the spirit itself have no special form'.

89. Henry More, *Immortality of the Soul* (1659), in *A Collection of Several Philosophical Writings*, 2nd ed. (London, 1662), (O'Shea no. 1377) pp. 167–68 (book III, ch. v, sections IX, X): 'the *Plastic* power'; '. . . Figure . . . appearance resemble . . . creature: But. . . .'; '. . . *Genii*'; 'into a different modification of the *Human shape*. [. . .] Not that the *Plastick* virtue [. . .] shall renew all the lineaments'; '. . . visible feature of . . . Person'.

90. John Philoponus, *Commentary on Aristotle, On the Soul*, tr. George Robert Stow Mead, in 'The Spirit-Body: An Excursion into Alexandrian Psycho-Psychology', *The Quest*, 1 (April 1910), (O'Shea no. 1298) 485: '. . . manifest, it . . . movement; or . . . of daimonic cooperation . . .' The paraphrased passage about Homer is not from Philoponus, but from Porphyry; Yeats's source is p. 481, note 2 by Mead.

91. Synesius (365–430?), Neoplatonic philosopher and (later) bishop of Ptolemais, was a correspondent of Hypatia (d. *c.* 415), Neoplatonic philosopher renowned for her beauty. Yeats closely paraphrases Synesius, *On Visions* (*c.* 404; before he became a Christian), 137D, tr. George Robert Stow Mead, in 'The Augoeides or Radiant Body', *The Quest* (London), 1 (July 1910), (O'Shea no. 1299) 717. That passage is also available in *The Chaldaean Oracles of Zoroaster*, ed. Sapere Aude [William Wynn Westcott], vol. VI of the Collectanea Hermetica series (London: Theosophical Publishing Society, 1895) pp. 37–38, no. 91: 'This Animastic Spirit which blessed men have called the Pneumatic

Soul, becometh a god, an all-various Daemon, and an Image (disembodied), and in this form of Soul suffereth her punishments. The Oracles, too, accord with this account; for they assimilate the employment of the Soul in Hades, to the delusive visions of a dream.'

92. Henry Cornelius Agrippa von Nettesheim (1486?–1535), German physician, theologian and occultist, wrote *Three Books of Occult Philosophy* (w. 1510), tr. John French (London, 1651), and (perhaps) *Henry Cornelius Agrippa, His Fourth Book of Occult Philosophy*, tr. Robert Turner (London, 1655). Yeats quotes from *Three Books of Occult Philosophy*, book III, ch. xli (pp. 479–80): 'to the plantastick reason'; '. . . the heaven falling . . . their head, sometimes of being consumed by the . . . a gulfe, sometimes . . . up into the . . . taken, and . . . by devils. . . .'; 'hags, and goblins'.

93. More, *The Immortality of the Soul*, book III, ch. iii, sections XI–XIII, in *A Collection*, p. 159.

94. More, *The Immortality of the Soul*, in *A Collection*, 182 (book III, ch. ix, section IV): '[their] comely . . . playing, with accents so . . . soft, as . . . imagine the Aire here of it self to . . . Lessons, and . . . Musical. . . .'; 183 (book III, ch. ix, section VIII) [likely source of 'a fleecy and milky light']: 'bounding their sight with such a white faint splendour as is discovered in the Moon'; 181 (book III, ch. ix, section IV): 'sing, and play, and . . . *Animal life* . . . World. For every thing . . . does as . . . were tast . . . cask, and . . . some coursness and foulness with it'; 119 (book II, ch. xiv, section VII): 'In the *Aëreal* the Soul . . . inhabit, as they define, many ages, and . . . the *Aethereal* for . . .'; 151 (book III, ch. ii, section II): '. . . *Round* . . . *Oval*. . . .'

95. The Noh play *Motome-zuka* (*The Maiden's Tomb*) (14th c.), attributed to Kiyotsugu. During the winter of 1913–14, while staying with Yeats at Stone Cottage, Coleman's Hatch, Sussex, Ezra Pound began working on the papers of Ernest Fenollosa (1853–1908), an American scholar who had spent eighteen years in Japan. The first published English translation was by Marie C. Stopes and Joji Sakurai, in *Plays of Old Japan: The 'Nō'* (London: Heinemann, 1913) pp. 39–52. See also p. 14 above, *V(A)* 225, *V(B)* 231 and *VPl* 777.

96. Thomas Lake Harris (1823–1906), English-born American spiritualist and founder of utopian communities. When Harris visited England in 1859, Laurence Oliphant (1829–88), English writer and politician, became his disciple. Harris subjected Oliphant to a severe probation as a manual labourer at Harris's community farm at Brockton, New York; later, when Oliphant married, Harris kept the couple apart for long periods. Oliphant eventually charged Harris with fraud and recovered much of the money he had entrusted to him. Even so, Oliphant continued to believe in Harris's psychic powers. The quotation is untraced.

97. Ernest Fenollosa, 'Fenollosa on the Noh' (*c.* 1906?), ed. Ezra Pound, in Ernest Fenollosa and Ezra Pound, *'Noh' or Accomplishment: A Study of the Classical Stage of Japan* (London: Macmillan, [t.p. 1916] January 1917), (O'Shea no. 1637) pp. 127, 129, 130: '. . . entangled—whose . . . dear? tangled up as . . . tangled in this. . . . are to-day our. . . .

sleep, and. . . .' (p. 127); 'vanished into the love-grave' [copy-text reads: 'slipped into the shadow of the cave'], 'spinning, and painted sticks', '. . . love promise of long perished incarnations' (p. 129); '. . . hill, where . . . the pines' (p. 130). The play is *Nishikigi* by Motokiyo, printed in Fenollosa and Pound, pp. 131–49, and in *Certain Noble Plays of Japan*, pp. [1]–16.

98. A brief, untitled Aran folktale collected by Lady Gregory (*V&B* I, 123; *V&B1970* 79). See also *E&I* 232 and *V(B)* 222.

99. In the opinion of T. G. Henry James, formerly Keeper of Egyptian Antiquities, British Museum, who worked in that collection from 1951 to 1988, the two references here might be (a)—for the august, public statue—the colossal red granite head (height 2.87 m.) of Amenophis III, which used to dominate the northern end of the main Sculpture Gallery, in front of the great doorway to the stairs (XVIII dynasty; exhibition no. 15; in 1909 it was thought to be of Thothmes III and was no. 360) and (b)—for the more naturalistic statue—a large painted limestone, standing statue (height 1.30 m.) of Nenkheftka (V dynasty; no. 1239, no. 33 in 1909). For illustrations, see T. G. H. James and W. V. Davies, *Egyptian Sculpture* (Cambridge: Harvard University Press, 1983) plate 36 (no. 15) (colour) and plate 20 (no. 1239); *A Guide to the Egyptian Galleries (Sculpture)* (London: British Museum, 1909) p. 105 ([no. 15 as] no. 360 'Thothmes III'); and I. E. S. Edwards, T. G. H. James and A. F. Shore, *A General Introductory Guide to the Egyptian Collections in the British Museum* (1964; repr. London: British Museum, 1971) p. 185, figure 65 (no. 1239) and 2nd ed., titled *An Introduction to Ancient Egypt* (New York: Farrar Straus Giroux, 1979) p. 200 (no. 1239).

100. Doneraile, Co. Cork, a village seven miles northeast of Mallow. The shepherd is also cited at pp. 72 and 208 above.

101. [Yeats's note] Herodotus has an equivalent tale. Periander, because the ghost of his wife complained that it was 'cold and naked', got the women of Corinth together in their best clothes and had them stripped and their clothes burned.[a]

101a. Periander, tyrant of Corinth (625–585 B.C.), in Herodotus, *History*, book V, ch. xcii, section VII, tr. Rev. Henry Cary, Bohn's Classical Library (London: Bell, 1912), (O'Shea no. 885) p. 344; see also *V(A)* 239.

102. Sir Thomas Browne, *Religio Medici*, I, xxx, in *Religio Medici, and Urn-Burial*, Temple Classics, ed. Israel Gollancz (London: Dent, 1896), (O'Shea no. 289) p. 45: '. . . they may assume, steal, or. . . .' See also *V(A)* 207 and *V(B)* 297.

103. *Paradiso*, XXX.124.

104. *The Odyssey of Homer*, XI.601–8, tr. Samuel Henry Butcher and Andrew Lang (1879; repr. London: Macmillan, 1918) pp. 190–91: '. . . gods, and . . . of great Zeus, and of Here of . . . flying every way in fear, and he like . . . Night, with . . . around, like. . . .' Hebe: Greek goddess of youth, daughter of Zeus and Hera (Here).

WITCHES AND WIZARDS AND IRISH FOLK-LORE

1. Adam Clarke (1760 or 1762?–1832), Irish Methodist preacher and orientalist. 'A family of *travelling tinkers*' showed him 'a copy of the three books of *Cornelius Agrippa's Occult Philosophy*' (*An Account of the Religious and Literary Life of Adam Clarke,* ed. J. B. B. Clarke, 3 vols. in 1 [1833; repr. New York: Mason and Lane, 1837] pp. 68–69 [vol. I, book I]). For Cornelius Agrippa, see p. 332, note 92 above.
2. The visionary friend probably was George William Russell ('AE'), who was born in Ulster but was not Unionist or a Freemason. The shepherd at Doneraile, Co. Cork, is also cited at p. 208 above. For 'Tetragramaton Agla', see p. 412, note 32 below.
3. *V&B* II, 267–68; *V&B1970* 288–89.
4. Joseph Glanvill (Glanvil), *Sadducismus Triumphatus*, part II, relation VIII (p. 326): '. . . Witness . . . Huntsman . . . out whith a Pack . . . Hounds . . . Hare . . . *Julian Cox* . . . House, he . . . Hare: The Dogs . . . Ring . . . Huntsman . . . Hare . . . spent, and making toward a . . . Bush . . . Bush . . . up, and . . . Dogs . . . Hands . . . *Julian Cox* . . . Head groveling on . . . Globes . . . he express'd it) upward: He . . . Hair . . . Head . . . Breath, that . . . Answer: His Dogs . . . up with full Cry . . . Game . . . and smelt at her, and . . . Hunting any farther. And . . . Huntsman . . . Dogs . . . presently, sadly. . . .'
5. Henry More letter to Joseph Glanvill, 26 December 1678, in Glanvill, *Sadducismus Triumphatus,* part II, advertisement to relation VIII (p. 331): '*ludicrous . . . Huntsman . . . Dogs . . . of an Hare . . . Form, and others . . . Body* . . . Julian . . . *Painters . . . Sky in an huge Landskip, so . . . Birds . . . Air. . . . Painters and Jugglers . . . Tricks of Leger demain, can . . . Feats . . . Sight . . . these airy invisible Spirits as far surpass them . . . such praestigious doings . . . Air . . . Earth for subtilty.*'
6. For this theory of Albert de Rochas, see p. 452, note 33 below; see also p. 315, note 49 above.

   Glanvill, *Sadducismus Triumphatus,* part I, section III (p. 9): '*Transformations* of *Witches . . . Shapes . . . Animals . . . conceivable* . . . Power of *Imagination . . . passive* and *pliable Vehicles . . . Shapes. . . .* when . . . Hurts . . . Bodies . . . *airy Vehicles* . . . Hurts of *those* . . . Bodies . . . *Diseases . . . Imagination . . . Fancy . . . Mother . . . Foetus* . . . Relations. . . .'

   For the French neurologist Jean Martin Charcot (1825–93), who experimentally demonstrated that stigmatisation could be induced under hypnosis, see p. 373, note 34 below.
7. Untraced.
8. John Heydon, *The Holy Guide, Leading the way to Unite Art and Nature,* book II, ch. xiii, section XXIII (London, 1662), (O'Shea 1920s list) p. 112: 'And *Socrates* lying in the field for quietness sake, being far from the noise of his brawling wife *Zantippe,* fell asleep, and being asleep, *Euripides* espied a thing come out of his mouth very lovely to behold, of a whitish colour, little, but made like a Cony running in

the grass, and at last coming to a Brook side, very buysily attempting to get over, but not being able, one of the standers by made a bridge for it of his sword, which it passed over by, and came back again with the use of the same passage, and then entered into *Socrates* his mouth, and they saw it no more afterwards; when he waked, he told how he dream'd he had gone over an iron bridge and other particulars answerable to what *Euripides* and his fellowes had seen before hand. . . .'

9. Jean Bodin (1530–96), French political economist, physician and theologian, author of *De la Démonomanie des sorciers* (Paris, 1580), which Yeats cites at p. 278 above.

Glanvill, *Sadducismus Triumphatus,* part I, section IV (p. 11): 'some *departed human Spirit,* forsaken . . .; part I, section X (p. 21): '. . . *Devil* is a Name for a *Body Politick*'. See also *V(A)* 228.

10. For the confession of Elizabeth Style, see Glanvill, *Sadducismus Triumphatus,* part II, relation III, section V (pp. 295–98). The quotations from the affidavit are from part II, relation III, section VII (p. 300): 'about Three . . . Clock . . . Morning . . . Head . . . Fly . . . Inch . . . length, which . . . Chimney, and. . . . He looking stedfastly . . . *Style* . . . and gastly, the Fire . . . *Thick* . . . *Read* conceiving . . . Poll . . . Hair . . . up, and . . . Fly . . . great Millar flew . . . place, and . . . Table board, and. . . . Examinant, and . . . persons looking . . . *Style's* Poll . . . Beef. . . . Poll . . . Butterfly . . . ask'd. . . . *Lambert* . . . not, I. . . . Informant . . . others looking . . . Poll. . . . Examinant demanded again . . . Fly . . . Familiar, and . . . Poll . . . time when her Familiar came to. . . .'

For devils taking the form of animals, see part II, relations III, VII, VIII (pp. 296, 319, 334).

11. Francis Hutchinson (1660–1739), bishop of Down and Connor, first published his history of witchcraft in 1718 (not 1730); the second edition, which Yeats used, is dated 1720, *An Historical Essay concerning Witchcraft. With Observations upon Matters of Fact; Tending to clear the Texts of the Sacred Scriptures, and confute the vulgar Errors about that Point. And also Two Sermons: One in Proof of the Christian Religion, the other concerning Good and Evil Angels,* 2nd ed. (London: Knaplock and Midwinter, 1720) pp. 86–87: '*Hopkins* . . . searching, and swimming the poor Creatures . . . Gentlemen . . . Indignation at the Barbarity . . . Thumbs . . . Toes, as . . . to tye others . . . Water, he. . . . clear'd . . . Country . . . him; and . . . was a great deal of Pity . . . Experiment. . . .'

12. *V&B* II, 247–48; *V&B1970* 277.

13. Testimony from the witchcraft trials of Elizabeth Clarke and of Anne West, 1645, at Chelmsford, Essex (thirty-five miles southwest of Manningtree, Essex), reported in H. F., *A true and exact Relation of the Several Informations, Examinations, and Confessions, of the late Witches, arraigned and executed in the county of Essex; who were arraigned and condemned at the late Chelmsford, before the right hon. Robert Earl of Warwick, and several of his majesty's justices of the peace, the 29th of July,* A.D. *1645. . . .* (1645), repr. in *A Complete Collection of State Trials and*

Proceedings for High Treason and Other Crimes and Misdemeanors from the Earliest Period to the Year 1783, ed. T. B. Howell (London: Longman, 1816) IV, cols. 814–58 (no. 176): 'The Information of Matthew Hopkins, of Mannintree, Gent. taken upon oath before us ['Sir Harbottell Grimston, Knight and Baronet, one of the Members of Honorable House of Commons; and Sir Thomas Bowes, Knight, another of his Majesties [*sic*] Justices of Peace for this County' (IV, col. 832)], the 25th day of March, 1645' (IV, col. 834): '. . . certain Mr. Edwards of Mannintree in . . . said Mr. Edwards . . . a jumpe, and . . . as shee had . . . informant made . . . thing about . . . bignesse of . . . standing aloofe from . . . white impe or kitlyn daunced about the said greyhound . . . to this informant . . . flesh torne from. . . . And this informant . . . That . . . thing, proportioned . . . informant; and . . . ran quite through . . . a paire of tumbrell strings . . . returned againe to. . . .'

'The Testimony of Sir Thomas Bowes, knight, which he spake upon the Bench, concerning the aforesaid Anne West, she being then at the Barre upon her Tryall' (IV, cols. 857–58): 'That . . . of Mannintree, whom . . . not speake an . . . Anne Weste's dore, about foure a clock, it . . . her dore to . . . house, and . . . the braines of . . . he tooke the . . . hand, and . . . it in another, and indeavoured to . . . head: and . . . of wooll; yet . . . not farre off . . . to drowne it: but . . . fell downe, and . . . not goe, but downe he fell againe, so . . . hand downe into . . . to his elbow . . . space, till . . . letting goe his . . . the aire, and. . . .'

14. Glanvill, *Sadducismus Triumphatus*, part II, relation I (p. 279): '. . . Wood . . . Chimney . . . Room . . . as of itself . . . Pistol . . . it, after . . . which, they . . . Drops of Blood . . . Hearth, and . . . Stairs.'
15. Yeats had recounted this anecdote in his essay 'The Prisoners of the Gods' (1898), *UP2* 85. For Odysseus in Hades, see p. 329, note 70 above.
16. Testimony of Matthew Hopkins, 18 April 1645, to Justices Grimston and Bowes (see note 13 above) at the witchcraft trial of Anne West, 1645, at Chelmsford, Essex, reported in H. F., *A true and exact Relation* (1645), repr. in *A Complete Collection of State Trials . . . to 1783*, IV, col. 842.
17. [Yeats's note] I have modernized the old lowland Scotch in these quotations from Pitcairn's *Criminal Trials.*[a]

17a. *Ancient Criminal Trials in Scotland*, compiled by Robert Pitcairn, 3 vols., Maitland Club Publication no. 19 (Edinburgh: Maitland Club, 1833), information from III, [appendix], 606, 610–11; quotations from III, 604; information from III, 611; quotations from III, 604 (Issobell Gowdie, Lochloy, 13 April 1662): '. . . put boosomes in . . . our husbandis, till ve return. . . . And than ve vold flie away, quhair ve vold, be ewin as strawes wold flie wpon an hie-way. We will flie lyk strawes quhan we pleas; wild-strawes and corn-strawes wilbe horses to ws, an ve put thaim betwixt our foot, and say, "Horse and hattok, in the Divellis nam!" An quhan any sies thes strawes in a whirlewind, and doe not sanctifie them selues, we . . . at owr pleasour'; 'bot ther bodies remains with ws, and will flie as horsis to ws, als small as strawes'.

18. Henry More uses the terms 'airy body' and 'animal spirits' frequently in *The Immortality of the Soul* (1659), in *A Collection*. See p. 327, Yeats's note 57 above.

19. Witchcraft trial of Alesoun Peirsoun (Alison Pearson), Byrehill, 28 May 1588, in *Ancient Criminal Trials in Scotland*, I, [part i], 161–65: '. . . for hanting and . . . the gude nychtbouris and Quene of Elfame, thir diuers zeiris bypast, scho had con fest be hir depositiounis, declaring that scho could nocht say reddelie how lang scho wes with thame; and that scho had freindis in . . . court quhilf wes of hir awin blude, quha had gude acquentance of the Quene of Elphane, quhilk mycht haif helpit hir: bot scho wes quhyles weill and quhyles ewill, and ane quhyle with thame and ane vthir quhyle away; and that sche wald be in hir bed haill and feir, and wald nocht wit quhair scho wald be or the morne.'

Agnes Sampsoune (Sampson), at her trial for witchcraft, 27 January 1590/1, confessed to James VI (1566–1625), King of Scotland (from 1567; and King of Great Britain, from 1603, as James I) (*Ancient Criminal Trials in Scotland*, I, [part II], 231–37). Many of the fifty-three separate items in her indictment concerned her curing of diseases; the quotation is a summary based on item 31 (I, 234): '. . . convict, for cureing of vmq[le] Robert Kerse in Dalkeyth . . . quhilk seiknes sche tuik vpoun hir selff, and kepit the samin with grit groining and torment quhill the morne . . . quhilk seikness sche caist of hir selff in the cloise . . . the samin wes laid vpoun Alexander Dowglas in Dalkeyth. . . .' See also item 43 (I, 237): '. . . convict, of the taking of the pane and seikness of the Lady Hirmestoune. . . .'

For Biddy Early, see p. 452, note 34 below.

20. Witchcraft confession of Isobel (Issobell) Gowdie, 15 May 1662, Auldearn, Scotland, in *Ancient Criminal Trials in Scotland*, III, [appendix], 611: 'Hair, hair, God send thé cair! / I . . . a hearis liknes now, / Bot I sall be an voman ewin now! / Hair, hair, God send thé cair!'

21. Cornelius Agrippa to the Abbot de Aqua Pendente, [24 September 1527], (*Epistles*, book V, epistle 14), in John Beaumont, *An Historical, Physiological and Theological Treatise of Spirits, Apparitions, Witchcrafts, and Other Magical Practices, with Refutation of Dr Bekker's World Bewitch'd* (London, 1705), (O'Shea no. 138) pp. 312–15 (ch. X). The passages to which Yeats, presumably refers are: '. . . many labour in vain, who pursue these most Secret *Arcana* of Nature, applying their Minds to the bare words as they lie; for by an unhappy *Genius*, being fall'n from a right understanding, and intangl'd in false Imaginations, by the craft of exteriour Spirits, they become dangerous Servants to those, over whom they might Rule, and not knowing themselves, they go forth after the Footsteps of their Herds, seeking without themselves, what they possess within them' (pp. 313–14) and 'He must die, die to the World and the Flesh, and to all his Senses, and the whole Animal Man, who would enter the recesses of Secrets; not that the Soul leaves the Body' (p. 315). See also pp. 62 and 328, note 64

above. The passage by Beaumont on the teachings of Arabian philosophers is from p. 321 (ch. x): '. . . Soul . . . Power . . . Imagination . . . Heav'ns . . . Elements . . . Mountains, raise Vallies to Mountains . . . Material Forms. . . .'

22. Chaucer, 'The Franklin's Tale', ll. 1189–92, 1198–1204, in *The Works of Geoffrey Chaucer*, ed. F. S. Ellis (Hammersmith: Kelmscott Press, 1896), (O'Shea no. 377) p. 166: '. . . with eye. / . . . knyghtes justyng in . . . / . . . swich plesaunce, / That . . . daunce, / On. . . .'
23. For Agrippa's *De Occulta Philosophia*, see pp. 74 and 332, note 92 above.
24. Ebenezer Sibly, *A Complete Illustration of the Celestial Science of Astrology; or, The Art of Foretelling Future Events and Contingencies, by the Aspects, Positions, and Influences of the Heavenly Bodies; Founded on Natural Philosophy, Scripture, Reason, and the Mathematics* (London: Green, 1784–88; separate title page for each section, but continuous pagination), (O'Shea no. 1912) pp. 1121–24: '. . . and that he . . . them, and . . . satisfaction' (p. 1122); '. . . the shape of . . . maidens, about . . . high. . . . voice, like. . . . bush, from . . . reed, but . . . managed, did. . . .' (p. 1123).
25. The eighteenth-century book is untraced. For other mentions of 'flocks of wool' see *UP2* 58 and *V&B* I, iii; II, 34, 112 (*V&B1970* 9, 164, 207).
26. Richard Hand to Adam Clarke, 2 December 1792, in *An Account of the Religious and Literary Life of Adam Clarke*, ed. J. B. B. Clarke, 3 vols. in 1 (1833; repr. New York: Mason and Lane, 1837) p. 263 (vol. II, book IV): 'he harms no one, but is every ingenious man's friend'; he transmutes lead into silver and then conjures, from a glass of water, 'a multitude of little live things like lizards'. Hand's two other letters, dated January 1793 and 13 May 1793, also describe this incident (pp. 264–66). The alchemist named Butler is unidentified.

PREFACE TO *ESSAYS 1931 TO 1936*

1. The four items he had collected in *Wheels and Butterflies* (1934) (Wade no. 175) were the preface (1924) to *The Cat and the Moon and Certain Poems*, the introduction (1931) to *The Words upon the Window-pane*, the introduction (1932–34) to *Fighting the Waves* and the introduction (1934) to *The Resurrection*.

   From among the essays Yeats had written since 1918 there are at least twelve candidates for the 'one or two' items that he omitted because they were 'notes rather than essays that seemed too slight in effort or in achievement': preface (1921) to John M. Synge, *Shingu Gikyoku Zenshu* (Collected Plays of Synge) (1923; *P&I* 145–46); introduction to Oscar Wilde, *The Happy Prince and Other Fairy Tales* (1923; *P&I* 147–51); preface to John Butler Yeats, *Early Memories: Some Chapters of Autobiography* (1923; *P&I* 152–53); preface (1923) to Oliver St John Gogarty, *An Offering of Swans and Other Poems* (1924; *P&I* 154–55); preface (1924) to Jean Marie Matthias Philippe Auguste

Count de Villiers de l'Isle-Adam, *Axel* (1925; *P&I* 156–58); introduction to Bryan Merriman and Donagh Rua Macnamara, *The Midnight Court and The Adventures of A Luckless Fellow* (1926; *P&I* 159–63); prefatory letter to the Medici Society, in William Blake, *Songs of Innocence*, illus. Jacynth Parsons (1927; *P&I* 164–65); preface (1929) to Oliver St John Gogarty, *Wild Apples* (1930; *P&I* 172–74); 'Plain Man's "Oedipus" ', *New York Times*, 15 January 1933, section IX, p. 1, cols. g-h; 'Anglo-Irish Ballads', by F. R. Higgins and W. B. Yeats, in *Broadsides: A Collection of Old and New Songs* (1935; *P&I* 175–81); introduction (1935) to *Selections from the Poems of Dorothy Wellesley* (1936; *P&I* 182–85) and introduction (1936) to Margot Ruddock, *The Lemon Tree* (May 1937; *P&I* 186–90).

He also omitted an additional fifteen other items that had not then been collected: 'If I were Four-and-Twenty' (1919; pp. 34 ff. above); 'A Memory of Synge' (1924; *UP2* 436–37); 'To All Artists and Writers,' (signed H. Stuart and Cecil Salkeld) (1924; *UP2* 438–39); 'Compulsory Gaelic: A Dialogue' (1924; *UP2* 439–49); 'An Undelivered Speech [on Divorce]' (1925; *UP2* 449–52); 'The Child and the State' (1925; *UP2* 454–61); 'The Need for Audacity of Thought' and 'Our Need for Religious Sincerity' (1926; *UP2* 461–65); 'A Defence of the Abbey Theatre' (1926; *UP2* 465–70); 'The Censorship and St Thomas Aquinas' (1928; *UP2* 477–80); 'Irish Censorship' (1928; *UP2* 480–85); introduction to *The Coinage of Saorstát Éireann* (1928; *P&I* 166–71); 'Ireland, 1921–1931' (1932; *UP2* 486–90); 'The Great Blasket' (1933; *UP2* 492–94) and 'The Growth of a Poet' (1934; *UP2* 495–99).

2. For bibliographical information on these items, see their individual textual introductions in this volume.

PARNELL

1. Henry Harrison (1867–1954), Irish nationalist and writer, graduated from Oxford in 1888. In 1889 he travelled to Ireland with his Balliol College tutor, Godfrey Benson, and quickly became a nationalist celebrity for fighting with Irish police in protest of evictions at Gweedore, Co. Donegal.
2. Henry Harrison, *Parnell Vindicated: The Lifting of the Veil* (London: Constable, 1931); he inscribed a copy to Yeats on 23 July 1936 (O'Shea no. 850). Charles Stewart Parnell (1846–91), Irish Nationalist leader in Parliament, was ruined politically in 1890 by being named as co-respondent in a divorce suit brought by Captain William Henry O'Shea, the husband of Parnell's long-time mistress, Mrs Katharine Woods O'Shea (1845–1921). Parnell married her in 1891. See also note 5 below.
3. R. C. K. Ensor, *England 1870–1914*, Oxford History of England (Oxford: Clarendon Press, February 1936) p. 564: '. . . main final. . . .'

4. This essay is dated August 1936 in *Essays 1931 to 1936.* Yeats sent the completed poem 'Come Gather Round Me Parnellites' (*P* 309) to Dorothy Wellesley in a letter dated 8 September 1936: 'I send you a ballad of mine which I propose to put [in *Broadsides*] with [W. J.] Turner's "Men fade like rocks." It has an interesting history; about three weeks or a month ago a man, Henry Harrison, an old decrepit man, came to see me. As a young Oxford undergraduate fifty years ago he had joined Parnell's party, and now had written a book to defend Parnell's memory. Mrs. O'Shea was a free woman when she met Parnell, O'Shea had been paid to leave her free, and if Parnell had been able to raise £20,000 would have let himself be divorced instead of Parnell. The Irish Catholic press had ignored his book. It preferred to think that the Protestant had deceived the Catholic husband. He begged me to write something in verse or prose to convince all Parnellites that Parnell had nothing to be ashamed of in her love. The result is the enclosed poem, and an historical footnote which I will reserve for my next book of essays. You will understand the first verse better if you remember that Parnell's most impassioned followers are now very old men.' (*L* 862–63)
5. Katharine O'Shea had lived separately from Captain O'Shea for a decade before Parnell met her in 1880; she and Parnell soon began living together and had three children. Katharine O'Shea and Captain O'Shea continued to receive separate allowances from Katharine's very elderly aunt, Mrs Benjamin Wood, a rich, pious, childless widow; divorce would have imperiled their expected inheritances. When the aunt died, at age ninety-seven in 1889, Captain O'Shea's allowance ceased and he received no inheritance. He then sued for divorce. Parnell was sure that Captain O'Shea would settle for £20,000 from the aunt's estate, but legal complications prevented Mrs O'Shea from receiving her inheritance soon enough to pay off Captain O'Shea before the divorce suit came to court. These details, and those in the next note, are available in Ensor, *England 1870–1914,* especially Appendix B: 'The Private Background of Parnell's Career', pp. 564–66, and are examined in F. S. L. Lyons, *Charles Stewart Parnell* (London: Oxford University Press, 1977) pp. 458–64.
6. Katharine O'Shea, *Charles Stewart Parnell: His Love Story and Political Life*, 2 vols. (London: Cassell; New York: Doran, 1914). The quotation is from Harrison, *Parnell Vindicated,* p. 238: '. . . hurtful in its aim, to Parnell's personal honour'. Richard Piggot, an Irish journalist, forged a letter in which Parnell condoned the Phoenix Park murders in May 1882; it was published by the *Times* in April 1887, at a crucial point in the Irish Home Rule debate.
7. 'In February 1886, when [Joseph] Biggar and [Timothy] Healy tried to prevent Parnell from procuring the by-election candidature of Captain O'Shea at Galway City, Biggar publicly stigmatized Mrs. O'Shea as "Parnell's mistress"; and though the phrase was kept out of the papers, it circulated among Irish politicians.' (Ensor, *England 1870–1914,* p. 183, n. 2.) Sir William Harcourt told the Cabinet on 17 May

1882; as Home Secretary, he was in charge of secret service men who watched Parnell (Ensor, *England 1870–1914*, p. 565).

8. William Ewart Gladstone (1809–98), prime minister (1868–74, 1880–85, 1886, 1892–94), leader of the Liberal party. George (later Sir George) Leveson-Gower, a nephew of Lord Granville, was one of Prime Minister Gladstone's private secretaries.

   Ensor, *England 1870–1914*, p. 183, n. 2: '. . . many mid-Victorians a particular aversion to . . . scandal) treated them as. . . .'
9. Untraced.
10. Wilfrid Scawen Blunt (1840–1922), English poet, traveller and ardent anti-colonialist, fell in love with Catherine 'Skittles' Walters (later Mrs Bailey) (1839–1920) in September 1863. His biographer observes that 'even those who ceased to be her lovers, remained, as Blunt did, her devoted friends'. Her Sunday parties 'were frequented by the Prince of Wales and other famous in England's public life. Even Gladstone, to the delight of Blunt and of Skittles herself, "came alone to take tea with her, having sent her beforehand twelve pounds of Russian tea"' (unidentified papers quoted by Edith Finch, *Wilfrid Scawen Blunt, 1840–1922* [London: Cape, 1938] pp. 44, 43). She was the 'Manon' of the first section of Blunt's *Love Sonnets of Proteus* (1881) and the 'Esther' of his sonnet sequence 'Esther, A Young Man's Tragedy', in *Esther, Love Lyrics, and Natalia's Resurrection* (1892). Yeats was a friend of Blunt and included two of the 'Esther' sonnets in *OBMV*; see also p. 395, note 4 below.
11. After the end of the Golden Age, Astrea (or Astraea), Greek goddess of justice, left the earth because of man's increasing impiety; she became the constellation Virgo. See *V(A)* 152, *V(B)* 243 and 'Two Songs from a Play' (*P* 213–14). In Yeats's poem 'The Cat and the Moon' (*P* 167–68), the cat's eyes are emblematic of the changing phases of the moon.
12. Untraced.
13. Ensor, *England 1870–1914*, p. 565: '. . . effect, a blackmailer'.

MODERN POETRY: A BROADCAST

1. Alfred Lord Tennyson died in October 1892; 'Modern Poetry' was broadcast 11 October 1936.
2. The Rhymers' Club was founded in early 1890 and last met in 1896 (Karl Beckson, 'Yeats and the Rhymers' Club', *Yeats Studies*, 1 [1971], 22, 41). Its usual meeting place was the Cheshire Cheese, 145 Fleet Street, London. Yeats listed its members as Lionel Johnson, Ernest Dowson, Victor Plarr, Ernest Radford, John Davidson, Richard Le Gallienne, Thomas William Rolleston, Selwyn Image, Edwin J. Ellis, John Todhunter, Arthur Symons and Herbert Horne, plus visitors Oscar Wilde, Francis Thomson and William Watson (*Au* 165); others were Aubrey Beardsley, George A. Greene, John Gray, A. C. Hillier and W. T. Peters.

3. Ernest Dowson (1867–1900), 'Villanelle of the Poet's Road' (1899), ll. 10–12, in *The Poetical Works*, ed. Desmond Flower (London: Cassell, 1934), (O'Shea no. 544) p. 74, ll. 10–12 and *OBMV* no. 90: 'Unto us they belong, / Us the bitter and gay, / Wine and woman and song.' See also pp. 184 above and 396, note 17 below.
4. For another mention of Lionel Johnson's (1867–1902) interest in the Fathers of the Church, respected ecclesiastical writers of Christian antiquity, see p. 97 above.
5. Lionel Johnson, 'By the Statue of King Charles at Charing Cross' (1889), in *Poems* (London: Mathews, 1895), (O'Shea no. 1020) pp. 12–13; *OBMV* no. 113.

   Lionel Johnson, 'Te Martyrum Candidatus' (1895), in *Ireland and Other Poems* (London: Mathews, 1897), (O'Shea no. 1019) pp. 101–2; *Poetical Works of Lionel Johnson* (London: Mathews, 1915), (O'Shea no. 1021) p. 252; and *OBMV* no. 111: '. . . companions . . . Christ!'
6. Lionel Johnson, 'The Church of a Dream' (1890), in *Poems* (1895) pp. 84–85: '. . . gray . . . / . . . / . . . long dead . . . / . . . / . . . saints . . . // . . . Priest . . . / . . . / . . . gray . . .'; *OBMV* no. 110 has the same variants as 'Modern Poetry'.
7. Inigo Jones (1573–1652), English architect who designed Lincoln's Inn Chapel and supervised the reconstruction of St Paul's Cathedral. For the Chapel of the Ascension (1892), Bayswater Road, near Albion Gate, designed by Herbert Percy Horne (1864–1916), architect and editor of the *Hobby Horse*, see p. 424, note 20 below.
8. This anecdote about Robert Browning is untraced.
9. Algernon Charles Swinburne (1837–1909), English poet; for Matthew Arnold (1822–88), English poet and critic, see pp. 199 above and 404, note 81 below, for excessive emphasis on psychology and / or moral fervour as evidenced in Arnold's excision of 'Empedocles on Etna' from his *Poems*, 1853, because of a concern for 'mental distress'.

   The French poet Paul Verlaine (1844–96) made this remark, in English, to Yeats in the spring of 1894. Yeats reported it in the *Savoy*, April 1896 (*UP1* 399); in a 1 March 1914 speech at the *Poetry* banquet, Chicago (see *Poetry*, 4 [April 1914], 26); in *Au* 342 (1922); and in *OBMV*, p. 183 above. Verlaine admired Tennyson's *In Memoriam* (1850) more than this remark suggests.
10. Catullus, first-century B.C. Roman lyric poet and epigrammatist, admired for his grace, simplicity and purity of style. The Palatine anthology of Greek poetic epigrams, compiled by an unknown Byzantine scholar(s) *c.* A.D. 980, contains 3,200 epigrams by some 300 poets. It was found in the Count Palatine's library at Heidelberg and was published in 1606. Among the Jacobean lyric poets, Yeats particularly admired John Donne (1572–1631) and Ben Jonson (1572–1637).
11. See p. 455, note 59 below.
12. Charles Ricketts (1866–1931), French-born English artist, with his friend Charles Shannon (1863–1937), assembled a remarkable collection of drawings, paintings and antiquities. Ricketts, who admired Dante Gabriel Rossetti, was a skilled wood-engraver. For the

influence of the French Romantic painter Eugène Delacroix (1798–1863), see Ricketts's oil painting *Bacchus in India* (117 x 95 cm.; Atkinson Art Gallery, Southport), illus. (monochrome) in Joseph Darracott, *The World of Charles Ricketts* (London: Eyre Methuen, 1980) p. 107. Yeats owned a framed, coloured reproduction (24 x 19 cm.) of another Ricketts oil painting, *The Betrayal* (*c.* 1904) (91 x 71 cm., Carlisle City Art Gallery), illus. in *The Studio* (London), 48, no. 201 (January 1910), 259, and T. Sturge Moore, *Charles Ricketts R.A.* (London: Cassell, 1933) plate 7. For a colour reproduction of another oil painting, *The Death of Montezuma* (*c.* 1905) (75 x 61 cm.), see Stephen Calloway, *Charles Ricketts: Subtle and Fantastic Decorator* (London: Thames and Hudson, 1979) colour plate 1, facing p. 24.

13. In 1898, Thomas Sturge Moore (1870–1944), English writer and wood-engraver, was introduced to Yeats by Laurence Binyon (1869–1943), English poet and art historian. In a review of Moore's first book of verse, *The Vine-dresser and Other Poems* (London: Unicorn Press, 1899), Binyon praised the book for disclosing 'a more remarkable gift than any first book of verse in recent years' ('Mr T. Sturge Moore's Poems', in *The Literary Year-Book and Bookman's Directory*, ed. Herbert Morrah [London: Allen, 1900] p. 54).
14. Thomas Sturge Moore, 'The Dying Swan' (1899), in *Selected Poems* (London: Macmillan, 1934), (O'Shea no. 1372) p. 48, and *OBMV* no. 124.
15. Under the joint pseudonym 'Michael Field', Edith Emma Cooper (1862–1913) and Katharine Harris Bradley (1846–1914) published sixteen tragic poetic dramas (1884–1903), a masque (1899) and a trialogue (1892); they published anonymously (1905–11) an additional seven tragic poetic dramas; four more were published posthumously (1913–19).
16. Michael Field [Edith Cooper and Katharine Bradley], 'Sweeter Far than the Harp, More Gold than Gold' (1889), in *A Selection from the Poems*, preface by T. Sturge Moore (London: Poetry Bookshop, 1923), (O'Shea no. 670) p. 35, and *OBMV* no. 66 (with a Greek epigraph).
17. Michael Field [Edith Cooper and Katharine Bradley], 'If They Honoured Me, Giving Me Their Gifts' (1889), ll. 1–8, in *A Selection from the Poems*, p. 36, and *OBMV* no. 67 (with a Greek epigraph).
18. Paul Verlaine, 'Art poétique' (dated 1874, publ. 1882), l. 20, in *Oeuvres complètes de Paul Verlaine* [Paris: Club du Meilleur Livre, 1959] I, 514: 'Prends l'éloquence et tords-lui son cou!' Yeats's source probably was Arthur Symons' essay 'Paul Verlaine', in *The Symbolist Movement in Literature* (London: Heinemann, 1899), (O'Shea no. 2068) p. 84: ' "Take eloquence, and wring its neck!" said Verlaine in his *Art Poétique*; and he showed, by writing it, that French verse could be written without rhetoric.'
19. A. E. Housman (1859–1936), *A Shropshire Lad* (1896); see p. 397, note 28 below. The three earliest of the four poems by Thomas Hardy (1840–1928) that Yeats chose for *OBMV* are ballad-like: 'Weathers'

(1922), 'The Night of Trafalgar' (from *The Dynasts*) (1903) and 'At Casterbridge Fair: 2. Former Beauties' (1902); the other poem is 'Snow in the Suburbs' (1925). Both of the poems by Rudyard Kipling (1865–1936) in *OBMV* are ballads: 'A St Helena Lullaby' (1910) and 'The Looking-glass: A Country Dance' (*OBMV* nos. 70, 71); see p. 397, note 22 below.

20. Frederick York Powell (1850–1904), English historian, scholar and translator of Icelandic, and Regius Professor of Modern History, Oxford, from 1894. Yeats's brother, the artist Jack Butler Yeats (1871–1957), often sketched boxing matches; for example, the drawings *Wonderland [14 February 1903, Whitechapel, London]* (1903–4) and *Boxing at an East-End Hall* (1904–5), illus. in *Jack B. Yeats 1871–1957: A Centenary Exhibition* (Dublin: National Gallery of Ireland and London: Secker & Warburg, 1971) nos. 3 and 4. Jack B. Yeats was the principal illustrator of *A Broad Sheet*, a series of twenty-four hand-coloured broadsides published monthly in 1902 and 1903 by Elkin Mathews, London.

Paul Fort, 'La Fille morte dans ses amours' (1894–96; prose poem), tr. Frederick York Powell, [untitled], in *A Broad Sheet*, no. 2 (London: Mathews, February 1902): '. . . church-yard: all . . . / . . . . / a-coffin'd in the day [*sic*]: / And . . . / . . . / . . . dead: in . . . lay; / . . . .' This translation was reprinted in Oliver Elton, *Frederick York Powell: A Life and a Selection from his Letters and Occasional Writings* (Oxford: Clarendon Press, 1906) II, 417; and in *OBMV* no. 31.

21. T. Sturge Moore, *The Centaur's Booty* (short poetic drama) (London: Duckworth, 1903); *The Rout of the Amazons* (short poetic drama) (London: Duckworth, 1903); 'The Gazelles' (1904), *OBMV* no. 129. See also p. 188 above.

Tristram and Isoult, from Arthurian legend, in Laurence Binyon (1869–1943), 'Tristram's End' (1897–1903), in *Collected Poems of Laurence Binyon* (London: Macmillan, 1931) I, 57–70, and *OBMV* no. 114.

The title character of Yeats's play *Deirdre* (perf. 1906; publ. 1907), from the ancient Irish tale; Yeats's plays about the Irish legendary hero Cuchulain are *On Baile's Strand* (1903), *The Green Helmet* (1910), *At the Hawk's Well* (perf. 1916; publ. 1917), *The Only Jealousy of Emer* (1919) (rewritten as *Fighting the Waves*, 1929) and *The Death of Cuchulain* (1939).

22. Thomas Sterns Eliot (1888–1965), *Prufrock and Other Observations* (London: Egoist, 1917), (O'Shea nos. 618, 619).

23. T. S. Eliot, 'Preludes: ii' (1915), ll. 1–5, 8–10; *OBMV* no. 253.

24. For Yeats's opinion of the poets of the First World War, see p. 199 above.

25. W. H. Auden (1907–73), Stephen (later Sir Stephen) Spender (1909–), Louis MacNeice (1907–63), C. Day Lewis (1904–72); for their interest in communism, see p. 405, note 86 below.

26. Cecil Day Lewis, 'Two Songs: 1.' ['I've heard them lilting at loom and belting'] (1935), ll. 1–8, in *A Time to Dance and Other Poems* (London: Hogarth Press, March 1935), (O'Shea no. 1114) p. 53: '. . .

day: / . . . // . . . are vanished away.' *OBMV* no. 353 has the same variants.

27. In a letter to Dorothy Wellesley, Yeats identified this 'poet of an older school' as his forty-year-old friend Frederick Robert Higgins (1896–1941), Irish poet, editor, Abbey Theatre director and later (from 1938) managing director (13 August [1936]; the name is omitted in *LDW* 97). F. R. Higgins and Yeats together produced *Broadsides: A Collection of Old and New Songs* (1935); see *P&I* 175–81.

28. Edith Sitwell (1887–1964), for a faun, see 'Colonel Fantock' (1924), l. 76, in *Troy Park* (London: Duckworth, 1925) p. 28 (*OBMV* no. 250, l. 7); for cats, see 'Trio for Two Cats and a Trombone' (1922, as 'Long Steel Glass') and 'The Cat' (1925, as 'Cendrillon and the Cat'), in *The Collected Poems of Edith Sitwell* (London: Duckworth; Boston: Houghton Mifflin, 1930), (O'Shea no. 1926) pp. 155–56, 146–47; for a columbine, see 'Ass-face' (1923), l. 6 (*OBMV* no. 251); for clowns, see 'Clown's Houses' (1916), title-poem in *Clown's Houses* (Oxford: Blackwell, 1918) and in *Collected Poems* (1930) pp. 151–53; for the wicked fairy Laidronette, see 'The Sleeping Beauty' (1924), ll. 105, 117, in *Collected Poems* (1930) pp. 5–6 (*OBMV* no. 247, l. 42 only).

Edith Sitwell's poem 'The Sleeping Beauty' (1924), in *The Sleeping Beauty* (London: Duckworth, 1924) and *Collected Poems* (1930) pp. 1–60, is excerpted (I, 1–42, 117–35; XV) as *OBMV* no. 247. *The Sleeping Beauty* (1889) by Peter Ilich Tchaikovsky; Nicholas II (1868–1918), czar of Russia.

Edith Sitwell, 'The Hambone and the Heart' (1927, rev. 1930) and 'The Lament of Edward Blastock' (1930), in *Collected Poems* (1930) pp. 91–97, 99–101 (*OBMV* no. 249).

29. The nursery rhyme 'Sing a Song of Sixpence', first printed in 1744, is of unknown age; see *The Oxford Dictionary of Nursery Rhymes*, ed. Iona and Peter Opie (Oxford: Clarendon Press, 1952) pp. 394–95, no. 486. In 1939 Yeats cited this nursery rhyme as an emblem of life, in opposition to abstract thought (*L* 922).

30. Edith Sitwell, 'Ass-face' (1923), in *The Collected Poems of Edith Sitwell* (London: Duckworth, 1930), ('Façade', section X) pp. 159–60, and *OBMV* no. 251: '. . . / Spiriting down / On sands. . . / . . . heard?" / . . . .'

31. Eesha Upanishad, 15, in *TPU* 16–17: '. . . bottle. Pull it, Lord! Let out reality.' For Yeats's fondness for this sentence, see his letter to Margot Ruddock, 25 December 1935 (*Ah Sweet Dancer* 65). It is also found in the Brihadāranyaka Upanishad (5.15.1), although not among the portions of that Upanishad excerpted in *TPU*.

32. Walter James Turner (1889–1946), *The Seven Days of the Sun: A Dramatic Poem* (London: Chatto & Windus, 1925) and excerpt in *OBMV* no. 270; Dorothy Wellesley, 'Matrix' (1928), in *Poems of Ten Years: 1924–1934* (London: Macmillan, 1934) pp. 306–24, and excerpts in *OBMV* no. 278; Herbert Read (1893–1968), 'Mutations of the Phoenix' (1923), in *Poems: 1914–1934* (London: Faber, 1935) pp. 144–51; T. S. Eliot's *The Waste Land* (1922), in *The Waste Land* (Lon-

don: Hogarth Press, 1923) and *Poems, 1909–1925* (1932, repr. London: Faber & Faber, 1933) pp. 63–99.

33. Dorothy Wellesley, 'Horses' (1925), in *Poems of Ten Years* (O'Shea nos. 2235, 2235a–c) p. 47, and *OBMV* no. 274; see also p. 198 above and p. 403, note 76 below.

    Walter James Turner, 'Romance' (1916), in *The Hunter and Other Poems* (London: Sidgwick & Jackson, 1916) pp. 9–10; *Modern British Poetry*, ed. Louis Untermeyer (New York: Harcourt, Brace and Howe, 1920) pp. 210–11; W. J. Turner, *The Dark Wind* (New York: Dutton, 1920), (O'Shea no. 2161) pp. 2–3; *W. J. Turner*, Augustan Books of Poetry series, ed. Edward Thompson (London: Benn, [1926]), (O'Shea no. 2172) p. 5; and *OBMV* no. 262: 'Popocatapetl' (ll. 7, 15, 23). The volcano Popocatepetl (elev. 17,887 feet) is forty miles southeast of Mexico City. Turner later wrote a novel entitled *The Duchess of Popocatapetl* (London: Dent, [1939]), (O'Shea no. 2162). 'Romance' also mentions an Ecuadorian mountain ('Chimborazo') and volcano ('Cotopaxi').

34. Immanuel Kant (1724–1804), German philosopher; see p. 353, note 33 below.

    Yeats's source is Henry Adams, who discussed the French mathematician and philosopher Jules Henri Poincaré (1854–1912) in *The Education of Henry Adams* (privately printed 1907; publ. 1918), ch. xxxi, 'The Grammar of Science' (1903). For details see p. 237 above and p. 434, note 80 below.

35. Nicholas of Cusa (1401–64), cardinal of San Pietro in Vincoli, *The Vision of God, or The Icon* (1453): 'The coincidence of opposites' is 'in the circle of the wall of Paradise . . . the coincidence of contradictories. . . .' (*The Vision of God,* tr. Emma G. Salter, intro. by Evelyn Underhill [London: Dent, 1928] pp. 46, 50 [ch. x] and 60 [ch. xiii].) See also *V(B)* 187, 247.

36. T. S. Eliot, 'Burnt Norton' (1936), section II, ll. 16–21, in *Collected Poems 1909–1935* (London: Faber & Faber, 1936), (O'Shea no. 611) p. 187.

37. Dorothy Wellesley, 'Matrix' (1928), section XIV, ll. 22–41, in *Poems of Ten Years: 1924–1934* (London: Macmillan, 1934) pp. 318–19: 'Where, then, are . . . / . . . / Cloud-wracks . . . / . . . forever? // . . . . // . . . Forever. . . .'

38. W. J. Turner, *The Seven Days of the Sun* (1925), 'Friday', section I, l. 20, in *The Seven Days of the Sun: A Dramatic Poem* (London: Chatto & Windus, 1925), (O'Shea no. 2170) p. 33; *OBMV* no. 270, section IV, l. 20: 'But we get intangled in a confusion of sensations.'

39. W. J. Turner, *The Seven Days of the Sun* (1925), 'Thursday', section II, in *The Seven Days of the Sun: A Dramatic Poem* (London: Chatto & Windus, 1925) pp. 25–26, and *OBMV* no. 270, section VII: '. . . paradise!'

40. John M. Synge (1871–1909), Irish playwright and poet; James Stephens (1882?–1950), Irish poet and novelist.

41. Oliver St John Gogarty, 'Dedication' (1933), in *Selected Poems* (New York: Macmillan, 1933), (O'Shea no. 756) p. 176 and *OBMV* no.

174; for his capture and escape in January 1923 and his subsequent presentation of two swans in April 1924, see p. 398, note 31 below; *P&I* 154–55 and Gogarty's poem 'To the Liffey with Swans' (1923), in *An Offering of Swans* (Dublin: Cuala Press, 1924 [colophon 1923]) p. 25 and *Selected Poems* (1933) p. 50.

42. Oliver St John Gogarty, 'Non Dolet' (1923), in *Selected Poems* (New York: Macmillan, 1933) p. 9 and *OBMV* no. 167; *An Offering of Swans* (Dublin: Cuala Press, 1924 [colophon 1923]) p. 1: '. . . home; // But. . . .'
43. William Morris (1834–96), English poet and artist, translated the Icelandic epic *The Story of Sigurd the Volsung and the Fall of the Niblungs* (1876).

BISHOP BERKELEY

1. Joseph M. Hone and Mario M. Rossi, *Bishop Berkeley: His Life, Writings, and Philosophy* (London: Faber & Faber, 1931). Mario Manlio Rossi had earlier translated and edited Berkeley's *Commonplace Book* in Italian: *Giorgio Berkeley, Gli Appunti* (Bologna: Cappelli, 1924).
2. For the decline of imagination after the death of Shakespeare (1616), see p. 401, note 59 below. Yeats admired the Dutch philosopher Baruch (or Benedict) Spinoza (1632–77) as a mystic for whom 'God and self are one' (*L* 650); see also *V(A)* 59 and *V(B)* 125–26. Yeats linked Spinoza with the German philosopher Georg Wilhelm Friedrich Hegel (1770–1831) in opposition to the materialism that stemmed from Newton and Locke. For Hegel and idealist philosophy, see p. 109 above and note 33 below.
3. William of Orange decisively defeated James II at the Battle of the Boyne in 1690, at the river Boyne, near Drogheda, Co. Louth.

   William Molyneux (1656–98), Irish philosopher and friend of Locke, translator of Descartes's *Meditations* (1680), member of Parliament (1692), scientist of optics. See his *The Case of Ireland's being bound by Acts of Parliament in English stated* (Dublin: Joseph Ray, 1698) pp. 12–17 and 147–49.
4. Samuel Molyneux (1689–1728), astronomer, member of Parliament (1715), First Lord of the Admiralty (1727), was secretary of the Philosophical Society, which Berkeley founded on 10 January 1705/6, at Trinity College, Dublin. The statutes of the society are included in the *Commonplace Book* (w. 1705–8; publ. 1871), although not in Berkeley's hand. See G. A. Johnston, *Development of Berkeley's Philosophy*, p. 17, and *Berkeley's Commonplace Book*, ed. G. A. Johnston (London: Faber & Faber, 1930), (O'Shea nos. 159 and 159a) p. 115, note 1. The quoted phrase is untraced.
5. *Berkeley's Commonplace Book*, aphorisms nos. 938–40, 944 (pp. 111–12).

   Sir Isaac Newton (1642–1727), English philosopher and mathematician; John Locke (1632–1704), English philosopher, known as the father of English empiricism. Yeats considered 'the mechanical philosophy of Newton, Locke and Hobbes' to have continued to dominate England, in opposition to 'Berkeley and the great modern idealist philosophy created by his influence' (*UP2* 458, 459).

6. William Morris (1834–96), English poet, artist, novelist and Socialist. Jonathan Swift (1667–1745), Irish satirist, dean of St Patrick's, Dublin (1713).

7. This portrait of Berkeley (undated, *c.* 1745?, oil on canvas, 74 x 61 cm.) in the Fellows' Common Room, Trinity College, Dublin, is by the Irish portrait painter James Latham (1696–1747). See Arthur Aston Luce, 'Iconography', in *The Life of George Berkeley Bishop of Cloyne* (London: Nelson, 1949) pp. 246–47 (painting no. 9), 249 (three engravings). However, because that portrait shows the bishop with sparkling eyes and even a hint of a smile, it does not accord well with Yeats's opinion here or in a diary entry of 15 September 1930 (*Ex* 322–23). The reference might instead be to another portrait of Berkeley (undated, *c.* 1734?, oil on canvas, 124 x 102 cm.), perhaps by John Vanderbank (Johan van der Banck) (1694–1739), which hangs in the Common Room hallway; in 1916 it hung in Regent House, Trinity College, Dublin, and was unattributed; the college had purchased it in 1870 (W. G. Strickland, *A Descriptive Catalogue of the Pictures, Busts, and Statues in Trinity College, Dublin, and in the Provost's House* [Dublin: University Press, 1916] p. 42; Luce, *Life of George Berkeley*, pp. 244–46 [painting no. 7]). See note 11 below for an engraving after another, similar portrait of Berkeley by John Vanderbank. The frontispiece of Hone and Rossi's book is an undated portrait, purchased by the National Gallery of Ireland (no. 895) in 1927 and attributed at that time to John Brookes (now 'Irish School'; oil on canvas, 113 x 91 cm.).

8. Thomas Phillips, portrait of William Blake (1807) (oil on canvas), 89.5 x 69.2 cm., National Portrait Gallery, London (no. 212; since 1866); illus. in *The Poetical Works of William Blake, Lyrical and Miscellaneous,* ed. William Michael Rossetti, Aldine edition (1874; repr. London: Bell, 1890), (O'Shea no. 212), frontispiece (engraved by C. H. Jeens); Geoffrey Keynes, *The Complete Portraiture of William & Catherine Blake* (London: Trianon Press, 1977) pp. 121–22 and plate 7 (Jeens engraving: p. 128 and plate 18).

Life mask of William Blake, taken by James S. Deville (July 1823), (plaster, 29.3 cm. height), Fitzwilliam Museum, Cambridge (M.7–1947). Yeats owned a photograph, a photogravure, and a lantern slide of this life mask. The photogravure had been published in *The Century Guild Hobby Horse,* 2, no. 5 (January 1887), facing p. 29, as an illustration to Herbert P. Horne's article 'The Life Mask of William Blake,' pp. 30–31. Another photograph of this same cast was published in *WWB* II, frontispiece. See also Keynes, *Complete Portraiture of Blake*, pp. 133–34 (cast no. 1) and plates 23ab, and Thomas Wright, *The Life of William Blake* (Olney, Bucks.: Wright, 1929) II, facing p. 45 (O'Shea no. 2297).

9. John Henry Foley (Irish sculptor, 1818–74), *Albert, Prince Consort* (1868?), bronze statue, Leinster Lawn, Dublin (until 1932 or later), present location unknown. See also a closely similar statement in Yeats's diary for 15 September 1930 (*Ex* 323): '. . . the mask of preposterous benevolence that prevailed in sculpture and painting down to the middle of the nineteenth century—the monument to the Prince Consort on Leinster Lawn. . . .' Foley also sculpted the colossal gilded bronze portrait statue (height 4.26 m.) of the Prince Consort in the National Albert Memorial, Hyde Park, London, posthumously completed in 1876, which shows him seated, holding a book titled *Great Exhibition of the Industry of all Nations,* and with an expression that the *Illustrated London News* dutifully characterised as 'intent meditation' (18 March 1876, p. 281; full-page illus., p. 284). Foley's well-regarded statues of Oliver Goldsmith (1728–74) and Edmund Burke (1729–97) are in front of Trinity College, Dublin.
10. *The Good-natur'd Man* (perf. 1768), comedy by Oliver Goldsmith (1730–74).
11. The small figures in the background, which Yeats mistook for 'gods and satyrs', are three workmen digging at broken cisterns; they appear, in the same pose, at the left edge of the oil portrait attributed to John Vanderbank at Trinity College, Dublin, and just left of the center of the engraving by W. Skelton (1763–1848) after another, similar portrait by Vanderbank, *The Right Revd George Berkeley, S.T.P. Late Lord Bishop of Cloyne in Ireland,* publ. London, 30 March 1800; the present location of the painting upon which the engraving is based is untraced. See Luce, *Life of George Berkeley,* pp. 243–44 (painting no. 6), 249 (engraving).

    For examples of Titian's portraits of women with elaborate sleeves, see *La Bella* (1536, Pitti Palace, Florence) and *Eleonora Gonzaga della Rovere, Duchess of Urbino* (1536–37, Uffizi Gallery, Florence), which includes the same small dog that he depicted in *Venus of Urbino* (1538, Uffizi Gallery).
12. Berkeley's manuscript commonplace book, written 1705–8, was discovered and published in 1871. *Berkeley's Commonplace Book,* aphorisms nos. 727–28 (p. 87: '. . . Church-men. Even . . . somewhat favourably of. . . .'), and aphorism no. 643 (p. 76: '. . . in yr. satyrical. . . .').
13. Berkeley's project for a mathematical system of ethics, in *Discourse on Passive Obedience* (1712), was first written as three sermons delivered in the chapel of Trinity College, Dublin. 'False reports of these sermons, Berkeley tells us were scattered broadcast, with the result that his loyalty to the House of Hanover came under suspicion. At that time "Passive Obedience" was a dangerous topic. . . . Berkeley thought it wise, with a view to dispelling these suspicions about his loyalty, to publish the sermons "under the form of one entire discourse." ' (G. A. Johnston, *The Development of Berkeley's Philosophy* [London: Macmillan, 1923] p. 298; page corner turned down in Yeats's copy, O'Shea no. 1025.)

14. William Thompson, Jonathan Rogers, James King and Robert Clayton, later Bishop of Killala, were among the five or six fellows of Trinity College, Dublin, who were engaged to serve in Berkeley's planned St Paul's College in Bermuda. See Berkeley's scale plans for 'The City of Bermuda Metropolis of the Summer Islands', in *The Works of George Berkeley* (Dublin: Exshaw, 1784), (O'Shea no. 160) II, 419, and his *A Proposal for the better supplying of Churches in our foreign plantations and for converting the savage Americans to Christianity* (1724–25). The men who accompanied Berkeley when he sailed for Rhode Island in 1728 were the portrait painter John Smibert (1684–1751) and two young men of means, John James (d. 1741) and Richard Dalton. For fox-hunters in Rhode Island, see Berkeley's *Alciphron* (1731), dialogue V, section I. The reference to 'immaterialist disciples' could be to Samuel Johnson (1696–1772), American philosopher, educator and Anglican minister, and perhaps also to Berkeley's role as a founder in 1730 of a literary and philosophical society in Newport, Rhode Island.

The Trinity College, Dublin, mission to Chota Nagpur, the southern portion of Bihar province, India, was established in 1892.

15. Berkeley advocated tar-water as a medicine for smallpox, gout, asthma, indigestion, fevers, etc. In *Siris: A Chain of Philosophical Reflections and divers other Subjects connected together and arising one from another* (1744), Berkeley's instructions for making tar-water are to dissolve a quart of tar (sap or pitch of pine, fir and other trees) in a gallon of cold water by stirring for five or six minutes, and then to let the tar settle for three days. The clear water is then bottled for use. He pointed out that the ancients knew of tar as a medicine, but did not know the method for 'rendering it an inoffensive medicine and agreeable to the stomach, by extracting its virtues in cold water'. Berkeley based his method on what he learned 'in certain parts of America' (*Siris,* sections IX and I, in *Works of Berkeley*, II, 477, 473). He encountered American Indians during his excursions from Rhode Island, 1729–31.

The Glorious Revolution (1688) and the Treaty of Limerick (1691) marked the end of a long period of religious and civil war and rebellion in England and Ireland. John Donne (1573–1631), English metaphysical poet, was raised as a Roman Catholic, took Anglican holy orders (1615) and was dean of St Paul's (from 1621). El Greco (Domingo Teotocópuli) (1548?–1614?), Greek-born Spanish mystical painter, favoured religious subjects. The Dutch philosopher Spinoza was excommunicated from his synagogue in 1656.

16. Yeats spoke on divorce, 11 June 1925 (*SS* 89–102), and on the condition of schools, 24 and 30 March and 28 April 1926 (*SS* 106–16). He had prepared a speech on divorce for 4 March 1925, but when the Senate did not discuss the topic, he published it in *The Irish Statesman*, 14 March 1925, pp. 8–10; repr. *SS* 156–60.

17. Burnham Beeches is three miles north of Slough, Berkshire. The friend is not identified. As a boy, Yeats had spent part of the summer of 1876 in lodgings at Farnham Common, near Farnham Royal

and Burnham Beeches, with his father and three other painters, named Farrar, Kennedy and Page (William M. Murphy, *Prodigal Father,* p. 110; information from William M. Murphy; *Au* 28–29; see also *CL1* 3).

18. John Locke, *An Essay Concerning Human Understanding* (1690), book II, ch. viii, sections VIII–X, ed. Peter H. Nidditch (Oxford: Clarendon Press, 1975) pp. 134–35: '. . . A Snow-ball having the power to produce in us the *Ideas* of *White, Cold,* and *Round,* the Powers to produce those *Ideas* in us, as they are in the Snow-ball, I call *Qualities.*' Primary qualities are such as 'are utterly inseparable from the Body, in what estate soever it be; such as in all the alterations and changes it suffers, all the force can be used upon it, it constantly keeps.' Primary qualities 'produce simple *Ideas* in us, *viz.* Solidity, Extension, Figure, Motion, or Rest, and Number'. Secondary qualities, such as colours, sounds, and tastes, 'are nothing in the Objects themselves', but rather are the 'various Sensations in us' produced by the primary qualities.
19. Edmund Burke (1729–97), Irish statesman and orator, took an active role in the investigation of the East India Company and urged the impeachment of Warren Hastings (1732–1818), English statesman and East India Company administrator, for corruption and cruelty. Burke opened the case in 1788 and delivered a nine-day speech in reply to Hastings's defence in 1794. Hastings was acquitted in 1795.
20. [Yeats's note] This cannot of course be less true of time-space than of the abstract space of Newton. The Russian mathematician Vasiliev in *Space, Time and Motion* calls Berkeley 'one of the most profound thinkers of all time' and adds 'It was Berkeley's immortal service that he decidedly rejected the external reality of space'.[e]

20a. Aleksandr Vasilevich Vasiliev (1853–1929), *Space Time Motion: An Historical Introduction to the General Theory of Relativity,* tr. H. M. Lucas and C. P. Sanger, intro. by Bertrand Russell (London: Chatto & Windus, 1924), (O'Shea no. 2191) pp. 79, 64.

21. In Edmund Spenser's *The Faerie Queene,* III.xi.54.8, Britomart, after seeing several signs that read *'Be bold',* sees a final sign that reads, *'Be not too bold'* (*Poems of Spenser,* p. 112).
22. Dmitri Svyatopolk-Mirsky, *Lenin,* Makers of the Modern Age series, ed. Osbert Burdett (London: Holme Press, 1931 [British Museum date-stamped 12 March 1931]) p. 67: '. . . of scientific Socialism'.
23. The verse is untraced. The line-division of the last two lines, in ballad (common) measure, presumably should be: 'And all thy great forefathers were / From Homer down to Ben.' Ben Jonson (1572–1637).
24. Jonathan Swift in part IV of *Gulliver's Travels* (1726) portrayed the country of the Houyhnhnms, horses characterised by rational behavior and moral perfection; in part III, Swift satirised Newtonian science and mechanical innovations.

    Oliver Goldsmith, Irish poet, playwright, essayist and novelist. Yeats consistently emphasized that Goldsmith wrote street ballads while a student at Trinity College, Dublin (*P&I* 54, 176).

    Edmund Burke (Irish politician, writer and orator), *Reflections on the Revolution in France* (1790), in *The Works of The Right Honourable*

Edmund Burke, Bohn's Standard Library (London: Bell, 1883), (O'Shea no. 306) II, 357; see also *SS* 172, *Ex* 318 and Donald T. Torchiana, *W. B. Yeats & Georgian Ireland* (Evanston: Northwestern University Press, 1966) pp. 190–93.

25. [Yeats's note] J. W. Dunne's experiments are of great value, his explanation is inconsistent. No heaping up of dimensions, what is successive in a lower dimension simultaneous in a higher, can bring him to the Pure Act or Eternal Instant, source of simultaneity and succession alike. His Infinite Observer is not Infinite.[a] McTaggart's exposition of a somewhat similar theory in the second volume of his *Nature of Existence*[b] is consistent with itself and with philosophical tradition.

25a. John William Dunne, *An Experiment with Time* (1927), 2nd ed. (London: Black, 1929), (O'Shea no. 588), used evidence from his dreams to assert that the conventional notion of 'serial time', with its rigid distinction between past, present and future action, can be surmounted. For Dunne, this explains prophetic dreams and suggests the simultaneity of absolute time, and further suggests 'the existence of a superlative general observer' (p. 207).

Yeats, in one of his two copies of *Bishop Berkeley,* marked 'His Infinite Observer is not Infinite' to be replaced by 'Because he believes in space, as something independent of the human mind his "infinite" observer is entangled in what Hegel called "The False Infinite" ' (O'Shea no. 911); that revision was not adopted in any printed text.

25b. John McTaggart Ellis McTaggart, *The Nature of Existence,* ed. C. D. Broad (Cambridge: Cambridge University Press, 1921 [vol. I], 1927 [vol. II]), (O'Shea no. 1202) II, especially pp. 9–31 (book V, ch. 33) and 271–81 (book VI, ch. 51).

26. For the creation, see *Berkeley's Commonplace Book,* aphorisms nos. 735, 351 (pp. 88, 40). For Berkeley's table, see *Principles of Human Knowledge* (1710), sections III, XXIII–XXIV, in *Works of Berkeley,* I, 24, 34–35.

27. [Yeats's note] Berkeley used common words on principle. They express perception with ease, he explains in the *Commonplace Book,*[a] but not those abstract ideas he derided.

27a. *Berkeley's Commonplace Book,* aphorism no. 764 (p. 93).

28. *Three Dialogues between Hylas and Philonous* (London, 1713). Plotinus (A.D. 205?–270), Egyptian Neoplatonic philosopher.

29. *Estrangement: Being Some Fifty Thoughts from a Diary Kept by William Butler Yeats in the Year Nineteen Hundred and Nine* (Dublin: Cuala Press, 1926) p. 37, entry no. LII (12 March 1909): '. . . sister, Lolly, dreamed. . . . somebody put. . . . J—— dreamed. . . . it, and. . . . sister, Lily, dreamed. . . .' Ruth Pollexfen is 'J——' (*Mem* 183).

30. In a letter to L. A. G. Strong, 4 December 1931, Yeats commented at length on this paragraph (*L* 787–88): 'I did not mean my allusion to "right and left" as a criticism of Dunne. I was merely suggesting an extension of his experiment. By "before and after" I meant past and future, and these Dunne had investigated with his experiments, and

by "right and left" I meant the relationship in space, not in time, which I am most anxious that he or somebody else should investigate. I won't go into the question now of the infinite observer, for I should have to look up Dunne again. I may perhaps write to you later about it. It happens to touch on a very difficult problem, one I have been a good deal bothered by. If I could know all the past and all the future and see it as a single instant I would still be conditioned, limited, but the form of that past and the form of that future, I would not be infinite. Perhaps you will tell me I misunderstood Dunne, for I am nothing of a mathematician.'

31. Epigraph to ch. xiii of *The Red and the Black* (1831) by Stendhal [Henri Beyle], who spuriously attributed it to a seventeenth-century historian, Abbé de Saint-Réal. It is left untranslated in the English edition that Yeats owned: *Scarlet and Black: A Chronicle of the Nineteenth Century*, tr. C. K. Scott Moncrieff, Everyman's Library (London: Chatto & Windus, 1927) I, 100: '*Un roman: c'est un miroir qu'on promène le long d'un chemin.* Saint-Réal.' A more literal translation is: 'A novel: it's a mirror that one carries along a road.'

32. Fourth-century Christian desert monastic hermits are associated with the Thebaid, the district of Thebes (25–45N/032–50E), ancient capital of Upper Egypt, and with Lake Mariotis (Mariut), just south of Alexandria. James O. Hannay, in a book that Yeats knew, *The Wisdom of the Desert* (London: Methuen, 1904), described those barren regions (pp. 5–10) and made extensive use of military imagery in recounting the spiritual battles of those early Christian monks with the devil, for example, in the introduction: 'The monks conceived themselves as fighting a final Armageddon with the already broken forces of the Prince of this world' (pp. 19–20; see also pp. 133, 140, 214 and 216). The quoted phrase is untraced; it is not from Gustave Flaubert, *The Temptation of Saint Antony*, tr. D. F. Hannigan (London: Nichols, 1895), (O'Shea no. 682). See Yeats's poem 'Demon and Beast' (1918; publ. 1920), ll. 43–50, *P* 187.

33. For the 'unconscious', see p. 299, note 61 above.

Georg Wilhelm Friedrich Hegel (1770–1831) sought to bridge the dualities such as nature and spirit, and to surmount the limitations of human knowledge that his fellow German philosopher Immanuel Kant (1724–1804) had considered inherent. Among Hegel's successors are Samuel Taylor Coleridge; the English philosophers Bernard Bosanquet (1848–1923), Frances Herbert Bradley (1846–1924) and John McTaggart (1866–1925); and the Australian philosopher Samuel Alexander (1859–1938).

The title character in Byron's dramatic poem *Manfred* (1817) is a remorseful, archly romantic young man. In Shelley's lyrical drama *Prometheus Unbound* (1820), the titan Prometheus, who defied Zeus by giving fire to mankind, finally is released from torturous punishment. Jean Valjean, an ex-convict, is the hero of Hugo's novel *Les Misérables* (1862). Pope Innocent XII (1615–1700, elected pope in 1691) is the most insightful and intuitive of the characters in Robert Browning's long poem *The Ring and the Book* (1868–69). The Wanderer, a philosophic pedlar, is a central character in William Wordsworth's long poem *The Excursion* (1814).

34. James Joyce had published the Anna Livia Plurabelle section of *Finnegans Wake* (I.viii), first as 'From Work in Progress' (1925), and then as a book, *Anna Livia Plurabelle* (New York: Crosby Gaige, 1928; London: Faber & Faber, 1930), (O'Shea no. 1040).

By the time Yeats wrote this introduction, Ezra Pound had published the first twenty-seven of his cantos: *A Draft of XVI Cantos* (Paris: Three Mountains Press, 1925) and *A Draft of the Cantos 17–27* (London: John Rodker, 1928). *A Draft of XXX Cantos* was published in Paris (Hours Press) in August 1930, but Yeats's copy of that book is the 1933 edition (London: Faber & Faber).

Marcel Proust (1871–1922), in his series of novels collectively titled *À la Recherche du temps perdu* (*Remembrance of Things Past*), emphasized detailed psychological analysis.

35. [Yeats's note] This definition is taken from M. W. Calkins' 'Introduction' to her selection from Berkeley.[a] Moore in his *Refutation of Idealism*, the manifesto of modern realism, merely affirmed the objectivity of the sense-data, the raw material from which mind fabricates the objects of sense. Of recent years he has however suggested that judgment may be a form of perception, and McTaggart has incorporated the suggestion in his idealistic system. Future philosophy will have to consider visions and experiences such as those recorded in *An Experiment with Time, An Adventure* and in Osty's *Supernormal Faculties*.[b] Events may be present to certain faculties, distant in time to others. Certain investigators[c] are convinced that they obtained through the mediumship of Mrs Crandon the finger-prints of a man dead some twenty years; and the terms idealist and realist may be about to lose their meaning. If photographs that I saw handed round in Paris thirty years ago can be repeated and mental images photographed, the distinction that Berkeley drew between what man created and what God creates will have broken down.[d]

35a. Mary Whiton Calkins, Introduction to *Berkeley: Essay, Principles, Dialogues with Selections from Other Writings*, ed. Mary Whiton Calkins (New York: Scribner's, 1929) p. xl. Calkins was professor of philosophy and psychology at Wellesley College.

35b. George Edward Moore, 'The Refutation of Idealism' (1903), collected in his *Philosophical Studies* (London: Kegan Paul, Trench, Trubner; New York: Harcourt, Brace, 1922) pp. 1–30. For McTaggart, see note 25b above; for *An Experiment with Time* by John William Dunne, see note 25a above. For *An Adventure* by Charlotte Anne Elizabeth Moberly and Eleanor Frances Jourdain, see p. 360, note 10 below. Eugene Osty (1874–1938), French physician and parapsychologist, director (1924–38) of the Institut Métapsychique International, Paris; Yeats refers here to Osty's study of clairvoyance, *Supernormal Faculties in Man*, tr. Stanley de Brath (London: Methuen, 1923).

35c. The 1931 version of this note had read 'Professor Schiller', a reference to Ferdinand Canning Scott Schiller (1864–1937), German-born tutor in philosophy, Corpus Christi College, Oxford (1897, 1903–26); president (1914) and vice-president (1920–28) of the Society for Psychical Research; professor of philosophy, University of Southern California (from 1929). Thumbprints that were claimed to have been produced from an ectoplasmic hand during séances by the famous Boston medium 'Margery', Mrs Mina Stinson Crandon (1888–1941), the Canadian-born wife of a Harvard Medical School surgeon, became the subject of considerable controversy from 1924 onwards. She never replied to damaging evidence, in 1932, that a Boston dentist had made the wax impressions of the thumbprints for her.

35d. Yeats elaborated on this sentence in letters to T. Sturge Moore, 15 February and 14 March [1926] (*LTSM* 69–70, 82), and identified the photographer as Commandant Darget, a French psychic investigator who made photographs of thoughts. See 'Actes de la Société Universelle d'Études psychiques: Les photographies de la pensée et des effluves humains, prises par le commandant Darget', *Annales des sciences psychiques* (Paris), 13 (January 1909), 20–26. In those letters to Sturge Moore, Yeats also referred to the spirit photograph of 'Little Stasia' taken by Julien Ochorowicz; see pp. 65 and 329, note 76 above. Spirit photographs received much attention from psychical researchers at the turn of the century. For a spirit photograph with Yeats, made probably in the late 1920s, see *Yeats and the Occult*, ed. George M. Harper (Toronto: Macmillan, 1975), plate 1, from the collection of Senator Michael Yeats. See also Charles Richet, *Thirty Years of Psychical Research; being A Treatise on Metaphysics*, tr. Stanley de Brath (London: Collins; New York: Macmillan, 1923), (O'Shea no. 1743) pp. 454 ff.; and James Coates, *Photographing the Invisible: Practical Studies in Spirit Photography, Spirit Portraiture, and other Rare but Allied Phenomena* (Chicago: Advanced Thought Publishing; London: Fowler, 1911).

36. Friedrich Nietzsche, *Thus Spoke Zarathustra* (part II, 1883), section XXXIX ('Poets'). Yeats used an identical translation in a letter to T. Sturge Moore, 26 June [1926] and a closely similar translation in an earlier letter to J. B. Yeats, 24 June [1918] (*LTSM* 103; *L* 650: '. . . I can give. . . .'). Yeats presumably adapted the wording of Thomas Common's translation, *Thus Spoke Zarathustra: A Book for All and None,* vol. XI [publ. as vol. IV] of *The Complete Works of Friedrich Nietzsche,* ed. Oscar Levy (Edinburgh and London: Foulis, 1909) p. 152 and *Thus Spake Zarathustra,* Modern Library (New York: Boni & Liveright, [1917]), (O'Shea 1920s list [probable identification]) p. 137: 'Should I not have to be a cask of memory, if I also wanted to have my reasons with me?' The passage does not appear in an earlier compilation by Thomas Common, *Nietzsche as Critic, Philosopher, Poet and Prophet* (London: Richards, 1901).

37. Samuel Taylor Coleridge, *Biographia Literaria* (1817), ch. vii, in *Biographia Literaria and Two Lay Sermons: 'The Statesman's Manual' and 'Blessed are Ye that Sow beside All Waters'*, new ed. (London: Bell, 1876), (O'Shea no. 401) p. 57: 'It is the mere quicksilver plating behind a looking-glass. . . .'

38. *Berkeley's Commonplace Book,* aphorisms no. 724–25 (p. 87: '. . . that wch is soul, & God . . . the Will alone. . . . will & understanding . . . mind; not. . . . *Mem.* Carefully to omit Defining of Person, or. . . .').

39. Plotinus, *Ennead,* IV.1 'On the Essence of the Soul', IV.3 and IV.9 'If All Souls are One'.

Berkeley's Commonplace Book, aphorism no. 726 (p. 87: 'Wt you . . . word—unite being no. . . .').

40. [Yeats's note] Berkeley has been called a utilitarian, even the first utilitarian, and the essay on Passive Obedience[a] would support that opinion were it more than a public plea where everything must be familiar and intelligible. In the *Commonplace Book* alone is Berkeley always sincere and there I find in paragraph 639 'Complacency seems rather to . . . constitute the essence of volition,'[b] which seems what an Irish poet meant who sang to some girl 'A joy within guides you', and what I meant when I wrote 'An aimless joy is a pure joy'.[c] Berkeley must have been familiar with Archbishop King's *De Origine Mali,* which makes all joy depend 'upon the act of the agent himself, and his election';[d] not upon an external object. The greater the purity the greater the joy. A Sligo countryman once said to me 'God smiles even when he condemns the lost'.[e] Berkeley deliberately refused to define personality and dared not say that man in so far as he is himself, in so far as he is a personality, reflects the whole act of God; his God and Man seem cut off from one another. It was the next step and because he did not take it Blake violently annotated *Siris* and because he himself did take it, certain heads—*Christ Blessing*—in Mona Wilson's *Life* for instance—have an incredible still energy.[f] It was not compatible from any point of view with Berkeley's external inanimate mask.

40a. *Discourse on Passive Obedience* (1712); see note 13 above.

40b. *Berkeley's Commonplace Book,* aphorism no. 639 (p. 75).

40c. Untraced. Yeats, 'Tom O'Roughley' (1918), l. 4 (*P* 141).

40d. William King, archbishop of Dublin, *An Essay on the Origin of Evil* (1702), ch. v, section II ('Where it is shown that Happiness consists in Elections'), tr. Edmund Law (1731), 5th ed. (London: Faulder; Cambridge: Merril, 1781) pp. 291–308 *passim*; the specific quotation is untraced.

40e. Untraced; see also p. 201 above.

40f. William Blake, annotations to Berkeley, *Siris* (1744), in Erdman, pp. 652–54. William Blake's painting *Christ Blessing* (*c.* 1810), 'fresco' (i.e., tempera) on canvas, 75 x 62 cm., Fogg Art Museum, Cambridge, Mass. (Martin Butlin, *The Paintings and Drawings of William Blake* [New Haven: Yale University Press, 1981], no. 670, plate 892) is reproduced in monochrome in Mona Wilson, *The Life of William Blake* (London: Nonesuch Press, 1927), (O'Shea no. 2285) plate 18, facing p. 228. See also p. 121 above.

41. [Yeats's note] I am thinking of his attack on Shaftesbury.[a]

41a. Anthony Ashley Cooper (1671–1713), third Earl of Shaftesbury, English moral philosopher, influenced by Deism; his principal work is

Characteristics of Men, Manners, Opinions, Times (1711, 1713). Hone and Rossi (pp. 175–76) acknowledge that Berkeley 'had a sort of peculiar animosity against this philosopher and shows in the *Alciphron* [1732] a pointed impatience with him, describing him as a man who under a fictitious enthusiasm for virtue endeavours to cover his fundamental amorality. Retaining always this prejudice or idea, Berkeley ignored the defence of Shaftesbury . . . and repeated against him the vague accusation of being simply an enemy of religion and a "plausible pretender . . . to Deism and Enthusiasm" (*Visual Language*, 3–5).'

42. The old hunter is thought to be Orion. The Greeks hid at Tenedos during the ploy of the wooden horse at Troy. Robert Browning, 'Pauline' (1833), ll. 323–25, in *The Poetical Works of Robert Browning*, ed. Ian Jack and Margaret Smith (Oxford: Clarendon Press, 1983) I, 47 (1887 text); Yeats quoted the same lines in *P&I* 127, *V(A)* 43 and *V(B)* 110.

43. Aeacus, in Greek legend, son of Zeus by Aegina, ruled the Myrmidons so justly that after his death he was appointed a judge of the underworld with Minos and Rhadamanthus. Pythagoras (6th c. B.C.), Greek philosopher and mathematician.

This is from a reply by the oracle at Delphi soon after the death of Plotinus, A.D. 270, in answer to 'Where has the soul of Plotinus gone?'; it was recorded by Porphyry, a disciple of Plotinus. Porphyry, *Life of Plotinus*, 22, in *Plotinus: The Ethical Treatises, Being the Treatises of the First Ennead with Porphyry's Life of Plotinus*, tr. Stephen MacKenna (London: Medici Society, 1917), (O'Shea no. 1589) pp. 22–23: '. . . wave-washed coast . . . Aeacus, and Plato, consecrated power, and stately Pythagoras and all else that form the Choir of Immortal Love'.

See also Yeats's poem 'The Delphic Oracle upon Plotinus' (1931; *P* 269–70) and H. W. Parke and D. E. W. Wormell, *The Delphic Oracle* (Oxford: Blackwell, 1956) II, 192–93 (no. 473) and Joseph Eddy Fontenrose, *The Delphic Oracle, Its Responses and Operations, with a Catalogue of Responses* (Berkeley and Los Angeles: University of California Press, 1978) pp. 264–65 (no. H69).

The oracle of Delphi was abolished by the emperor Theodosius in A.D. 390.

44. *The Battle of the Books* (1704), in *The Works of the Rev. Dr Jonathan Swift, Dean of St Patrick's, Dublin*, ed. Thomas Sheridan, new ed. 17 vols. (London: Strahan, 1784), (O'Shea no. 2043) II, 291–97. For a modern edition see *The Prose Works of Jonathan Swift*, ed. Herbert Davis (Oxford: Blackwell, 1939) I, 149–51. In Swift's satirical parable, the spider, who '*Spins and Spits wholly from Himself*' (Davis, I, 149), represents the Moderns, and the bee, who visits the best in nature, represents the Ancients. See also p. 205 above.

45. Giambattista Vico (1668–1744), Italian philosopher, in *Principles of a New Science of Giambattista Vico concerning the Common Nature of Nations* (1725, 1730, 1744), paras. 198, 203, 205 (book I, sections XLIII, XLVI, XLVII), 403 (book II, section II, ch. i), 820 (book III, section I, ch.

v, part x). See also Benedetto Croce, *The Philosophy of Giambattista Vico,* tr. R. G. Collingwood (London: Latimer, 1913), (O'Shea no. 445) pp. 160–61 and 180–81.

46. *Berkeley's Commonplace Book,* aphorisms nos. 782, 544 (pp. 94, 64).

47. William Blake, *The Marriage of Heaven and Hell* (1790–93?), plate 11, in *PWB* 183 (Erdman, p. 37: 'enlarged & numerous . . .').

48. Thomas Lake Harris (1832–1906), English-born American spiritualist and patriarch of a religious utopian community, studied the visionary writings of the Swedish religious writer, philosopher and scientist Emanuel Swedenborg (1688–1772). Then in 1857 Harris wrote, through what he claimed was dictation from an angel, the lengthy *Arcana of Christianity: An Unfolding of the Celestial Sense of the Divine Word, through T. L. Harris* (New York: New Church Publishing Association, 1858), in which he explained that Swedenborg's range of perception had surpassed the 'natural' world, but was limited to an intermediate, 'spiritual' level; Harris himself claimed to be the first mortal to attain the higher, 'celestial' level (pp. 43, 281, 285). Yeats's quotation is a paraphrase from a later book by Harris, *The Wisdom of the Adepts: Esoteric Science in Human History* (Fountain Grove, Santa Rosa, CA: Privately printed, 1884) p. 263 (para. 648): 'Being but half a man, the seer [Swedenborg] also glimpsed at heaven with but half a sight, heard of heaven with but half an ear, tasted of heaven with but half a taste. . . .' See also *SB* 69–73 and notes 95, 98, 99.

49. See Arthur Waley, *An Introduction to the Study of Chinese Painting* (London: Benn, 1923), (O'Shea no. 2215) p. 226: 'Through Zen we annihilate Time and see the Universe not split up into myriad fragments, but in its primal unity.' Compare Yeats to Thomas Sturge Moore, 5 February [1926], *LTSM* 68: 'Zen art was the result of a contemplation that saw all becoming through rhythm a single act of the mind.' Yeats admired Chinese painting for being 'full of rhythm', as opposed to abstraction (Yeats to J. B. Yeats, 14 March [1916?], *L* 608–9). For Zen, see also p. 392, note 22 below.

50. For this contrast between Juliet's nurse and Hamlet, see, for example, Samuel Taylor Coleridge, *Lectures and Notes on Shakespere [sic] and Other English Poets,* ed. T. Ashe (1883; repr. London: Bell, 1908) pp. 85–86 and 323–24 (the nurse), and 159–60 (Hamlet).

51. Unidentified.

52. The Young Ireland movement, founded in 1842, had fostered political and cultural Irish nationalism through a weekly newspaper, *The Nation,* and a series of inexpensive books in the Duffy's Library of Ireland series. Beginning in 1891 Yeats worked to organise the Irish Literary Society in London, the National Literary Society in Dublin, and the New Irish Library, a series of books on Irish topics. For Yeats's account of those efforts, see *Au* 199–250.

MY FRIEND'S BOOK

1. In *Song and its Fountains* (London: Macmillan, 1932), George Russell ('AE') (1867–1935) gives autobiographical settings and discussions for a selection of his poems. AE began writing it in February or March 1929 and finished in December 1931. When the book was published, 16 February 1932, he was in mourning for his wife, who died February 3. Yeats and AE first met in May 1884 when they were students at the Metropolitan School of Art, Dublin. They were estranged from 1905 until 1913. Since 1922, Yeats had lived at 82 Merrion Square; AE worked at 84 Merrion Square, in the offices of the Irish Agricultural Organisation Society, as editor of *The Irish Homestead* and then, from 1923 to 1930, of *The Irish Statesman*. In 1933 AE described Yeats as 'my oldest friend and enemy' (*Letters from AE*, ed. Alan Denson [London: Abelard-Schuman, 1961] p. 201).
2. St John the Baptist spent many years in the desert (Luke 1:80). Leonardo da Vinci (1452–1519), Florentine painter, sculptor, architect and engineer; AE mentioned him in *Song and its Fountains* (p. 31). For Emanuel Swedenborg (1688–1772), Swedish scientist, mystic and religious writer, see p. 394, note 31 below.
3. Two Rock Mountain (elev. 1,699 feet), Co. Dublin, four miles south of Dundrum and six miles southwest of Dun Laoghaire pier; see also *Au* 249.
4. Yeats added a few details to this anecdote in his journal, but did not name the 'strange mad pious student who used to come in sometimes with a daisy chain round his neck' (*Mem* 150, *Au* 468).
5. Matthew 27:26; Mark 15:15; John 19:1.
6. Parzival, when he first attended the banquet of the Grail, at the court of Anfortas (the wounded 'Fisher King'), saw the Bleeding Lance and the Grail, received a sword from Anfortas, and failed to ask the question that would have restored the fertility of the land (Wolfram von Eschenbach [d. *c.* 1220], *Parzival: A Knightly Epic*, v.1–258, tr. Jessie L. Weston [London: Nutt, 1894], I, 129–37). See Jessie L. Weston, *The Quest of the Holy Grail* (London: Bell, 1913) pp. 1–49, and Arthur E. Waite, *The Hidden Church of the Holy Graal: Its Legends and Symbolism Considered in their Affinity with Certain Mysteries of Initiation and other Traces of a Secret Tradition in Christian Times* (London: Redman, 1909), (O'Shea 1920s list) pp. 79–165.
7. That is, sense (or sensation) as a single faculty distinct from intellect or will. In John Locke's *An Essay Concerning Human Understanding* (1690), book II, ch. i, section II, the marginal summary reads: '*All* Ideas *come from Sensation or Reflection*' (ed. Peter H. Nidditch [Oxford: Clarendon Press, 1975] p. 104). Baron Gottfried Wilhelm von Leibnitz (1646–1716), German philosopher and mathematician, in *New Essays concerning Human Understanding* (w. 1703–5, publ. 1765) II.i.2, commented in response to that section in Locke: 'You oppose to me this axiom received by the philosophers, *that there is nothing in the soul*

which does not come from the senses. But you must except the soul itself and its affections. *Nihil est in intellectu, quod non fuerit in sunsu,* excipe: *nisi ipse intellectus.*' (Tr. Alfred Gideon Langley [New York: Macmillan, 1896] p. 111.)

8. Henry More (1614–87), English philosopher of the Cambridge Platonist school. In *The Immortality of the Soul* (1659), book III, ch. vii, section III, More offers two examples to show that 'the *Soul of the World* has to doe with all Efformations of either *Plants* or *Animals*' (in *A Collection,* p. 174). In book III, ch. vi, sections VII–VIII, he explains that the Soul of the World assists in the formation of the foetus, especially in its general design: 'For what rude inchoating the *Soul of the World* has begun in the Matter of the *Foetus,* this *Signature* is comprehended in the whole design, and after compleated by the presence and operation of the particular *Soul of the Infant,* which cooperates conformably to the pattern of the Soul of the World. . . .' (p. 172)
9. See Henry More, *The Immortality of the Soul,* book III, ch. xii, sections VIII–IX, in *A Collection,* pp. 200–1.
10. Charlotte Anne Elizabeth Moberly (1846–1937) and Eleanor Frances Jourdain (*c.* 1866–1924) described their visions of the court of Marie Antoinette in *An Adventure,* which they published under the pseudonyms 'Elizabeth Morison' and 'Frances Lamont' (London: Macmillan, 1911). Moberly was principal of St Hugh's College, Oxford, from 1886 to 1915; Jourdain became vice-principal of the same college in 1902 and then succeeded her as principal from 1915 to 1924. For other mentions of their book, see p. 354, note 35 above; p. 452, note 36 below; *V(A)* 168; *V(A)CE* note to p. 168, ll. 2–5; *V(B)* 227, n. 2; *VPl* 970. For John William Dunne, *An Experiment with Time* (1929), see p. 352, note 25 above.
11. AE continued to paint visionary landscapes throughout his life, in oils and in pastels.
12. George Russell, 'The Squandering of National Feeling', *Irish Statesman,* I, no. 7 (27 October 1923) 197–99. The general hunger strike began 13 October 1923 in Mountjoy Prison, Dublin, with 424 men (including ten members of the Dáil). It quickly spread to Kilmainham Prison and other prisons and camps. On 23 November 1923, when the hunger strike was called off, two men had died (on 20 and 22 November 1923) and 167 men had remained on hunger strike since its first week.
13. William Sharp (1855–1905) wrote novels and short stories in a Celtic Renaissance style, from 1894, under the pseudonym Miss Fiona Macleod.
14. *Song and its Fountains,* pp. 3 (daffodils and a 'magic sword' with a silver hilt and a blue blade), 4 (primroses and lilies), 7–8 (a dying woman who wept because 'she was unable to rise and nurse a sick neighbour').
15. *Song and its Fountains,* p. 45: '. . . and a tragic . . . concentration on that. . . .'
16. *Song and its Fountains,* p. 48.

17. AE, 'Recollection' (1904–13), ll. 13–16, in *Song and its Fountains*, p. 48: '. . . the wandering soul . . . yet, / And. . . .'; *Collected Poems* (London: Macmillan, 1913), (O'Shea no. 1800) and (London: Macmillan, 1926), (O'Shea no. 1801) p. 196; and *Selected Poems* (London: Macmillan, 1935), (O'Shea no. 1811) p. 98: '. . . know, when . . . immortal, I . . . / . . . the wandering soul . . . fair: / . . . crumbled, and . . . yet, / . . . broken, and. . . .'
18. Ralph Cudworth (1617–88) and Henry More (see note 8 above) were prominent members of a seventeenth-century English philosophical school, the Cambridge Platonists, which advocated idealist and spiritual views.

    Joseph Glanvill (Glanvil) (1636–80), English clergyman and philosopher, in *Lux Orientalis* (1662) defended belief in the pre-existence of souls.
19. *Song and its Fountains*, p. 114: '. . . The spirit . . . infinite vision . . . knowing it was all about me. . . .'
20. 'Will o' the Wisp' (1931) (ll. 20–23 and 27–30); Yeats quotes from the untitled revised version in *Song and its Fountains*, p. 115: '. . . flying fishes, a. . . .'

PROMETHEUS UNBOUND

1. Yeats began writing 'The Philosophy of Shelley's Poetry' in July 1899, and he published its first part, later subtitled 'His Ruling Ideas', in the May–July 1900 issue of *The Dome* (new ser. 7, 75–83). In it he praised Shelley's *Prometheus Unbound: A Lyrical Drama in Four Acts* (1820) as a 'sacred book' (75). The second part of the essay, subtitled 'His Ruling Symbols', was added in *Ideas of Good and Evil* (1903); the complete essay was reprinted (with slight revisions) in 1908, 1924 and 1961 (*E&I* 65–95).
2. Shelley, *Prometheus Unbound* (w. 1818–19; publ. 1820), II.iv.3–4, *The Poems of Percy Bysshe Shelley*, ed. C. D. Locock (London: Methuen, 1911), (O'Shea no. 1905) I, 289. For the sphere of Parmenides, fifth-century B.C. Greek philosopher, compare a revised passage for *V(B)* 211 and note 1: 'When Shelley's Demogorgon—eternity—comes from the centre of the earth it may so come because Shelley substituted the earth for such a sphere [of eternity, a Thirteenth Sphere].' Yeats explained in a note: 'Shelley, who had more philosophy than men thought when I was young, probably knew that Parmenides represented reality as a motionless sphere.' In *V(A)* 133, Yeats had here quoted the assertion of Parmenides that all that exists is finite and within a sphere: 'Where then it has its furthest boundary it is complete on every side, equally poised from the centre in every direction like the mass of a rounded sphere, for it cannot be greater or smaller in one place than another . . . and there is not, and never shall be any time, other than that which is present, since Fate has chained it so as to be whole and immoveable.' Yeats found the quotation in John

Burnet, *Early Greek Philosophy* (London: Black, 1892), (O'Shea no. 307) p. 187 (ll. 103–6, 96–98; slightly modified); Parmenides, as quoted in Burnet, then contrasted that view to the cosmology believed by others, at the centre of which 'is the divinity that directs the course of all things' (ll. 128–29; p. 188).

3. Shelley, 'Adonais' (1821), LII.3–4, in *Poems of Shelley*, ed. Locock, II, 37: 'Life, like a dome of many-coloured glass, / Stains the white radiance of Eternity'; see *E&I* 72.
4. *Prometheus Unbound,* III.i.56.
5. Shelley assented 'to the conclusions of those philosophers', notably the idealist George Berkeley (see pp. 103 ff. above), 'who assert that nothing exists but as it is perceived'. Shelley particularly praised William Drummond's *Academical Questions* (1805) as a 'clear and vigorous statement of the intellectual system' (Shelley, 'On Life' [essay fragment, 1815?, publ. 1832], in Shelley, *Essays and Letters,* ed. Ernest Rhys, Camelot Classics [London: Scott, 1886], [O'Shea no. 1902] pp. 75, 73).
6. Shelley, 'On Life', in *Essays and Letters,* p. 76: 'Mind . . . cannot create, it can only perceive'; see *E&I* 84.
7. *Prometheus Unbound,* II.v.108.
8. Tír-na-nÓg: the Country of the Young, the Irish folk paradise; see Yeats's definition and his note, quoted from Douglas Hyde (*P&I* 20–21, 242 n. 57). The quatrain is from Shelley's 'The Sensitive Plant' (1820), Conclusion, ll. 17–20, in *Poems of Shelley*, ed. Locock, I, 467: '. . . Lady . . . / . . . / . . . truth have . . . away: / 'Tis we, 'tis ours, are. . . .'
9. *Prometheus Unbound,* II.iii.2, 4–5.
10. Asia, a symbol of love in *Prometheus Unbound,* was the wife of Prometheus (Herodotus, *Histories,* IV.45). Urania is the muse of Astronomy. Prince Athanase, the title character of Shelley's poetic fragment written in 1817, is a Platonist. Mrs Shelley recorded, in a note to her 1839 edition of *The Poetical Works of Percy Bysshe Shelley,* that a draft title of the poem had been 'Pandemos and Urania' and that in Shelley's first sketch of it, 'Athanase seeks through the world the One whom he may love. He meets . . . a lady who appears to him to embody his ideal of love and beauty. But she proves to be Pandemos, or the earthly and unworthy Venus; who, after disappointing his cherished dreams and hopes, deserts him' (*Poems of Shelley,* ed. Locock, I, 576).
11. William Blake, *The Marriage of Heaven and Hell* (1793), plate 14, in *PWB* 185: '. . . with his flaming . . . at [the] tree . . . life, and . . . does, the. . . .' (Erdman, p. 38: '. . . with his flaming . . . at tree . . . life, and . . . does, the . . . consumed, and . . . infinite. and holy whereas . . . finite & corrupt.')
12. Elizabeth Hitchener (not Hutchinson), a schoolmistress in Sussex with feminist and republican views, was Shelley's acquaintance from June 1811 to November 1812, when she left his household. The quotation is from Shelley's letter to Thomas Jefferson Hogg, 3 December 1812: '. . . Brown Demon. . . .' (*Letters 1812 to 1818,* ed. Roger Ing-

pen, vol. IX of *The Complete Works of Percy Bysshe Shelley*, ed. Ingpen and Walter E. Peck, Julian Edition [London: Benn, 1926] p. 27.)

13. Shelley, *Oedipus Tyrannus; or, Swellfoot the Tyrant. A Tragedy in Two Acts* (1820).
14. Shelley, *The Cenci: A Tragedy in Five Acts* (1819; perf. 1886).
15. Yeats knew the English artist Aubrey Beardsley (1872–98) and owned reproductions of eleven of Beardsley's fifteen ink drawings (1894) illustrating Oscar Wilde's drama *Salome* (1894). Yeats had praised one of those drawings, *The Climax* (Salome with the head of John the Baptist), to Beardsley as his best work. Stanley Weintraub suggests that the quotation about Priapus, phallic Greek god of fruitfulness, is perhaps based on Beardsley's drawing in 1895 for the prospectus and inside front cover of *The Savoy*, showing John Bull with a hint of small erection in his very large trousers; see Weintraub, *Aubrey Beardsley: Imp of the Perverse* (University Park and London: Pennsylvania State University Press, 1976) pp. 155–56 and illus. p. 154. For the *Salome* drawings, some of which were replaced or modified for respectability, see Weintraub, pp. 54–79.
16. Alexander Gilchrist, *Life of Blake, 'Pictor Ignotus'* (London: Macmillan, 1863) p. 128, and *Life of William Blake*, 2nd ed. (London: Macmillan, 1880) I, 125.
17. *Paradiso*, III.85: 'E'n la sua volontade è nostra pace.' (In His will is our peace.)
18. *Gods and Fighting Men*, p. 312 ('Oisin's Children'): '. . . It used to be said by the Fianna that the music that was best with Finn was what happened'; earlier in the same volume Lady Gregory gave a richly elaborated version (pp. 286–87, 'The Wedding at Ceann Slieve'). See also *P&I* 132 and 280 n. 53.
19. The ten Sephiroth of the Cabbalistic Tree represent the successive emanations from God (crown, wisdom, understanding, greatness or goodness, strength, beauty or grace, victory, honour, foundation or peace, and kingdom). The fifth element or quintessence is philosophic mercury. The five elements are earth, water, air, fire and the immaterial quintessence.
20. Ramakrishna (1834–86), a revered Hindu yogi who was averse to books and Western ideas. Jacob Boehme (1575–1624), German theosophist and mystic.
21. A character in William Morris's *The Well at the World's End* has a 'lucky look' in his eyes and is told that 'whatsoever thou dost, that thou dost full well' (*The Collected Works of William Morris* [London: Longmans, Green, 1913], XVIII, 29 [book I, ch. V] and 306 [book I, ch. XXXV]; XIX, 215 [book IV, ch. XXVI]. See p. 403, note 75 below and *V(A)CE* note to p. 249, ll. 9–11.
22. Blake, 'The Divine Image' (*Songs of Innocence*, 1789), ll. 11, 15, in *PWB* 54–55 (Erdman, pp. 12–13); see also 'A Divine Image' (*Songs of Experience*, 1794, plate b only), l. 3, in *PWB* 82 (Erdman, p. 32).
23. *Prometheus Unbound*, IV.400.
24. Blake, *Christ Blessing* (*c.* 1810), tempera on canvas, 75 x 62 cm., Fogg Art Museum, Cambridge, Mass.; see p. 356, note 40f above.

25. Yeats might have intended the phrase 'Shelley would not' to read 'Shelley could not'. The manuscript (dated 30 July [1932], NLI Ms. 30,512) clearly reads 'could'; the typescript (NLI 30,033), which was typed by Mrs Yeats, has 'could', but with the 'c' as a strikeover correction for 'w'; and the first published version (*The Spectator*, 17 March 1933) has 'could'. On the other hand, all subsequent versions, beginning with the Cuala Press *Essays 1931 to 1936* (1937) read 'would'.

    The quotation 'from a multitude of opinions' perhaps is based on Shelley's essay fragment 'On Life' (1815?, publ. 1832), in *Essays and Letters*, p. 75: 'Thus feeling and then reasonings are the combined result of a multitude of entangled thoughts, and of a series of what are called impressions, planted by reiteration.'
26. Blake, 'Infant Joy' (*Songs of Innocence*, 1789), ll. 6, 12, in *PWB* 59–60 (Erdman, p. 16); 'Several Questions Answerd' (Notebook, 1793?–1818?), l. 9, in Erdman, p. 466: '. . . deceit & Idleness'; 'Introduction' to *Songs of Experience* (1794), ll. 4–5, in *PWB* 65: '. . . Word / That walked. . . .' (Erdman, p. 18: '. . . Word, / That walk'd among . . .').
27. Byron, *Manfred, A Dramatic Poem* (1817), I.176.
28. The poet John Keats (1795–1821) and playwright Christopher Marlowe (1564–93).
29. Honoré de Balzac (1799–1850) sought to include a full spectrum of French society in his *Comédie humaine*; see pp. 123 ff. above.
30. The English artist John Trivett Nettleship (1841–1903) was a friend of J. B. Yeats. The drawing 'God Creating Evil' (1869 or before) is not extant; for a contemporary description by John Todhunter, see William M. Murphy, *Prodigal Father: The Life of John Butler Yeats (1839–1922)* (Ithaca: Cornell University Press, 1978) pp. 61–62.
31. Blake, 'The Tyger' (1794), l. 20, in *PWB* 75 (Erdman, p. 25: '. . . he . . . Lamb . . .').

LOUIS LAMBERT

1. Honoré de Balzac's novella *Louis Lambert* (1832–35), in *Séraphita*, tr. Clara Bell, *Comédie humaine*, ed. George Saintsbury (London: Dent Edition, 1895–98), repr. as vol. XXXIV of Temple Edition (New York: Macmillan, 1901), (O'Shea no. 106).
2. Balzac was a schoolboy at the Collège de Vendôme, Vendôme, of the Oratorian fathers. Its sizable library included a wide variety of books plundered during the Revolution; see *Louis Lambert*, in *Séraphita*, p. 162.
3. St Bonaventure (*c*. 1217–74), Italian scholastic philosopher and mystic; for the multiplicity of light, see his *Commentary on the Sentences of Peter Lombard* (*Sententiarum Petri Lombardi*) (1250–51), II. 13.3.2, in *S. Bonaventurae Opera Omnia*, ed. Collegii a S. Bonaventura (Quaracchi, Italy: Typographia Collegii S. Bonventurae, 1885) II, 329.

4. Robert Grosseteste (*c.* 1175–1253), chancellor of Oxford University and bishop of Lincoln, 'On Light' (*c.* 1225–28), opens: 'The first corporeal form which some call corporeity is in my opinion light.' (*On Light* [*De Luce*], tr. Clare C. Riedl [Milwaukee: Marquette University Press, 1942] p. 10.) Riedl's translation in 1942 was the first in English, but Yeats could have known the French translation in Pierre Duhem, *Le Système du monde: histoire des doctrines cosmologiques de Platon à Copernic* (Paris: Librairie Scientifique Hermann, 1917), v, 356 (ch. ix, section 4H): '*Cette forme première que certains nomment corporéité, dit-il c'est, je pense, la lumière. La lumière . . . en sorte qu'à partir du point lumineux, une sphère de lumière.*' For the Latin text, see Ludwig Baur, ed., *Die philosophischen Werke des Robert Grosseteste, Bischofs von Lincoln* (Münster, 1912) p. 51.
5. In 1871, William (later Sir William) Crookes (1832–1919) postulated the existence of a 'Psychic Force' through which physical phenomena are produced in séances. See his 'Experimental Investigation of a New Force' and 'Some Further Experiments on Psychic Force', *Quarterly Journal of Science,* 8 (1 July and 1 October 1871) 339–49 and 471–93, repr. in his *Researches in the Phenomena of Spiritualism* (London: Burns, [1874]), (O'Shea no. 449) pp. 9–43.

   Balthasar Claës, the Flemish scientist in Balzac's *The Quest of the Absolute* (1834), tr. Ellen Marriage, *Comédie humaine,* ed. George Saintsbury (London: Dent Edition, 1895–98), repr. as vol. XXXI of Temple Edition (New York: Macmillan, 1901), (O'Shea no. 103), spends twenty years searching for the 'Absolute', the 'Primitive Element' that is common to all chemical elements and the 'Agency' that is 'the common principle of positive and negative electricity' (pp. 77–78).
6. See, for example, George Berkeley, *Siris: A Chain of Philosophical Reflexions and Inquiries concerning the Virtues of Tar-Water* (1744), sections 151, 157, in *Works of Berkeley,* II, 553, 535: '. . . The whole permeated by pure aether, or light, or fire: for these words are used promiscuously by ancient philosophers. . . . This pure spirit or invisible fire is ever ready to exert and shew itself in its effects.'
7. René Descartes (1596–1650), French philosopher and scientist.
8. Balzac, while a schoolboy at the Vendôme College, perhaps drafted a 'Treatise upon the Will' that was confiscated and burned by a schoolmaster. In *Louis Lambert* the title character, also at the Vendôme College, writes such a treatise (pp. 198–215), which is confiscated; it is excerpted in the novel (pp. 270 ff.).
9. For example, *Séraphita* (1834–35), ch. vii, 'The Assumption'. For Yeats's visions in colour, see p. 300, note 65 above.

   Lucien Chardon de Rubempré, the poetic dreamer of *Lost Illusions* (1837–43), in the moment before his suicide in prison in 1830 at age twenty-nine, sees the Conciergerie precincts and the Palais de Justice in their former mediaeval beauty (Part III ['The End of Evil Ways'] [1846] of *A Harlot's Progress* [1838–47], tr. James Waring, in *Comédie humaine,* ed. George Saintsbury [London: Dent Edition, 1897], repr.

as vol. XVIII of Temple Edition [New York: Macmillan, 1901], [O'Shea no. 90b] p. 116).

10. Emanuel Swedenborg (1688–1772), Swedish scientist, mystic and religious writer.

11. [Yeats's note] I think it probable that Éliphas Lévi found his 'Astral Light' not, as he said, in Saint-Martin, where the one deep student of that eighteenth-century mystic[a] known to me has searched for it in vain, but in *Louis Lambert*.

11a. Éliphas Lévi (Alphonse Louis Constant, 1810–75), *The History of Magic, Including a Clear and Precise Exposition of its Procedure, its Rites and its Mysteries* (1860), tr. Arthur Edward Waite (London: Rider, 1913) p. 39: '. . . There is a composite agent, a natural and divine agent, at once corporeal and spiritual, an universal plastic mediator, a common receptacle for vibrations of movement and images of form, a fluid and a force. . . . By the mediation of this force every nervous apparatus is in secret communication together; hence come . . . dreams, hence the phenomena of second sight and extranatural vision. This universal agent of Nature's works is . . . the Astral Light of the Martinists. . . .' Waite here commented in a footnote (p. 39n): 'Saint-Martin recognises the existence of an astral region, which is apparently that of sidereal rule. There is, in his view, a certain science of this region, and of this the active branch is theurgic, while the passive engenders somnambulism. These divisions constitute the elementary science of the astral, but above these there is one which is more fatal and dangerous, of which he refuses to speak. There is no Martinistic doctrine concerning the Astral Light, understood as an universal medium. Éliphas Lévi seems to have used the term Martinism in a general sense. . . . Modern French Martinism has read it into Saint-Martin's rather ridiculous "epico-magical poem" or allegory, called *Le Crocodile*, much as another school of experiment might find therein a veiled account of the Akasic records and the mode of their study.'

Louis-Claude de Saint-Martin (1743–1803) was a French author on occultism and mysticism. The 'student' to whom Yeats here refers was Arthur Edward Waite (1858–1942), occultist, member of the Golden Dawn, translator of Éliphas Lévi and author of *The Life of Louis Claude de Saint-Martin: The Unknown Philosopher and the Substance of his Transcendental Doctrine* (London: Wellby, 1901), where Waite compared the attitudes of Saint-Martin and Éliphas Lévi toward the astral activity and the astral region, but without mentioning astral light (p. 107). For Éliphas Lévi and astral light, see also p. 453, note 40 below.

12. *Siris*, section 166, in *Works of George Berkeley*, II, 539: '. . . is supposed something . . . in a human. . . . Doth this not seem . . . spirit, flowing . . . darting through. . . .'

Plato, *Timaeus*, 45–46, in *The Dialogues*, tr. Benjamin Jowett, 2nd ed. (Oxford: Clarendon Press, 1875), (O'Shea no. 1586) III, 628–29.

13. *Siris*, section 211, in *Works of George Berkeley*, II, 558: '. . . we may believe . . . fire, which had somewhat divine. . . . heaven . . . situation, as . . . heaven . . . Ficinus.'

Diogenes Laërtius (fl. *c.* 222–35?), 'Pythagoras', in *Lives of Eminent Philosophers,* book VIII, ch. i, section XXVII, tr. R. D. Hicks (London: Heinemann; New York: Putnam's, 1925) II, 343.

Marsilio Ficino (1433–99), Italian philosopher who made Latin translations of Plato and several Neoplatonists.

14. In Balzac's novel *Ursule Mirouët* (1841), chs. 6–7, an unnamed woman medium, during a séance in Paris, is able to observe scenes forty miles away, at Nemours. She is employed by a Mesmerist magnetizer who is a disciple of Swedenborg. For mesmerism (animal magnetism), see note 19 below.
15. For Desplein and Bianchon, physicians in Balzac's fiction, see note 30 below. Hereward H. L. Carrington, *Vitality, Fasting and Nutrition: A Physiological Study of the Curative Power of Fasting, together with a New Theory of the Relation of Food to Human Vitality,* book III, ch. iv (New York: Rebman, 1908) pp. 332–50 (esp. p. 335); Dr Carrington (1880–1958), English-born psychical researcher and author who moved to the United States in 1899, wrote many books on spiritualism.
16. The reference probably is to Julien Ochorowicz, 'Les Phénomènes lumineux et la photographie de l'invisible', *Annales des Sciences Psychiques,* 13 (1909), 199; for an English translation by James Hyslop, see 'Experiments of Dr Ochorovics: Report of a Commission of Naturalists', *Journal of the American Society for Psychical Research,* 5 (1911), 710. See also p. 325, note 52b above.
17. Honoré de Balzac, *Louis Lambert* (1832–35), in *Séraphita,* pp. 196–97.
18. Kate Fox (1841–92) and Margaret Fox (1838–93), American spiritualist mediums. See also p. 394, note 34 below.
19. Franz Anton Mesmer (1733–1815), a Viennese physician who arrived in Paris in 1778, began a sustained vogue for animal magnetism or mesmerism. For references to mesmerism see Honoré de Balzac, *Séraphita* (1834–35) (ch. iii), *Ursule Mirouët* (1841) (see note 14 above), *Le Cousin Pons* (1847) (ch. xiii), and *Louis Lambert* (1832) and Alexandre Dumas (père), *Mémoires d'un médecin: Joseph Balsamo* (1888) (chs. vi ff.); see also p. 180 above. George Sand (1804–76) also alluded to mesmerism; see Robert Darnton, *Mesmerism and the End of the Enlightenment in France* (Cambridge: Harvard University Press, 1968) p. 151, note 16, and Maria M. Tatar, *Spellbound: Studies on Mesmerism and Literature* (Princeton: Princeton University Press, 1978).

    The former society coquette Antoinette, Duchesse de Langeais (not Longuet), plays the organ at a Spanish Carmelite convent in which she is living as Soeur Thérèse, in Balzac's 'The Duchesse de Langeais' (1833) in *The Thirteen,* tr. Ellen Marriage, in *Comédie humaine,* ed. George Saintsbury (London: Dent Edition, 1895–98), repr. as vol. XXXV of Temple Edition (New York: Macmillan, 1901), (O'Shea no. 107) pp. 149–56.

    For the physicians Desplein and Bianchon, see note 30 below.
20. *Louis Lambert,* meditation no. VIII, in *Séraphita,* p. 272.
21. See *Séraphita* (1834–35) and *Louis Lambert,* aphorisms nos. X–XIII, in *Séraphita,* pp. 109–10, 278.

22. For example, James Abbott McNeill Whistler, 'Propositions—No. 2', in *The Gentle Art of Making Enemies*, 2nd ed. (1892; repr. London: Heinemann, 1909) p. 115: 'The work of the master . . . is finished from its beginning.'
23. Novelists Jane Austen (1775–1817), Sir Walter Scott (1771–1832) and Henry Fielding (1707–54).
24. Charles Darwin (1809–82) published *On the Origin of Species by Means of Natural Selection* in 1859; Balzac died in 1850.
25. Catherine de Medici (1519–89) was queen of France in 1159, and then regent (1560–63) for her son Charles IX and controlled him during his reign (1560–74); she remained influential during the reign of another son, Henry III (1574–89). Balzac defended her for preserving the monarchy at the expense of the Huguenot party and Calvinists: *About Catherine de' Medici* (1842–43), tr. Clara Bell, in *Comédie humaine*, ed. George Saintsbury (London: Dent Edition, 1895–98), repr. as vol. I of Temple Edition (New York: Macmillan, 1901), (O'Shea no. 76).

    Napoleon Bonaparte (1769–1821), emperor of France (1805–14), whom Balzac admired as a superman: 'The Vendetta', in *At the Sign of the Cat and Racket* (1830), tr. Clara Bell, in *Comédie humaine*, ed. George Saintsbury (Dent Edition, 1895–98), repr. as vol. II of Temple Edition (New York: Macmillan, 1901), (O'Shea no. 77) and in *A Gondreville Mystery* [*Une ténébreuse Affaire*] (1841), tr. Ellen Marriage, in *Comédie humaine*, ed. George Saintsbury (Dent Edition, 1895–98), repr. as vol. XV of Temple Edition (New York: Macmillan, 1901), (O'Shea no. 89).

    John Calvin (1509–64), French theologian and religious reformer, banished from Paris in 1533 for his support of the Reformation; for Calvin and the war of ideas with the State, see the preface to 'The Calvinist Martyr' in *About Catherine de' Medici*, p. 11: '. . . there were two vast armies to contend with—that of ideas and that of men. Royal power perished in the struggle. . . .'; see also pp. 9–10, 210.
26. Balzac, *Eugénie Grandet* (1833), tr. Ellen Marriage, in *Comédie humaine*, ed. George Saintsbury (London: Dent Edition, 1895–98), repr. as vol. XIII of Temple Edition (New York: Macmillan, 1901), (O'Shea no. 87) pp. 154 (Charles departs), 206–8 (description of Charles making his fortune in the East Indies, Africa, St Thomas, Lisbon and the United States), 208 (Charles returns to France).
27. The arch-criminal Vautrin in Balzac's *Old Goriot* (*Le père Goriot*) (1834–35) and 'Vautrin's Last Avatar' ('La dernière Incarnation de Vautrin') (1847), in *Scenes from a Courtesan's Life* (*Splendeurs et Misères des Courtisanes*).

    Séraphita-Séraphitus, the Swedenborgian angel of *Séraphita* (1834–35).

    The fictional 'Association of Thirteen' or 'Devourers', a Parisian aristocratic criminal secret society, is portrayed in 'Ferragus', 'The Duchesse de Langeais' and 'The Girl with the Golden Eyes', in *The Thirteen* (1833–35).

28. Divisionism (or Chromo-luminarism, Pointillism), especially as in the French Neo-Impressionists Georges Seurat (1859–91) and Paul Signac (1863–1935).
29. Yeats read Count Leo Tolstoi's novel *Anna Karenina* (1875–77) in *c.* 1890 (*Au* 193), and he mentioned it and *War and Peace* (1866) in 1901 (*UP2* 263). The records of Yeats's library do not include any books by Tolstoi, but Yeats owned three books, dated 1913 and 1916, by the Russian novelist Fëdor Dostoevski (1821–81) (O'Shea 1920s list) and four books, dated 1895 to 1910, by the French novelist Gustave Flaubert (1821–80) (O'Shea nos. 679–82).
30. The Balzac novels and stories to which Yeats here refers include *Séraphita* (1834–35), *Old Goriot* (1834–35) for the young Horace Bianchon as a medical student and then, with the free-thinking doctor (later Baron) Desplein, in 'The Atheist's Mass' (1836) (in *The Atheist's Mass*). Each of those doctors is mentioned in several other works by Balzac; Desplein as a young man is in *La Rabouilleuse* (1841–43) and *Cousin Pons* (1847).
31. For this description of a novel as a mirror, in Stendhal's *Le Rouge et la noir* (1831), see p. 353, note 31 above.
32. The English poets Abraham Cowley (1618–67), William Blake (1757–1827), John Keats (1795–1821), Robert Browning (1812–89) and Wilfrid Scawen Blunt (1840–1922).
33. Balzac, *The Quest of the Absolute* (1834), tr. Ellen Marriage, in *Comédie humaine,* ed. George Saintsbury (London: Dent Edition, 1895), repr. as vol. XXXI of Temple Edition (New York: Macmillan, 1901), (O'Shea no. 103) p. 32: '. . . imperfect, for . . . kingdom . . . love.' In the next paragraph Balzac gives a list of 'the best loved women in history', from Cleopatra to Madame de Pompadour, who 'have been by no means perfectly beautiful for ordinary eyes' (p. 33).
34. Dante Alighieri (1265–1321). Most of the French kings were crowned at the cathedral at Rheims and buried at Saint-Denis.
35. Yeats was a friend of the English poet Lionel Johnson (1867–1902) during the 1890s. Yeats arrived in New York on 26 October 1932 and departed on 22 January 1933. He owned *The Book of the Thousand Nights and One Night* in the English translation by E. Powys Mathers from the French edition of J. C. Mardrus, 4 vols. (London: Casanova Society, 1923), (O'Shea no. 251). For William Morris and the Icelandic sagas, see p. 347, note 43 above, and p. 435, note 86 below.

INTRODUCTION TO *AN INDIAN MONK*

1. Yeats's introduction to *Gitanjali,* by Rabindranath Tagore, is dated September 1912; see pp. 165–70 above.
2. Shri Purohit Swāmi (born Shankar Gajanan Purohit, 1882–1941) arrived in London from India on 28 February 1931. Yeats met Purohit Swāmi on 6 June 1931 at the home of Thomas Sturge Moore (1870–1944), English artist and poet, and long-time friend of Yeats. In the

acknowledgments to *An Indian Monk*, Shri Purohit Swāmi thanked Sturge Moore for giving 'much time and labour to the clarifying and arranging of this book' (*IM* vii); see John Harwood, 'Yeats, Shri Purohit Swami, and Mrs Foden', appendix to 'Olivia Shakespear: Letters to W. B. Yeats', *YA6*, ed. Warwick Gould (London: Macmillan, 1988) pp. 102–3.

3. The Bengali Swāmi Vivekānanda (1863–1902) visited America to attend the World Parliament of Religions, in Chicago, during the World's Fair of 1893. Purohit Swāmi calls him 'the first exponent of Hindu philosophy to the West' (*IM* 169).
4. See *IM* 192 for the Hindu shrines and for the quotation: 'The . . . Bhārat Dharma . . .'. Swāmi Gyananand ji Maharaj (1847–1952) had founded the Bharat Dharma Mahāmandal ('Organisation of various Hindu sects'), in Varanasi (Benaras), in 1867. (Information from Shalini Sikka.)
5. John Masefield (1878–1967) became poet laureate in 1930.
6. Henry James (1843–1916), American novelist. The attaché from the Egyptian legation is unidentified.
7. Wilfrid Scawen Blunt (1840–1922), English poet and traveller, supported Indian nationalism and had visited India in 1878 and 1883–84; he raised Arabian horses at his country house, Newbuildings Place, Southwater, Horsham, Sussex. Yeats probably is referring to Dr Syed Mahmud (1889–1971), an Indian student from a wealthy Sunni Muslim family. Dr Mahmud often visited Blunt during 1909–12, while a student at Cambridge and the University of Münster, where he received a Ph.D. degree in 1911. He was called to the Bar in June 1912 from Lincoln's Inn, and later that year returned to India, where he had a long career in nationalist politics, punctuated by several imprisonments for his opposition to British rule. He was general secretary of the Congress (1923, 1929–36) and minister of state in the Ministry of External Affairs (1952–57). Blunt's published diaries mention only two visits by Yeats to Newbuildings Place, however, in June 1902 and 18 January 1914, after Syed had left England.
8. Dr D. N. Maitra (1878–1950); see p. 385, note 1 below. In the manuscript version the 'Indian leader' is identified as 'the famous Vivekānanda'; see note 3 above.
9. Chloride of lime: bleaching powder.
10. See p. 411, note 25 below.
11. William Wordsworth, 'Poems dedicated to National Independence and Liberty: VII: To Toussaint L'Ouverture' (1802; publ. 1803), l. 11–12, in *The Poetical Works of William Wordsworth*, ed. Edward Dowden, Aldine Edition of the British Poets (London: Bell, 1892), (O'Shea no. 2292) III, 130; see also p. 414, note 55 below.
12. His pilgrimage to Mount Girnār (elev. 3,666 feet), in the Gir Hills, just east of Junagadh (21–34N/070–30E), is described in *IM* 70–73. Nearly seven thousand granite steps lead to the sacred footprints of the god Dattātreya impressed on a stone slab. For Dattātreya, see pp. 139–40 above and p. 387, note 2 below.

   Later, probably at Mount Māhur, a hill outside the town of Māhur

(Mahor), forty miles south-southwest of Nagpur, Purohit Swāmi found a small temple with a bed to which the Lord Dattātreya is said to come at night. The tapping of Lord Dattātreya's golden pattens (shoes) makes measured music as he walks across the temple floor (*IM* 87–88); on the third night Purohit Swāmi 'heard the creaking noise of the bed as if someone was lying down on it' (*IM* 89).

13. This continuous praying, known as the Jesus prayer, is described in the Greek *Philokalia* ('Love of Spiritual Beauty'), a collection of mystical and ascetic writings of spiritual masters of the Eastern Orthodox Church, from the fourth through the fifteenth centuries. The *Philokalia* was compiled by St Nicodemus (Nikodimos) of the Holy Mountain of Athos (1748?–1809) and St Macarius (Makarios) of Corinth (1731–1805); it was first published in 1782 in Venice. The writers whom Yeats mentions are St Simeon the New Theologian or Metaphrastis ('Translator') (949–1022), a monk in Constantinople; Callistus of Xanthopoulos, Patriarch of Constantinople and his close friend and fellow-worker Ignatius of Xanthopoulos (14th c.). See *Writings from the Philokalia on Prayer of the Heart,* tr. E. Kadloubovsky and G. E. H. Palmer (London: Faber, 1951).

14. [Yeats's note] The Rev. R. M. French has translated his autobiography into English and calls it *The Way of a Pilgrim.* 'Of the pilgrim's identity nothing is known', he writes; 'in some way his manuscript, or a copy of it, came into the hands of a monk on Mount Athos, in whose possession it was found by the Abbot of St Michael's Monastery at Kasan.'[a]

14a. [Rasskazui Otkrovennuie], *The Way of a Pilgrim,* tr. [from the Russian] R. M. French (London: Philip Allan, 1930) pp. 8–9: '. . . the Pilgrim's identity. . . .' The book was first printed in 1884 at Kasan (Kazan), Russia, from that manuscript copy. The anonymous pilgrim dates probably from the first half of the nineteenth century. Mount Athos (the Holy Mountain) (elev. 2,073 feet), eighty miles east-southeast of Thessalonica, Greece, lies at the end of a peninsula that is dotted with monasteries.

15. See *The Way of a Pilgrim,* p. 26: 'It was as though my lips and my tongue pronounced the words entirely of themselves without any urging from me. . . . I easily finished my twelve thousand prayers by the early evening.'

16. [Yeats's note] Swami comments, 'Some of the yogis of India practise Ajapā-japa Mantram. Ajapā-japa is very short and easy. They repeat "Soham" as they draw in the breath and "Hamsah" as they breathe it out. Soham Hamsah means, "I am that Hamsa"—the eternal self or soul.'

17. *IM* 70: '. . . mantram, and became so. . . . others, my . . . muttering: "We . . . Supreme . . . divine Being; may. . . .'

18. For Mount Athos, see note 14a above. The quoted phrase is untraced.

19. *IM* 71: '. . . time. My. . . .'

20. This anecdote of Saint Bernard of Clairvaux (1090–1153), from the *Vita prima Bernardi* (*Opera,* ed. Mabillon, 2nd ed. [1690] ɪɪ, col. 1118, repr. J. P. Migne, ed., *Patrologiae . . . Latinae* [Paris: Migne, 1855]

CLXXXV, col. 306) is noted by Robert Burton in *The Anatomy of Melancholy* (1621), part I, section II, member 3, subsection 15, ed. Rev. A. R. Shilleto, Bohn's Libraries (London: Bell, 1912), (O'Shea no. 311) I, 353; by Edward Gibbon in *The History of the Decline and Fall of the Roman Empire* (1776–88), ed. J. B. Bury, World's Classics (London: Methuen, 1912), (O'Shea no. 746) VI, 346 and note 34; and by James Cotter Morison in *The Life and Times of Saint Bernard, Abbot of Clairvaux* (London: Macmillan, 1868) p. 68.

21. From the Gāyitri (Gāyatri) Mantra (*IM* 50: '. . . that Divine Being'; *IM* 103: '. . . that divine Being').
22. Hagia Sophia (Santa Sophia), Istanbul, constructed 532–37.
23. Yeats first used this notion in the 1900 version of his novel *The Speckled Bird,* where the autobiographical hero explains, 'Christ, being the perfect man, had alone the perfect measurements. . . . It is an idea the people have' (*SB* 99). Then another character in the novel dreams of Christ, who points to his crown and says to her, 'There is among the birds one that is perfect and among the fish one that is perfect and among the beasts one that is perfect, and if I were not among men none would know the perfect' (*SB* 101). See *Gods and Fighting Men,* p. 8: 'For it was a law with the Tuatha de Danaan that no man that was not perfect in shape should be king.' See also Callan, *Yeats on Yeats,* p. 50, note 35, for a passage from John Rhys, *Lectures on the Origin and Growth of Celtic Heathendom* (1888), (O'Shea no. 1741), on the blending of Druidism with Christianity, for the possible attribution of the quotation to St Columba, and for a Druid requirement that kings be unblemished in body.
24. Untraced.
25. Among the paintings by Sandro Botticelli that make prominent use of flowers, Yeats could have been thinking of *The Primavera* (*c.* 1478) or *The Birth of Venus* (*c.* 1486) (Uffizi, Florence).
26. The poetry of Edmund Spenser (1552?–99); Samuel Taylor Coleridge's poems 'Christabel' (1797, 1800; publ. 1816) and 'Kubla Khan: A Vision in a Dream' (1797, publ. 1816). For the pedlar in William Wordsworth's *The Excursion,* see p. 353, note 33 above; in Percy Bysshe Shelley's poetic drama *Hellas* (1821, publ. 1822), Ahasuerus is a wandering Jew who possesses great wisdom and can summon visions.
27. John 10:30.
28. Shri Purohit Swāmi records that, prior to his pilgrimage to Mount Girnār, 'the great truth dawned upon me that all gods are one. . . . God, in whatever form you worship him, is willing to manifest himself according to the wishes of the devotee.' Thus 'every man is free to worship the god who . . . is for him the most perfect way of approaching divinity' (*IM* 58). Purohit Swāmi twice mentions (*IM* 63, 69) that his worship of Dattātreya is helped by a photograph of a life-size oil painting of the god by an artist named Bhat in the late 1890s, at Wādi, a town and place of pilgrimage 100 miles southeast of Bombay; in 1931 the painting was in Bombay. Purohit Swāmi recounts the 'wonderful story' of the 'very curious circumstances' of the

painting having been accomplished entirely during a vision that lasted three days and nights, while the artist suffered a very high temperature from a plague. (*IM* 75–76)

29. Purohit Swāmi was born at Badnerā (20–47N/077–15E), a town six miles south-southwest of Amrāoti, Berar. For his singing, see also *L* 794 and Olivia Shakespear to Yeats, 29 April 1932, in 'Olivia Shakespear: Letters to W. B. Yeats', ed. John Harwood, *YA6,* ed. Warwick Gould (London: Macmillan, 1988) pp. 81–82.
30. See p. 345, note 29 above.
31. Shalini Sikka has examined the typescripts of these four lyrics, which are in two of Purohit Swāmi's unpublished collections of lyrics in English, among his papers at the Nehru Memorial Library, New Delhi; the published versions reflect considerable verbal revision. The first lyric, from *The Harbinger of Love* (1914), opens, 'His eyes are sweet, his looks are sweet' (song no. 54). The other three lyrics are from *At Thy Lotus Feet* (*c.* 1914–15); their opening lines are: 'I know I am the sinner great, / But the remedy there is none' (song no. 60); 'And now shall I do this, / And again shall I do that' (song no. 62); 'What a wonderful miracle thou hast worked? / Thou art the lord of all the powers great' (song no. 103).

   Purohit Swāmi recorded (*IM* 130) that he was instructed to write by Dattātreya: 'I obeyed, took pencil and paper, and to my surprise began to write in English *In Quest of Myself, The Harbinger of Love* and *The Song of Silence.* Each was complete in a week.' Those were followed by two more collections of verse in English, *The Honey-Comb* and *At Thy Lotus Feet* (*IM* 131). He brought his writings to Europe in 1931: 'I had my Sanskrit, Hindi and English writings with me, and I read them before appreciative audiences. They had slept for many years, but appealed to the devout.' (*IM* 193) The only collection published was *The Song of Silence,* which contains 108 short lyrics in English (Poona City: V. S. Chitale, n.d., British Museum date-stamped 9 May 1931).
32. *IM* 36, 35, 197–98.
33. The *Urna* or 'third eye' is one of the magic marks (*laksanā*) of the Buddha. Similarly, the Hindu god Siva is usually shown with a vertical third eye, on his forehead. See Yeats's commentary at p. 374, note 15.
34. Jean Martin Charcot (1825–93), French neurologist, a founder of modern neuropathology, professor at the Sorbonne and director of a neurological clinic at the Salpêtrière, Paris, studied hysteria and hypnotism. He experimentally demonstrated that stigmatisation could be induced under hypnosis.

INTRODUCTION TO *THE HOLY MOUNTAIN*

1. For Patanjali, *Aphorisms of Yôga,* see pp. 175 ff. above.
2. Honoré de Balzac's comprehensive view of French life in the novels

and stories collected as *Comédie humaine* (1st series, 1842; publ. posthumously in 47 vols.).

3. For the travels of Purohit Swāmi, see pp. 130 ff. above. For Bhagwān Shri Hamsa (formerly Shri Nātēkār Swāmi), see the biographical note, pp. 291 ff. above.
4. Honoré de Balzac's Swedenborgian novel *Séraphita* (1834–35).
5. The verse is untraced.
6. The biographical details, here and in the following two sections, on Shri Purohit Swāmi and his worship of Dattātreya are from Purohit Swāmi's autobiography, *IM*; see pp. 130 ff. and notes above.
7. *IM* 63; *Bhagavad-Geetā* (*Bhagavad-Gita*): a sacred text in the form of a philosophical dialogue, in the *Mahābhārata,* a Sanskrit Hindu epic (*c.* 200 B.C.). In *c.* 1913 Purohit Swāmi made a verse translation of the *Bhagavad-Gita* into his native Marāthi and wrote a commentary; he later prepared an English translation, which he dedicated to Yeats, *The [Bhagavad] Geetā: The Gospel of the Lord Shri Krishna,* tr. Shri Purohit Swāmi (London: Faber and Faber, July 1935), (O'Shea nos. 738–38d).
8. Of the Gāyitri (Gāyatrī) (*The Hymns of the Rgveda,* III.lxii.10), Purohit Swāmi records, 'I repeated the Gāyitri, the most sacred mantram, and became so habituated that even in my dreams I continued. When talking with others, my mind went on unconsciously muttering: "We meditate on the Supreme splendour of that divine Being; may it illuminate our intellects" ' (*IM* 103). In an earlier passage the capitalisation in the quoted passage varies slightly: '. . . supreme . . . Divine. . . .' (*IM* 50).
9. The village of Narsoba Vādi (Wādi) (16–43N/074–40E) on the River Krishna, twenty-five miles east of Kolhapur, is the site of a large annual festival.
10. *IM* 59: '. . . stairs of the Keertikar's building . . . Swāmi who . . . sitting on a . . . skin rose, our. . . .'
11. *IM* 60: '. . . after such a . . . time!'
12. Brahmāvarta: the region (29N/076E), in the eastern Punjab, between the ancient divine rivers Sarasvatī and Drsadvatī.
13. The Lady of the Mat is unidentified.
14. *IM* 70–73; for the quotation see p. 371, note 17 above. The remainder of this paragraph is drawn from information not given in *IM*.
15. See p. 373, note 33 above. The typescript (SUI 76/1/5, p. 3) had a fuller explanation before Yeats revised it: '. . . when he felt his forehead, he found in the centre, the first trace of that small mound, the sculptors show upon the forehead of the Buddha, the outward sign of the third eye, the soul's eye, an intuition that is above the antinomies as that mound is above the two eyes, the two ears, the two nostrils. He had attained. . . .'
16. As Yeats explains later, the four stages of the *Savikalpa-Samādhi* system of meditation are (1) selection of some place, object or image, as the theme of meditation; (2) mutual transformation, the drawing, as it were, together, of theme and thought, fact and idea; (3) *Sushupti* or unconscious *Samādhi,* a dreamless sleep; and (4) *Turiyā* (or *Tureeyā*),

the greater or conscious *Samādhi*. See pp. 147–49, 158 and 177 above and *AY* 32–33, 62.

17. *IM* 71–72.
18. The bright-eyed man is not mentioned in *IM*. Purohit Swāmi reported only that in his vision at the top of the hill, he saw Dattātreya 'in that same form on which I meditate' (*IM* 73).
19. For *Savikalpa-Samādhi, Turiyā* and *Samādhi,* see note 16 above. For Mount Kailās (Mount Meru), see note 22 below.
20. The verse is untraced.
21. Elements of Byzantine abstraction and the newer Gothic expressiveness are co-present in the paintings of early fourteenth-century Sienese masters Duccio (e.g., *Maestà*, 1308–11) and Simone Martini (e.g., *Maestà*, 1315 and repainted 1321).
22. Mount Kailās (elev. 22,030 feet), in the Himalayan range, Tibet (31–15N/081–10E); it is called Mount Meru in the epic *Mahābhārata* and in the Vedas. See also p. 163 above and *IM* 78.
23. Sven Anders Hedin, *Trans-Himalaya: Discoveries and Adventures in Tibet* (London: Macmillan, 1909), (O'Shea no. 867) II, 198 (ch. li).
24. For references to Kailās in the works of Kalidās (Kālidāsa), the great Sanskrit poet and dramatist of fifth-century India, see the opening of his drama *Vikramorvaśīya* and his poems *Kumārasambhava* (canto I) and *Meghadūta* (or *Meghasandeśa*) (stanzas 110–21).

    According to the Hindu epic *Mahābhārata*, the Ganges begins from the roots of a great jujube tree on the summit of Mount Kailās, and then flows to Lake Manasarowar, where it provides the source of the Brahmaputra, Sutlej and Indus rivers.
25. Yeats's translation is correct; Hedin had translated the name Manasarowar as 'the holy lake' (*Trans-Himalaya*, II, 432, 110–11).
26. The Dehrā Dun (Dehrādun) district, in the Himalaya foothills, between the Ganges and Yamuna (Jumna) rivers (30–24N/078–05E); *HM* 48–49.
27. Ekai Kawaguchi, *Three Years in Tibet* (Adyar, Madras: Theosophist Office; Benares and London: Theosophical Publishing Society, 1909).
28. See *AY* 90 for an illustration of Baddha-Padmāsana (Lotus-lock posture).
29. *HM* 131–35.
30. *HM* 146 has only 'from the west'; Yeats added 'the direction of Mount Kailās', despite the more accurate statement available at *HM* 140: 'Mount Kailās lies north-west, north of Mānas'.
31. For 'AUM' see also pp. 157–58 above.
32. *HM* 145–49.
33. *HM* 150–61, 165–67.
34. *HM* 168: '. . . Grace. . . . said: "Achhā, Vatsa, Uthake baitho" (My . . . up).'
35. On the northeast side of the mountain. *HM* 177: 'Gaurikund stands at a height of about 20,000 feet above sea-level, and is a natural lake about four furlongs in circumference. The peak of Kailās seems to be about 10,000 feet above this lake.'

36. *HM* 167–73.
37. *HM* 180: '. . . child! O . . . dear!'
38. Giri: mountain or height. Sanyāsin (Sannyāsin): a religious mendicant who has relinquished all worldly attachments and values and has chosen a life of religious contemplation or asceticism. He is assumed to have attained a state of holiness and thus become immortal; his death is regarded simply as the trance-state *samādhi* (*Harper's Dictionary of Hinduism*, p. 267).
39. *HM* 173–82.
40. For the dating of these works, see also p. 176 above.
41. Thomas Hobbes (1588–1679), English philosopher, was narrowly rationalistic and held that all human knowledge begins with the senses.

    The intense interest and debate during the 1920s and early 1930s among Soviet philosophers over the relation of Spinoza (1632–77) to Marxism centered on the Mechanists (L. I. Axelrod and A. I. Varyash), who rejected Spinoza as an idealist, and the Deborinites (A. M. 'Deborin' Ioffe, N. Karev and I. K. Luppol), who valued Spinoza as a dialectician and materialist and who spoke of Spinoza as 'Marx without a beard'. In April 1929 the Second All-Union Conference of Marxist-Leninist Scientific Institutions condemned the Mechanist position as 'revisionist'. Yeats's reference may have been to that or to the June 1930 First All-Union Philosophical Conference, at which the anti-Mechanist Luppol read a paper on Spinoza. See *VPl*; George L. Kline, *Spinoza in Soviet Philosophy* (London: Routledge and Kegan Paul, 1952) pp. 15–16; and John Somerville, *Soviet Philosophy* (New York: Philosophical Library, 1946) pp. 213–21.

    For the German philosopher Arthur Schopenhauer (1788–1860), 'will' is the true reality, an unconscious force in nature, known to man only through intuition.
42. [Yeats's note] 'Subtler',[a] 'finer', because it penetrates all things. Ordinary matter cannot go through the wall, mind can.
42a. The first version of this note, which Yeats wrote in the margin of the typescript (SUI 76/1/5, p. 8), was more tentative: 'In my slight study of Indian thought I have never discovered what "subtle" used in this context means. How does "Matter" seen in dreams differ from "Matter" seen with open eyes?'
43. In the *Sāmkhya* philosophy, *tamas*, *rajas* and *satva* (*sattva*) are the three constituents of *prakrti*, an eternal unconscious principle which is always changing. *Tamas* is the principle of passivity or negativity; *rajas* is the principle of activity; and *satva* is the subtle principle which determines the qualities of light, knowledge, intellect and the emotions. (*Harper's Dictionary of Hinduism*, p. 264.) Yeats and Purohit Swāmi used a variety of terms for these: 'ignorance' (*AY* 64, 82) and 'heaviness, exhaustion' (p. 161 above) for *tamas*; 'passion' (*AY* 64, 82) and 'passion, violence, movement' (p. 161 above) for *rajas*; 'purity' (*AY* 64, 82) and 'wisdom, peace, beauty' (p. 161 above) for *satva*.
44. Probably book I, section XLI (*AY* 42). In the next sentences Yeats

draws on several of the commentaries, especially book I, sections XXIV, XXXV, XXXVII (*AY* 37–38, 40–41).

45. Blake, *Milton* (1804–8?), plate 2, l. 10, in Erdman, p. 95: '. . . vegetated'; *AY* 40 (no. 35).
46. Māndookya-Upanishad, in *TPU* 59–61; see *AY* 33 (no. 17).
47. [Yeats's note] The tongue represents colour and sound, perhaps because the ascetic can see the point of nose or tongue, but not his eyes or ears.
48. *AY* 32 (no. 17) and 42 (no. 41).
49. Untraced.
50. See note 16 above.
51. The Pythagoreans regarded ten, the Decad, as the perfect number and also as the last number. John Burnet explained this in *Early Greek Philosophy* (London and Edinburgh: Black, 1892), (O'Shea no. 308) p. 318, n. 51: 'The Pythagorean view was that, after ten, the numbers were simply repeated.' For the Decad as defining Nature, see Porphyry, *The Life of Pythagoras* 52, in *The Pythagorean Sourcebook and Library: An Anthology of Ancient Writings Which Relate to Pythagoras and Pythagorean Philosophy,* compiled and tr. Kenneth Sylvan Guthrie (1920), ed. David R. Fideler (Grand Rapids, MI: Phanes Press, 1987) p. 133: 'Since the Decad comprehends every reason [or ratio] of numbers, every proportion, and every species—why should Nature herself not be denoted by the most perfect number, Ten? Such was the use of numbers among the Pythagoreans.' See also Philolaus the Pythagorean, of Croton (5th c. B.C.), *The Fragments of Philolaus* 18A (Stobaeus, 1.3.8) (Diels-Krans, *Fragmente der Vorsokratieker* 11), in *Pythagorean Sourcebook and Library,* p. 171: 'The power, efficacy and essence of Number is seen in the Decad; it is great, it realizes all its purposes, and it is the cause of all effects. The power of the Decad is the principle and guide of all life, divine, celestial, or human into which it is insinuated; without it everything is unlimited, obscure, and furtive.' The significance of the Decad for the Pythagoreans is discussed in Thomas Taylor, *Theoretic Arithmetic . . . [with] a Specimen of the Manner in Which Pythagoreans Philosophized about Numbers; and a Development of Their Mystical and Theological Arithmetic,* book III, ch. xii (1816; repr. as *The Theoretic Arithmetic of the Pythagoreans,* Los Angeles: Phoenix Press, 1934) pp. 204–7.
52. Samuel Taylor Coleridge, 'What is Life' (1805), ll. 1–5, in *The Poetical Works of Samuel Taylor Coleridge,* ed. James Dykes Campbell (1903; repr. London: Macmillan, 1925), (O'Shea no. 404) p. 173: '. . . was deem'd of . . . / . . . shade / By encroach of . . . made?—'
53. In chapter ix of *The Tale of Genji* by Lady Murasaki (978?–1031?), Lady Rokujō, mistress of Prince Genji, kills the Prince's wife, Lady Aoi. See *The Tale of Genji,* tr. Arthur Waley (London: Allen and Unwin, 1925), (O'Shea no. 1403) pp. 263–73, especially pp. 265–66.
54. See Purohit Swāmi's commentary in *AY* 71: 'I saw a Mahātmā . . . [who] went to Benāres from Nāgpur [a distance of 370 miles] with the speed of thought through air and dissolved his body in the Ganges.'

Purohit Swāmi gives a fuller account at *IM* 39. For Christ's empty tomb, see Matthew 28:6, Mark 16:6, Luke 24:3 and John 20:2.

55. See Plato, *Timaeus,* 45E–46A and *Republic,* 571C ff.
56. Henry Vaughan, 'The Night. John iii.2' (1650), ll. 49–54, in *The Works of Henry Vaughan,* ed. Leonard Cyril Martin (Oxford: Clarendon Press, 1914), (O'Shea no. 2192) II, 523: '. . . God (some say) / A deep, but dazling darkness; / As . . . / . . . clear; / . . . night! where I . . . / . . . dim.'
57. Buddha's Nirvana could be defined as nothingness attained by the non-self (*an-atman*); the Vedānta philosophy, derived from the teachings of the Upanishads, unites the individual's essence or real self (*ātman*) with the cosmic self (*brahman*).
58. Georg Wilhelm Friedrich Hegel (1770–1831) first delivered his lectures on the philosophy of history in 1820; they were compiled and published posthumously in 1837. For the references here, see *The Philosophy of History,* tr. J. Sibree (1858), rev. ed. (New York: Colonial Press, [1889]) pp. 199 (part I, section III, ch. iii, 'Egypt'), 220–21 (part I, section III, ch. iii, 'Transition to the Greek World': 'What is that which in the morning goes on four legs, at mid-day on two, and in the evening on three?'), 108–9 ('Classification of Historic Data'), 54–79 (Introduction, section III, 'The Course of the World's History'), 103 and 105 ('Classification of Historic Data').
59. That era could have begun with the eleventh century. Raphael (1483–1520) and Michelangelo (1475–1564) were Italian artists of the sixteenth century; Romanesque architecture prevailed in western and southern Europe from the ninth through the thirteenth centuries.
60. In 1509–11, Raphael decorated the *Stanza* (or *Camera*) *della Segnatura,* in the Vatican Palace, with frescoes of *Parnassus, School of Athens, Disputation on the Holy Sacrament, Three Cardinal Virtues, Civil Law* and *Canon Law*. The popes from the Medici family were Leo X (Giovanni de' Medici, pope 1513–21); Clement VII (Giulio de' Medici, pope 1523–34); Pius IV (Giovanni Angelo Medici, pope 1559–65); Leo XI (Alessandro Ottaviano de' Medici, pope in 1605).
61. [Yeats's note] Hegel's lectures[a] were not published until 1837, seven years after the publication of the *Peau de chagrin*. Balzac probably derived his thought from classical sources. It is more like Vico's than Hegel's.
61a. For Hegel's lectures on the philosophy of history, see note 58 above. For Giambattista Vico, *Principles of a New Science* (1725, 1730, 1744), see p. 357, note 45 above; see also p. 432, note 61 below.
62. In Balzac's short tale *La Peau de chagrin* (*The Wild Ass's Skin*) (1831), a reckless young man finds a wild-ass's skin with magical power to grant his wishes, which are for individual, material happiness. However, the magic skin inexorably decreases in size with every wish, and when it disappears, he dies. In the historical novel *Sur Catherine de Médicis* (*About Catherine de' Medici*) (1842–43), Balzac expresses his admiration of Catherine de' Medici (1519–89) for having tried to stem the tide of individualism and rationalism that would overturn the

monarchy; see also p. 127 above. Both of those works are part of Balzac's *Comédie humaine.*

The abbey and fortress of Mont-Saint-Michel, on the coast of Brittany, date from the eighth century; the Gothic cathedral at Chartres, southwest of Paris, dates from the twelfth century. Dante Alighieri began the *Divina Commedia c.* 1307.

Yeats's reference to an open letter to Madame de Castries here and in *On the Boiler* (p. 233 above) probably is to the opening paragraph of 'Gaudissart the Great' ('L'Illustre Gaudissart') (1833), a story that Honoré de Balzac dedicated to the Duchesse (later Marquise) Henriette de Castries. In Yeats's copy of *Parisians in the Country,* tr. James Waring, *Comédie Humaine,* ed. George Saintsbury (London: Dent Edition, 1895–98), repr. as vol. XXVII of Temple Edition (New York: Macmillan, 1901), (O'Shea no. 99) p. 11, the dedication, 'To Madame la Duchesse de Castries', is printed immediately above the first paragraph, which is not a letter; that opening paragraph reads: 'Is not the commercial traveller—a being unknown in earlier times—one of the most curious types produced by the manners and customs of this age? And is it not his peculiar function to carry out in a certain class of things the immense transition which connects the age of material development with that of intellectual development? Our epoch will be the link between the age of isolated forces rich in original creativeness, and that of the uniform but levelling force which gives monotony to its products, casting them in masses, and following out a unifying idea—the ultimate expression of social communities. After the Saturnalia of intellectual communism, after the last struggles of many civilizations concentrating all the treasures of the world on a single spot, must not the darkness of barbarism invariably supervene?' The second part of *Parisians in the Country,* 'The Muse of the Department', does open with a dedicatory letter, but to le Comte Ferdinand de Gramont. For the identification of this passage, see also *V(B)* 301 and Paul Scott Stanfield, *Yeats and Politics in the 1930s* (London: Macmillan, 1988) pp. 127–28 and 208–9, note 53.

63. Victor-Marie Hugo (1802–85), French Romantic poet and novelist.
64. Jean-Jacques Rousseau (1712–78), French philosopher and writer, advocated the political authority of the people in *Du Contrat social* (1762).
65. Presumably Yeats's reference is to Arthur Schopenhauer, 'The Metaphysics of the Love of the Sexes' (1844), in *The World as Will and Idea,* tr. R. B. Haldane and J. Kemp (London: Routledge & Kegan Paul, 1883) III, 336–75 (ch. xliv, supplement to the fourth book).
66. Prashna Upanishad, 1.5, 1.9–10, 1.12, in *TPU* 40–41: 'Sun is life, Moon matter. . . . There are two paths, the southern and the northern. Those that are content with alms-giving and ritual preferring the life of the family, go to their ancestors by the southern path, attain the lunar world and are born again. All there is matter. But those who seek the Self through austerity, continence, faith, knowledge, go by the northern path, attain the solar world. It is living, immortal, beyond fear; it is the goal. . . . The month too is the Creator, its bright half is life, its dark half matter. Wise men perform their rituals in the

bright half; fools in the dark. . . . Let all things find their food, thrive, rejoice. . . . Fire itself, Eater, Master! All the world your food, Father in Heaven!'

67. For soma, see p. 392, note 19 below. The quotation from Count de Villiers de l'Isle-Adam's drama *Axël* (publ. 1890, perf. 1894), part IV, scene 2 ('The Supreme Choice'), is from the translation by Arthur Symons, 'Villiers de L'Isle-Adam' in *The Symbolist Movement in Literature* (London: Heinemann, 1899), (O'Shea no. 2068) p. 56; Yeats quoted it often (*UP2* 117; *P&I* 112, 156; pp. 33 and 307, note 136 above; *Au* 305).
68. Untraced; see also p. 153 above.
69. John Burnet, *Early Greek Philosophy* (London: Black, 1892), (O'Shea no. 307) pp. 163–64, note 65, remarked, of 'the Great Year' that the 'statements as to the precise duration of this cycle vary very much', and he mentioned 10,800 years and 18,000 years. In the subsequent editions (1908, 1920 and 1930) of *Early Greek Philosophy*, he added: 'The period of 36,000 years was Babylonian' (4th ed. [London: Black, 1930] p. 157).
70. Proclus (A.D. 410–85), Greek Neoplatonic philosopher (born in Constantinople, lived in Athens from 430). For his interpretation of the Great Year, see *V(B)* 202 and 248, from Pierre Duhem, *Le Système du monde: histoire des doctrines cosmologiques de Platon à Copernic* (1913; repr. Paris: Librairie Scientifique Hermann, 1954) I, 290 (ch. V, section VII) (1913 ed.: III, 49). For the Great Year in India, see *Ex* 395–96/*VPl* 933–34, where Yeats cites Duhem, I, 67–68.
71. Philolaus the Pythagorean, of Croton (5th c. B.C.). Pseudo-Plutarque, *De Placitis philosophorum* (book II, ch. V, section III), tr. and quoted in Pierre Duhem, *Le Système du monde: histoire des doctrines cosmologiques de Platon à Copernic* (1913; repr. Paris: Librairie Scientifique Hermann, 1954) I, 77 (ch. ii, section X): 'De quoi se nourrit le Monde—Philolaüs dit que la destruction se produit de deux manières . . . le feu du ciel . . . l'eau lunaire . . . de ces deux éléments sont formés les aliments gazeux du monde.' See also *V(B)* 247.
72. For Raphael, see notes 59 and 60 above; Leonardo da Vinci (1452–1519). Yeats, 'Old Tom Again' (1932): 'Things out of perfection sail, / And all their swelling canvas wear. . . .' *P* 269. See also Yeats's manuscript notes (*c.* 1928) quoted in Richard Ellmann, *The Identity of Yeats*, 2nd ed. (London: Faber and Faber, 1964) p. 221: 'Philosophy has always explained its moment of moments in much the same way; nothing can be added to it, nothing taken away; that all progressions are full of illusion, that everything is born there like a ship in full sail.'
73. Yeats, tr., *Sophocles' King Oedipus: A Version for the Modern Stage* (perf. 1926) ll. 686–90, 696–700, spoken by the chorus [*VPl* 832–33], (London: Macmillan, 1928) p. 29, which Yeats cited here in the manuscript ('Quote 1st & last verses Page 28 [*sic*] King Oedipus leaving out the words "all men honour such" '): '. . . Zeus, and that high . . . Empyrean, / Fashioned. . . . holy images, the . . . blessed perchance, / Why should we honour the gods . . . dance?'

74. Shri Purohit Swāmi, *An Indian Monk: His Life and Adventures,* intro. W. B. Yeats (London: Macmillan, 1932); see p. 130 ff. above.
Bhagwān Shree (Shri) Patanjali, *Aphorisms of Yôga,* tr. from Samskrit with commentary by Shree (Shri) Purohit Swāmi, intro. W. B. Yeats (London: Faber and Faber, June 1938); see p. 175 ff. above.
James Haughton Woods, tr., *The Yoga-System of Patanjali: Or the Ancient Hindu Doctrine of Concentration of Mind,* Harvard Oriental Series (1914; repr. Cambridge: Harvard University Press, 1927), (O'Shea no. 1536); see p. 390, note 1 below.

INTRODUCTION TO 'MANDUKYA UPANISHAD'

1. The vision at Gaurikund, a little lake high up on Mount Kailās, is described in *HM* 179–82. For Yeats's mention of it in his introduction (1934), see p. 146 above; see also p. 375, note 35 above.
2. William (later Sir William) Crookes reported that he measured the pulse and heard the heartbeat of a materialised spirit named Katie King at a séance with the English medium Miss Florence Cook (1856–1904). The spirit sometimes appeared standing close to the medium. See William Crookes, 'The Last of Katie King: The Photographing of Katie King by the Aid of the Electric Light' and 'Spirit-Forms', *The Spiritualist,* 3 April and 5 June 1874, repr. in Crookes, *Researches in the Phenomena of Spiritualism* (London: Burns, [1874]), (O'Shea no. 449) pp. 119–21, 126. The incident is also mentioned in Cesare Lombroso, *After Death—What?,* pp. 334–35.
3. George Russell ('AE') (1867–1935) saw visions of an Irish avatar, beginning in 1896. AE had wanted to go around Ireland to announce it (AE to Sarah Purser, 27 January 1897, in 'Letters from George William Russell [AE], Selected, Transcribed and Edited by Alan Denson', no. 46, NLI Ms. 9967–69). Yeats and Patrick Hanon recommended AE to Horace Plunkett's Irish Agricultural Organisation Society, which Russell joined in November 1897 as a travelling organiser of rural cooperative banks. See Henry Summerfield, *That Myriad-Minded Man: A Biography of George William Russell "A.E." 1867–1935* (Gerrard's Cross: Smythe; Totowa, NJ: Rowman and Littlefield, 1975) pp. 77–79, 84–85.
4. AE to Yeats, [? June 1897]: 'The Celtic adept whom I am inclined to regard as the genius of the renaissance . . . lives in a little whitewashed cottage. I feel convinced it is in Donegal or Sligo. There is a great log a tree with the bark still on it a few feet before the door. It is on a gentle slope. He is middleaged has a grey golden beard and hair (more golden than grey) face very delicate and absorbed. Eyes have a curious golden fire in them, broad forehead.' ('Letters . . . Denson', no. 50, NLI Ms. 9967–69 and, dated [shortly after 2 June 1896], quoted by Richard Ellmann, *Yeats: The Man and the Masks,* 3rd ed. [New York: Norton, 1979] p. 124.)

5. For Emanuel Swedenborg (1688–1772), Swedish scientist, mystic and religious writer, see p. 394, note 31 below.
6. Slievenamon (elev. 2,368 feet), a mountain in southeastern Co. Tipperary, is numbered among Yeats's 'old sacred places' (*Mem* 124) as the site of a house of Irish gods; as Sidhe Femen it was the home of Bodb Dearg, a Tuatha de Danaan king; see *Gods and Fighting Men*, pp. 73–74.

   Standish James O'Grady (1846–1928), Irish novelist and editor of the weekly *All-Ireland Review* (1900–7), 'Slievenaman' repr. in O'Grady, *Selected Essays and Passages*, Every Irishman's Library (Dublin: Talbot Press; London: Unwin, [1918]) pp. 334, 337: 'This mountain, a *mons fabulous* if ever there were such. . . .' 'Slievenaman, in East Tipperary . . . is one kindred with Olympus, and Ida, and Delphi, and Hymettus, and all the famous Hellenic mountains—famous for thirty centuries, and all the world over. . . . And Slievenaman may yet—all depends on our poets—be more famous than ever was Olympus, or Delphi, or Ida.'
7. Yeats often visited with his uncle George Pollexfen (1839–1910), a strong Unionist, in Sligo.
8. For Mount Kailās, see p. 375, note 22 above.
9. *HM* 146.
10. Māndukya Upanishad, 1.1, in *TPU* 59. The wording of translation here is much more direct than in *TPU*, although still by Purohit Swāmi; it is from *The Criterion: A Literary Review*, 14 (July 1935) 556: '. . . Imperishable. . . . is its manifestation. . . . future—everything is *Aum*. And . . . transcends these three divisions of Time. . . .' The passages that follow are from *Criterion* 557–58, *TPU* 60–61.
11. For this reference to Patanjali, *Aphorisms of Yôga*, see pp. 177–78 and 377, note 44 above.
12. For parallel summaries, see pp. 142 and 374, note 16 above.
13. Daniel 3:25, when Nebuchadnezzar sees the angel in the fiery furnace with Shadrach, Meshach and Abednego.
14. *HM* 178–81: '. . . crying, "Victory. . . . Siddhāsana. . . . mantra. . . .'
15. The specific source of this quoted phrase is untraced.
16. The specific source of this quoted phrase is untraced.
17. *HM* 181: '. . . Buddhi, Chitta, Antahkaran [*sic*] and Manas—all. . . .'

   In *TPU* 59–60, note 2, Purohit Swāmi and Yeats used some variant translations: 'Discursive mind (Manas), Discriminative mind (Buddhi), Mind-Material (Chitta)'.

   Brahmā (masc. form of *brahman*), the Hindu Creator, is a mental image of the abstract *brahman*, the eternal, all-pervading, self-existent Universal Principle.
18. See p. 376, note 43 above, and *AY* 64, 82.
19. According to Jacob Boehme, the universe consists of three worlds. The 'Dark World' and the 'Light World' are opposite to one another and are eternal. The third world is our temporal 'world of four Elements, which is produced out of the two Inward Worlds, and is a Glass of them, wherein Light and Darkness, Good and Evil are mixed'

(*The Clavis* [w. 1624; Eng. tr. 1647], verse 132, in *The Works of Jacob Behmen, The Teutonic Theosopher* [London, 1764], [O'Shea no. 239] II, 17 [separately paginated]). Lightning is emblematic of the third world and its creation from darkness and light; see Boehme, *The Treatise of the Incarnation* (w. 1620; Eng. tr. 1659) part II, ch. viii, vv. 81, 83–84 and William Law, 'An Illustration of the Deep Principles of Jacob Behmen, the Teutonic Theosopher, in Thirteen Figures', in *Works* (London, 1764) II, illus. no. VI.

20. Karma (Sanskrit: action): 'causation, or . . . the unbroken linked series of causes and effects that make up all human activity' (Annie Wood Besant, *The Ancient Wisdom: An Outline of Theosophical Teachings* [London: Theosophical Publishing Society, 1897], [O'Shea 1920s list] p. 242).

21. William Blake, 'A Divine Image' (1790–91), l. 3, and also 'The Divine Image' in *Songs of Innocence* (1789), ll. 11, 15, both in *PWB* 82, 55, and Erdman, pp. 32, 12–13: 'the human form divine'.

22. Yeats's first recording of the phrase 'Unity of Being' was in the automatic script, on 3 September 1918. In 1919, Yeats used the phrase in 'If I were Four-and-Twenty' (p. 46 above), and then, on 13 October 1919, his wife and he were instructed by the automatic script to read Dante's *Il Convito* (*Il Convivio*) (see Harper, *Making of A Vision,* II, 78, 73, 329). The first of Yeats's ten published statements linking Unity of Being with *Il Convito* was in November 1919, in 'A People's Theatre' (*Ex* 250); others followed in 1921 (*Au* 190, 246, 291), 1925 (*V[A]* 202), 1931 (*Ex* 356), 1935 (here), 1937 (*V[B]* 258, 291) and 1938 (p. 179 above).

George Bornstein has suggested that Yeats conflated two passages from Dante's *Convito*: 'Amongst the effects of the divine wisdom man is the most marvellous, seeing how the divine power has united three natures in one form, and how subtly his body must be harmonised for such a form, having organs for almost all its powers. [The translation in Yeats's other copy, by Elizabeth Price Sayer, 1887, differs: 'It is organized for all his distinct powers.'] Wherefore, because of the complex harmony amongst so many organs which is required to make them perfectly answer to one another, few of all the great number of men are perfect' (treatise III, ch. viii) and 'the beauty of the body results from the members, in proportion as they are duly ordered' (treatise III, ch. xv) (*The Convivio of Dante Alighieri,* tr. Philip H. Wicksteed, Temple Classics [1903; repr. London: Dent, 1909], [O'Shea no. 467; Mrs Yeats's copy] pp. 178, 219–20; these passages are on uncut pages in Yeats's other copy, *Il Convito: The Banquet of Dante Alighieri*, tr. Elizabeth Price Sayer [London: Routledge, 1887], [O'Shea no. 466] pp. 126, 156). See Bornstein, 'Yeats's Romantic Dante,' *Colby Library Quarterly,* 15 (1979), 107; collected in his *Poetic Remaking: The Art of Browning, Yeats, and Pound* (University Park: Pennsylvania State University Press, 1988) p. 89.

George M. Harper and Walter K. Hood in *V(A)CE* (note to p. 18, ll. 12–13) add a third passage from *Il Convito*: 'And when it [the body] is well ordained and disposed, then it is beauteous as a whole and in its parts; for the due order of our members conveys the pleasure of a certain wondrous harmony; and their right disposition, that is their health, throws over them a colour lovely to behold. And so, to say that the noble nature beautifies its body and makes it comely and alert, is to say not less than that it adjusts it to the perfection of order.' (Treatise IV, ch. XXV, p. 358.)

23. Blake, *The Marriage of Heaven and Hell,* plate 16, in *PWB* 186, and Erdman, p. 39: '. . . of his delights'.
24. Percy Bysshe Shelley, *Adonais* (1821).
25. *HM* 180.
26. Tantra: an esoteric literature of a religious and practical nature. In Tantricism, both Hindu and Buddhist, truth is best realised through the human body, and the physical union of male and female can be emblematic of the unity of the ultimate reality; some Tantric yoga practices involve sexual relations.
27. *Parzival,* a German Grail romance by Wolfram von Eschenbach (d. *c.* 1220), was adapted from the French *Perceval le Gallois; Conte du Graal* (*c.* 1175) of Chrétien de Troyes. For these incidents see Eschenbach, *Parzival: A Knightly Epic,* tr. Jessie L. Weston (London: Nutt, 1894) I, 171 (book VI, ll. 385–86; verse 301) (Gawain's wound); I, 160–71 (book VI, ll. 37–398; verses 282–302) (Parzival's wife is Kondwiranmur [Condwiramurs, Condwîr âmûrs]; he overcomes Segramor [Segramors] and Kay [Keye]); II, 140 (book XV, ll. 151–77; verses 743–44).
28. Here and at p. 56 above, Yeats cites Chrétien de Troyes, twelfth-century French poet (see note 27 above); however, the imprisonment of Merlin is not described by Chrétien. Yeats's source, as in *V(A)* 197, is William Wells Newell, *King Arthur and the Table Round: Tales Chiefly after the Old French of Crestien of Troyes with an Account of Arthurian Romance, and Notes* (London: Watt, 1897) II, 139; see *V(A)CE* note to p. 197, ll. 18–32.
29. Perhaps F. Max Müller (1823–1900), in *A History of Ancient Sanskrit Literature so far as it Illustrates the Primitive Religion of the Brahmans* (1859; 2nd ed., London: Williams and Norgate, 1860) p. 14: '. . . and as no other language has carried off so large a share of the common Aryan [linguistic] heirloom . . . it is natural to suppose that, though perhaps the eldest brother, the Hindu was the last to leave the central home of the Aryan family.' Müller subscribed to the opinion, widely accepted by mid-nineteenth-century linguists, that the Aryans originated in the region between the Aral Sea and the Himalayas. Yeats owned a copy of Isaac Taylor's *The Origin of the Aryans: An Account of the Prehistoric Ethnology and Civilisation of Europe,* Contemporary Science Series, ed. Havelock Ellis (London: Scott, 1889), (O'Shea 1920s list), which opens with a summary of that view.

    For Kailās, or Mount Meru, in the Tibetan Himalayas, see p. 375, note 22 above.
30. For Lake Manasarowar, see p. 375, notes 24–25 above.

GITANJALI

1. Dr D. N. Maitra (1878–1950), resident surgeon, Mayo Hospital, Calcutta. See Mary M. Lago, ed., *Imperfect Encounter: Letters of William Rothenstein and Rabindranath Tagore 1911–1941* (Cambridge: Harvard University Press, 1972) p. 55, note 4. See also pp. 131 and 177 above, and p. 392, note 16 below. The typescript at first read 'Calcutta Indian' rather than 'Bengali'; the change was at the suggestion of Tagore (William Rothenstein to Yeats, 16 September 1912, SUNY-SB formerly 1.10.21).
2. Richard II reigned 1377–99. The Italian poet Petrarch (1304–74) settled in Milan, in the province of Lombardy, in 1353. Dante (1265–1321) was banished from his native Florence *c.* 1302 and died in Ravenna.
3. In 1881, at age twenty, Tagore began work on his first novel, *Bau-Thakuranir Hat* (*The Young Queen's Market*), published 1882 in Bengali. Plays written soon after this include *Prakritir Protishodh (Nature's Revenge)* and *Mayar Khela* (*The Play of Illusion*), both of which remain popular, as are his more than two thousand songs.
4. Tagore encountered a series of tragic events beginning, at age forty-one, with the death of his wife in 1902, and followed by the deaths of a daughter and of an admired young teacher in 1903, his father in 1905, and a son in 1907. From that time he began to regard his work as an offering to God, hence the title *Gitanjali* (*Song Offerings*) for his collection of poems published in Bengali in 1911. However, in 1884, at age twenty-two, he had been deeply saddened by the suicide of a twenty-five-year-old sister-in-law to whom he was a devoted friend. Tagore commented: 'My encounter with death at the age of twenty-four [*sic*] was a lifelong one, its memory linking itself to each succeeding bereavement. . . .' (*Jivan-smriti,* quoted and tr. by Krishna Kripalani, *Rabindranath Tagore: A Biography* [New York: Grove Press, 1962] p. 114.) Yeats was worried about not having accurate knowledge of the chronology of Tagore's life and told William Rothenstein: 'I have given what Indians have said to me about Tagore—their praise of him and their description of his life. What I am anxious about—some fact may be given wrongly. . . . My essay is an impression, I give no facts except those in the quoted conversation.' (Yeats to William Rothenstein, 7 September 1912, *L* 570.)
5. The Brahma Samaj, a monotheistic Hindu sect founded in 1859 by Tagore's father, continued the traditions established in 1825 by the famous Indian social reformer Raja Rammohun Roy (1772–1833). Tagore was much acclaimed during his fiftieth year, as, for example, at his public reception on 28 January 1912 in the Town Hall of Calcutta.
6. Tagore's father, Devendranath Tagore (1817–1905), was born into a wealthy, aristocratic family, but his religious interests led him to shun luxury. His disciples called him 'Maharishi' (great sage). Although an able manager of practical matters and a zealous social reformer, he

spent much time in meditation. In his autobiography the Maharishi recounts several experiences in which he was lost in meditative trances while contemplating nature, but he does not mention this particular instance (*The Auto-Biography of Maharishi Devendranath Tagore,* tr. Satyendranath Tagore and Indira Devi [London: Macmillan, 1914], [O'Shea 1920s list]).

7. Tagore was the uncle of the artist-brothers Gaganendranath Tagore (1867–1938) and Abanindranath Tagore (1871–1951). Tagore's oldest brother, Dwijendranath Tagore (1840–1926), was an accomplished poet, musician and mathematician as well as a theological philosopher.
8. See, for example, Friedrich Nietzsche, *The Will to Power,* sections 314, 532, tr. Anthony M. Ludovici, vols. XIV and XV of *The Complete Works of Friedrich Nietzsche,* ed. Oscar Levy (Edinburgh: Foulis, 1909–10), (O'Shea nos. 1440–41) XIV, 254 and XV, 47; and *Thus Spake Zarathustra,* section XXXV ('The Sublime Ones'), tr. Thomas Common, vol. XI of *The Complete Works of Friedrich Nietzsche,* ed. Oscar Levy (Edinburgh: Foulis, 1909), (O'Shea 1920s list) pp. 139–41.
9. Laurence Binyon (1869–1943) was Keeper of Oriental Prints and Drawings in the Department of Prints and Drawings, British Museum. For a more detailed version of this anecdote, see *Au* 548.
10. Robert Bridges wrote to Yeats, 20 April 1913, praising this introduction, but also suggesting that he should alter the phrase 'Four-fifths of our energy is spent in the quarrel with bad taste' when the popular edition was published. Yeats replied, 'You are quite right about that fraction and if I should ever reprint the essay (the popular edition is out) I will change it' (25 April [1913]; *L* 580 and 580, n. 1).
11. Geoffrey Chaucer wrote the narrative poem *Troilus and Criseyde* in *c.* 1380–86.
12. These are found in Rabindranath Tagore, *Gitanjali* (*Song Offerings*), tr. Rabindranath Tagore (London: Macmillan, 1913), (O'Shea nos. 2084–85), nos. XXIV and XII (pp. 14 and 7–8), LII (p. 33) and LI (p. 32), respectively.
13. These images appear throughout *Gitanjali*. The lute player mentioned in LXXIV (p. 50) is probably the god Krishna.
14. Sonnets 49–52 (1869) in Dante Gabriel Rossetti's sonnet sequence *The House of Life*.
15. See p. 371, note 20 above.
16. *Gitanjali,* no. XCIII (pp. 61–62).
17. Thomas à Kempis (1380–1471), the German ecclesiastic, and Saint John of the Cross (1542–91), the Spanish mystic. In a speech at a dinner honoring Tagore, 10 July 1912, Yeats elaborated on the difference between Tagore and Thomas à Kempis: 'When I tried to find anything Western which I might compare with the work of Mr. Tagore, I thought of 'The Imitation of Christ' by Thomas à Kempis. It is like, yet between the work of the two men there is a whole world of difference. Thomas à Kempis was obsessed by the thought of sin; he wrote of it in terrible imagery. Mr. Tagore has as little thought of sin as a child playing with a top. In Thomas à Kempis there is no place

for the love of visible nature; into his great austere nature such a love did not enter. But Mr. Tagore loves nature.' ('Dinner to Mr Rabindra Nath Tagore', [at the Trocadero restaurant, London], *Times* [London], 13 July 1912, p. 5, col. f.)

18. *Gitanjali*, no. XCV (p. 63).
19. *Gitanjali*, no. XLIII (pp. 25–26).
20. Saint Francis of Assisi (*c.* 1181–1226), renowned for humility, gentleness and simplicity. Yeats had emphasized William Blake's serene, saintlike death (*P&I* 99–100), even though Blake also served as a model for 'an old man's frenzy' in Yeats's poem 'An Acre of Grass' (w. 1936, publ. 1938; *P* 301–2).
21. *Gitanjali*, no. XLI (p. 24).
22. *Gitanjali*, no. LXXXIX (pp. 59–60).
23. Tristram and King Pellinore in Malory's *Morte d'Arthur* (1469–70, publ. 1485).
24. *Gitanjali*, no. LX (p. 39).

THE TEN PRINCIPAL UPANISHADS

1. Shree (Shri) Purohit Swāmi (born Shankar Gajanan Purohit, 1882–1941) renounced his worldly ties and possessions in 1923; see his autobiography, *IM*, with an introduction by Yeats (p. 130 ff. above).
2. Chapters x and xi of *An Indian Monk* recount Purohit Swāmi's decision to worship Dattātreya, a Brāhmin saint who is believed to be an incarnation of the god Vishnu—or a composite of Vishnu, Brahma and Siva. Purohit Swāmi translated the Avadhoota Geetā into English and sent Yeats a copy which arrived from India *c.* June 1937; the translation was not published until 1979. See Mokashi-Punekar's introduction to the *Avadhoota Gita* (New Delhi: Munshiram Manoharlal, 1979), which incorporates his 'Introduction to Shri Purohit Swami and the Avadhoota Geeta', *Literary Criterion* (Mysore, India), 11, no. 3 (1974) 95–97.
3. The Sadguru Upanishad (i.e., 'divine knowledge received from the holy teacher') was probably knowledge that Purohit Swāmi received from his teacher, Bhagwān Shri Hamsa. Purohit Swāmi's use of the word 'Upanishad' in reference to his own composition is uncommon, but not without precedent (Information from Shalini Sikka). Purohit Swāmi, in his autobiography, mentioned 'singing the Sadguru Upanishad' and 'my Sanskrit hymns' (*IM* 143, 152). Yeats's sentence was clearer in the manuscript version: '. . . two Upanishads the Mandookya and one of his own composition' (NLI Ms. 30,530). Yeats used the variant transliteration 'Māndookya' (for 'Māndukya') throughout this introduction.
4. Like Yeats, George Russell ('AE') was introduced to Hindu philosophy through theosophy and by Mohini Chatterji, who visited Dublin in 1885. Charles Johnston, a Dublin friend of both Russell and

Yeats, studied the Upanishads and dedicated to Russell a translation of excerpts (Charles Johnston, ed. and tr., *From the Upanishads* [Dublin: Whaley, 1896, and Portland, Maine: Mosher, 1913], [O'Shea no. 716]).

5. Robert Ernest Hume, tr., Brihad-āranyaka Upanishad, 6.3.1, in *The Thirteen Principal Upanishads,* 2nd ed. (London: Oxford University Press, 1931), (O'Shea no. 2122) p. 164.
6. Aristotle (348–322 B.C.) in *The Art of Rhetoric,* book III, recommends appropriate diction. Lady Gregory's specific reference, which Yeats had cited twice before, in 1934 (*Ex* 371/*VPl* 567, *Au* 395), is untraced.
7. Yeats and Purohit Swāmi worked on this translation in Majorca, December 1935 to April 1936; Yeats was very seriously ill with nephritis and an irregular heartbeat in January, but had recovered by March.
8. George Russell ('AE') died in England, 17 July 1935.
9. The distinguished British scientists Sir Oliver Joseph Lodge (1851–1940) and Sir William Crookes (1832–1919) were convinced of the reality of spiritual mediumship. The continental investigators to whom Yeats refers here include Enrico A. Morselli (1852–1929), professor of psychiatry at the University of Genoa, and Théodore Flournoy (1854–1920), professor of psychology at the University of Geneva. Morselli, in *Psicologia e 'Spiritismo'* (1908), and Flournoy, in *Esprits et Médiums: Mélanges de Métapsychique et de Psychologie* (1911; abridged Eng. tr. Hereward Carrington, *Spiritism and Psychology* [New York and London: Harper, 1911]), fully agreed with Lodge that the phenomena achieved by the famous medium Eusapia Palladino (1854–1918) were authentic, but both Morselli and Flournoy explained the material phenomena as the products of Eusapia Palladino's mind 'without any intervention from "the Beyond" ' (*Spiritism and Psychology,* p. 218). Flournoy recounts that according to Morselli's theory of psychodynamism, 'the medium has the faculty of exteriorizing a force capable of plastically molding, in space, the figures produced by her imagination' and of transmitting them by telepathy (*Spiritism and Psychology,* p. 261). Yeats could also be thinking of Henri Bergson (1859–1941), French philosopher and president of the Society for Psychical Research (1913–14), who signed a report of the Institut Général Psychologique, Paris, 1908, that guardedly attested to the validity of Eusapia Palladino's phenomena.
10. This theme of unity between the individual soul and the Absolute appears throughout the Upanishads. See p. 180 above, where Yeats cited the Chāndogya (Chhāndôgya) Upanishad, 8.3.2, in *TPU* 109: 'A wise man sees in Self, those that are alive, those that are dead; and gets what this world cannot give.'
11. *The Waste Land* (1922) and 'The Hollow Men' (1925).
12. The first of Buddha's four Noble Truths is 'All life is suffering'. In Huxley's novel *Those Barren Leaves* (London: Chatto & Windus, 1925), the principal character, Mr Calamy, realises that 'sooner or later every soul is stifled by the sick body' (p. 334); he retreats to the mountains for a life of contemplation.

13. The German philosopher Arthur Schopenhauer (1788–1860) was influenced by Anquetil Duperron's Latin translation of fifty Upanishads, *Oupnek'hat* (2 vols., Strassburg: Levrault, 1801–2), the first translation into a European language. It was based on a translation into Persian from 1656–57. Schopenhauer, seeking an escape from materialism, advocated the finding of reality through ascetic renunciation or through art.
14. For Walter James Turner (1889–1946), *The Seven Days of the Sun* (1925); Dorothy Wellesley (1889–1956), 'Matrix' (1925); and Herbert Read (1893–1968), 'The Mutations of a Phoenix' (1923), see pp. 195–98 above and *P&I* 184.
15. C. Day Lewis (1904–72), Louis MacNeice (1907–63), W. H. Auden (1907–73) and Laura Riding (1901-91).
16. Louis MacNeice, 'An Eclogue for Christmas' (December 1933; publ. April 1934), ll. 118–19, in *Poems* (London: Faber, 1935), (O'Shea nos. 1199b) p. 18, and in *OBMV* (no. 366).
17. In the introduction to *OBMV* these three poets of the 1890s are twice mentioned as having found emotional satisfaction in the traditions of Christianity (pp. 191–92, 202 above).
18. *The Golden Bough* (12 vols.; 1890–1915), Sir J. G. Frazer's massive anthropological compilation of beliefs and social institutions, shows Christianity to have parallels with many myths.
19. Pound, who had begun to read Confucius as early as 1907, renewed his study of him in January 1915, while staying with Yeats. Pound published translations of Confucian texts in 1928 and 1938.
20. In W. J. Turner's comic novel *Blow for Balloons: Being the First Hemisphere of the History of Henry Airbubble* (London: Dent, 1935), (O'Shea no. 2160), the young Henry Airbubble finds this statement (p. 106) in a letter written in 1864 by his grandfather, the old Henry Airbubble, to an obnoxious English missionary in Hong Kong, where the grandfather managed the branch office of Messrs Blow & Blow, balloon manufacturers.
21. The date of Buddha's birth is variously calculated at *c.* 568 B.C. and *c.* 623 B.C.; for the forest sages, see p. 392, note 17 below.
22. The 'Song of Triumph', composed by Amergin, a poet of the first Milesian invaders of Ireland, perhaps *c.* 1000 B.C., opens: 'I am the wind which breathes upon the sea, / I am the wave of the ocean. . . .' Douglas Hyde translated it in his *A Literary History of Ireland* (London: Unwin, 1899), (O'Shea no. 941), where he described it as 'very ancient and very strange' and as 'the oldest surviving lines in the vernacular of any country in Europe except Greece alone' (pp. 243–44 and 244, n. 1). Hyde's chapter on Druidism calls Amergin a druid (p. 82) and points to the ancient Irish pagan belief in metempsychosis (p. 104). In finding the poem to be pantheistic, Hyde agreed with Henri d'Arbois de Jubainville, *Cours de littérature celtique: II: Le cycle mythologique irlandais et la mythologie celtique* (Paris: Thorin, 1884), (O'Shea no. 1047) pp. 243, 246.
23. [Yeats's note] All Indian clerks in Government offices have just been ordered to wear trousers, so at any rate declares a London merchant,

an exporter to India, who has decided to specialise in trouser-stretchers. It follows the flag.

24. The Vedas, which were composed probably between 1500 and 1000 B.C., are the oldest Hindu scriptures. They are hymns in an archaic form of Sanskrit. The unusual transliteration 'Weda' was preferred by Purohit Swāmi; see p. 390, note 2 below.

25. Narayan Hegde, in his dissertation 'W. B. Yeats and Shri Purohit Swami: A Study of Yeats's Last Indian Phase' (SUNY Stony Brook, 1980) pp. 90–92, has pointed out that although the translation omits ritualistic and repetitive passages, it also leaves out some passages that would have interested Yeats, for example, Brihadāranyaka Upanishad, 5.2 (which T. S. Eliot had used in the final lines of *The Waste Land*) and Brihadāranyaka Upanishad, 6.4 (which refers to sexual intercourse). On the latter of those examples, Shalini Sikka points to its ritualistic emphasis (see S. Radhakrishnan, *The Principal Upanisads* [London: Allen and Unwin, 1953] p. 322: 'The sexual act is explained as a kind of ritual performance').

APHORISMS OF YOGA

1. James Haughton (not Horton) Woods, tr., *The Yoga-System of Patanjali: Or the Ancient Hindu Doctrine of Concentration of Mind*, Harvard Oriental Series, no. 17 (1914; repr. Cambridge: Harvard University Press, 1927), (O'Shea no. 1536). His meticulously accurate rendering of the original text is widely respected, but is technical and difficult. Professor Woods (1864–1935), who taught history, philosophy, anthropology and comparative religion at Harvard, took a strictly academic and historical view of Patanjali's system.
2. While a graduate student at Harvard, T. S. Eliot spent two years studying Sanskrit and one year (1912–13) studying Patanjali's yoga system under James Woods, whose translation was published in 1914.
   When Purohit Swāmi read the proofs of the introduction he suggested the transliteration 'Samskrit' for Yeats's 'Sanskrit'. He also suggested 'Nirwāna' (for 'Nirvāna'), 'Tureeya' (for 'Turīya') and 'Wedic' (for 'Vedic') (Purohit Swāmi to Yeats, 25 January 1938, SUNY-SB formerly 3.9.150).
3. The Ajantā cave temples, 200 miles northeast of Bombay, date from the second through the seventh centuries; Yeats owned some reproductions of their famous wall paintings.
4. The Buddhist worship hall cut into the rock in the Western Ghats at Kārlē, fifty miles southeast of Bombay, was begun in 80 B.C. Wooden ribs are attached to the vaulted rock dome above the two aisles. Its two rows of columns are adorned with bell-shaped, lotus-flower capitals.
5. *Yoga-Sutra*, I. 50, from Woods's translation (p. 96): '. . . the subliminal-impression produced by this [super-reflected balanced-

state]'. Purohit Swāmi's translation reads: '. . . the impression remaining after this illumination' (*AY* 44).

6. Throughout his translation, Woods uses 'predicate relations' for the Sanskrit 'vikalpa', which Purohit Swāmi translates as 'delusions'.
7. Purohit Swāmi and Yeats worked on the translation of *TPU* in Majorca, December 1935 to April 1936. For Yeats's introduction to it, see p. 171 ff. above.
8. After renouncing his worldly possessions and becoming a disciple of Bhagwān Shri Hamsa, Purohit Swāmi travelled all over India, visiting holy places and preaching. Purohit Swāmi gives full accounts of those experiences in his autobiography, *IM* (1932); for Yeats's introduction to that book, see p. 130 ff. above.
9. Lady Elizabeth Jocelyn Pelham (1899–1975), daughter of the sixth Earl of Chichester, later Mrs Charles M. Beazley; Yeats mentioned her in several letters to Purohit Swāmi during 1937 and 1938 (quoted in Shankar Mokashi-Punekar, *The Later Phase in the Development of W. B. Yeats* [Dharwar, India: Karnatak University, 1966] pp. 264–65, 267).
10. See p. 131 above.
11. Woods translated two commentaries: *Yoga-bhāsaya*, written between 650 and 850, and *Tattva-vāicārdī*, written *c.* 850.
12. Brihadāranyaka Upanishad, 2.5.12, in *TPU* 134.
13. Although most of Vedic hymns were composed before the time of Yājnavalkya (Yādnyawalkya), a renowned thinker and teacher who is mentioned in several Upanishads, Yeats uses the dating he found in Hermann Schneider's *History of World Civilization: From Prehistoric Times to the Middle Ages,* tr. Margaret M. Green, 2 vols. (London: Routledge, 1931), (O'Shea no. 1853), which he cites in note 15 below.
14. Pythagoras (6th c. B.C.), Greek philosopher and mathematician; see also pp. 149 and 377, note 51.

    Yeats marked a relevant passage in his copy of Robert Ernest Hume's introductory essay to his scholarly translation, *The Thirteen Principal Upanishads,* 2nd ed. (London: Oxford University Press, 1931), (O'Shea no. 2122) p. 58: 'Because of the theoretical importance of knowledge in that period of speculative activity, and also because of the discrediting of the popular polytheistic religion by philosophical reasoning, there took place in India during the times of the Upanishads a movement similar to that which produced the Sophists in Greece, namely, a re-adjustment of the accepted ethics and a substitution of philosophic insight for traditional morality. [Here Yeats wrote in the margin: 'Not necessarily a substitute'.] Knowledge was the one object of supreme value, the irresistible means of obtaining one's ends. This idea of the worth and efficacy of knowledge is expressed again and again throughout the Upanishads not only in connection with philosophical speculation, but also in the practical affairs of life.'
15. [Yeats's note] See *History of World Civilization* by Hermann Schneider, translated by Marjorie Green, vol. 2, page 706.

16. Dr D. N. Maitra (1878–1950), resident surgeon, Mayo Hospital, Calcutta (Mary M. Lago, ed., *Imperfect Encounter: Letters of William Rothenstein and Rabindranath Tagore: 1911–1941* [Cambridge: Harvard University Press, 1972] p. 55, n. 4); the quotation presumably is from conversation. See also pp. 165 and 385, note 1 above. Malabar: coast of southwestern India.
17. The forest Brahmins (Brāhmans) dedicated their lives to the pursuit of truth, renounced their worldly possessions and lived in the forest.
18. Like Yājnavalkya (Yādnyawalkya), Patanjali taught that the individual soul is one with the Absolute; his yoga system is an eight-step process involving physical and mental disciplines through which one comes to the realisation of this truth.
19. Juice of the soma plant was used as an intoxicant in ancient Indian religious ceremonies; the mescal plant has been similarly used in Mexico. Cesare Lombroso, *After Death—What?* (p. 152) observed, 'The Hindu priest is called a drinker of soma' and quoted the *Rig Veda*, VIII.48: ' "We have drunk the soma; we became immortal; we entered into the light." '
20. See pp. 374, note 16; 147–49; 158 above and *AY* 32.
21. [Yeats's note] To Aristotle and to Christian orthodoxy only God has value in Himself, even Spirit is contingent. At the fall of Hellenism and its exaltation of personality, instinct demanded an extreme objectivity. Man had to annihilate himself. Spirit alone has value, Spirit has no value. Eternity expresses itself through contradictions.[a]

21a. In this elliptically phrased antinomy, Yeats opposes the Hellenic celebration of the individual to the Christian denial of the self.

22. Zen Buddhism, which originated in China as a reaction against the scholasticism and systematic logic of the Indian Buddhist texts, emphasizes spontaneous, intuitive knowledge rather than abstract speculation. Zen exerted a major influence on Chinese painting during the Sung period (960–1270) and on Japanese painting during the fourteenth and fifteenth centuries, when Japanese artists began to emulate Chinese masters. These landscape paintings reflect the Zen spirit in their simple techniques, especially their forceful brush strokes, and in their Impressionist-like attempts to produce an instantaneous perception of nature.
23. 'Gutei's Finger' is one of the forty-eight Zen koans (paradoxes) in the *Mumonkan* (*Wu-men-kuan*) (*Gateless Gate*) (1229), written by the Chinese master Ekai (Hui-k'ai) (1183–1260). Gutei (Chuh-chih) was a disciple of Tenryu (T'ien-lung), probably towards the end of the T'ang dynasty (618–907). Yeats could have known this koan from Daisetz Teitaro Suzuki's introduction to his *Essays in Zen Buddhism: First Series* (London: Luzac, 1927), (O'Shea no. 2033) p. 23n: '. . . Gutei did or said nothing but just holding up a finger to all the questions that might be asked of him concerning Zen. There was a boy in his temple, who seeing the master's trick imitated him when the boy himself was asked about what kind of preaching his master generally practised. When the boy told the master about it showing his lifted little finger, the master cut it right off with a knife. The boy

ran away screaming in pain when Gutei called him back. The boy turned back, the master lifted his own finger, and the boy instantly realised the meaning of the "one finger Zen" of Tenryu as well as Gutei.'

24. Adapted by Yeats from a verse by the Zen Master Yengo (Yüan-wu, 1063–1135), translated in Daisetz Teitaro Suzuki's essay 'On Satori—The Revelation of a New Truth in Zen Buddhism', in *Essays in Zen Buddhism (First Series)* (London: Luzac, 1927), (O'Shea no. 2033) p. 234. Elsewhere, Yeats used these verses from Yengo, acknowledging (though misspelling) his source and noting, 'I have substituted here and there better-sounding words' (*V[B]* 215). Yengo's verse reads: '. . . No more issues odorous smoke behind the brocade screens, / Amidst flute-playing and singing, he retreats, thoroughly in liquor and supported by others: / A happy event in the life of a romantic youth, / It is his sweetheart alone that is allowed to know.'
25. Goethe's romance *Wilhelm Meisters Lehrjahre* (1796) and *Wilhelm Meisters Wanderjahre* (1821–29); Yeats owned Thomas Carlyle's translation, *Wilhelm Meister* (O'Shea 1920s list). For Honoré de Balzac's *Comédie humaine*, see p. 313, note 24 above.
26. *Faust*, ll. 1224–37 (part I, Act I [scene 3; in Faust's study]). Thomas E. Webb, tr., *The First Part of the Tragedy of Faust* (1880, titled *Faust*), 2nd ed. (with 'The Death of Faust from the Second Part') (London: Longmans, Green, 1898), (O'Shea no. 753) p. 73: '. . . *Word!* . . . *Act!*' Thomas Webb, LLD, was Queen's Counsel, sometime fellow of Trinity College, and, in 1880, Regius Professor of Laws, and Public Orator in the University of Dublin.
27. *Faust*, ll. 11581–82 (part II, Act V [scene 6; in the great forecourt of the palace]); see p. 299, note 57 above.
28. For Dante and 'unity of being', see p. 383, note 22 above.
29. Giovanni Gentile (1875–1944) argued that the act of thinking was the only real act and that there was no distinction between subject and object: 'This act [of thinking] we can never absolutely transcend since it is our very subjectivity, that is, our own self: an act therefore which we can never in any possible manner objectify' (*The Theory of Mind as Pure Act* [1911], 3rd ed., tr. H. Wildon Carr [London: Macmillan, 1922], [O'Shea no. 742] p. 6).
30. The German mystic Jacob Boehme (1575–1624) had lengthy visionary experiences, and in the account of his second vision he specifically mentions that he walked during the vision (Abraham von Frankenberg [d. 1652], *Memoirs of the Life, Death, Burial, and Wonderful Writings of Jacob Behmen*, tr. Francis Okely [Northampton: Dicey, 1780] p. 8).

    Boehme wrote that his inspiration came like a shower-burst of rain ('*Platzregen*') (*Theosophical Letters*, no. 10 [1620], para. 45, in *Sämtliche Schriften* [facsimile of 1730 edition] [Stuttgart: Frommanns, 1956] IX [XXI], 40). The only book in Yeats's library that contains that passage is Franz Hartmann's *The Life and Doctrines of Jacob Boehme: The God-Taught Philosopher: An Introduction to the Study of his Works* (London: Kegan Paul, Trench, Trübner, 1891), (O'Shea no. 853) p. 53, where the passage is translated: 'The inspiration comes like a shower of rain.' Yeats on two earlier occasions had used closely similar wording, first in his anonymous review of Charles G. Leland, *Gypsy Sorcery* (London: Unwin, 1891), in the *National Observer: A Record and Review*, new ser. 5, no. 126 (18 April 1891) p. 569, col. 1, and then in the play *The Unicorn from the Stars* (1908) (*VPl* 650).

31. Emanuel Swedenborg (1688–1772), Swedish scientist and Christian visionary, wrote vivid accounts of his visions of the spiritual world and conversations with angels, spirits and God. Because Swedenborg was fully conscious during these experiences, Yeats attributed only an impure *samādhi* to him. In judging the mystical visions of St Theresa (1515–82) perhaps Yeats considered that her practical accomplishments in reforming the Carmelite order were evidence of a less than complete loss of self during her visions. *Baisers,* a French genre of short erotic poems about kissing, enjoyed a vogue during the second half of the sixteenth century; see *Dictionnaire des lettres françaises: Le Seizième Siècle,* ed. Georges Grente (Paris: Fayard, 1951) I, 80. For soma drinkers, see note 19 above.
32. Adapted (see note 24 above) by Yeats from a verse by Chōkei (Chang-ching, d. 932), in Suzuki's essay 'On Satori—The Revelation of a New Truth in Zen Buddhism', in *Essays in Zen Buddhism (First Series),* p. 234: ' "What religion believest thou?" you ask. / I raise my hossu [fly whisk, a symbol of religious authority] and hit your mouth.'
33. See p. 367, note 19 above.
34. In America, the many reports of unexplained material phenomena during the mid-nineteenth century led to the widely accepted belief in spiritualism, beginning especially with the mediumship of the Fox sisters, Kate (1841–92) and Margaret (1838–93), in 1848. For the debate between supporters of spiritism and animism, see p. 388, note 9 above.
35. Chāndogya (Chhāndôgya) Upanishad, 8.3.2, in *TPU* 109: 'A wise man sees in Self, those that are alive, those that are dead; and gets what this world cannot give.'

INTRODUCTION TO *THE OXFORD BOOK OF MODERN VERSE*

1. *OBMV* includes Gerard Manley Hopkins (1844–89), who died three years before Tennyson, but whose work—except for a few poems that were posthumously anthologised in 1893 and 1915—was virtually unknown until 1918, when a small first edition of his poems was published. When Yeats began work on the anthology, he explained in a letter to T. Sturge Moore, 'My period is from the death of Tennyson; this enables me to put Hopkins among the Victorians' (12 July [1935], *LTSM* 182). The 'two or three' Victorian poets who are not

in *OBMV* probably are George Meredith (1828–1909), A. C. Swinburne (1837–1909) and perhaps John Davidson (1857–1909) or William Morris (1834–96) or Coventry Patmore (1823–96). The four earliest poets in *OBMV* are Wilfrid Scawen Blunt (1840–1922), Thomas Hardy (1840–1928), Robert Bridges (1844–1930) and Hopkins; in addition, the anthology opens with a prose sentence by Walter Pater (1839–94) set as *vers libre*.

2. Yeats was twenty-one (not seventeen) years old when he met Hopkins, in 1886. Hardy's first volume of poems was published in 1898.
3. Bridges published four slim volumes, each titled *Poems*, between 1873 and 1884. He gained critical favour in 1890 with his collected *Shorter Poems* and was appointed Poet Laureate in 1913.
4. Wilfrid Scawen Blunt, poet and ardent publicist of nationalist causes, was also an amateur painter and sculptor. He travelled widely in Africa, the Near East and India. In 1888, during Blunt's two months of imprisonment for actions in support of Irish tenants, Yeats published an article on Blunt's sonnets and essays (*UP1* 122–30). The first collected edition of Blunt's poems was published in 1898.
5. William Ernest Henley (1849–1903) edited the weekly *National Observer* (1888–94) and the monthly *New Review* (1895–97). He was crippled from age twelve by bone tuberculosis; one foot was amputated when he was eighteen. Clement K. Shorter (1857–1926) edited the *Illustrated London News* (1891–1900), the *Sketch* (1893–1900) and the *Sphere* (1900–26). Yeats contributed to both of Henley's journals and to the *Sketch*.
6. Oscar Wilde, *The Ballad of Reading Gaol* (1898), part I, stanzas vii–viii; the poem closes with a variant of the first of these stanzas. None of the three stanzas is among the 38 (of 105) stanzas in *OBMV*. (*Works* [London: Methuen, 1908] XI, 316–17: '. . . word, / '.)
7. Pater's death on 30 July 1894 was, in fact, noted by the London *Times* in an obituary on the next day. The sentence, which Yeats titled 'Mona Lisa', set as *vers libre* and slightly misquoted, is from 'Leonardo da Vinci' (1869), in *The Renaissance: Studies in Art and Poetry* (1873, 1877, 1888, 4th ed. 1893; repr. London: Macmillan, 1935), (O'Shea no. 1539) p. 116.
8. 'In Hospital', a series of twenty-eight poems dated 'The Old Infirmary, Edinburgh, 1873–75', which Henley published in *A Book of Verses* (1895).
9. Walter James Turner (1889–1946) and Ezra Pound (1885–1972), whom Yeats discusses in sections xii and x, respectively.
10. Hugh MacDiarmid (Christopher Murray Grieve) (1892–1978), 'O wha's been here afore me, lass', ll. 1–2, in *Selected Poems* (London: Macmillan, 1934), (O'Shea no. 1175) p. 36.
11. For this remark that the French poet Paul Verlaine (1844–96) made to Yeats, in English, in 1894, see p. 343, note 18 above.
12. Catullus, Roman lyric poet (1st c. B.C.) and epigrammatist, was admired for his grace, simplicity and purity of style. For the Jacobean writers, see p. 342, note 10 above. Charles Baudelaire (1821–67), French poet.

The Palatine anthology of Greek poetic epigrams, compiled by an unknown Byzantine scholar(s), *c.* 980, contains 3200 epigrams by some 300 poets. It was found in the library of Count Palatine at Heidelberg and was printed in 1606.

13. 'Conclusion' (1868), in *The Renaissance: Studies in Art and Poetry* (1873, [omitted 1877], 1888, 1893) (London: Macmillan, 1935), (O'Shea no. 1539) p. 236: 'this hard, gem-like. . . .'
14. The 1890s generation is here contrasted with their fathers' admiration for Giuseppe Garibaldi (1807–82), the Italian patriot, and John Bright (1811–89), an MP who had advocated free trade, election reform and religious freedom. Bright denounced the Crimean War and supported the North in the U.S. Civil War.
15. Yeats attended a dinner, *c.* 1894, at the house of Count Stanislaus Eric Stenbock (1860–95), a poet and short story writer. For Yeats's descriptions of the dinner, see *SB* 263–64 and 77n.
16. See *Mem* 35, where Yeats recorded (*c.* 1915) that his friend the poet Lionel Johnson (1867–1902) 'had taken from Walter Pater certain favourite words which came to mean much for me: "Life should be a ritual" '. That aphorism also appeared in George Yeats's automatic writing (21 March 1920, quoted in Harper, *Making of A Vision*, II, 390).
17. Ernest Dowson, 'Villanelle of the Poet's Road' (1899), ll. 10–12, in *The Poetical Works*, ed. Desmond Flower (London: Cassell, 1934), (O'Shea no. 544) p. 74 and *OBMV* no. 90: '. . . belong, / Us the. . . .' In a letter to Dorothy Wellesley, Yeats stated that the 'true poetic movement of our time is towards some heroic discipline', and he quoted these lines to illustrate that 'heroic ecstasy' or 'heroic mood', as opposed to the despair that he said prompted Auden and Spender to look to Marxism (6 July 1935, *LDW* 8).
18. For the Rhymers' Club, see p. 341, note 2 above.
19. Wilfrid Meynell (1852–1948), editor of the monthly *Merry England*, had searched out the impoverished and opium-addicted Francis Thompson (1857–1907) in 1888. Thompson's 'Ode to the Setting Sun' was first published in 1893.
20. There was a series of Sunday afternoon processions from the East End to mass meetings of workmen at Hyde Park during the London dock strike of 13 August–16 September 1889 (e.g., *The Times*, 9 September 1889, p. 4, col. c). From 1887 to the early 1890s Yeats attended Sunday evening Socialist lectures at the Hammersmith Club, adjacent to the home of William Morris (1834–96); see p. 315, note 44 above. Yeats reported the anecdote about the woman in 1908 (*Ex* 239) and also used it in 'Lapis Lazuli' (*P* 294), which he began writing in 1936. Southampton Row, WC1, is a half mile northeast of Trafalgar Square.
21. Percy Bysshe Shelley to Henry Reveley, 28 October 1819; to John and Maria Gisborne, 6 November 1819; and to John Gisborne, 16 November 1819 and 10 April 1822, in Percy Bysshe Shelley, *Essays and Letters*, ed. Ernest Rhys (London: Scott, 1886), (O'Shea no. 1902) pp. 298–300, 304, 370.

22. Kipling (1865–1936) was born in Bombay and worked as a journalist in India (1882–89). 'Danny Deever' (1890) had been Yeats's original single selection for the anthology, but at a last-minute suggestion from Dorothy Wellesley, he replaced it with 'A St Helena Lullaby' (1910) and 'The Looking-glass: A Country Dance' (*OBMV* nos. 70, 71) (Humphrey Milford, Oxford University Press, memo to 'J. M.', 14 August 1936, cited by Edward O'Shea, 'Yeats as Editor' [diss., Northwestern University, 1976] p. 202); see also O'Shea no. 2235a (inside back cover), *L* 877 and *LDW* 72.
23. William Watson (1858–1935) published his first book of poems, *The Prince's Quest,* in 1880. See p. 291 above for Yeats's explanation that Watson was not included in the anthology because his executors did not give permission. When Yeats submitted a preliminary list of poets for the anthology, an Oxford University Press editor commented that 'there may be some difficulty' about using William Watson poems because 'Lady Watson does not, I think love the Oxford Press' (Charles Williams to Yeats, 11 October 1935, quoted by Jon Stallworthy, 'Yeats as Anthologist', in *In Excited Reverie: A Centenary Tribute to William Butler Yeats: 1865–1939,* ed. A. Norman Jeffares and K. G. W. Cross [New York: Macmillan, 1965] p. 180).
24. For this statement by Paul Verlaine in 'Art poétique' (dated 1874, publ. 1882), see p. 343, note 18 above.
25. Seven of William Archer's translations of social realistic plays by Henrik Ibsen were produced in London between 1889 and 1897.
26. William Watson, 'To a Strenuous Critic', ll. 9–12, in *Retrogression and Other Poems* (London and New York: Lane, 1917) p. 31: 'bar, / . . . . / . . . star.' Watson's previous collection, *The Muse in Exile: Poems* (1913), had received considerable adverse criticism.

    Watson, 'Melancholia', ll. 13–14, in *For England: Poems Written during Estrangement* (New York and London: Lane, 1903 [title page 1904]) p. 29: 'night, / '.
27. The Irish poets Joseph Campbell (1879–1944) and Padraic Colum (1881–1972).
28. None of the five poems by A. E. Housman (1859–1936) in *OBMV* is from *A Shropshire Lad* (1896) because, from early in the century, Housman consistently refused all anthologists (*LTWBY* 579).
29. James Stephens (1882?–1950) translated and adapted Gaelic poems in *Reincarnations* (London: Macmillan, 1918), (O'Shea nos. 2004, 2004a). Frank O'Connor (Michael O'Donovan) (1903–66) translated many Gaelic poems. The quoted lines are from James Stephens's 'Egan O Rahilly' (after O'Rahilly) (ll. 6–14), one of his adaptations from the Irish in *Reincarnations* (*Collected Poems* [London: Macmillan, 1931], [O'Shea no. 1997] p. 191 and *OBMV* no. 210): 'even-tide . . . dish! // The . . . said /—This . . . seemly! Bring. . . . O Rahilly! / . . . place he holds his tongue / '.
30. Lady Gregory died 22 May 1932. The book by C. Day Lewis (1904–72) was probably *From Feathers to Iron* (London: Hogarth Press, 1931), (O'Shea no. 1112).

31. Oliver St-John Gogarty (1878–1957), surgeon and wit, is the 'distinguished Irish poet' to whom Yeats alludes. Seventeen poems by Gogarty are in *OBMV*. While serving as an Irish Free State senator, Gogarty was abducted by Republicans on 12 January 1923, during the Irish Civil War. Yeats attended the ceremony at which Gogarty's two swans were presented, 26 April 1924. For Yeats's prefaces to two volumes of poems by Gogarty, *An Offering of Swans and Other Poems* (1924) and *Wild Apples* (1930), see *P&I* 154–55, 172–74.
32. For these subjects see the following poems in *OBMV*: William Henry Davies (1871–1940), 'Joy and Pleasure' (1908), 'Truly Great' (1908), 'Leisure' (1911), 'The Sluggard' (1910), 'School's Out' (1908), *OBMV* nos. 116–17, 119–20, 122; John Masefield (1878–1967), 'Sea-Change', '"Port of Many Ships"', 'A Valediction (Liverpool Docks)' and 'Trade Winds' (all 1902); 'Cargoes' (1903), 'Port of Holy Peter' (1910), *OBMV* nos. 176–81; Laurence Binyon (1869–1943), 'Tristram's End' (1897), *OBMV* no. 114; T. Sturge Moore (1870–1944), 'The Gazelles' (1904), *OBMV* no. 129; and Walter De la Mare (1873–1956), 'The Listeners' (1912), 'Winter' (1912), 'The Scribe' (1918), 'All That's Past' (1912), 'Echo' (1906), 'The Silver Penny' (1902), *OBMV* nos. 143–48. The quotation is from De la Mare's 'All That's Past', ll. 7–8, in *Poems: 1901 to 1918* (London: Constable, 1932) I, 142 and *OBMV* no. 146: '. . . rose.'
33. Edith Cooper (1862–1913), who with Katharine Bradley (1846–1914) wrote as 'Michael Field'. Their nine poems in the anthology are from *A Selection from the Poems of Michael Field* (London: Poetry Bookshop, 1923), (O'Shea no. 670). Yeats omitted the final three stanzas of 'If They Honoured Me, Giving Me Their Gifts' (*OBMV* no. 67; *Selection*, p. 36). T. Sturge Moore, in his preface to *A Selection from the Poems of Michael Field* (p. 15), highly praised their poem 'And on my Eyes Dark Sleep by Night' (*OBMV* no. 64) as rivalling and even surpassing 'the very best' poems of Walter Savage Landor (1775–1864). For the Greek anthology see note 12 above.
34. Sacheverell Sitwell's (1897–1988) 'Agamemnon's Tomb', in *Canons of Giant Art: Twenty Torsos in Heroic Landscapes* (London: Faber, 1933), (O'Shea no. 1936) pp. 101–9 and p. 208n: 'The first half of the poem deals with the horrors and the hopelessness of death.' It is his only poem in *OBMV* (no. 322).
35. Robert Bridges (1844–1930) was widely recognised for his technical accomplishments in the lyric and for his prosodic experimentation with classical meters.
36. James Abbott McNeill Whistler (1834–1903), expatriate American Impressionist painter.
37. Robert Bridges, *Achilles in Scyros* (1890), ll. 1599–600 (London: Bell, 1892), (O'Shea no. 274) p. 64: 'The glitter . . . pleasure, / . . . tomb.' In 1897 Yeats described this passage from Bridges's verse drama as 'placid and charming' (*E&I* 200).
38. Robert Bridges, 'I Heard a Linnet Courting' (1873; rev. 1931), ll. 1–7, in *The Shorter Poems of Robert Bridges* (Oxford: Clarendon Press, 1931) p. 9, and *OBMV* no. 16: '. . . spring: / '.

39. Dante Gabriel Rossetti, *The House of Life*, sonnet 74, 'Old and New Art—I. St Luke the Painter' (w. 1849; publ. 1881), l. 11, in *The Collected Works*, ed. William M. Rossetti (London: Ellis and Elvey, 1897), (O'Shea no. 1789) I, 214.
40. Yeats was probably thinking of 'Said King Pompey' (1923) and 'Madam Mouse Trots' (1923), two poems in the 'Façade' series by the English poet Edith Sitwell (1887–1964). 'Said King Pompey' ends (ll. 13–14): ' "That elephantiasis / The flunkeyed and trumpeting Sea!" ' (*The Collected Poems of Edith Sitwell* [London: Duckworth, 1930], [O'Shea no. 1926] p. 163.) 'Madam Mouse Trots', ll. 5–6, reads: 'The elephant-trunks / Trumpet from the sea . . . [her ellipsis]'(*Collected Poems* [1930] p. 156). Additionally, 'Metamorphosis' (1929) has the phrase 'elephant trunks of the water' (l. 169, in *Collected Poems* [1930] p. 76).
41. The boldly stylised designs of Léon Bakst (1866?–1924) contributed to the vogue for Diaghilev's Russian Ballet (from 1909). Aubrey Beardsley's (1872–98) famous drawings for *Salome* (1894) are characteristic of his later style. For Bakst and Beardsley, see also *P&I* 183. The Jacobean dramatist John Webster is best known for his tragedies *The White Devil* (*c.* 1608) and *The Duchess of Malfi* (*c.* 1614).
42. Edith Sitwell, 'Metamorphosis' (1929), ll. 279, 67, in *Collected Poems* (1930) pp. 81, 72. See also 'The Hambone and the Heart' (1927, rev. 1930), l. 13, in *Collected Poems* (1930) p. 91: 'That terrible Gehenna of the bone.' Yeats printed 'The Hambone and the Heart' in *OBMV* no. 248.
43. T. S. Eliot (1888–1965), 'Whispers of Immortality' (1918), ll. 15–16, in *Poems: 1909–1925*, 2nd ed. (1932; repr. London: Faber, 1933), (O'Shea no. 617a) p. 72, and *OBMV* no. 255.
44. Elinor Hoyt Wylie (1885–1928) lived in England 1910–21. The quotation is from 'The Eagle and the Mole', ll. 19–24, in *Nets to Catch the Wind* (1921; repr. London: Knopf, 1928), (O'Shea no. 2300) p. 4: '. . . mole; / Go . . . underground. // . . . source, / '.
45. Yeats here refers to the aesthetic theories of the English art critics Clive Bell (1881–1964) and Roger Fry (1855–1934), who jointly organised the influential London exhibitions of Post-Impressionist art in 1910 and 1912. In prefaces to the catalogue of the 1912 exhibition, Fry said that Post-Impressionist artists 'do not seek to imitate form, but to create form', and Clive Bell stated that a Post-Impressionist artist 'simplifies, omits details . . . to concentrate on . . . the significance of form' (*Second Post-Impressionist Exhibition*, Grafton Galleries, London [London: Ballantyne, 1912] pp. 14, 10). Bell defined 'significant form' as 'lines and colours combined' so as to 'stir our aesthetic emotions' rather than to 'recount anecdotes, suggest ideas, and indicate the manners and customs of an age': 'In primitive art you will find no accurate representation; you will find only significant form.' ('The Aesthetic Hypothesis', in *Art* [London: Chatto and Windus, 1914] pp. 8, 18, 22.) Bell acknowledged a debt to Roger Fry's 'An Essay in Aesthetics' (1909; repr. 1920 in *Vision and Design*).

46. This might have been Dorothy ('Dolly') Travers-Smith Robinson (*c.* 1902–77), a landscape artist and a designer of sets and costumes at the Abbey Theatre, where her husband, Lennox Robinson, was a director (from 1923); she married Lennox Robinson on 8 September 1931. Yeats owned an oil landscape by her, 'Riversdale, Rathfarnham', dated 1937[? or perhaps 1934], which shows the grounds of his home in summer (collection of Anne Yeats).
47. Yeats's source is Henry Adams, who discussed the French mathematician and philosopher Jules Henri Poincaré (1854–1912) in *The Education of Henry Adams* (privately printed 1907; publ. 1918), (O'Shea nos. 17–18), ch. xxxi, 'The Grammar of Science' (1903). For details see p. 237 above and p. 434, note 80 below.
48. Dorothy Wellesley, 'Matrix' (1928), section XXI, ll. 10–12, in *Poems of Ten Years: 1924–1934* (London: Macmillan, 1934), (O'Shea nos. 2235–2235c) p. 324, and *OBMV* no. 278: '. . . womb, / Womb . . . bones, / '.
49. For example, 'Preludes' (1915) (*OBMV* no. 253) and *The Waste Land* (1922), section III, 'The Fire Sermon'.
50. Edith Sitwell, in her biography *Alexander Pope* (London: Faber, 1930), (O'Shea no. 1924), lauded Pope as a 'great and—at his best—flawless poet' (p. 7), but she paid little attention to 'An Essay on Man' (1733–34).

    William Blake, who complained that Pope and Dryden 'did not understand Verse', described Dryden's *The State of Innocence, and Fall of Man* (1677) as 'Monotonous Sing Song Sing Song from beginning to end' ('Public Address' [*Notebook*, pp. 39, 20], in Erdman, pp. 564, 570). Keats thought Pope 'was no poet, only a versifier' (Henry Stephens to George Felton Mathew, March 1847 [reminiscence of 1815 or 1816], quoted in Sidney Colvin, *John Keats: His Life and Poetry, His Friends, Critics and After-Fame* [London: Macmillan, 1917] I, 31; for a modern edition see Walter Jackson Bate, *Keats* [Cambridge, Mass.: Harvard University Press, 1966] p. 49). In 'Sleep and Poetry' (1817; ll. 185–86) Keats extended that criticism to eighteenth-century poets in general: 'They sway'd about upon a rocking horse, / And thought it Pegasus.' (*The Poetical Works*, ed. William T. Arnold [1884; repr. London: Kegan Paul, Trench, 1888], [O'Shea no. 1056] p. 56.)
51. *The Waste Land* (1922), section III, 'The Fire Sermon', ll. 253–56, in *Poems: 1909–1925,* 2nd ed. (1932; repr. London: Faber, 1933), (O'Shea no. 617a) p. 98: '. . . She smoothes her. . . .'
52. The French artists Edouard Manet (1832–83), an Impressionist; Henri Rousseau (1844–1910), a modern Primitive; and Gustave Courbet (1819–77), a Realist.
53. 'Sweeney Among the Nightingales' (1918), ll. 33–40, in *Poems 1909–1925,* 2nd ed. (1932; repr. London: Faber, 1933), (O'Shea no. 617a) p. 80, and *OBMV* no. 256.
54. 'The Hollow Men' (1925) (*OBMV* no. 257) and especially 'Ash Wednesday' (1927–30) mark Eliot's conversion in 1927 from secularism to Anglicanism. John Gray (1866–1934), English decadent poet,

converted to Catholicism in 1890 and was ordained a priest in 1901; *OBMV* has none of his poems. For Francis Thompson, see note 19 above; his powerful poem 'The Hound of Heaven' is *OBMV* no. 49. Lionel Johnson's poem 'The Dark Angel' (1895) is *OBMV* no. 108.

55. The opening speech by Thomas Becket in *Murder in the Cathedral* (London: Faber and Faber, 1935), (O'Shea no. 616) p. 21 (but with the second line omitted): '. . . exaltation. / They know and do not know, what it is to act or suffer. / They. . . .'
56. Cantos I–III had been published in 1917, IV in 1919, V–VII in 1921, VIII–XVI in 1925, XXVIII–XXX in 1930, XXXI–XLI in 1934, XLV in February 1936 and XLVI in March 1936. Dionysus is mentioned in Canto II and also in Canto XVII (*OBMV* no. 236). The descent of Odysseus into Hades is described in Canto I and is mentioned in Canto XXXIX. The petty frauds at Gibraltar are in Canto XXII.
57. In section XVI, Yeats discusses C. Day Lewis, Charles Madge (1912–), Louis MacNeice (1907–63), Stephen (later Sir Stephen) Spender (1909–) and—without naming him—W. H. Auden (1907–73).
58. Ezra Pound, 'The Return' (1912), ll. 1–14, in *Personae: The Collected Poems of Ezra Pound* (New York: Boni & Liveright, 1926), (O'Shea no. 1628) p. 74: '. . . back; / These . . . Inviolable. // Gods. . . .' In a speech at the *Poetry* banquet in Chicago, 1 March 1914, Yeats recited this poem and called it 'the most beautiful poem that has been written in the free form' and 'one of the few' with 'real organic rhythm' (*UP2* 414).
59. Sir John Falstaff, the good-humoured, extravagant braggart in Shakespeare's *King Henry IV, Parts I and II* (*c.* 1597). As early as 1902, Yeats said that 'Merry England' ended with Shakespeare, and that the modern England of 'the puritan and the merchant' began with Oliver Cromwell (1599–1658), Lord Protector of England (1653–58) (*E&I* 364). The friend is unidentified.
60. Christopher Smart's poem was published in 1763; Byron died in 1824.
61. Stendhal [Marie-Henri Beyle], *The Red and the Black* (1831), epigraph to ch. xiii; see p. 353, note 31 above.
62. Robert Browning, *The Ring and the Book* (1868–69), and Alfred Lord Tennyson, *Idylls of the King* (1859–85). In 1889 Tennyson said of King Arthur, the hero *of Idylls of the King*: 'I intended Arthur to represent the Ideal Soul of Man coming into contact with the warring elements of the flesh.' (Quoted by Hallam Tennyson, ed., *The Poetical Works of Alfred, Lord Tennyson* [New York: Macmillan, 1908] III, 443n.)
63. The novel by Joris Karl Huysmans was published in 1898; Hemingway's novel *A Farewell to Arms* was published in 1929.
64. Walter James Turner, Australian-born music critic of the *New Statesman*, poet, novelist and playwright in England. See the excerpt in *OBMV* (no. 270) from Turner's *The Seven Days of the Sun: A Dramatic Poem* ('Thursday', section IV, ll. 1–2), (London: Chatto & Win-

dus, 1925), (O'Shea nos. 2170, 2170a) p. 27: 'I had watched the ascension and decline of the Moon / And did not realize that it moved only in my mind.'

65. The comedy is *The Man Who Ate the Popomack: A Tragic-Comedy of Love in Two Acts* (1922); Yeats saw a performance in London during November 1935. 'Snivelling majorities' is a misquotation of *The Seven Days of the Sun* ('Saturday', section III, l. 1) p. 44: 'O the horror of this life among snivelling mediocrities'.
66. In Turner's novel *The Aesthetes* (London: Wishart, 1927), a character based on Lytton Strachey announces that the extravagant ostentatiousness of a female character modelled on Lady Ottoline Morrell 'is merely a by-product of thwarted sex' and that she 'is more masculine than feminine' (p. 40).
67. Turner's mathematical training did not extend beyond his one year as a mining student, but *The Seven Days of the Sun* includes an algebraic formula ('Saturday', section II) and makes frequent use of terminology from geometry ('Thursday', section II and 'Friday', section III).
68. *The Seven Days of the Sun* ('Thursday', section III, ll. 8–21) p. 27 and *OBMV* no. 270, section VI.
69. In Honoré de Balzac's story 'The Unknown Masterpiece' (1832), the mysterious old artist, Master Frenhofer, announces that in his portrait of Catherine Lescault, *La Belle Noisseuse*: 'I have succeeded in reproducing Nature's roundness and relief on the flat surface of the canvas. . . . I have not marked out the limits of my figure in hard, dry outlines . . . for the human body is not contained within the limits of line. Nature's way is a complicated succession of curve within curve. Strictly speaking there is no such thing as drawing. . . . A line is a method of expressing the effect of light upon an object; but there are no lines in nature, everything is solid.' *(The Unknown Masterpiece [Le Chef-d'oeuvre inconnu] and Other Stories,* tr. Ellen Marriage, in *Comédie humaine,* ed. George Saintsbury [London: Dent Edition, 1896], repr. as vol. XXXVII in Temple edition [New York: Macmillan, 1901], [O'Shea no. 109] pp. 15–16.)
70. Turner refers to the 'Dark Lady' of Shakespeare's sonnets (nos. 127–54) in *The Seven Days of the Sun* ('Friday', section I) pp. 32–34 and *OBMV* no. 270, section IV.
71. W. J. Turner, *Pursuit of Psyche* (Canto IV, ll. 1–8) (London: Wishart, 1931) p. 21.
72. George Berkeley, *Siris: A Chain of Philosophical Reflexions and Inquiries concerning the Virtues of Tar-Water* (1744); see pp. 123 and 365, note 6 above. Robert Grosseteste (*c.* 1175–1253), chancellor of Oxford University and bishop of Lincoln, 'On Light'; see p. 365, note 4 above.
73. Herbert Read (1893–1968), 'The Mutations of the Phoenix' (1923) (section V, last stanza; section VI, ll. 1–5, 11), in *Poems: 1914–1934* (London: Faber, 1935), (O'Shea no. 1728) p. 148; section VI begins at 'The phoenix burns spiritually'.
74. Dorothy Violet Wellesley (1889–1956), Duchess of Wellington, 'Matrix' (1928), (section XIV, ll. 28–31), in *Poems of Ten Years: 1924–1934*

(London: Macmillan, 1934), (O'Shea nos. 2235–2235c) p. 319: '. . . loam, / . . . / . . . rock: / '.

75. For the character Ralph in William Morris's *The Well at the World's End*, see p. 363, note 21 above. Dorothy Wellesley discussed this attribute in a letter to Yeats, 18 July 1936 (*LDW* 80).
76. Dorothy Wellesley, 'Horses' (1925), ll. 1–9, in *Poems of Ten Years: 1924–1934*, p. 47 and *OBMV* no. 274. Yeats first read the poem in May or June 1935.
77. For Nicholas of Cusa, *The Vision of God, or The Icon* (1453), see p. 346, note 35 above.
78. Herbert Read, *The End of a War* (1931–32, publ. in 1933), *OBMV* no. 305.
79. Siegfried Sassoon (1886–1967) (*OBMV* nos. 242–45) fought with exceptional bravery, won a Military Cross (which he threw away in 1917) and was recommended for the Distinguished Service Order. Other officer-poets included Edmund Blunden, M.C. (1896–1974) (*OBMV* nos. 307–12); Rupert Brooke (1887–1915) (*OBMV* no. 246); Robert Graves (1895–1985); Julian Grenfell, D.S.O. (1888–1915) (*OBMV* no. 260); Robert Nichols (1893–1944) (*OBMV* nos. 296–304); Wilfred Owen, M.C. (1893–1918); Herbert Read, M.C., D.S.O. (*OBMV* no. 305); Edward Shanks (1892–1953) (*OBMV* nos. 289–92); and Charles Hamilton Sorley (1895–1915). Wilfrid Wilson Gibson (1878–1962) (*OBMV* nos. 155–58) and Isaac Rosenberg (1890–1918) were enlisted men and were not decorated.

    OBMV has eight poems about the First World War: Wilfrid Wilson Gibson, 'Breakfast' (1916; written before he enlisted) (*OBMV* no. 155); Julian Grenfell, 'Into Battle' (1915) (*OBMV* no. 260); Herbert Read, *The End of a War* (1931–32, publ. 1933) (*OBMV* no. 305); Siegfried Sassoon, 'On Passing the New Menin Gate' (1928) (*OBMV* no. 244); and Edward Shanks, 'Sleeping Heroes' (1915), 'Drilling in Russell Square' (1915), and 'The Winter Soldier', sections I: 'To be Sung to the Tune of High Germany' (dated August 1914) and V: 'Going in to Dinner' (*OBMV* nos. 289–92). Yeats had at first selected two additional war poems, 'In the Grass: Halt by the Roadside' and 'Nearer', from *Ardours and Endurances* (1917) by Robert Nichols, but eventually replaced them with other, later poems by Nichols (Edward O'Shea, *Yeats as Editor* [Dublin: Dolmen Press, 1975] p. 71; see also Nichols to Yeats, 26 October 1935, *LTWBY* 581, and letters quoted by Jon Stallworthy, 'Yeats as Anthologist', in *In Excited Reverie: A Centenary Tribute to William Butler Yeats: 1865–1939*, ed. A. Norman Jeffares and K. G. W. Cross [New York: Macmillan, 1965] pp. 182–83).
80. Sassoon's statement to his commanding officer in July 1917 was widely published: 'I have seen and endured the sufferings of the troops, and I can no longer be a party to prolong these sufferings for ends which I believe to be evil and unjust. . . . On behalf of those who are suffering now I make this protest.' (*Bradford Pioneer*, 27 July 1917; Robert Graves, *Good-Bye to All That: An Autobiography* [London: Cape, 1929] pp. 320–21; and Sassoon, *Memoirs of an Infantry*

Officer [London: Faber, 1930], [O'Shea no. 1843] p. 308.) Yeats was probably also thinking of Wilfred Owen's poem 'Strange Meeting', ll. 24–25 ('. . . the truth untold, / The pity of war, the pity war distilled') and his preface published in *Poems* (London: Chatto & Windus, 1920) p. vii: 'Above all, this book is not concerned with Poetry. The subject of it is War, and the pity of War. The Poetry is in the pity.' In 1933, W. H. Auden quoted that last sentence in the closing stanza of his poem 'Here on the cropped grass of the narrow ridge I stand': ' "The poetry is in the pity," Wilfred said' (collected in *Look, Stranger* [London: Faber, 22 October 1936], [O'Shea no. 64] p. 46). C. Day Lewis quoted that sentence three times in his essays in *A Hope for Poetry* ([Oxford: Blackwell, 1934], [O'Shea no. 1113] pp. 2, 14, 15). Stephen Spender, in an essay on Owen, titled 'Poetry and Pity', which mentions Yeats, quoted Owen's 'Preface' and praised him as 'the most useful influence in modern verse' (in *The Destructive Element: A Study of Modern Writers and Beliefs* [London: Cape, 1935] pp. 217, 220).

81. In his preface to *Poems* (London: Longman, Brown, Green, and Longmans, 1853), Arnold explained that he withdrew 'Empedocles on Etna', which had been the title poem of his 1852 collection, because it was 'poetically faulty', and because 'no poetical enjoyment can be derived' from the representation of situations 'in which the suffering finds no vent in action; in which a continuous state of mental distress is prolonged, unrelieved by incident, hope, or resistance' (p. viii). Dorothy Wellesley recalled that during August 1935, when Yeats was selecting poems for the anthology, he refused to reconsider 'his decision to omit nearly all the war poets, including Wilfred Owen': 'On this point he remained adamant, holding that "passive suffering was not a subject for poetry". . . . The creative man must impose himself upon suffering' (*LDW* 21; see also *LDW* 124–26, 129).

82. Aeschylus, *The Persians* (475 B.C., set in 480 B.C.); Michael Drayton, 'Ballad of Agincourt' (1606–19, set in 1415); and the anonymous 'Ballad of Chevy Chase' (probably fifteenth century), published by Thomas Percy in *Reliques of Ancient English Poetry* (1765). For Yeats's motif of tragic joy, see, for example, p. 213 above and 'Lapis Lazuli' (*P* 294–95).

83. Florence Farr (Mrs Emery) (1860–1917), actress, occultist and novelist. The Connacht Rangers was an Irish regiment (disbanded 1922) of the British Army; the Boer War ended in 1902.

84. Patrick Street, in the Liberties section of Dublin, is roughly the equivalent of London's Cockney slums. Kilmainham Jail, Dublin, was built in 1787. 'Luke Caffrey's Kilmainham Minit' or 'The Kilmainham Minuet (or Minut)' is a late-eighteenth-century Irish street ballad written in thieves' cant; it was printed by James Edward Walsh in *Sketches of Ireland Sixty Years Ago* (Dublin: McGlashan, 1847) pp. 86–89.

'Johnny, I hardly knew ye!', another Irish street ballad, dates from the early nineteenth century, 'when Irish regiments were so extensively raised for the East India Service', according to a note in Halliday Sparling's *Irish Minstrelsy: Being a Selection of Irish Songs, Lyrics, and Ballads* (London: Scott, 1888), (O'Shea no. 1967) p. 512. *Irish Minstrelsy*, which included a poem by Yeats, was the first publication of the full version of 'Johnny, I hardly knew ye!' (pp. 491–93). Yeats used that version in *A Book of Irish Verse* (London: Methuen, 1895) pp. 238–41, and in *A Broadside*, new series 9 (September 1935).

The 'medieval *Dance of Death*' (or *La Danse macabre*) is a pictorial or literary representation of dead persons, usually shown as skeletons, leading a procession or dance of living persons to the grave. Yeats specified 'medieval' perhaps to preclude any confusion with Auden's play *The Dance of Death* (publ. 1933, perf. 1934).

85. For the Russian Ballet, see note 41 above. '*Mare tranquillum*' is from Turner's *The Seven Days of the Sun* ('Thursday', section III, l. 13) p. 27, quoted on p. 196 above, and *OBMV* no. 270, section VI, l. 13).

'Heraclitus added fire' is from Dorothy Wellesley's poem 'Fire: An Incantation' (1936), ll. 67, 72, 98 (*Selections from the Poems of Dorothy Wellesley* [London: Macmillan, 1936], [O'Shea nos. 2236–2236b] pp. 7–8 and *OBMV* no. 273). The references to moths, horses and snakes are to poems in her sequence 'Lost Lane, or Poetry of Every Day' (1925), in *Poems of Ten Years: 1924–1934* (London: Macmillan, 1934), (O'Shea nos. 2235–2235c) pp. 83–85, 47–49, 68–69: 'Trilogy VI: Summer Night' [poem 2]; 'Trilogy II: Dinner Party' [poem 3], (*OBMV* no. 274 and excerpted on p. 198 above); and 'Trilogy IV: Sight-seeing' [poem 3].

Pound's Canto I (1917) describes the descent of Odysseus into Hades (*A Draft of XVI Cantos* [1925]); Pound's Chinese translations are in *Cathy* (1915).

86. *OBMV* includes several poets who were attracted, some only briefly, to communist ideas: W. H. Auden, C. Day Lewis, Hugh MacDiarmid, Louis MacNeice, Charles Madge, Michael Roberts (1902–48) and Stephen Spender. Only MacDiarmid, Roberts and Spender joined the Communist party, but they did not remain members; MacDiarmid rejoined in 1957, after an absence of two decades.

87. See p. 376, note 41 above.

88. Irish Protestant parades commemorating the 1690 victory of William of Orange over James II at the Battle of the Boyne.

89. Untraced; see also Yeats's note, p. 356, note 40 above.

90. Stephen Spender, who deplored the 'aristocratic individualism' in Yeats's poem 'A Prayer for My Daughter' (1919), called for 'the artist to discover a system of values that are not purely subjective and individualistic, but objective and social'. To find 'beliefs . . . we must turn back to the past, or we must exercise our imaginations to some degree, so that we live in the future'. Spender urged artists to reject the 'complete unbelief' that characterised the works of Henry James, Yeats and T. S. Eliot. (*The Destructive Element: A Study of Modern Writers and Beliefs* [London: Cape, 1935] pp. 203, 222–24.)

91. W. H. Auden, '[This lunar beauty]' (1930), ll. 1–7, in *Poems*, 2nd ed. (London: Faber, 1933), (O'Shea no. 66) p. 67, no. XVII; *OBMV* no.

368. It was printed in *OBMV* with another Auden poem, '[Before this loved one]' (1930), mistakenly appended to it without any break. Yeats gave the printer, as copy-text, pages cut from a copy of Auden's *Poems* (1933), in which those two consecutive, untitled poems are recto and verso of the same page; Auden simply numbered them 'XVII' and 'XVIII'. Yeats may or may not have intended to include both poems. His preliminary count, dated 9 October 1935, of poems for *OBMV* gave Auden three poems; *OBMV* has four Auden poems, counting '[Before this loved one]'. See Edward O'Shea, *Yeats as Editor* (Dublin: Dolmen Press, 1975) p. 80, note 141. The poems remained mistakenly run together in the first three British issues. Then, after Yeats mentioned the error in a letter to the Oxford University Press in March 1937, the poems were separated (and renumbered as 368 and 368a) in the 1938 issue, only to have the error reinstated in the 'corrected' reissue in 1966, although '[This lunar beauty]' was retained in the index. The poems were never separated in the New York edition. See p. 483 below.

92. Hopkins, *Poems*, ed. Robert Bridges (London: Milford, 1918), took ten years to sell 750 copies; the second edition was published in 1930 (London: Oxford University Press).
93. In Milton's *Sampson Agonistes* (1671) the speeches of the chorus are in irregular verse, as Milton noted in his preface: 'The measure of Verse used in the Chorus is of all sorts, called by the Greeks *monostrophic*, or rather *apolelymenon* ["free"].' (John Milton, *Paradise Regained Sampson Agonistes and Other Poems*, ed. W. H. D. Rouse, Temple Classics [London: Dent, 1898], [O'Shea no. 1322] p. 76.)
94. See note 78 above.
95. The anthology includes only 'The River Merchant's Wife: A Letter' (*OBMV* no. 234) from Pound's Chinese translations, *Cathay* (1915). Yeats had considered printing also 'A Ballad of the Mulberry Road' and 'South-Folk in Cold Country' (O'Shea, *Yeats as Editor*, pp. 66 and 79 n. 137, and O'Shea no. 1628); see also *LDW* 25. Pound's freely adapted versions were based on literal translations by Ernest Fenollosa of Japanese translations of the Chinese originals.

    Arthur Waley (1889–1966) translated many volumes of Oriental prose; his translation (1918) of 'The Temple' (814), by Po Chü-i, is in *OBMV* (no. 237).

    See p. 165 above for Yeats's enthusiastic introduction to Rabindranath Tagore's *Gitanjali: Song Offerings* (1912), a collection of his Bengali religious poems. Tagore then dedicated to Yeats a collection of secular poems, *The Gardener*, published in 1913. The following year, Yeats wrote an introduction to Tagore's short play *The Post Office* (*P&I* 144). Although Yeats's esteem for Tagore had markedly declined by 1935, *OBMV* has five poems from *Gitanjali* and two from *The Gardener*, all in prose translations by Tagore (*OBMV* nos. 53–59).
96. The eight poems by George Russell ('AE') (1867–1935) in *OBMV* (nos. 100–7) reflect only indirectly his study of Indian religion.
97. Translations from the Irish account for all five of the poems by Lady

Gregory in *OBMV*, four of the eight by James Stephens, and all seven by Frank O'Connor (*OBMV* nos. 35–39, 208–11, 338–44).

98. Richard Hughes (1900–77), an Oxford-educated English traveller who is best known for his novel *A High Wind in Jamaica* (1929), had published two books of poems (1922, 1926); eight of his poems are in *OBMV* (nos. 324–31).

Robert Nichols (1893–1944), an Oxford-educated poet and minor playwright, served in the First World War and was professor of English literature at Tokyo University (1921–24); nine of his poems are in *OBMV* (nos. 296–304).

On p. 183 above, Yeats quoted two lines from a Scottish dialect poem by Hugh MacDiarmid without naming him (see note 10 above). That poem and one other dialect poem are in *OBMV*, along with two poems by him not in dialect (nos. 281–84).

99. George Barker (1913–91) is the youngest poet in *OBMV*. On 8 September [1935] Yeats wrote to Dorothy Wellesley, 'I delight in a young poet called George Barker . . . a lovely subtle mind and a rhythmical invention comparable to Gerard Hopkins' (*LDW* 25). Yeats's preliminary count of poems for *OBMV*, dated 9 October 1935, had eight poems by Barker, but only four were printed (nos. 375–78; Jon Stallworthy, 'Yeats as Anthologist', in *In Excited Reverie: A Centenary Tribute to William Butler Yeats: 1865–1939*, ed. A. Norman Jeffares and K. G. W. Cross [New York: Macmillan, 1965] p. 179).

100. William Force Stead (1884–1967) was chaplain of Worcester College, Oxford, from 1927 until 1933, when he became a Roman Catholic. *OBMV* has two of his poems (nos. 226–27).

Margot Ruddock (1907–51) had never published a poem prior to July 1936, when Yeats introduced six of her poems in the *London Mercury* (see *P&I* 186–90, 336); all six, plus one very short additional poem, are in *OBMV* (nos. 356–62).

101. Mrs Yeats selected the fourteen poems by Yeats in *OBMV* (nos. 76–89; *LDW* 127). The selection begins with five poems from his latest collection, *The Winding Stair and Other Poems* (1933): 'After Long Silence', 'Three Things', 'Lullaby', 'Symbols', and 'Vacillation' (section VIII), followed by the opening poem of *The Tower* (1928), 'Sailing to Byzantium'. Next comes the patriotic Irish 'The Rose Tree' (1920), as a preface to 'On a Political Prisoner' (1920) and 'In Memory of Eva Gore-Booth and Con Markiewicz' (1929), which was the opening poem in *The Winding Stair and Other Poems*. Then follow four poems associated with Lady Gregory: 'To a Friend whose Work has come to Nothing' (1913), 'An Irish Airman Foresees his Death' (1919), 'Coole Park, 1929' (1931), and 'Coole and Ballylee, 1931' (1932). The last poem in the selection is the closing poem of the 'A Man Young and Old' series, 'XI: From *Oedipus at Colonus*' (1927).

102. The advice was from T. S. Eliot, as Yeats told Charles Williams, an Oxford University Press editor, in a letter of 24 October 1935. Williams had suggested that Yeats add the Americans H.D., Robert

Frost and either Stephen Vincent Benet or William Rose Benet (Jon Stallworthy, 'Yeats as Anthologist' in *In Excited Reverie: A Centenary Tribute to William Butler Yeats: 1865–1939*, ed. A. Norman Jeffares and K. G. W. Cross [New York: Macmillan, 1965] p. 181). The only three American-born poets in *OBMV* are T. S. Eliot, who had been a British subject since 1927; Ezra Pound, who had left the U.S.A. in 1907; and W. Force Stead, who had been a resident of England since 1908.

INTRODUCTION [PUBL. 1961 AS 'A GENERAL INTRODUCTION FOR MY WORK']

1. Sir Walter Raleigh, 'The Lie' (1593–96?), l. 18, in *The Poems of Sir Walter Ralegh*, ed. Agnes Latham (London: Constable, 1929) p. 45: 'giue Potentates the lie'.
2. Percy Bysshe Shelley, 'Julian and Maddalo' (1819, p. 1824), ll. 449–50, in *Poems of Shelley*, ed. Locock, I, 229: '. . . oppressions of this earth'.
3. George Gordon, Lord Byron, 'So, we'll go no more a roving' (1817, p. 1830), ll. 5–7, in *The Poetical Works of Lord Byron*, Chandos Classics series (London: Warne, 1889) p. 661: 'For the sword outwears its sheath, / And the soul wears out the breast, / And the heart must pause to breathe'.
4. Tiresias, the legendary blind Theban seer, in *Antigone* and *Oedipus the King* by Sophocles, and *Bacchae* and *The Phoenician Maidens* by Euripides; Rosalind in *As You Like It* and the 'Dark Lady' of Shakespeare's sonnets (nos. 127–54).
5. Prashna Upanishad, 4.6, in *TPU* 45: '. . . lost in that happiness'. Chāndôgya Upanishad, 8.3.2, in *TPU* 109: '. . . alive, those . . . dead; and . . . what this world. . . .'
6. Yeats was twenty when, in 1885, he met John O'Leary (1830–1907), who had only recently returned to Ireland after five years in prison and fifteen years of exile. O'Leary had been convicted for treason as editor of the Irish Republican Brotherhood ('Fenian') journal, *The Irish People*.
7. Yeats's pastoral play influenced by Edmund Spenser's *The Faerie Queene* (1590–96) and Ben Jonson's pastoral play *The Sad Shepherd or A Tale of Robin Hood* (unfinished, publ. 1641) could be *The Island of Statues: An Arcadian Faery Tale—in Two Acts* (1885) or else the very brief 'The Seeker: A Dramatic Poem—in Two Acts' (1885) (*P* 453–83, 484–87).
8. Yeats's 'two plays' that were influenced by Percy Bysshe Shelley's *Prometheus Unbound* (1820) are perhaps two versions of an unfinished play from 1886 that was variously titled *Blind*, *The Blindness*, *Sans Eyes* and *The Epic of the Forests*. Its early version is set probably in the Caucasus and its later version mentions craters of the moon. David R.

Clark further points out, however, that the phrase 'somewhere in the Caucasus' might be a loose reference to Yeats's other major early unpublished play, *Love and Death*, from which the poem 'Love and Death' (publ. 1885; *P* 483–84) developed.

9. Thomas Davis (1814–45) and James Clarence Mangan (1803–49) were the best poets who published in *The Nation*, founded 1842, the journal of the Young Ireland movement, which sought to foster Irish cultural nationalism as well as political independence. Among its many lesser poets were John de Jean Frazer (1810?–50?), John Kells Ingram (1823–1907), Denis Florence MacCarthy (1817–82), Mary (or 'Mary of *The Nation*') [Ellen Mary Patrick Downing] (1829–69) and Richard D'Alton Williams (1822–62).
10. See p. 357, note 44 above.
11. Standish James O'Grady's (1846–1928) influential early books were *History of Ireland: The Heroic Period*, 2 vols. (1878) and *Cuchulain and His Contemporaries* (1880); Yeats owned several other of his Irish books published between 1889 and 1894 (O'Shea nos. 1490–93). Eugene O'Curry (1796–1862), professor of Irish history and archaeology at the Catholic University of Ireland, *Lectures on the Manuscript Materials of Ancient Irish History, Delivered at the Catholic University of Ireland, during the Sessions of 1855 and 1856* (1861, repr. 1872), (O'Shea no. 1477) and *On the Manners and Customs of the Ancient Irish: A Series of Lectures*, 3 vols. (posthumously, 1873), (O'Shea no. 1478); both of the O'Curry works are thought to have been given to Yeats by John O'Leary.
12. John Mitchel (1815–75), Irish journalist and patriot, wrote for *The Nation* from 1845 until 1848; his most famous work is *Jail Journal* (1854).
13. The scholars George Petrie (1790–1866), John O'Donovan (1809–61) and Eugene O'Curry worked in the Ordnance Survey of Ireland's historical department during the 1830s.
14. Yeats explained (*P&I* 16): 'The *banshee* (from *ban* [*bean*], a woman, and *shee* [*sidhe*], a fairy) is an attendant fairy that follows the old families, and none but them, and wails before a death. Many have seen her as she goes wailing and clapping her hands.' John O'Donovan reported that when his grandfather died in 1798 a banshee had cried (quoted by Yeats, 1889, *UP1* 136–37), but see O'Donovan's highly sceptical account of an aristocratic Irish friend's encounter in 1820 with a banshee (quoted in William G. Wood-Martin, *Traces of the Elder Faiths of Ireland: A Folklore Sketch: A Handbook of Irish Pre-Christian Traditions* [London: Longmans, Green, 1902] I, 370–71; see also I, 364). See Edward Callan, *Yeats on Yeats*, p. 46, note 20.
15. The Irish round towers, such as at Glendalough, were thought to be related to Persian fire-worship, according to the theories of General Charles Vallancey (*Essay on the Antiquity of the Irish Language*, 1772; 3rd ed., 1818) and John Windele (*Historical and Descriptive Notices of the City of Cork and its Vicinity*, 1839). George Petrie overturned those speculations in *The Ecclesiastical Architecture of Ireland . . . The Origin*

and Uses of the Round Towers of Ireland (1833, 2nd ed. [Dublin: Hodges and Smith, 1845] pp. 12–109).

16. This Church of Ireland rector (born *c.* 1740s) is unidentified except as having been a friend of Oliver Goldsmith (1730–74) and, as Yeats adds, 'a connection and close friend of my great-grandmother' Grace Armstrong Corbet (*c.* 1768–1861) 'and though we spoke of him as "Uncle Beattie" in our childhood, no blood relation' (*Au* 23). The portrait drawing is not extant.
17. In November 1841, Daniel O'Connell (1775–1847), leader of the movement for repeal of the union with England, was elected Lord Mayor of Dublin, and his Repeal Association was rapidly gaining strength. The Office of Ordnance, which ran £2,788 over budget for 1841–42, cancelled the funding of the Ordnance Survey of Ireland's historical department in 1842 as an economy measure; the Survey was then within four years of publishing the last county map. Sir Robert Peel's Conservative government, which had been elected in 1841, rejected the recommendation of a commission in 1843 that the historical department be continued. The historical and topographical information collected during the survey is principally preserved in the library of the Royal Irish Academy, Dublin.
18. For O'Grady's reference to Slievenamon (elev. 2,368 feet), a mountain in southeastern Co. Tipperary, and Mount Olympus, home of the Greek gods, see pp. 157 and 382, note 6 above. Slievenamon is numbered among Yeats's 'old sacred places' (*Mem* 124) as the site of a house of Irish gods; as Sidhe Femen it was the home of Bodb Dearg, a Tuatha de Danaan king; see *Gods and Fighting Men*, pp. 73–74.
19. Standish Hayes O'Grady (1832–1915) compiled the first volume of the *Catalogue of Irish Manuscripts in the British Museum*, continuing the work begun by Eugene O'Curry in 1849. The Irish Literary Society, which Yeats helped to found in London in 1891, supported Irish cultural nationalism but sought to be apolitical.
20. The quoted phrases are characteristic of Standish Hayes O'Grady's English translations in *Silva Gadelica (i.–xxxi.): A Collection of Tales in Irish with Extracts Illustrating Persons and Places* (London: Williams and Norgate, 1892), but not all of the quotations are exact. The first phrase, 'fractured her heart', is not in *Silva Gadelica*. O'Grady used 'ascended', 'apex' and 'eminence' (ii, 222, 219, 392), but not together. Caoilte, one of the last of the Fianna, says, 'I used to vibrate a sharp javelin hardily' (ii, 192). Cian's son Teigue sees the 'colossal Ocean's superficies' (ii, 387).
21. For Yeats's introductions to Lady Gregory's *Cuchulain of Muirthemne: The Story of the Men of the Red Branch of Ulster* (1902) and *Gods and Fighting Men* (1904), see *P&I* 119–34. Lady Charlotte Guest translated Welsh heroic tales in *The Mabinogion, from . . . The Red Book of Hergest* (1838–49, repr. London: Quaritch, 1877), (O'Shea no. 1166).
22. For Thomas Carlyle, see p. 307, note 128 above.
23. Rosses Point is a village on Sligo Bay where the Yeats family spent summer holidays. A prominent burial cairn atop Knocknarea (elev. 1,078 feet), a hill three miles west of Sligo, is popularly assigned to

Maeve (or Medh), a legendary queen of Connacht; Yeats knew that she would have been much more likely to have been buried at the royal site, Cruachan, thirty-five miles south of Sligo, near Tulsk, Co. Roscommon.

24. In the introduction to *Fairy and Folk Tales of the Irish Peasantry* (1888), Yeats objected that T. Crofton Croker (1798–1854) and Samuel Lover (1797–1868) 'saw everything humorised' (*P&I* 7). He included both authors in that folklore anthology and in his *Representative Irish Tales* (1891); he worked on those anthologies in the Reading Room of the British Museum.

25. Yeats accompanied Lady Gregory in collecting local folklore from 1897 onwards. He amalgamated some three hundred of her items into a series of six lengthy articles published between November 1897 and April 1902. Lady Gregory herself used some of the material in *V&B* (1920), to which Yeats contributed essays and notes; see pp. 47 ff., 74 ff. and 258 ff. above.

26. See p. 372, note 23 above.

27. Francis Crawford Burkitt (1864–1935), professor of divinity, Cambridge University, gave Yeats an off-print of his review of Rev. John Roche Ardill, *St Patrick—A.D. 189* (London: Murray, 1931), (O'Shea no. 49), in *The Journal of Theological Studies*, 33 (July 1932), (O'Shea no. 307) 404–8. In that review, Professor Burkitt acknowledges that modern scholars place St Patrick's mission to Ireland in the fifth century, but finds that Ardill 'has made out a strong case which deserves serious consideration' (405). On the same page, Burkitt mentions that in the fourth and fifth centuries the Irish determined the date of Easter differently from the Roman method. The Irish method was officially ended by the Synod of Whitby in 664, but conformity was not achieved until at least sixty years later. See the commentary of Standish Hayes O'Grady to 'Fragmentary Annals: 704', in *Silva Gadelica*, II, 444. A third-century date for St Patrick had been proposed by R. Steele Nicholson in *Saint Patrick: Apostle of Ireland in the Third Century: The Story of his Mission by Pope Celestine in A.D. 431 . . . Proved to be a mere Fiction* (Dublin: McGlashan and Gill, 1868).

28. Dionysus (Bacchus): Greek god worshipped in orgiastic rites.
The slowness of Irish Christians to abandon the Druidic style of tonsure in favour of the Roman style was an issue at the Synod of Whitby (664). There is some uncertainty about the precise nature of the Druid tonsure, but probably only the front part of the head was shaved, from ear to ear. See J. B. Bury, *The Life of St Patrick and his Place in History* (London: Macmillan, 1905) pp. 142–43, 239–43.

29. Early Irish Christian bishops often lacked a fixed see and did not have settled boundaries to their territory; abbots headed the monasteries and often had the support of the local ruler. See J. B. Bury, *The Life of St Patrick and his Place in History*, pp. 174–84, 375–79, cited by Arnold Toynbee in *A Study of History*, 2nd ed. (London: Oxford University Press, 1935), (O'Shea no. 2157) II, 326, n. 2.

30. James G. Frazer, *The Golden Bough: A Study of Magic and Religion* (1st ed., 2 vols., 1890; 2nd ed., 3 vols., 1900; 3rd ed., 12 vols., 1907–15).

Frederic W. H. Myers, *Human Personality and its Survival of Bodily Death* (1903); see also p. 324, note 52a above. St Patrick's 'Creed', in the second paragraph of 'The Confession of St Patrick, or His Epistle to the Irish', says that Christ 'is soon [*mox*] about to be the judge of the quick and the dead' (tr. R. Steele Nicholson, *Saint Patrick: Apostle of Ireland in the Third Century* [Dublin: McGlashan and Gill, 1868] pp. 82, 116). See Callan, *Yeats on Yeats*, p. 52, notes 40–41.

31. See p. 388, note 10 above.
32. The Tetragrammaton (four Hebrew letters representing the name of God) and Agla (an acrostic of four Hebrew words meaning 'Thou are powerful and eternal, Lord') are extensively used in Cabbalism and in ritual magic, as for example in S. L. MacGregor Mathers's introduction and tr., *The Kabbalah Unveiled* (London: Redway, 1887), (O'Shea nos. 1292, 1292a) pp. 9 *et passim* (for Tetragrammaton) and 31 (for Agla). The village of Doneraile, Co. Cork, is seven miles northeast of Mallow. See also p. 74 above.
33. Baroque and rococo: the elaborated styles of the seventeenth and eighteenth centuries, respectively. *Yeats on Yeats* (p. 53, n. 44) mentions the manuscript version's reference here to sectarian religious persecution: '. . . the scientific and theological dogmatist that accompanied Baroque and Rococo remained aloof, we had but wars of blood and iron' (NLI Ms. 30,798).
34. John Synge's play *The Well of the Saints* (1905); James Stephens, Irish poet and novelist (1882?–1950); for George Russell (AE) and the Hindu Upanishads, see p. 387, note 4 above.
35. Executions of Padraic Pearse, Thomas MacDonagh and other leaders of the Easter Rising.
36. Cuchulain, legendary warrior of the Red Branch (or Ulster) heroic tales.
37. George Chapman, 'Hymnus in Noctem', *The Shadow of the Night* (1594), in *The Works of George Chapman* (London: Chatto & Windus, 1904), (O'Shea no. 370) II, 7: '. . . heaven, in . . . hurl'd, / And cleanse this beastly . . . of the world'.
38. The Gaelic League, founded in 1893 to promote the Irish language. As Edward Callan has pointed out, the house plant aspidistra was a familiar emblem of middle-class respectability (*Yeats on Yeats*, p. 55, n. 52). Jesse, the father of King David.
39. For this anonymous Irish street ballad from the early nineteenth century, see p. 404, note 84 above and *P&I* 301, note 9.
40. The quotations that follow are from Arnold Toynbee, *A Study of History* (Oxford: Clarendon Press, 1934), (O'Shea no. 2157) II, 424–26 (Annex III. 'The Extinction of the Far Western Christian Culture in Ireland'): '. . . The process of extinction. . . . in the ecclesiastical sphere . . . was completed in the twelfth century, with the thoroughgoing . . . Church. In . . . spheres, it was completed in the. . . . nitch . . . society. . . . of Ancient Ireland . . . Modern Ireland has made up her mind, in our generation, to . . . in our workaday Western World.' See also II, 322–40. For the Synod of Whitby, see note 27 above.

41. Charles Stewart Parnell (1846–91). Lord Edward Fitzgerald (1763–98), who died from wounds received when he was arrested a few days before he was to have led the United Irishmen in the Rising of 1798.
42. See pp. 47 ff., 74 ff. and 258 ff. above for Yeats's two essays, 'Swedenborg, Mediums, and the Desolate Places' (dated 14 October 1914), 'Witches and Wizards and Irish Folk-lore' (dated 1914) and forty-six notes for *Visions and Beliefs in the West of Ireland* by Lady Gregory (New York: Putnam's, 1920).
43. For Yeats's earlier mentions of this anecdote, see p. 47 above and *Mem* 126.
44. Shri (Shree) Purohit Swāmi, tr., *The Holy Mountain: Being the Story of a Pilgrimage to Lake Mānas and of Initiation on Mount Kailā in Tibet* by Bhagwān Shri Hamsa (London: Faber, 1934); see p. 139 ff. above. *The Ten Principal Upanishads,* tr. Shree Purohit Swāmi and W. B. Yeats (London: Faber, 1937); see p. 171 ff. above.
45. For the deer at Coole Park, Lady Gregory's estate, see *V&B,* ɪɪ, 249; *V&B1970* 278. For the priest, see *UP2* 104. Raths, which are circular, prehistoric hill-forts, are traditionally inhabited by fairies.
46. For St Patrick's Creed, see note 30 above. For 'Unity of Being', see p. 383, note 22 above.
47. Blake often called imagination 'the Divine Body of the Lord Jesus' (for example, *Jerusalem,* plate 5, ll. 58–59; plate 24, l. 23; plate 60, l. 57; plate 74, l. 13; in Erdman, pp. 147, 168, 209, 227).
48. Yeats misspelled 'immanent' (as 'imanent') in the manuscript (p. 12; NLI Ms. 30,798), but allowed 'imminent' to stand in both typescript versions (corr. Ts., p. 12; NLI Ms. 30,798) (Scribner's Ts., p. 11). See Callan, *Yeats on Yeats,* p. 59, note 67, and plates 5 (Ms.) and 6 (corr. Ts.).
49. Ingredients in the witches' cauldron, in *Macbeth,* ɪᴠɪ.i.14: 'Eye of newt and toe of frog'.
50. *A Vision* (1925, rev. 1937) applies elaborately schematised diagrams to Yeats's theories of personality and history.
51. William E. H. Lecky, *A History of Ireland in the Eighteenth Century,* 5 vols. (London: Longmans, Green, 1892) ɪ, 5–10.
52. As Edward Callan has pointed out, the manuscript (NLI Ms. 30,798) here reads: 'Quote first verse of Curse of Cromwell' (*Yeats on Yeats,* p. 62, n. 70). The corrected Ts. (pp. 13–14; NLI Ms. 30,798) has approximately ten blank lines here, but the Scribner's Ts. (p. 11) closed up that space. (See Callan, *Yeats on Yeats,* plates 7 [Ms.], 8–9 [corr. Ts.].) Yeats said of 'The Curse of Cromwell': 'I speak through the mouth of some wandering peasant poet in Ireland' (Yeats to Dorothy Wellesley, 8 January 1937, *LDW* 131). The first stanza of 'The Curse of Cromwell' (*P* 304) reads:

You ask what I have found and far and wide I go,
Nothing but Cromwell's house and Cromwell's murderous crew,
The lovers and the dancers are beaten into the clay,
And the tall men and the swordsmen and the horsemen where are they?

And there is an old beggar wandering in his pride
His fathers served their fathers before Christ was crucified.
O what of that, O what of that
What is there left to say?

53. William Morris (1834–96), English poet, designer and painter.
54. Unidentified.
55. Jonathan Swift, *Gulliver's Travels* (1726). For the epitaph see Yeats's versified translation, 'Swift's Epitaph' (*P* 245–46).
56. The occasion, which is untraced, perhaps was associated with the Indian poet Rabindranath Tagore's seventieth birthday, in 1931. Yeats gives nearly these same opinions in an undated letter to William Rothenstein, quoted in *Since Fifty: Men and Memories, 1922–1938: Recollections of William Rothenstein* (London: Faber, 1939) pp. 111–12; see also *P&I* 175. This was not the dinner given in Yeats's honour by the Irish Literary Society, London, on 3 April 1932.
57. William Wordsworth, 'Poems dedicated to National Independence and Liberty: VII: To Toussaint L'Ouverture' (1802; publ. February 1803), ll. 11–12, in *The Poetical Works of William Wordsworth*, ed. Edward Dowden, The Adline Edition of the British Poets (London: Bell, 1892), (O'Shea no. 2292) III, 130. Pierre-Dominique Toussaint L'Ouverture (1743–1803), Haitian rebel leader, died in a French prison after resisting Napoleon's edict re-establishing slavery. Edward Dowden's note in Yeats's copy (III, 380) remarks that Toussaint was imprisoned June 1802 and that Wordsworth wrote the sonnet probably in August 1802. Robert Emmet (1778–1803) was hanged for leading an abortive Irish rebellion in 1803. William E. H. Lecky, in *A History of Ireland in the Eighteenth Century* (London: Longmans, Green, 1892), described the weeks of martial law just prior to the Rising of 1798 as 'a scene of horrors hardly surpassed in the modern history of Europe' (IV, 265): 'Torture was . . . systematically employed to discover arms. Great multitudes were flogged . . . picketed and half strangled' (IV, 271). The torture of Irish republicans who wore short hair (the 'croppies') in the manner of French republicans 'soon became a popular amusement among the soldiers. Some soldiers of the North Cork Militia are said to have invented the pitched cap of linen or thick brown paper, which was fastened with burning pitch to the victim's head and could not be torn off without tearing the hair or lacerating the skin.' (IV, 272)
58. Dante Gabriel Rossetti, 'The Stream's Secret' (w. 1870) has 234 lines; Algernon Charles Swinburne, 'Dolores' (1866) has 368 lines. Robert Burns (1759–96). James Thomson (1700–48) is best known for his long poem *The Seasons* (1726–30) (5541 lines) and William Cowper (1731–1800) for his long poem *The Task* (1785) (5185 lines). The Thames River valley.
59. William Wordsworth, 'Preface to *Lyrical Ballads*' (1800), in *The Poetical Works of William Wordsworth*, ed. Edward Dowden, Adline Edition of the British Poets (London: 1893), (O'Shea no. 2292) V, 219: '. . . a selection of language really used by men'.

60. Yeats included free verse by Ezra Pound (1885–1972), W. J. Turner (1889–1946) and D. H. Lawrence in *OBMV*.
61. Sir Thomas Browne (1605–82), English physician whose *Religio Medici* (1642) has a highly elaborated prose style.
62. This general reference would include George Chapman's Homer (1616) and perhaps William Cowper's Homer (1791), each of which, although not widely admired, is simpler in style than the elevated diction and heroic couplets of Alexander Pope's *Iliad* (1720) and *Odyssey* (1726); for Yeats's dislike of Pope see p. 191 above. Yeats also objected to the prose style of Thomas Taylor's (1758–1835) translations of Plato and Neoplatonic texts (Kathleen Raine, 'Thomas Taylor in England', in *Thomas Taylor the Platonist: Selected Writings*, ed. Kathleen Raine and George M. Harper [Princeton: Princeton University Press, 1969] p. 18). Yeats might perhaps have heard of John Ozell's *Iliad* (1712) in blank verse set as prose.
63. In December 1929 or January 1930, when Yeats had Malta fever (Yeats to T. Sturge Moore, April 1930, *LTSM* 160); Callan has pointed out that the manuscript (NLI Ms. 30,798) first read 'Malta fever' (*Yeats on Yeats*, p. 66, n. 80). George Moore (1852–1933), Irish novelist. For salt as a symbol of eternity, see pp. 278 above and 455, note 53 below; for salt in alchemy, see also p. 300, note 66 above.
64. John Milton, 'Il Penseroso' (*c.* 1631), ll. 85–92; Percy Bysshe Shelley, 'Prince Athanase' (1817), ll. 69, 189; Samuel Palmer (1805–81), 'The Lonely Tower' (illustration to 'Il Penseroso' by Milton) (etching, 1879, publ. 1880, repr. in *The Minor Poems of Milton* [London: Seeley, 1889]).
65. *Macbeth*, v.iv.17 (Macbeth speaking of Lady Macbeth); *Anthony and Cleopatra*, IV.xv.20 (Anthony speaking to Cleopatra): 'Of many thousand kisses, the poor last'; *Hamlet*, v.ii.334 (Hamlet to Horatio); *Anthony and Cleopatra*, v.ii.308 (Cleopatra, of the asp).
66. For the association of cold winds with psychic phenomena, see Cesare Lombroso, *After Death—What?*, pp. 94–95, 249.

    For Yeats's view of tragedy as a joy to the man who dies, see, for example, p. 199 above. The specific occasion for the remark by Lady Gregory is untraced.
67. The Queen's Maries: four ladies named Mary who served Mary Queen of Scots (1542–87).
68. 'The Fisherman' (w. 1914; publ. 1916), ll. 39–40 (*P* 149). The letter from J. B. Yeats is untraced.
69. *The Countess Cathleen* (publ. 1892; perf. 1899). *The Green Helmet* (1910) is in iambic heptameter, a long line that can be equivalent to ballad meter if split (as Yeats's is not) into halves of four- and three-stress lines.
70. Deirdre, the lover of Naoise, in *Deirdre* (perf. 1906; publ. 1907). Yeats used the warrior hero Cuchulain in two of the highly stylized 'dance' plays based on Japanese Noh drama, *At the Hawk's Well* (perf. 1916; publ. 1917) and *The Only Jealousy of Emer* (1919), and in a later dance play, *The Death of Cuchulain* (1939). Cuchulain was also used in

On *Baile's Strand* (1903, prose) and *The Green Helmet* (1910, verse revision of *The Golden Helmet* 1908, prose).

71. Jonah 2:10. Paul Fort, 'La Reine à la Mer' (The Queen in the Sea) (1894–96), l. 23, tr. Frederick York Powell, as 'The Sailor and the Shark' (1900), in *A Broad Sheet,* no. 5 (May 1902), (London: Mathews) and repr. as 'A Ballad of the Sea: A Song from the French of Paul Fort', in Oliver Elton, *Frederick York Powell: A Life and a Selection from his Letters and Occasional Writings* (Oxford: Clarendon Press, 1906) II, 418; see also Elton, II, 296.
72. Robert Bridges (1844–1930), English poet. See, for example, 'Letter to a Musician on English Prosody' (1909 and 1914): 'In classical prosody the quantities were the main prosodial basis . . . with the speech-rhythms counterpointed upon it' (*Collected Essays, Papers, &c of Robert Bridges* [London: Oxford University Press, 1933], VII, 75 [essay no. 15]).
73. The poem is not known to be extant.
74. Perhaps W. H. Auden, *Paid on Both Sides: A Charade,* in *Poems,* 2nd ed. (London: Faber & Faber, 1933), (O'Shea no. 66) p. 13 (Chorus's first speech): '. . . wake / Our dream of waking . . . / . . . . / By your bright day / See clear what we were doing, that we were vile.' Or perhaps C. Day Lewis, 'The Magnetic Mountain' (1933), in *Collected Poems 1929–1933* (London: Hogarth Press, 1935), (O'Shea no. 1111) p. 149: 'Make us a wind / To shake the world out of this sleepy sickness / Where flesh has dwindled and brightness waned!' or *A Hope for Poetry* (Oxford: Blackwell, 1934), (O'Shea no. 1113) p. 35, where he deplored the 'the narcotic and unnerving' social effects on poetry of shallow education, 'advertisement and cheap publicity of every description. . . . the newspaper, the wireless, the mass-produced novel, the cinema. . . .'
75. Probably C. Day Lewis (1904–72), who taught at Cheltenham Junior School, Cheltenham (a spa rather than a cathedral town) from 1930 to 1935, after having taught at Summer Fields, Oxford (1927–28) and at Larchfield School, Helensburgh, Dumbartonshire, Scotland (1928–30). D. H. Lawrence (1885–1930) lived in Capri and Sicily in 1920 and 1921. W. H. Auden and Christopher Isherwood describe, in a verse section of a play published in September 1936, an office worker who commutes by suburban train from a 'tawdry new estate' (*The Ascent of F6,* I.i, [London: Faber & Faber, 1936] p. 18). Tube: (London) underground railway.
76. Ezra Pound did this *c.* 1910. See Yeats's speech at the *Poetry* magazine banquet, in Chicago, 1 March 1913: 'When I returned to London from Ireland, I had a young man go over all my work with me to eliminate the abstract. This was an American poet, Ezra Pound.' (*UP2* 414)
77. Stéphane Mallarmé (1842–98), French poet. See Arthur Symons, 'Stéphane Mallarmé', *The Symbolist Movement in Literature* (London: Heinemann, 1899), (O'Shea no. 2068) p. 136: 'The doctrine which . . . had been divined by Gérard de Nerval; but what, in Gérard, was pure vision, becomes in Mallarmé a logical sequence of meditation.'

78. *TPU* 30.
79. For Leonardo da Vinci, see pp. 314, note 35 and 359, note 2 above.
80. In central Dublin.
81. This remark by the French Romantic writer Victor Marie Hugo (1802–85) is untraced. In '*Postscriptum de ma vie*' Hugo used the linnet's song as an example of natural beauty (*Victor Hugo's Intellectual Autobiography*, ed. L. O'Rourke [New York and London: Funk & Wagnalls, 1907] p. 177), and Yeats quoted from that collection in 1934 in another context (*VP* 836 and *P* 709n.). See also p. 225 above.

INTRODUCTION TO ESSAYS

1. Only a few of the specific paintings and drawings can be identified for this list of Yeats's favourites in the mid-1890s. Among the many portraits by the English painter George Frederic Watts (1817–1904), the only one that Yeats mentioned in print is of William Morris (1870, oil, National Portrait Gallery, no. 1078); he owned a reproduction of it in 1921. Yeats approved of Watts's 'ecstatic and picturesque . . . subtle inspiration', probably in the pictures of beautiful women, but gave no examples ('William Blake and his Illustrations to the Divine Comedy', *The Savoy*, no. 3 [July 1896] p. 41; omitted from *E&I* 116). The National Gallery of Ireland acquired in 1887 Watts's oil sketch of Mrs Caroline Norton.

   Watts, who was called 'England's Michelangelo', enjoyed popular acclaim for his allegorical paintings such as *Hope* (1886), in which a blindfolded woman, seated atop a globe, plucks a lyre of which only one string is unbroken. For Yeats's dislike of those allegorical paintings, see his lecture, 25 January 1906, at a Royal Hibernian Academy exhibition in memory of Watts (*UP2* 344); for Yeats on allegory in the poetry of Edmund Spenser (1552?–99), see *E&I* 368–69.

   Yeats admired *Sardanapalus and Myrra* (which Yeats called *Dream of Sardanapalous*; *UP1* 185) by the English painter Ford Madox Brown (1821–93), an associate of the Pre-Raphaelites.

   The early or Pre-Raphaelite period of the English painter John Everett Millais (1829–96) ended after his election as Associate of the Royal Academy in 1853. Yeats liked Millais's oil painting *Ophelia* (1852, Tate Gallery, London) and his drawing *The Fireside Story* (1855, in William Allingham, *The Music Master, A Love Story; and Two Series of Day and Night Songs* [London: Routledge, 1855], facing p. 216 and as frontispiece to William Allingham, *Life and Phastasy* [London: Reeves and Turner, 1889], [O'Shea no. 35]), an illustration for William Allingham's poem of that name. In 1919 Yeats was given a reproduction of a drawing for *Christ in the House of His Parents* (1850, oil, Tate Gallery); the drawing belonged to his friend Charles Ricketts.

   Yeats particularly admired the English Pre-Raphaelite painter and poet Dante Gabriel Rossetti (1828–82). Only a few of his paintings and drawings that Yeats mentioned elsewhere have 'several figures engaged in some dramatic action': *The Beloved* (1865–66, oil, Tate Gallery); *Mary Magdalene at the Door of Simon the Pharisee* (1857, ink, Fitzwilliam Museum, Cambridge), which Yeats's friend Charles Ricketts found in a shop in the Brompton Road, London, during the late-1890s; one of the Dantean Beatrice designs, probably *Dante's Dream at the Time of the Death of Beatrice* (1856; 1871, oil replica, Walker Art Gallery, Liverpool) or perhaps *Paolo and Francesca da Rimini* (1855, water-colour triptych, Tate Gallery); and perhaps *The Maids of Elfen-Mere,* drawing to illustrate William Allingham's poem of that name, in *The Music Master, A Love Story, and Two Series of Day and Night Songs* (London: Routledge, 1855), facing p. 202 and repr. as *Day and Night Songs; and The Music Master, A Love Story, and Two Series of Day and Night Songs* (London: Bell and Daldy, 1860), facing p. 202.

Yeats's favourites among the prints by William Blake (1757–1827) are likely to have included most of the following engravings and etchings, of which, in the 1890s, he owned originals or reproductions: *The Ancient of Days* (*c.* 1794, reproduction of relief etching and water-colour); *The Soul exploring the recesses of the Grave* (1808, reproduction of engraving); and *[Illustrations to Dante's Inferno]* (1827, full set of seven unfinished engravings; and reproduced in 1922, O'Shea no. 202). Later he also acquired facsimile reproductions of all of Blake's woodcuts (1902, O'Shea no. 218) and *Illustrations to the Book of Job* (1825, full set of twenty-one engravings, owned by Mrs Yeats, O'Shea no. 200; and a facsimile set, 1902, O'Shea no. 201). In 1917 he purchased lantern slides of the following additional engravings and colour prints: *Job* (1793); *Ezekiel* (1794); *Pity* (1795, colour print with water-colour and ink); *Hecate* (1795, colour print with water-colour and ink); *Chaucer's Canterbury Pilgrims* (detail, 1810, engraving); and *[Illustrations to Thornton's Virgil]* (1820–21, wood-engravings, nos. 2, 3, 5–8, 10).

2. Mrs Patrick Campbell (1865–1940), English actress, had been a friend of Edward Burne-Jones (1833–98) during the mid-1890s and often sat to him. Her house at 33 Kensington Square, London, was decorated with reproductions of Burne-Jones paintings, of which *The Last Sleep of Arthur at Avalon* (1881–98, Museo de Arte, Ponce, Puerto Rico) was her favourite. One of her fondest possessions was an ink caricature sketch by Burne-Jones of her with her dog (collection of Patrick Beech; illus. in Margot Peters, *Mrs Pat: The Life of Mrs Patrick Campbell* [New York: Knopf, 1984] plate 19b). The German connoisseur is unidentified; Mrs Campbell visited Dresden in December 1903. A likely date for the anecdote would be *c.* 1904 or *c.* 1908.
3. Ezra Pound, '*Yeux Glauques*' (sea-green eyes), ll. 6, 9–10, Part I, section VI of 'Hugh Selwyn Mauberley' (1920), in *Personae: The Collected Poems* (New York: Boni and Liveright, 1926), (O'Shea no. 1628) p. 192; 'faun's head' alludes to Rimbaud's poem '*Tête de Faune*'. Pound uses the French spelling 'cartons' (for 'cartoons', drawings).

The next two lines in Pound's poem refer to Burne-Jones's painting *King Cophetua and the Beggar Maid* (1884, Tate Gallery), in which the young woman's eyes are very striking; the model was the painter's wife, Georgiana Macdonald Burne-Jones. Yeats's allusion might also include Mrs Patrick Campbell, whose dark eyes were much admired.

Robert Williams Buchanan (1841–1901) attacked the Pre-Raphaelites in a review of the fifth edition of D. G. Rossetti's *Poems*. In that pseudonymous review, 'The Fleshly School of Poetry', *Contemporary Review*, 43 (October 1871), 334–50, Buchanan did not specifically mention any paintings or women, but he did quote (340) the two opening stanzas of Rossetti's 'The Blessed Damozel', of which lines 3–4 are 'Her eyes were deeper than the depth / Of water stilled at even'.

4. None of the four odalisques painted by Auguste Renoir (1841–1919) fits this description, although corpulent female nudes were among his favourite subjects.
5. Probably Ezra Pound.
6. Yeats defended John Synge's *The Playboy of the Western World* before a noisy audience at the Abbey Theatre on 29 January 1907 and again at a public debate in the Abbey Theatre on 4 February 1907. He addressed the Abbey Theatre audience for Sean O'Casey's *The Plough and the Stars* on several evenings in February 1926.
7. Edward Bulwer-Lytton (1803–73), the Victorian novelist and Conservative politician, was the son of a general and graduated from Cambridge; his historical novels and aristocratic station as Baron Lytton would be antithetical to the contemporary novelist H. G. Wells (1866–1946), who was a Socialist and the son of a poor tradesman.
8. Professor Craig R. Thompson explains that 'tradition' and 'deposit of faith' are terms closely allied, and sometimes virtually synonymous, in writings of early Christian theologians. St Paul uses the Greek word for 'deposit' (*paratheke*) three times in the New Testament, referring to the spiritual heritage (1 Timothy 6:20; 2 Timothy 1:12, 14). See 'Deposit of Faith' in *New Catholic Encyclopedia* (New York: McGraw-Hill, 1967) IV, 780. John Henry Cardinal Newman discussed *paratheke*, as 'tradition', and cited St Paul, in *Prophetical Office of the Church Viewed relatively to Romanism and Popular Protestantism* (1837), Lecture X ('On the Essentials of the Gospel'), section XI, in *The Via Media of the Anglican Church: Illustrated in Lectures, Letters, and Tracts Written between 1830 and 1841* (3rd ed., 1877, repr. London: Longmans, Green, 1918) I, 250. Newman again referred to it in his influential *An Essay on the Development of Christian Doctrine* (1845), 2nd ed. (London: Toovey, 1846) p. 116 (ch. ii, section II, 'On the Probability of a Developing Authority in Christianity').
9. Walter Pater, 'Style' (1888), in *Appreciations: With an Essay on Style* (1889; repr. London: Macmillan, 1910) p. 38.
10. The title character of Gustave Flaubert's romantic novel *Salammbô* (1862) is a priestess and the daughter of the leader of Carthage after the first Punic war. In a letter to the critic Charles A. Sainte-Beuve, 23–24 December 1862, Flaubert said that no one could say whether or

not Salammbô was portrayed realistically because it is impossible to get to know an Oriental woman since one cannot spend time in her company. (Gustave Flaubert, *Correspondance: cinquième série [1862–1868]* [Paris: Conard, 1929] p. 58.)

11. Probably Elisabeth Bergner (1900–86), Austrian-born English actress who enjoyed great success in the title role of the first German production of Shaw's *Saint Joan*, Deutsches Theatre, Berlin, 1924.
12. For T. S. Eliot and Christian symbolism, see p. 173 above. Dame Ninette de Valois [Edris Stannus] (1898–), the distinguished Irish dancer and choreographer, was a soloist with Diaghilev's Russian Ballet, 1923–25; at Yeats's invitation she founded the Abbey School of Ballet in 1927. She choreographed and danced in productions of Yeats's plays in 1928 and 1929. Later she founded and directed the Vic-Wells (later, Sadler's Wells Theatre, and Royal) Ballet (1931–63).
13. Among the three Bolognese artists named Carracci, Agostino (1557–1602) and Annibale (1560–1609) were brothers; Lodovico (1555–1619) was their cousin. According to a tradition which was still current in 1937, Annibale Carracci's painting *Butcher Shop* (*c.* 1582–83, oil, Christ Church College, Oxford) depicts himself, Agostino and Lodovico as butchers amid carcasses of meat. The painting sometimes has been attributed to Agostino. See Donald Posner, *Annibale Carracci: A Study in the Reform of Italian Painting around 1590* (London: Phaidon, 1971) II, 3–4 (no. 4) and plates 4ab.
14. Walt Whitman's 'Song of Myself' (1855) opens, 'I celebrate myself, and sing myself.' Yeats advocated artistic expression of self at least as late as 1906, in a lecture on the painter G. F. Watts (*UP1* 344).
15. Throughout the 1850s D. G. Rossetti avidly pursued strikingly beautiful women to sit as models. These 'stunners' included Elizabeth Siddal, whom he met in 1850, Fanny Cornforth [Cox] in 1856 and Jane Burden in 1857, among others. Yeats's reference may be to a waitress whom Rossetti and William Allingham nicknamed *la belle sauvage* because Rossetti had discovered her at the Bell Savage Inn, Ludgate Hill, London, in 1854 (George Birkbeck Hill, *Letters of Dante Gabriel Rossetti to William Allingham: 1854–1870* [New York: Stokes, 1897], [O'Shea no. 1791] p. 28).
16. 'Lillie' (Mrs Emilie Charlotte Le Breton) Langtry (1853–1929), the famous English society beauty, actress and mistress of the Prince of Wales. G. F. Watts painted a portrait of her in 1880 (*The Dean's Daughter*, Watts Gallery, Compton, Surrey; illus. in Jeremy Birkett and John Richardson, *Lillie Langtry: Her Life in Words and Pictures* [Poole, Dorset: Blandford Press, 1979] p. 23). Mrs Langtry enjoyed sitting to the 'soft-voiced, gentle-mannered' Watts, with whom she 'always felt at rest'. In her memoir she recalled, with what would be irony to Yeats, how she pleased Watts by telling him of his physical resemblance to Titian: 'It produced in him the ingenuous pleasure of a child. How simple are the great! And such charming simplicity!' (Lillie Langtry, *The Days I Knew* [New York: Doran, 1925] p. 56.) Lady Gregory's husband, Sir William Henry Gregory (1817–92), was a long-time friend of Watts.

17. Arthur Rimbaud, '*Les Chercheuses de poux*' (The Ladies who Look for Lice) (1882–83). Yeats's friend T. Sturge Moore wrote an English version of Rimbaud's poem ('The Lice-Finders', *The Poems of T. Sturge Moore: Collected Edition* [London: Macmillan, 1932], [O'Shea no. 1369] II, 195). The Silver Age, which succeeds the simple and patriarchal Golden Age, was characterised by the Greek poet Hesiod as voluptuous and godless (8th c. B.C.; *Works and Days*, 127–42); see also Ovid, *Metamorphoses*, I.113–24. Peter Paul Rubens (1577–1640), Flemish painter.
18. Julius Caesar was assassinated in 44 B.C.; Alexander the Great died of fever in Babylon in 323 B.C.
19. See *V(A)* 181. Boehme's phrase is untraced, but compare these three characteristic statements: 'The Author's Preface', verses 15–16, *Mysterium Magnum* (w. 1623; Eng. tr. 1654), in *The Works of Jacob Behmen, The Teutonic Theosopher* (London, 1772) III, 9: '*But we have wrote nothing for the proud and haughty Wiselings who know enough already; and yet indeed know nothing at all. . . . But we desire to be clearly and fundamentally understood by the Children of God*' and part III, ch. 78, v. 8 (*Works*, III, 507): 'This is a *brief* summary Explanation . . . which we have faithfully imparted, in a co-operating Member-like Love and Care, to our dear *Fellow Brethren*, that shall read and *understand* this'; and *Four Tables of Divine Revelation* (w. 1623; Eng. tr. 1655), in *Works* (1772) III, 8 [separately paginated]): 'Thus you have a brief Intimation of the first Table, and of all the Author's Writings; faithfully imparted, out of a good Christian Affection to his loving Friends, and as an A, B, C, to Beginners.' Compare *V(A)* xii ('my old fellow students').

ON THE BOILER

1. *Beltaine: The Organ of the Irish Literary Theatre*, nos. 1–3 (May 1899–April 1900), ed. W. B. Yeats, and *Samhain: An Occasional Review*, [nos. 1–7] (October 1901–November 1908), ed. Yeats. John M. Synge, *Riders to the Sea*, in *Samhain*, [no. 3] (September 1903) pp. 25–33. Lady Gregory, *Spreading the News. (A Comedy)*, in *Samhain*, [no. 5] (November 1905) pp. 15–28 and *Hyacinth Halvey*, in *Samhain*, [no. 6] (December 1906) pp. 15–35. Yeats, *Cathleen ni Houlihan* (as *Cathleen ni Hoolihan*), in *Samhain*, [no. 2] (October 1902) pp. 24–31. *Purgatory* was first published in *On the Boiler*, following this essay.
2. Rosses Point, Co. Sligo, five miles northwest of Sligo.
3. Repr., titled 'Why should not Old Men be Mad?', in *Last Poems & Plays* (London and New York: Macmillan, 1940); *P* 585–86.
4. Alderman Alfred Byrne had been Lord Mayor since 1930. The Mansion House, Dawson Street, was built in 1705 by Joshua Dawson and, since 1715, has been the Lord Mayor's residence. This Queen Anne house was built in brick but was modified in the nineteenth century; the Round Room next to it was erected in 1821.

5. The Catholic University, St Stephen's Green, Dublin, was founded in 1854; it was renamed University College, Dublin, in 1882 and is part of the National University of Ireland, established in 1908.

   The penal laws, an intricate series of severe restrictions on the education, ownership of property and political activity of Catholics in Ireland, were instituted 1695–1727. Their enforcement eased during the second half of the eighteenth century, and the laws were rescinded by a series of relief acts in 1782, 1793 and 1829.
6. Firbolgs: An early Irish people in mythological times, prior to the Tuatha de Danaan (see *VP* 795); their descendants are described very unflatteringly in Duald Mac Firbis, *Book of Genealogies* (1650), quoted in Douglas Hyde, *A Literary History of Ireland: From Earliest Times to the Present Day* (London: Unwin, 1899), (O'Shea no. 941) p. 563. Christopher Moore's statue (1857) of the Irish poet Thomas Moore (1779–1852), cast by Elkington Mason and Co., stands on a pedestal—next to a Dublin Corporation public urinal—in the intersection of Westmoreland Street and College Street, near Trinity College, Dublin. The statue had been moved there by 1862.
7. The hypocrites, in the eighth circle of Dante's *Inferno,* XXIII.
8. 'Books in Galway Libraries: Shaw is on the Banned List', *The Irish Times,* 20 December (not October) 1937, p. 8, col. a, describing the 18 December 1937 meeting of the Galway County Library Committee. Nothing came of the suggestion to burn offensive books. The reference to the mob is in William Kirkpatrick Magee ('John Eglinton'), *A Memoir of A.E.: George William Russell* (London: Macmillan, 1937) p. 198.
9. William Makepeace Thackeray reported this scene, which is set in Cork (not Dublin), in *The Irish Sketch Book of 1842* (1843), ch. vii: 'Two boys almost in rags: they were lolling over the quay balustrade, and talking about *one of the Ptolemys*! and talking very well too.' (*The Works of William Makepeace Thackeray* [London: Smith, Elder, 1911] XXIII, 88.) Ptolemy was the name of fourteen (or sixteen) kings of Egypt (fourth through first centuries B.C.), and also of the second-century A.D. astronomer, mathematician and geographer.
10. Peter Keegan at the opening of Act II of *John Bull's Other Island* (1904), in *The Bodley Head Bernard Shaw Collected Plays with their Prefaces,* II, 923.
11. William Gladstone (1809–98), as British prime minister (1868–74, 1880–85, 1886, 1892–94), supported the Land Law (Ireland) Act of 1881, which Charles Stewart Parnell (1846–91), Irish nationalist leader in Parliament, vigorously attacked as too limited. Limerick successfully withstood siege by William of Orange in 1690, but fell in a second siege by Williamite forces in 1691.
12. Yeats was among the thirty senators appointed to a six-year term (1922–28) in the Irish Free State Senate by William Cosgrave (1880–1965), president of the Executive Council; thirty other senators were elected for a three-year term by the lower house (Dáil). Andrew Jameson (1855–1941), a prominent southern Unionist, was chairman of John Jameson & Son, Ltd, distillers. In the Irish Free State Senate

(1922–36), he chaired a loosely knit independent group of senators who consulted together but were not pledged to vote as a block; the independent group had twelve members in 1928.

13. Kevin O'Higgins (1892–1927), Irish Free State vice-president of the Executive Council and Minister of Justice and External Affairs (1922–27). Rory O'Connor (1883–1922), who had been best man at O'Higgins's wedding, was opposed to the treaty and was a leader of a Republican garrison at the Four Courts, Dublin, in April 1922. He was captured 28 June 1922, when the government attacked that garrison at the start of the eleven-month Civil War. O'Connor was one of the four Republicans executed on 8 December 1922 under orders from O'Higgins, as Minister for Home Affairs, in reprisal for the assassination, on the previous day, of Sean Hales, T.D.
14. Yeats's friend Oliver St John Gogarty (1878–1957), Irish physician, poet and wit, was appointed to the Senate in 1922 and remained until 1936.
15. The Easter Rising, 1916, centered on the General Post Office, Dublin; the Pilgrims sailed to America on the *Mayflower* in 1620.
16. See p. 216 above.
17. The Abbey Players left Ireland 18 September 1937 and were on tour in America until 28 May 1938.
18. Máire O'Neill played Deirdre in the first performance of John Synge's unfinished *Deirdre of the Sorrows,* at the Abbey Theatre, Dublin, 13 January 1910. This speech, near the end of Act III, reads: 'Draw a little back with the squabbling of. . . .' (*Deirdre of the Sorrows: A Play* [Churchtown, Co. Dublin: Cuala Press, 1910] p. 76; *The Works of John M. Synge* [Dublin: Maunsel, 1910], [O'Shea no. 2076] II, 194.)

J. M. Kerrigan and Máire O'Neill created the roles of the 'innocent' Davideen and his sister, Cracked Mary, in Lady Gregory's *The Full Moon* (1910). At their exit, Davideen takes his sister's hand and sings:

Oh! don't you remember
What our comrades called to us
And they footing steps
At the call of the moon?
Come out to the rushes,
Come out to the bushes,
Where the music is called
By the lads of Queen Anne!

The stage direction reads: 'They look beautiful. They dance and sing in perfect time as they go out.' (Lady Gregory, *The Full Moon: A Comedy in One Act* [Dublin: published by the author at the Abbey Theatre, 1911], [O'Shea no. 793] pp. 41–42.) In an unpaged note at the end of the book, Lady Gregory printed the air to Davideen's song and explained, 'The Queen Anne in it was not English queen, but, as I think, that Aine of the old gods at whose hill mad dogs were used to gather, and who turned to grey the yellow hair of Finn of the Fianna of Ireland.'

Francis John (Frank J.) Fay (1870–1931), Irish actor, created the part of the wandering friar in John M. Synge's *The Well of the Saints* at the Abbey Theatre, 4 February 1905. His brother William George Fay (1872–1947) created the part of the fool, Barach, in Yeats's one-act play *On Baile's Strand,* at the Abbey Theatre, 27 December 1904.

Mrs Patrick Campbell played the title role in a much praised revival of Yeats's *Deirdre* (1906) at the Abbey Theatre, 9–14 November 1908, and in London at the New Theatre, 27 November–11 December 1908, and at the Court Theatre, 22–26 June 1909; during the intervening months she toured provincial cities with that production. See Robert Hogan and James Kilroy, *The Abbey Theatre: The Years of Synge 1905–1909* (Dublin: Dolmen Press, 1978) pp. 230–31 and Mrs Patrick Campbell [Beatrice Stella Cornwallis-West], *My Life and Some Letters* (New York: Dodd, Mead, 1922) pp. 301–2.

Dame Ninette de Valois (1898–), Irish ballet dancer and choreographer, played Fand in the first production of Yeats's dance play *Fighting the Waves,* at the Abbey Theatre, 13 August 1929; see p. 420, note 12 above.

19. Honoré de Balzac, French novelist (1799–1850). John Ruskin in *Unto this Last* (1860, in *Cornhill Magazine*) called for radical changes in attitudes to art, religion and economics to correct the social injustices caused by application of the theories of political economy supported by John Stuart Mill (1806–73), English philosopher and economist. Compare the account in *Mem* 19.

20. Heraclitus (6th–5th c. B.C.), frag. 67, tr. John Burnet, *Early Greek Philosophy* (London and Edinburgh: Black, 1892), (O'Shea no. 308) p. 138: 'Mortals are immortals and immortals are mortals, the one living the other's death and dying the other's life.' See also pp. 234 and 236 above, *Mem* 216 and a note by Harper and Hood in *V(A)CE* note to p. 130, l.9.

Herbert Percy Horne (1864–1916) designed (1889–90) the Chapel of the Ascension (1892), Bayswater Road, near Albion Gate, on a narrow site adjacent to a disused burial ground. The chapel, which was decorated with symbolic murals by Frederic Shields (1833–1911), was heavily damaged during the Second World War and was pulled down in 1969. See Ian Fletcher, 'Herbert Horne: The Earlier Phase', *English Miscellany: A Symposium of History, Literature and the Arts* (Rome), 21 (1970), 138–39; see also pp. 92 and 455, note 59 above. Horne's book on Botticelli, *Alessandro Filipepi, Commonly Called Sandro Botticelli, Painter of Florence* (London: Bell, 1908), is still highly regarded.

21. Charles Ricketts (1866–1931), English illustrator, book designer, typographer, painter, sculptor, art critic and scenic designer, greatly admired the French Romantic painter Ferdinand Victor Eugène Delacroix (1799–1863). Yeats owned a framed coloured reproduction of an oil painting by Ricketts, *The Betrayal* (*c.* 1904; exhibited 1908; Carlisle City Art Gallery), probably given to him by Ricketts. It fits the description Yeats gives here. For a coloured reproduction see Joseph Darracott, *The World of Charles Ricketts* (London: Eyre Methuen, 1980) p. 65.

The intense, passionately exaggerated acting style of the renowned French tragedian François-Joseph Talma (1763–1826) was well suited for being described in metaphors of thunder and lightning, as, for example, by Edmond and Jules Goncourt in *Histoire de la société française pendant la directoire* (1855): '. . . Stressing with sudden lightning flashes the poet's thought and with everything unleashed for the vital lines.' Talma described his own style thus in *Quelques réflexions sur Lefain et sur l'art théâtral par Talma* (1825): 'Gesture, bearing, facial expression, must of necessity forestall words as the lightning flash precedes the thunder clap.' (Tr. and quoted in Herbert F. Collins, *Talma: A Biography of an Actor* [New York: Hill and Wang, 1964] pp. 105, 354; with frontispiece portrait by Delacroix of Talma in the role of Néron in *Britannicus* by Racine.)

22. John M. Synge, *The Aran Islands* (Dublin: Maunsel, 1907), (O'Shea no. 2073) p. 76: 'The nullity of the rich and the squalor of the poor'. Yeats had quoted the same passage in a review, 'The Great Blasket', in 1933 (*UP2* 492).
23. In 1902–6 Yeats wrote *On Baile's Strand* (publ. 1903; perf. 1904), *The King's Threshold* (perf. 1903; publ. 1904) and *Deirdre* (perf. 1906; publ. 1907).
24. Untraced. The first sinking by a Japanese torpedo had been in 1894, from a cruiser commanded by Captain Heihachiro Togo (1846–1934); ten years later, as a vice-admiral during the Russo-Japanese War, Togo was in charge of the attack on Port Arthur (February 1904) and the crushing victory over the Russian Baltic fleet in the Battle of Tsushima Strait (May 1905). Another early candidate is Sukeyuki Ito (1843–1914), who commanded the Japanese fleet in 1895 during the Sino-Japanese War, as a vice-admiral, and during the Russo-Japanese War (1904–5), as an admiral. Vice-Admiral Hikonojo Kamimura (1849–1916) defeated the Russian Vladivostok fleet off Ulsan in August 1904. The only major naval engagement from then until the mid-1930s was the capture of the German port at Tsingtao in October and November 1914.
25. Proverbial for keeping silent for some weighty reason (from Aeschelus, *Agamemnon*, 36: 'He has an ox on his tongue') (*The Oxford Dictionary of English Proverbs*, 3rd ed., ed. F. P. Wilson [Oxford: Clarendon Press, 1970] pp. 604–5).
26. Robert Burton, *The Anatomy of Melancholy* (1621; 6th ed. 1651–52); for details, see note 33 below.
27. Jean Fernel, *Pathologiae* (I, iii), book VII of *Medicina* (Paris: Wechel, 1554). See Sir Charles S. Sherrington, *The Endeavour of Jean Fernel* (Cambridge: Cambridge University Press, 1946) pp. 20–21.

    Burton continues this passage from Fernel in the next two sentences, of which the latter is a translation of the Latin, *quanto . . . observandum*.
28. In a note here, Burton observed, *'Infantes infirmi praecipitio necati'* (feeble infants are killed immediately) and cited Aubanus Bohemus (Albertus Bohemus, Albert von Beham, Albert Behaim, Albert Böhme) (1180?–1260), papal legate in Bavaria. Burton followed with a generalised reference to the writings of Spartans (*'apud Laconas olim'*) and a quotation from Justus Lipsius (Joest Lips) (1547–1606), Flemish

scholar, in a letter (no. 85) to Dionysio Villerio, 10 July 1601, on the killing of deformed newborn infants, in *Epistolarum Selectarum, Centuria Prima ad Belgas, Opera Omnia postremum ab ipso Aucta et Recensita* (Antverpiae, 1637) II, 411: '*Si quos [insignes, aut] aliqua membrorum parte inutiles notaver[u]nt, necari jubent*' (If they notice anyone [extraordinarily or] in any degree feeble, they order them to be killed).

29. Quintus Curtius Rufus (fl. *c.* 43), Roman rhetorician and historian, from his *History of Alexander the Great of Macedon*, IX.i.XXV, in the description of the realm of an Indian king, Sopithes.

30. Hector Boece (Boyce, Boethius) (1465?–1536), *Scotorum Historiae a prima gentis origine* (*Histories of the Scots from the Origin of the Race*) (Paris, 1526) fol. 12^r, ll. 4–10 ('*De Scotorum Priscis Recentibusque institutis ac moribus Parenesis Hectoris Boethii accommodatissima*'). Burton, in a footnote to his English translation of the passage here, gave the Latin text, which he titled '*Lib. I. De veterum Scotorum moribus*' (in fact, it is from an introductory essay that precedes book I). The Latin text in Burton's footnote (*Anatomy of Melancholy*, ed. A. R. Shilleto [O'Shea no. 311] p. 246, n. 7) varies in many details from Boece. For John Bellenden's translation of Boece into Scots, see *The Chronicles of Scotland* (1533), 2 vols. (1536; repr. Edinburgh: Tait, 1821) I, lviii.

31. Loosely based on John Barclay (1582–1621), Scottish satirist and Latin poet, *Euphormionis Lusinini Satyricon (Euphormio's Satyricon)* (1605–7), part I, ch. iv: '*inesse in ijs semina paternae claritudinis*' ('the seed of the father's glory were in the children'), tr. David A. Fleming (Nieuwkoop: De Graaf, 1973) pp. 16 (Latin), 17 (English).

32. 'Our fathers the cause of our ruin', as translated by A. R. Shilleto, in a footnote in Yeats's copy of *The Anatomy of Melancholy* (O'Shea no. 311). In another note, Shilleto mentioned the parallel with Horace, *Odes*, book III, ode 6, ll. 46–48: 'Our parents' age, worse than our grandsires', has brought forth us less worthy and destined soon to yield an offspring still more wicked' (*The Odes and Epodes*, tr. C. E. Bennett, Loeb Library [Cambridge: Harvard University Press; London: Heinemann, 1978] p. 203).

33. [Yeats's note] *The Anatomy of Melancholy* by Robert Burton, edited by the Rev. A. R. Shilleto, M.A., published by G. Bell & Sons, London, 1912. Part. I, Sect. 2, Mem. II, Subs. VI.[a]

33a. The quotation is on pages 246–47 of the first volume in that three-volume edition (O'Shea no. 311). Yeats's citation should be to Member I (not II); he perhaps was confused by that edition's running title for page 247, which reads 'Member II' because Member II begins later on that page. Shilleto's edition was first published in 1893; it is based on the sixth edition (1651–52) of *The Anatomy of Melancholy* (1st ed., 1621). The text in Shilleto's edition reads: '. . . many several ways . . . *Fernelius* . . . saith *it is the greatest part of our felicity to be well born, & it were happy for human kind, if only such parents as are sound of body & mind should be suffered to marry*. An . . . best & choicest . . . horse, except. . . . *Indians* . . . *Curtius*, & many. . . . *Scotland* . . . *Hect. Boethius, if any were visited with the falling sickness, madness, gout, leprosy, or any such dangerous disease, which was likely to be progagated* [sic] *from the father to the son, he was instantly gelded: a woman kept from all company of men; and if by chance, having some such disease, she were found to be with child, she with her brood were buried alive.* . . . used amongst Christians. . . . maimed, unable, intemperate . . . inheritance: it. . . .'

34. See, for example, Charles Wicksteed Armstrong, *The Survival of the Unfittest* (1927), 2nd ed. (London: Daniel, 1931) pp. 24–43 (ch. i: 'Is Degeneration a Fact?'); Raymond B. Cattell, 'Is National Intelligence Declining,' *The Eugenics Review* (London), 28 (October 1936), (O'Shea no. 643) 181; and Ferdinand C. S. Schiller, 'Eugenics and Politics' (1914) in *Eugenics and Politics: Essays* (London: Constable, 1926) p. 14.

35. [Yeats's note] I have deduced this rough definition of intelligence from the general nature of the 'intelligence tests' and from *The Measurement of Intelligence* by Lewis M. Terman (pages 44–47).[a] I am indebted to the Secretary of the Eugenics Society for a long typed extract from this book. I am, indeed, indebted to his patience and courtesy for much of my information.[b]

35a. Lewis Madison Terman (1877–1956), American psychologist, professor of education at Stanford University. In *The Measurement of Intelligence: An Explanation of and a Complete Guide for the Use of the Stanford Revision and Extension of the Binet-Simon Intelligence Scale* (London: Harrap, 1919), Terman briefly discusses Alfred Binet's 'conception of general intelligence' as having three characteristics: to maintain a definite direction, to adapt and to auto-criticise (pp. 44–46). He then sketches 'other conceptions of intelligence', including Ebbinghaus (combining activity), Meumann (invention and error avoidance), Stern, Spearman and Hart (pp. 46–47) and 'guiding principles in choice and arrangement of tests' (pp. 47–48).

35b. Dr Carlos (Charles) Paton Blacker (1895–1975), general secretary of the Eugenics Society, London. Yeats's membership began in November 1936; the five extant letters relating to his inquiry about intelligence tests are dated from 30 November 1937 to 17 January 1938 (NLI Ms. 30,583).

36. Yeats could have found much of this general information in his copies of two works by Raymond Bernard Cattell (b. 1905), Ph.D., Leonard Darwin Research Fellow and psychologist to the Leicester Education Authority: 'Is National Intelligence Declining,' *The Eugenics Review* (London), 28 (October 1936), (O'Shea no. 643) 181–203 and *The Fight for Our National Intelligence* (London: King, 1937), (O'Shea no. 353) pp. 18–38 (ch. iii: 'Intelligence Produced by Environment or Breeding?'). See also Yeats's note 44 below.

37. Bluebeard, who murdered his several wives, is the title character of a French popular tale ('La Barge bleue') recorded by Charles Perrault (1628–1703), and is sometimes identified with Baron Gilles de Retz (or Rais) (1404–40), infamous for atrocities and necromancy.

St Augustine (354–430).

Thomas Gray, 'Elegy Written in a Country Church-yard' (1751), l. 59: 'Some mute inglorious Milton here may rest'.

38. [Yeats's note] A test of this kind with three hundred Glasgow children was summarised by Shepherd Dawson in an address to the British Association in 1934. On re-examination eighteen months after removal to better surroundings they did show 'a just appreciable improvement'. Cattell considers this seeming 'improvement' the result of tests which did not sufficiently exclude acquired knowledge. Shepherd Dawson, a cautious man, while considering it encouraging to philanthropists, says that it was so small that those who initiate 'social welfare schemes may have to rely on the formation of habits that have to be learned, rather than on any improvement in intelligence'.[a] Cattell, with later and fuller information from his own exhaustive investigations in Devonshire and in the town of Leicester, would say not 'may' but 'must'.[b]

38a. Shepherd Dawson (1880–1936), 'Psychology and Social Problems' [Psychology Section (J) presidential address, 7 September 1935], in *British Association for the Advancement of Science: Report of the Annual Meeting, 1934* (London: British Association, 1934) pp. 183–94; the quoted passages are from p. 189: '. . . of new habits of thought, feeling and action, habits that will have. . . .' Dawson tested 289 children, aged five to nine, who were relocated in a slum-clearance scheme and a control group of 56 who stayed in the slum. They were retested after twelve to eighteen months; see also Shepherd Dawson, 'Environmental Influence on Mentality', *The British Journal of Psychology (General Section)*, 27, part II (October 1936) 132, 134.

38b. For Raymond B. Cattell, see note 36 above.

39. [Yeats's note] A well-known authority writes in answer to a question of mine: 'We have no statistics for the leisured classes, owing to the difficulty of getting them into groups for examination.'[a] It is a pity, for I want to know what happens to the plant when it gets from under the stone.

39a. Carlos P. Blacker, general secretary of the Eugenics Society, London, to Yeats, 17 January 1938 (NLI Ms. 30,583): 'I know of no observations as to intelligence quotients among the leisured classes living on unearned incomes. Such person would be very difficult to get hold of in any organized body.'

40. [Yeats's note] The physical degeneration is the most easy to measure. In England since 1873 the average stature has declined about two inches, chest measurement about two inches and weight about twenty pounds. In almost all European countries, especially those where Catholicism encourages large families among the poor, there has been an equal or greater decline. Military standards have been lowered almost everywhere; Spain has lowered hers four times in the last forty years. Holland seems the one exception, and there, presumably because the poor have reduced the size of their families, the average stature has risen with astonishing rapidity. I summarise from Cattell's *Psychology and Social Progress*, pages 102 and 112.[a]

40a. Raymond Bernard Cattell, *Psychology and Social Progress: Mankind and Destiny from the Standpoint of a Scientist* (London: Daniel, 1933) pp. 102 (England), 112n (other European countries). For the comparison of the English populace in 1883 (not 1873) with 1917–19, Cattell (p. 102) cites Eldon Moore, 'Social Progress and Racial Decline', *The Eugenics Review* (London), 18, nos. 26–27 (April 1926–January 1927) 124: 'Between 1883 and 1919 there was an average decline for the whole country from 67.4 to 65.7 inches in stature, from 36.4 to 32.75 inches in chest girth, and of 148.7 to 128.4 pounds in body weight.' Cattell (p. 102) also cites Charles Wicksteed Armstrong, *The Survival of the Unfittest* (1927), 2nd ed. (London: Daniel, 1931) p. 30, whose data 'for this country' are from the Anthropometrical Committee of the British Association (1883) and a 'report of the Ministry of National Service' (1917–19), as follows:

	1883	1917–19
Height (inches)	66.9	65.1
Chest girth (inches)	34.2	32.2
Weight (pounds)	131	116.5

41. See Raymond B. Cattell, *The Fight for Our National Intelligence* (London: King, 1937), (O'Shea no. 353) p. 62: 'A considerable number of very able people are willing, granted a pittance and the minimum of comfort, to devote themselves to social, religious, artistic and scientific endeavours; whilst less-developed characters of lower intelligence accumulate far greater wealth through an obsessional concentration on it. . . . Consequently the correlation of capability and earnings is much closer below a salary of, say, £240 [not £140] a year than above; for above that figure the better abilities often set out on quite other goals than earning money.'
42. The specific source of this data is untraced, but the general information was available to Yeats in the Galton Lecture, 16 February 1928, of Charles John Bond, *Some Causes of Racial Decay: An Inquiry into the Distribution of National Capacity in the Population* (London: Eugenics Society, [1928]), (O'Shea no. 241; inserted in Yeats's copy of Cattell, *The Fight for Our National Intelligence*) and repr. in *Essays and Addresses: Sociological, Biological and Psychological* by 'A Surgeon' [C. J. Bond] (London: Lewis, 1930) pp. 134–36.
43. William Richard Morris, first Viscount Nuffield (1877–1963), English automobile manufacturer, in 1936 donated a £2 million endowment to the medical school at Oxford and in 1937 gave another large gift to establish Nuffield College, Oxford, for social, economic and political research.
44. [a][Yeats's note] I recommend to my readers Cattell's *Fight for the National Intelligence*, a book recommended by Lord Horder and Leonard Darwin.[b] I have taken most of the facts in this section, and some of the arguments and metaphors that follow, from this book.
44a. Bernard Shaw's remark, from the 'Epistle Dedicatory' (1903) to *Man and Superman* (*Prefaces by Bernard Shaw* [London: Constable, 1934] p. 159), is quoted by Raymond Bernard Cattell, *The Fight for Our Na-*

tional Intelligence, p. 58, note 1: 'Bernard Shaw confesses: "I do not know whether you have any illusions left on the subject of education, progress, and so forth. I have none. Any pamphleteer can shew the way to better things; but when there is no will there is no way. My nurse was fond of remarking that you cannot make a silk purse out of a sow's ear; and the more I see of the efforts of our churches and universities and literary sages to raise the mass above its own level, the more convinced I am that my nurse was right. . . ." '

44b. Cattell's *The Fight for Our National Intelligence* has separate introductions by Lord Horder (pp. v–vi) and Major Leonard Darwin (pp. vii–xi), both of whom were honorary presidents of the Eugenics Society. Thomas Jeeves Horder (1871–1955), first Baron of Ashford, K.C.V.O, M.D., F.R.C.P., was Physician in Ordinary to the King, president of the National Birth Control Association, chairman of the Anti-Noise League and vice-president of the Cremation Society. Major Leonard Darwin (1850–1943), Sc.D., author of *The Need for Eugenic Reform* (1926) and president of the Eugenics Education Society (1911–28), was the fourth son of Charles Darwin and was president of the Royal Geographical Society (1908–11).

45. Yeats's phrase at p. 224 above.

46. Julian the Apostate (Flavius Claudius Julianus Augustus) (331–63), emperor of Rome (361–63), was well educated from study in philosophical schools at Athens. He was highly successful in a series of campaigns in Gaul, 356–59, and was greatly admired by his troops for sharing their hardships in the field. His troops proclaimed him emperor in 361. He was an enemy of Christianity and publicly announced his conversion to paganism in 361. Yeats owned the first volume of *The Works of the Emperor Julian* (O'Shea no. 1049).

David Lloyd George (1863–1945), first Earl Lloyd-George of Dwyfor, British Prime Minister (1916–22). Lloyd George, born the son of a schoolmaster-farmer, was raised in a shoemaker's household. He entered Parliament (1890) and won recognition as a debater. During the First World War he was Minister of Munitions (1915–16), Secretary of State for War (1916) and then Prime Minister (1916–22).

47. Cattell, *The Fight for Our National Intelligence*, p. 79: 'The Americans sorted their recruits by intelligence tests: we used some of the best brains from civilian life to stop bullets in front-line trenches.'

The Government of India Act, 1935, provided a bicameral federal legislature, for which the first elections were held in February 1937.

48. See Cattell, *The Fight for Our National Intelligence*, p. 116: '. . . The inauguration of indiscriminate family allowances such as has occurred in France, Russia, Germany and Italy. . . . We may well laugh at these latter schemes, for their net effect is to increase the birth rate of the less capable, of those who can earn money in no other way than by going to bed. Stalin's bonus of £80 per annum for the eighth and subsequent children in a family may be justifiable in Russia, which has great amounts of low-grade work to be done, but not in Atlantic civilisations. Even in Russia it may prove a short-sighted policy. . . .'

49. Karl Marx (1818–83), founder of modern socialism and author of the *Communist Manifesto* (1847; with Friedrich Engels) and *Das Kapital* (1867–85; completed by Engels); Thomas Babington Macaulay, first Baron Macaulay (1800–59), English writer and statesman, author of *History of England* (1848, 1855, 1861). Cattell in *The Fight for Our National Intelligence* (p. 87) emphasized 'Macaulay's preoccupation with material improvement' and noted that 'the crescendo of improvement which so impressed, for example, Macaulay in the last century has already faltered'.
50. See Cattell, *The Fight for Our National Intelligence*, pp. 121–22: '. . . In Sweden, where birth control has for decades been universally accepted, where the birth rate of the poor has fallen, and the birth rate of the higher-income group has already appreciably risen in response.' For slaves in Plato's ideal state, see *The Republic*, 433d (book IV).
51. Clifford Hugh Douglas (1879–1952), English engineer and social economist, founder of the theory of Social Credit, under which production was to be freed from the price system, while remaining under private ownership.
52. Rear-Admiral Sydney Stewart Hall, introduction to *By Guess and by God: The Story of the British Submarines in the War* (Garden City, NY: Doubleday, 1930; London: Hutchinson, 1931) p. x, quoted by Cattell, *The Fight for Our National Intelligence*, p. 79, note 1: 'Germany had some four hundred submarine captains during the war, but over sixty per cent of the damage they did was accomplished by but twenty-two [not twenty-four] of these four hundred officers.'
53. Gangrel: (Scottish) vagrant.
54. According to the Stoic school of Greek philosophers, founded by Zeno *c.* 310 B.C., the end of each cosmic cycle occurs in a conflagration (*ekpyrosis*), in which everything is changed into fire (Zeno of Citium, frag. 107; Cleanthes of Assos, frags. 510–12; Chrysippus of Soli, frags. 585–620, in H. von Arnim, ed., *Stoicorum Veterum Fragmenta* [Leipzig: Teubneri, 1903–5] I, frags. 107, 510–12; II, frags. 585–620).

    The Battle of Thermopylae (480 B.C.). The quoted speech by the fictional character Michael Robartes is from *Stories of Michael Robartes and his Friends* (1931), reprinted in the front matter to *V(B)* 52–53: '. . . Test art . . . by Thermopylae; make. . .'
55. Raymond B. Cattell, in *Psychology and Social Progress: Mankind and Destiny from the Standpoint of a Scientist* (London: Daniel, 1933), assigns the western half of Ireland to the 'Mediterranean' race and the eastern half to the 'Nordic' race (chart, facing p. 37); he says that among the European races, the 'Mediterranean' race has the lowest average intelligence (IQ 85) and the 'Nordic' has the highest (IQ 105) (pp. 52–53).
56. Probably John Quinn (1870–1924).
57. The specific source of this statistic is untraced.
58. Achill Island, Co. Mayo, off the west coast of Ireland.
59. The Canadian artist is unidentified.

    [Yeats's note] Since I wrote this passage a friend[a] has described to me Mayo boys and girls looking at a film or magazine page for the first time. It takes some little time before they understand that black and white splashes or black lines can represent natural objects. If it is a magazine page, some one will presently say 'That is a horse,' or, 'That is a man.'

59a. The anecdote about Mayo children could have come from Yeats's friend Frederick Robert Higgins (1896–1941), poet and Abbey Theatre director, who was from Co. Mayo and had a strong interest in Irish folk materials.

60. See note 18 and p. 420, note 12 above.

61. Giambattista Vico, *The Most Ancient Wisdom of the Italians* (1710), ch. i, section I; see H. P. Adams, *The Life and Writings of Giambattista Vico* (London: Allen and Unwin, 1935) p. 92: 'Vico proclaims that nobody knows anything he has not made.' See also Benedetto Croce, *The Philosophy of Giambattista Vico,* tr. R. G. Collingwood (London: Latimer, 1913), (O'Shea no. 445) p. 5 ('The universal principle' of Vico's theory of knowledge is 'that the condition under which a thing can be known is that the knower should have made it, that the true is identical with the created: *verum ipsum factum*'); and pp. 23, 29, 241, 279–301 and *V(B)* 207.

62. Jonathan Swift, *A Discourse of the Contests and Dissensions between the Nobles and the Commons in Athens and Rome, with the Consequences they had upon both those States* (London, 1701).

63. [Yeats's note] Hegel's historical dialectic[a] is, I am persuaded, false, and its falsehood has led to the rancid ill-temper of the typical communist and his incitements or condonations of murder. When the spring vegetables are over they have not been refuted, nor have they suffered in honour or reputation. Hegel in his more popular writings seems to misrepresent his own thought. Mind cannot be the ultimate reality seeing that in his *Logic*[b] both mind and matter have their ground in spirit. To Hegel, as to the ancient Indian Sages, spirit is that which has value in itself.

63a. Georg Wilhelm Friedrich Hegel, *The Philosophy of History* (posthumously publ. 1830), tr. J. Sibree (1858); see p. 378, note 58 above.

63b. *Science of Logic,* I: *Objective Logic* (2 vols., 1812–13) and II: *Subjective Logic* (1816); and the first part of Hegel's system, in *Encyclopedia of the Philosophical Sciences in Outline* (1817; 2nd ed., 1827). Yeats owned *Hegel's Logic of World and Idea: A Translation of the Second and Third Parts of the Subjective Logic,* tr. Henry S. Macran (Oxford: Clarendon Press, 1929), (O'Shea no. 868) and *The Logic of Hegel: Translated from the Encyclopaedia of the Philosophical Sciences,* tr. William Wallace (1873), 2nd ed. (Oxford: Clarendon Press, 1892), (O'Shea no. 869: vol. 1 of 2).

64. For Balzac's 'open letter' to the Duchesse de Castries, and for his short tale *The Wild Ass's Skin* (*La Peau de chagrin*) (1831) and historical novel *About Catherine de' Medici* (*Sur Catherine de Médicis*) (1842–43), see p. 378, note 62 above.

65. Heraclitus (frag. 67); see note 20 above.

66. Count Baldassare Castiglione (1478–1529), Italian diplomat and writer, was at Urbino 1504–16 and described in *The Courtier* (1528; Eng. tr. 1561, Sir Thomas Hoby) the ideals of courtly life at Urbino, first under Duke Guidobaldo da Montefeltro and then, from 1508, Francesco Maria della Rovere, Duke of Urbino (1490–1538). Yeats owned a 1900 edition of the Hoby translation (O'Shea no. 351); he read the translation by Leonard E. Opdycke, *The Book of the Courtier* (London: Duckworth, 1902); see Harper and Hood, *V(A)CE* note to p. 42, ll. 9–11.
67. Titian (1477–1576), Venetian painter; Sir Anthony Van Dyck (1599–1641), Flemish painter.
68. *Apocrypha*, Ecclesiasticus 25:24 reads: 'The wisdom of a learned man cometh by opportunity of leisure.'
69. Unidentified.
70. Castletown House, Celbridge, Co. Kildare, twelve miles west of Dublin, is the largest and most palatial eighteenth-century house in Ireland. Its exterior was designed in 1718 by Alessandro Galilei (1691–1737), a Florentine architect, during a visit to Ireland; Sir Edward Lovett Pearce (*c.* 1699–1733) supervised its construction (1722–32). Its owner was William Conolly (d. 1729), Speaker of the Irish House of Commons (1715–29). Berkeley was abroad, mostly in Italy, from 1716 to July 1721; he returned to Dublin in October 1721. See Hone and Rossi, *Bishop Berkeley*, p. 108, note 1.
71. Sir William (not Richard) Temple (1628–99) in his 'Essay upon the Ancient and Modern Learning', in *Miscellanea* (1690; vol. II), praised certain of the epistles of Phalaris (Sicilian tyrant, 6th c. B.C.), in an edition by Charles Boyle (1676–1731). During 1697–99, Richard Bentley (1662–1742) proved the letters spurious. Jonathan Swift, while serving as secretary to Temple in 1697, wrote *The Battle of the Books* (publ. 1704), which treats the controversy with satirical humour.
72. Jonathan Swift, 'Ode to the Honorable Sir William Temple' (w. 1689; publ. 1745), section III (complete), in *The Works of the Rev. Dr Jonathan Swift, Dean of St Patrick's, Dublin,* ed. Thomas Sheridan (London: W. Strahan, *et al.*, 1784), (O'Shea no. 2043) VII, 4: '. . . tablebook . . . / . . . she died./ Confine. . . .'; for a modern edition, see *The Poems of Jonathan Swift,* ed. Harold Williams, 2nd ed. (Oxford: Clarendon Press, 1958) I, 27.
73. Unidentified.
74. *Liadain and Curithir: An Irish Love-Story of the Ninth Century* [*Comrac Liadaine Ocus Cuirithir*], ed. and tr. Kuno Meyer (London: Nutt, 1902) pp. 14 (' "Why should not we two unite, Liadain?" saith Curithir. "A son of us two would be famous." ') and 27.
75. See Patrick Kennedy, 'How Fion Selected a Wife', in *Legendary Fictions of the Irish Celts* (London: Macmillan, 1866) pp. 222–23.
76. [Yeats's note] In a fragment from some early version of *The Courting of Emer*, Emer is chosen for the strength and volume of her bladder. This strength and volume were certainly considered signs of vigour. A woman of divine origin was murdered by jealous rivals because she made the deepest hole in the snow with her urine.[a]

76a. Yeats's source for this information about Emer, wife of Cuchulain, is untraced. The woman murdered by jealous rivals was Derbforgill, daughter of the king of Norway and wife of Lugaid of the Red Stripe. For details, see the note to '[Crazy Jane on the Mountain]', ll. 15–17, in *P* 711–12; see also note 101 below.

77. Friedrich Nietzsche, *The Antichrist* (section LXI), in *The Case of Wagner. Nietzsche Contra Wagner. The Twilight of the Idols*, tr. Thomas Common (1896; repr. London: Unwin, 1899), (O'Shea no. 1444) p. 347: '. . . *what* the Renaissance was? The *transvaluation of Christian values,* the attempt, undertaken with all means, with all instincts, with all genius, to bring about the triumph of the *opposite* values, the *noble* values. . . .'

78. For example, Christ in the *Procession of the Martyrs,* Sant'Apollinare Nuovo (right wall) or *Christ Blessing,* Sant'Apollinare in Classe (triumphal arch), both in Ravenna, which Yeats had visited in 1907. For the phoenix, see p. 301, note 69 above.

79. See *V(B)* 253: 'When the trumpet sounded in the sky in Sulla's time the Etruscan sages, according to Plutarch, declared the Etruscan cycle of 11,000 years at an end. . . .' The earlier version in *V(A)* 153 reads: 'Plutarch records a trumpet shrilling from the sky to announce the Ninth Age, Sulla's rise. . . .' Harper and Hood, in *A Critical Edition of Yeats's A Vision (1925)* (note to pp. 153–54, ll. 30 ff.), identify Yeats's source as Joseph B. Mayor, 'Sources of the Fourth Eclogue', in Mayor, W. Warde Fowler and R. S. Conway, *Virgil's Messianic Eclogue: Its Meaning, Occasion, & Sources* (London: Murray, 1907) pp. 121–22: 'Plutarch (*Vita Sullae,* 7), speaking of the signs which foreboded the rise of Sulla, mentions in particular the piercing and terror-striking sound of a trumpet which came from a clear sky, and was understood to announce the end of the eighth stage of the great year. Censorinus (*De Die Natali,* 17) adds that the Etruscan soothsayers believed that, when the tenth stage was completed, there would be an end of the Etruscan name.' Lucius Cornelius Sulla, Felix (138–78 B.C.), Roman general and politician, established the first Roman military colony in Etruria, leading to the destruction of the independent national character of the Etruscans.

80. The French mathematician and philosopher Jules Henri Poincaré (1854–1912), *Science and Hypothesis* (1902), ch. viii, is quoted by Henry Brooks Adams (1838–1918), American historian, in *The Education of Henry Adams* (privately printed 1907; publ. 1918), ch. xxxi, 'The Grammar of Science' (1903): 'In short, the mind has the faculty of creating symbols' (*The Education of Henry Adams: An Autobiography* [Boston: Houghton Mifflin, 1918], [O'Shea no. 17] p. 455). See also Poincaré's *Science and Hypothesis*, tr. William J. Greenstreet [London: Scott, 1905] pp. xxv (preface) and 51–71 ('Space and Geometry') and his *Science and Method*, tr. Francis Maitland (London: Nelson, [1914]) pp. 116 ('the space bequeathed to us by our ancestors') and 286 ('our far-off ancestors . . . constructed for us our instinctive notion of space').

81. William Blake to George Cumberland, 12 April 1827, in *The Letters of William Blake*, ed. Archibald G. B. Russell (London: Methuen, 1906), (O'Shea no. 203) p. 222; Erdman, p. 707.
82. [Yeats's note] For a modern re-statement, see Boyce Gibbons' translation from Husserl's *Ideas*, pages 128, 129 and elsewhere.[a]
82a. Edmund Husserl, *Ideas: General Introduction to Pure Phenomenology* (1913, in German), tr. W. R. Boyce Gibson (London: Allen & Unwin; New York: Macmillan, 1931), section 40 ('"Primary" and "Secondary" Qualities. The Bodily Given Thing "Mere Appearance" of the "Physically True"') (pp. 128–29) and section 41 ('The Real Nature of Perception and its Transcendent Object') (pp. 129–32).
For *Anima Mundi* and Henry More, see pp. 20 ff. and 300, note 67 above. For George Berkeley and Jonathan Swift, see pp. 103 ff. and 348, note 6 above, respectively.
83. Title and refrain of a poem written by Yeats in 1929 (*P* 265–66).
84. Jacob used a stone as his pillow when he had his dream vision of a ladder reaching from earth to heaven (Genesis 28:11–18).
85. For Hegel, see p. 378, note 58 above.
86. William Morris, *The Story of Sigurd the Volsung and the Fall of the Niblungs* (1876), (book II, ll. 57, 61, 65–68), in *The Collected Works of William Morris* (London: Longmans Green, 1911), (O'Shea no. 1389) XII, 63: '. . . child hath gazed . . . beholdeth,—and . . . part!' For Yeats's praise of this description of Hiordis giving birth to Sigurd, king of the Volsungs, see *L* 816. He was the grandson of Volsung, and the son of Sigmund, who was slain in battle before the birth of Sigurd. Morris twice translated the Icelandic prose *Volsunga Saga* (12th c.), in prose (1870) and here, in verse. This saga is the oldest form of the Teutonic epic, the story of Siegfried (or Sigurd) and the Niblungs, best known through the *Nibelungenlied*. See also *UP1* 125 and note 1.
87. Daniel Corkery (1878–1964), professor of English, University College, Cork, from 1931, was a long-time and often fanatical supporter of the Irish language. In his view, the survival of the vernacular Irish culture depended on Ireland not having been overwhelmed by the Renaissance; see his *Hidden Ireland: A Study of Gaelic Munster in the Eighteenth Century* (Dublin: Gill, 1925) p. 153: 'Whatever of the Renaissance came to Ireland met a culture, so ancient, so widely-based and well-articulated, that it was received only on sufferance'. Sean O'Faolain quoted that passage in 1936 and commented, 'There is only one word for this—rubbish' ('Daniel Corkery', *The Commonweal: A Weekly Review of Literature, The Arts and Public Affairs*, 25, no. 2 [6 November 1936] 37). Monsignor Patrick Browne, a mathematician and classical scholar at Maynooth College, was from Galway and was fluent in Irish, as well as German and French. He was a friend of Yeats and of Oliver St John Gogarty, especially during the 1910s; in 1926, Yeats had asked for Father Browne to be appointed to the Irish Free State committee to select new coinage designs. However, the committee, which was chaired by Yeats, did not include Father Browne.

88. Squiffer: Concertina.
89. Marie Henri d'Arbois de Jubainville (1827–1910), French archaeologist and philologist, professor of Celtic language and literature at the Collège de France (from 1882), founder of the *Revue celtique* and author of *Cours de littérature celtique* (12 vols., 1883–1902). For his interest in parallels between ancient Irish and Greek mythology, see his *Le Cycle mythologique irlandais et la mythologique celtique* (1884), (O'Shea no. 1048); *The Irish Mythological Cycle and Celtic Mythology*, tr. Richard Irvine Best (Dublin: Hodges, Figgis, 1903), chs. i–ii *et passim* and *La civilisation des Celtes et celle de l'épopée homérique*, vol. VI of *Cours de littérature celtique* (Paris: Fontemoing, 1899) *passim*.
90. In 1926–27, Yeats translated *Sophocles' Oedipus at Colonus: A Version for the Modern Stage*; it was first produced 12 September 1927, at the Abbey Theatre by Lennox Robinson.
91. Frank O'Connor (Michael O'Donovan, 1903–66) and Lady Augusta Gregory (1852–1932). See Yeats's introductions to Lady Gregory's *Cuchulain of Muirthemne* and *Gods and Fighting Men* (*P&I* 119–34) and to *OBMV* (p. 202 above).
92. For an early statement of this opinion by Yeats about George Chapman (1559?–1634), see *UP1* 325.
93. See *L* 780, Yeats to Olivia Shakespear, 27 December [1930], when Anne Yeats was eleven years old and Michael Yeats was nine: 'Anne and Michael have a French governess every morning and are plainly very fluent. I wish I could send Michael to a school at Cambridge where Greek and Latin are learned in the same way and spoken, but we must keep him under our eyes for a couple of years yet, and by that time I shall have submitted to the local influences or he will be too old to pick up languages without knowing it.' The Perse School, Cambridge, pioneered what became known as the 'Direct Method' of language teaching, in which all conversations were conducted in Greek or Latin.
94. [Yeats's note] This was written before de Valera's London agreement.[a]
94a. The Anglo-Irish Agreements signed by Eamon de Valera in London, 25 April 1938, gave Ireland control of the ports that had been retained by Britain in the 1922 Treaty.
95. Edmund Burke (1729–97), Irish statesman and orator. Henry Grattan (1746–1820), Irish statesman and orator in support of Irish independence and Catholic emancipation. Kevin O'Higgins (1892–1927), vice-president of the Irish Free State Executive Council and Minister of Justice, was assassinated; he is the only Roman Catholic among the list of eight names.
96. Jonathan Swift made the remark in a letter [July–2 August 1732] to Sir Charles Wogan (*c.* 1698–*c.* 1752), an Irish soldier who fled to France in 1716 and later was a brigadier-general in the Spanish army and governor of LaMancha: '. . . I cannot but highly esteem those gentlemen of Ireland, who, with all the disadvantages of being exiles and strangers, have been able to distinguish themselves by their valour and conduct in so many parts of Europe, I think above all other

nations . . .' (*The Works of the Rev. Dr Jonathan Swift,* ed. Thomas Sheridan [London, 1784], [O'Shea no. 2043] XII, 452–53); see also *VP* 837 and *P* 708. In 1607, after the Irish defeat at the battle of Kinsale (1603), the Earl of Tirconnell (O'Donnell) and the Earl of Tyrone (O'Neill) left for the continent with their followers (the Flight of the Earls); after the defeats of 1689–91, Irish soldiers (the Wild Geese) fled Ireland to serve in foreign armies.

97. The last royal visit to Dublin had been on 8–12 July 1911, by King George V, Queen Mary, the Prince of Wales and Princess Mary. The royal yacht had arrived at Kingstown (Dun Laoghaire) escorted by a fleet of twenty-seven warships; during the visit the king reviewed 16,000 troops in Phoenix Park.

98. David Lloyd George (British Prime Minister, 1916–22) mentioned this rumour in his memoirs, but asserted that the offer never was withdrawn (*The War Memoirs of David Lloyd George* [London: Nicholson & Watson, 1934] III, 1637–46). Nicholas II (1868–1918), czar of Russia from 1894, abdicated 15 March 1917; he was a cousin of King George V (1865–1936). Lloyd George's War Cabinet offered asylum in England to Nicholas and his family on March 22. As early as March 30, George V, worried by the antimonarchical mood of British labour, opposed the offer, preferring instead that Nicholas go to France or Denmark. On April 13 the British ambassador at Petrograd delivered the British government's verbal retraction of the offer of asylum. Nicholas, his wife and children were executed by the Bolsheviks on the night of 16–17 July 1918. See Harold Nicolson, *King George the Fifth: His Life and Reign* (London: Constable, 1952) pp. 298–302, and Lloyd C. Gardner, *Safe for Democracy: The Anglo-American Response to Revolution, 1913–1923* (New York and Oxford: Oxford University Press, 1984) pp. 132–33. See also 'Crazy Jane on the Mountain' (w. 1938), ll. 7–10, p. 243 above and *P* 586.

99. Untraced. George V's twenty-fifth year as king was celebrated in 1935; he died 20 January 1936.

100. *Sophocles' King Oedipus: A Version for the Modern Stage* (perf. 1926; publ. 1928) ll. 686–90, in *VPl* 832–33, *CPlays* 499 and *P* 568: '. . . high clear. . . .'

101. 'Crazy Jane on the Mountain' (w. July 1938), *P* 586; for 'great bladdered Emer', see also Dorothy Wellesley's notes of Yeats's conversations during 1938 (*LDW* 188–89).

102. George Shiels, *Cartney and Kevney* (perf. 29 November 1927); the Abbey Theatre previously had produced six of his popular 'kitchen comedies', beginning in 1921. Yeats saw *Cartney and Kevney* during a revival at the Abbey Theatre, 8–20 November 1937; only unusually popular plays enjoyed runs of longer than one week.

103. Yeats wrote, 8 February 1921, of Allan Wade's production at Oxford of Ben Jonson's *Volpone; or The Fox* (perf. 1606, publ. 1607) (*L* 665): '*Volpone* was even finer than I expected. I could think of nothing else for hours after I left the theatre. The great surprise to me was the pathos of the two young people, united not in love but in in-

nocence, and going in the end their separate way. The pathos was so much greater because their suffering was an accident, neither sought nor noticed by the impersonal greed that caused it.'

104. Yeats participated in the selection of plays for the Abbey Theatre (opened 1904) from its earliest beginnings in 1897 with the Irish Literary Theatre. He remained influential in the theatre's management until his death; see note 107 below.

Dion Boucicault (1820?–90), Dublin-born dramatist of popular, thrilling melodramas. The Queen's Royal Theatre, Great Brunswick Street, Dublin, had specialised in melodrama, especially during J. W. Whitbread's management (1883–1906).

105. Beginning in 1920, British silver coins, including the sixpence, were debased to half silver and half base metal. The Irish Free State sixpence, first minted in 1928, was made of nickel.

106. The Irish Free State Executive Council (1922–37), comprised of the principal government ministers, exercised the executive authority of the Irish Free State. Its presidents were William T. Cosgrave (1922–32) and Eamon de Valera (1932–37).

107. Yeats probably had in mind Paul Vincent Carroll's *Shadow and Substance,* which was hailed as the start of a new phase in the history of the Abbey Theatre, where it premiered on 25 January 1937. (See David Sears, review in the *Irish Independent,* quoted in Hugh Hunt, *The Abbey: Ireland's National Theatre 1904–1978* [Dublin: Gill and Macmillan, 1979] pp. 157–58; Frank O'Connor [Michael O'Donovan] speech, September 1937, quoted in Peter Kavanagh, *The Story of the Abbey Theatre* [New York: Devin-Adair, 1950] pp. 172–73; and *The Irish Times,* 26 January 1937, p. 8, col. e: ' "Shadow and Substance" is a brilliant play, splendidly acted. . . .') Until 1934 the Abbey Theatre's board of directors had consisted only of Yeats and two others. By the end of 1935 the board had been expanded to seven members, and Yeats no longer took an active part. In 'Advice to Playwrights who are Sending Plays to the Abbey, Dublin' (*c.* 1907), issued by the Abbey Theatre, Yeats had suggested that the achievement of artistic unity by 'a long shaping and reshaping of the plot, is the principal labour of the dramatist, and not the writing of the dialogue' (quoted in Liam Miller, *The Noble Drama of W. B. Yeats* [Dublin: Dolmen Press, 1977] p. 135).

108. *Hamlet,* v.ii.1–59; the first quarto (1603) omits this entirely.

109. King Fortinbras, of Norway, father of Prince Fortinbras. *Hamlet,* I.i.80–86; see also *E&I* 215–16.

110. Yeats perhaps heard this while sitting for a portrait by the American artist John Singer Sargent (1856–1925), in London in April 1908. For the 'unconscious', see p. 299, note 61 above.

111. Yeats included the forty-six-line poem 'Santorin (A Legend of the Aegean)' (1913) by James Elroy Flecker (1884–1915), English poet and playwright, in *OBMV* (no. 218).

In summer 1913, Flecker moved to Switzerland on his doctor's advice; he died there of consumption in January 1915, at age twenty-eight. His play *Hassan: The Story of Hassan of Bagdad and how he came to make the Golden Journey to Samarkand: A Play in Five Acts* (London: Heinemann, 1922) ran for 282 performances in London, 20 September 1923–24 May 1924. The Abbey Theatre production, directed by Hugh Hunt, 1–6 June 1936, was unsuccessful, despite enthusiastic advance praise from the *Irish Times* (30 May 1936, p. 4, col. e) for the Abbey's decision to give Dubliners a chance to see this 'delightful', large-scale example of 'an entertainment from the Arabian Nights'. The subsequent review in that same newspaper (2 June 1936, p. 8, col. f) focused on the difficulty of mounting so large a production on the tiny stage of the Abbey and suggested that the play be trimmed in length so that playgoers would not miss the last tram. The reviewer, who might have been staring at his watch during the last half of the play, made only a glancing mention of the play's extreme cruelty, which Yeats addresses later in this paragraph. The action of the entire last half of the play focuses on the ghastly torture that the caliph of Bagdad (Harun al-Rashid) inflicts upon his young slave maiden and her lover, who had tried to rescue her. The title character calls the caliph a 'hideous tyrant, torturer from Hell!' (v.ii; p. 159) and then flees Bagdad for distant Samarkand.

112. The cultural nationalism of the Young Ireland movement (1842–48) centered on the newspaper *The Nation,* founded by Thomas Davis, Charles Gavan Duffy and John Dillon.

113. Matthew Arnold, preface and introduction (1873) to *Literature & Dogma: An Essay towards a Better Apprehension of the Bible* (London: Smith, Elder, 1873) pp. xxxiii ('. . . culture is: *To know the best that has been thought and said in the world* . . .'), 8 ('. . . acquainting oneself with the best which has been thought and said in the world . . . make acquaintance with the best which has been thought and uttered in the world . . .').

114. Harun al-Rashid (al Raschid) (764?–809), caliph of Bagdad (from 786) and famed as the caliph in many of the tales in the *Arabian Nights* (collected *c.* fourteenth to sixteenth centuries). The particular reference might be 'The Tale of Ala al-Din Abu al-Shamat', in which Harun al-Rashid sends one of his slave-girls, Kut al-Kulub, to the young widower Ala al-Din, but eventually settles for giving him money with which he buys another slave-girl, Jessamine (*A Plain and Literal Tranlation of the Arabian Nights' Entertainments, now Entituled The Book of the Thousand Nights and a Night,* tr. Burton [1885; repr. with illus. London: Burton Club (*c.* 1900)] IV, 64–67 [nights 261–62]). In each of three tales a man other than Harun al-Rashid sets free a slave-girl to marry (or return to) her lover: 'Abdallah bin Ma'amar with the Man of Bassorah and his Slave-Girl' (V, 69) (night 383), 'The Loves of Abú Isá and Kurrat al-Ayn' (V, 145–52) (nights 414–18) and 'The Ruined Man and his Slave-Girl' (IX, 28–32) (nights 898–99). See also Yeats's poem 'The Gift of Harun Al-Rashid' (1924), *P* 445–50.

115. *Hamlet,* III.iv; v.ii.358: '. . . felicity a while'; v.i.278 ff.; *Anthony and Cleopatra,* v.ii; *King Lear,* III.ii. *Sophocles' Oedipus at Colonus: A Ver-*

sion for the Modern Stage (1934), in *VPl* 897 (l. 1518), *CPlays* 573.

116. This might be based, although very loosely, on Alain René Lesage (1668–1747), French novelist and playwright, *Le Diable boiteux* (1707), ch. xiv (xv in some later editions; 'Of the Broil betwixt a Tragick and Comick Author'), which Yeats mentioned in 'The Tragic Theatre', an essay he wrote in 1910 (*E&I* 242 and *UP2* 387). According to Lesage, tragedy deals with 'serious Problems' (p. 214), is supported by the 'majestick Grandeur of the Subject' (p. 218), inspires 'noble Thoughts' and is praised by the Learned (p. 214), while comedy needs 'an ingenious Subject, which turns on the Manners of Men' (p. 215), and uses characters of low class. Farce is lumped together with comedy (p. 216). *Le Diable Boiteux; or, The Devil upon Two Sticks,* [tr. anon.] (London: Tonson, 1708).

    William Blake, *The Marriage of Heaven and Hell* (1790–93), plate 4, in *PWB* 178: 'Energy is eternal delight.' (Erdman, p. 34: '. . . Eternal Delight.')

117. For this reference to St Thomas Aquinas in Villiers de l'Isle Adam's drama *Axël,* see p. 301, note 70 above.

118. *A Broadside,* new ser., nos. 1–12 (January–December 1935), ed. W. B. Yeats and F. R. Higgins, musical ed. Arthur Duff; published monthly at the Cuala Press, Dublin; collected as *Broadsides: A Collection of Old and New Songs* (1935). *A Broadside,* new ser., nos. 1–12 (January–December 1937), ed. Dorothy Wellesley and W. B. Yeats; published monthly at the Cuala Press, Dublin; collected as *Broadsides: A Collection of Old and New Songs* (1937).

    Frederick Robert Higgins (1896–1941), Irish poet, editor and director at the Abbey Theatre. Dorothy Violet (née Ashton) Wellesley, Duchess of Wellington (1889–1956), English poet.

119. The famed Irish lyric tenor John McCormack (1884–1945) included Irish songs in each of the concerts and recitals in which he specialised from 1914 onwards. A large portion of his recordings, the first of which were in 1904, are Irish ballads. He recorded two songs with words by Padraic Colum (1881–1972), 'A Cradle Song' ('O men from the fields!') and 'She Moved thro' the Fair'; one with words by Joseph Campbell (1879–1944), 'My Lagan Love'; and two with words by Yeats, 'Down by the Salley Garden' and 'The Cloths of Heaven'. See L. F. X. McDermott Roe, *John McCormack, the Complete Discography* (London: Jackson, 1956) pp. 35–36, 47, 53.

120. The Irish Academy of Letters was founded by George Bernard Shaw and Yeats in 1932 with twenty members (from a planned total of thirty-five). Milton's masque *Comus* (publ. 1637) was performed in 1634 to celebrate a reunion of the Egerton family at Ludlow Castle, seat of the Earl of Bridgewater, president of the Council in the Marches of Wales.

121. For Yeats's diary entry, 12 March 1909, see pp. 108 and 352, note 29 above.

122. For a life of knowledge and contemplation rather than of action and glory; W. H. Auden and Christopher Isherwood, *The Ascent of F6,* II.i (London: Faber & Faber, 1936) p. 72.

123. Jack B. Yeats's expressionistic novel *The Charmed Life* (London: Routledge, 1938).
124. In June 1936 the English artist William Rothenstein had recommended Diana Murphy, a young Irish designer in England. In April 1937, Yeats commissioned from her a design illustrating his poem 'The Lake Isle of Innisfree' (1890, *P* 39). He rejected her first version as unsuitably symbolic, but in August accepted a second version. By then she also had designed an embroidery titled 'The Land of Youth', which was worked by Lily Yeats at Cuala Industries (completed September 1937). For its subject, see Yeats's introduction titled 'T'yeer-na-n-Oge' (Tír-na-nÓg, 'the Country of the Young') in *Folk and Fairy Tales of the Irish Peasantry* (1888) (*P&I* 20–21). Her other design was an illustration to 'The Happy Townland' (1903, *P* 85–86). Yeats subsidised his sister's embroidery work with advance payments, first of £5 to the designer and then, when the embroidery had been worked, of £5 5s. to Lily Yeats. These advances were to be repaid to him when and if the work was sold. On 3 March 1938, Yeats sent payment for the embroidery 'Innisfree', worked by Lily Yeats (silk thread on linen, 60.5 x 41.0 cm. [worked area], now in the collection of Anne Yeats). In his letter he mentioned that he had finished the first number of *On the Boiler* and had put in a note about the embroideries, adding, 'Some rich American may buy the lot' (unpublished letter, transcription by John Kelly). In December 1938 Diana Murphy was at work on an illustration to 'Sailing to Byzantium' (1927), *P* 193–94 and/or 'Byzantium' (1932; *P* 248–49), depicting 'an ideal country' (Yeats to William Rothenstein, 29 December 1938, in William Rothenstein, *Since Fifty: Men and Memories, 1922–1938: Recollections* [New York: Macmillan, 1940] p. 305).
125. For this quotation from Dante Gabriel Rossetti, see p. 399, note 39 above.
126. Pierre Puvis de Chavannes (1824–98), French decorative painter.
127. According to Yeats's scheme of history, Greek art changed from a stylized, delicate Ionic or 'Eastern' (Persian) style to a naturalistic, athletic Doric or 'Western' style by the middle of the fifth century B.C. In 480 B.C., at the naval battle of Salamis, an island near Athens, the Greeks defeated the invading forces of the Persian Xerxes. For Pythagoras, compare pp. 149 and 377, note 51 above. For parallels with Yeats's poem 'The Statues' (1938), see A. Norman Jeffares, *A New Commentary on the Poems of W. B. Yeats* (London: Macmillan, 1984) pp. 412–17 and Thomas R. Whitaker, *Swan and Shadow: Yeats's Dialogue with History* (Chapel Hill: University of North Carolina Press, 1964) pp. 235–45.
128. Yeats lived in Rapallo, on the Italian Riviera, during winters from 1928 to 1930 and returned briefly in June 1934.
129. Sir (later St) Thomas More (1478–1535) wrote his *Utopia* (1516) after he entered Parliament in 1504; he became Privy Councillor in 1518.
130. '[Avalon]' (also titled 'A Statesman's Holiday'), *P* 586–87 and 712 (notes to A128). Yeats used the title 'Avalon' in three typescripts of

On the Boiler, but cancelled the title. The title 'A Statesman's Holiday' was added, probably by Mrs Yeats, on a set of page proofs for the second edition of *On the Boiler* (Wade no. 202) that were used for the Macmillan 'Coole Edition' in July 1939 (BL Add. Ms. 55881). In the typescripts, the penultimate line is 'And nothing else to sing!' and the poem is dated April 1938 (NLI Mss. 30,552 and 30,553). The poem was not included in the Cuala Press *Last Poems and Two Plays* (1939) or in the two-volume *Poems* (1949); it was titled 'A Statesman's Holiday' in the Macmillan *Last Poems and Plays* (1940) and in *Collected Poems* (1950).

APPENDIX 1

'Epilogue' to *Per Amica Silentia Lunae*

1. For St Patrick's Purgatory, see p. 310, note 13 above.
2. Curtis Bradford, in an unpublished typescript transcription at Grinnell College, deciphered this manuscript passage differently: '. . . say that [it] is an expedient[?] since God. . . .'
3. St Thomas Aquinas (1225?–74), Italian scholastic philosopher, discussed God as the first efficient cause in *Summa Theologica*, part I, questions 1–4, and the Trinity in his *Treatise on the Theological Virtues*, question 2, article 8.
4. Curtis Bradford's transcription reads: '. . . we are span-long. . . .'
5. Curtis Bradford transcribed this word as 'summer'.

APPENDIX 2

Alternative ending for 'If I were Four-and-Twenty'

1. Spoil-five: One of the oldest card games and particularly popular in Ireland.
2. Laurence, Marquise de Cinq-Cygne, an aristocratic royalist in Balzac's *A Gondreville Mystery* (*Une Ténébreuse Affaire*), *The Member for Arcis* (*Le Député d'Arcis*) and *A Princess's Secrets* (*Les Secrets de la Princesse de Cadignan*). Raoul Nathan, journalist, man of letters and dramatist who figures in fourteen novels and stories by Balzac. For the chiropodist Publicola Masson in Balzac's 'The Unconscious Mummers' ('*Les Comédiens sans le savoir*') see pp. 40 and 313, note 33 above.

   Karl Marx and Friedrich Engels published the *Communist Manifesto* in 1848.
3. Gregor Johann Mendel (1822–84), Austrian botanist and Augustinian abbot who developed Mendel's Law on the inheritance of character-

istics in plants and animals from his experiments with peas in the monastery garden. Mendel's Law, although published in 1865, was not widely recognised until after 1900.

St Thomas Aquinas (1225?–74), Italian scholastic philosopher.

4. See p. 353, note 32 above.
5. The Abbé Vachère at Mirebeau told Yeats, in May 1914, that the stigmatised German religious seeress Rosalie Putt had visited Mirebeau in spirit. See p. 256 above; p. 454, note 49 below; and an untitled essay by Yeats, ed. George M. Harper, in '"A Subject of Investigation": Miracle at Mirebeau', in *Yeats and the Occult*, ed. Harper (Toronto: Macmillan, 1975) p. 188 and note 12.
6. The hermit and barrister from Sri Lanka (Ceylon) are untraced.
7. *Civitas Dei*: City of God.
8. Untraced.
9. Robert Burton, author of *The Anatomy of Melancholy* (1621; 6th ed. 1651–52), ed. Rev. A. R. Shilleto (1892; repr. London: Bell, 1912), (O'Shea no. 311) and a Latin comedy *Philosophaster* (1606; perf. 1618); the specific reference is untraced.
10. See pp. 49 and 318, note 8 above.
11. For the traditional ferocity of the unicorn, see Aelian, *Historia Animalium* (3rd c.), XVI, 20 and, for example, Edmund Spenser, *The Faerie Queene* (1590–96), II.v.10.2 ('prowd rebellious unicorne'). Seventeenth-century authors of studies on the unicorn, in Latin (or translated into Latin), include Caspar Bartholinus, his son Thomas Bartholinus the Elder and grandson Caspar the Younger, Ulysses Aldrovandus, Johann Frederick Hubrigk, George Caspard Kirchmayer and Christian Vater; for summaries, see Odell Shepard, *The Lore of the Unicorn* (1930; repr. New York: Harper and Row, 1979) pp. 175–82. Of those accounts, the only one available to Yeats in English translation was Hubrigius [Hubrigk], *De Monocerote seu Unicornu* (Wittenberg, 1660), reprinted by Kirchmayer as his own in *Hexas Disputationum Zoologicum* (1661) and then collected and translated by Edmund Goldsmid in his *Un-Natural History; or Myths of Ancient Science*, 4 vols. (Edinburgh: privately printed, 1886); he reported that the unicorn is 'incapable of being tamed' (II, 5) and then quoted Job 39:9: 'Will the unicorn be willing to serve thee . . .?' (II, 7).

    Curtis Bradford, in his freely edited unpublished transcription at Grinnell College, cancelled the paragraph division here and continued the rhetorical quotation to include the next sentence.
12. Thomas à Kempis (Thomas Hamerken, 1380–1471), German monk and writer, is famed as the probable author of *The Imitation of Christ*, but he is not a saint.
13. See Yeats to the editor, *United Ireland*, 17 December 1892, *CL1* 338 and note 1. Yeats was a founder of the National Literary Society, Dublin, in the summer of 1892; Douglas Hyde's inaugural address as president of the society, on 25 November 1892, was titled 'The Necessity for De-Anglicising Ireland'. That influential speech was reprinted in *The Revival of Irish Literature: Addresses by Sir Charles Duffy*,

K.C.M.G., Dr George Sigerson, and Dr Douglas Hyde (London: Unwin, 1894) pp. 117–61.

14. Yeats had moved to 4 Broad Street, Oxford, in October 1919.

APPENDIX 3

NOTES TO *VISIONS AND BELIEFS IN THE WEST OF IRELAND*

1. Robert Kirk (*c.* 1641–92), *Secret Commonwealth, or, A Treatise displayeing the Chiefe Curiosities as they are in Use among diverse of the People of Scotland to this Day; Singularities for the most Part peculiar to that Nation* ('1691'; probably Ms.), repr. as *An Essay on the Nature and Actions of the Subterranean (and, for the most Part,) Invisible People, heretofioir going under the name of Elves, Faunes, and Fairies, or the like among the Low Country Scots, as they are described by those who have the second sight. . . .* [ed. Sir Walter Scott? and Robert Jamieson?] (London: Longman, Rees, Orme & Brown, 1815) (printed in Edinburgh by J. Ballantyne). Yeats quoted the 1815 title as reproduced in his copy of an 1893 edition, with commentary by Andrew Lang, *The Secret Commonwealth of Elves, Fauns, & Fairies: A Study in Folk-Lore & Psychical Research* (London: Nutt, 1893), (O'Shea no. 1068; gift from Lady Gregory) p. [1]: '. . . The Nature and Actions of . . . Subterranean (and, for . . . Part,) Invisible People, heretofioir going . . . the name of Elves, Faunes, and Fairies'. Yeats accepted Lang's judgment (p. x) that the 1691 date of *The Secret Commonwealth* refers to its manuscript and that the first printed edition was in 1815, despite Sir Walter Scott's assertion, in 1830, that it 'was printed with the author's name in 1691, and reprinted, Edinburgh, 1815, for Longman & Co.' (Sir Walter Scott, *Letters on Demonology and Witchcraft, Addressed to J. G. Lockhart* [1st ed. (London: Murray, 1830), (O'Shea no. 1860; inscribed Georgie Hyde-Lees, 1914) and] 4th ed., Morley's Universal Library [London: Routledge, 1899], [O'Shea no. 1860a] p. 137.) For the bibliographical history, see Lang's introduction and postscript to *The Secret Commonwealth*, 1893 ed., pp. ix–x, 89–92.
2. 'Light of the Irish language'; Latin misquoted from Andrew Lang, introduction to *The Secret Commonwealth* (1691), by Robert Kirk (London: Nutt, 1893), (O'Shea no. 1068; gift from Lady Gregory) p. xii: 'Linguae Hiberniae Lumen'.
3. Walter Yeeling Evans-Wentz, a young American scholar at Oxford, recorded these interviews with the Reverend William M. Taylor and with Mrs Margaret MacGregor in his *The Fairy-Faith in Celtic Countries: Its Psychical Origin and Nature* (London: Oxford University Press, 1911), (O'Shea no. 2242) pp. 89–90; the book is dedicated to AE and Yeats.
4. Andrew Lang, introduction (1893) to *The Secret Commonwealth*, pp. xii–xiii ('Grahame of Duchray', p. xii). The incident is also recounted

by Sir Walter Scott in *Letters on Demonology and Witchcraft, Addressed to J. G. Lockhart*, pp. 138–39; Scott cites Rev. Dr Grahame of Aberfoyle, *Sketches of Perthshire* (Edinburgh, 1812). A third source, also in Yeats's library, is Walter Yeeling Evans-Wentz, *The Fairy-Faith in Celtic Countries: Its Psychical Origin and Nature* (London: Oxford University Press, 1911), (O'Shea no. 2242) p. 89, citing Lang's introduction to *The Secret Commonwealth*.

5. Kirk, *The Secret Commonwealth*, pp. 18 (ch. i, section vii) 'those subterranean People'; 7 (ch. 1, section ii) 'that abstruse People'; 73 ('A Succint Accompt of My Lord Tarbott's Relations, in a letter to the Honourable Robert Boyle, Esquire, of the Predictions made by Seers, Whereof himself was Ear and Eye-witness', question 2) '. . . and dregy Bodies. . . .'; 77 ('Succint Accompt', question 3) 'especially of the more spirituall and hautie Sins'; 25 (ch. i, section xi) 'whatever . . . Laws be, sure, according . . . ours, and Equity, natural, civil, and reveal'd' . . . their stealling of Nurses . . . their Children, and . . . our Children away, (may . . . Estate . . . Dominions,) which never returne. For . . . Inconvenience . . . Succubi, who . . . Men, it . . . abominable; but . . . Swearing . . . Intemperance, they . . . to those Irregularities, as . . . Envy, Spite, Hypocracie, lieing, and Dissimulation.'; 17 (ch. 1, section vii) '. . . sore Sicknesses, but . . . Period, all . . . Age'; 77 ('Succint Accompt', question 4) '. . . pass (after . . . healthy Lyfe) into . . . Orb . . . Receptacle fitted for their Degree, till . . . general Cognizance of the . . . Day'; [5]–6 (ch. i, section i) '*Sleagh Maith*, or . . . Good People . . . Dint . . . ill Attempts . . . a midle Nature betuixt Man . . . Angel . . . intelligent studious Spirits . . . light changable Bodies, (lyke those . . . Astral,) somewhat . . . Nature . . . Cloud, and . . . Twilight. Thes Bodies be so plyable thorough the Subtilty of . . . Spirits . . . them, that . . . disappear att Pleasure. . . . Bodies . . . Vehicles so spungious, thin, and desecat, that . . . Liquors, that peirce lyke pure Air and Oyl: others feid more . . . the Foyson or . . . Corns . . . Liquors, or Corne it selfe that grows on the Surface . . . Earth, which these Fairies steall away . . . Grain, as do Crowes and Mice.'

For Father Lodovico Maria Sinistrari of Ameno (1622–1701), Franciscan theologian, see note 11 below.

For Kirk citing the Scriptures in *The Secret Commonwealth*, see the 1893 edition, pp. [3] (title page of the 1815 edition); 27–29 (ch. i, section xii); [39]–78 ('Succint Accompt', *passim*).

Pelagius, British monk and theologian (360?–420?), who was accused (but acquitted) of heresy in 415, argued that baptism was not essential for infants. St Augustine insisted on the orthodox position that any infants who do not receive baptism would be denied salvation.

6. *V&B* ii, 218; *V&B1970* 262.

7. Kirk, *The Secret Commonwealth*, pp. 6–7 (ch. i, section i) 'When . . . plenty, they . . . Scarcity . . . Homes . . . the contrarie (for . . . are empowred to . . . Prey . . . please,) . . . There Bodies of congealled Air are some tymes carried . . . whiles grovell in different Schapes,

and . . . any Cranie or Clift of . . . Earth . . . Air enters, to . . . Dwellings; the Earth being full . . . Cavities . . . Cells, and . . . Place . . . Creature . . . Animals (greater . . . lesser) living . . . Inhabitants; and . . . Wilderness . . . Universe. . . . People, as weill as. . . . Lodgings . . . Beginning . . . Quarter . . . Year . . . Doomsday, being imputent and [impotent of?] staying . . . Place, and . . . Ease . . . purning [Journeying] and . . . Habitations. Their chamaelion-lyke Bodies . . . Air . . . Earth . . . Bag and Bagadge'; 18 (ch. i, section vii) 'What . . . Revolution . . . them, when . . . are lock't up . . . Condition . . . frolic Fitts of Mirth, 'tis . . . the constrained grinning . . . a Mort-head. . . . Observations'; 7 (ch. 1, section ii) '. . . People'; 18 (ch. i, section vii) '. . . subterranean People . . . Souls, attending . . . State, and . . . Bodies procured throwgh their Almsdeeds in this Lyfe; fluid, active, aetheriall Vehicles . . . them, that . . . scatter, or wander, or . . . Totum, or their first Nothing . . . Alms, they . . . Souls . . . do depairt, they . . . an unaictve State . . . the terrestriall Bodies'.

8. See Jacob Boehme, *The Treatise of the Incarnation, in Three Parts* (w. 1620, Eng. tr. 1659), part i, ch. 13, v. 94 in *The Works of Jacob Behmen, The Teutonic Theosopher* (London: Richardson, 1764), (O'Shea no. 239) iii, 83, 159 (separately paginated) and *Forty Questions concerning the Soul* (w. 1620, Eng. tr. 1650), questions 21–23, 26, 30, 37, in *Works* (1764) ii, 75–82, 86–89, 91–98, 109–12 (separately paginated). '*Turba magna*': Great turmoil (or wrath).
9. The Irish god Lug (Lugh) was the father of Cuchulain. Mongan, a legendary king of Ulster and son of the sea-god Manannan Mac Lir, is once described by Caoilte as a reincarnation of Finn Mac Cool, leader of the Fianna.
10. Glanvill, *Sadducismus Triumphatus*, part ii, relation xviii (pp. 356, 358): '. . . Gentleman . . . *Ireland* . . . of *Orrery's* Seat, sending . . . Butler . . . Afternoon . . . Cards . . . Field . . . People . . . Table . . . good chear before . . . of the Field. . . . *Do nothing this Company invites you to*. . . . Table . . . Table . . . Company . . . Musical Instruments . . . Butler . . . working any . . . feasting or dancing . . . Butler. . . .' '. . . dead, said . . . Spectre . . . Ghost, seven years, and. . . . have I been . . . Condition . . . Company . . . saw, and . . . be to the day. . . .' The date 1674 is mistaken, although Glanvill's book on witchcraft had been published in a series of earlier forms and titles in 1666, 1667, 1668 and 1676 before the posthumous first edition titled *Saducismus Triumphatus* . . . in 1681; see also p. 328, note 65 above.
11. The manuscript *De Daemonialitate, et Incubis, et Succubis* (*c*. 1700), by Father Lodovico Maria Sinistrari of Ameno (1622–1701), Franciscan theologian, was first published in 1875 in Paris by Isidore Liseux (1835–94), in Latin and with an anonymous French translation, *De la Démonialité et des animaux incubes et succubes*. In 1879, Liseux issued the Latin text with an anonymous English version on the facing pages, *Demoniality; or, Incubi and Succubi: A Treatise wherein is shown that there are in existence on earth rational creatures besides man, endowed like him with a body and a soul, that are born and die like him, redeemed by our Lord*

Jesus-Christ, and capable of receiving salvation or damnation (Paris: Isidore Liseux), from which Yeats quotes (p. 163, section 77): ' "*I am a mortal,*" replied he, "*and one of the inhabitants of the Wilderness, whom Gentility, under its varied delusions, worship under the names of Fauns, Satyrs and Incubi; I am on a mission from my flock: we request thee to pray for us unto the common God, whom we know to have come for the salvation of the world, and whose praises are sounded all over the earth.*" Rejoicing at the glory of Christ, St Anthony, turning his face towards Alexandria, and striking the ground with his staff, cried out, "Woe be unto thee, thou harlot City, who worshipest animals as Gods!" '

12. 'The Priest and the Fairy' (1889), *P* 523–26.
13. St Jerome (Latin: Hieronymus) (340?–420), *Vita Pauli* (*Life of St Paul, the First Hermit*) (374–79), in J. P. Migne, ed., *Patrologiae Cursus Completus . . . Series Latina* (Paris: Migne, 1883) XXIII, col. 23; Sinistrari, *Demoniality* (1879) pp. 160–61 (section 77), with '*homunculum*' translated as 'a little man, almost a dwarf'.

    Rath: circular, prehistoric hill-fort, traditionally inhabited by faeries.
14. Sinistrari, *Demoniality* (1879), p. 173 (section 84): 'whom *the Gentiles*, blinded by *error, call Fauns, Satyrs and Incubi*'; see also p. 163 (section 77). For Sinistrari, see note 11 above.
15. For the Sidhe as Tuatha De Danaan, see, for example, 'The Destruction of Da Derga's Hostel' and 'The Intoxication of the Ulaid', from the *Book of the Dun Cow* (before 1106) and the *Book of Leinster* (*c.* 1160), which Yeats dated as eleventh century (*UP2* 221); see also *V&B* II, 214; *V&B1970* 260: 'the old inhabitants of Ireland'. For the Sidhe as fallen angels, see *P&I* 10 and 233, note 33; *UP1* 137; *V&B* I, 192; II, 70, 130, 136, 148, 172; *V&B1970* 117, 182, 212, 216, 223, 238. In *V&B* the someone who said that Christ might empty the whole paradise is variously identified as St Michael the Archangel (II, 151, 172; *V&B1970* 225, 238) or St Peter (II, 176, 178; *V&B1970* 240, 241).
16. Sinistrari, *Demoniality* (1879): '*And other sheep I have, which are not of this fold: them also I must bring, and they shall hear my voice, and there shall be one fold and one shepherd*' (p. 191, section 96); pp. 193–201 (sections 97–100); 'rational Creatures or animals . . . Himself, or through the Apostles' (p. 201, section 100); pp. 203–7 (section 102); p. 225 (section 115); '. . . more subtile . . . degrade, but rather dignifies his nature' (p. 223, section 114); '. . . *hoc modo homo* . . . Incubo . . .' (p. 222, section 114); p. 223 (section 114); p. 205 (section 102); p. 137 (section 70); pp. 175–77 (section 87); pp. 213–15 (sections 109–10); '. . . Theologian . . . man to . . . despite the exorcisms' . . . 'the crowd of relics and other holy objects' (p. 141, section 71); '. . . long-pepper, caryophylleae, cinnamon . . . mace, nutmegs, calamite storax, benzoin, aloes-wood and roots, one . . . of triasandalis, and . . .' (p. 143, section 71); p. 145 (section 72) 'Carthusian Friary' (vice 'priory'); p. 143 (section 71) 'Peruvian balsam' (vice 'bark'); '. . . Angel . . . with the figure . . . Friars. . . . *Verbus caro factum est*. . . . least, aerial . . . water-lily, liver-wort, spurge. . . .' (pp. 145–49, section 72); p. 51 (section 28) 'the threshold of the church' (vice 'the

steps of the Cathedral altar') and 'in a gust of wind' (vice 'by invisible hands').

Cubeb: dried berry of *Piper Cubeba*, a Sumatran climbing pepper shrub, used in medicine and cooking. Aristolochies: Aristolochia genus of shrubs, including the Common Birthwort. Cardamom: capsules of several tropical plants of the ginger family, which form an aromatic, pungent spice. Long Pepper: spice from the immature fruit-spikes of the allied plants *Piper officinarum* and *Piper longum*; formerly supposed to be the flower or unripe fruit of *Piper nigrum*. Caryophylleae: clove pink. Calamite Storax: dried resin of *Styrax officinalis*, formerly used as a medicine. Benzoin: gum benjamin, the aromatic and resinous juice of *Styrax Benzoin*, a tree of Java and Sumatra, used in perfumes and incense, and in friar's balsam. Aloes-wood and roots: eaglewood heart-wood and roots. Triasandalis: presumably related to sandalwood oil, used in perfumes.

Certosa di Pavia, friary founded in 1396.

Exsurgat Deus: 'Let God arise', Psalm 67 (Vulgate, 68 in King James version). *Qui habitat*: 'He that dwelleth', Psalm 90 (Vulgate, 91 in King James version).

Verbum caro factum est: 'the Word was made flesh' (John 1:14).

Liverwort: green nonflowering plants of the class Hepaticae, forming with the mosses the Bryophyta, formerly used for diseases of the liver.

17. Plutarch, 'Life of Numa' (IV.3–4) in *The Lives of the Noble Grecians and Romanes* [*sic*], tr. Thomas North (1579) (Stratford-upon-Avon: Shakespeare Head Press, 1928), (O'Shea no. 1597) I, 168: '. . . to beleeve the goddes have carnall knowledge, and doe delight . . . outward beawtie of . . . to carie a very harde beliefe. Yet . . . Egyptians thincke it . . . the spirite of the goddes hath geven originall of . . . and doe beget fruite of . . . bodies: howbeit . . . no corporall companie with. . . .'
18. For Cuchulain and the Morrigu, a Tuatha de Danaan queen and goddess of battle, see *Cuchulain of Muirthemne*, pp. 211–12, and John Rhys, *Lectures on the Origin and Growth of Religion as Illustrated by Celtic Heathendom* (1888), 2nd ed. (London: Williams and Norgate, 1892), (O'Shea no. 1741) p. 468.
19. Yeats earlier had praised the beauty of this song, in which 'the god Midhir sings to Queen Etain' (*P&I* 130); it is from the third section of 'The Wooing of Étaín', in *The Book of the Dun Cow*. Yeats quotes the version in *Gods and Fighting Men*, p. 96 ('Midhir and Etain'): 'O. . . . there, beautiful . . . flag-flower . . . fox-glove. . . . there; the . . . warm, sweet . . . and of wine . . . sorrow on any. . . .' For other examples of mortals and fairies as lovers, see *V&B* I, 100, 107, 114; *V&B1970* 68, 70, 74.
20. Dame Alice Kyteler of Co. Kilkenny was prosecuted for sorcery in 1324. Yeats had the date right in his note (1921) to 'Nineteen Hundred and Nineteen', ll. 126–30 (*P* 599). Her sacrifice of 'nine red cocks and nine peacocks eies' (tail feathers) to her incubus, Robert Artisson, was reported in Raphael Holinshed's *Chronicle of Ireland* (entry for

1323), apparently based in part on the account in a fifteenth-century compilation, *Annales Hiberniae* (*'novem gallos rubeos'*). The charges described her incubus as *'ex pauperioribus inferni'* (*A Contemporary Narrative of the Proceedings against Dame Alice Kyteler, Prosecuted for Sorcery in 1324, by Richard de Ledrede, Bishop of Ossory*, ed. Thomas Wright, Camden Society Publications, no. 24 [London: Camden Society, 1843] p. 2; the accounts in Holinshed and *Annales Hiberniae* are quoted on p. 46).

21. Yeats himself reported having seen spirit light during a séance in Wimbledon on 9 May 1912 with Mrs Etta Wriedt (1860–1942), an American medium who was visiting England: 'I saw a light very distinctly and without any possibility of being mistaken straight in front of me. It was not bright; it was the usual phosphorescent glow and about the size and shape of a sixpenny loaf.' (Quoted in Steve L. Adams and George M. Harper, 'The Manuscript of "Leo Africanus" ' in *YA1* 20.)

In the *Grettis saga*, Grettir the Strong (996–1031), an Icelandic outlaw, saw flames burning 'above hid treasure' (*The Story of Grettir the Strong*, ch. xviii ['Of Grettir at Haramsey and his dealings with Karr the Old'], tr. William Morris and Eirikr Magnusson [1869; repr. in *The Collected Works of William Morris* (London: Longmans, Green, 1911), (O'Shea no. 1389; purchased in 1919)] VII, 39).

Hereward the Wake, English outlaw who led a rising of the English against the Normans in 1070. The specific reference is untraced. *Gesta Herwardi* mentions the young boy Hereward's blond hair (in *Rerum Britannicarum Medii Aevi Scriptores, or The Chronicles and Memorials of Great Britain and Ireland during the Middle Ages*, Master of the Rolls Series, no. 91 [London: Eyre and Spottiswoode, 1888] I, 341 [in Latin]).

Baron Karl von Reichenbach (1788–1869), German scientist, conducted a scientific study of several hundred 'sensitives', persons who could see emanations from crystals and magnets in total darkness and could see an aura surrounding the human body. See his *Researches on Magnetism, Electricity, Heat, Light, Crystallization, and Chemical Attraction, in their relations to the Vital Force* (1849; 2nd ed., 1850), tr. William Gregory (London: Taylor, Walton and Maberly, 1850) and, as *Physico-Physicological Researches on the Dynamics of Magnetism . . .*, tr. John Asburner (London: Baillière, 1851); for a briefer account see his *Od Force: Letters on a Newly Discovered Power in Nature, and its Relation to Magnetism, Electricity, Heat and Light* (1852), tr. J. George Guenther (Boston: Mussey, 1854).

William Holman Hunt, *The Triumph of the Innocents* (1883, signed 1884), oil on canvas, 62 x 100 in., Tate Gallery, London (no. 3334); illus. in Timothy Hilton, *The Pre-Raphaelites* (London: Thames and Hudson, 1970; New York: Praeger, 1974) plate 155.

22. George Russell ('AE') at Coole in the late 1890s (*Mem* 131).

23. *Gods and Fighting Men*, p. 113 ('His [Manannan's] Call to Bran').

24. For example, Swedenborg, *Heaven and . . . Hell*, no. 481 (p. 256).

George Russell ('AE') noted that he saw in his first vision, during the mid-1880s, when he and Yeats were students at the Metropolitan School of Art, Dublin, 'palaces of light, and the winds were sparkling and diamond clear, yet full of colour as an opal, as they glittered' (*The Candle of Vision* [London: Macmillan, 1918], [O'Shea no. 1799] p. 9).

See Annie Besant, *The Ancient Wisdom: An Outline of Theosophical Teachings* (London: Theosophical Publishing Society, 1897), (O'Shea 1920s list) pp. 73–78 (the vividness of colour increases with the spiritual development of a person's astral body), 112 ('The vibrating life of the Thinker' in the highest spiritual planes produces 'the most exquisite and constantly changing colors. . . . Every seer who has witnessed it, Hindu, Buddhist, Christian, speaks in rapturous terms of its glorious beauty').

25. On 3 June 1871, the English mediums Frank Herne and Charles Williams, in a séance at 61 Lamb's Conduit Street with several witnesses, are reported to have transported Mrs Samuel (Agnes Nichol) Guppy, II (d. 1917) from her home in 1 Morland Villas, Highbury Hill Park (renamed Drayton Park), Highbury (not Hampstead), two miles away. According to the written testimony of one of the eleven sitters, there was 'a heavy bump on the table. . . . A match was struck, and there was Mrs. G[uppy], standing on the centre of the table. . . . She had one arm over her eyes, with a pen in her hand, and an account-book in her other hand. . . .' (Letter to the editor, *Echo*, 8 June 1871, quoted in Frank Podmore, *Modern Spiritualism: A History and a Criticism* [London: Methuen, 1902] II, 82; Podmore cites parallel accounts in the *Medium and Daybreak: A Weekly Journal Devoted to the History, Phenomena, Philosophy, and Teachings of Spiritualism*, 15 June 1871, [O'Shea no. 1301]; *Spiritual Magazine*, July 1871; and the *Spiritualist*, 15 June 1871 [signed by all eleven persons present].)

Daniel Dunglas Home (or Hume) (1833–86), Scottish medium, was famous for his levitations. He was based in the United States 1842–84, but resided in England during the 1860s for several extended periods. The levitation to which Yeats refers took place on 16 December 1868 at 5, Buckingham Gate, London, with Home, Viscount Adare (later Earl of Dunraven), his cousin Captain Wynne, and the Master of Lindsay (later Earl of Crawford). Reports of it by Lindsay and by Adare are quoted in Frank Podmore, *Modern Spiritualism: A History and a Criticism* (London: Methuen, 1902) II, 255–56. Lord Dunraven (Windham Thomas Wyndham-Quin, fourth Earl of Dunraven and Mount-Earl and Viscount Adare) (1841–1926) later was chairman of the Irish Land Conference and served with Yeats as an Irish Free State senator. William (later Sir William) Crookes described Home as the most remarkable medium he had studied ('Experimental Investigation of a New Force', *Quarterly Journal of Science*, 8 [1 July 1871], 340, repr. in his *Researches in the Phenomena of Spiritualism* [London: Burns, (1874)], [O'Shea no. 449] p. 15).

In 1905, two brothers aged eight and ten, Paolo and Alfredo Pansini of Ruvo, Puglia, Italy, were mysteriously transported several times, for distances of several miles. On one of those occasions they found themselves in front of a Capuchin convent in Molfetta. The boys' mother took them to seek the aid of Monsignor Berardi Pasquale, bishop of Ruvo and Bitonto, but while she was talking with the bishop both boys mysteriously disappeared from the room. These events were recorded by Giuseppi Lapponi, physician to Pope Leo XIII and Pope Pius X, in his book *Ipnotismo e Spiritismo: Studio Medico-Critico* (1906 and 2nd ed. augmented, 1906), tr. by Mrs Philip Gibbs, as Joseph Lapponi, *Hypnotism and Spiritism: A Critical and Medical Study* (New York: Longmans, Green, 1907) pp. 128–33. Lapponi's account is cited in a book Yeats owned, Cesare Lombroso, *After Death—What?*, pp. 168, 176–77, 336; Yeats marked pages 176 and 336 in his copy. I have not located the account 'in a spiritualistic paper'.

26. Sinistrari, *Demoniality* (1879), p. 34 (Latin) (section 26). The English translation (p. 35) reads: '. . . and it happens not merely with women, but also with mares; if they readily comply with his desire, he pets them, and plaits their mane in elaborate and inextricable tresses; but if they resist, he ill-treats and strikes them, smites them with the glanders, and finally puts them to death, as is shown by daily experience.'

    Glanders: A malignant, contagious, and fatal disease of the horse and ass (and man), showing itself especially on the mucous membrane of the nose, upon the lungs, and on the lymphatic system. (*Chambers's Twentieth Century Dictionary*)

27. John Heydon, *The Holy Guide, Leading the way to Unite Art and Nature: In which is made plain All things past, present, and to come* (London, 1662), (O'Shea 1920s list [titled there: *The Holy Guide, leading the way to the wonder of the world (A Complete Physitian). Teaching the Knowledge of all things past, present, and to come etc.*]), title page: 'A . . . Secretary . . . Nature'. John Heydon, *The Holy Guide*, book VI [with separate title page and separate pagination, but same foliation as *The Holy Guide*], *The Rosie Cross Uncovered* . . . (London, 1662) p. 4: 'a *Heroes* [*sic*] a *Daemon*, or good *Genius*, of a *Genius* a . . . Divine things, and . . . Companion . . . Company . . . Souls . . . Angels, and according . . . Vehicles, a . . . themselves, *Proteus*-like, into. . . .'; and in 'An Apologue for an Epilogue', sig. Zz[6]r: '*a* Heroes [*sic*] *a* Daemon, *or good* Genius, *of a* Genius *a partaker of Divine things, and a companion of the holy company of unbodied Soules and immortal Angels, and according to their* vehicles *a versatile life, turning themselves,* Proteus-like, *into any shape.*'

28. Annie Wood Besant (1847–1933), *The Ancient Wisdom: An Outline of Theosophical Teachings* (London: Theosophical Publishing Society, 1897), (O'Shea 1920s list) p. 59.

29. William Wordsworth, 'The White Doe of Rylstone: Shape Changers' (1815), ll. 268, 274, in *The Poetical Works*, ed. Edward Dowden, Aldine Edition of the British Poets (London: Bell, 1893), (O'Shea no. 2292) IV, 13: 'Shepherd-lord' (l. 268); '. . . She. . . .' (l. 274).

30. Milton, *Paradise Lost*, I.423–31, illus. William Blake (Liverpool: Liverpool Booksellers, 1906), (O'Shea no. 1321) pp. 16–17: '. . . . / Not tied or. . . .'

31. An Aran Islander; *V&B* II, 81; *V&B1970* 186.

32. For this report by Mrs Sheridan (pseudonym), an old woman who lived near Coole Park, see *V&B* I, 79–80; *V&B1970* 55.
33. Albert de Rochas, 'The Fluidic Hands of Eusapia' (1908 in French), *The Annals of Psychical Science*, 8 (April–June 1909) 226–27; see also his *L'Extériorisation de la motricité: recueil d'expériences et d'observations* (1896), 4th ed. (Paris: Bibliothèque Chacornac, 1906), (O'Shea no. 1175). Yeats owned a clipping (NLI Ms. 30,005) of Hereward Carrington's illustrated article, 'Fluidic Hands: The Latest in Medium Photography', *New York Times*, 28 July 1912, part v, p. 8. For materialisation phenomena during séances, see also p. 302, note 81 above.
34. In *V&B*, the section on 'Seers and Healers' opens with many accounts (I, 35–69; *V&B1970* 31–50) of Biddy Early, who lived between Feakle and Tulla, Co. Clare, thirteen miles southeast of Coole Park, in the early and mid-nineteenth century. For her bottle, see *V&B* I, 40, 46–48, 53, 56, 64, 69, 97; *V&B1970* 33, 36–38, 41–42, 47, 50. Camberwell, in southeast London, contrasts with the elegant West End areas near Bond Street.
35. For an example of a knowledgeable man communicating with his dead sister, see p. 20 above. 'Rochester rappings' were knocking sounds that gave spirit information, by counting out numbers or letters, to the American spiritualists the Fox sisters, Kate (1841–92), Margaret (1838–93) and Leah (1814–90), first in Hydesville, New York, in March 1848 and then in nearby Rochester, New York. For Plutarch's daemon, see p. 330, note 78 above.
36. [Yeats's note, signed W.B.Y. and dated October 1918] Since writing the above the authors of *An Adventure*[a] have shown me a mass of letters proving that they spoke of the visions to various correspondents before the corroboration, and showing the long and careful research that the corroboration involved.
36a. For *An Adventure*, by Charlotte Anne Elizabeth Moberly and Eleanor Frances Jourdain, see p. 360, note 10 above.
37. William Denton (1823–83), *The Soul of Things; or, Psychometric Researches and Discoveries* (Boston: Walker, Wise, 1863), includes Elizabeth M. F. Denton, 'Questions, Considerations, and Suggestions'.
38. Agrippa, *Three Books of Occult Philosophy*, book I, ch. vi (p. 14): 'This is a vitall spirit, passing . . . Beings, giving life, and subsistence to . . . things. . . . It immediately . . . into it self the influencies of all Celestiall bodies, and then communicates . . . Elements, as . . . all mixt bodies: Also . . . into it self, as . . . Looking-glass, the . . . well naturall, as artificiall'; '. . . Impression . . . them, as . . . sleep, as . . . they be awake, and . . . matter for divers . . . Dreams . . . Divinations. Hence they say it is, that . . . slain, or the Carkase newly hid, is moved with fear . . . the Aire in . . . the dreadfull species . . . Man-slaughter, doth, being . . . species. . . . Whence . . . is, that . . . Philosophers . . . that Aire is. . . .'
39. See Henry More, *The Immortality of the Soul*, book III, ch. vi, section VII, in *A Collection*, pp. 172–73; and More's letter to Joseph Glanvill in Glanvill, *Saddучismus Triumphatus*, part II, advertisement to relation VIII (pp. 330–32).

40. Éliphas Lévi (Alphonse Louis Constant, 1810–75), *Dogme et rituel de l'haute magie* (1856), tr. Arthur E. Waite, in *The Mysteries of Magic: a Digest of the writings of Éliphas Lévi with Biographical and Critical Essay* (1886) and in *Transcendental Magic: Its Doctrine and Ritual: A complete translation of Dogme et Rituel de la Haute Magie* (London: Redway, 1896), (O'Shea no. 1109) p. 62 (ch. v) *et passim*; the astral light is one of the forms of what Lévi called the 'Universal Agent' (p. 42) (ch. ii) or 'Great Magical Agent' (p. 52) (ch. iv). For Éliphas Lévi and the Astral Light, see also p. 366, notes 11–11a above.

Helena Petrovna Blavatsky (1831–91), Russian theosophist.

41. Agrippa, *Three Books of Occult Philosophy*, book III, ch. xli (pp. 475, 476):

> *Four things of man there are; Spirit, Soul, Ghost, Flesh;*
> *These four fowre places keep and do possess.*
> *The earth covers flesh, the Ghost hovers o're the grave.*
> Orcus *hath the soul, Stars do the spirit crave.*

Agrippa quoted these lines as by Ovid (43 B.C.–A.D. 17?), but they are not now attributed to Ovid; lexical evidence suggests that the Latin text quoted by Agrippa is from the fourth century or later. Yeats's quotation from Agrippa is from p. 476: '. . . Hell . . . spirit, and . . . image'.

42. Lady Gregory's source is Mrs Dennehy, in *V&B* II, 91; *V&B1970* 191: '. . . wandering, and . . . is weak, and. . . .'

43. Yeats met William James (1842–1910), the distinguished American psychologist and philosopher, on 1 December 1903 at Harvard University, where James was professor of philosophy, and where Yeats delivered a lecture during his first American lecture tour. Yeats owned two copies of James's Ingersoll Lecture on Immortality (1897, publ. 1898), *Human Immortality: Two Supposed Objections to the Doctrine*, 2nd ed. (Boston: Houghton, Mifflin, 1899) and an almost wholly uncut 4th ed. (Westminster: Constable, 1899), (O'Shea nos. 1008–9). In that book James cites evidence of psychical phenomena (pp. 24–27 and 66, n. 7) and praises the anti-materialist views of Ferdinand C. S. Schiller (pp. 29 and 66–69, n. 9). James's view is that all individuals are transmitters of 'the eternal Spirit of the Universe'—or of a God whose 'scale is infinite in all things' (pp. 41–43). James had been interested in psychical research since 1884, and the Society for Psychical Research, London, had appointed him as its honorary president in December 1893.

44. 'The Sensitive Plant' (1820), Conclusion, ll. 17–24, in *Poems of Shelley*, ed. Locock, I, 467: '. . . Lady . . . never past away: / 'Tis . . . changed; not. . . . // . . . change; their might / Exceeds. . . .'

45. W. K. Sullivan, intro. to *On the Manners and Customs of the Ancient Irish: A Series of Lectures*, by Eugene O'Curry (London: Williams and Norgate, 1873), (O'Shea no. 1478) I, ccxcvii: '. . . in *Duns*, and *Stone Caiseals*, and . . . probably, in. . . .'

46. George Petrie (1790–1866), Irish antiquarian, topographical artist and musicologist, 'On the History and Antiquities of Tara Hill', *Transactions of the Royal Irish Academy*, 18 (1837), part III, 185: 'Its length,

taken from the road is 759 f., and its present breadth at the bottom is 46 f., but its original breadth must have been about 90.'

47. '*De exorcizandis obsessis a Daemonio*' and '*De visitatione et cura Infirmorum*, in *Rituale Romanum* (Baltimore: Murphy, 1873) pp. 385–412, 143–56. The specific passages referred to read: '*Sacras imagines Christi Domini crucifixi, beatae Mariae virginis, et Sancti, quem aeger praecipue veneratur, ob oculos ejus apponi curabit*' (p. 144); '([rubric:] *tres Cruces sequentes fiant in pectore daemoniaci*' (p. 394); '*Recede ergo in nomine Patris [*CROSS SYMBOL*], et Filii [*CROSS SYMBOL*], et Spiritus [*CROSS SYMBOL*] Sancti*' (p. 393); '*Adjuro ergo te, draco nequissime, in nomine Agni immaculati, qui ambulavit super aspidem et basiliscum, qui conculcavit leonem et draconem, ut discedas ab hoc homine*' (pp. 395–96); '*Sacerdos imponat dexteram manum super caput infirmi, et dicat*:' '*Super aegros manus imponent, et bene habebunt. Jesus Mariae Filius, mundi salus, et Dominus, meritis et intercessione sanctorum Apostolorum suorum Petri et Pauli, et omnium Sanctorum, sit tibi clemens et propitius*' (p. 155).
48. Demon-possessed swine that rushed into the sea (Matthew 8:28).
49. This conversation with Abbé Vachère (d. 1921), priest at Mirebeau, near Poitiers, France, occurred on 12 May 1914, during an investigation of the Abbé's miraculous bleeding oleographs of the bleeding heart. The Abbé was excommunicated by 1916. The Italian nun was a Benedictine, Benedetta of Viterbo, who died in 1913; the living holy woman, whom Yeats described as 'a Belgian holy woman', was 'the stigmatised German religious seeress Rosalie Putt' (Untitled essay by Yeats, ed. George M. Harper, in '"An Subject of Investigation": Miracle at Mirebeau' in *Yeats and the Occult*, ed. George M. Harper [Toronto: Macmillan, 1975] p. 188 and n. 12).
50. Albert de Rochas, *L'Extériorisation de la sensibilité: Étude expérimentale & historique* (1894), 6th ed. (Paris: Bibliothèque Chacornac, 1909), (O'Shea no. 1776) pp. 147–59 (ch. v, sections I–III); see also his pp. 122–33 (ch. iv, sections II–III). He quotes from Pierre Le Lorrain de Vallemort, *La Physique occulte, ou traité de la baguette divinatoire, et de son utilité pour la découverte des sources d'eau, des minières. . . . Augmenté en cette édition, d'un traité de la connaissance des causes magnetiques des cures sympathiques*, 2nd ed. (Amsterdam: Braakman, 1696), ch. ix; the first edition was published in 1693. De Rochas variously prints the Latin '*mumia*' (p. 150) and two spellings in French, '*mommie(s)*', '*mumie*' and '*mumiques*' (pp. 150, 151, 165, 166, 169). The French phrase ('the spirits which reside in the blood') is quoted by de Vallemort from Robert Fludd (De Rochas, p. 150).

    De Rochas describes the experiments of Dr Babinski, '*chef de clinique de M Charcot à la Salpêtrière*' (p. 160) on pp. 160–62 (ch. v, section IV) and quotes, at length, on pp. 163–65 (ch. v, section IV) a lecture, 10 February 1894, by Dr Luys, of the *Hôpital de la Charité*. Jacques Arsène d'Arsonval (1851–1940), mentioned by Dr Luys, was a French physicist. The English translations given by Yeats might have been made by Lady Gregory; see also note 52 below. For Jean Martin Charcot and *la Salpêtrière*, see p. 373, note 34 above.
51. *motu proprio* (Latin): of his own accord.

52. Albert de Rochas, *L'Extériorisation de la sensibilité*, 6th ed. (Paris: Bibliothèque Chacornac, 1909), (O'Shea no. 1776) p. 165 (ch. v, section IV) (in French). Yeats's manuscript of this passage cites another French edition, in which these quoted passages are on pp. 174–76 (NLI Ms. 13,575[3], p. 13b).
53. Jean Bodin, *De la Demonomanie des Sorciers* (Paris, 1580); its German translation (1581) used the Latin title, *De Magorum Daemonomania*. The specific reference in Bodin is untraced. In alchemical texts from that period salt is one of the elements and thus 'incorruptible' and 'inalterable' (OED); Yeats described salt as 'the symbol of eternity' (Yeats to T. Sturge Moore, 7 April 1930, *LTSM* 160).
54. For this anecdote, which is reported in *The Tour of the French Traveller M. de la Boullaye le Gouz in Ireland, A.D. 1644*, see *P&I* 21 and 237, n. 58.
55. Giraldus Cambrensis, *The Topography of Ireland* (1187), tr. Thomas Forester, in *The Historical Works of Giraldus Cambrensis*, ed. Thomas Wright (London: Bell, 1887) pp. 73–74 (ch. xii).
56. In the opening section of '*De exorcizandis obsessis a Daemonio*', in *Rituale Romanum* (Baltimore: Murphy, 1873) p. 385: '*Signa autem obsidentis daemonis sunt*: . . . *Vires supra aetatis seu conditionis naturam ostendere*. . . .' (Signs of possession are the following: . . . display of powers which are beyond the subject's age and natural condition. . . .)
57. John Rhys, *Lectures on the Origin and Growth of Religion as Illustrated by Celtic Heathendom*, Hibbert Lectures 1886 (1888; repr. London: Williams and Norgate, 1892), (O'Shea no. 1741) pp. 256–57 (Lecture III), 558 (Lecture V, part II), 372–73 (Lecture IV).

    Alfred Nutt, *The Legends of the Holy Grail*, Popular Studies in Mythology, Romance and Folklore, no. 14 (London: Nutt, 1902), (O'Shea no. 1467) p. 116 ('the cauldron of the Dagda').
58. John Rhys, *Celtic Heathendom* (1888), pp. 596–97 (Lecture VI).

    Sporran: ornamental pouch worn in front of the kilt by the Highlanders of Scotland.
59. Swedenborg, *Conjugial Love*, no. 44, section IX. The wording ('day-spring of their youth') that Yeats used here, in *Au* 311, in a letter to T. Sturge Moore (*LTSM* 114) and in 'Modern Poetry' (p. 92 above), is closer to the translation by Samuel M. Warren, rev. Louis H. Tafel (1910; repr. New York: Swedenborg Foundation, 1954) p. 54 ('the springtime of their youth'), than to the translation by A. H. Searle (1876), rev. R. H. Tafel (1891), which Yeats owned (London: Swedenborg Society, 1891), (O'Shea no. 2038) p. 48 ('their vernal youth'). See also p. 319, note 20 above. For parallel statements by Swedenborg, see *Heaven and . . . Hell*, no. 414 (p. 209): 'The inhabitants of heaven are continually advancing towards the spring-time of life. . . .'; *Arcana Coelestia*, nos. 1854, 4676 (II, 395; VI, 349): '. . . They are constantly verging toward the life of early manhood and of youth' (no. 1854); 'into the bloom of youth' (no. 4676).
60. Mrs Fagan, wife of a local fairy doctor, described her husband's dead sister to Lady Gregory and Yeats: 'Twenty years she's gone, but she's

not dead yet, but the last time he saw her he said that she was getting grey' (*V&B* I, 106; *V&B1970* 70); see also p. 301, note 73 above.

61. Lombroso, *After Death—What?*, p. 231: '. . . hour. "Remigio," on . . . are all in. . . . hour, and. . . .' Professor Aureliano Faifofer (1843–1909), Italian mathematician, psychical researcher and author of textbooks on algebra, geometry and trigonometry. Giosuè Carducci (1835–1907), Italian poet and Nobel laureate for literature (1906).

62. A. J. (not I.) Smart (dated 10 June 1877 and signed by ten other witnesses), 'Materialisation Phenomena at Cardiff: A Spirit Assumes the Form, Partakes of Food, and Vanishes from Sight', *The Medium and Daybreak: A Weekly Journal Devoted to the History, Phenomena, Philosophy, and Teachings of Spiritualism* (London), 8, no. 376 (15 June 1877) 369–71.

63. Mrs Leonora E. Piper (1859–1950), American medium whose séances in Boston from 1884 through 1927 were extensively studied by the American Society for Psychical Research and by the Society for Psychical Research, London. She visited England in 1889–90, 1906–7 and 1909–11. Yeats's source here is Mrs Henry Sidgwick, 'A Contribution to the Study of the Psychology of Mrs Piper's Trance Phenomena', *Proceedings of the Society for Psychical Research* (London), 28 (1915), part LXXI, (O'Shea no. 1643) 25, 'She would say, namely, that the sitter, when she first saw him, had looked to her very small and a long way off, as if she sometimes described it, she had been looking at him through the wrong end of an opera glass.' Yeats noted in the margin: 'Mary Battle on faeries.' Yeats mentioned that 'much of my *Celtic Twilight* is but her daily speech' (*Au* 71).

64. See pp. 70–71 and 332–33, notes 97–98 above.

65. John Heydon, *The Holy Guide*, book VI: *The Rosie Cross Uncovered* . . . (London, 1662) p. 3: 'the . . . of the great King'; and in 'An Apologue for an Epilogue', sig. Zz[6][r]: '*the eyes and ears of the great King*'. For additional bibliographical details, see note 27 above.

66. The medium Mrs Piper (see note 63 above), after awakening from trance, did not remember her contact with the spirit world. In 1901, after eighteen years of mediumship, she said that she simply did not know if 'spirits of the dead have spoken through me when I have been in the trance state. . . . It may be that they have, but I do not affirm it' (*New York Herald*, 20 October 1901, quoted in Nandor Fodor, *Encyclopaedia of Psychic Science* [1934; repr. University Books, 1966] p. 286).

67. John L. Nevius, *Demon Possession and Allied Themes* (1894; repr. Chicago: Revell, 1896); for examples of Christian exorcism, see his pages 13, 51, 71 and 145; for examples of Chinese exorcism by burning paper money or offerings, pricking with needles or burning the feet, see his pages 50, 54 and 68.

68. Michael Cleary was convicted of manslaughter in July 1895 and sentenced to twenty years of penal servitude for burning his wife, Bridget, to death, thinking that she was a fairy changeling. Convicted with him were her father, her aunt, four of her cousins, and two other

neighbours at Ballyvadlea, between Cloneen and Millinahone, Co. Tipperary. The inquest, inquiry and trial were summarised in 'The "Witch-Burning" at Clonmel', *Folk-Lore: Transactions of the Folk-Lore Society*, 6, no. 4 (December 1895), 373–84, from reports in the *Irish Times*, 26–28 March; 2, 3, 6 and 8 April; 6 July 1895.

69. Percival Lowell, *Occult Japan; or, The Way of the Gods: An Esoteric Study of Japanese Personality and Possession* (Boston: Houghton, Mifflin, 1895) pp. 2–8. This episode occurred in August 1891; the stick with zigzag paper is a *gohei*-wand.

70. The twelfth-century Irish manuscript *The Book of the Dun Cow* is the oldest extant version of *Táin*. John Rhys, *Lectures on the Origin and Growth of Religion as Illustrated by Celtic Heathendom*, Hibbert Lectures 1866, 2nd ed. (London: Williams and Norgate, 1892), (O'Shea no. 1741) p. 468 (Lecture v, 'The Sun Hero', part I).

Cuchulain of Muirthemne, ch. xiv, 'The Only Jealousy of Emer', summary of pp. 276–93; quoted passages from pp. 276–78: '. . . to-day? . . . with the women of Ulster; for . . . to-day. . . . said. "Is it because . . . women?" "You . . . while, as to me, no. . . ." . . . him, and smiled at him, and she gave. . . . then, and smiled at him, and . . . turn, till. . . .'

71. John Rhys, *Celtic Heathendom* (1888), p. 346 (Cúchulainn and the Sons of Dóel Dermait [Beetle of Forgetfulness], pp. 342–46; Lecture IV).

72. Caesarius of Heisterbach, *Dialogue on Miracles* (1220–35), VII.xxxiv.

73. 'Pwyll Prince of Dyved' in *The Mabinogion, from the Welsh of the Llyfr Coch O Hergest (The Red Book of Hergest)*, tr. Lady Charlotte Guest, 2nd ed. (London: Quaritch, 1877), (O'Shea no. 1166) pp. 339–65; see also John Rhys, *Celtic Heathendom* (1888), pp. 337–42.

74. This Norse legend about the chief god Odin (Woden) is untraced; Yeats had first mentioned it in 1902 (*UP2* 282).

75. For Boehme, see p. 393, note 30 above.

76. 'Going to Mass by the will of God', quoted in Yeats, 'Dust Hath Closed Helen's Eyes' (dated 1900, 1902), in *The Celtic Twilight*, 2nd ed. (1903) (*Myth* 24–25), with each verse of Lady Gregory's prose translation set as a quatrain. Lady Gregory, 'Raftery' (1900, 1902), in *Poets and Dreamers: Studies & Translations from the Irish* (Dublin: Hodges, Figgis, 1903), (O'Shea no. 807) pp. 4, 23–25 (two of eleven prose verses), and titled 'Raftery's Praise of Mary Hynes' in *The Kiltartan Poetry Book: Prose Translations from the Irish* (Churchtown, Dundrum, Co. Dublin: Cuala Press, 1918) pp. 5–6 (prose verses, complete), repr. in *The Kiltartan Poetry Book: Translations from the Irish* (London: Putnam's, 1919) pp. 31–33, and in *The Kiltartan Books comprising The Kiltartan Poetry, History and Wonder Books*, Coole Edition (Gerrard's Cross, Berks.: Smythe, 1971) p. 27.

77. *V&B* I, 189; *V&B1970* 262. For Mary Battle, see p. 281 above.

78. Reverend William Stainton Moses (1839–92), English medium and religious teacher, produced many physical phenomena during séances in the 1870s. See, for example, 'Extracts from Mr Moses' Note-Books', in Frederic W. H. Myers, 'The Experiences of W. Stainton

Moses', *Proceedings of the Society for Psychical Research*, 11 (1895), part XXVII, 26, 29: 'Copious scent fell from the ceiling' (31 December 1873), 'We had cool waves of scented air during the evening' (31 December 1873), 'We had masses of scent—verbena, sandalwood, rose, musk' (2 January 1874). Full accounts of those séances were also published, beginning in 1892, in *Light*, the journal of the London Spiritualist Alliance, of which Reverend Moses was the editor. Moses's notebooks, along with typed transcriptions, were available from the mid-1890s at the London Spiritual Alliance. Yeats owned a sizable typescript copy of them (George M. Harper, *Yeats and the Occult*, pp. 7–8). Reverend Moses, who published under the pseudonym 'M.A. Oxon', was a founding member of the Society for Psychical Research, resigned in 1886, and was the founder and president of the London Spiritualist Alliance.

79. George Russell ('AE').
80. This Gaelic poem is variously titled '*Faeth Fiada*' (The Deer's Cry), 'St Patrick's Lorica' (or Breastplate), and 'Patrick's Hymn'. William G. Wood-Martin, in his *History of Sligo* (Dublin: Hodges, Figgis, 1882) I, 140, accepted the now-repudiated popular attribution of the poem to St Patrick and noted that the line that mentions the 'spells of women and *smiths*' is 'the only blot' of paganism in this otherwise Christian poem. The translation closest to that used by Yeats here and in *SB* 128 is by J. Whitley Stokes, *The Tripartite Life of Patrick* (1887; repr. New York: Kraus, 1965) I, 49–51, and *Luireach Phádruig: St Patrick's Breastplate* (London: Catholic Truth Society, n.d. [*c.* 1905]. Other, similar translations are by George Petrie, in his essay 'On the History and Antiquities of Tara Hill', *Transactions of the Royal Irish Academy*, 18 (1837), part III, 67–69 (with specific attention to the phrase 'against the spells of women, smiths, and Druids'); by James Clarence Mangan, as 'St Patrick's Hymn before Tara' (1848), *Poems of James Clarence Mangan (Many Hitherto Uncollected)*, ed. David James O'Donoghue (1903; repr. Dublin: Gill, 1918) pp. 44–48; and by Lady Gregory in *A Book of Saints and Wonders* (London: Murray, 1907) pp. 62–64.

APPENDIX 4

Deleted 'Introduction' of 'Swedenborg, Mediums, and the Desolate Places'

1. Lady Gregory reported that in each household of fairies, 'the greatest power belongs to their fool, the Fool of the Forth, Amadan-na-Briona. He is their strongest, the most wicked, the most deadly; there is no cure for any one he has struck.' (*V&B*, I, iv; *V&B1970* 9) See also the section of *V&B* on 'The Fool of the Forth' (*V&B*, II, 195–204; *V&B1970*, 250–54).
2. For Robert Kirk (*c.* 1641–92), see p. 458, note 1 above.

3. Shelley, *Prometheus Unbound*, IV.86.
4. Ballisodare, Co. Sligo. See *Au* 16.
5. Melusine: French water-sprite fairy. The Virgin Mary.
6. Lady Gregory mentions 'the Golden Mountain, Slieve nan-Or, "where the last great battle will be fought before the end of the world"' (*V&B* 36; *V&B*1970 31); a village Slieveanore, Co. Clare, in the Slieve Aughty mountains, is ten miles east-southeast of Coole Park.
7. See William Blake, '[Vision of the Last Judgment]' (Notebook, p. 87), in *PWB* 252 (as 'Prose Fragment: Why Men enter Heaven') and Erdman, p. 554.
8. See William Blake, annotation to Berkeley, *Siris* (p. 219), in Erdman, p. 654: 'God is Man & exists in us & we in him'; see also John 17:21–23.

   The quotation 'God is an abode of spirits' perhaps echoes Blake's ['A Vision of the Last Judgment'], pp. 69–70: 'All Things are comprehended in their Eternal Forms in the Divine body of the Saviour . . .' (Erdman, p. 545) or *Jerusalem*, 'To the Christians', plate 77: 'Is God a Spirit who must be worshipped in Spirit & in Truth and are not the Gifts of the Spirit Every-thing to Man? . . . . What is Immortality but the things relating to the Spirit, which Lives Eternally! What is the Joy of Heaven but Improvement in the things of the Spirit?' (Erdman, p. 229).

APPENDIX 6

Biographical note in *The Holy Mountain*

1. Dhuliā, city (21–00N/074–56E), 185 miles northeast of Bombay.
2. See p. 374, note 7 above.
3. Dehu, a town (18–43N/073–45E), nineteen miles north-northwest of Poona.
4. See p. 374, note 8 above.

APPENDIX 7

Final Paragraph of Introduction to *The Oxford Book of Modern Verse*

1. For Graves and Riding see *LTWBY* 579–81 and 609–11, and *LDW* 40, 64 and 66–67. Laura Riding (1901–91), an American, had lived in England and on the Continent since 1925.
2. John Hayward, reviewing for *The Spectator*, 20 November 1936, complained that 'Kipling and Pound are poorly represented because the Clarendon Press would not pay for their work' (p. 3). Yeats replied,

in a letter to the editor: 'The book has been immensely expensive because all the contents are copyright. As I had a fixed sum for payment of authors I decided on my own responsibility that I could not afford more of these expensive writers' (*The Spectator*, 157 [4 December 1936], 995). On 26 April 1936 Yeats had told Dorothy Wellesley, who assisted him in selecting poems by Kipling: 'I have already over spent by about fifty pounds the five hundred pounds the Oxford Press set aside to pay authors. The fifty pounds must come out of my own pocket & that is almost empty' (*LDW* 67). For Yeats's selection of Pound's poems, see p. 406, note 95 above.

TEXTUAL INTRODUCTIONS

Per Amica Silentia Lunae (1917). Appendix: alternate epilogue (1917).

Per Amica Silentia Lunae was written in early 1917, and was originally titled *The Alphabet*. 'Anima Hominis', the first of its two principal sections, is dated 25 February 1917. The other section, 'Anima Mundi', for which Yeats considered the titles 'Spiritus Mundi' and 'The Orders', is dated 9 May 1917 in the manuscript. The prologue (dated 11 May 1916 [*sic*, 1917]) of the final manuscript was moved and retitled as the epilogue in the published version, where it displaced an undated alternative epilogue that Yeats left in manuscript (NLI Ms. 30,532). That alternative epilogue (printed here as Appendix 1) is written on the same variety of paper as the 'Anima Mundi' section. In the published version, both the prologue and epilogue are dated 11 May 1917. In every edition of *Per Amica Silentia Lunae* the poem 'Ego Dominus Tuus' (w. 1915; publ. October 1917; *P* 160–62) is reprinted immediately following the prologue. Another poem, 'The Moods' (1893; *P* 56), is reprinted in the 'Anima Mundi' section.

In a letter written the day after he completed the book, still titled *The Alphabet*, Yeats described it as 'a little philosophical book' that he would publish in the autumn alongside a book of verse, *The Wild Swans at Coole*, since 'reviewers find it easier to write if they have ideas to write about'.[1] A few days later, when he promised to send the manuscripts of *The Alphabet* and *The Wild Swans at Coole* to John Quinn, Yeats described the essay as 'an elaborate bit of writing'.[2]

In June 1917 he changed the book's title to *Per Amica Silentia Lunae*, which he translated, in a letter to Lady Gregory, as 'through the friendly silences of the moon'.[3] In July or August 1917 Yeats approved the front cover design of a rose in a geometrical frame, drawn by his friend T. Sturge Moore.[4]

Per Amica Silentia Lunae was published by Macmillan on 18 January 1918, in both London (Wade 120) and New York (Wade 121, labelled: 'Printed in U.S.A.'). An errata slip tipped in at least some copies of the London edition gave four corrections,[5] all of which were incorporated in the 1924 version, which is the copy-text for this edition.

Yeats's library has nine copies of the 1918 edition, five from London (O'Shea nos. 2392–2392d) and four from New York (O'Shea nos. 2393–

2393c). Edward O'Shea has recorded that one copy (O'Shea no. 2392) of the London edition has six revisions, two of which are mentioned by the errata slip and were incorporated in the 1924 edition. One revision needlessly called for more space between two sentences (p. 9, l. 28: 'sun. The'). The three other revisions marked in Yeats's copy, although substantive, were not adopted in the 1924 edition or in any of the posthumous copy-editing, and are not used in the text of this edition, but they are recorded here for interest:

P. 4, ll. 9–10 above: 'among images of good and evil, crude allegories?' CHANGED TO 'amid wooden allegories painted in black and gold and vermillion?'

P. 6, l. 33 above: 'slake' CHANGED TO 'appease'.

P. 9, l. 17 above: 'can never be a portion of our being, "Soon got, soon gone", as the proverb says.' CHANGED TO 'stays not in our being but as the proverb puts it "ill got, soon gone." '

Per Amica Silentia Lunae was slightly revised for *Essays* (London: Macmillan, 6 May 1924), (Wade 141), the fourth volume of Macmillan's 'Collected Edition of the Works', pp. 477–538. The four corrections from the 1918 errata slip were adopted, and Yeats added three footnotes (dated 1924): p. 297, note 43 (dated February 1924); 302, note 78 (dated 1924) and 305, note 105 (dated 1924) above. The New York edition of *Essays*, which was published five months later, 14 October 1924, was typeset separately, using the London edition as its copy-text, but introducing two typographical errors: 'de' (p. 521) instead of 'do', and p. 538: '*Charitè*' (p. 538) instead of '*Charité*'. A signed, limited edition of 250 copies was issued 26 October 1924 by Macmillan, New York.

Per Amica Silentia Lunae was included in a Macmillan, London, typescript list of contents, 27 October 1936 (NLI Ms. 30,202), for volume v, *Essays*, in Macmillan's planned collected 'Coole Edition'. It was also included in a typewritten list of contents that Yeats prepared in January 1937 for Charles Scribner's Sons, New York, for their planned collected 'Dublin Edition', volume v, *Essays*. Yeats instructed Scribners to use the text of *Essays*, London, 1924.[6] By 23 June 1937, the New York firm had followed those instructions, using pages from the London 1924 edition, with no copy-editing other than a query of the misspelled name 'Douthenday' (rather than 'Dauthendey') on page 536 (HRC Texas, Scribners papers, box 2, vol. VIII). Scribners printed three sample versions of a page from 'Anima Hominis', section v (HRC Texas, Scribners papers, slip-case dated 1937).

Soon after Yeats's death, the planned Macmillan 'Coole Edition' had expanded to eleven volumes, with *Per Amica Silentia Lunae* in volume VIII, *Mythologies*, along with *The Celtic Twilight*, *The Secret Rose*, *Stories of Red Hanrahan*, 'Rosa Alchemica', 'The Tables of the Law' and 'The Adoration of the Magi'.[7] In New York, Scribners similarly increased its planned 'Dublin Edition' to eleven volumes, with volume VIII titled *Mythologies* and having the same contents as the Macmillan 'Coole Edition'.[8] Neither of the editions was published.

Macmillan, London, eventually published, 12 March 1959, a heavily copy-edited version of *Mythologies* (Wade 211P), including *Per Amica Si-*

lentia Lunae, pp. 319–69; the American issue was published by Macmillan, New York, on 28 July 1959 (Wade 211Q). Some 128 of the posthumous copy-editing revisions from *Mythologies* go beyond the bounds of the textual emendation policies of the present edition and have not been adopted here.[9]

If I were Four-and-Twenty (1919). Appendix: alternative ending (1919–20?).

'If I were Four-and-Twenty' was written in July 1919 and was published in the next month. The first manuscript draft, dated July 1919, is titled 'If I were Twenty' (NLI Ms. 18,750 photocopy). It was followed by a second, complete manuscript draft that has only limited revisions and is dated July 21 (NLI Ms. 30,493). A few pages survive from a carbon copy of a typed transcription of the opening of that manuscript (NLI Mss. 30,814 and 30,298). The copy-text for the present edition is the first periodical publication of the essay, in two consecutive weekly issues of *The Irish Statesman*, 23 and 30 August 1919.[10] Yeats's copies of those issues (O'Shea nos. 984–85) are unmarked.

Yeats had spent July and August at Ballylee, Co. Galway, and in Dublin. He had received an invitation in July 1919 to come to Japan, and in the published essay he mentions that he is 'about to move to the Far East' (p. 46, ll. 7–8 above). But instead of moving to Japan he moved to 4 Broad Street, Oxford, where he settled in October 1919. At some time from then until he moved back to Ireland in March 1922, Yeats returned to this essay and wrote a completely new, expanded version of the closing few sections; the alternate ending probably was meant to take over at the end of the first paragraph of section VIII (p. 44, l. 22 above). In the alternate ending, he described himself as 'of late settled in a Cathedral City' (p. 258, ll. 1–2 above). A lightly revised manuscript draft of that alternative ending and a typed transcription of it are extant (NLI Ms. 30,493), along with a carbon copy of a subsequent six-page typescript (NLI Ms. 30,794), which is printed for the first time as Appendix 2 of this edition.

The only reprinting of 'If I were Four-and-Twenty' during Yeats's lifetime was in the 4 October 1920 issue of *The Living Age*, a small-circulation American weekly magazine that specialised in republishing articles from British periodicals.[11] *The Living Age* (p. 33, col. 1) acknowledged *The Irish Statesman* as the source of its text. Yeats did not revise the text and is unlikely even to have seen proofs from the American magazine. Its only variants are from minor copy-editing and four new typographical errors.

Yeats, probably in 1938, considered collecting this essay or perhaps using it in a planned series of *On the Boiler* miscellanies, but he did not reach a final decision. An inaccurately typed transcription was prepared from *The Irish Statesman*, possibly by Mrs Yeats, either in 1938 or perhaps in March or April 1939, when she was assembling materials for the Macmillan and Scribners collected editions (see p. 464 below). A carbon copy of that uncorrected typescript is extant (NLI Ms. 30,277); its major errors are the skipping of portions of two sentences.[12]

Mrs Yeats recalled, in a letter to Harold Macmillan on 14 June 1939 (NLI Ms. 30,248), that 'about a year ago' her husband 'had dug . . . up' this essay and another, 'Ireland, 1921–1931' (1932), 'for possible use in the Scribner edition . . . but was doubtful about them'. She added, 'He thought of them in connection with *On the Boiler.*' Yeats had planned to have two issues per year of *On the Boiler*, and he finished a full draft of the first (and only) issue in March 1938. The two essays that Mrs Yeats mentioned would have been available for publication, perhaps after some recasting, in a future issue of *On the Boiler*; see p. 488 below. Those two essays are not mentioned in any of the correspondence with Charles Scribner's Sons, are not included on any of the lists of contents for the Scribners 'Dublin Edition', and are not extant among the material sent to Scribners. In her letter of 14 June 1939, Mrs Yeats recommended to Harold Macmillan that the two essays be withdrawn from consideration for inclusion in the Macmillan 'Coole Edition', and she asked him to return them to her. Someone has written a faint 'NO' in thick red pencil in the top margin of the first page of the typescript carbon copy of 'If I were Four-and-Twenty'.

Later, the same inaccurate typescript was used as copy-text for a Cuala Press book, *If I were Four-and-Twenty*, finished in the first week of September 1940 and published 28 September 1940 (Wade 205). The title essay, which comprises the first one-third of the book, is paired with 'Swedenborg, Mediums, and the Desolate Places' (pp. 47–73 above). Sometime after June 1939, probably Mrs Yeats deleted the opening four sentences, which refer directly to *The Irish Statesman*. That cut is not marked on the typescript, but had been made prior to the printing of the page proofs. A complete set of corrected page proofs is extant (NLI Ms. 30,212), as well as another, uncorrected set.

That posthumous printing failed to correct many of the errors from the typescript, notably the two truncated sentences.[13] It introduced several new errors of spelling and punctuation, while also correcting (or partially correcting) errors from the earlier text.

When the text was collected in the Macmillan, London, volume *Explorations*, pages 263–80, published 23 July 1962 (Wade 211Y), the copy-text was the Cuala Press *If I were Four-and-Twenty*. All of the major errors from the typescript that were retained in the Cuala Press book were repeated in *Explorations.*[14]

Despite the statement on the title page and dust jacket of *Explorations* that its contents had been selected by Mrs Yeats, the choices were made largely at Macmillan, London, by Lovat Dickson and/or the recently retired Thomas Mark. Mrs Yeats eventually did provide a list of contents, but only quite late in the process of production. The earliest documentary evidence of the *Explorations* project is an undated and unsigned pencil draft of a letter to Mrs Yeats (BL Add. Ms. 55896), written in late 1959 or early 1960, about the corrections to be made on the autumn 1959 page proofs of *Essays and Introductions*. The letter mentions Thomas Mark several times, in the third person, and thus probably was written by Lovat Dickson, although Thomas Mark occasionally had written letters to Mrs Yeats that were signed by Harold Macmillan. The draft letter gives a tentative list of contents that does not mention either 'If I were Four-and-Twenty' or

'Swedenborg, Mediums, and the Desolate Places'. The draft letter concludes: 'We have not yet gone into this proposal officially, but it naturally interests me greatly, and I shall look forward to hearing what you think of it and whether you have anything else you would like to include. If the book were put in hand, T.[homas] M.[ark] says he would be very happy to join you in seeing it through the press.'

Those two essays, 'If I were Four-and-Twenty' and 'Swedenborg, Mediums, and the Desolate Places', again were not mentioned in what perhaps was Lovat Dickson's next letter to Mrs Yeats on this project, 11 August 1960 (NLI Ms. 30,755). The Macmillan editor wrote, 'I shall look forward with great interest to seeing your list of material that might appear in *Explorations.*' He sent her the 1939 proofs of 'The Irish Dramatic Movement 1901–1919' and 'A Packet for Ezra Pound', plus a marked copy of *Pages from a Diary 1930*, and a copy of *On the Boiler* marked with suggested cuts. He also returned Yeats's personal copy of Hone and Rossi's *Bishop Berkeley*, from which Macmillan had taken the introduction used in *Essays and Introductions*. At the end of this letter, Lovat Dickson added, after mentioning that Thomas Mark sends his regards, 'We are both delighted, as everyone here is, that you are prepared to make up a list of material to appear in *Explorations* and I will look forward to hearing from you about this at your convenience.'

Eight months later, on 19 April 1961, Lovat Dickson still had not received a list of contents from her: 'I hear indirectly that you are distressed about the cuts suggested in the marked copy sent to you of *On the Boiler*. I don't know whether this is the reason why I haven't heard from you in reply to my letters of last August and January of this year, but if it is I wish that I had known that. We are perfectly read[y] to print *On the Boiler* without any alterations at all. The suggested cuts were indeed only suggestions, and they can be ignored altogether.' He went on to plead, 'Do let us get on with *Explorations*. The other books have done very well, and it is a pity not to add this valuable material to W.B.Y.'s published work.' (NLI Ms. 30,755)

Two Macmillan lists of contents are extant (BL Add. Ms. 55896) that presumably can be dated between that letter of 19 April 1961 and the galley proofs of *Explorations*, which are date-stamped 24 November 1961. The first list is written in blue-black ink with a ball-point pen, perhaps by Thomas Mark. It has the first mention of 'If I were Four-and-Twenty', but still lacks 'Swedenborg, Mediums, and the Desolate Places'. The list has 'Cuchulain', 'Gods and Fighting Men', 'If I were Four and Twenty', 'The Midnight Court', 'Pages from a Diary 1930' and 'On the Boiler'. At the bottom is a later notation referring to the Macmillan editor T. M. Farmiloe: 'given to T.M.F. to go back to Mrs. Yeats. May 23, 1962'.

The other list of contents was written by Mrs Yeats, in blue ink with a ball-point pen, and coincides exactly with the contents as published in *Explorations*. The list, which is headed '*Explorations*', contains 'Cuchulain of Muirthemne 1902', 'Gods and Fighting Men 1904', 'Swedenborg, Mediums, and the Desolate Places 1914', 'The Irish Dramatic Movement 1901–1919', 'If I were Four and Twenty 1919', 'The Midnight Court 1926', 'Pages from a Diary Written in 1930', 'Introduction to The Words upon

The Window Pane', 'Fighting the Waves (play & introduction)', 'The Resurrection', 'The Cat and the Moon 1934' and 'On the Boiler 1939'. Below this list, in another hand, is the comment: 'If cuts necessary remove Swedenborg &/or If I were Four & Twenty'.

No such cuts were needed. *Explorations* was published by Macmillan, London, on 23 July 1962 (Wade 211Y) and by Macmillan, New York, on 1 April 1963 (Wade 211Z).

Swedenborg, Mediums, and the Desolate Places (1914), and Witches and Wizards and Irish Folk-Lore (14 October 1914), in *Visions and Beliefs in the West of Ireland* by Lady Gregory (New York: Putnam's, 1920) II, 295–339 and I, 247–62, respectively. Appendices: Notes (1914–15), *V&B* I, 265–93 and II, 343; and deleted section I, 'Introduction', from the manuscript of 'Swedenborg, Mediums, and the Desolate Places' (w. 1911–14).

Yeats's essays and notes for Lady Gregory's two-volume collection of folklore, *Visions and Beliefs in the West of Ireland*, can be traced back to 1897, when Lady Gregory began taking him along while she collected folklore in the vicinity of Coole Park. Between November 1897 and April 1902 he published six lengthy articles that made extensive use of that folklore (*UP2* 54–70, 74–87, 94–108, 167–83, 219–36 and 267–82). After publishing the first three of those articles, Yeats wrote to Lady Gregory, on 22 December 1898:

> I forgot to ask you something which I have long meant to ask you. Would you agree to collaborate with me in the big book of folk lore? One hand should do the actual shaping and writing—apart from peasant talk—and I would wish to do this. In some cases my opinions may be too directly mystical for you to accept. In such cases I can either initial the chapters containing them or make a general statement about them in the preface. If you agree to this, all future essays can either appear over our two signatures or I can add a footnote saying that a friend, whose name I do not give, because it is easier to collect if one is not known to be writing, is helping me throughout. Please agree to this arrangement as I dislike taking credit for what is not mine and it will be a great pleasure to do this work with you. (*L* 305)

None of the six articles refers to Lady Gregory except as an anonymous 'friend', but she presumably agreed to work with him on the proposed 'big book'. In the revised version of *The Celtic Twilight*, published in July 1902, Yeats announced, 'I shall publish in a little a big book about the commonwealth of faery, and shall try to make it systematical and learned enough to buy pardon for this handful of dreams.'[15] Nine years later, he told his father that he had 'started with Lady Gregory putting into final shape the big book on Fairy Belief that we have been doing for years. My part is to show that what we call Fairy Belief is exactly the same thing as English and

American spiritism except that Fairy Belief is very much more charming' (9 May 1911, *L* 558).

In 1912 he began writing the introductory essay 'Swedenborg, Mediums, and the Desolate Places'. In January he lectured in Dublin on psychical research, 'A New Theory of Apparition',[16] and on 5 March 1912 he wrote to his father:

> I have been lecturing on the Other World and am now writing the lecture as an introduction to Lady Gregory's big book of Fairy Belief. I think I have made the first philosophic generalization that has been made from the facts of spiritism and the facts of folk-lore in combination. I have got nearly all the thought down now on paper, but I shall have to spend a long time making it vivid to the senses and making it emotionally sincere. It is always such a long research getting down to one's exact impression, one's exact ignorance and knowledge. . . . I shall probably spend a good deal of time the next two or three months trying to give my readers an exact measure in these things. (*L* 567–68)

Rather than finishing the essay in two or three months, he took two years. Several manuscripts survive that are associated with the early stages of this project (NLI Mss. 13,575 and 30,172). The only extant complete manuscript of 'Swedenborg, Mediums, and the Desolate Places' ends with Yeats's signature and the date 14 October 1914. Its opening three-page section (or perhaps of the entire essay) was originally titled 'Introduction', and was retitled as 'Swedenborg, Mediums, and the Desolate Places' in a holograph revision to the first typescript (NLI Ms. 13,575).

That opening section was dropped from the second typescript version, which opens with the former section II. The deleted section had provided two of the three mentions of 'the desolate places' that are part of the title of Yeats's essay; the section is printed here as Appendix 4. Lady Gregory might have used it as a starting point for her preface to *Visions and Beliefs in the West of Ireland* (I, iii–vi), which is signed by her and dated February 1916.

The second typescript was prepared in London at the typewriting office of Misses Jacobs & Oldroyd; its ribbon copy (Berg NYPL) has occasional pencil corrections and queries, probably by Lady Gregory; a carbon copy (NLI Ms. 30,623) has revisions by Yeats on two pages. A different commercial typist then prepared a final typescript of 'Swedenborg, Mediums, and the Desolate Places' and 'Witches and Wizards and Irish Folk-Lore', together with Yeats's note 1 to *Visions and Beliefs in the West of Ireland*.[17] The other forty-five notes occupied him until the middle of 1915; on 24 June 1915 he reported to John Quinn, 'I have . . . nearly finished my Notes for Lady Gregory's book, and that has laid the ghosts for me.' He added, very unprophetically, 'I am free at last from the obsession of the supernatural, having got my thoughts in order and ranged on paper' (*L* 595).

Visions and Beliefs in the West of Ireland was printed in the United States and published by G. P. Putnam's Sons, New York, in two volumes. Lady Gregory had begun correcting proofs by 5 March 1916 (*L* 608). The galley proofs of 'Witches and Wizards and Irish Folk-Lore' (galleys 1–5) and 'Swedenborg, Mediums, and the Desolate Places' (galleys 6–18) have very faint date-stamping from 1916 (NLI Ms. 30,276). Yeats corrected the galleys and pointed out, unsuccessfully, that 'Swedenborg, Mediums, and the Desolate Places' should come before 'Witches and Wizards and Irish Folk-Lore'. He wrote a note at the top of galley 1: '"Witches & Wizards" etc (galleys 1 2 3 4 5) comes after "Swedenborg, Mediums and the Desolate Places" but before the notes. WBY'. The printer, however, left 'Witches and Wizards and Irish Folk-Lore' in volume one and 'Swedenborg, Mediums, and the Desolate Places' in volume two.

Those two essays were part of a group of manuscripts that, on 16 May 1917, Yeats offered to send to John Quinn as soon as the seas were safer.[18] The book's publication was delayed until September 1920.[19] 'Swedenborg, Mediums, and the Desolate Places' was printed at the end of volume two (pp. 295–339) and was followed by two notes (p. 343). 'Witches and Wizards and Irish Folk-Lore' was printed at the end of volume one (pp. 247–62) and was followed by forty-four notes (pp. 265–93). It is the copy-text for the present edition. The copy-text for the posthumous Cuala Press printing of 'Swedenborg, Mediums, and the Desolate Places' in *If I were Four-and-Twenty* (1940) was a compilation of two carbon copies of a typescript (NLI Mss. 30,623 and 30,271), which was made from *Visions and Beliefs*. Both these carbon copies were copy-edited, sometimes differently, and the Cuala text incorporates readings from each, plus three changes that are not from the typed copies. Yeats's library now has only volume one of the book (O'Shea no. 811); that copy has markings, probably by Mrs Yeats, that suggest some consideration was given to including 'Witches and Wizards and Irish Folklore' along with 'Swedenborg, Mediums, and the Desolate Places' in the posthumous printing by the Cuala Press in 1940 of *If I were Four-and-Twenty*. Yeats's copy of volume two might perhaps have been mislaid at the press. For the Cuala Press book, *If I were Four-and-Twenty*, finished in the first week of September 1940 and published 28 September 1940 (Wade 205), see p. 464 above. For the reprinting of the Cuala Press texts of 'If I were Four-and-Twenty' and 'Swedenborg, Mediums, and the Desolate Places' in *Explorations* (pp. 30–70), published 23 July 1962 (Wade 211Y), see pp. 464–66 above. *Explorations* was set without consulting *Visions and Beliefs*, as shown by the compounding of a Cuala Press error.[20] *Visions and Beliefs* was reprinted in 1970 as volume one of the 'Coole Edition of the Works of Lady Gregory'.[21]

Preface to *Essays 1931 to 1936* (1937)

The brief preface to the Cuala Press *Essays 1931 to 1936* is undated, but probably was written in September or the first week of October 1937. The manuscript (NLI Ms. 30,462) is supplemented by an inserted revision that was written on the verso of a loose sheet (NLI Ms. 30,395) that concludes the manuscript draft of 'Introduction to Plays', completed by early October 1937, for the Scribners 'Dublin Edition'. The preface was published in *Essays 1931 to 1936* (Dublin: Cuala Press, finished in the last week of October 1937, published 14 December 1937) (Wade 194) sig. A4^r. That is the copy-text for the present edition. The preface was never reprinted, and was omitted from a set of corrected page proofs of *Essays 1931 to 1936* that

Mrs Yeats sent, via J. Hansard S. Watt on 15 October 1937, to Scribners as copy-text for the 'Dublin Edition' volume v, *Essays* (see note 24 below).

Parnell (1936)

Henry Harrison, author of a book defending Thomas Parnell, called on Yeats in August 1936. That visit led to Yeats's poem 'Come Gather Round Me Parnellites' (dated August 1936) and this essay, which he described as 'an historical footnote' to the poem. For Yeats's description of that meeting and the subsequent composition of the poem and the essay, see p. 340, note 4 above. A manuscript (NLI Ms. 30,494) and a typescript (NLI Ms. 30,497) are extant. On 8 September 1936, Yeats sent the poem to Dorothy Wellesley, his co-editor for a new series of Cuala Press broadsides, but said that he would hold the essay—which was too lengthy for the broadside format—for his 'next book of essays' (*L* 863). The poem was published, with an illustration by Jack Yeats and with four staves of music, but without the essay, in the Cuala Press *A Broadside*, January 1937. Yeats did not include the essay in a list of contents for the Scribners 'Dublin Edition' volume v, *Essays*, sent, via Yeats's agent on 28 January 1937, to Charles Scribner's Sons, New York,[22] but within a few months the essay had been added.

The essay was first published by the Cuala Press in *Essays 1931 to 1936* (Wade 194), where it was the lead item (pp. 1–4) and was accompanied by the poem 'Come Gather Round Me Parnellites' (pp. 4–6). A first, nearly complete set of page proofs of *Essays 1931 to 1936* (NLI Ms. 30,021), which Yeats and perhaps Mrs Yeats marked, was printed before 22 June 1937.[23] Mrs Yeats sent a later set of corrected page proofs to Scribners, via the literary agent A. P. Watt & Son on 15 October 1937, as copy-text for the 'Dublin Edition', volume v, *Essays*.[24] At that same time Scribners was sent the three introductions that Yeats wrote for the 'Dublin Edition' and also copies of his introductions to *Gitanjali* and *The Oxford Book of Modern Verse*. The Cuala Press published *Essays 1931 to 1936* on 14 December 1937. That was the last version seen by Yeats, and it is the copy-text for the present edition.

In June 1939 Mrs Yeats sent a bound copy of *Essays 1931 to 1936* to Scribners as duplicate copy-text for their 'Dublin Edition', the plans for which had expanded by then from seven to eleven volumes, although none of its volumes was ever typeset.[25]

The equivalent for the expanded Macmillan 'Coole Edition', volume XI, *Essays*, probably is a bound copy of *Essays 1931 to 1936* (BL Add. Ms. 55880) with pencilled, preliminary copy-editing by a Macmillan editor. At least two of the emendations written in its margins of the Cuala text (pp. 75 and 105) have been identified as the hand of Thomas Mark,[26] and the large size of the pencilled copy-editing marks is not characteristic of Yeats or Mrs Yeats. Furthermore, the copy-editing is more tentative than would be expected of Yeats or Mrs Yeats, as in a passage where the Cuala text (p. 118) had mistakenly failed to delete a cross-reference ('described in the following pages') to the main text of *An Indian Monk*. Here the copy editor, perhaps Thomas Mark, was content to underscore the words 'the following pages' and write a question mark in the margin, instead of simply deleting the extraneous phrase.

I have found nothing to support an unattributed remark, mentioned in the British Library cataloguing of this item at the British Library, that the corrections are 'said to be' by Yeats. In that copy of *Essays 1931 to 1936*, the copy-editing of each of the four earliest published essays was negated with a later, pencilled comment: 'Not wanted Already in'.[27] Those four essays, 'Bishop Berkeley' (1931), 'My Friend's Book' (1932), 'An Indian Monk' (1932) and 'Prometheus Unbound' (1933), were the only ones in *Essays 1931 to 1936* that had been on Macmillan's 27 October 1936 typewritten list of contents for the Macmillan 'Coole Edition' volume v (as then numbered), *Essays*.[28] For the five other essays in *Essays 1931 to 1936* Macmillan apparently did use that pencilled preliminary copy-editing for the 'Coole Edition', volume XI, *Essays*, of which the page proofs are date-stamped 19 July 1939 (BL Add. Ms. 55895).

The contents, arrangement and copy-texts in those 19 July 1939 proofs of the Macmillan 'Coole Edition', volume XI, *Essays*, are as follows (pp. 1–170 are *Ideas of Good and Evil* and *The Cutting of an Agate*):

'Bishop Berkeley' (1931) pp. 171–86—from Yeats's unmarked copy (O'Shea no. 911a) of Joseph Hone and Mario Rossi, *Bishop Berkeley* (London: Faber & Faber, 1931) pp. xv–xxix, but supplemented with some of the revisions from *Essays 1931 to 1936*.

'My Friend's Book' (1932) pp. 187–93—from a missing typescript or a copy of *The Spectator*, 9 April 1932, pp. 503–4, where it was first published.

'Louis Lambert' (1934) pp. 194–203—from a marked copy of *Essays 1931 to 1936* (BL Add. Ms. 55880).

'Prometheus Unbound' (1933) pp. 204–10—from ts., Macmillan Archive, Basingstoke.

'Parnell' (w. 1936; publ. 1937) pp. 211–14—from a marked copy of *Essays 1931 to 1936* (BL Add. Ms. 55880).

'Gitanjali' (1912) pp. 233–41—probably from a Macmillan copy of *Gitanjali: Song Offerings*, by Rabindranath Tagore (London: Macmillan, 1913 or a later issue) pp. vii–xvi.

'An Indian Monk' (1932) pp. 243–54—probably from a Macmillan copy of *An Indian Monk: His Life and Adventures*, by Shri Purohit Swāmi (London: Macmillan, 1932) pp. xv–xxvi.

'The Mandukya Upanishad' (1935) pp. 255–66—from a marked copy of *Essays 1931 to 1936* (BL Add. Ms. 55880).

'The Holy Mountain' (1934) pp. 267–92—from a marked copy of *Essays 1931 to 1936* (BL Add. Ms. 55880).

'The Ten Principal Upanishads' (w. 1936; publ. 1937) pp. 293–7—from copy-edited ts. 'B', Macmillan Archive, Basingstoke.

'Aphorisms of Yoga' (1937) pp. 298–304, [305 not extant]—from copy-edited ts. 'A', Macmillan Archive, Basingstoke.

'The Midnight Court' (1926) (*P&I* 159–63) pp. [306–11 not extant]—untraced.

'Dorothy Wellesley (1935; publ. 1936) (*P&I* 182–85) pp. [312–16 not extant]—from copy-edited ts. 'C', Macmillan Archive, Basingstoke.
'The Oxford Book of Modern Verse' (1936) pp. [317–20 not extant], 321–48—from copy-edited ts. 'D', Macmillan Archive, Basingstoke.
'The Coinage of Saorstat Eireann' (1928) (*P&I* 166–71) pp. 349–56—from copy-edited ts., Macmillan Archive, Basingstoke.
On the Boiler (w. 1938; publ. 1939) pp. [357]–[409]—from marked and copy-edited page proofs (revised state) (BL Add. Ms. 55881) of *On the Boiler* (Wade 201).

The Macmillan page proofs of volume XI are date-stamped 19 July 1939. A month earlier, 12 June 1939, Thomas Mark at Macmillan had asked for Mrs Yeats's help in answering queries on the proofs for the 'Coole Edition' (BL Add. Ms. 55825): 'I should feel more at ease if you would let me send you my marked proofs of all the volumes before they go to press, as there are always one or two points on which I should like your advice.' Mrs Yeats agreed, but she pointed out that after mid-July she would be busy with a move from Riversdale, Willbrook, Rathfarnham, to 46 Palmerston Road.[29] By 26 June, Thomas Mark had sent her the page proofs of nine of the eleven volumes, and by 14 July she had returned eight of them. The two volumes that she had not yet received were volume V (*Plays* III) and volume XI (Essays II), which contained the essays of interest here.

Thomas Mark sent her the proofs of volume V (*Plays* III) on 4 August, together with the proofs of *Last Poems and Plays*, but unlike before, she did not return them promptly. Thomas Mark became concerned over the delay, and on 31 August he sent another set of those proofs to her, this time via her literary agent (BL Add. Ms 55828). Britain declared war on Germany 3 September 1939, and on 17 October 1939, Harold Macmillan announced the postponement of *Last Poems and Plays* and of the 'Coole Edition' (BL Add. Ms. 55830).

Only then did Mrs Yeats return the proofs of *Last Poems and Plays* and of volume V (*Plays* III). When Thomas Mark wrote on 19 October 1939 to acknowledge receipt of those proofs, he repeated that 'the Coole Edition has to wait for better times', but went on to ask, 'Perhaps you will not mind letting me know if I may now send the proofs of Volume XI, with the typescript of all the new Introductions, and "ON THE BOILER". I understand that there is no difficulty about sending the material to Ireland, but I should like to know that it will be convenient for you to look at it now' (BL Add. Ms. 55830). She, however, did not reply to that request or to his follow-up letter twelve weeks later. After almost six more weeks, on 12 February 1940, he wrote to the literary agent A. S. Watt: 'I wonder if you think that you could do anything by wiring to Mrs. Yeats. I have written to her several times about some outstanding proofs of the big edition of her husband's works, but have had no reply' (BL Add. Ms. 55834). On 20 February 1940, Lovat Dickson of Macmillan, London, informed Charles Kingsley of Scribners, New York, that publication of the 'Coole Edition' had been postponed 'indefinitely', probably 'until after the war'.[30] That apparently was that.

Twenty years later, in 1959, when Macmillan, London, began preparing *Essays and Introductions*, Mrs Yeats was sent the 19 July 1939 page proofs from the 'Coole Edition' (BL Add. Ms. 55895) which were copy-edited (or re-copy-edited) by Thomas Mark, who retired in 1959, and/or by Lovat Dickson, who replaced him at Macmillan, although Mark continued to assist with the production of Yeats texts. Mrs Yeats replied to the queries written on the proofs.

The results of that copy-editing were incorporated in page proofs of *Essays and Introductions* printed in September and October 1959.[31] On 5 May 1960, Lovat Dickson sent a marked set of the 1959 proofs to Mrs Yeats (NLI Ms. 30,775), who replied to queries and paid much attention to improving the accuracy of Yeats's quotations. She returned pages 1–384 (*Ideas of Good and Evil* and *The Cutting of An Agate*, including a section titled 'Explorations') in May 1960, and then returned the other half (pp. 385–532, 'Introductions') at the end of July 1960. At the request of Mrs Yeats, 'A General Introduction' (which was retitled 'A General Introduction for my Work') and 'An Introduction for my Plays' were moved from the opening of the 'Introductions' section (pp. 387 ff.) to the end of the volume (pp. 509 ff.). *Essays and Introductions* (Wade 211T) was published by Macmillan, London, on 16 February 1961, and by Macmillan, New York, on 31 May 1961 (Wade 211U).

Modern Poetry: A Broadcast (1936)

On 21 July 1936 Yeats accepted a request from the British Broadcasting Corporation (BBC) to deliver the eighteenth lecture in the National Programme's Sunday evening 'Broadcast National Lectures' series, for a fee of £1000.[32] The forty-five-minute lecture was closely based on his introduction to *The Oxford Book of Modern Verse*, which he had completed in typescript in December 1935, but even so the surviving manuscript drafts are heavily revised (NLI Ms. 30,327 and NLI Ms. 30,386). The BBC Written Archives Centre, Caversham, Reading, has a typescript[33] that is close to the text that Yeats used when he broadcast the lecture from London on 11 October 1936, 9:05–9:50 P.M., but that typescript does not have a page division at p. 95, l. 7 ('. . . book. // No . . .'), where the turning of a page can be heard on the BBC archival phonograph record. According to the BBC's then standard practice of recording only randomly selected, brief portions of broadcasts, the single archival record contains only one-fifth of the broadcast.[34]

The BBC published the lecture, with minor variants, as 'Modern Poetry', in its magazine *The Listener*, 14 October 1936 (697–99, 739–40), from which it was reprinted in America by *The Living Age*, 351 (December 1936), 330–39, still titled 'Modern Poetry', but with American editorial conventions adopted by that journal; see p. 463 above. Yeats revised the lecture for its publication, in December 1936, by the BBC in a booklet series of the Broadcast National Lectures (Wade 188).

In 1937, when Yeats collected the lecture in *Essays 1931 to 1936*, he deleted an opening announcement about recently having completed an anthology of modern poetry, and he revised the new first sentence and made two additional local verbal revisions. But in what was presumably simply an oversight on his part, he did not use the revised text from the BBC booklet, *Modern Poetry*, and instead reverted to the earlier version from *The Listener*. Thus the text in *Essays 1931 to 1936* ignores all eighteen instances of verbal revision from the BBC booklet, as well as several revisions of punctuation. *Essays 1931 to 1936* was published by the Cuala Press on 14 December 1937, with this essay on pp. 6–29. That was the last version seen by Yeats, and it is the copy-text for the present edition. It was also the copy-text for the Scribners 'Dublin Edition' and the Macmillan 'Coole Edition'. For details of the publishing history of *Essays 1931 to 1936*, and for the subsequent history of this essay in the never-published 'Dublin' and 'Coole' editions, and then in *Essays and Introductions* (1961), see pp. 469–72 above.

Bishop Berkeley (1931)

Bishop Berkeley: His Life, Writings, and Philosophy, published in October 1931, was co-authored by the Irish biographer Joseph Maunsel Hone, who had been a founder of the publishing firm Maunsel and Co. (1905–25) and who later wrote biographies of Thomas Davis (1934), Swift (1934), George Moore (1936), Henry Tonks (1939) and Yeats (1942). His co-author for the biographies of Berkeley and Swift was Dr Mario Manlio Rossi, an Italian teacher of philosophy in Bologna and Naples, who spent the summer of 1931 in Ireland. Hone was the principal author of the Berkeley book; Rossi was the principal author of *Swift or the Egoist* (London: Gollancz, 1934).[35] Yeats had agreed to write an introduction to *Bishop Berkeley* and had received a copy of Hone's portion of the main text prior to 20 November 1930 (*L* 779). Hone, in his biography of Yeats, reported that Yeats wrote the introduction during that winter, in Killiney,[36] ten miles south of Dublin, where Yeats lived from February 1931. Yeats finished the introduction in the first half of July 1931;[37] the extensive manuscript drafts (NLI Ms. 30,516) are undated, and no typescript is extant. The introduction is dated July 1931 in page proofs, which are date-stamped 19 August 1931 (NLI Ms. 30,027). A bibliographical note by Hone and Rossi is dated Killiney, July 1931 (*BB* 273). The book was published in October 1931 in London by Faber & Faber (Wade 280) and in New York by Macmillan, also in 1931. The introduction (pp. xv–xxix) was titled 'Berkeley: An Introduction' and was followed by a signed, undated postscript (p. xxix) that is printed here as Appendix 5 because it was dropped when the introduction was later collected. In that postscript Yeats announces that he had completed the introduction before he read Rossi's contributions, which are about the philosophy and for which Yeats expresses admiration. In a letter to T. Sturge Moore on 25 October 1931, soon after the publication of the book, Yeats gave it measured praise: 'Get Hone and Rossi's *Berkeley* if you subscribe to some library; it is a fine book and I think I have done a fine introduction. It is in part Irish polemics aimed at fools and bigots at home but for all that it is, I am certain, the best Berkeley there is' (*LTSM* 169–70).

When this essay was collected in the Cuala Press *Essays 1931 to 1936*, the text received extensive local revision and the postscript was deleted; those revisions began with pencilled markings added on an old set of Faber & Faber page proofs for *Bishop Berkeley* (date-stamped 19 August 1931, NLI Ms. 30,027), which in 1931 had been marked in ink. *Essays 1931 to 1936* was published by the Cuala Press on 14 December 1937, with this essay on pp. 29–46. That was the last version revised by Yeats and is the copy-text for the present edition. For details of the publishing history of *Essays 1931 to 1936* and for the subsequent history of this essay in the never-published 'Dublin' and 'Coole' editions, and then in *Essays and Introductions* (1961), see pp. 469–72 above. The copy-text for this essay in the 'Dublin Edition' was *Essays 1931 to 1936*, but the 'Coole Edition' page proofs in July 1939 (XI, 171–86) and then also *Essays and Introductions* (pp. 396–411) mistakenly were based on the 1931 text of the essay and were only partially corrected to reflect the 1937 version; see p. 000, note 27 below.

My Friend's Book (1932)

Yeats completed this review of *Song and its Fountains*, by George William Russell ('AE'), on 4 March 1932 at Coole Park. AE's book, which gives autobiographical settings and discussions for a selection of his poems, was published in London by Macmillan on 16 February 1932, while AE was in mourning for the death of his wife on 3 February 1932. Yeats had known AE for nearly fifty years. Since 1922 Yeats had lived at 82 Merrion Square, near the offices of the Irish Agricultural Organization Society at 84 Merrion Square, where AE worked as editor of the *Irish Homestead* and then, from 1923 to 1930, of *The Irish Statesman*; Yeats had been a director of *The Irish Statesman*. In 1933 AE aptly described Yeats as 'my oldest friend and enemy'.[38]

The manuscript (NLI Ms. 30,518) is dated 4 March 1932, although the typescript ribbon copy and carbon copy are undated. The typescript (University of Kansas library, P. S. O'Hegarty collection, Ms. 25.Wc.2), probably typed by Mrs Yeats, has one sentence added in the margin; that revision was not entered on the carbon copy kept by Yeats (NLI Ms. 30,115). The ribbon copy has additional markings by the London journal *The Spectator*, where the essay was first published, as 'My Friend's Book', 9 April 1932, pp. 503–4. Yeats read proof in London after 26 March and presumably at that time made a small revision to the added sentence. The essay was collected (with two minor corrections) in *Spectator's Gallery: Essays, Sketches, Short Stories & Poems from The Spectator 1932*, eds. Peter Fleming and Derek Verschoyle (London: Cape, June 1933) pp. 335–41. Yeats's copy of *The Spectator*, 9 April 1932 (O'Shea no. 1970), was the copy-text when the essay was collected in the Cuala Press *Essays 1931 to 1936*. The essay had seven minor changes in *Essays 1931 to 1936*, which was published by the Cuala Press on 14 December 1937 (pp. 47–54). That was the last version revised by Yeats and is the copy-text for the present edition. For details of the publishing history of *Essays 1931 to 1936* and for the subsequent history of this essay in the never-published 'Dublin' and 'Coole' editions, and then in *Essays and Introductions* (1961), see pp. 469–72 above.

The copy-text for 'My Friend's Book' in the 'Dublin Edition' was *Essays 1931 to 1936* (pp. 47–54). The copy-text for the 'Coole Edition' page proofs in July 1939 (XI, 187–93), and then also for *Essays and Introductions* (pp. 412–18) probably was *The Spectator* or a missing typescript.

Prometheus Unbound (w. 1932; publ. 1933)

Yeats wrote 'Prometheus Unbound' in 1932, and dated its complete manuscript 30 July (NLI Ms. 30,512). Mrs Yeats prepared the typescript (NLI Ms. 30,033). 'Prometheus Unbound' was first published in the London journal *The Spectator*, 17 March 1933 (pp. 366–67), with six minor errors. When the essay was collected in *Essays 1931 to 1936*, published by the Cuala Press on 14 December 1937 (pp. 55–62), those errors were corrected, two revisions of words and seven minor changes of punctuation and capitalisation were introduced, along with four new typographical errors. That was the last version revised by Yeats and is the copy-text for the present edition. For details of the publishing history of *Essays 1931 to 1936* and for the subsequent history of this essay in the never-published 'Dublin' and 'Coole' editions, and then in *Essays and Introductions* (1961), see pp. 469–72 above. The copy-text for 'Prometheus Unbound' in the 'Dublin Edition' was *Essays 1931 to 1936* (pp. 55–62). The copy-text for the 'Coole Edition' page proofs in July 1939 (XI, 204–10), and then also *Essays and Introductions* (pp. 419–25), was a typescript that is in the Macmillan Archive, Basingstoke. Mrs Yeats probably sent that typescript to Macmillan in June 1939 (see p. 480 below).

Louis Lambert (w. 1933; publ. 1934)

In a letter to Olivia Shakespear on 21 February 1933, Yeats announced that he had reread Balzac's *Louis Lambert* and was thinking of writing an 'annotation' of it, perhaps in the voice of the character Michael Robartes (*L* 805). He finished the essay on 4 March.[39] The two revised typescript versions are both titled 'A Note on *Louis Lambert*', although the second has an additional title page that reads 'Notes on Louis Lambert'. The first typescript was prepared by Mrs Yeats, and its second half (pp. 8–11) was replaced with a revised set of pages that were typed on another typewriter and with a different variety of paper.[40]

Either a missing third typescript was prepared or, more likely, Yeats revised the essay in the proofs for its first publication, titled simply 'Louis Lambert', in *The London Mercury*, 30, no. 177, July 1934 (pp. 231–35). A set of pages torn from *The London Mercury*, with five handwritten corrections of spelling, was the copy-text (NLI Ms. 30,152) for the reprinting, with only minor editorial corrections, in *Essays 1931 to 1936*, which was published by the Cuala Press on 14 December 1937 (pp. 63–74). That was the last version revised by Yeats and is the copy-text for the present edition. For details of the publishing history of *Essays 1931 to*

1936 and for the subsequent history of this essay in the never-published 'Dublin' and 'Coole' editions, and then in *Essays and Introductions* (1961), see pp. 469–72 above. The copy-text for 'Louis Lambert' in the 'Dublin Edition' was *Essays 1931 to 1936* (pp. 63–74). The copy-text for the 'Coole Edition' page proofs in July 1939 (XI, 204–10), and then also *Essays and Introductions* (pp. 419–25), was the Macmillan copy of *Essays 1931 to 1936* (BL Add. Ms. 55880).

Introduction to *An Indian Monk* (1932)

Shri Purohit Swāmi and Yeats were introduced on 6 June 1931 at the home of T. Sturge Moore.[41] Yeats wrote to Moore from Coole Park on 13 October 1931, asking for information about the autobiography that Purohit Swāmi was writing. Yeats had not seen any of the work, but he assumed, probably from his prior experience with Rabindranath Tagore, that Purohit Swāmi would need editorial assistance. Yeats asked if Moore was revising the book, and he offered to help 'if it was too great a task for one' (*LTSM* 168). Purohit Swāmi was working swiftly and by 23 October had completed thirty-nine chapters.[42] Moore and then Yeats, in turn, quickly refused to take the lead as editor; they then joined forces in asking George Russell (AE), who refused in December 1931 (*LTSM* 169–70; *LTWBY* 527). By January or February 1932 Moore had agreed to help Purohit Swāmi with the text, and Yeats agreed to write the introduction and to recommend the book to his publisher, Macmillan.[43] His admiration for the content of Purohit Swāmi's book outweighed his considerable distress with Purohit Swāmi's Anglo-Indian prose style.[44]

On 12 April 1932, Yeats delivered the main text of Purohit Swāmi's autobiography to Macmillan, who accepted the book at the start of June 1932 and made plans to publish it in early September.[45] In early August, Yeats was still waiting to receive a proof copy of the autobiography and had not decided whether the introduction would be short or long. Purohit Swāmi wrote to him on 6 August 1932, anxiously asking for a long introduction:

> The least thing that you can do is to interpret in your introduction the spiritual tradition of the West, and draw a parallel—I am sure you can do it. The world expects it from you, along with me. Your introduction to Dr. Tagore's Gitanjali was a fine gesture, but the world expects something more from you, and your introduction to my book ought to be a concrete contribution to the better understanding of the cultures of the two hemispheres. If you feel an urge to write at length, please do it for Heaven's Sake. . . . (*LTWBY* 540–41)

The introduction, which Yeats signed on 5 September 1932, turned out to be only about twenty-five percent longer than his 1912 introduction to *Gitanjali* (see pp. 165–70 above). A complete manuscript is extant (NLI Ms. 30,506) and a complete, uncorrected, smooth typescript (NLI Ms. 30,042), plus two carbon copies (NLI Ms. 30,042). *An Indian Monk: His Life and Adventures*, by Shri Purohit Swāmi (Wade 281), was published by

Macmillan, London, in November 1932, with the introduction on pages xv–xxvi.

The essay was reprinted, as 'Introduction to "An Indian Monk" ', in *Essays 1931 to 1936*, published by the Cuala Press on 14 December 1937 (pp. 74–88). The Cuala Press text had some twenty minor changes of single words, spelling and punctuation, which include six corrections and changes marked in one of Yeats's own copies of *An Indian Monk: His Life and Adventures* (O'Shea no. 2035), but the Cuala Press introduced several typographical errors, one of which was the omission of an entire line of verse. That was the last version seen by Yeats, and is the copy-text for the present edition. For details of the publishing history of *Essays 1931 to 1936* and for the subsequent history of this essay in the never-published 'Dublin' and 'Coole' editions, and then in *Essays and Introductions* (1961), see pp. 469–72 above. The copy-text for 'An Indian Monk' in the 'Dublin Edition' was *Essays 1931 to 1936* (pp. 74–88). The copy-text for the 'Coole Edition' page proofs in July 1939 (XI, 243–54), and then also for *Essays and Introductions* (pp. 426–37), was probably a Macmillan copy of their *An Indian Monk* (pp. xv–xxvi).

Introduction to *The Holy Mountain* (1934)

On 17 August 1933, in a letter to Olivia Shakespear, Yeats announced his introduction to Shri Purohit Swāmi's translation of his master Bhagwān Shri Hamsa's *The Holy Mountain*: 'If you see the Swāmi tell him that I have now finished study of various authorities and am about to start my essay upon his master's journey in Tibet' (*L* 813). The heavily revised manuscript (NLI Ms. 13,566) is titled 'Mount Meru' and lacks only the postscript and the biographical note. Nine weeks later he reported to Olivia Shakespear that he planned to come to London in November 'to go through my essay on the Tibetan travels of his Master with the Swāmi. This essay—seven or eight thousand words—has taken me two months at least, has grown to have great importance in my scheme of things' (24 October [1933], *L* 815). That matches the word count (8,086) of a heavily revised typescript, titled 'The Holy Mountain', which is now in the H. Lytton Wilson Collection at Southern Illinois University.[46] On 11 November 1933, Yeats was waiting for his Dublin typist to complete 'the corrected copy' of the 'already dictated essay'. I have not located that smooth typescript, which presumably was finished before Yeats travelled to London in early December.

Faber and Faber, London, accepted the book in January 1934 (*L* 819). Yeats saw the final proofs for the entire book in May 1934, and he praised it to Olivia Shakespear:

> It seems to me one of those rare books that are fundamental. For generations writers will refer to it as they will to *An Indian Monk*. The Swāmi will fulfill the prophecy of his astrologers 'Preach to the whole world'. . . . Two such books will shift for those, who move others, the foundations of their thought, but it will take years. ([postmark 1 June 1934], *L* 823)

In September 1934, Faber and Faber published *The Holy Mountain: Being the Story of a Pilgrimage to Lake Mānas and of Initiation on Mount Kailās in Tibet*, by Bhagwān Shri Hamsa, translated by Shri Purohit Swāmi from the Marāthi (Wade 282). Yeats's contributions were the introduction (pp. 11–41), signed 'W.B.Y.'; an unsigned postscript (p. 41); and 'A Biographical Note' (p. 43), signed 'W.B.Y.' I have not found any manuscripts or typescripts for the postscript or the biographical note.

In July 1934, two months before Faber and Faber published the book, a slightly earlier version of Yeats's introduction appeared as the lead article in a journal also published by Faber and Faber, *The Criterion: A Literary Review*, 13, pp. 537–57. In that version, titled 'Initiation upon a Mountain', section IV had not yet been divided into the new sections IV and V that are used in the book and all subsequent printings. The *Criterion* text included the postscript but not the biographical note. It also lacked numerous local changes that were adopted in the book version, notably a major revision of a parenthetical comment, from '(I think of Schopenhauer's essay upon Love)' (TS f. 13; *Criterion* 553) to '(Schopenhauer's essay upon Love reversed)' (*HM* 37 and in all subsequent printings). Yeats considered that particular revision to be important enough for it to be the only correction that he entered on a set of pages removed from a bound copy of the *Criterion*, perhaps for use as an off-print.[47]

The introduction, postscript and biographical note were reprinted from *The Holy Mountain*, with minor changes,[48] in the Cuala Press *Essays 1931 to 1936*, published on 14 December 1937 (pp. 88–118). That was the last version revised by Yeats and is the copy-text for the present edition. For details of the publishing history of *Essays 1931 to 1936* and for the subsequent history of this essay in the never-published 'Dublin' and 'Coole' editions, and then in *Essays and Introductions* (1961), see pp. 469–72 above. The copy-text for 'The Holy Mountain' in the 'Dublin Edition' was *Essays 1931 to 1936* (pp. 88–118). The copy-text for the 'Coole Edition' page proofs in July 1939 (XI, 267–92), and then also *Essays and Introductions* (pp. 448–73), was the Macmillan copy of *Essays 1931 to 1936* (BL Add. Ms. 55880).

Introduction to 'Mandukya Upanishad' (1935)

Shri Purohit Swāmi's two-page translation of the Mandukya Upanishad was published July 1935 with a nine-page introduction by Yeats, as 'Mandookya Upanishad with an Introduction by William Butler Yeats', in *The Criterion*, 14, pp. 547–56 (introduction) and 556–58 (text). Two manuscripts of the introduction are extant, a partial draft (NLI Ms. 30,507) and a revised final version (NLI Ms. 30,505), from which a missing typescript presumably was transcribed.

Faber and Faber, publishers of *The Criterion*, also published *The Ten Principal Upanishads* (1937), which included a much revised version of the text of the Mandukya Upanishad, with a different introduction by Yeats (see p. 480 below).

Yeats's introduction to 'Mandukya Upanishad' was reprinted with only minor changes in *Essays 1931 to 1936*, which was published by the Cuala Press on 14 December 1937 (pp. 118–32). That was the last version revised by Yeats and is the copy-text for the present edition. For details of the publishing history of *Essays 1931 to 1936* and for the subsequent history of this essay in the never-published 'Dublin' and 'Coole' editions, and then in *Essays and Introductions* (1961), see pp. 469–72 above. The copy-text for 'Mandukya Upanishad' in the 'Dublin Edition' was *Essays 1931 to 1936* (pp. 118–32). The copy-text for the 'Coole Edition' page proofs in July 1939 (XI, 255–66), and then also *Essays and Introductions* (pp. 474–85), was the Macmillan copy of *Essays 1931 to 1936* (BL Add. Ms. 55880).

Gitanjali (1912)

Yeats first met the Indian poet Rabindranath Tagore on 27 June 1912 in London, at the home of William Rothenstein.[49] That summer Rothenstein and Yeats helped to select and edit Tagore's prose translations of his Bengali poems. Yeats volunteered to donate an introduction,[50] and he finished the second of two complete manuscript drafts of it in the first week of September 1912. Mary Lago has pointed out that the introduction echoes Yeats's remarks when toasting Tagore at an India Society dinner, 10 July 1912.[51] A typewritten transcription of the manuscript was made 7–9 September, and Yeats then revised the typescript before sending it to Rothenstein.[52] In a letter to Rothenstein on 7 September, Yeats mentioned that he was anxious about the accuracy of biographical information in the opening section of his introduction.[53] On 16 September, Rothenstein wrote to tell Yeats that Tagore suggested two changes, which were adopted: revision of 'Calcutta Indian' to 'Bengali' in a reference to Dr D. N. Maitra, and deletion of 'Raja Sourendra Tagore, a musician' from a list of great men in Tagore's family.[54] *Gitanjali (Song Offerings): A Collection of Prose Translations Made by the Author from the Original Bengali* was published by the Chiswick Press, London, in November 1912 for the India Society (Wade 263); Yeats's introduction (pp. vii–xvi) is dated September 1912. When Macmillan, London, published the first public edition (Wade 264) in March 1913, the introduction (vii–xxii) was very lightly revised, perhaps by the publisher, and it acquired a few typographical errors. The two most prominent errors (an omitted closing quotation mark at p. xiii, l. 6, and 'tops' rather than 'top' at p. xiii, l. 10) were corrected prior to the Macmillan, London, reissue in 1931, from which Yeats sent unmarked pages (vii–xxii) in 1937 to Scribners, New York, as copy-text for the never-published 'Dublin Edition' (HRC Texas, Scribners papers, box 4, vol. XI). Those pages are the copy-text for the present edition.[55] The copy-text for the Macmillan 'Coole Edition' page proofs in July 1939 (XI, 233–41), and then also for *Essays and Introductions* (pp. 387–95), was probably a Macmillan, London, copy of a 1930s reissue of *Gitanjali (Song Offerings)* (pp. vii–xvi). Perhaps because of Macmillan's frequent reprintings of *Gitanjali*, spurred especially by the award of a Nobel Prize for Literature to Tagore in November 1913, this introduction was not collected in *Essays* 1924 (Wade 141–42) or in *Essays 1931 to 1936*. For details of the publishing history of this essay in the never-published 'Dublin' and 'Coole' editions, and then in *Essays and Introductions* (1961), see pp. 469–72 above.

The Ten Principal Upanishads (w. 1936; dated and publ. 1937)

In July 1935, when Shri Purohit Swāmi's English translation of the Mandukya Upanishad and an introduction by Yeats were published, Yeats had already made plans to spend the winter with Purohit Swāmi in 'some warm place' and to 'put his translation of the *Upanishads* into good English'.[56] Purohit Swāmi and Yeats worked on the translations in Palma de Majorca from December 1935 until April 1936, with an interruption during January and February, when Yeats was seriously ill. On 19 April 1936, Yeats announced to Dorothy Wellesley that during the remaining month or so of his stay in Palma he would write a preface to *The Ten Principal Upanishads* (*LDW* 65 and *L* 853). A signed but undated manuscript is extant (NLI Ms. 30,530). Later that same month, Purohit Swāmi and he had begun work on a new project, Purohit Swāmi's translation of the *Aphorisms of Yôga* by Patanjali.[57] Yeats left Palma on 26 May 1936, a week after Purohit Swāmi had left for India.

Faber and Faber accepted *The Ten Principal Upanishads* in August. Yeats read the galley proofs in November 1936 and page proofs in February 1937. The book, with Yeats's preface on pages 7–12, was published in London in April 1937 (Wade 252) and in New York by Macmillan, also in 1937 (Wade 253).[58] In March 1938, Faber and Faber issued a second edition of *The Ten Principal Upanishads* that corrected some minor errors; it is the copy-text for the present edition.

Probably in April or May 1939, Mrs Yeats or a typist whom she hired prepared a group of transcriptions of four essays that had not been included in *Essays 1931 to 1936*. She sent the typed transcriptions to Macmillan and Scribners in June 1939, when they were assembling materials for their collected editions of Yeats's works.[59] In that set of typewritten transcriptions, the preface to *The Ten Principal Upanishads* was labelled with a typewritten 'B' at the top left corner. The other three essays, labelled 'A', 'C' and 'D', were 'Aphorisms of Yoga' (1938), 'Selections from the Poems of Dorothy Wellesley' (publ. 1936)[60] and 'The Oxford Book of Modern Verse' (1936). The ribbon copy of each was sent to Macmillan, London, for the 'Coole Edition' (Macmillan Archive, Basingstoke); one carbon copy of each was sent to Scribners, New York, for the 'Dublin Edition' (HRC Texas, Scribners papers, box 4, vol. XI); and Mrs Yeats kept one carbon copy of each.[61] Macmillan, London, copy-edited all four of those typewritten transcriptions and used them as copy-texts for the 'Coole Edition' volume XI proofs (date-stamped 19 July 1939).[62]

In the set of four typewritten transcriptions, the preface to *The Ten Principal Upanishads* mistakenly was made from a copy of the 1937 first edition (O'Shea no. 2114) rather than the revised second edition of March

1938. That oversight might simply have been the result of Mrs Yeats not having a copy of the second edition readily at hand, since Yeats's library has four copies of the first edition (O'Shea nos. 2114–2114Aa), but none of the second edition.

For the subsequent history of this preface in the 'Dublin Edition' and the 'Coole Edition', see pp. 469–72 above. 'The Ten Principal Upanishads' was not reprinted in *Essays and Introductions* (1961) or *Explorations* (1962).

Aphorisms of Yoga (1938)

During April and May 1936, in Palma de Majorca, Yeats helped Shri Purohit Swāmi with his translation of *Aphorisms of Yôga*, by Bhagwān Shree Patanjali. Yeats then returned to Ireland and Purohit Swāmi went on to India. In May 1937, Faber and Faber accepted the book, and Yeats agreed to write the preface, at the suggestion of T. S. Eliot, the editor at Faber and Faber.[63]

Yeats began the preface probably in October 1937, before he had received the corrected proofs of the book, which Purohit Swāmi mailed from Bombay on 11 November 1937.[64] When the proofs arrived, Yeats recast his first draft of the preface so that it 'took a completely different track', as he told Dorothy Wellesley on 1 December (*LDW* 165). Some fragments and a complete manuscript are extant, along with two revised typescripts.[65] Yeats mailed a copy of the second typescript version of the preface to Purohit Swāmi, in Bombay. Then, on 25 January 1938, Purohit Swāmi sent to Yeats a list of spelling suggestions for Indian words and pointed out an error in a name; Yeats adopted all of those corrections.

Aphorisms of Yoga was first published in June 1938 by Faber and Faber, London (Wade 286), with the preface (pp. 11–21) dated 'Dublin 1937'. That was the last version revised by Yeats and is the copy-text for the present edition. It was also the copy-text for 'Aphorisms of Yoga' in a carelessly typed transcription, made probably in April or May 1939 (see p. 480 above), and for the Macmillan 'Coole Edition' page proofs (XI, 298–[305]; p. 305 is missing) in July 1939. For the subsequent history of this preface in the 'Dublin Edition' and the 'Coole Edition', see pp. 469–72 above. The preface to *Aphorisms of Yoga* was not reprinted in *Essays and Introductions* (1961) or *Explorations* (1962).

Introduction to *The Oxford Book of Modern Verse* (1936)

Yeats accepted the editorship of *The Oxford Book of Modern Verse* in October or November 1934,[66] and he chose the poems for the anthology from wide reading during February through October 1935. He completed a manuscript draft of the introduction (NLI Ms. 30,522) probably before mid-October. Mrs Yeats prepared a series of three typescripts that Yeats revised extensively; the second has a typewritten date of 15 November 1935.[67] Soon afterwards he added the lengthy first paragraph of section

XVIII ('That I might follow a theme . . .'), for which a heavily revised manuscript is extant (NLI Ms. 30,295). On 27 November he reported in a letter to Charles Williams, editor at the Oxford University Press office in London, 'I have finished my introduction (about thirty pages) finished except for verbal revisions which I will do in Majorca. My wife thinks it is [the] best bit of prose I have written for years. I leave for Majorca to-morrow.'[68] Two weeks later he mailed the corrected third typescript to Mrs Yeats from Majorca.[69]

The Oxford University Press received the introduction and text of the anthology, complete except for the acknowledgements, on 30 April 1936. The page proofs of the introduction were date-stamped 4 June 1936 by the Clarendon Press, Oxford (NLI Ms. 30,522). Yeats and his wife were still reading proofs in August 1936. The introduction, which had been dated 15 November 1935 in the second typescript, and which was undated in the third typescript and in the 4 June 1936 page proofs, was published with the date September 1936. Yeats announced, in a letter of 12 November to Olivia Shakespear, that the book had not yet been released because 'trouble about some omitted acknowledgements to publishers has made an errata slip necessary' but that the advance orders were double the size of the entire first edition (*L* 866). *The Oxford Book of Modern Verse* (Wade 250) was published 19 November 1936 at the Clarendon Press, Oxford, with a pasted-in sheet (pp. xlvii–xlviii) that corrected some omissions from the acknowledgements list (Wade 259).

The book attracted immediate, wide notice, with many complaints about the idiosyncrasy both of Yeats's opinions in the introduction and of his choice of poems. On 9 December he reported somewhat gleefully to Dorothy Wellesley: 'The Oxford University Press has congratulated me on my "courage" in stirring up "such a hornet's nest" and offers me a further advance on royalties.' (*LDW* 121–22) Jon Stallworthy has cited as an 'admirably balanced review', that of Stuart H. Hampshire in *The Oxford Magazine*: 'It is the prose, not the verse, which makes this book magnificent and exciting. The Introduction is a contribution to any future anthology of English prose, the rest does not even afford the raw material for an adequate anthology of modern verse.'[70]

The first American edition (Wade 251), which was published in November or early December 1936 by the Oxford University Press, New York, was a completely different typesetting from the Oxford edition and was printed in the U.S.A. The American edition corrected a missing full stop at the end of section XV, but also introduced two typographical errors: 'filagreed' (rather than 'filigreed'; p. 197, l. 1 above) and 'descent in Hades' (rather than 'descent into Hades'; p. 200, l. 4 above). It completely revised the acknowledgements.

Fifteen thousand copies were sold in the first three months (*LDW* 146), and seventeen years later the British sales continued at 2,000 to 3,000 copies a year.[71] The British reprints began with an urgent order, dated 25 November 1936 and annotated: 'Corrections as per working copy. New copy for acknowledgement follows today'.[72] That second issue was published in December 1936, and Yeats owned four copies of it (O'Shea nos. 2454b–e).

The introduction to *The Oxford Book of Modern Verse* was to be included in both the never-published Scribners 'Dublin Edition' and Macmillan 'Coole Edition'. Two of Yeats's copies of the Oxford, December 1936 issue (O'Shea nos. 2454b,c) were revised in pen-and-ink to cancel the introduction's title and last paragraph. From one of those marked copies (O'Shea no. 2454c), Yeats removed the introduction pages and sent them to Scribners, New York, in October 1937, as part of a packet of copy-texts for what was then volume v, *Essays*, in the Scribners collected edition.[73] Those pages are the copy-text for the present edition.

Despite the mention of 'corrections as per working copy' in six of the thirteen British reprinting orders prior to a resetting in 1972,[74] the printing errors were never consistently eliminated. For example, in the introduction the British editions in 1972 and 1978 continued to lack a full stop at the end of section xxxv. Among the poems in the anthology, two of W. H. Auden's untitled poems, which begin 'This lunar beauty' and 'Before this loved one', were mistakenly run together as a single poem in the first three British issues. Then, after Yeats mentioned the error in a letter to the Oxford University Press in March 1937, the two poems were separated (and renumbered as 368 and 368a) in the 1938 issue, but the error was reinstated in 1966 and remains in the resetting in 1972 and in the 1978 reissue (see p. 405, note 91 above), although 'Before this loved one' was retained in the index of first lines. The error was never corrected in the five reprintings of the New York edition to 1966.

The second of Yeats's identically marked copies of the Oxford, December 1936 issue was the copy-text for a typewritten transcription that was prepared, probably in April or May 1939, as part of a set of typescripts[75] of four essays that had been published subsequent to those collected in the Cuala Press *Essays 1931 to 1936* (published 14 December 1937). That typewritten transcription was copy-edited at Macmillan, London, and was then used as the copy-text for 'Coole Edition' page proofs (xi, [317–20 not extant], 321–48) date-stamped 19 July 1939 (BL Add. Ms. 55895). The introduction was not reprinted in *Essays and Introductions* (1961) or *Explorations* (1962).

Introduction [1961 title: A General Introduction for my Work] and Introduction to Essays (w. 1937; publ. 1961)

Charles Scribner's Sons, New York, buoyed by the success of their limited editions of Shelley and of Eugene O'Neill, began planning in October 1935 for a similar edition of Keats and then, if Macmillan would consent, a collected edition of Yeats.[76] At lunch on 7 November 1935, George P. Brett, Jr., president of Macmillan, New York, agreed to the proposal for a limited definitive edition, from which Macmillan would receive ten percent. The specific plans, as settled during the next month, were for a collected edition, as yet unnamed, in 750 sets of eight volumes at $10 per volume, with Yeats to sign one sheet and write three short introductions 'of a page or two' for 'the three natural divisions of the set—namely, Poems, Plays, and Essays'.[77] On 24 February 1936, after Yeats already had received information on the 'business details' of the project, John Hall Wheelock, an editor at Scribners, New York, wrote to Yeats to encourage him to write a large number of prefaces for this 'beautiful, limited edition of your complete works': 'We have published some twenty or thirty authors, perhaps, in this form, among them a few contemporary writers, and the list contains such names as Shelley, Stevenson, Kipling, Barrie, Galsworthy. The idea would be that you would sign each of the seven hundred and fifty sets, and we think that the set would run to eight or ten volumes. I feel very strongly that a brief introduction or preface especially written by you for each volume would greatly enhance the value of the set. It is the sort of thing that you do better than any one else. The work contained in each volume would naturally fall into classifications, such as "Early Poems", "Later Poems", etc., and the prefaces would embody, in brief compass, whatever you had in mind to say regarding these general divisions of your work.'[78] Yeats countered with an offer to write an introduction for the set, but not for each volume.[79] During the next several months an agreement was settled for three or four introductions, in the form of 'an introductory or general preface to the Edition, and brief prefaces to the poems, the plays, and the essays'.[80]

On 11 April 1937, when Yeats began writing the general introduction, he mentioned to Dorothy Wellesley that the introduction 'may develop into an essay on the nature of poetry or into that in part' (*LDW* 148). The ambitious extent of that general introduction had the advantage of allowing him to avoid writing a separate introduction to the poems, thus reducing the total number of introductions to three. He twice mentioned the project during May 1937, reporting to Ethel Mannin on May 24 (*L* 889): 'I have been busy and bothered. I am writing a general introduction and short prefaces for an expensive American collected edition of my works and I hate writing prose. The only kind of prose I can write is a great toil.' By June 22 he perhaps had finished the manuscript draft of the general introduction (NLI Ms. 30,395 and NLI Ms. 30,798) and had moved on to manuscript drafts of the introductions to essays (NLI Ms. 30,395) and to plays (NLI Ms. 30,395). By the end of the summer he had extensively revised a typescript (NLI Ms. 30,798) prepared from the manuscript of the general introduction, and another typescript (NLI Ms. 30,628) that was dictated from the manuscript of the introduction to essays. On 5 October 1937 Yeats told his literary agent that a smooth copy of each of the three introductions was being typed; Mrs Yeats prepared those from the revised typescripts.[81] The smooth typescript of the introduction to essays was extensively revised in pen-and-ink before it was mailed by Mrs Yeats to the literary agent, A. P. Watt & Son, London. On 15 October 1937 the three typewritten introductions were forwarded to Charles Kingsley, the London representative of Scribners.[82]

The Scribners editor in New York, presumably John Henry Wheelock, did nothing except to label the typescripts in black pencil 'General Introduction to Yeats' and, on the introduction to essays, 'Vol V—Yeats'. Those marked typescripts then were stored in a safe, together with the rest of the copy-texts for the Scribners 'Dublin Edition', where they remained throughout 1938, while work proceeded on assembling a set of frontispiece illustrations. On 24 June 1938 John Henry Wheelock, Scribners, New York, notified Yeats's literary agent that the 'Dublin Edition' would follow their limited, eight-volume 'Hampstead Edition' of John Keats, which was published 1938–39.[83] As of 5 January 1939, some three weeks prior to Yeats's death, Scribners planned to begin work on the layout and general format in March 1939 and to publish the 'first volume or so' in autumn 1939.[84]

When Yeats died on 27 January 1939, Scribners expanded their plans for the 'Dublin Edition' by adding all of Yeats's works published since 1937, so that the edition increased to eleven volumes. Macmillan, London, began moving vigorously with its 'Edition de Luxe', which later that spring was named the 'Coole Edition' and expanded to eleven volumes. Scribners and Macmillan, London, sparred and feinted—in the decorously gentlemanly manner that still reigned in publishers' business correspondence—over the three unpublished introductions, which were in the possession of Scribners, and which Macmillan, London, had never seen. On 21 April 1939, Thomas Mark, the editor at Macmillan, London, sent Mrs Yeats a revised prospectus (BL Add. Ms. 55890) that announced the 'Coole Edition' would be published in autumn 1939 in 350 sets, royal octavo, bound in blue buckram with gilt tops, at sixteen and one-half guineas. In his letter he mentioned, 'By the way, Scribners refer in a letter to three or four brief prefaces which Mr. Yeats wrote for their Dublin Edition. Are they exclusively for that edition or will they also appear in ours?'[85] A month later, John Hall Wheelock at Scribners, New York, received an inquiry from Macmillan, London: 'We should be interested to see the general introduction and the three [*sic*] prefaces which Mr Yeats supplied for your edition if you would be good enough to send us proofs of these.'[86] Scribners was not disposed to share the introductions. Harold Macmillan tried once again with Mrs Yeats about the introductions, on 2 June 1939: 'In a recent letter Messrs. Scribners say "As you probably know, Mr. Yeats wrote for our edition a general introduction of about 28 pp. and three [*sic*, two] prefaces of about 7 or 8 pp. each, which are of very great value as casting light upon his theory of poetry and his methods of composition." I wonder if this material relates exclusively to The Dublin Edition or whether we might also have it for ours. I am sorry to trouble you with all these matters, but there is still so much to be done as regards The Coole Edition, and the autumn will all too soon be on us.'[87] Then, on 13 June 1939, Thomas Mark composed a letter, signed by Harold Macmillan, to Mrs Yeats: 'As regards the Prefaces written specially for the Scribner edition, I have come to the conclusion that The Coole Edition might very well dispense with them, especially as they will no doubt contain some token of the particular purpose for which they were written.'[88]

In the autumn of 1939, both the Macmillan and the Scribners editions were postponed, and then eventually abandoned, because of the unfavorable economic condition of the book market.[89] But the Scribners introductions continued to have a life of their own. Morton Dauwen Zabel, a University of Chicago professor who was a friend of John Hall Wheelock, obtained photostatic copies of the three introductions from Scribners in February 1941, and mentioned them in a Yeats commemorative issue of

The Southern Review (Winter 1941–42).[90] In 1946 two more scholars, Richard Ellmann and Marion Witt, were allowed to read the introductions, but not to quote from them.[91]

Scribners retained some hope of publishing the 'Dublin Edition' as late as 1949, and then gave 'a good deal of consideration to the possibility' of using their supply of autographed sheets and illustrations for the 'Dublin Edition' in a limited edition of 'a small volume which would contain the three Prefaces, hitherto unpublished' with one or two of the illustrations and an autographed flyleaf.[92] But in January 1953 they unsuccessfully offered the materials to Macmillan, New York, for $4,000 and then, in September, sent photostatic copies of the introductions to Macmillan, New York, who replied that they had no immediate prospect for using the introductions.[93] But the next year, Macmillan, New York, considered adding the general 'Introduction' to a projected new edition of *Collected Poems*. At that time, John Hall Wheelock at Scribners checked his company's files for any record of whether Yeats had been paid an advance. However, Wheelock mistakenly searched the files for 1934 instead of 1935, when Yeats first had agreed to the project, or 1936, when Scribners reached an accord with Macmillan, London. Finding nothing, he generously suggested that any payment for publication of the introductions should go to the Yeats estate rather than to Scribners.[94]

Meanwhile in Dublin, Curtis Bradford, an American scholar working at the home of Mrs Yeats, had prepared extensively edited transcriptions of the three introductions, and Mrs Yeats gave permission for him to offer the edited versions to *Encounter* in England and to the *Kenyon Review* in America. However, when he wrote to Scribners on 6 September 1955 about the introductions, Scribners simply referred him to Macmillan, New York, and Bradford's project stopped.[95]

The next step in the introductions' labored passage into print began in New York on the morning of 27 September 1955, when probably Macmillan, New York, prepared a set of photostatic copies from their September 1953 photostatic copies of the typescripts held by Scribners. The new photostatic copies, which included the few markings made by the editor at Scribners in 1937–39, were sent to Macmillan, London, where they received extensive copy-editing, first in black pencil and then in blue ball-point pen, and finally were marked in green pencil by the printer of the first version of *Essays and Introductions* in 1959.[96]

The Macmillan, London, copy-editing revisions of the general 'Introduction' (retitled 'A General Introduction') and 'Introduction to Essays' (retitled 'Introduction') for the 1959 page proofs of *Essays and Introductions*,[97] although frequent (172 in the general 'Introduction' and 43 in 'Introduction to Essays'), were mostly straightforward corrections and regularisations that could have been made without any need to consult an earlier typescript or manuscript. However, a few emendations in 'A General Introduction', as mentioned on p. xi above, presumably came from a preliminary typescript and a manuscript in the possession of Mrs Yeats. I have not found explicit evidence of the date when Mrs Yeats provided those emendations, but they were marked on the copy-edited photostatic copy from which the 1959 page proofs of *Essays and Introductions* were set.

On 5 May 1960, Lovat Dickson, editor at Macmillan, London, sent Mrs Yeats a complete set of the 1959 page proofs of *Essays and Introductions*, 'together with the photostats of the three new Introductions which were sent us from America'. In a conversation with Lovat Dickson, prior to the preparation of this volume, she had discussed the selection of its contents, but this was her first view of the printed text of the Scribners introductions. Lovat Dickson continued, 'I do not think that the first part of the book will give you much trouble'—that portion of the volume was reprinted from the Macmillan *Essays* (1924)—'but there are a good many points to be settled in the second part, the Introductions. This part contains the material which you approved when we had a talk about the volume'. He made advance arrangements to pick up the proofs from her and to 'answer any queries' she might have about the proofs, on 22 May, when he would be travelling through Dublin.[98] On 11 August 1960, when Lovat Dickson returned from holiday, he wrote Mrs Yeats to thank her for an additional correction to a quotation from Toynbee (p. 209, ll. 17–21 above) and told her, 'We will, of course, use your version' (NLI Ms. 30,755).

Most of the editorial emendations (100 of 107) that I have made to the general 'Introduction' also had been used in *Essays and Introductions*. In 'Introduction to Essays', 30 of the 36 emendations that I have made were also used in *Essays and Introductions*. On the other hand, I have not adopted 82 other editorial emendations that were made in *Essays and Introductions* to the text of the general 'Introduction' and 14 emendations to 'Introduction to Essays'. Perhaps most of those unadopted posthumous emendations carry the authority of Mrs Yeats's opinion, but, on the other hand, none of those unadopted emendations was made sooner than twenty years after the last time that Yeats had worked on these texts.[99]

E&I was published 16 February 1961 by Macmillan, London (Wade 211T), and on 31 May 1961 by Macmillan, New York, with 'Introduction to Essays' (retitled 'Introduction') on pp. vii–xi and the general 'Introduction' (retitled 'A General Introduction for my Work') on pp. 509–26.

Both introductions, together with 'Introduction for my Plays', were published with explanatory annotation in an edition by Edward Callan, *Yeats on Yeats: The Last Introductions and the 'Dublin' Edition*, New Yeats Papers 20 (Mountrath, Portlaoise: Dolmen Press, 1981; Atlantic Highlands, NJ: Humanities Press, 1981) pp. 40–73, 77–80. That edition usefully includes twenty letters, written between 1935 and 1953, about arrangements for the 'Dublin Edition'.[100]

On the Boiler (w. 1938; publ. 1939)

In November 1937, Yeats began planning *On the Boiler*, which was to be a semi-annual miscellany with its first issue in spring (Beltaine) 1938. At that time the Cuala Press urgently needed to increase its income. The practical necessity of producing revenue for the Cuala Press did nothing to quiet Yeats's increasing relish for controversy, and the example of strong sales by his *Oxford Book of Modern Verse* could even have encouraged him to think of *On the Boiler* as parallel to John Ruskin's outspoken miscellany,

Fors Clavigera (1871–84). On 17 December 1937, when Yeats was beginning the manuscript of *On the Boiler*, he announced in a letter to Dorothy Wellesley: 'For the first time in my life I am saying what are my political beliefs. . . . I shall lose friends if I am able to get on to paper the passion that is in my head. I shall go on to poetry and the arts, and shall be not less inimical to contemporary taste' (*LDW* 166 and *L* 902). And in another letter written that same day, he told Ethel Mannin: 'I must in the first number discuss social politics in so far as they affect Ireland. I must lay aside the pleasant paths I have built up for years and seek the brutality, the ill breeding, the barbarism of truth. Pray for me, my dear, I want an atheist's prayers, no Christian can do me any good' (*L* 903).

He had finished an early portion of the manuscript by 4 January 1938 and completed a full draft by 3 March 1938.[101] Yeats was in the south of France from early January through 19 March 1938. The first typescript, dictated to Mrs Yeats, contains an early version of 'To-morrow's Revolution' and of the first two sections of 'Private Thoughts' (pp. 226–33 above); a carbon copy is extant of that central portion of *On the Boiler* (NLI Ms. 30,551). By 8 March, a full typescript had been completed and corrected (NLI Ms. 30,461). After nearly completing *On the Boiler* Yeats turned to writing the play *Purgatory*, which occupied him in the second half of March and continued through April and into May 1938.[102] From 23 March he was in London and Sussex, where he visited with Edith Shackleton Heald at Steyning and with Dorothy Wellesley at Penns in the Rocks.

In the first week of May he added three short new sections to *On the Boiler*.[103] A smooth typescript was made after 13 May 1938, when he returned to Ireland (NLI Ms. 30,552). In 1954–55 and 1960 at the home of Mrs Yeats, the late Curtis Bradford studied the extant partial manuscript and three typescripts, plus carbon copies with some separate revisions; he published a carefully detailed account of those materials in 1965.[104]

Yeats's friend F. R. Higgins, a poet and director of the Abbey Theatre, returned to Dublin at the end of May with the Abbey Players, who had been on an eight-month tour in America. Higgins probably was the source for at least one of the two footnotes that Yeats added on pasted-in slips to the smooth typescript (pp. 432, note 59 and 433, note 76 below). In mid-June, while on a visit to England, Yeats confidently announced that the first number of *On the Boiler* would be published 'in about a month', and he began to talk about its second number.[105] Then, before Yeats left on 8 or 9 July 1938 for a month in England, he made some more additions, such as the poem 'I am tired of cursing the Bishop' (p. 243 above), which became section IV of 'After the Revolution', and probably a footnote that refers to the Anglo-Irish Agreements that were signed 25 April 1938 (p. 436, note 94 above).

Yeats left the typescript of *On the Boiler* with F. R. Higgins, who was to send it to the printer.[106] *On the Boiler* was to be produced by a commercial printer and then be published under the imprint of the Cuala Press, thus avoiding the limited print runs, higher production costs and slower speed of the hand-operated printing press at the Cuala Press. But, in an act that Yeats later described as 'pure eccentricity', Higgins chose a small, relatively inexperienced printing firm, Longford Printing Press, in Longford, seventy miles from Dublin.[107] The result was a series of delays and very poorly executed work at every phase, from design through typesetting and printing. On 4 September 1938, Yeats reported that *On the Boiler* had 'at last gone to the press' (*L* 915), and sometime during September or October he corrected its galley proofs, which are not extant.[108] At the end of October he left Ireland for England and then the south of France, where Mrs Yeats and he corrected the first state of the page proofs (NLI Ms. 30,154), probably during the last week of December 1938 or in early January 1939. He sent one set of marked proofs to Higgins, with an undated cover letter; but, according to Richard J. Finneran's plausible conjecture, Higgins, probably in poor health and overworked with Abbey Theatre business, returned the proofs to Yeats and withdrew from the project.[109] On 10 January 1939, Yeats mailed those marked proofs (or perhaps the duplicate set) directly to the Longford Printing Press, and he requested that a set of revised page proofs be sent to him when the corrections had been made.[110] Two marked sets of the first state of the page proofs are extant, a set (NLI Ms. 30,485) that the printer probably returned to Mrs Yeats with the revised page proofs, and a duplicate set onto which Yeats or Mrs Yeats had copied all the corrections.[111]

Yeats died on 28 January, before the Longford Printing Press completed the revised page proofs. Probably Mrs Yeats read those revised page proofs; one set is extant (BL Add. Ms. 55881). The Cuala Press advertised that *On the Boiler* would be ready in May, but encountered further delays in the printing by the Longford Printing Press, so that on 9 June 1939 the Cuala Press described the planned date of publication of *On the Boiler* as still 'two weeks' away.[112]

Soon after Yeats's death, both Macmillan and Scribners had begun plans to add recent and posthumous works to the 'Coole' and 'Dublin' collected editions. At the start of June, Macmillan needed copy immediately for the 'Coole Edition' because *On the Boiler* was scheduled for volume VIII (*Autobiographies II*), which reached page proofs by 21 June. Thus when Harold Macmillan asked Mrs Yeats, on 2 June, for a copy of *On the Boiler*, she promptly sent him the page proofs of the revised state.[113] That set of page proofs, marked by Mrs Yeats to correspond with the still not yet published book (Wade 201), then was copy-edited by Thomas Mark at Macmillan. In the middle of June, *On the Boiler* was moved to volume XI (*Essays*), of which the page proofs are date-stamped 19 July 1939 (BL Add. Ms. 55895).[114]

Scribners also wanted *On the Boiler*, but their first volume, planned for October 1939, was *Poems*. During the spring Mrs Yeats therefore concentrated on providing them the additional poems needed for that volume, rather than sending copy for *On the Boiler*, which was planned for volume VII in the expanded Scribners 'Dublin Edition'. She certainly would have expected to have been able to furnish Scribners a copy of the published book, rather than page proofs. But when she sent Scribners a large packet of copy for additional essays and introductions for the 'Dublin Edition', shortly before 19 June 1939, she resorted, presumably only as a temporary measure, to sending the duplicate set of the first state of the page proofs.[115]

When *On the Boiler* finally arrived from the Longford Printing Press, the quality of the finished book was found to be very poor: all the page numbers in the table of contents are wrong; the type in much of the book has poor clarity, especially in the extensive footnotes; the opening line of a section is left widowed at the bottom of a page; very wide gaps are left between words; and Latin text is not set in italics. As Mrs Yeats later told Allan Wade, 'only about four copies of this edition had been issued when it was decided to reprint the book; the whole remainder of the edition was then destroyed and the new edition substituted'.[116] A year later, a Dublin waste paper firm hauled away the copies of the withdrawn edition.[117]

The replacement was printed by Alex Thom & Co., Dublin, and was published by the Cuala Press prior to 6 September 1939, when the British Library date-stamped its copy (Wade 202). The New York office of Scribners received its copy (HRC Texas, Scribners papers, box 2, file vol. VII) before 19 September.[118] For the subsequent history of *On the Boiler* in the 'Dublin Edition' and the 'Coole Edition', see pp. 469–72 above.

For the general publishing history of *Explorations* (1961), in which *On the Boiler* was excerpted, see pp. 464–66 above. An undated and unsigned pencil draft of a letter to Mrs Yeats in late 1959 or early 1960, presumably written by Macmillan's Lovat Dickson, suggested that *Explorations* include 'selections of *general* interest from *On the Boiler*', and proposed a 'tentative list' that would have cut 'Preface'; 'Preliminaries', section I; 'To-morrow's Revolution', sections II–V; 'Ireland after the Revolution', all five sections; and 'Other Matters', sections V and VIII (BL Add. Ms. 55896).

The copy-text for *Explorations* was a copy of *On the Boiler* (Wade 202) that was marked at Macmillan with copy-editing, cuts and queries. It was sent in August 1960 to Mrs Yeats for her to answer the editor's queries (NLI Ms. 38,461). She did not return it until at least eight months later, sometime after 19 April 1961, when Lovat Dickson wrote to her about the cuts and about her delay (quoted on p. 465 above). Those suggested cuts (and the result in *Explorations*) were as follows: 'Preface' (cut); 'Private Thoughts', sections I–IV (printed), section V (cut); 'Ireland after the Revolution', sections IV–V (cut); 'Other Matters', last paragraph of section II (printed), sections III–IV (printed), section V (cut); sections VI–VII (printed); and the play *Purgatory* (cut).

Mrs Yeats did return the marked book, which then was used by the printer for galley proofs dated 24 November 1961 (BL Add. Ms. 55896). *Explorations* was published in London on 23 July 1962 (Wade 211Y) and in New York the next year (Wade 211Z).

The copy-text for the present edition is the marked page proofs of the first state from the Longford Printing Press, as the last version seen by Yeats (NLI Ms. 30,485). As we have seen, however, that text, even after another revise of its page proofs, was so inexpertly printed that the Cuala Press chose not to publish the book until it had been completely reprinted, by a different printer. Thus I have allowed an additional measure of authority to the posthumous evidence in a set of marked page proofs (revised state) that Mrs Yeats sent to Macmillan in June 1939, in the first printing (Wade 201), and in the second printing (Wade 202).

Of some 228 emendations to *On the Boiler* in the present edition, 205 are parallel to those in *Explorations*, and 12 are to sections that were omitted in

Explorations. However, *Explorations* has 93 other posthumous copy-editing emendations that exceed the textual emendation policies of the present edition and thus have not been adopted. Nearly half of the posthumous copy-editing changes that I have not adopted from *Explorations* probably were made at the sole initiative of the publisher, since those emendations are not marked on the copy of *On the Boiler* (Wade 202) that Macmillan, London, sent to Mrs Yeats in August 1960 (NLI Ms. 38,461). Seven of the unadopted emendations from *Explorations* were corrections to quotations and references. The only six unadopted emendations of wording from *Explorations* are listed in the note here, together with a brief summary of the other unadopted emendations.[119]

NOTES TO TEXTUAL INTRODUCTIONS

1. Yeats to J. B. Yeats, 12 May 1917, *L* 624–25.
2. Yeats to John Quinn, 16 May [1917], Berg NYPL, and quoted in B. L. Reid, *The Man from New York: John Quinn and his Friends* (New York: Oxford University Press, 1968) p. 306. He mailed them to Quinn on 11 July 1919; they are now in the Harry Ransom Humanities Research Center, University of Texas. On 27 May 1920, during a visit to John Quinn's apartment in New York, Yeats wrote on the cover sheet, 'This is the complete MS set in order for John Quinn', and added an imperfect transcription of the closing sentence of the published epilogue, noting that it had been 'corrected to the following in proof'. Some early drafts and fragments of *Per Amica Silentia Lunae* are at the National Library of Ireland (NLI Mss. 30,368; 30,500 and 30,532).
3. 28 June [1917], NLI Ms. 18,735.
4. Pen and black ink, with green wash, on white card, 20 x 12.4 cm., University of London Library, illus. in Malcolm Easton, *T. Sturge Moore (1870–1944): Contributions to the Art of the Book & Collaboration with Yeats: Catalogue of an Exhibition* (Hull: University of Hull, 1970), no. 48 and p. 37; Yeats to T. Sturge Moore, [Summer 1917], *LTSM* 28 and 29 (illus.).
5. See the copy (London: Macmillan, 1918) in the Forbes Library, Northampton, Mass., and another described in Peter A. Bologna Rare Books Ltd, Kilbrittain, Bandon, Co. Cork, catalogue 4, item no. 593.
6. [January 1937], enclosure to letter, J. Hansard S. Watt, A. P. Watt & Son, London, to John Hall Wheelock, Charles Scribner's Sons, New York, 28 January 1937, CSS Princeton University Library, author files I, box 174, Yeats folder 1. For details of the Scribners 'Dublin Edition', see pp. 483–86 above.
7. BL Add. Ms. 55890; 'Preliminary Notice: The Collected Edition of the Works of W. B. Yeats', enclosure to letter, Harold Macmillan to

John Hall Wheelock, 27 March 1939, Macmillan letter-book, BL Add. Ms. 55821.

8. Handwritten table of contents, [summer or autumn 1939], HRC Texas, Scribners papers, box 3, vol. x.
9. Sixty-eight of those unadopted posthumous emendations are to punctuation, for example, forty-five commas added and seventeen deleted; fifty-eight are minor changes in spelling, including twenty-eight shifts in capitalisation, eight changes in hyphenation and eighteen instances of changing to a variant spelling of a word or name, such as 'Connaught' changed to 'Connacht'. The two posthumous copy-editing changes of wording that have not been adopted here are (a) one word misquoted by Yeats from a poem by Shelley: 'And live like' (p. 28, l. 2 above; with the correct quotation from Shelley in note 116, p. 306) emended in *Mythologies* to 'And move like' (p. 360); and (b) correction of the case of a pronoun: 'it is not him who sleeps' (p. 32, l. 6) emended in *Mythologies* to 'it is not he who sleeps' (p. 366).
10. *The Irish Statesman* (Dublin) 1, no. 9 (23 August 1919) 211–13 and no. 10 (30 August 1919) 236–37.
11. *The Living Age*, 16, no. 787 (4 October 1920) 25–33.
12. It mistakenly skips, in mid-sentence (at p. 39, l. 4 above), one complete line from *The Irish Statesman* (213: 'fittest, [LINE DIVISION] though as a creator of social, not of biological, [LINE DIVISION] species'), so that the typescript (p. 9) reads: 'fittest, species'. Also the typescript (p. 17) mistakenly skipped the last five words of a sentence from *The Irish Statesman* (237; p. 43, l. 40 above): '. . . suffering, above all in eternal suffering.'
13. Pp. 39, l. 4 and 43, l. 40 above; Cuala pp. 9, 17.
14. For example, the two badly truncated sentences (see note 12 above) are left unrepaired (*Ex* 270, 277).
15. 'This Book' (section dated 1902), *The Celtic Twilight*, 2nd ed. (London: Bullen, 1902) p. 3.
16. Reported in the *Irish Times*, 13 January 1912, p. 9, col. f.
17. Carbon copy, NLI Ms. 30,623 ('Swedenborg, Mediums, and the Desolate Places'). Carbon copy, NLI Ms. 30,041 ('Witches and Wizards and Irish Folk-Lore'); this is the only extant typescript of 'Witches and Wizards and Irish Folk-Lore'. Carbon copy of note 1, NLI Ms. 30,114; and another carbon copy NLI (SUNY-SB formerly 23.10.72–88). NLI Ms. 30,269 is a typescript of an earlier version of note 1, perhaps dictated to a typist.
18. Yeats to John Quinn, 16 May 1917, in B. L. Reid, *The Man from New York: John Quinn and his Friends* (New York: Oxford University Press, 1968) p. 306.
19. Wade 312; a copy in the Princeton University Library is date-stamped 14 October 1920.
20. *V&B* 307, l. 26: 'man." They'; *If I were Four-and-Twenty* (Cuala Press) p. 35, l. 1: 'man." they'; *Ex* 41, l. 20: 'man', they'.
21. Foreword by Elizabeth Coxhead (Gerrard's Cross: Smythe; New York: Oxford University Press, 1970).

22. Enclosure, contents list of vol. v (*Essays*), CSS Princeton, author files I, box 174, Yeats folder 1.
23. Mrs Yeats noted on a list of contents, dated 22 June 1937, for the Scribners 'Dublin Edition' that the text for volume v, *Essays*, 'will be delayed owing to final proofs of new essays not yet ready' (Ts., ribbon copy, NLI Ms. 30,202). A carbon copy of the list and a transcription of a letter from Mrs Yeats to [J. Hansard S.] Watt, 22 June 1937, that repeats the comment and date are both in CSS Princeton, author files I, box 174, Yeats folder 1.
24. HRC Texas, Scribners papers, box 4, Miscellaneous vol. This particular set of page proofs of the Cuala Press *Essays 1931 to 1936*, which lacks only the front matter, has a typewritten label that mistakenly reads 'ESSAYS 1926–1936' (with '1926' rather than '1931') pasted on its first page; that error is mirrored in the letters of transmittal and receipt to and from Scribners in October 1937 (A. S. Watt, A. P. Watt & Son, London, to Charles Kingsley, Scribners, London, 15 October 1937 [transcription], with excerpts from two undated letters of Mrs Yeats to Watt; CSS Princeton, author files I, box 174, Yeats folder 1). The colophon of these page proofs announces that the book was finished 'in the third week of October'; the colophon of the published book there reads 'in the last week of October' 1937.
25. HRC Texas, Scribners papers, box 4, vol. XI.
26. Information from Warwick Gould, 7 December 1990.
27. The quoted comment, 'Not wanted Already in' is for 'Bishop Berkeley' (p. 27); the other three each is marked 'Already in': 'My Friend's Book' (p. 47), 'Prometheus Unbound' (p. 55) and 'An Indian Monk' (p. 74).
28. Enclosure to letter from Macmillan, London, [unsigned] to A. Hansard S. Watt, A. P. Watt & Son, London, 27 October 1936, BL Add. Ms. 55786.
29. Mrs Yeats to Thomas Mark, 22 June 1939, BL Add. Ms. 55825 and Thomas Mark to Mrs Yeats, 26 June 1939, BL Add. Ms. 55826. Her change of address announcement postcard had an effective date of 26 July 1939 (CSS Princeton, author files I, box 174, Yeats folder 2).
30. Lovat Dickson, Macmillan, London, to Charles Kingsley, Scribners [London, but mistakenly addressed and mailed to New York], 20 February 1940, (transcription) CSS Princeton, author files I, box 174, Yeats folder 2.
31. BL Add. Ms. 55882; the first gathering, date-stamped 22 September 1959, is filed in BL Add. Ms. 55895 with the 1939 page proofs. A paper-bound advance copy of those proofs for *Essays and Introductions*, labelled 'Uncorrected Proof Copy' and dated 1959 on the title page and copyright notice, is in the collection of George M. Harper.
32. Yeats to Dorothy Wellesley, 21 July 1936, *LDW* 90.
33. Ts. 15 pages plus title page: '*NATIONAL LECTURE* / MODERN POETRY / by / *W.B.YEATS* / *NATIONAL PROGRAMME Sunday, October 11th* [*hand-written addition: , 1936*] *9.5–9.50 p.m.*'
34. 78-rpm coarse-groove disc BBC no. 1235E, 2 sides (4 min. 5 sec. and

4 min. 22 sec.); copied 12 February 1985 onto tape 8888WR, National Sound Archive, London. It contains from 'The pretty maid . . .' (p. 94, l. 23 above) to '. . . Cain and Abel fighting' (p. 96, l. 39 above). The thirteen verbal variants in that 1,429-word excerpt probably were simply nervous slips; at one point, Yeats hesitated momentarily and then apologised to his radio listeners, 'I'm sorry to delay you for a moment.'

35. For more information on Rossi and his collaboration with Hone, see Hone's preface to *Pilgrimage in the West*, by Mario M. Rossi, tr. J. M. Hone (Dublin: Cuala Press, 1933) sigs. A2-A3.
36. J. M. Hone, *W. B. Yeats: 1865–1939*, 2nd ed. (London: Macmillan, 1962) p. 420.
37. Yeats to Olivia Shakespear, 2 August [1931], *L* 782.
38. *Letters from AE*, ed. Alan Denson (London: Abelard-Schuman, 1961) p. 201.
39. Date typed at the end of the typescript (NLI Ms. 30,432, p. 11); Yeats to Olivia Shakespear, 9 and 14 March [1933], *L* 807–8.
40. 'A Note on *Louis Lambert*', typescript pp. 1–7 (typed by Mrs Yeats) and pp. 8–11 (revised version, on another typewriter), H. Lytton Wilson Collection, Southern Illinois University at Carbondale, Morris Library, collection 76, box 1, folder 8. That composite typescript is marked with word counting, done probably by Yeats himself, after he had revised the typescript, just as with a typescript of 'The Holy Mountain' that was typed on the same two typewriters used in this 'A Note on *Louis Lambert*' and that is also in the H. Lytton Wilson Collection. The typescript's pages 8–11 that were replaced in the composite typescript are in Dublin (NLI Ms. 30,432). A manuscript insert is reported in Yeats's white vellum notebook that was begun 23 November 1930 (Partial List of Mss., no. 545, formerly in the collection of Michael B. Yeats; not sighted).

    The second typescript, also corrected and revised in Yeats's hand, is NLI Ms. 30,054.
41. John Harwood, 'Yeats, Shri Purohit Swāmi, and Mrs Foden', appendix to 'Olivia Shakespear: Letters to W. B. Yeats', *YA* 6 (1988), p. 102.
42. Harwood, p. 102.
43. T. Sturge Moore to Yeats, 9 February 1932, *LTSM* 171–72.
44. Yeats to Edith Shackleton Heald, 6 August [1937], *L* 896.
45. Harwood, p. 103; Yeats to T. Sturge Moore, 4 June [1932], *LTSM* 173.
46. Morris Library, collection 76, box 1, folder 5. The word count was done probably by Yeats himself, after he had completed the revisions. This typescript was typed on the same two typewriters used in a typescript of 'A Note on *Louis Lambert*' that is also in the H. Lytton Wilson Collection; see note 40 above.
47. NLI Ms. 30,106. The only other marking on that set was his incomplete revision, in the postscript (p. 556), from *Yugi Sutras* to *Yuga-Sutras* (p. 556); in the book and in all subsequent printings it was changed to *Yoga-Sutras*.

48. These were one rephrasing, one correction, several changes of punctuation, seven new typographical errors and one editorial oversight. The rephrasing (p. 148 above) was from 'In Patanjali and his commentaries there is a detailed . . .' (*HM* 27) to 'In one of the Patanjali commentaries there is detailed . . .' (*Essays 1931 to 1936*, pp. 103–4).
49. Yeats to Florence Farr, 27 June [1912], *L* 569.
50. Yeats to William Rothenstein, 14 November [1912], in Mary M. Lago, ed., *Imperfect Encounter: Letters of William Rothenstein and Rabindranath Tagore: 1911–1941* (Cambridge: Harvard University Press, 1972) p. 43. *Imperfect Encounter* is an important and reliable source of information on Yeats and Tagore. See also William Rothenstein, *Men and Memories: Recollections of William Rothenstein: 1900–1922* (London: Faber and Faber, 1932) pp. 262–69.
51. Lago, *Imperfect Encounter*, p. 40, citing the report in *The Times* (London), 13 July 1912, p. 5, col. f.
52. Berg NYPL folders 64B5978 (first Ms.), 64B5977 (second Ms.) and 64B5979 (Ts.).
53. Rothenstein, *Men and Memories: 1900–1922*, pp. 266–67 and *L* 570.
54. NLI (SUNY-SB formerly 1.10.21); see pp. 165 and 385, note 1.
55. The American and Indian issues of *Gitanjali* have no direct textual interest concerning Yeats's introduction. The Macmillan, New York, edition in 1914 (Wade 265) was a resetting that followed the Macmillan, London, 1913 text (including its errors at p. xiii, ll. 6 and 10) and introduced a new error at p. xix, l. 15 (comma at the end of a sentence). The International Pocket Library edition (Boston, [*c.* 1920]) was very carelessly set; at two places the printer skipped a full line of text (p. 9, l. 34 and p. 11, l. 24). The 'Indian Edition' (Wade 266) was issued by Macmillan, Calcutta, in 1919.
56. Yeats to Dorothy Wellesley, [8 July 1935], *LDW* 9.
57. Yeats to Olivia Shakespear, 26 April [1936], *L* 854.
58. The New York 1937 issue corrected an error ('deduced' corrected to 'deduce') (p. 172, l. 39 above), but later American issues reverted to the London reading, 'deduced'.
59. Harold Macmillan (signed; letter composed by Thomas Mark) to Mrs Yeats, 8 June 1939, Macmillan letter-book, BL Add. Ms. 55825. Charles Kingsley, Scribners, London, to John Hall Wheelock, Scribners, New York, 19 June 1939, CSS Princeton, author files I, box 174, Yeats folder 1.
60. The dating and description of this typescript at *P&I* 335 should be revised to agree with those here.
61. NLI Mss. 30,043 ('Aphorisms of Yoga'); 30,130 ('The Ten Principal Upanishads'); 30,151 ('Selections from the Poems of Dorothy Wellesley') and 30,038 ('The Oxford Book of Modern Verse').
62. BL Add. Ms. 55895; see pp. 470–72 above. Probably Thomas Mark wrote a query in pencil at the start of 'The Ten Principal Upanishads': 'Not to be used?'; this preface and the six essays that follow it in the 1939 proofs (see pp. 470–71 above) were omitted from *Essays and Introductions* (1961).

63. Shri Purohit Swāmi to Yeats, 21 May 1937, NLI (SUNY-SB formerly 3.9.168).
64. Purohit Swāmi to Yeats, 11 November 1937, NLI (SUNY-SB formerly 3.9.154).
65. NLI Mss. 30,462 (drafts); 30,400 (complete Ms.) and 30,148 (Tss.). For the typewritten transcription in 1939, see p. 480 above.
66. For the selection of Yeats by Oxford University Press and for other details of the project, see Jon Stallworthy, 'Yeats as Anthologist', in *In Excited Reverie: A Centenary Tribute to William Butler Yeats 1865–1939*, ed. A. Norman Jeffares and K. G. W. Cross (London: Macmillan, 1965) pp. 171–92 and Edward O'Shea, *Yeats as Editor*, New Yeats Papers no. 12 (Dublin: Dolmen Press, 1975) pp. 57–72.
67. NLI Ms. 30,797; NLI Ms. 30,295 (ribbon copy), labelled 'Final version', and its carbon copy (NLI Ms. 30,625), which was revised subsequently to the ribbon copy; and NLI Ms. 30,522, labelled 'Corrected copy Not to be given away!!'
68. Quoted by Jon Stallworthy, 'Yeats as Anthologist', in *In Excited Reverie*, p. 185.
69. Yeats to Dorothy Wellesley, 16 December [1935], *LDW* 47.
70. Published 4 February 1937; Stallworthy, 'Yeats as Anthologist', in *In Excited Reverie*, p. 192.
71. November 1953 note from the files of Oxford University Press, in Frances Whistler, Oxford University Press, to Colin Smythe, 2 September 1983.
72. See note 74 below.
73. Marked pages, HRC Texas, Scribners papers, box 4, Miscellaneous vol. A. S. Watt, of A. P. Watt & Son, London, to Charles Kingsley, London representative of Scribners, 15 October 1937 (transcription), CSS Princeton, author files I, box 174, Yeats folder 1. Mrs Yeats had sent the materials to Watt after 6 October 1937. In a detailed listing of contents, prepared by a Scribners editor in black pencil, for the seven-volume arrangement of the Scribners 'Dublin Edition', the introduction to *The Oxford Book of Modern Verse* is the final item in volume v, *Essays*, pp. 689–726 (HRC Texas, Scribners papers, box 4, Miscellaneous vol.). In an undated, typewritten list of contents, *c.* June 1939, for a volume titled *Additional Essays and Introductions* in the expanded, posthumous version of the Scribners 'Dublin Edition', the introduction to *The Oxford Book of Modern Verse* is the final item, and is annotated '(subject to the permission of the Oxford University Press)' (HRC Texas, Scribners papers, box 4, Miscellaneous vol.).
74. Oxford University Press reprint orders dated 25 November 1936, 10 December 1937, 1 February 1947, 20 May 1950 and 20 August 1965 (quoted in Frances Whistler, Oxford University Press, to Colin Smythe, 2 September 1983). The British reissues were published December 1936, January 1937, 1938, 1939, 1941, 1942, 1947, 1950, 1953, 1955, 1960, 1966 and 1970. On 22 February 1972, Oxford University Press ordered a resetting and printing of the book from Richard Clay and Co., Ltd, although the colophon in 1972 shows the University Press, Oxford; a 1978 issue was printed by J. W. Arrowsmith Ltd,

Bristol. American reprints by Oxford University Press, New York, were in January 1937, 1947, 1960, 1962 and 1966.

75. Ribbon copy: Macmillan Archive, Basingstoke. Carbon copy: NLI Ms. 30,038. Carbon copy: 'D', HRC Texas, Scribners papers, box 4, vol. XI. See p. 480 above.

76. [Charles Scribner] to Charles Kingsley, London representative of Charles Scribner's Sons (carbon copy), CSS Princeton, author files I, box 17, Kingsley folder 1932–1936. For accounts of the Scribners 'Dublin Edition', see also Finneran, *EYPR* 12–23; Edward Callan, *Yeats on Yeats: The Last Introductions and the 'Dublin' Edition*, New Yeats Papers 20 (Mountrath, Portlaoise: Dolmen Press, 1981) pp. 87–103; and Warwick Gould, 'The Definitive Edition: a History of the Final Arrangements of Yeats's Work', in *Yeats's Poems*, ed. A. Norman Jeffares (London: Macmillan, 1989) pp. 709–49.

77. Charles Scribner, Scribners, New York, to George P. Brett, Jr., president, Macmillan, New York, 7 November 1935 (carbon copy); Charles Scribner memo to C. B. Merritt, Scribners, New York, 17 December 1935 (carbon copy); and Charles Scribner to George P. Brett, Jr., 27 December 1935 (carbon copy); all CSS Princeton, author files I, box 174, Yeats folder 1. The quoted passages are from 17 and 27 December, respectively.

78. (Carbon copy), CSS Princeton, author files I, box 174, Yeats folder 1. John Hall Wheelock (1886–1978), a poet, had joined Scribners in 1911 and had been an editor since 1926; he became a senior editor in 1947 and retired in 1957.

79. J. Hansard S. Watt, A. P. Watt & Son, London, to John Hall Wheelock, Scribners, New York, 9 June 1936, CSS Princeton, author files I, box 174, Yeats folder 1.

80. [John Hall Wheelock], Scribners, New York, to J. Hansard S. Watt, A. P. Watt & Son, London, 9 February 1937 (carbon copy), CSS Princeton, author files I, box 174, Yeats folder 1.

81. Conversation of Yeats and [A. S.] Watt, 5 October 1937, reported in Charles Kingsley, Scribners, London, to John Hall Wheelock, Scribners, New York, 6 October 1937, CSS Princeton, author files I, box 174, Yeats folder 1. The smooth typescript of the general introduction has misreadings and corrections by the typist at two places that were heavily revised in the earlier typescript (Ts. pp. 8, l. 13 and 10, l. 19; see NLI Ms. 30,798, Ts. pp. 10 and 12). The smooth typescripts sent to Scribners, New York, are now at the HRC Texas (Scribners papers, box 4, slip-case dated 1937).

82. A. S. Watt, A. P. Watt & Son, London, to Charles Kingsley, London representative of Charles Scribner's Sons, New York, 15 October 1937 (transcription), CSS Princeton, author files I, box 174, Yeats folder 1.

83. *The Poetical Works and Other Writings of John Keats*, ed. H. Buxton Forman, rev. by Maurice Buxton Forman, intro. John Masefield, 8 vols., The Hampstead Edition, 1,025 sets (New York: Scribners, 1938–39), bound in blue half morocco, stamped in gold, top edges gilt, price $27.50.

84. John Hall Wheelock, Scribners, New York, to Charles Kingsley, London representative of Scribners, 5 January 1939 (carbon copy), CSS Princeton, author files I, box 174, Yeats folder 2.
85. Macmillan letter-book, BL Add. Ms. 55822.
86. Drafted by Thomas Mark and signed by H.[?] Macmillan, 19 May 1939, Macmillan letter-book, BL Add. Ms. 55824.
87. Macmillan letter-book, BL Add. Ms. 55824.
88. Macmillan letter-book, BL Add. Ms. 55825.
89. In 1938–39 Scribners had published its 'Hampstead Edition' of John Keats at only about one-third the price that had been mentioned in December 1935 when the Yeats edition was planned. See p. 483 and note 83 above.
90. John Hall Wheelock, Scribners, New York, to Morton Dauwen Zabel, 28 February 1941 (carbon copy), CSS Princeton, author files I, box 174, Yeats folder 1. Morton Dauwen Zabel, 'The Thinking of the Body: Yeats in the Autobiographies', *The Southern Review*, 7 (Winter 1941–42) 564, n. 1: '. . . . I have also had the privilege of reading the prefaces written by Yeats in the last year of his life [*sic*, 1937], on his prose, poetry, and drama, for the complete authorized edition of his works which is to be issued in New York sometime in the future by Charles Scribner's Sons; this edition will be an invaluable authority on the texts. For access to these unpublished prefaces I am indebted to Mr. John Hall Wheelock; they have been neither quoted or paraphrased here, but are important summaries of Yeats's thought and motives.'
91. John Hall Wheelock to Marion Witt, Hunter College, New York, 29 May 1946 (carbon copy), CSS Princeton, author files II, box 37, Yeats folder 1.
92. [John Hall Wheelock, Scribners, New York] to George Brett, president, Macmillan, New York, 22 January 1953 (carbon copy), CSS Princeton, author files II, box 37, Yeats folder 1.
93. John Hall Wheelock, Scribners, New York, to George Brett, president, Macmillan, New York, 16 and 22 January 1953 (file copies). George Brett to John Hall Wheelock, 20 January 1953. John Hall Wheelock, Scribners, New York, to Randall Williams, Macmillan, New York (carbon copy); Roland L. De Wilton, assistant editor-in-chief, Macmillan, New York, to John Hall Wheelock, 24 August 1953; John Hall Wheelock to Roland L. De Wilton, 11 September 1953 (carbon copy); J. Randall Williams, III, vice-president, Macmillan, New York, to John Hall Wheelock, 25 September 1953. All CSS Princeton, author files II, box 37, Yeats folder 1.
94. [John Hall Wheelock, Scribners, New York] to Roland L. De Wilton, assistant editor-in-chief, Macmillan, New York, 12 March 1954 (carbon copy), author files II, box 37, Yeats folder 1.
95. Curtis Bradford, ed., 'Three Introductions Intended for the Scribner's Edition', in 'Unpublished Prose of W. B. Yeats, III. Works Completed but Never Published', Tss. pp. 1–20 (Introduction), 21–24 (Plays) and 25–29 (Essays), Grinnell College Library, Grinnell, Iowa, call no. 64.2/B72u/Vault. Curtis Bradford to T. J. B. Walsh, direc-

tor, college department, Scribners, New York, 6 September 1955; John Hall Wheelock, Scribners, New York, to Curtis Bradford, 13 September 1955 (carbon copy), both in CSS Princeton, author files II, box 37, Yeats folder 1.

96. 'A General Introduction' has some markings in blue pencil and red pencil. Typescripts: HRC Texas, Scribners papers, box 4, slip-case dated 1937. Photostatic copy time-date-stamped 27 September 1955 on verso, copy-edited by Macmillan, London, and then sent to Mrs Yeats on 5 May 1960: NLI Mss. 30,798 ('A General Introduction') and 30,628 ('Introduction to Essays').

97. BL Add. Ms. 55882 and an advance review copy (uncorrected page proofs) in the possession of George M. Harper. It was typeset in 1959 from the Macmillan copy-edited photostatic copy (NLI 30,798) that had been made 27 September 1955.

98. Lovat Dickson, Macmillan, London, to Mrs Yeats, 5 May 1960, NLI Ms. 30,755.

99. The eighty-two unadopted posthumous emendations in *Essays and Introductions* for the general 'Introduction' can be characterised as follows. Half are changes in punctuation, including six new sentences made by splitting Yeats's original sentences, seven new semicolons and three new dashes. Nine are corrections to improve the accuracy of Yeats's quotations. Eight are changes in capitalisation and ten are changes of spelling. One-quarter are avoidable emendations that have no documentary support from the manuscript or earlier typescript. Typical examples of these are: 'drawn round him' (p. 205, l. 9) changed to read 'drawn around him' (*E&I* 510); 'I was but eighteen or nineteen and I had' (p. 205, ll. 9–10) changed to read 'I was but eighteen or nineteen and had' (*E&I* 510); 'more important than' (p. 209, l. 29) changed to read 'more famous than' (*E&I* 512); and 'it, I think' (p. 208, ll. 7–8) changed to read 'it and think' (*E&I* 514).

Of the fourteen unadopted posthumous emendations in *Essays and Introductions* for 'Introduction to Essays', five are changes in punctuation (with one new sentence division), four are changes in spelling, and five are avoidable emendations that have no documentary support from the manuscript or earlier typescript. That last category includes the addition of a signature and date, a revision of the title, and one change of wording: 'Renoir perhaps or an' (p. 217, l. 18) changed to 'Renoir or perhaps an' (*E&I* vii).

100. I have reviewed the Callan edition in *YA2* (1983) 109–10.

101. Curtis B. Bradford, *Yeats at Work* (Carbondale and Edwardsville: Southern Illinois University Press, 1965) p. 378. Yeats to Lily Yeats, 3 March [1938], transcription John Kelly, and quoted by Sandra Siegel, *Purgatory: Manuscript Materials Including the Author's Final Text* (Ithaca: Cornell University Press, 1986) p. 16; see also note 108 below. The manuscripts are NLI Mss. 30,391 and 30,486.

102. See *L* 907 and Yeats to Mrs Yeats, 6 April 1938, cited by Siegel, *Purgatory*, p. 15.

103. The new material might have been the first half of the preface (al-

though in a subsequent typescript Yeats signed and dated the preface 'July 1938'); the poem '[Why should not old men be mad?]' (p. 221 above); 'Ireland after the Revolution', section III (pp. 242–43 above); and the second paragraph of 'Other Matters', section VII (pp. 244–45).

104. Bradford, *Yeats at Work*, pp. 377–85.

105. Yeats to Maud Gonne MacBride, 16 June [1938], *L* 910. Yeats to Dorothy Wellesley, 22 June 1938, *LDW* 182 and *L* 410–11.

106. Yeats to Dorothy Wellesley, 13 July 1938, *LDW* 199 and *L* 912.

107. Yeats to Ethel Mannin, 23 December [1938], *L* 921.

108. Richard J. Finneran, in *EYPR* (1990) pp. 140–45, provides a detailed account of the complex, fragmentary chronology of the publishing history of *On the Boiler* from July 1938 until Yeats's death in January 1939; that chronology supersedes the earlier versions by Finneran in *Editing Yeats's Poems* (London: Macmillan, 1983) pp. 113–16, and by Sandra Siegel in *Purgatory*, pp. 14–20.

109. Yeats to F. R. Higgins, undated, HRC Texas; excerpts printed in Finneran, *EYPR* 142 and Siegel, *Purgatory*, pp. 18–19.

110. Yeats to Longford Printing Press, 10 January 1939, NLI Ms. 30,513; printed in Finneran, *EYPR* 142.

111. HRC Texas, Scribners papers, box 4, Miscellaneous case, (lacks 'Preface') pp. 3–31, 33 upper one-third of page; NLI Ms. 30,461, p. 32 (single sheet filed with a typescript); NLI Ms. 8771, pp. 33 (lower two-thirds of page)–43 (*Purgatory*).

112. Elizabeth C. Yeats, Cuala Press, to Charles Kingsley, Scribners, London, 9 June 1939 (transcription), CSS Princeton, author files I, box 174, Yeats folder 2.

113. 2 June 1939, Macmillan letter-book, BL Add. Ms. 55824. The proofs are BL Add. Ms. 55881.

114. Harold Macmillan (signed; letter composed by Thomas Mark) to Mrs Yeats, 13 and 19 June 1939, Macmillan letter-books, BL Add. Ms. 55825. See also p. 471 above.

115. HRC Texas, Scribners papers, box 4, Miscellaneous case (that set of page proofs lacks p. 32, which is misfiled among the corrected typescript in NLI Ms. 30,461). Charles Kingsley, Scribners, London, to John Hall Wheelock, Scribners, New York, 19 June 1939, CSS Princeton, author files I, box 174, Yeats folder 2.

116. Wade 201. Extant copies: Emory University, Wesleyan University, George M. Harper (formerly in the collection of Senator Michael Yeats), and Dublin Municipal Library (mentioned by Wade).

117. Cuala Press diary, 25 June 1940, cited in Liam Miller, *The Dun Emer Press, Later the Cuala Press* (Dublin: Dolmen Press, 1973) p. 122.

118. [John Hall Wheelock] memorandum to Harold Cadmus, 19 September 1939, (carbon copy), CSS Princeton, author files I, box 174, Yeats folder 2.

119. Five of those six unadopted verbal emendations in *Explorations* were marked in the copy of Wade 202 that Mrs Yeats saw in 1960: 'its' (p. 222, l. 28 above), 'their' (*Ex* 410); 'a' (p. 223, l. 13 above), 'the' (*Ex* 411); 'tinkers' (p. 237, l. 12 above), 'tramps' (*Ex* 435); 'deaths' (p. 245, l. 29 above), 'death' (*Ex* 446); 'disease of which' (p. 246, l. 18

above), 'disease from which' (*Ex* 447). The other unadopted verbal emendation is found only in *Explorations*: 'a Dublin' (p. 233, l. 2 above), 'an Irish' (*Ex* 428).

Apart from the emendation of wording, *Explorations* created one section division (*Ex* 432; p. 235, l. 31 above) to compensate for a section division elsewhere that mistakenly was omitted in early page proofs; one paragraph division (p. 228, l. 32 above) was dropped (*Ex* 420); and two sentences (p. 249, l. 24) were combined (*Ex* 451). Seventeen of the unadopted changes were minor alterations of spelling. The rest were local changes in punctuation, often to add commas.

COPY-TEXTS USED FOR THIS EDITION

Per Amica Silentia Lunae (9 and 11 May 1917). Copy-text: 'Per Amica Silentia Lunae', in *Essays*, vol. IV of the Collected Edition (London: Macmillan, 6 May 1924), (Wade 141) pp. 477–538.

'If I were Four-and-Twenty', *The Irish Statesman*, 1, nos. 9 and 10 (23 and 30 August 1919) 211–13 and 236–37.

'Swedenborg, Mediums, and the Desolate Places' (14 October 1914), in *Visions and Beliefs in the West of Ireland*, by Lady Gregory (New York and London: G. P. Putnam's Sons, September 1920), (Wade 312) II, 295–339.

'Witches and Wizards and Irish Folk-Lore' (1914), in *Visions and Beliefs in the West of Ireland*, by Lady Gregory (New York and London: G. P. Putnam's Sons, September 1920), (Wade 312) I, 247–62.

Preface to *Essays 1931 to 1936* (Dublin: Cuala Press, December 1937), (Wade 194) sig A4^{r}.

'Parnell' (with the poem 'Come gather round me Parnellites', dated August 1936), in *Essays 1931 to 1936* (Dublin: Cuala Press, December 1937), (Wade 1941) pp. [1]–6.

'Modern Poetry: A Broadcast' (1936): (BBC London, National Programme, 9:05–9:50 P.M., 11 October 1936). Copy-text: *Essays 1931 to 1936*, pp. 6–29.

'Bishop Berkeley': Introduction (July 1931) to *Bishop Berkeley: His Life, Writings, and Philosophy*, by Joseph M. Hone and Mario M. Rossi (London: Faber and Faber, October 1931), (Wade 280). Copy-text: *Essays 1931 to 1936*, pp. 29–46.

'My Friend's Book' (1932): Review of *Song and its Fountains*, by AE (George Russell): First published in *The Spectator*, 9 April 1932. Copy-text: *Essays 1931 to 1936*, pp. 47–54.

'Prometheus Unbound' (w. 1932; publ. 1933): First published in *The Spectator*, 17 March 1933. Copy-text: *Essays 1931 to 1936*, pp. 55–62.

'Louis Lambert' (w. 1933; publ. 1934): First published in *The London Mercury*, July 1934. Copy-text: *Essays 1931 to 1936*, pp. 63–74.

'Introduction to *An Indian Monk*': Introduction (5 September 1932) to *An Indian Monk: His Life and Adventures*, by Shri Purohit Swāmi (London: Macmillan, November 1932), (Wade 281). Copy-text: *Essays 1931 to 1936*, pp. 74–87.

'Introduction to *The Holy Mountain*': Introduction to *The Holy Mountain: Being the Story of a Pilgrimage to Lake Mānas and of Initiation on Mount Kailās in Tibet*, by Bhagwān Shri Hamsa, tr. (from Marāthi) Shri Purohit Swāmi (London: Faber and Faber, September 1934), (Wade 282). Copy-text: *Essays 1931 to 1936*, pp. 88–117.

'Introduction to "Mandukya Upanishad" ': First published as introduction to 'Māndookya Upanishad', tr. (from Sanskrit) Shri Purohit Swāmi, in *The Criterion: A Literary Review*, July 1935. Copy-text: *Essays 1931 to 1936*, pp. 118–[132].

'Gitanjali': Introduction (September 1912) to *Gitanjali* (*Song Offerings*), by Rabindranath Tagore (London: Chiswick Press for the India Society, 1912), (Wade 263). Copy-text: pages vii–xxii torn from a copy of *Gitanjali* (*Song Offerings*), by Rabindranath Tagore (London: Macmillan, 1931), (later issue of Wade 264), with no corrections; supplied by Yeats in 1937 for the Charles Scribner's Sons never-published 'Dublin Edition' of W. B. Yeats. HRC Texas, Scribners papers, box 4, vol. XI.

'The Ten Principal Upanishads': Preface (w. 1936; dated 1937) to *The Ten Principal Upanishads*, tr. Shree Purohit Swāmi and W. B. Yeats (London: Faber and Faber, April 1937), (Wade 252). Copy-text: 2nd ed. (London: Faber and Faber, March 1938), pp. 7–12 [2nd ed. not recorded by Wade].

'Aphorisms of Yoga': Introduction to *Aphorisms of Yôga*, by Bhagwān Shree Patanjali, tr. (from Samskrit) Shree Purohit Swāmi (London: Faber and Faber, June 1938), (Wade 286) pp. 11–21.

'Introduction to *The Oxford Book of Modern Verse*' (September 1936). Copy-text: pages v–xlii, corrected by Yeats, torn from a bound copy of *The Oxford Book of Modern Verse*, ed. W. B. Yeats, 2nd ed. (Oxford: Clarendon Press, December 1936), (Wade 250) (O'Shea no. 2454c); supplied by Yeats in 1937 for the never-published Charles Scribner's Sons 'Dublin Edition' of W. B. Yeats. HRC Texas, Scribners papers, box 4, vol. XI.

'Introduction' [w. 1937, publ. 1961 as 'A General Introduction for my Work']. Copy-text: TS with corrections, probably by the typist, supplied by Yeats in 1937 for the never-published Charles Scribner's Sons 'Dublin Edition' of W. B. Yeats. HRC Texas, Scribners papers, box 4, Miscellaneous vol.

'Introduction to Essays' [w. 1937; publ. 1961]. Copy-text: TS with extensive holograph revision by Yeats, supplied by him in 1937 for the Charles Scribner's Sons never-published 'Dulin Edition' of W. B. Yeats. HRC Texas, Scribners papers, box 4, Miscellaneous vol.

On the Boiler (October 1938). Copy-text: Corrected page proofs (first state) of *On the Boiler* (NLI Ms. 30,485), marked by Yeats in late December 1938–early January 1939. Yeats died prior to receipt of the second state of page proofs for this edition (Wade 201), printed by the Longford Printing Press for the Cuala Press; it was completed, but had so many errors that Mrs Yeats withdrew it in mid-1939. A completely reset edition was published before 4 September 1939 (Dublin: Cuala Press; Wade 202).

Textual Appendices

'Epilogue' (unadopted manuscript, *c.* 1917) to *Per Amica Silentia Lunae*. NLI Ms. 30,352.

Alternative ending (unadopted typescript, 1919–20?) for 'If I were Four-and-Twenty'. NLI Ms. 30,794.

Notes (1914–15) to *Visions and Beliefs in the West of Ireland*, by Lady Gregory (New York and London: Putnam's, September 1920), (Wade 312) I, 265–93; II, 343.

Deleted typescript section I, 'Introduction', of 'Swedenborg, Mediums, and the Desolate Places', perhaps originally intended to introduce the entire collection *Visions and Beliefs in the West of Ireland* (w. 1911–14; dated 14 October 1914). Copy-text: corrected typescript, pp. [1]–3, NLI Ms. 13,575.

P.S. to the introduction (July 1931) to *Bishop Berkeley: His Life, Writings, and Philosophy*, by Joseph M. Hone and Mario M. Rossi (London: Faber and Faber, October 1931), (Wade 280) p. xxix.

'A Biographical Note', in *The Holy Mountain: Being the Story of a Pilgrimage to Lake Mānas and of Initiation on Mount Kailās in Tibet*, by Bhagwān Shri Hamsa, tr. (from Marāthi) Shri Purohit Swāmi (London: Faber and Faber, September 1934), (Wade 282). Copy-text: *Essays 1931 to 1936*, pp. 117–18.

Final paragraph of introduction (September 1936) to *The Oxford Book of Modern Verse*, ed. W. B. Yeats (Oxford: Clarendon Press, December 1936), (Wade 250) p. xlii.

EMENDATIONS TO THE COPY-TEXTS

In addition to the abbreviations listed on pp. 000–00 above, the following special abbreviations are used in the list of emendations.

BB revise:	*Bishop Berkeley* (NLI Ms. 30,027) page proofs revised for Cuala Press *Essays 1931 to 1936* (1937)
BBC:	*Modern Poetry: The Eighteenth of the Broadcast National Lectures delivered on 11 October 1936* (London: British Broadcasting Corporation, 1936)
BBC Ts.:	'National Lecture: Modern Poetry by W. B. Yeats', typescript, British Broadcasting Company Written Archives Centre, Caversham Park, Reading
BL 55880:	Pencilled copy-editing for an early state of Macmillan 'Coole Edition' vol. XI, before July 1939, in bound copy of *Essays 1931 to 1936* (BL Add. Ms. 55880)
BL 55881:	Page proofs of the second state of *On the Boiler* (Dublin: Cuala Press, [1939]), (Wade 201), with copy-editing by Mrs Yeats and Thomas Mark (BL Add. Ms. 55881)
BL 55895:	Macmillan 'Coole Edition' vol. XI page proofs date-stamped 19 July 1939 (BL Add. Ms. 55895)
CP 1933:	*The Collected Poems of W. B. Yeats* (London: Macmillan, 1933), (Wade 172)
Criterion 1934:	'Initiation upon a Mountain', *The Criterion: A Literary Review*, 13, no. 53 (July 1934) 537–56
Criterion 1935:	'Māndookya Upanishad: Introduction' by W. B. Yeats, *The Criterion: A Literary Review*, 14, no. 57 (July 1935) 547–56
Essays NY 1924:	*Essays and Introductions* (New York: Macmillan, 1924)
GY:	Mrs Yeats
GY 55881:	Copy-editing very probably by Mrs Yeats in May–June 1939 in BL 55881 for Macmillan, London, to use as copy for BL 55895
IS:	'If I were Four-and-Twenty', *The Irish Statesman*, 1, no. 9 (23 August 1919) 211–13 and no. 10 (30 August 1919) 236–37
LA:	'If I were Four-and-Twenty', *The Living Age*, 16, no. 787 (4 October 1920) 25–33
LA 1936:	'Modern Poetry', *The Living Age*, 351 (December 1936) 330–39
Listener:	'Modern Poetry', *The Listener*, 16, no. 405 (14 October 1936) 697–99, 739–40
LM:	'Louis Lambert', *The London Mercury*, 30, no. 177 (July 1934) 231–35

London 1912:	Rabindranath Tagore, *Gitanjali* (*Song Offerings*) (London: Chiswick Press for the India Society, 1912), (Wade 263)
SIU 76/1/5:	'The Holy Mountain', corrected typescript, H. Lytton Wilson Collection of William Butler Yeats, Southern Illinois University, Carbondale, Ms. 76/1/5
SIU 76/1/8:	'A Note on Louis Lambert', corrected typescript, H. Lytton Wilson Collection of William Butler Yeats, Southern Illinois University, Carbondale, Ms. 76/1/8
Spectator 1932:	'My Friend's Book', *The Spectator* (London), 9 April 1932, pp. 503–4
Spectator 1933:	'Prometheus Unbound: An Essay', *The Spectator* (London), 17 March 1933, pp. 366–67
Spectator's Gallery:	'My Friend's Book', in *Spectator's Gallery: Essays, Sketches, Short Stories & Poems from The Spectator 1932*, ed. Peter Fleming and Derek Verschoyle (London: Cape, 1933) pp. 335–41
TPU London 1937:	*The Ten Principal Upanishads*, tr. Shree Purohit Swāmi and W. B. Yeats (London: Faber and Faber, 1937), (Wade 252)
TPU New York 1937:	*The Ten Principal Upanishads*, tr. Shree Purohit Swāmi and W. B. Yeats (New York: Macmillan, 1937), (Wade 253)
W201:	*On the Boiler* (edition withdrawn in June 1939 prior to publication) (Wade 201)
W202:	*On the Boiler* (Dublin: Cuala Press, 1939) (Wade 202)

KEY TO FORMAT OF ENTRIES

Page.Line in this edition: Reading in this edition] Reading in copy-text }Contemporary authority for emendation [posthumous and other auxiliary evidence for emendation is given in square brackets].

• *Per Amica Silentia Lunae* 1.18 stream] }*CP* 1933. 1.20: beside] above }*CP* 1933. 1.21: moon] moon, }*CP* 1933. 1.22: And] And, }*CP* 1933. 1.22: life] life, }*CP* 1933. 2.8: yet] yet, }*CP* 1933. 2.10: himself] himself, }*CP* 1933. 2.15: himself] himself, }*CP* 1933. 2.18: and] And }*CP* 1933. 2.21: face] face, }*CP* 1933. 2.22: Bedouin's] Beduin's }*CP* 1933. 2.22: roof] roof, }*CP* 1933. 2.24: camel-dung] camel dung }*CP* 1933. 2.25: stone.] stone; }*CP* 1933. 2.32: war,] war; }*CP* 1933. 2.32: men] men, }*CP* 1933. 2.32: happiness] happiness, }*CP* 1933. 2.36: popular] popular, }*CP* 1933. 2.36: influence,] influence; }*CP* 1933. 2.37: write,] write }*CP* 1933. 2.37: action:] action, }*CP* 1933. 3.4: have] have, }*CP* 1933. 3.5: dream] dream }*CP* 1933. 3.7: yet] yet, }*CP* 1933. 3.8: world;] world, }*CP* 1933. 3.11: schoolboy] schoolboy, }*CP* 1933. 3.12; sweet-shop] sweetshop }*CP* 1933. 3.13: grave] grave, }*CP* 1933. 3.14: unsatisfied,] unsatisfied; }*CP* 1933. 3.17: livery-stable] livery stable }*CP* 1933. 3.21 sands] sand }*CP* 1933. 3.22: toil] toil, }*CP* 1933. 3:24: book.] book; }*CP* 1933. 3.28: edge of the stream] water's edge, }*CP* 1933. 3.32: And] And, }*CP* 1933. 3.32: characters] characters, }*CP* 1933. 5.25–26: Post-/Impressionist }copy-text hyphen. 7.34: Cino] Gino }Ms. HRC Texas; name; quoted text. 14.21–22: *Séraphita*] *Seraphita* }Title. 14.37 Cabbala] Caballa }Conventional spelling of name. 18.15: Cabbalistic] cabalistic }Conventional spelling of name. 18.16–17: never-/published]copy-text hyphen. 20.9: Guaïta] Gaeta }Name. 26.13: day;] day. }*CP* 1933. 26.14: one] one, }*CP* 1933. 26.15: moods] moods, }*CP* 1933. 27.4: memories] memories, }Ms. HRC Texas. 28.18: winding path] Winding Path }Ms. HRC Texas; p. 28, 1.26 above. 31.36–37: Daemon] daemon }All 15 instances in *PASL* except 2 in quoted texts. 32.23: Guaïta] Gaeta }Name. 32.24–25: Dauthendey] Douthenday }Name. 32.35; l'Isle] L'Isle }Name; *Essays* NY 1924. 33.1: *Axël*] *Axel* }Title. 33.4 and 8: Axël] Axel }Name. 33.21: Péguy's] Peguy's }Name. 33.25–26: charcoal-/burners }COPY-TEXT HYPHEN. 33.26–27: self-/teaching }COPY-TEXT HYPHEN. • IF I WERE FOUR-AND-TWENTY 34.5: review] Review }None. 34.13–14: four-and-/fifty }COPY-TEXT HYPHEN. 35.7: Mont-Saint-Michel] Mont St. Michel }Name. 35.20: Huysmans'] Hauptmann's }Name; Ms. NLI 30,493. 35.28: cries: 'The] cries: "the }None. 35.32: obstinacy, 'The] obstinacy, "the }None. 36.8: *faite*] *fait* }Ms. NLI 30,493; title. 37.24: Neo-Platonism] neo-platonism }None. 38.22: Sinn Féin] *Sinn Féin* }Ts. NLI 30,277. 38.31: Utopian] utopian }Ms. NLI 30,493. 38.39: Nietzsche] Neitzche }Name. 39.17: Utopian] utopian }Ms. NLI 30,493. 40.12: *'Fourieristes'*] *Fourieristes* }Name. 40.17: chiropodist] Chiropedist }[Ts. NLI 30,277: 'chiropedist']. 40.32: Leonardo] Leonardi }Ms. NLI 30,493. 40.34: preoccupation] pre-occupation }None. 41.26: dry] dry, }Ts. NLI 30,277. 41.37: Certainly] Certainly, }Ts. NLI 30,277. 42.29: preoccupation] pre-occupation }Ms NLI 30,493. 43.8: crotchety] crochety }None. 43.10: not] not, }Ts. NLI. 30,277. 43.20: mind] Mind }Ms. NLI 30,493. 43.20–21: shadowiness] shadowyness }Ms. NLI 30,493. 45.10: Chinese] Chinean }Name. • SWEDENBORG, MEDIUMS, AND THE DESOLATE PLACES 48.24–25: Allan Kardec] Allen Cardec }Name. 49.22: Immanuel] Emmanuel }Name. 53.37: Slieve Ochte] Sleive Ochta }Name; [Ms. NLI 30,623: Slieve Ochta; Ts. NLI (SB 29.5.233); Slieve Ochte]. 55.14: *Coelestia*] *Celestia* }Title. 57.5: faeries] fairies }All four other instances here. 57.18 and 59.11: Allan Kardec] Allen Cardec }Name. 60.38–39: seventeenth-/century }COPY-TEXT HYPHEN. 61.34: rummaging] rumaging }None. 64.9: hypnosis] hypnoses }Ms. NLI 13,575; next line. 66.14: Scot] Scott }Name. 67.6: Mead] Meade }Ts. NLI (SB 29.5.252); name. 67.18: Mead] Meade }Name. 72.35: *Odyssey*] Odyssey }Convention for title. 72.38: Zeus and Here] Zeus, and Hero }Ts. NLI (SB 29.5.259) • WITCHES AND WIZARDS AND IRISH FOLK-LORE 76.10: Heydon] Haydon }Name; p. 268, n. 10, l. 5 and p. 281, n. 37, ll. 1–2 above. 77.29 and 78.11: Manningtree] Manintree }Name. 78.35: Mompesson] Monpesson }Name in quoted text. 80.19: I] I. }Ms. NLI 13,575. 80.23: today] to-/day }Ms. NLI 13,575; consistent usage in *V&B*. • PREFACE TO ESSAYS 1931 TO 1936 84.18: 1932,] 1932. }None. 84.20: recall,] recall. }None. • PARNELL 86.8: sycophantic] syphophantic }Ms. NLI 30,494. 86.12: Leveson-Gower] Levison Gower }Name; [Ms. NLI 30,494: 'Leveson Gower']. 87.12: man,] man; }*New Poems* 1939. 87.13: awhile,] awhile; }*New Poems* 1938. 87.14: can,] can }*New Poems* 1938. 87.16: underground;] underground. }*New Poems* 1938. 87.19: reason] reason, }*New Poems* 1938. 87.22: poor,] poor; }*New Poems* 1938. 87.30: mind] mind, }*New Poems* 1938. 88.6: glass,] glass; }*New Poems* 1938. 88.7: country] country, }*New Poems* 1938. 88.8 his] a }*New Poems* 1938. • MODERN POETRY: A BROADCAST 90.1: START OF PARAGRAPH When] AMBIGUOUS PARAGRAPHING When }Ms. NLI 30,327; BBC Ts.; *BBC*. 90.3–4: self-/possession }COPY-TEXT HYPHEN. 90.27: penitential] penitential, }Ms. NLI 30,327; BBC Ts.; *Listener; LA* 1936; *BBC*. 91.10: remembrances] rememberances }BBC Ts.; *Listener; LA* 1936; *BBC*. 94.3: written:] written; }BBC Ts.; *Listener; LA* 1936; *BBC*. 94.33 and 95.12: Isoult] Iseult }[Spelling in Binyon's poem]; BBC Ts.; *Listener; BBC;* [p. 188, l. 2 above]. 94.35: Cuchulain] Cuchullain }Conventional spelling of name. 96.24: 'Ass-face'] *Ass-Face* }Title [and text] of work; *Listener; LA* 1936; *BBC*. 96.28: Ass-face] Ass-Face }Title [and text] of work; *Listener; LA* 1936; *BBC;* and all seven following instances, pp. 96–97 above. 97.26–27: pre-/suppositions }COPY-TEXT HYPHEN. 98.14–15: see-/saw }COPY-TEXT HYPHEN. 98.35–36: no.//They] NO STANZA DIVISION }[Text of the poem in *Poems of Ten Years: 1924–1934* (London: Macmillan, 1934) p. 319]. 99.34–35: stars.//The] NO STANZA DIVISION }[Text of the poem in *The Seven Days of the Sun: A Dramatic Poem* (London: Chatto & Windus) p. 26]; BBC Ts.; *BBC; OBMV* no. 270, section vii. 100.11–12: lips—//*Pain*] NO STANZA DIVISION }[Text of the poem in

Seven Days of the Sun, p. 26; *OBMV* no. 270, section vii]. 100.26–27: bad-/tempered }COPY-TEXT HYPHEN. 101.3–4: Self-/possessed }COPY-TEXT HYPHEN. 101.11: changed:] changed.: }BBC Ts.; *Listener; LA* 1936; *BBC*. 102.13: *Sigurd] Sigard* }Title; Ms. NLI 30,327; *BBC*. • BISHOP BERKELEY 104.27: one's] ones }*BB*. 104.31: incredulity] increduality }*BB* revise. 106.19: comprehensive,] comprehensive }*BB* revise. 106.37: shall prevail] shall not prevail }[BL 55880; Thomas Mark circled 'shall prevail' and asked in a query 'shall not prevail in copy, but?' in BL 55895 p. 176, and Mrs. Yeats did not respond; *E&I* proofs 1959; *E&I*]. 108.7: Philonous,] Plotinus; }Title; *BB* revise. 108.19: J—] J . . . }Convention. 108.37: Thebaid] Thebiad } Name; *BB*. 109.8: pedlar] peddlar }Ms. NLI 30,516. 109.11–12: self-/assertion }COPY-TEXT HYPHEN. • MY FRIEND'S BOOK 113.9: known] kown }Ts. NLI 30,115; *Spectator* 1932; *Spectator's Gallery*. 113.26: Mountain] Mountains }Name. [*Au* 249]. 114.10: reminiscences] reminisences }Ts. NLI 30,115; *Spectator* 1932; *Spectator's Gallery*. 115.5: Dunne's] Dunn's }Name. 115.15: Swedenborg,] Swedenborg }Ts. NLI 30,115; *Spectator* 1932; *Spectator's Gallery*. 116.16 begun] began }Ts. NLI 30,115; *Spectator's Gallery*. 116.37: Platonists] Platonist }Ts. NLI 30,115; *Spectator* 1932; *Spectator's Gallery*. • PROMETHEUS UNBOUND 118:7: Demogorgon] Demo-gorgon }Name; Ms. NLI 30,512. 118.13: purified. Shelley] purified, Shelley }Ms. NLI 30,512: 'purified PAGE DIVISION Shelly'; Ts. NLI 30,033 has a comma followed by the four spaces used by that typist for a sentence division; *Spectator* 1933. 118.27: Tír-na-nÓg] Tir n'an og }Conventional spelling of name. 118.27–28: country-/woman }COPY-TEXT HYPHEN. 119.1: Demogorgon] Demo-gorgon }Name; Ms. NLI 30,512. 119.6: 'Athanase'] *Athanais* }Title. 119.13: Demogorgon] Demo-gorgon }Name; Ms. NLI 30,512; correction in page proofs for Cuala *Essays 1931 to 1936* NLI 30,021. 119.34–35: a like] alike }Ts. NLI 30,033; *Spectator* 1933. 120.23: sole] soul }Ts. NLI 30,033; *Spectator* 1933. 120.28; Purpose] purpose }Ts. NLI 30,033; *Spector* 1933; p. 120, l. 33 and p. 121, l. 2 above. 120.37: touches] to chase }Ts. NLI 30,033: 'to ches' *[sic]; Spectator* 1933. 121.35: contrary,] contrary, }Ts. NLI 30,033; *Spectator* 1933; page proofs of *Essays 1931 to 1936* NLI 30,021. • LOUIS LAMBERT 123.39: Claës] Claes }Name. 124.9 *upon*] *Upon* }Ts. SIU 76/1/8. 124.12: *Séraphita*] *Seraphita* }Title. 124.19: Lucien] Lucian }Name; Ts. SIU 76/1/8. 124.30: *Timaeus*] Timaeus }Convention for title; Ts. SIU 76/1/8. 124.33: *Séraphita*] *Seraphita* }Title. 124.36: Laërtius] Laertius }Name. 125.2: Ficinus] Facinus }Name; [quoted text]. 125.10: *Mirouët*] *Mirouet* }Title. 125.11: Bianchon] Biancon }Name; [see also entry below for 128.8]. 126.3: Séraphita] Seraphita }Name. 126.5: Bianchon] Biancon }Name; [see also entry below for 128.8]. 126.18: Séraphita] Seraphita }Name. 126.24: suggestion,] suggestion }None. 126.24–25: bull-/necked }COPY-TEXT HYPHEN. 126.35–36: dramatist's] dramatist }*LM;* Ts. NLI 30,054. 127.27 and 128.5: Séraphita] Seraphita }Name. 128.8: Bianchon] Biancon }Name; Yeats holograph revision in Ts. SIU 76/1/8. 129.11: *Arrabian Nights*] Arabian Nights }Convention for title. • INTRODUCTION TO *AN INDIAN MONK* 130.10: religious] religii-/ous }Ts. NLI 30,042; *IM;* Cuala page proofs NLI 30,021. 130.29: Mohammedans] Mahommedans }Name; *IM*. 131.6: Wilfrid] Wilfred }Name. 131.7: Mohammedan] Mahommdan }Name; *IM*. 131.14: leader:] leader. }None. 132.55: listener.] listener }*IM;* Yeats copy-editing on Cuala page proofs NLI 30,021. 134.4: Nails] nails }*IM*. 134.22: Ahasuerus in *Hellas,*] *Ahasuerus* in Hellas }Name and title; *IM*. 135.6: an] any }Ts. NLI 30,042; *IM*. 135.36: sweet,] sweet. }*IM*. 136.17: nothing./Never will I do anything,/ Never,] nothing./Never, }Ts. NLI 30,042; *IM*. 136.30: All] all }*IM*. 137.36: Saints] saints }Ts. NLI 30,042; correction in an unidentified hand in both copies of *IM* in Yeats's library (O'Shea nos. 2035–2035a). • INTRODUCTION TO THE HOLY MOUNTAIN 139.15: philosophise] philosophize }*Criterion* 1934. 139.21: Bhagwān] Bhagwām }Name; *HM*. 139.22: *Séraphita*] *Seraphita* }Title. 139.26–27: QUOTATION IN ROMAN] QUOTATION IN ITALIC }*Criterion* 1934. 140.27: foreseeing] forseeing }*HM*. 140.32: despair] de-/pair }*HM*. 141.31: disturbed;] disturbed }*HM*. 141.34–35: upon the instant] upon the the instant }*HM*. 141.38: Master] master }*HM*. 142.2: 25] 25th. }*HM*. 142.11: *Samādhi*] *Samdāhi* }*HM*. 143.1: Master's] master's }*HM*. 143.1–2: first-/class }COPY-TEXT HYPHEN. 143.20–24: QUOTATION IN ROMAN] QUOTATION IN ITALIC }Ts. SIU 76/1/5; *Criterion* 1934. 144.3 and 12–3: *Mahābhārata*] *Mahabharata* }Title: }*HM*. 144.4: Mont] Mount }Name; Ms. NLI 13,566. 144.35: Kawaguchi's] Kavizuchi's }Name; Ms. NLI 13,566. 145.7: Yoga] Yogi }None. 145.8: *Padmāsan*] *Padmasan* }*HM; AY* 90. 145.18: robbers,] robbers }*HM*. 145.27: Māndukya Upanishad's [*Mandukya Upanishad's* }Title; convention; Ms. NLI 13,566. 146.25: He] he }*HM*. 146.31: Māndukya Upanishad] *Mandukya Upanishad* }Title; convention. 148.9: '*Tomas*', darkness] "*Tamas*, darkness }*HM*. 148.9: '*Rajas*'] *Rajas* }*HM*. 148.9: '*Satva*'] *Satva* }*HM*. 148.24: attain] attains }None.. 148.29–30: Upanishads] *Upanishads* }Convention; MS. NLI 13,566. 148.39: 'seedless'] seedless }Ts. SIU 76/1/5; p. 149, l. 18 and p. 150, l. 20 above. 149.7–11: QUOTATION IN ROMAN] QUOTATION IN ITALIC }*Criterion* 1934. 149.19: life after life] Life after Life }Ms. NLI 13,566. 149.21: life] Life }Ts. SIU 76/1/5. 150.9–10: dreaming-/sleep }COPY-TEXT HYPHEN. 150.16: *Turiyā*] *Turiyā*, }Ms. NLI 13,566; *Criterion* 1934. 151.3–8: QUOTATION IN ROMAN] QUOTATION IN ITALIC }*Criterion* 1934. 151.15: is,] is }*HM*. 151.30: Sphinx] sphinx }*HM*. 151.31: What] what }*HM*. 152.10–11: mid-moment] mid moment }None. 152.18–19: Camera della Segnatura] *Camera Signatura* }Name. 152.23: hatching,] hatching }*Criterion* 1934. 152.23: *Catherine de*] *Catherine ae* }Title; *HM*. 152.26: Mont-Saint-Michel] Mont Saint Michel }Name. 152.29: Duchesse] Duchess }Title. 152.30: foretell] fortell }*HM*. 152.37: whit] wit }*HM*. 153.7 and 22: Upānishads] *Upanishads* }Ts. SIU 76/1/5. 153.15: penitential] penetential }*HM*. 154.8: Self and Not-Self] self and not self }For capitalisation: p. 142, ll. 17 and 22; p. 148, l. 17; p. 149, l. 17; p. 150, l. 29 above. For hyphenation: none. 152.22: solemnised] soleminsed }*HM*. 154.36: XI] II }Section numbering in all other published texts. 155.1: Philolaus] Philaus }Name. 155.16: civilisation,] civilisation }*HM*. 155.20–29: QUOTATION IN ROMAN] QUOTATION IN ITALIC }*Criterion* 1934. 155.22: Olympian] Olymdian }*HM*. • INTRODUCTION TO 'MANDUKYA UPANISHAD' 156.18: START OF PARAGRAPH Forty] AMBIGUOUS PARAGRAPHING Forty }*Criterion* 1935. 157.5: review] Review }Ms. NLI 30,505. 157.16: A.M.] a.m. }None. 157.25: Māndukya] Mandukya }[Quoted text; p. 157, l. 19 above, in quoted text]. 157.28: START OF PARAGRAPH Two] ambiguous paragraphing Two }*Criterion* 1935. 157.31: "*Aum*"] *Aum*, }Ms. NLI 30,505; [quoted text]. 158.1: whereto] where to }*Criterion* 1935. 159.32: realisation] realization }[Quoted text; p. 158, ll. 28–29 above]. 160.9: unforeseen] unforseen }*Criterion* 1935. 160.13: sleeping,] sleeping }*Criterion* 1935. 161.21: place] space }Ms. NLI 30,505. 161.29: events] events, }Ms. NLI 30,505. 162.1: Discursive] Discoursive }*Criterion* 1935; p. 161, l. 30 above. 162.3–4: concentration] concentratian }*Criterion* 1935. 162.14–15: self-/creating }COPY-TEXT HYPHEN. 162.36: recognise] recognize }P. 162, ll. 3–4 above; [Ms. NLI 30,505: 'recognises']. 163.38: Mānas] Manas }*Criterion* 1935. • GITANJALI 165.4: I] NO SECTION NUMBER }None. 165.14: day;] day, }None. 165.17: Second,] Second }London 1912. 165.17: Burma] Burmah }Name. 166.3: 'Words] "words }None. 166.28: Gaganendranath] Gogonendranath }Name. 166.37: museum] Museum }Convention; [holograph revision (from 'curator at the British Museum' to 'curator of a Museum') in Ts. NYPL Berg]. 167.35: *Criseyde*] *Cressida* }Conventional spelling of title. 169.38: me] me, }London 1912; Ts. NYPL Berg; [quoted text]. 170.13: Tristram] Tristan }Conventional spelling of name; p. 94, l. 33 and p. 95, l. 11 above. 170.13: Pellinore }Conventional spelling of name. • THE TEN PRINCIPAL UPANISHADS 171.[3 and] 8: Shree NO EMENDATION] Shree }'Shree' here, in *AY* and *V(B)* 260 (Holograph correction [Connie K. Hood, 'The Remaking of *A Vision*', *Yeats*, 1 (1983) 60]); 'Shri' in Purohit Swāmi's three other English books: *IM*, *HM* and *The Geetā*. 171.19: ('AE')] (A.E.) }Name. Ms. NLI 30,530. 171.27: English—] English: — }Ms. NLI 30,530. 172.14: drunk,] drunk; }Ts. HRC Texas. 172.24–25: miracle-

/working }COPY-TEXT HYPHEN. 172.39: deduce] deduced }*TPU* (London & New York 1937). 173.14: half-Asiatic] half-asiatic }None. 174.9–10: Yajur-/Weda }COPY-TEXT HYPHEN. 174.11: Chāndôgya-Upanishad] Chhāndôgya-Upanishad]Ts. HRC Texas. 174.13–141: Brihadāranyaka-/Upanishad }COPY-TEXT HYPHEN. 174.21: *1937*] NO DATE }Ts. HRC Texas. • APHORISMS OF YOGA 175.3: Shree NO EMENDATION] Shree }See entry above for 171.[3 and] 8. 175.21: reflective] repetive }[Quoted text, p. 50, reads: 'super-reflected'; Ms. NLI 30,400 reads either 'refective' or 'repetive'; Tss. NLI 30,148 and HRC Texas read 'repetive']. 176.22–23: Brihadāranyaka-/Upanishad }COPY-TEXT HYPHEN. 177.24: analogous] analagous }None. 178.34: Yôga] Yôgi }P. 180, ll. 14 and 22 above. 179.24–25: punching-/ball }COPY-TEXT HYPHEN. 179.37: Baisers] basarid }Name; Ms. NLI 30,400: 'Bais*re*'. 180.14: Yôga] Yôgi }P. 180, ll. 14 and 22 above. 180.12–13: fore-/knowledge }COPY-TEXT HYPHEN. • INTRODUCTION TO *THE OXFORD BOOK OF MODERN VERSE* 181.7–8: long-/lived }COPY-TEXT HYPHEN. 182.3–4: crutch-/supported }COPY-TEXT HYPHEN. 182.19: *Ballad*] Ballad }None. 183.37 and 184.2: hard] [CANCELLED: pure] hard }[Ink correction on the copy-text, not in Yeats's hand; quoted text]. 184.22: the] The }Ts. NLI 30,625; uncorr. proofs NLI 30,522. 185.12: it:] it; }None. 185.20–21: rhetoric,'] rhetoric' }None. 188.2: Isoult;] Isoult: }Ts. NLI 30,522; uncorr. proofs NLI 30,522. 188.3: picture;] picture: }None. 189.12–14: self-/control }COPY-TEXT HYPHEN. 191.6: the] The }Title; Ts. NLI 30,522; uncorr. proofs NLI 30,522. 191.17–18: middle-/tint }COPY-TEXT HYPHEN. 191.31R14.12: 'Ash Wednesday'] *Ash-Wednesday* }Title. 192.2–3: self-/surrender }COPY-TEXT HYPHEN. 193.20–21: self-/control }COPY-TEXT HYPHEN. 194.12–13: pre-/occupation }COPY-TEXT HYPHEN. 194.21: *to*] *of* }Title: New York 1936. 194.28: the] *The* }Title. 195.5–6: stone-/built }COPY-TEXT HYPHEN. 195.23: Platonic] platonic }None. 196.17–20: Chef-/d'oeuvre }COPY-TEXT HYPHEN. 199.33: *Death.*] *Death* }New York 1936; Oxford Jan 1937. 200.2: *tranquillum*] *Tranquillum* }P. 196, l. 6 above; quoted text. 201.5: *deus ex machina*] *Deus ex Machina* }None. 202.16–17: on-/rush] onrush }NO EMENDATION. 202.28: AE] AE. }New York 1936. 202.34: Upanishads] *Upanishads* }None. 203.17: Field';] Field': }None. 203.19: talent,] talent }None. • INTRODUCTION FOR THE NEVER-PUBLISHED CHARLES SCRIBNER'S SONS 'DUBLIN EDITION' OF W. B. YEATS 204.9–10: loneliness;] loneliness, }None. 204.17: sheath',] sheath'' }None. 204.20: incoherence,] incoherence [COMMA ADDED PERHAPS BY TYPIST OR AT SCRIBNERS] }Ts. NLI 30,798. 204.26 and 28: Self',] Self'' }None. 204.28: Chāndôgya] Chandogya }P. 180, l. 23 above. 204.29: Upanishad, 'those] Upanishad''[CANCELLED:—] those }Ts. NLI 30,798. 205.4: Subject-Matter] Subject Matter }Ts. NLI 30,798. 205.11: *Queenie*] *Queen* }Title. 205.20: eighteenth-century] eighteenth century }None. 205.22: spoke] spoke, }Ts. NLI 30,798. 205.26; bowels;] bowels, }None. 205.26–27: ever growing] evergrowing }None. 205.27: view;] view, }None. 206.2: Royal Irish Academy] *Royal Irish Academy* }Convention for name of organisation; }Ms. NLI 30,798. 206.8: ordnance] ordinance }None. 206.13: the Royal] The Royal }Ms. NLI 30,798. 206.15: Christian—thought] christian; thought }None. 206.15: commemoration] commemmoration }Ts. NLI 30,798. 206.22: surveyed] surveyed }Ts. NLI 30,798. 206.24: support;] support, }None. 206.26: began,] began }None. 206.34: although] allthough }None. 206.37: eighteenth-century] Eighteenth century }None. 206.38: frenzy;] frenzy,; }Typing error. 207.5: *Cuchulain*] *Cuchullain* }Title. 207.9: Anglo-Irish] Anglo1/2Irish }Ts. NLI 30,798. 207.20: But] But PAGE DIVISION But }Ts. NLI 30,798. 207.36: Dionysus] Dionysius }Name. 207.40: clans] classes }Ts. NLI 30,798. 207.41: monk] Monk }Ms. NLI 30,798. 207.41: bishop] Bishop }Ms. NLI 30,798. 208.2: head,] head }None. 208.10: the words] the word }Ms. NLI 30,798. 208.11: Agla] agla }P. 74, l. 17 above; }Ms. NLI 30,798. 208.13: come] scome }Ts. NLI 30,798. 208.14: abstraction—it] abstraction it }None. 208.24: part,] part }None. 208.27: Cuchulain] Cuchullain }Conventional spelling of name. 208.32–33: not of what the newspapers call my] not what the newspapers call of my }Ts. NLI 30,708.

208.34: aspidistra] aspidestra }Ts. NLI 30,798: 'Aspidistra']. 208.38: attempted,] attempted }None. 208.40 and 209.6: seventeenth] Seventeenth }Ts. NLI 30,798 (second instance only). 209.14: Mr] Mt }Ts. NLI 30,798. 209.16: Far Western] far-Western }Ms. NLI 30,798; [usage of cited text]. 209.18: twelfth] Twelfth }None. 109.21: seventeenth] Seventeenth }Ms. NLI 30,798. 209.27: find] ind }Ts. NLI 30,798. 209.35: the 'Irishry'] "the Irishry" }P. 209, l. 30 and p. 210, ll. 32–33 above. 209.49: in] is }Ts. NLI 30,798. 210.5: 'That] "that }Ts. NLI 30,798. 210.5: ages,'] ages" I }None. 210.6: Swāmi] Swami }None. 210.6: nor] not }Ts. NLI 30,798. 210.11: priest] Priest }Ts. NLI 30,798. 210.11: hell] Hell }Ts. NLI 30,798. 210.12: rath] Rath }None. 210.28: understandable,] understandable }None. 210.32: *Vision,*] *Vision* }Ts. NLI 30,798. 210.34: sixteenth] Sixteenth }Ts. NLI 30,798. 210.34: seventeenth] Seventeenth }Ts. NLI 30,798. 210.34: centuries,] centuries }None. 210.35: extermination;] extermination, }None. 210.37: altogether] alltogether }Ts. NLI 30,798. 210.39: alive;] alive, }None. 211.1: that,] that }None. 211.2: line,] line }None. 211.20: speak] pseak }Ts. NLI 30,798. 211.21: compliments;] compliments, }None. 211.27: Santo] San }Name. 211.34 preceded] preceeded }None. 211.39: bywords] bye-words }None. 212.13: Thomson] Thompson }Name. }Ms. NLI 30,798. 212.15: speech [would] be] speech [CANCELLED BY TYPIST: is] be }None. 212.27: you,'] you" }None. 213.1: subject-matter] subject matter] }None. 213.7: midway] mid-way }Ms. NLI 30,798. 213.10: pneumonia] pnewmonia }Ts. NLI 30,798. 213.18: shepherds] shapherds }Ts. NLI 30,798. 213.25: 'She] "she }None. 213.26: last] lass }Ms. NLI 30,798; [quoted text]. 213.27: awhile'; they] awhile", "they }Ts. NLI 30,798. 213.28: pelican, 'My] pelican", "My }Ts. NLI 30,798. 213.36: some play] someplay }Ts. NLI 30,798. 214.8: fitted] fitte }Ts. NLI 30,798. 214.11: Cuchulain] Cuchullain }Conventional spelling of name. 214.16: past.] past* I }Typing error (copy-text has two spaces rather than the four spaces it uses at a sentence division). 214.23: singers 'Of] singers "Of }None. 214.23: mán's] NO ACCENTS IN THIS QUOTATION OR IN THE TWO FOLLOWING QUOTATIONS }Ms. NLI 30,798 (except that in this first quotation 'fruit' has no accent); all of the Tss. omit all of the accents; Mrs Yeats must have consulted the manuscript (or perhaps a copy of Curtis Bradford's edited transcription) for the accents that were added to the photocopy that was copy-edited at Macmillan, London; *E&I* 1959 page proofs omit the accent on 'and' in the first quotation and omit the accent on 'first' in both the second and third quotations; *E&I* 1961 prints the accents as here. 214.27; there,] there }None. 214.30: and] an }Ts. NLI 30,798. 214.34: line:] line }None. 214.36: syllabic] syllablic }Ts. NLI 30,798. 214.37: elisions] ellisions }None. 215.1: Cuchulain] Cuchullain }Conventional spelling of name. 215.2: belly.] belly. PAGE DIVISION belly. }Ts. NLI 30,798. 215.14: cathedral] Cathedral }None. 215.17 and 23: Tube] tube }None. 215.22: intellect,] intellect }None. 215.24: objective] o jective }Ts. NLI 30,798. 215.24: kill the] kill thw }Ts. NLI 30,798. 215.25: Leonardo;] Leonardo, }None. 215.26–27: the 'Irishy'] "the Irishry" }Ts. NLI 30,798; p. 209, l. 30 and p. 210, ll. 32–33 above. 215.31: half-light] half light }None. 215.33: form,] form }None. 216.7: Nation] Nationa }Ts. NLI 30,798. • INTRODUCTION TO ESSAYS FOR THE NEVER PUBLISHED CHARLES SCRIBNER'S SONS 'DUBLIN EDITION' OF W. B. YEATS 217.7: pictures—had] pictures, had }None. 217.7: Spenser)] Spenser }None. 217.7: four] for }Ms. NLI 30,395. 217.8: Millaises] Millais' }None. 217.10: action;/] action, }None. 217.11: Blake,] Blake }None. 217.14: Burne-Joneses] Burne-Jones' }None. 217.24: connoisseur's] connoiseur's }None. 217.26: myself,] myself }Ms. NLI 30,395. 218.4: Bulwer-Lytton] Bulwer Lytton }Name. 218.5: yes,] yes }None. 218.6: me,] me }None. 218.7: away.] away }Ts. NLI 30,628. 218.10 and 15: subject-matter] subject matter }P. 218, l. 14 above. 218.17: born; NO EMENDATION.] born;[?] }(Copy-text has indecipherable pen-and-ink emendation of the typescript punctuation); }Ms. NLI 30,395. 218.23: theme:] theme., in }None. 218.26: writers;] writers, }None. 218.26: without] with/out }None. 218.27: people;] people, }None.

218.29: *Salammbô*] *Salambo* }Title 218.32: 'Bernard Shaw'. 218.35: poet's] poet }None. 218.36: engine-driver] engine driver }None. 218.40: subject-matter] subject matter }P. 218, 1. 14 above. 219.2: Carracci] Caracci }Name. Ms. NLI 30,395. 219.8: view,] view: }Ms. NLI 30,395. 210.15: justified [not] by] justified PAGE DIVISION by }[Extensive pen-and-ink revision at the start of the new page in the copy-text]. 219.18: life,] life }None. 219.26: desirable] desireable }Ms. NLI 30,395. 219.30: touch,] touch. }Incomplete authorial revision. 219.31: goddesses] godesses }Ms. NLI 30,395. 219.31: Rubensesque] Rubenesque }None. 219.31: exaggeration,] exagerration }For spelling: None. For punctuation: }Ts. NLI 30,628. 219.34: exhausted] created }Ts. NLI 30,628: 'exausted' *[sic]*. 219.39: *Vision,*] VISION }None. 219.40: Boehme's,] Boehme's }None. • *On the Boiler* 220.6: Lady] lady }[Ts. NLI 30,552: 'Lay'; W202]. 220.7: *Cathleen*] Kathleen }[W202]. 220.11: *Purgatory*] Purgatory }Ms. NLI 30,486; [W202]. 220.13: Boy.] Boy. The "Three Marching Songs" were printed in my "Full Moon in March" in a form that I have come to think neither readable nor singable. In their present form they seem to fulfill this purpose. }[W201; W202; the 'Three Marching Songs' (*P* 333–35) were retained in the posthumous revised state of the page proofs for W201, but were omitted from all published texts of *On the Boiler*]. 220.15: October] July }[W201; W202]. 220.18: such-and-such] such and such }]GY 55881]. 220.21: sake,] sake }[GY 55881; W202]. 220.27: boat,] boat; }[GY 55881]. 220.24 and 29: eighteenth-century] eighteenth century }[55881]. 221.28: cast-iron] cast iron }[GY 55881]. 221.32: Ireland,] Ireland }Ts. NLI 30,552; [W202]. 221.34; its] it }Ts. NLI 30,552; [GY 55881; W202]. 221.35: window-panes] window panes }[GY 55881]. 221.37–222.1: gin-palace] Gin Palace }[GY 55881]; [EMENDED] COPY-TEXT HYPHEN. 222.4: amiable,] amiable }[W202]. 222.8: crèches] creches }[GY 55881]. 222.15: Shakespearean] Shakesperian }Name. [GY 55881: 'Shakespearian']. 222.18–19: semi-/hypocritical }COPY-TEXT HYPHEN. 222.22: the] *The* }Ts. NLI 30,461; [GY 55881]. 222.23: committee] Committee }Ts. NLI 30,461; p. 223, l. 5 above; (W202]. 223.1: them] them, }[GY 55881; W202]. 223.6: nephew,] nephew }[GY 55881]. 223.9: government-appointed] government appointed }[GY 55881]. 223.9: dunce,] dunce }[W202]. 223.37: Senator's] senator's }[GY 55881]. 223.38: Ministers] ministers }[GY 55881]. 224.5: Senators] senators }[GY 55881]. 224.6: Ministers] ministers }None; see entries for 223.38 above and 224.15 below]. 224.10–11: self-possession] self possession }Ts. NLI 30,461; [GY 55881: W202];[EMENDED] COPY-TEXT HYPHEN. 224.11: board-room] board room }[GY 55881]. 224.15: Ministers] ministers }[GY 55881]. 224.24: descendants,] descendants }Ts. NLI 30,461; [GY 55881; W202]. 224.28: *Mayflower*] Mayflower }Name of ship; [GY 55881; W202]. 224.33: mother,] mother }Ts. NLI 30,461; [GY 55881; W202]. 225.3: else,] else }[GY 55881]. 225.5: thousand,] thousand }[GY 55881; W202]. 225.6: itself.'] itself. }Ts. NLI 30,461. 225.10–11: nineteenth-century] nineteenth century }[GY 55881]; [EMENDED] COPY-TEXT HYPHEN. 225.33: actors,] actors }Ts. NLI 30,461; [GY 55881; W202]. 225.36: theirs] their's }Ts. NLI 30,552; [GY 55881; W202]. 226.5–6: English-/speaking }COPY-TEXT HYPHEN. 226.5: ecstasy,] ecstasy }Ts. NLI 30,461; [GY 55881]. 226.11: arm's] arms }[GY 55881]. 226.13: quarrelling] quarreling }Ts. NLI 30,552; [W201 2nd proofs; W201; W202]. 226.16: Boys] boys }[GY 55881]. 226.27: I was] UNINKED S }Ts. NLI 30,552; [HRC Texas W201 proofs; W201]. 226.27–28: twenty-/three }COPY-TEXT HYPHEN. 226.28: *Last,*] UNINKED }(Ts. NLI 30,553; [HRC Texas W201 proofs; W201]: 'Last" ';[GY 55881]. 226.32: quarrelled] quarreled }[GY 55881]. 226.36: bore,] bore }[GY 55881]. 227.7–8: slow-/moving }COPY-TEXT HYPHEN. 227.18: Shakespearean] Shakesperian }Name; [GY 55881: 'Shakespearian']. 227.27: plagued] pledged }Ts. NLI 30,552; [quoted text]. 227.31: marry."] marry. }[Quoted text]. 227.36–37: LATIN SET IN ITALIC] LATIN SET IN ROMAN }[GY 55881; W202]. 228.17: grievous] grievious }[W202; quoted text]. 228.21: LATIN SET IN ITALIC] LATIN SET IN ROMAN }[GY 55881; W202]. 228.25: LATIN SET IN ITALIC] LATIN SET IN ROMAN }[GY

55881; W202]. 228.38: especially,] especially }Ts. NLI 30,461; [W202]. 229.6: time:] time; }Ts. NLI 30,552. 229.12: Furthermore,] Furthermore }Ts. NLI 30,551; [W202]. 229.15: men,[39] there] men. (*3) There }Ts. NLI 30,552; }[GY 55881]. 229.27–28: may, or must,] may or must }[W202]. 229.32: labour,] labour }[GY 55881]. 229.33: end,] end }Ts. NLI 30,551; [GY 55881; W202]. 230.1: and, I am convinced,] and I am convinced }[GY 55881; W202]. 230.9: preoccupation] pre-occupation }Ts. NLI 30,552. 230.10: chimpanzee'. Any] chimpanzee." BLANK LINE Any }Ts. NLI 30,552; }[GY 55881; W202]. 230.10: eighteenth-century] eighteenth century [GY 55881]. 230.16–17: practice; and] practice, and }Ts. NLI 30,461. 230.24: baby,] baby }[W202]. 230.31: city:] city; }[GY 55881]. 230.37: increase, too,] increase too }[GY 55881; W202]. 231.2: reorganisation] re-organisation }[GY 55881]. 231.12: cent] cent. }Ts. NLI 30,552. 231.23–24: Thermopylae] Thermophylae }Name; [*V(B)* 52]. 231.33–34: Irish-/American }COPY-TEXT HYPHEN. 232.3–4: unintelligent] un-intelligent }[GY 55881; W202]. 232.4: Government] government }[GY 55881; see also entry below for 239.16]. 232.5: gets] get }Ts. NLI 30,461. 232.6: confession-box] confession box }[GY 55881]. 232.19: child having] ch UNINKED ing }Ts. NLI 30,552; [HRC Texas W201 proofs; BL 55881; W201]. 232.20: lack of] la UNINKED }Ts. NLI 30,552; [HRC Texas W201 proofs; BL 55881; W201]. 232.26: said,] said }[GY 55881; W202]. 232.30: fellow-traveller] fellow traveller }[GY 55881]. 232.32: said,] said: }None. 232.34–35: I said,] I said: }None. 232.35: He said,] he said }[GY 55881; W202]. 232.36: said,] said }[GY 55881; W202]. 232.40: theatre; pity,] threats, pity {For 'theatre': Ts. NLI 30,552. For punctuation: [W202]. 232.41: experience,] experience }[W202]. 233.11: JOURNALISTS.)] JOURNALISTS). }Ts. NLI 30,552; [W202]. 233.17: Such-and-such] Such and such }[GY 55881]. 233.18 and 19: such-and-such] such and such }[GY 55881]. 233.19: deliberately,] deliberately }Ts. NLI 30,461. 233.24: this] that }[GY 55881; W202]. 233.30: Swift,] Swift }[GY 55881; W202]. 233.32: experience,] experience }Ts. NLI 30,461; [W202]. 233.32: *History*,] History"; }Ts. NLI 30,461. 233.33: Castries] Castris }Name. 233.34: *La*] "Le }Title; [GY 55881]. 233.37: found,] found }Ts. NLI 30,461; [Perhaps GY in 55881; W202]. 234.2: it,] it }Ts. NLI 30,461; [GY 55881; W202]. 234.10: lacks;] lacks, }None; [1939 Macmillan copy-editing in 55881]. 234.11: nature,] nature }[GY 55881]. 234.14: were,] were }[GY 55881; W202]. 234.18: II] BLANK LINE (SECTION NUMBERING OMITTED) }Ts. NLI 30,461. 234.22: Court] court }[GY 55881]. 234.29: Dyck] Dyke }Name; [GY 55881]. 234.30: written,] written }[W202]. 234.39: façade] facade }None; [1939 Macmillan copy-editing in 55881]. 234.39: Conolly's] Connolly's }Name. 234.39: Celbridge,] Celbridge }Ts. NLI 30,461; [GY 55881]. 235.2: notoriety:] notoriety; }[GY 55881]. 235.3: distinguished] dis-/distinguished }Ts. NLI 30,552; [W202]. 235.4: genuineness] genuiness }[W202]. 235.4: Phalaris,] Phalaris }[GY 55881]. 235.6: sufficed,] sufficed }[GY 55881; W202]. 235.7: Swift,] Swift }[W202]. 235.7: boy,] boy }[W202]. 235.17–18: book;/Think] book;//Think }Ts. NLI 30,552; [quoted text]. 235.23: purchase] purshase }Ts. NLI 30,461; [quoted text; GY 55881; W202]. 235.23: expense] expence }[W202; quoted text]. 235.25–26: fools;/Affect] fools;//Affect }Ts. NLI 30,552; [quoted text]. 235.34: butcher's] butchers }[GY 55881; W202]. 236.10: Finn,] Fionn }[W202]. For punctuation: [GY 55881]. 236.10: body,] body }[GY 55881; W202]. 236.17: Nietszche's] Nietsche's }Name: [W202]. 236.32: beneficent] beneficient }Ts. NLI 30,552; [GY 55881; W202]. 237.1: Poincaré] Poincare }Name; [GY 55881; W202]. 237.3: meaning, I conclude,] meaning I conclude }[GY 55881; W202]. 237.7: alike,] alike }[W202]. 237.9: measure,] measure }[GY 55881]. 237.9–10: inhabitants] inhabitant }None. 237.10: space, men were told,] space men were told }[GY 55881]. 237.12–13: perception] preception }Ts. NLI 30,552; [W202]. 237.13: is unique,] is unique }[GY 55881]. 237.14–15: measureable. PARAGRAPH DIVISION A] measureable. BLANK LINE PARAGRAPH DIVISION A }Ts. NLI 30,552; [W202]. 237.19: four,] four }[W202]. 237.22: society,] society }[W202]. 237.22:

different,] different }[W202]. 237.22–23: democracy;] democracy, }[GY 55881; W202]. 237.23–24: *Anima Mundi*] Anima Mundi }[GY 55881]. 237.25: Whiggish] whiggish }Ts. NLI 30,552. 237.26: he] be }Ts. NLI 30,552; [perhaps GY in 55881; W202]. 237.28: new] new, }Ts. NLI 30,552. 237.28: listen,] listen }Ts. NLI 30,552; [GY 55881]. 237.35: unique] unieu }Ts. NLI 30,552; [GY 55881; W202]. 237.38: grave-diggers] grave diggers }[GY 55881]. 237.39–40: mind. PARAGRAPH DIVISION When] mind. BLANK LINE PARAGRAPH DIVISION When }Ts. NLI 30,552; [W202]. 238.17: prevision] pre-vision }None; [1939 Macmillan copy-editing in 55881]. 238.19: Asia,] Asia }[W202]. 238.33: gazed] gazen }Ts. NLI 30,552; [perhaps GY in 55881]. 239.12: come, not as an inspiration] come not as an inspiration, }[W202]. 239.16: Government] government }Ts. NLI 30,461; [see also entry above for 232.5]. 239.19–20: parcel-/making }COPY-TEXT HYPHEN. 239.20: tin-can-soldering] tin can soldering }[W202]. 239.20: door-knob-polishing] door-/knob polishing }None. 239.21: coat-cleaning] coat cleaning }[GY 55881; W202]. 239.22: squiffer] Squiffer }None; [1939 Macmillan copy-editing in 55881]. 239.29–30: priest, doctor or lawyer] Priest, Doctor or Lawyer }[GY 55881]. 239.31: D'Arbois] D'Arblay }Name. 240.11: bottom,] bottom }Ts. NLI 30,552; [GY 55881]. 240.11: no top] on top }Ts. NLI 30,552; [1939 Macmillan copy-editing in 55881]. 240.12–13: co-/ordination }COPY-TEXT HYPHEN. 240.14: man,] man,] man }[W202]. 240.15: drama,] drama }[W202]. 240.19: Shakespearean] Shakesperian }Name; Ts. NLI 30,461; [W202]. 240.24–25: myself,] myself }[GY 55881; W202]. 240.28: wheel,] wheel }[GY 55881; W202]. 240.31: certainty] certainity }[GY 55881; W202]. 240.34: mimics,] mimics }[GY 55881; W202]. 241.1: India,] India }[GY 55881; W202]. 241.6–7: mother-/tongue }COPY-TEXT HYPHEN. 241.33: bridge-playing] bridge playing }[GY 55881; W202]. 242.10: Crown] crown }[GY 55881]. 242.24: educational] Educational }Ts. NLI 30,552; [GY 55881]. 242.26: question,] question }[W202]. 242.27: answered,] answered }[Perhaps GY in 55881; W202]. 242.36: Fashioned] Fashioed }Ts. NLI 30,552; [quoted text; W202]. 243.2: still,] still }[GY 55881]. 243.23: Cuchulain] Cuchullain }Conventional spelling of name; [GY 55881; W202. 244.14: demerits] de-merits }[GY 55881; W202]. 244.28: doom,] doom }[GY 55881; W202]. 244.34: priest] Priest }Ts. NLI 30,461; [GY 55881]. 245.7: inscriptions] instriptions }Ts. NLI 30,552; [W202]. 245.11: grammar] grammar }Ts. NLI 30,552; [GY 55881; W202]. 245.11: vain,] vain }[W202]. 245.16: talk,] talk }Ts. NLI 30,552; [GY 55881]. 245.19: home,] home }[GY 55881; W202]. 245.23: study,] study }[W202]. 245.24: visibility—] visibility; }[GY 55881]. 245.25: peep-show?—] peep-show, }[GY 55881]. 245.29: Guildenstern] Gildenstern }Name: [GY 55881]. 245.35: concerned] cencerned }Ts. NLI 30,552; [GY 55881; W202]. 246.6: art,] art }[W202]. 246.18: petulance] petulence }Ts. NLI 30,552. 246.21: folk-feeling] folk feeling }[GY 55881; W202]. 246.28–29 and 30: subject-matter] subject matter }[GY 55881]; [EMENDED] COPY-TEXT HYPHEN. 246.30: subject-matter] subject matter }[GY 55881]. 246.33: at] as }Ts. NLI 30,552; [W202]. 246.34: the] "The }[GY 55881]. 247.20: will,] will }Ts. NLI 30,552; [HRC Texas W201 proofs; W201]. 247.24: l'Isle] L'Isle }Name; [GY 55881]. 247.30: by modern Irish poets] by mod UNINKED h poets }Ts. NLI 30,552; [HRC Texas W201 proofs; BL 55881; W201]. 247.31: by modern Irish and] by UNINKED and]Ts. NLI 30,552; [HRC Texas W201 proofs; BL 55881; W201]. 247.32: accompaniments,] accompaniments }[GY 55881; W202]. 247.37–38: McCormack's] MacCormack's }Name; [1939 Macmillan copy-editing in 55881]. 248.14: We,] We }Ts. NLI 30,552; [GY 55881; W202]. 248.15: heterogeneous] heterogenous }[W202]. 248.17: McCormack] MacCormack }Name; [1939 Macmillan copy-editing in 55881]. 248.27: space,] space }[GY 55881]. 248.34: book,] book }[W202]. 248.38: purpose,] purpose }[GY 55881. 249.16: heavy,] heavy }[GY 55881; W202]. 249.23: broad-backed] broad backed }[GY 55881; W202]. 249.26: Riviera] riviera }Name; [GY 55881; W202]. 249.30: There, too,] There too }[GY 55881]. 249.31: flesh-tints] flesh tints }[GY 55881]. 249.32: body,] body }[GY

55881; W202]. 249.33: woman,] woman }[GY 55881; W202]. 249.38: *Utopia*] Utopia }Title; [GY 55881]. 249.38: that we could] UNINKED ld }Ts. NLI 30,552; [HRC Texas W201 proofs; BL 55881; W201]. 250.1: think that artists] thin UNINKED ts }Ts. NLI 30,552; [HRC Texas W201 proofs; BL 55881; W201]. 250.3: Carlo,] Carlo }[W202]. 250.3: writing,] writ UNINKED }Ts. NLI 30,552; [HRC Texas W201 proofs; BL 55881; W201]: [W202]. 250.4: sort of] s UNINKED }Ts. NLI 30,552; [HRC Texas W201 proofs; BL 55881; W201]. 250.13: troop] troup }[GY 55881; W202]. 251.[9]: NO DATE] April, 1938 }[BL 55881; W201; W202] • 'EPILOGUE' TO *PER AMICA SILENTIA LUNAE* 253.4: brother] brother, }None. 253.10: fire. The] fire; and the }None. 253.10: monk [wanted] to] monk to }[CANCELLED VERSION: '. . . knight was old and wanted to be left in peace to watch']. 253.12–13: THE MANUSCRIPT HAS NO PARAGRAPH DIVISIONS. 253.13: said,] said }None. 253.14: Son] Sun }Name. 253.15: power,] power }None. 253.16 and 18: Father] father }Convention. 253.16: Son] son }Convention. 253.16: Holy] holy }Convention. 253.17: world.'] world" }None. 253.18: sin', said the pilgrim,] sin" said the pilgrim }None. 253.19: Son] sun }Name. 253.19: redeems us] redeems [?CANCELLED: or] us }None. 253.20: Holy Spirit] holy spirit }Convention. 253.20: good.'] good" }None. 253.21: sin,' said the monk,] sin" said the monk }None. 253.24: Damascus, said the pilgrim,] Damascus said the pilgrim }None. 253.26: whatever age,] what[? which?] ever age }None. 253.28: born, whereas if we] born where as[? or?] if if we }None. 253.32: birth [are] fanciful] birth [CANCELLED: are very] fanciful]None. 253.33: Pollycarte[?],] Pollyc**** }Name: Final four letters of character name are undeciphered; Curtis Bradford transcription reads 'Pollycarte'; Punctuation: None. 253.34: ear?'] ear. }None. 254.1: said,] said }None. 254.7: know,'] know" }None. • ALTERNATIVE ENDING FOR 'IF I WERE FOUR-AND-TWENTY' 254.11: [. . .] and] and }None. 255.4: eighteenth-century] eighteenth century }None. 255.15: Cinq-Cygne] Ceng-Cygne }Name. 255.16: Raoul] Raol }Name. 256.8: from] fomm }None. 256.19: So',] So" }None. 256.23: hermit',] hermit" }None. 256.24: once,] once }None. 256.27: *Civitas Dei*] Civitas Dei }Convention. 256.32: woman] women }None. 256.33: conquest,] conquest }None. 256.35–36: moralize] moralise }None. 256.38: some] so e }None. 257.1: author] Author }None. 257.2: *Melancholy*] Melancholy", }None. 257.4: Immanuel] Emmanuel }Name. 257.5: proof,] proof }None. 257.12: foresee] forsee }None. 257.17: re-organizing] re-organising }[P. 256, l. 35 above: 'organize']. 257.21: feeding] fe ding }None. 257.26: seventeenth-century] seventeenth century }None. 257.26: author] Author }None. 257.27: serve.'] serve. }None. 257.31–32: Thomas à Kempis] Thomas-a-Kempis }Name. 257.34: XII] XI }None. 257.39: four-and-fifty] four and fifty }[P. 34, l. 1 above]. • NOTES TO *VISIONS AND BELIEFS IN THE WEST OF IRELAND* 258.19: Aberfoyle] Abberfoyle }Name; Sir Walter Scott, *Letters on Demonology and Witchcraft, Addressed to J. G. Lockhart* (1830), 4th ed., Morley's Universal Library (London: Routledge, 1899), (O'Shea no. 1860A) p. 16 *et passim* [and 1st ed., London: Murray, 1830, O'Shea no. 1860; inscribed Georgie Hyde-Lees, 1914]. 258.28–29: Grahame of Duchray] Graham of Ducray }Name in all three of Yeats's possible sources (Lang, Scott and Evans-Wentz; see p. 444, nn. 1 and 3 above). 259.4: Pelaginism] Plaginism }Name. 260.7: [impotent?] [impotent?] }NO EMENDATION. 260.8: [turning]] [turning] }NO EMENDATION. 260.33: seventeenth-century] seventeenth century }None. 260.37: Cabbalistic] Cabalistic }Conventional spelling of name. 260.41: seventeenth-century] seventeenth century }None. 262.31–32: eleventh-/century }COPY-TEXT HYPHEN. 263.1: X,] X., }None. 263.25: venial] venal }None. 264.13: cardamom] cardamon }Name. 264.13: caryophylleae] caryophylias }Ts. NLI 30,269; [quoted text]. 264.14: nutmegs, calamite storax] nutmeg, calamite, storax }Ts. NLI 30,269; [quoted text]. 264.14–15: aloes-wood and roots] aloes wood root }Ts. NLI 30,269; [quoted text]; [EMENDED COPY-TEXT HYPHEN. 264.15: triasandalis] triasandates }Ts. NLI 30,269; [quoted text]. 264.18: friary] priory }Ts. NLI 30,269; [quoted text]. 264.20: Peruvian balsam] peruvian bark }Ts. NLI 30,269; [quoted text]. 264.29–30: '*Verbum caro factum est*'] *Verbum caro factum est* }None. 265.7: Plutarch] PLUTARCH }Ts. NLI 30,269. 265.28: Kyteler] Kettler }Name; [*P* 210]. 267.1: modern] Modern }P. 268, l. 14 above. 267.24–29: LATIN SET IN ITALIC] LATIN SET IN ROMAN }None. 267.25–26: *commiscetur*] commicetur }[Quoted text]. 267.29: *experientia*] experienta }[Quoted text]. 270.10: Macmillan] Mac- PAGE DIVISION Millan }Name. 271.17–18: looking-/glass }COPY-TEXT HYPHEN. 271.34: Éliphas] Élephas }Name. 271.36: *l'haute*] *la Haute* }Title. 272.10: Orcus] Oxos }Name; [quoted text]. 273.1: "Duns"] *Duns* }None. 273.1–2: "stone caiseal"] *stone caiseal* }None. 273.3: cases,] cases }[Quoted text]. 273.3: houses.'] houses." }None. 273.3: "Bo Aires"] *Bo Aires* }None. 273.13: IV,] IV., }None. 274.16–17: so-/ and-so }COPY-TEXT HYPHEN .274.35: Vallemort] Vellemort }Name. 275.7: la] La }Convention for title. 275.9: d'Arsonval] D'Arsonval }Name. 275.32: led] lead }None. 276.14: d'Arsonval's] D'Arsonval's }Name. 276.26 and 277.2: d'Arsonval] D'Arsonval }Name. 280.14: Faifofer] Faffofer }Name; [quoted source]. 281.11: servant,] servant }None. 284.23: rite] right }None. 286.24–25: spell-/breaking }COPY-TEXT HYPHEN. 287.2: *Mabinogion*] Mabinogion }Title. 287.21: Ballylee] Bally Lee }Name. 287.27: said:] said; }None. 287.31: glamour',] glamour" }None. 288.2: séance] Séance }P. 280, n. 29, 1. 3 above. 288.3: Stainton] Stanton }Name. • DELETED 'INTRODUCTION' OF 'SWEDENBORG, MEDIUMS, AND THE DESOLATE PLACES' 288.26: Faeries] Faerys }Ms. NLI 13,575; copy-text has 'Faery' with holograph 's' added. 289.10: knowledgeable] knowledgable }None; [copy-text is a holograph correction from 'knowledgible']. 289.19: Forth,] Forts }Spelling: Ms. NLI 13,575; punctuation: none. 289.23: remnant] remant }Ms. NLI 13,575. 289.35: of] by }Ms. NLI 13,575. 290.6–7: hedge-/row }COPY-TEXT HYPHEN. 290.15: Slieve-na-nOr] Sleive-na-Nore }None; [Ms. NLI 13,575 has 'Sleive-nan-[CANCELLED: Org*]Ore'] 290.20: faeries,] faeries }None. • BIOGRAPHICAL NOTE IN *THE HOLY MOUNTAIN* 291.1: A Biographical Note] UNTITLED }*HM*. 291.3: 15th] 15th. }*HM*. 291.4: Tātyā] Tatyā }*HM*. 291.4–5: well-/known }COPY-TEXT HYPHEN. • SWEDENBORG, MEDIUMS, AND THE DESOLATE PLACES [YEATS'S NOTES] 318 n. 17.1: Noh] *Noh* }Ts. NLI 30,271; p. 69, l. 26 above. 323 n. 52.1: Aksakof] Atsikof }Name. 323 n. 52.2: de] De }Name. 323 n. 52.4: Dr Ochorowicz] D'Ochorowicz }Name. 324.1: *Sciences*] *Science* }Title of periodical. 327 n. 57.3: Hippocrates] Harpocrates }P. 20, l. 25 above; [name in cited text]. • WITCHES AND WIZARDS AND IRISH FOLK-LORE [YEATS'S NOTE] 336 n. 17.2: Pitcairn's] *Pitcairn's* }Title. • BISHOP BERKELEY [YEATS'S NOTES] 351 n. 20.2: mathematician] Mathematician }Ms. NLI. 352 n. 25.4: source] sourse }*BB* revised. 354 n. 35.1: Calkins'] Catkins' }Name. 354 n. 35.10: *Faculties.* Events] Faculties" Events }*BB* revise. • LOUIS LAMBERT [YEATS'S NOTE] 366 n. 11.1: Éliphas Lévi] Eliphas Levi }Name. 366 n. 11.2: Saint-Martin] Saint Martin }Name. • INTRODUCTION TO *AN INDIAN MONK* [YEATS'S NOTE] 371 n. 16.4: Hamsa"—] Hamsa,— }*IM*. 390.1–2: trouser-stretchers {COPY-TEXT HYPHEN. • APHORISMS OF YOGA [YEATS'S NOTES] 391 n. 15.1: *Civilization*] Civilisations }Title of book. 392 n. 21.3: personality,] personality }Ms. NLI 30,400. • *ON THE BOILER* [YEATS'S NOTES] 426 n. 33.3: Part.] Part }[Abbreviation of 'Partition'; 1939 Macmillan copy-editing in 55881]. 426 n. 33.3: I,] I }[W202]. 426 n. 33.3: 2, Mem.] 2. Mem }[W202]. 428 n. 38.2 and 7: Shepherd] Shephard }Name; Ms. NLI 30,551; Ts. NLI 30,551. 428 n. 38.2: the] The }None; [1939 Macmillan copy-editing in 55881]. 428 n. 38.4: just] just, }Ms. NLI 30,551; [quoted text]. 428 n. 39.2: mine:] mine; }[GY 55881; W202]. 428 n. 40.11: *Progress,*] Progress" }Ts. NLI 30,461; [W202]. 432.5: That] that }[Same word in preceding clause; GY 55881]. 433 n. 76.2: *Emer,* Emer] Emer." Emer }[No sentence division in holograph footnote on Ts. NLI 30,552]. 435 n. 82.2: Husserl's] Russerl's }Name; Ts. NLI 30,552; [W201; W202]. 436 n. 94.1: de] De }Name; Ts. NLI 30,461; [W202].

INDEX

www.ingramcontent.com/pod-product-compliance
Lightning Source LLC
Chambersburg PA
CBHW010748310726
48980CB00003B/366
9780026327022